D1715594

CYCLOPS

CYCLOPS

RANKO MARINKOVIĆ

TRANSLATED BY VLADA STOJILJKOVIĆ

EDITED BY ELLEN ELIAS-BURSAĆ

YALE UNIVERSITY PRESS ■ NEW HAVEN & LONDON

A MARGELLOS
WORLD REPUBLIC OF LETTERS BOOK

The Margellos World Republic of Letters is dedicated to making literary works from around the globe available in English through translation. It brings to the English-speaking world the work of leading poets, novelists, essayists, philosophers, and playwrights from Europe, Latin America, Africa, Asia, and the Middle East to stimulate international discourse and creative exchange.

Yale University Press books may be purchased in quantity for educational, business, or promotional use. For information, please e-mail sales.press@yale.edu (U.S. office) or sales@yaleup.co.uk (U.K. office).

Set in Electra and Nobel types by Keystone Typesetting, Inc.
Printed in the United States of America.

Library of Congress Cataloging-in-Publication Data
Marinković, Ranko, 1913–2001
[Kiklop. English]
Cyclops / Ranko Marinković, ; translated by Vlada Stojiljković ; edited by Ellen Elias-Bursać.
    p.   cm. — (A Margellos world republic of letters book)
Originally published in Serbo-Croatian as: Kiklop.
ISBN 978-0-300-15241-8 (hardcover : alk. paper)
1. World War, 1939–1945—Yugoslavia—Fiction. 2. Zagreb (Croatia)—Fiction.
I. Stojiljković, Vlada, 1938– II. Elias-Bursać, Ellen. III. Title.
PG1618.M28K513 2010
891.8′235—dc22
2010024516

A catalogue record for this book is available from the British Library.

This paper meets the requirements of ANSI/NISO Z39.48-1992 (Permanence of Paper).

10 9 8 7 6 5 4 3 2 1

Making his way through a crowded Zagreb square one evening on the eve of World War II, Melkior Tresić catches sight of a priest with familiar, jutting ears. The priest, we learn, had taught him catechism during his childhood in Dalmatia. The fleeting glimpse of the Dalmatian priest in the opening pages of this quintessentially Zagreb novel is Ranko Marinković's nod to his native Dalmatia. The nod tells us that Melkior Tresić is an outside insider, someone who, like Marinković, came to the city as a student, and who sees Zagreb as someone born there never could. Marinković captures Zagreb's crowds, the shysters, the army barracks, and the seedy neighborhoods in one of the most famous fictional portraits of the city, yet he peoples the novel with a closely knit group whose playful jibes and cheerful ignorance of the portentous events taking shape around them have a certain resonance with the insular Mediterranean culture in which he was raised.

When Marinković set out to write *CYCLOPS* in the early 1960s he was thinking big. In shaping his plot he reached for the big writers, such as Joyce (whose *Ulysses* had first been translated into Croatian in 1957), Homer, Shakespeare, and Dostoyevsky. For all the influence of other literatures, however, the novel is anchored firmly in a more local context. The story unfolds on the streets between the Zagreb main square and the Opera House, and the streets and cafés are inhabited by the poets, actors, and other public figures of Marinković's student years in Zagreb. Along with the readily identifiable references to Hamlet and Leopold Bloom, the narrative and dialogue are interwoven with allusions to various Croatian writers and their characters and to verses of Croatian poets—all unfamiliar to American readers, including Ivan Gundulić,[1] Ivan Brlić-Mažuranić,[2] a character of Krleža's,[3] and lines of verse by Vladimir Nazor,[4] Vladimir Vidrić,[5] Ivo Vojnović,[6] and Tin Ujević,[7] —as well as mentions of equally unfamiliar Serbian writers such as Simo Pandurović[8] and Jovan Dučić.[9] The panorama of Zagreb life in the opening pages of the novel, the MAAR street advertisements, the vendors selling shoelaces, are authentic images of Zagreb life of the late thirties, and *Jutarnji List* (*Morning News*) is still hawked by vendors on Zagreb's streets.

There are many comparisons that can be drawn between *CYCLOPS* and other works of literature, most obviously *Ulysses*, the *Odyssey*, and *Hamlet*. But the irreverence, irony, and satire with which Marinković dissects Zagreb cultural life on the eve of World War II also resonate with Joseph Heller's *Catch-22* (1961). Heller's biography affords a surprisingly productive comparison with Marinković's. They both were playwrights and short-story writers, as well as novelists, and they were close in age. Heller fought in active combat in World War II, unlike Marinković, who spent the war as an internee and refugee, but both of them were the first, for their respective readerships, to write of World War II in a darkly humorous vein. And they were each known chiefly for their first novel, each of which became a huge best seller, never to be outshone by anything else they later wrote.

The year *CYCLOPS* was published (1965) was pivotal for postwar Yugoslavia. It followed on a period of furious economic growth during the late 1950s and a repressive spell that came after Yugoslavia's break with Cominform in 1948. There were major economic reforms in 1965, and the next year saw the dismissal of the Minister of the Interior, Aleksandar Ranković, over a wiretapping scandal, which became the symbolic end of the immediate postwar period. The Yugoslav government began allowing its citizens to travel abroad freely in 1966, thereby setting itself apart from the

Eastern European countries that were still "behind the iron curtain," and these political and economic reforms were accompanied by a thaw in culture. After a brief spell of socialist realism in the early fifties, the literatures in Yugoslavia had asserted a modicum of artistic independence, but only within limits (there could be no mention of the Goli Otok and other prison camps, or articulation of nationalist and separatist sentiments, or scurrilous mention of the person of Josip Broz Tito). The limits relaxed somewhat in the 1960s, which was a decade for ferment in all the arts.

Marinković's CYCLOPS, published in the midst of all this, and *Death and the Dervish*, by Meša Selimović, which appeared a year later, were groundbreaking novels that brought new intellectual depth to the treatment of controversial issues, such as, in CYCLOPS, the use of irony and satire in the treatment of the recent war, and, in *Death and the Dervish* the nature of repressive authority. As soon as it appeared, CYCLOPS was showered with accolades, including the NIN award—the most prestigious recognition for literary works in the former Yugoslavia,[10] and the same happened with *Death and the Dervish* the following year.

To say that Marinković raised eyebrows with his ironic treatment of the war theme in CYCLOPS is not to suggest that there had been no antiwar Croatian prose before him. Miroslav Krleža, in particular, is famous for his antiwar stories after World War I. Where Marinković broke new ground was in his use of irony and satirical humor to transgress the various strictures imposed by the victorious Partisans on how the conflict would be described in the years following the war. But it was precisely the madcap brand of humor, the sly nicknames used by the denizens of Zagreb's cafés, the fantastical tales of shipwrecked sailors confronted by cannibalistic natives in the South Pacific, the ingenuity with which Melkior Tresić keeps himself out of combat, that gave the novel its irresistible charm and steered it through the sensitive political waters of the day.

Marinković studied psychology at Zagreb University in the 1930s. He was intrigued by the psychology of the artist and was drawn, in particular, to Tin Ujević's verse and the workings of the poet's psyche. While still a student, he published three brief articles[11] on Ujević,[12] in which he remarks on "something mysterious, special and remarkable, almost unintelligible" in Ujević's personality.[13] Marinković credits Dostoyevsky with having a formative influence on Ujević's preoccupation with suffering, humiliation, and pain. He wonders whether Ujević's bohemian eccentricity is a form of mental illness, and concludes that with an ear for the right resonance one could enter into this complex, chaotic psychology. Marinković also describes the way Ujević represents love and the feminine in his verse, saying that Ujević is a poet of "spiritual love, the erotic turned mystical, stripped of its sexuality, love that is felt with a sixth sense, like music,"[14] a poet who perceives woman as a symbol of "creative mystery."[15] Marinković and Ujević got to know each other later, and there are several Zagreb anecdotes stemming from their relationship, particularly that Marinković dubbed Ujević the Baudelaire from Vrgorec, while Ujević's nickname for Marinković was the Voltaire from Vis (each man's respective birthplace).

Only a few chapters in CYCLOPS feature the Ujević-like character Maestro, but Maestro's spirit and his relationship with Tresić permeate the entire novel. For all his curmudgeonly manner, Maestro has an abiding fondness for Tresić, and chooses him as the only person from their circle he can trust. Theirs is the principle emotional relationship of CYCLOPS. Another vestige of Ujević's is the mystique attached to the name "Viviana," which personifies the feminine "creative mystery" in Ujević's poetic.

In the immediate postwar years Marinković was one of the rising stars in Zagreb cultural life, active in the theater and in publishing and teaching, while in the same period Ujević was working only as a literary translator, having been banned for five years by the Writers' Association from publishing his own poetry and essays—punishment for accepting employment from the fascist regime as a translator during the war. Marinković was among those who saw to it that Ujević always had enough translation work to support him during this time. Harold Bloom alerts us to the dynamic that often shapes relations between younger generations of writers and the powerful figures of previous generations. Ranko Marinković was not a poet, so he was not competing directly with Ujević's looming influence, but this dynamic is also worth keeping in mind when parsing his portrait of Ujević in the character of Maestro.

Marinković is frequently hailed for his irony and the psychological and social analysis he brings to his stories, novels, and plays, but, as several recent critics have remarked, there is room for more scholarship on his work. As one scholar comments, "*CYCLOPS*, the novel by Ranko Marinković published in 1965, is regularly accorded a distinguished place in critical and historical surveys of Croatian literary modernism, but this claim is supported by a somewhat tautological argumentation. Namely, instead of insisting on the stylistic excellence of Marinković's writing and the vivid elaboration of the characters, Croatian criticism hardly ever moves beyond discussing the plot."[16]

On the other hand, a critic notes, "*CYCLOPS* will continue to be read for pure pleasure for a long time to come . . . It is a great urban novel. Academic critics, in speaking of *CYCLOPS*, insist on the theme of fear and other things which are certainly relevant, but which sidestep the 'details' that make even high school students enjoy this novel . . . *CYCLOPS* will survive because it takes place on the street and in the smoke of cafés, because it is promiscuous, witty and full of fools."[17]

A new generation of scholars is rediscovering Marinković's writing, bringing the precepts of literary theory to bear on his themes, characters, and structures in a variety of productive and engaging ways. Aside from the two articles cited here, there is very little critical writing available in English on Marinković's work. The entry in the *Dictionary of Literary Biography* is a valuable general overview of his opus.

Aside from delighting generations of high school students, Ranko Marinković and *CYCLOPS* have entered into the cultural parlance with a television series and a 1982 film based on the novel *CYCLOPS* (directed by Antun Vrdoljak), and *Kiklop* [*CYCLOPS*] is the name of the most prestigious cultural award conferred annually in Croatia to winners in categories such as best editor, best prose work, best book of essays, best first book, best children's book, best translation, etc. The *Vjesnik* newspaper also confers a "Ranko Marinković" best short story award.

I knew Ranko Marinković only briefly, late in his life, when he and I occasionally ran into each other at a Zagreb publishing company. Always the gentleman, Magritte-like in his impeccable gray coat and bowler hat, a twinkle in his eye, he'd raised his hat in greeting, and it is in this pose, hat in hand, eyes twinkling, that I will always remember him. Vlada Stojiljković I never met, but several friends of mine knew him well and tell of his fascination of many years with CYCLOPS, his commitment to the translation, the quandaries he regaled them with, and the solutions he devised for the book's countless quips, puns, and verses. Hats off, then, to Yale University Press for bringing this marvelous novel to American readers!

Notes

1. Gundulić's dream (510) refers to the scene painted by Vlaho Bukovac on the stage curtain of the Croatian National Theater in Zagreb.

2. "Stories from the Olden Days" (432), the title of a popular collection of children's stories.

3. Leone from Krleža's *Glembays*, 132.

4. "We drank the blazing sun . . ." (42); "Each beech . . ." (527).

5. "Zeus was a wonderful god . . ." (42); "a Pompeiian scene" (113); and "I have been on a cloud . . ." (145).

6. "You are our leader!" (379), from the *Dubrovnik Trilogy*. The original line reads, "Gulls and clouds will ask us: who are you? what do you seek? . . . and our sails will reply: Dubrovnik sails! Dubrovnik seeks a barren reef, to hide her Liberty thereon."

7. "to be pure, to be pure . . ." (38); "a little smile on dear lips, a bunch of flowers in a water glass" (65); "and his feet are bloody . . ." (305); "A star on his forehead, a sparkle in his eye . . ." (512).

8. See page 436.

9. "to the queen of all women . . ." (456).

10. The NIN award is still given out today for Serbian writers in Serbia.

11. Ante Stamać reprinted the three articles (*Republika* 11, no. 4 [2004]: 38–63) as part of a discussion of Marinković's understanding of Ujević and his development of the character of Maestro.

12. Tin Ujević figured large on the Yugoslav cultural scene during the first half of the twentieth century, as much for his scandalous behavior as for his poetry. He dedicated his life to art and became a legend in his own time, the archetype of the bohemian figure in the cafés of Split, Belgrade, Sarajevo, and Zagreb, a quixotic public personality. Having spent most of the thirties in Sarajevo, Ujević moved to Zagreb in 1937, where he died of cancer in 1955, ten years before *CYCLOPS* came out.

13. "Esej o pjesniku rezignacija," *Republika* 11, no. 4 (2004): 50.

14. Ibid., 53.

15. "Jeka 'Ojađenog zvona,'" *Republika* 11, no. 4 (2004): 57.

16. Morana Čale, " 'The Fraction Man': Anthropology of *CYCLOPS*," *Slavica Tergestina* n. 11–12. *Studia slavica III,* Scuola Superiore di Lingue Moderne per Interpreti e Traduttori, May 2004, 83.

17. Robert Perišić, "Ranko Marinković, on the Occasion of His Death," *Relations,* 3–4 (2004): 295–296.

Ellen Elias-Bursać

CYCLOPS

"MAAR . . . MAAR . . ." cried a voice from the rooftop. Melkior was standing next to the stair railing leading down below ground; glowing above the stairway was a GENTS sign. Across the way another set of stairs angled downward, intersecting with the first, under the sign of LADIES. A staircase X, he thought, reciprocal values, the numerators GENTS and the numerators LADIES (cross multiplication), the denominators ending up downstairs in majolica and porcelain, where the denominators keep a respectful silence; the only sounds are the muffled whisper of water, the hiss of valves, and the whirr of ventilators. Like being in the bowels of an ocean liner. Smooth sailing. Passengers make their cheery and noisy way downstairs as if going to the ship's bar for a shot of whiskey. Afterward, they return to the promenade deck, spry and well satisfied, and sip the fresh evening potion from MAAR's air.

MAAR conquers all. When the darkness falls, it unfurls its screen high up on the rooftop of a palace and starts yelling, "MAAR Commercials!" After it finishes tracing its mighty name across the screen using a mysterious light, MAAR's letters go into a silly dance routine, singing a song in unison in praise of their master. The letters then trip away into the darkened sky while giving a parting shout to the dumbstruck audience, "MAAR Movietone Advertising!"

Next there appears a house, miserable and dirty, its roof askew, its door frame battered loose, wrinkled and stained shirts, spectral torsos with no heads or legs, jumping out of its windows in panic. To *danse macabre* music, the ailing victims of grime proceed to drag themselves toward a boiling cauldron bubbling with impatient thick white foam. With spinsterish mistrust, wavering on the very lip of the cauldron (fearful of being duped), the shirts leap into the foam . . . and what do you know, the mistrust was nothing but foolish superstition, for here they are, emerging from the cauldron, dazzlingly white, one after another, marching in single file and singing lustily, "*Radion* washes on its own." Next, a sphinx appears on the screen and asks the viewers in a far-off, desert-dry voice: "Is this possible?" and the next instant a pretty typist shows that two typewriters cannot possibly be typed at once. "And is this possible?" the sphinx asks again. No, it is also not possible for water to flow uphill. It is equally impossible to build a house from the roof down, or for the Sun to revolve around the Earth . . . "but it *is* possible for Tungsram-Crypton double-spiraled filament lightbulbs to give twice as much light as the ordinary ones for the same wattage . . ." and on goes a lightbulb, as bright as the sun in the sky, the terrible glare forcing the viewers to squint. Then a mischievous little girl in a polka-dot dirndl prances her way onto the screen and declaims, in the virginal voice of a girl living with the nuns, "*Zora* soap washes clean, cleaner than you ever saw . . . you've ever seen," she hastens to correct her mistake, too late, the viewers chuckle. The little girl withdraws in embarrassment. She is followed by a traveler carrying a heavy suitcase in each hand, the road winding behind him in endless perspective. The sun beats him with fiery lashes from above, but his step is spry and cheery; with a sly wink at the audience he whispers confidentially, "You go a long way without tiring thanks to Palma heels" and displays the enormous soles of his feet: sure enough, Palma heels! Next comes a mighty horde of cockroaches, fleas, bedbugs, and other horrible pests, afforded air support by dense formations of moths and flies and escorted by speedy mosquito squadrons . . . but suddenly there is a clatter of heavy hooves and a Flit grenadier comes galloping into the fray, armed with the dreaded Flit spray can. Before long the battlefield is littered with dead bodies (of the pests). From the platen of a Remington grows the legendary portrait of the great Napoleon with a curl of hair, drunkard-like, down his forehead. As Napoleon grows so does the Remington, and when the two have covered the entire globe the Remington types across the equator the historic words "We have conquered the world" ". . . and ended up on St. Helena," muttered Melkior, "don't give yourself airs." Afterward a Singer uses Eurasia and America to stitch a many-colored coat for portly Mr. Globe; it fashions black trousers from Africa, and a white cap from Greenland, and Mr. Globe chortles with glee. Bata asks a passerby tottering along with lightning bolts flashing from his corns, "Is that necessary?" "No," replied Melkior, "not if you buy your shoes at Bata's. Shoes are an Antaean bond with Mother Earth, the pedestrian's secret power . . ." And there is Brill kissing human footwear with its polishes, two long-haired brushes curling and cuddling like two sly cats around a pedestrian's feet; he walks on tall and proud, his shoes shining!—Kästner & Öhler's, the Balkan's largest department store, has spilled unbelievable and magic objects, "even the kitchen sink" out of its horn of plenty, and the viewers' imagination pecks away among the luxuries. Julio Meinl desires to fill everyone to the brim with Chinese, Ceylon, and even Russian tea; as for coffee, Haag is the brand—it caters to your heart. Sneeze if you can after a Bayer aspirin! Darmol works while you sleep, and Planinka Tea has the patriotic duty to cleanse Aryan blood. Elida Cream looks after your complexion. Intercosma swears to afforest your denuded head sooner than possible. Kalodont is the arch enemy of tartar, while VHG asks you, rather saucily, if you are a man. Finally, First Croatian Splendid Funerals Company takes the respectful liberty of reminding you of your dignity and . . . well, see for yourself: black varnished hearses with baroque gold angels, horses with glossy black coats, a comfortable coffin, attendance of ideally sober personnel in admirals' hats, making your death another success and a thing of almost poetic beauty . . .

From the tall roof MAAR announced *urbi et orbi* its glittering standard of living. Its mighty acoustics had all but drowned out a blind peddler's feeble supplication issuing from a dark doorway, "Shoelaces, black, yellow—two dinars; ten envelopes, letter paper inside—six dinars . . ." The blind man's monotonous litany sounded tired and unconvinced; the pathetic bit of verbal advertising aspired only to mask the begging, that much and no more.

Melkior took refuge in the doorway with the blind man and fell to watching: what can this MAAR thing hope to accomplish? The viewer stands entranced with his head thrown back and drinks in, henlike, the filmed comfort of well-being. From his earthbound condition he watches MAAR's looming mirage, listening to this voice "from the other world" and is already intoxicated by the luxurious illusion of his eternal longing to be pampered—and then there comes the voice of the accursed petty things—the shoelaces, black, yellow, for two dinars . . . and he fingers his two dinars in his pocket and his petty need for shoelaces, black or yellow as the case may be. Tungsram-Crypton's glare has dimmed . . . and what do I need the Flit grenadier for . . . and I see this business with Napoleon is just a ruse. . . . The evening has gone down the drain. To think that he was actually willing to die for the sake of First Croatian! Can't they have blind people weaving baskets or something instead of letting them beg like this? Melkior felt the thought himself, through irritation with the beggar's plea. Why indeed can't they open a center with heating provided, for the poor blind people to gather, think of the savings on electrical lighting . . . he made to redress his cruel thought, even bought a pair of yellow shoelaces (although he needed black) and generally cast about for a way to help the blind man. . . . He dropped a silver piece on the ground, picked it up again, and asked him, "You lost this coin, didn't you?" "Could be, I've got a hole in my pocket," replied the blind man half-jokingly, just in case, but he did, eagerly, accept the coin.

The quaint act of charity moved a person nearby. A clerical collar around his neck, the man had cast only a passing, sadly indifferent glance up at MAAR's magic tricks as he squeezed through the throng. Then his spirits soared with a "true glow" when Melkior found a way (and how Christian a way!) of being charitable to the blind man. "When giving alms, no need to make a show of it." He patted Melkior on the shoulder and, giving him an approving smile, dipped into the crowd again. Melkior only managed to catch a glimpse of his head, wrinkled, sad, wrung between the hands of some terrible misfortune, and a pair of large ears thereupon, jutting grimly out on either side. He was astounded by how oddly large they were, so similar to a very familiar and well-remembered pair. . . . But back in those days the head had been ruddy and full, young and terrifying, with those selfsame batwing ears amid waves of thick hair which protected them from ridicule.

"That pale scrawny neck!" cried Melkior in a low voice, "is it possible?"

After him, then! He had to see those ears again!

But who is to know whether or not ears have a hiding place for their memories? A secret spring-catch drawer from which at night, when they burrow into solitude, they take out trinkets to caress and sob over?

Melkior launched into a romantic tale about the mysterious soul of a priest roaming through the urban hustle and bustle seeking peace and salvation. . . . But the romantic tale is something else. . . . Those ears carry with them a different secret, one that darkened his entire childhood. He still wears the catechistic slaps, riddlelike, on his cheeks. And all that subsequently befell Dom Kuzma was cobbled together by his imagination into a story of a man apart. He was even ready to proclaim Dom Kuzma a martyr, for all that the martyr had whacked a pair of red-hot slaps on his darling cheeks. (The older ladies used to say at the time how "that child" had such darling cheeks—and they would kiss him, even nibble at his cheeks, the old maids.)

All the pupils in Melkior's school, including the tiny first-graders who didn't even know how to write an *i*, knew how to draw an ear. They all, everywhere and at every opportunity, drew ears. Ears on the blackboard, on the classroom desktop, on the floor, on the roadbed, on fences, on walls, on any wall near which they happened to have a piece of charcoal handy. All the books, the notebooks, were doodled over with ears. Ears on agave leaves, on the beach sand. There sprang into being a secret sect of otosists, aurists, ear maniacs, in hoc signo vinces. Ears everywhere, like early-Christian fish. A large, huge, outsize ear on any potatolike head. The head did not matter, what mattered was the ear . . . to draw it as well as possible. To master the technique and the cliché. The older lads did the Charleston in trendy bell-bottomed trousers; the small boys drew ears fanatically. They did not know why it had to be the ear. Their parents, their teachers, asked, "Why ears?" "Everyone is drawing them," the child would reply, puzzled that this, too, should be forbidden. "An epidemic," people shrugged, "the measles." And the local gendarmerie post received a telegram from higher up: had the phenomenon anything to do with the Communists?

The silly puerile manias. Collecting stamps was all right—adults did it, too, philatelists, postal-oriented thinkers. But carob beans!— that was for seminarians (the independent faction). Melkior had kilos of the things. He threw the lot away when sock knitting caught on. The socks naturally never reached the length of the heel; the boys were ignorant of either the utility or the futility of work.

The ear-drawing was an outburst and it spread like the plague. Later on, measures were taken (by the educational authorities), but they served only to fan the epidemic: they helped to reveal the meaning of *The Ear* . . . which previously no one might have divined.

When he learned the reason Melkior thought it seriously insulting and undignified, and he never drew an ear again. But Dom Kuzma's hand eventually reached him nevertheless. After the physical pain subsided he felt ashamed before the catechist, he claimed his part of the guilt. Shame made him stop going to school, lest he meet Dom Kuzma again. Which he did not . . . until tonight. (But in such pathetic shape!)

Dom Kuzma brought too much passion to his struggle to prevail. What he did was senseless, even mad; he seemed to want to wipe all those provocative "ears" around him with his bare hands (or, slaps). He went in for mindless collective face slapping in his classes, for purely preventive reasons. His vengeful fervor, brandishing a heavy hand, reached everywhere, like God's punishment.

Vengefully, he gave every pupil a zoological nickname. Or two, in tandem. He used the names of curious animals so that he could ridicule a person, to provoke laughter. . . . But there was no laughter, only the low cunning of children: how to weather the blows.

Dom Kuzma spied a bumpkin sitting at his desk and, wiping his avian nose on his sleeve, the thatch of his hair overgrowing his neck and (remarkably large) ears:

"What is hope? . . . you there, Andean Condor!"

The ornithological individual felt the two bright swords of Dom Kuzma's gaze on his avian countenance and promptly identified with that large predatory bird of the Andes.

"Ho- . . . hope is . . . hope is when . . ."

"Come here, I'll whisper it . . . in your ear."

The Condor approached the lectern, hand on ear (as though unsure of his hearing), but Dom Kuzma smacked him on the other ear with his meaty hand. A boy with a funny nose, which gave him a permanent grin, instinctively flinched at the blow to the Condor's ear. That is why Dom Kuzma chose him:

"And what is love, you . . . Duckbilled Platypus?"

"L-love . . . love is . . . when . . ."

". . . when you get one across that snotty duckbill," Dom Kuzma finished for him, while the Platypus's nose made a wet and hollow sound under the blow, letting out a trickle of blood as proof of its virginity.

"Now then. I want you, Seal Penguinsky, to tell him what love is." It was a shortish attentive boy who could not open his mouth for terror. His large eyes suspiciously followed the movement of Dom Kuzma's hands: he was mustering all his scanty cunning to dodge the blow. . . . But it suddenly happened that the boy resolutely raised his head and fixed an impertinent stare on Dom Kuzma's ear. The ear was clearly ashamed at the stare. It began to change color, going pale, reddening, more and more violently, angrily red, into scarlet, purple, the colors of a stormy sky. Thunder and lightning were imminent. The entire class dropped their eyes, hugged their desks, they knew what was coming next. In their minds they were each drawing a terrible, vengeful, murderous ear: everyone knew, now, what was behind the ear-drawing craze. . . . But the ear began to darken into a leaden blue-gray, to a gloomy indigo: the rage had died inside it, leaving only dead, beaten blood. Dom Kuzma let his hands drop to his sides, turned around, and went out of the classroom.

Melkior nearly applauded. What an example of human greatness! He felt curiously unburdened of a grueling thought about Dom Kuzma: all the cruelty of the man's fate was revealed to him in an instant, dimly and darkly. It was indeed the first time that the word had made itself known inside him; soundlessly he said *Fate* and felt moved almost to tears.

"And God saith . . . ," Dom Kuzma was saying majestically; he was creating the world before their very eyes. "And there was light!" Again saith the Lord . . . but Adam and Eve ate the apple and God banished them from Paradise. Dom Kuzma was personally banishing them from the classroom, pointing his forefinger at the door. In the sweat of thy face shalt thou eat bread! And that was where human suffering began. Cain slew his brother Abel; Absalom rebelled against his father David; Jacob fled from his brother Esau and his brothers sold his son Joseph to the Egyptians; Potiphar's wife tempting Joseph; Joseph testing his brothers; Benjamin. The three young men in the fiery furnace; Daniel in the lion's den; Jonah in the whale's belly; David slaying Goliath; the terrible story of Samson who slew thousands upon thousands of Philistines with an ass's jaw but was subdued by a fallen woman who delivered him to the mercy of his enemies. At the point where the accursed Delilah was shearing Samson's hair Dom Kuzma's face was transformed, his words hobbled by bitterness, his eyes veiled with sorrow. Melkior pictured Dom Kuzma standing shorn and blinded in the center of the Philistine temple, his ears protruding in solitude among the pillars. . . . But then Samson, in desperation, called unto the Lord and said, Oh Lord God, remember me, I pray thee, and strengthen me, I pray thee, only this once, Oh God, that I may be at once avenged on the Philistines for my two eyes. And Samson took hold of the two middle pillars upon which the house stood, and on which it was borne up, of the one with his right hand, and of the other with his left. And Samson said, Let me die with the Philistines. And he bowed himself with all his might; and the house fell upon the lords, and upon all the people who were therein. So the dead which he slew at his death were more than they which he slew in his life.

Melkior saw tears of vengeance in his Bible teacher's eyes and, moved and overwhelmed by the story, driven by a passionate desire for the vengeance to be complete and terrible to the end, he asked excitedly in innocent elation, purely out of a feeling of justice:

"Was Delilah there in the temple, too?"

That was when his darling cheeks were slapped.

Melkior interrupted his primary education. He did not want to face Dom Kuzma again. Because of the shame and the humiliation. Because of the fatal misunderstanding. He had not meant to mock the tears in Dom Kuzma's eyes, which may have been there, after all, only in his imagination. . . . But how was he to explain that now? How was he to say, having been slapped in the face, "I was feeling sorry for Samson myself, Father. I only wanted that cow Delilah to be punished, too. That's why I asked . . . Why did you hit me?"

But something strange happened to Dom Kuzma shortly thereafter and he mysteriously disappeared. Gossip had it that he had been dispatched to Rome for a rigorous confession, since only a cardinal (indeed, according to others, the Holy Father himself) could absolve him from certain abominable sins. Later on the word went around that he was with the Benedictines at Monte Cassino, doing penance, and later still that he had been "seen" at the Trappist convent in Mostar, wearing a white rope girdle with severe-denial knots, mortifying his flesh by hunger, thirst, and vigils, and making the fabled Trappist cheese in absolute silence.

Melkior had himself heard a thing or two about the cheese . . . as well as some other things which had elevated Dom Kuzma to biblical martyrdom. Delilah's identity was never fully established. Some suspected the pretty tobacconist who smiled secretively at men; others said it was the spinster schoolmistress who had fallen in love with Dom Kuzma's virility (which she made no effort to conceal).

Then again, perhaps neither of them was the despicable traitress. It may have been a third woman, angel-faced, who snipped off seven locks of Dom Kuzma's hair while he slept and sent them to the bishop himself, with a letter in her own hand, as evidence of his sinful ways. The letter is supposed to have said, "Look how his bare ears stick out now." A terrible piece of mockery.

But why seven locks, no more and no less? Why seven? Might Dom Kuzma have told her, too, in love's sated ease, chuckling with his masculine superiority, how perfidious Delilah stripped Samson of his strength? The omnipotent male would have had his fun while in the arms of the fragile female, relaxed his tired strength, and cynically launched into the story of the mighty Samson and the scheming little bitch . . . and fallen asleep. And she, the tobacconist or the schoolmistress . . . or the third . . . would have leaned over the sleeper's repose and thought: "Look how helpless my Samson is now! Why don't I . . ." and she would have found in the story a wonderful recipe for her long-contemplated revenge. On top of which she might have been after that silly superiority poor females fall prey to only too often . . .

The unknown woman had thus deprived him of all his strength, exposed him to horrible shame. And there he was, the wretch, plodding along in the autumn dusk, emaciated and pale as if he had spent all the intervening years in a dark basement, sharing his crust of black bread with mice and asps and drenching it in bitter tears. His once-strong neck whose veins would writhe furiously when he was angry was now a thin, fragile twig bearing its wrinkled desiccated fruit with the two vast ears as though doing penance.

Melkior moved with effort through the dense throng that spilled across the city on this pleasant warm evening. The fragrance of autumn made itself felt in the freshness of ripe fruit coming from the open windows of fruit stands: odors wafted down the streets like a mild hint preceding a momentous farewell. A yellowed leaf or two fell in the alley, rustling sadly like an old letter from a past happy romance.

Autumn, autumn . . . To the tune of the season's hit the summer had danced away—*Addio, mare*. Autumn had come in on little cat feet over the lawns and greens, the wilted courtesan in rustling silks had walked the parks, her breath making the birches shy like innocent little girls.

Melkior plunged insolently into the warm torrent of bodies, words, smells, looking impatiently for Dom Kuzma's scrawny neck. Using his elbows and shoulders, he forced his way through the thick, tough dough of evening strollers, receiving insults and threats and "underwater" blows to the ribs. But he scarcely minded them. The pathetic soul adrift in the town so occupied his attention that he nearly yelled out loud when all of a sudden he discovered in front of him his poor corporeality preparing to cross the street. Dom Kuzma first cast a cautious look to either side and then, hesitating for a moment as if about to step into crocodile-infested waters, hurriedly crossed the insecure riverbed waving his arms about in a curious way as if really walking on water.

"How prudent he is, the restless soul!" Melkior thought with compassion as he crossed the street with more caution than Dom Kuzma himself.

"Trams are not what kill you nowadays, my dear sir!" remarked a passing stranger to him. He was not drunk, nor was he a meddling sneerer; holding his evening paper open, he was frightened and desperate, and wished to impart his condition to someone. Melkior decided to ignore the man. Of late, since reserve-training calls to the older age groups had begun to multiply, grifters using the "psychological" approach had appeared in town. An operator of that kind would casually cast his hook at a passerby, gauging from afar the extent of the man's generosity. The gullible and considerate mark would easily swallow the bait, and the expert would proceed to hustle him: he had been called up, not that it mattered so much except that there were the wife, the children, the aging parents, the ailing mother-in-law (an angel!), not to mention the rent that was due and he stone broke, and winter on its way . . . God, I'm at my wits' end! And he would flail his arms about in desperation, and his words would flow easily and convincingly and in the blink of an eye he would mesmerize his victim and break any attempt at resistance.

Only the other day a man had been hurrying down the street, striding along at a fast purposeful clip. Topped by a greasy floppy hat, his shoes Chaplinian—each pointing in its own direction—his face stubbly and sad, his look worried, he acknowledged Melkior with a casual, absentminded, and almost careless greeting, as if meeting him for the fifth time that day.

"Hello there, Filipović," and strode on without looking back.

Surprised, Melkior stopped in his tracks and turned. The man did not turn around right away: he merely registered that Melkior had halted. Only a moment later, still hurrying, he looked back a little, out of sheer curiosity, gave Melkior a casual wave of his hand, "Hey there," and a pleasant smile. He was in a hurry though, he had no time for friendly banter on life and health. Melkior was still standing there, sheepishly: he couldn't recall any previous encounter with the face. On the other hand, he knew he had not returned the man's greeting and feared the man might take offense. He was even about to run after him, to explain himself, to apologize. But the man knew what was up, knew Melkior had stopped and was looking after him, so he, too, stopped and looked at Melkior with the smile of someone who was in no mood for smiling. Wagging his head slightly in disapproval, he made toward Melkior at a slow and seemingly patient pace. His whole behavior (when he came close) reflected embarrassment at "such an appearance" before a friend who had not even recognized him in *such a state*.

"Four Eyes," he enunciated with a feeling of utter embarrassment, mourning his cruel fate by way of his sobriquet. "I've changed, sure," he added in elegiac tones, gazing mournfully into his past. His eyes actually went moist . . . or so it seemed to Melkior.

"I really . . . can't . . ." stammered Melkior, himself ashamed for some reason.

"What? You don't remember? Junior year of grammar school, two desks behind you . . . Four Eyes. Rotten grades in Latin the whole time. Ipse dixit, I was so sure I'd fix it—but I couldn't. You went on, I lagged behind. I can still see you as you were then, your clever little head. You had sitting next to you that little . . . what was his name now? . . . Wait, it was something to eat . . ."

"Tokay?"

". . . or drink, see? I knew it had to do with . . ."

Melkior felt ill at ease. For all that he had never in his life known anyone called Four Eyes, this fellow was quite at home in their conversation, had even grasped him by the elbow and was shaking it in the manner of a close friend, waking boyhood memories inside him.

Melkior fell to rummaging in his memory to see if he could winkle out this man Four Eyes from somewhere after all. Perhaps Four Eyes had really existed at some desk behind him as a modest, unobtrusive little schoolboy who was in no way remarkable? Meanwhile Four Eyes was eyeing him hopefully.

"Well? Remember how we put horse chestnuts in the stove in wintertime, the noise they made cracking in class?"

We did indeed . . . only my name isn't Filipović!—and Melkior communicated his reservation to Four Eyes out loud.

"Filipović?" he said in surprise and smacked himself on the forehead. "God, yes, you're right! I've got it all mixed up, it's been years, you know. God, yes, Filipović used to sit next to me, he was always writing riddles, making crosswords, reading words backwards, *tractor—rot cart* . . . Of course, you can't be Filipović when you're . . . er . . ."

"Tresić," Melkior blurted out imprudently.

"But of course, Tresić-Pavičić! Christ, I've got it all . . ."

"No, just Tresić. I'm just Tresić."

"That's it! Why, we even called you Distressić, remember?" said Four Eyes, delighting in his own memory, so much so that Melkior unconsciously confirmed it with a nod, although he had no recollection of anyone ever calling him Distressić. "There must've been others who called you Tresić-Pavičić, too, and you telling them 'Just Tresić,' and it came out 'Distressić.' Somehow or other it just rolls off the tongue together, Tresić-Pavičić, like Rolls-Royce. As if Rolls could not stand on his own without Royce. Silly, isn't it?"

"Yes, it is silly," Melkior agreed and shifted his weight from one foot to the other, which Four Eyes interpreted as impatience and showed fear.

"In a hurry, old boy? Now me, I'm fresh out of the hospital. The old kidney problem. The doctor said, 'We must have it out'—Four Eyes made a sharp gesture as if slicing his own side with his thumb— and I said, 'Not so fast, doc! I'm not having my kidney pickled in alcohol,' I said. And so, my dear Distressić, I lost a nice little job with First Croatian. I went to see the Old Man this morning. 'The Board of Directors meets tomorrow,' he said, 'kindly have your resignation in by then.' 'With a government stamp?' 'Government stamp and all.' 'The usual? The one that costs seventy-five in change?' 'Seventy-five in change.'

"Short and sweet. Goodbye—Goodbye. While I was in hospital, the wife pawned all we had. If only I had something to pawn! . . . but there's nothing left. No job—no credit. I needn't tell you, do I, you know well enough what our damned Scrooges are like. Got money to burn while you may as well croak for want of a piddling seventy five in change!"

Four Eyes fell silent, hanging his head in expectation. It was only out of the corner of his eye that he followed, animal-like, Melkior's embarrassed dive into the inside breast pocket, where wallets are usually stored. And surely enough Melkior took out his wallet . . .

"No, please, I didn't mean . . ." and Four Eyes made a belated attempt to stop his arm . . . "I only told you as an old . . . I've got no one to share my troubles with."

"Unfortunately, I . . ." Melkior stammered shyly. "This is all I've got," he offered Four Eyes a silver fifty-dinar piece and displayed his empty wallet, "Look."

"Heaven forbid!" Four Eyes cried out, flinching as if frightened. "Take a fellow's last penny? Never! I'm not that kind of guy!"

"But it's not my last," Melkior was almost pleading, "I've got some coming tomorrow."

"Are you sure?"

"Quite sure."

"Well then . . . But listen, I don't want you lying to me! If you're lying, then this is charity, and I won't have that!" Four Eyes asserted with pride and added in a confidential tone, "And look, I'd like to ask you as a favor, let's keep this between ourselves, shall we? By the way, where can I find you to pay you back?"

"No problem, we'll be in touch . . ."

"Distressić, old boy, I can't thank you enough. I'll never forget it, so help me God!" He gave Melkior a hurried handshake, looking him in the eyes with sincere gratitude. "Bye then. I'm off to buy the stamps," and he took off at the same hurried purposeful clip with which he had come into view a little while before.

Melkior knew that Four Eyes had duped him, but had been unable to resist the extraordinary form of the effrontery. He then wisely resolved never to heed again any baited hooks thrown his way. So he now thought he'd ignore the Trams-are-not-what-kill-you-nowadays man with the newspaper and to hurry after Dom Kuzma; he had lost him again among the passersby. Nevertheless he cast a glance at the man with the newspaper out of some sort of curiosity. The other perceived the glance as a door that was opened a crack and scuttled right inside:

"It's not the trams that kill you these days, my dear sir, it's this!" and he nodded at the bold headlines in the newspaper.

Melkior read, BOMBS HIT LONDON IN WAR'S WORST RAID and, underneath, "Six Hours of Hell and Horror—Entire Quarters in Flames" . . . But he could picture nothing specific behind those alarming words, no dead child, crushed skull, man despairing over his demolished home and slaughtered family, none of those terrible scenes which were really there behind headlines. Melkior remained indifferent, which seemed to offend the man:

"What do you say to that? Hardly a traffic accident, eh?" he was saying with a bitter smile, proud at being able to comprehend the extent of the horror in the headlines.

"What can I say? You could have read the same thing yesterday and the day before . . ."

"Yesterday and the day before . . . If it was there yesterday and the day before, does that make today less appalling?" the man asked sternly. "You don't have to be a doctor to see that. But of course, doctors see only what it's like to be ill when they get sick themselves. Now, what about when those people over there"—he gestured vaguely with his head—"read about us in the papers one day? When a California doctor starts muttering that the headlines are boring, always the same as yesterday, and the day before? Just because you and yours were spared yesterday and the day before, does that mean you'll be saying today and tomorrow that everything's the same?"

Melkior was finding the conversation strange. . . . And why the devil had this man picked on no one but him?

"Yes, well, people are funny that way," he said, merely to end the unexpected encounter.

"What way?"

"Well . . . if one of us were to be run over by a tram they would be more upset about it than about those thousands killed in the ruins in London. Not because they like us more—simply because they don't want to expend their imagination on things like that."

The man didn't understand what Melkior was on about, and the word *imagination* struck him as downright offensive.

"Imagination?" he asked sternly. He knitted his eyebrows and looked Melkior in the eye with unconcealed disapproval. "Conscience, not imagination! What's there to imagine? Shall I pretend I'm not afraid of war? No, not for myself! Nor for the wife! I told them this morning at the Mobilization Office . . . They gave me papers for Apatin . . . I said, I'm not talking about my wife . . . If there's got to be a war, I said, you won't be canceling it for my wife's sake. Right? But how can I look my fourteen-year-old boy in the eye and pretend to be as full of cheer as if I were going bowling when the child reads the papers and knows that the Jerries broke through the Maginot Line and took France in a month? Children are no longer babes these days. The boy knows where I'm going and he never says a word . . . And I hear the little ones talk: Daddy's going to drive a tank, they say. That's what things have come to!" and the man spread his arms, showed that they were holding nothing, empty helpless arms.

"So you've been . . ." but the man didn't let him finish.

"Called up!" he cried sharply as if cursing God. "There, see for yourself: youngsters strutting about free as birds, picking up girls, while they go calling us up, the class of nineteen hundred! They told me—because I'm a driver with Impex—they told me I'd been reclassified as a tank driver. But I've only seen tanks in the cinema! How on earth am I going to drive one? And Russian—because they say the Russians are going to give us the tanks—Russian tanks are not designed for our kind of terrain, no sir, not by a long shot! That's something for those bigwigs up in Belgrade to sort out, not for a simple driver like myself, right?"

Melkior had been looking in all directions in search of Dom Kuzma and scarcely listened to the argument about the tanks. He asked the man offhandedly, only to be polite:

"Not for our kind of terrain, you say?"

"By no means! Those are steel fortresses, weighing upwards of ninety tons, what use can they be up our hills? This is a mountainous country."

"How strange . . ." said Melkior quite absentmindedly. He was overcome by an odd kind of queasiness at the word *mobilization.* "Mobilizing, aren't they?"

"You bet they are! My best friend's been in since last Tuesday. Class of nineteen hundred, same as me. He's all right, he's a tailor, they didn't post him, he's stitching great coats, sleeping at home. They didn't even cut his hair. And me they're sending to Apatin!"

The man had softened with self-pity, so much so that his eyes went moist. Melkior felt the pointless need to offer consolation which humans resort to when failing to find a better or more sincere feeling.

"Who knows? Perhaps it's only exercises. After all, there's a war on in Europe, nobody wants to be caught by surprise."

"That's just it!" cried the driver with desperation as if Melkior has guessed what he feared most. "That's what Hitler is counting on—surprise!"

Coming quite close to Melkior, he said in a confidential whisper, "There are Jerry spies and fifth columnists everywhere. They've been paddling about in rubber boats since nineteen thirty-seven, photographing the natural wonders. Tourists," and he laughed with bitter irony as if he had found some relief in a shot of stiff drink.

"But you're busy," he added, self-conscious, having noticed Melkior's impatience. "Yes, well, we've all got our worries. Goodbye," and off he went, opening his paper again with an air of importance, like a caring man among the lot of happy-go-lucky fools.

Melkior remained where he was. What was his rush? His pity over Dom Kuzma's fate struck him now as ridiculous. The word *mobilization* had filled him with a feeling of unbearable dread, the restlessness of a terrible anticipation had come over him. This was now something he would have to live with. . . . There appeared (childish, of course) images of deserted streets, of doors and shops boarded up. . . . The dead city has shut itself into its walls, with not a sound to be heard, not a light to be seen. Behind closed shutters cautious matches were struck, papers burned in stoves, things piled into suitcases: people packing, hurrying, leaving. . . . The streets were deserted and silent. The eerie quiet was disturbed only by an occasional government motorcar driving past at breakneck speed; it carried urgent orders: burn the documents . . . submit the report. . . . The echoes of horses' hooves in the night, the whisper of mysterious words among the sentries, top military secrets.

Unrealistic and childish, like Dom Kuzma's Samson story in Melkior's boyhood. Nevertheless Melkior found serious, military pathos in those images. He pictured himself as a muscular, strapping soldier decked out in full army gear (isn't that what they call it) standing at attention in a column of awesome Samsons about to slay the Philistines with the jawbone of an ass. . . . All they were waiting for is the order from the officer on the white charger . . .

Reflected in the plate glass window, among the shoes on display, was Melkior's thin, unprepossessing silhouette, a poorly built city dweller. The slanting image reflected in the shop window triggered a crafty sneer inside Melkior, and the word *mobilization* suddenly found itself in autumn mud churned by a squelching olive drab monotony of dejected strangers on some endless trek; there was the bluster of angry sergeants, the tired voice of sodden boots, and the mysterious word "aide-de-camp." Here was born a fear of the new events around him: the driver bound for Apatin to drive a tank . . . across our mountainous country. . . . Oh for a mountain and a forest in which to go quiet and still like an insect curled deep inside the bark of an indestructible tree: I'm not here . . . and to live, to live. . . . How to conceal one's existence, steal from the world one's traitorous body, take it off to some endless isolation, conceal it in a cocoon of fear, insinuate oneself into temporary death?

Dom Kuzma had no idea that he might be the object of envy. . . . Arriving at a weighing machine tended by an invalid in a passageway, he doffed his hat, ran his handkerchief over his small moth-eaten head with ears—as if two angels were carrying it, ran his handkerchief over his thin sweaty neck and the inside of his hat, donned the hat, put the handkerchief in his pocket and stepped up onto the platform.

The invalid was waiting only for him (it was getting very dark): he stirred obligingly and made a hurried stomp with his wooden leg, put on his thread-reinforced glasses and weighed Dom Kuzma with what might have been due reverence. By all appearances, Dom Kuzma was a good regular customer who had long since earned the man's full confidence. The question of confidence was key here.

The patient whose life depends on testimony from a common weighing machine is likely to have little confidence in a commercial device (which was after all invented for the purpose of deceiving), and even less in its master. He is suspicious and thinks everyone is out to con him, to do him out of several precious decagrams, of the last thing supporting his life—his very life, my friend!

Dom Kuzma waited anxiously for the fateful amount which meant *to be or not to be*. He actually fiddled with the arms of the scale and had some words with the invalid, brushing the latter's hand away impatiently, but calmed down eventually and made his peace with the scale, collected his ticket and went away, worried.

It seemed to Melkior that he was witnessing a crafty rite designed to test the grace of God, if not His actual existence. With intellectual embarrassment, as if he were extending his palm to be read by a palm-reading neighbor, he stepped onto the platform with an anxious heart. Apatin is a town on the Danube, he thought, or the brand name of an anti-apathy drug. . . .

"How much?" he asked the invalid, faking a casual tone.

"Sixty-one kilos, seven hundred and eighty grams."

"It can't be!" he cried in alarm.

"Oh yes it can," replied the invalid with self-confidence. He was used to the bickering of skinny clients.

"What? Why, I'm . . ."

"You're skinny enough to weigh that much," said the invalid with a doctor-like cynicism. "My machine does not steal," he added for the sake of his reputation. "Don't worry, we earn our bread fair and square."

"I'm not worrying about it stealing," he used a smile to explain his meaning. "What I'd like to know is, does it give a little?"

"Neither. The true weight whatever the freight."

"And that . . . that priest fellow . . . how did he fare?"

"Same as this morning."

"You mean he was here this morning as well to . . . ?"

"Oh yes. Twice a day he shows up." The invalid had visibly had enough of the pointless conversation; he was finding Melkior's curiosity a bit suspicious: "This fellow's too nosey by half . . ."

"Could it be a case, then, of mortification of the flesh?" insisted Melkior. "He may be trying to become a saint for all you know."

"I don't know what saints you have in mind, but he's a subscriber, if you must know. Pays in advance by the month, he does. Third year running."

"Third year? And he weighed more then—three years ago, I mean—than he does now, didn't he?"

"Not up to anything funny, are you?" the invalid shot a glance at the newspaper in Melkior's hand. "He tipped them at eighty-plus to begin with. He was so strong his eyes flashed. Now he barely makes fifty-six. And that's with my help."

"Your help?" Melkior felt fear at the technical term. So the scrawny neck did not come of the cellar and penance at Monte Cassino? To the invalid he said hypocritically, "Well, there you are, it's like I said: he's bound for sainthood."

"Ahh," the invalid waved his hand compassionately, "he's bound for Mother Earth, that's where he's bound. He's got this wasting disease, poor man, and every single gram he's lost has been registered by me—and my old gal," and he gave the machine's iron neck a chummy slap. "The twenty-six kilos he's lost so far, that's nothing. He never noticed how I slashed them, I did it all little by little. He knows I took them away, of course he does, but he's not said a word to me about it. But when it's a question of ten grams . . . you're killing me, he mutters, you're killing me indeed."

Melkior thought back: perhaps it was all due to the loss of those seven locks while he was sleeping?

"And now I have to drop him by over eight hundred grams a month. The man's dying on my machine, as it were, before my eyes, and I have to keep a record of it day in and day out. I'm having a hard time of it, but what can I do?" The invalid was not lying, he genuinely felt for Dom Kuzma. "I give him anything up to sixty grams of an evening, to set him up nicely for bed, but come morning I bring him down by a hundred and twenty. He hangs his head, there are tears in his eyes, he doesn't believe me; you're lying, he says, how could I have possibly lost so much overnight? Your machine's out of whack, he says, get it fixed! I'm a human being, don't forget! and he cries with fear. He goes to the blind colleague over there on the corner, who consoles him—by mutual agreement, shall we say—with a couple of grams. But then he won't believe him either, and comes back to me again, the pest.

"Your machine's good, he says, all things considered. On second thought, he says, you *can* lose weight overnight, through the digestive process and so on. . . . All the same you should keep an eye on it, you should indeed! As for that man on the corner, his contraption's no good at all. If you ask me, he says, his license should be revoked. Chose a corner position, no less! You think he's really blind? That's their cover, no doubt about it. . . . And I have no choice but to say yes. Now then, he says, let's have another go in the name of God. So I weigh him again, pressing a wee bit, to reassure him. I've driven this here nail into my peg leg for him special, and I press the bottom bar, careful like, as if I am squeezing drops into his eye. But he smells a rat, thinks the measure's now too good all of a sudden, and he won't believe me. Go on, he says, press your scale! There will be somebody to press the scale for you, too, when your soul is weighed before God! And off he goes, all angry and unhappy. He was unhappy just now, too, over weighing the same as he did this morning. He'd had the feed of his lifetime, he said . . . he even showed me his belly. There he is now, over at the other fellow's, he may yet be back here again. I feel sorry for him, you might say. The man's wasting away like a leaf in autumn, and all I can do is look on. Not to mention that he still owes me over two kilos."

"Oh, you give credit then?" Melkior joked to hide his feeling of shock. The invalid did not like the joke and let it pass with a sigh:

"Ahh, he's to be pitied, believe me."

"Pitied indeed," Melkior echoed in all sincerity, but presently hastened to undo it, "and yet conceivably he can retrieve his kilos, while you can't get your leg back. Your loss is greater than his."

"But he's going to die!" the invalid cried didactically.

"Meaning you won't? Haven't you in fact been at death's door, weren't you dying in Galicia when the Russian Emperor's brotherly shell kissed your leg? And later on, in the field hospital in Káposvár or somewhere, bedbugs eating you as punishment, as if you'd invented war! 'Wasting away,' indeed! Come off it, man!"

Without bothering to collect his ticket, Melkior hurried over to the corner where Dom Kuzma was standing on the blind man's weighing machine, leveling the arms himself, seeking a balance for them. His fingers were trembling in the prayer wherein he supplicated God to stretch forth his arms and show His mercy by way of the arms of the scale. And, lo and behold, God lent him a hand, Dom Kuzma stepped down, elated, and began hurriedly emptying his pockets, as if preparing to rob himself. He piled his keys, wallet, watch, coin purse, breviary, and handkerchief and other odds and ends on the small bench next to the scale. He even took off his hat—and stepped back up. The inspired machine mercifully overlooked the fact that the client had divested himself of a thousand grams and showed his previous weight with a smile. In vain did the priest and the blind man shake and whack it (Dom Kuzma actually struck it)—it stood firmly by its statement, suffering for the truth.

Dom Kuzma took offense at the act of consolation. What was the point of sprucing up reality so stupidly? "Damn you," he said and decided to weigh himself once again, with all his possessions back in place.

The scale now gave a joyous leap of a full one thousand two hundred grams and stood steadfastly by its assertion. It bore all the torture unleashed upon it by its frightened rider, stubbornly repeating what it had said before. The martyr. Its beaklike weights were seeking each other with the yearning of amorous birds, to come together in an everlasting kiss of equilibrium, harmony, and peace.

"At last!" Dom Kuzma sighed with relief and gave his blessing to the innocent kiss. "See?" he said to the blind man. "Obviously it got it wrong the first time. It's not without reason that I keep telling you to have it fixed. Oh well, third time's a charm, as they say . . ." He paid the blind man twice as much as usual, but warned him before leaving, "Anyway, you'd do well to have it checked. You'll lose your customers, my friend!" and away he went, his faith shaken in all the scales in the world.

"How interesting," thought Melkior, himself feeling a weakened confidence in the invalid's machine. Dom Kuzma's mistrust was weighing on him; God only knew how many tricks of the trade those people had up their sleeves. . . . Nevertheless he stepped onto the blind man's machine.

"Oh Eustachius the Long Lost! Oh Ineffable Eustachius!" called out a clarion voice behind his back. Melkior broke out in goose bumps: he had a sudden feeling of standing stark naked on the scale watched by all the passersby. He pretended the cries had nothing to do with him: he went on talking with the blind man.

"Defies the imagination, gentlemen, defies the imagination!"

The man with the clarion voice was laughing an ugly laugh, baring front teeth pocked with large dark fillings. "An intellectual, a Schweik, speculating on the weighing machine. Look at him! Take a good look, all you sharp-eyed people! The military speculator! Heh, heh, heh . . . Going to the blind man! Good-looking people!"

Passersby stopped and watched with interest. Somebody asked his neighbor: What did he steal? You were here when it started, weren't you?

No one knew anything about the curious incident, nor was anyone able to make sense of it. Was there going to be a brawl?

The drunkard had come right up to Melkior and was touching his ears, his chin, displaying him to the audience as if he were a carnival barker showing off a freak dwarf, a two-headed pig, a shark that had devoured a Swedish tourist . . .

The blind man extended both hands to fend off the drunkard, but the other pressed a two-dinar coin into each: "Not a lot, but it's the gesture that counts," and patted them.

The audience was now expecting an amusing spectacle: the man was totally drunk. . . . Having got his first laughs, the drunkard went on with his makeshift show.

"So, dear bard," he addressed the blind man, "how heavily does the fear of war weigh upon the mind of this Eustachius the Peaceable?"

"What's this nonsense? You're mad!" Melkior whispered in his ear.

"How about you, *Monsieur Boulechite?*" the drunkard addressed a short stout man who was grinning with glee and stroking his ear with pleasure. "What do you think of my madness?"

"Listen, you . . . !" the short fatty took offense. "Watch it or I'll box your ears in, you . . . !"

"Oh, that I will, you . . . Stroking your ear, I see? Is that ear your breadwinner by any chance, working in the capacity of eldest son for May I See Your ID Card Ltd? If so, please treat it paternally; such an ear is worth more than seven plump cows. Also, by all means protect it from contact with heavy fists wearing bulky rings."

Fatty had not been able to pull the right strand out from that tangle of words: he was thrown off by "ID card" and "heavy hands." He plunged sensibly in among the overcoats and umbrellas, muttering unlikely threats.

The drunkard meanwhile leapt onto the platform of the weighing machine, waved his hat and shouted: "Drive on, *izvoshchik!*" He had one arm around Melkior's neck, waving with the other and clucking his tongue: driving horses . . . and, closing his eyes, enraptured, he began reciting Yesenin:

. . . a troika is dashing across the field
but I'm not on it—someone else is instead . . .
My joy and my happiness, where have you fled? . . .

and tears welled in his eyes. He kept repeating "My joy and my happiness, where have you fled?" as tears streamed down his cheeks.

The onlookers watched as he wildly drove the troika on the weighing machine, tears flowing from his eyes, and someone whispered respectfully, "He's crying." And he, perhaps having heard the whisper of sympathy with his grief, suddenly jumped off the machine and bared his dark fillings in a grin.

"Eustachius Equivalentovich, I haven't got a kopeck to my name, you pay the *izvoshchik*," he said to Melkior. "Citizen Ferdyshchenko, I think it's time to shut up shop," and on the overcoat button of a curious passerby who had just stopped to see what was going on he surreptitiously hung a CLOSED sign he had kept tucked under his overcoat, having apparently lifted it from a shop door. The curious citizen had no idea anything was hanging down his belly and was laughing with the others. Meanwhile Melkior was still standing on the scale sweating in dismay. He'll slink away as soon as Ferdyshchenko spots the sign, and then Ferdyshchenko will take it out on me . . .

"Tell me, Ugo," he said pleasantly, "where might I find you later on?"

"Ugo, quoth he! Have you forgot my Giventakian moniker?"

"Parampion, I mean. Where will you be later this evening?" Melkior corrected himself patiently.

"Now you're talking! At Hotel Pimodan, dear Eustachius, of

course, at Hotel Pimodan . . . or, in our parlance, at the Give'nTake. Everybody will be there. They are looking for you. . . . Maestro the Mad Bug has been asking after you for months. Over and over he asks: where's our sagacious Eustachius? Don Fernando will be there, too, for a change. Do come."

"I'll be right behind you. There's just a thing or two I . . ."

But Ugo was no longer listening. He had already turned around to face the audience and was bowing to someone in Spanish ceremonial style:

"My humble respects to the noble hidalgo!" It was the choleric tobacconist who was busily closing his little corner kiosk for the night and had looked back to see what the monkey business was all about. "Your generosity, señor, will surely harvest a cigarette on the tobacco island o'er which you rule?"

The tobacconist took this as an insult. He resolutely dropped his keys into his pocket, muttering angrily, "Damned spongers." And spat as he left.

"But, sir, what if the tuberculosis you just spat out comes back to your daughter on the eve of her marriage as her paternal dowry? You cannot be too careful. Therefore, no spitting on the floor, gentlemen! Right, Comrade?" he said to a man with a bicycle putting up posters.

"Right," said the cyclist, proud at being addressed.

"And what are these, swastika posters? Not by any chance working for the German consulate, are you, von Velocitas? Dropping hooks among us, eh?"

"No," the cyclist laughed artlessly, "I work for Franck-O."

"For Franco? Well, well! I *said* you were up to some Fascist business. Working for the Caudillo himself! So how's General Queipo de Llano? Getting old, isn't he? Hemorrhoids, confession, come over all holy?"

"Listen, you!" the bill-sticker went serious. "A joke is a joke, but this . . . ! Me and the Fascists? Think I'm crazy, do you?" The last sentence was directly linked with his right hand, which had already handed the bicycle to the left . . .

But Parampion . . . was his grinning mug to be punished for the mischievous little game of the harlequin who was performing his silly show inside his head?

"Bicycletissime!" he cried with delight and went on in a sober, bright, and solemn tone, "May I, before the honorable folk of this ancient, royal, free, capital city, firmly shake your hand for your proud and manly revulsion at the idea of being in any way connected with mankind's greatest enemy, illiterate Fascism!" and he grabbed the cyclist's abovementioned right hand, all ready to do a job of another kind, and pumped it thoroughly to mark "eternal friendship." There was even a kiss to the man's brow, the seal on the covenant.

The well-pleased employee of Franck-O, whose job it was to stick up posters advertising the Franck factory's chicory coffee substitute, was happily excited over the public proclamation of his political integrity.

"And now, gentlemen," Ugo addressed the audience, "I'm off . . . perhaps to Pampeluna. This concludes our Street Treat Show for today. We wish our listeners a very pleasant goodnight. The anthem —and we're done. A *propos*, *bicycletissime*, would Your Velocipederasty happen to have a cigarette to spare?"

"Make it two, make it two," and the cyclist took out a large pigskin cigarette case, filled to bursting. "Here you are, help yourself."

"I thank you from the heart of my bottom! No, no, only one, for what the Ragusan gentry called *harmonious memory*. Then again . . . perhaps another one for my Eustachius. No, not a parrot, it's that friend of mine on the weighing machine. Certain specialists he has been seeing prescribe smoking for his condition. Look, I've got him riled, heh, heh . . . Right, thanks a million and a half. Such a velocipederastic gesture shall never be forgotten. Hail, fair knight!" exclaimed Ugo.

Taking three steps backward he made a flourish with his hat, bowing to the cyclist in a ceremonial manner. He then shot Melkior a quick glance and burst out laughing.

"Hah, good-looking people, pay attention, he's angry. No, both

smokes are for me actually, and the third . . . if I may, bicycletissime"
—and he slipped one more cigarette from the posterer's case—"the
third I will give him tonight at the Give'n Take. He's ashamed of me
for the moment, but as a rule I enjoy his affection and respect. And
you, honorable Mr. Ferdyshchenko . . . open Sesame!"—and he
surreptitiously lifted the CLOSED sign from Nosey's belly. Nosey took
offense at the drunkard handling his person for a second time and
calling him what could only be an insulting name, but he wanted to
be sensible and only said in a cautious mutter:

"Wonder who these scoundrels mooch off."

"And now, gentlemen, hah . . . you thought I was off to a place
called Pampeluna? No, they were wrong! I am now off to Pantogegone. And Pantogegone is . . . nothing. Zero, *nihil, nitchevo!*
Adieu, perhaps *pour toujours*, you never can tell . . ."

Ugo elbowed his way through the crowd toward a passerby on the
other side of the street, cadged a light off of him and went on his way
singing *Auprès de ma blonde* without a care in the world.

Melkior remained alone before the crowd of disappointed spectators, like a culprit who was now to answer for the letdown. They
were looking at him as if he had invited them to a show which had
not amused them and they would now ask him to explain. Indeed,
he began behaving as though he had really wronged the disgruntled
mob . . .

"All I want to know is, who these scoundrels mooch off?" repeated the curious citizen with the CLOSED sign. His question had
now been asked aloud of all those present; they were duty-bound to
supply an answer. "Hah!" shrugged one of those who sees through
everything, in a scandal-mongering tone. "Clear enough, isn't it?
Couldn't you see how they did it? Making like that Mexican general
was his pal, all the 'bicycletimus,' 'bicycletimus' hocus-pocus, a real
circus, the sneak, with this guy on the weighing machine playing his
second, making a fool of the poor blind man. . . . It's all stage-
managed, gentlemen, and now you may as well check your pockets
and see if you're missing anything. Well, I'm not; I've been to Mexico, I know all their tricks."

Like marionettes linked to a single string pulled by the experienced Mexican, all those present went through identical swift and anxious motions. There was a round of nervous patting of chests, sides, hips, all the places where pockets are to be found. One man even checked whether his wedding ring was still on his finger . . .

There was a sudden "Oh no!"—a cry of utter dismay. All arms stopped dead and all eyes stared at the desperate man. He stood there like a man stunned, his arms in an X across his chest, patting his empty pockets; his eyes rolling from one bystander to another seeking help.

Melkior looked at the victim of the theft: naturally, everyone could see his astonishment at recognizing the man as Four Eyes! His innocent idea to slip away unnoticed (he had no wish to be present when the pickpocket was nabbed) now turned out to have been naïve. It soon became clear to him that he had been, at the Mexican's suggestion, tacitly proclaimed a thief himself! A thief or partner to a thief.

Under the accusation of those terrible looks which demanded that he come clean, Melkior quite foolishly stared at Four Eyes in tense expectation of . . . what? Proof of his innocence?

He himself did not know what he had expected of Four Eyes. He might possibly have been hoping against hope that Four Eyes hadn't yet recognized him . . . the business the other day . . . the Distressić thing . . . Meanwhile Four Eyes was giving him a tearful, tragic look, one full of pleading and martyrlike forgiveness (which did not go unnoticed). Then, turning his uncertain and confused gaze somewhere aside, he said in a voice so tearful as to be almost inaudible (but it *was* audible) . . . for he was accusing no one, it was only that his paternal heart was breaking:

"I was going to buy shoes for my boy . . . Daddy, he said, make them one size too big, I'm growing. The poor little fellow, that he should have to think about such things. And here's autumn coming, the rains . . . The child will be off to school soon."

The scoundrel's been reading Dostoyevsky, Melkior thought hastily.

"Did you lose much?" somebody asked in a voice moved nearly to tears.

"My wallet with twelve hundred inside. And all my papers." Then he added, after a well-measured pause, crying out from the bottom of his heart, appealing to all of mankind, "If only he would let me have my ID back! These are serious times."

It was touching. A woman's eyes filled with tears. The poor man, his child walking around barefoot and all he wants back is his ID card! Someone hit on the idea of notifying the police. . . . But Four Eyes didn't care much for that idea: he opposed it vigorously, going on at very suspicious lengths: "No, no, please! Fair's fair, we must show some understanding . . ."

"Listen, you!" spoke up the cyclist all of a sudden, angrily grabbing Four Eyes by the elbow. "Who d'you think you're kidding? You never had a wallet to begin with. Listen folks, he only showed up here a second ago, right after the bloke from Mexico asked what might be missing from our pockets."

"Good heavens, me?" Four Eyes rolled his eyes, the very picture of a martyred saint appealing to God to be his witness. "I who have been here all along? Here, this gentleman will tell you whether I've been standing behind him or not! Didn't you accidentally tread on my foot and very politely say you were sorry? Here, look, the footprint's still there."

The Mexican was the gentleman who had accidentally trod on his foot. He confirmed it with a nod.

"The footprint's still there my eye! I'll give you a footprint across your thieving mug! He only got here a minute ago, and the first thing he did was to ask me if the coppers had been around! As if I didn't know you, you lush! You'd barter God's child's shoes for booze, you would! What will he think of next, the creep!"

"Did you hear him, folks?" moaned the grief-stricken Four Eyes. "As if robbing you blind wasn't enough, they call you a drunk in the bargain!"

"Clear enough, isn't it? That's their method all right," said the Mexican grimly, terribly disappointed by something in this world.

"Tell the truth and they'll say you're a drunk; tell a lie and they'll buy you a drink. Ptui!" he spat out vehemently and began to push his way out of the circle around the weighing machine. "Let me through before I ram someone's teeth down their throat . . ." and so saying he gave Melkior another once-over glance.

Melkior's knees buckled for an instant. The Mexican's threat had met with approval, and Four Eyes' unheard-of nerve had found a home with the guardians of the sanctity of private property. Melkior decided it was time he lit out from the circle of these highly honorable men, even at the risk of having them yell "Stop thief!" after him. He stepped down from the weighing machine and tried to elbow through by way of the (so-called) "Mexican's Passage," but there was instantly a general mumbling . . . and a closing of the passage. They meant to have the thief identified (and should there be a brawl as well, so much the better).

This emboldened Four Eyes. The cyclist had failed to shake his reputation. . . . Impertinently he stepped out in front of Melkior:

"Hey, not so fast, young man! What about my money? Someone's got to answer for it!"

"You go ahead," and the cyclist gave Melkior a protective nod. He then let his left hand take charge of the bicycle, putting his right on his hip and facing Four Eyes:

"All right, *I'll* answer for it!"

"H-how do you mean . . . you'll answer for it?" stammered Four Eyes, his courage evaporating. "I'm only asking that my money be searched for, no offense meant. . . . We're only human, aren't we? No need to get all hot and . . . But it's got to be fair!"

Melkior then made a gesture of utterly stupid magnanimity: he took out his wallet with several hundred-dinar notes stacked in it and offered one to Four Eyes.

"Here you are. I'm sure the others will want to give you something, too, but please leave me alone."

Four Eyes extended a greedy hand for the money, but the cyclist pushed it aside, scarcely bothering to choose the kindest way of doing so.

"Why?" wondered Four Eyes. "You can see the gentleman is willing to give it to me. Is that how to be?" he said with mild reproach and made another try to take hold of the note.

Angered by his manner, the cyclist slapped his outstretched hand and compounded the act by making a fist and pushing it up under his nose.

"Go on, have a sniff," he said generously, as if offering him an orange, but the other turned his head aside with a grimace of irritation and disgust.

"Queasy, eh? But other people's money smells nice, is that it?"

"What other people's? I was robbed . . ." But this sounded like retreat.

Four Eyes was indeed backing down, defending himself with a muffled mutter of what sounded like curses. Once outside the circle, he heaved a soul-deep sigh of "Oh, the honest man's burden!" and went away at his habitual businesslike clip.

The audience, too, began to disperse, disappointed.

"Rogues, all of them, I'm telling you, one as bad as the other. It's anyone's guess whether he was robbed or not."

That was the ear-stroking citizen, disgruntled at the matter having been left unsettled.

"He'd have hardly spoken like that if he hadn't been, would he?"

"Oh come on, it's only thieves nowadays who shout 'Stop thief.'"

Only Melkior and the cyclist remained. The blind man was there, too, but he was pottering about his machine, covering it with its oilcloth cover (for the night), and was so intent on it as to be actually absent.

Melkior felt the uneasy accident of his position and said "There" and, a little later, "Thank you" and, in his confusion, buttoned his raincoat up wrong.

"Yes, well," said the cyclist, ill at ease himself, but then he remembered Four Eyes: "The thieving scoundrel! The shoes old Owl says he wants to buy his boy . . . when the rotten lush hasn't got a cat to call his own."

"Owl?" Melkior voiced his surprise. "But isn't his name . . . ?"

"Nah! Everybody calls him Owl. God knows what his real name

might be. He does the rounds of the bars at night, rolling the drunks, and sleeps in attics by day. The other day he nearly set our book-keeper's house on fire. He was playing with matches, some old papers caught fire . . . the firemen had a job getting him out of the smoke."

The cyclist was silent for a moment, then shyly asked:

"That other fellow . . . is he a friend of yours?"

"Yes. Don't mind his behavior, he was a bit . . ."

"Mind?" said the cyclist genially. "I like his kind. He made fun of us all and went away singing. He can't be a bad man." He then asked in a confidential tone:

"Do you by any chance have any connections with the news-papers?"

"Yes I do. I write for one."

"Well, uh . . . what's the word about us getting into the war?"

"I don't write anything political . . . but they say we might . . ." Melkior shuddered as if they were invoking the devil.

"Well, it wouldn't surprise me at all if Hitler bit off more than he can chew here in the Balkans! Mark my words!" said the cyclist with fervid conviction. "We may meet again somewhere. You're an honest man," he added with a cheery laugh, then mounted his bicycle and, tossing Melkior a "Bye now!" sped off down the street.

What's this? The words were thought soundlessly and had a blind man's meaning of: Where am I? All of a sudden everything seemed strange: the streets, the trams, the houses, the people . . . even the human faces themselves. He had been transported here in his sleep, he had woken up on the corner by the weighing ma-chine. . . . He felt ashamed, naked as he was, he feared they might be watching him, those passersby and those women up there leaning out of windows and laughing in such a . . .

"You didn't pay for the weighing!" The blind man's rude voice brought him back to familiar relationships. He paid the fee. The small task reminded him of his other duties. In his pocket he still had a ticket for a film with von Stroheim and Viviane Romance, but instead of going to see it he had followed Dom Kuzma down the path of childhood memories. . . . And ended up by the weighing machine . . . weight control . . . *Ta-ta-taaa, ta-ta-taaa, ta-ta-ta-ta-ta-taaa* . . . the bugler from the barracks was announcing the sad taps of army life. He started down the dark alley of the 35th Regiment, and the sad go-to-sleep tune robbed him of any desire to go up to his rooms across from the barracks.

He was treading on autumn leaves. The leaves rustled with a withered voice . . . *and I remembered my sweet dreams; happy days, where are you now?* the song inside him complemented the rustling of leaves underfoot. He was supposed to do a review of the film that night in time for the next day's issue. Beautiful Viviane Romance played debauched vamps. He was overcome with sadness every time he saw a film of hers. And his heart fluttered inside him for Viviana, the woman he had so dubbed for the sake of purging his love, sad and hopeless . . .

The autumnal melancholy. The aimless streets, the web of tangled dreams. A warm south wind caressing his features with a harlot's breath; he ran his hand over his face, revulsed.

On the corner glowed the letters of the Give'nTake, blinking on and off, winking to the passerby, "Come on in, have a drink, have a laugh." Melkior, too, understood their wink. He had passed the place twice already, the blue Give'nTake winking to him from above: "Come on in, don't sulk, Viviana's here."

Viviana, here? That was why he was not going in. How many times lately had he responded to the hint by defying the malicious destiny beckoning to him. "Come on in, come on in, she's here." He had resisted, letting time heal . . . or however it was that the saying went. But tonight it had extended its magical finger, tracing Viviana's name in the dust . . .

Behind the steamy glass panels there was an orgy of laughter and, surely enough, Ugo's voice.

"They are having a good time of it," he said like a miser watching others squander their fortunes, and decided to move on. But suddenly he spun around and in he went. The bell above the door (fitted to chime after the fleeing drunkard) dutifully announced Melkior's entrance.

Another drunken night, smoke and antics, he thought with a touch of malice. Where's it all going to end? But Maestro was already wheezing in a cloud of smoke—"Ah, at last, here comes Eustachius the Sagacious!"—and Ugo was rushing up to meet him and showering kisses on both cheeks, one of them planted on the eyebrow "for the pure mind." The entire bar had to hear that Eustachius had returned from his splendid isolation. Using sweeping oratorical gestures and most scrupulously chosen words—with a special bow to the cash-register girl, *"Madam!"*—all according to Giventakian ritual, Ugo delivered an *éloge* in honor of his friend.

Melkior made his shy way through the clamor and rhetoric and headed for the familiar table at the foot of the bar, where the full complement of the "boys" was sitting.

"Approach, Eustachius the Lampion, approach the Parampion Brethren," howled Maestro, pulling Melkior down into the chair next to him. "I'm no longer the Mad Bug, I'm the Inspired Bug—a new title, acquired during your absence," he confided. His nose tonight was like a ripe plum and his hands were shaking badly.

A man not too old but already dissipated, a brandy-soaked drunk, the City Desk editor. His fingers and teeth were black with nicotine, his mouth reeked with the odor of an animal's lair. He got ahold of Melkior's neck and blew the horrible breath into his face.

Melkior coughed, expelling Maestro's "inspiration," and nearly choked with revulsion. He longingly remembered his peaceful room with his books; the blank white sheets of paper passionately offering themselves—"Write upon us"—he, watching the play of the flames in the cast iron stove and saying, "Wait until I've come up with the right words for you, my chaste little virgins."

Female titters at the "virgins" splashed upon the play of the flames and put them out. She was here! He also knew that she was with Freddie: the man's cloying breakfast-spread voice was clearly audible. He was just in the process of generously presenting her and that other female at the table with the outer leaves of his cabbagelike wit. Melkior monitored the voices from *the other* table with both ears and transmuted them into the evil and bitter flowers of his envy.

Ugo spoke movingly, with tears in his eyes, about Melkior's "return" and finally asked the owner of the Give'nTake to pronounce a word or two of welcome.

"And now it is your turn, Papa Thénardier, to welcome the return of your favorite customer."

"Oh, nonsense, I'm not much at making speeches," stalled the owner with a dismissive wave of his hand. "I have no favorites among you, it's a pleasure to welcome any and all of you here . . ." which actually meant: I am over the moon . . .

Nevertheless he put up with the "Parampion Brethren," even encouraged them, as a kind of advertisement for his establishment. He was aware of the tongue-in-cheek mockery of their dubbing him Thénardier, but business was business, damn it. The unruly gang, "artsy types and bohemians," drew the theatrical and journalist crowd; the masterful pranks, the salvos of laughter, who wouldn't down a drink just to watch them! Mouths cramped with leering, throats scratchy with laughter, let's have another round, by God, this beats the circus any day of the week!

Ugo's inspired scenes were more useful than the blue neon tubes flashing *Give'nTake* above the entrance; knowing this, Thénardier even took some pride in his "arty moniker." They all had funny nicknames, well, it was apparently the thing to do with this crackpot set, and he permitted himself, for the sake of business, to act the role of "Papa Parampion, otherwise known as honorable Thénardier," as Ugo had once proclaimed him to be. All the same, he kept a Thénardierian eye on things, seeing to it that glassware breakage was kept to a minimum and the bills duly settled—or at least entered on a tab—and a zero or two was even added to the bill when the brethren went too heartily into their frolicking.

"No, no, Papa Thénardier, I want you to tell it straight: who is your absolute favorite?" insisted Ugo, shoving the man's long equine head toward Melkior's. "As Christ said of the lost sheep: he rejoiceth more of that sheep than of the ninety and nine which went not astray. Say it, Papa, like Christ in the Bible: I rejoice most in Melkior Tresić, the lost one."

"Eustachius Lampion the Ineffable!" Maestro wheezed professorially, as if Ugo had got a historical name wrong.

"No, Maestro, sorry! For the moment he's still Melkior Tresić the Apostate. There's rehabilitation in the offing, before full privileges may be restored. . . . For half a year (rhetorical pathos) he has been purifying his mind of Give'nTake smoke, inhaling inspirations from the fragrant ozone of the soul's storms, fattening his head with sagacious volumes. . . . Shutting himself away in his room and himself, not answering the door, hiding out like a culprit or someone with bad debts, veiling himself like a nun or a lovely doe-eyed virgin from the lustful looks of this low and crass world . . . Given up smoking, started going to the blind invalid to weigh his hermit's body prior to boarding the next God-bound aeroplane. . . . In short: he entered a loftier sphere of being and opted for the miserable life of a solitary sage dwelling in silence and contemplating his mortal navel with tear-filled eyes. . . . He has quite possibly fallen in love . . . (her laughter and Melkior's saintly pallor) but we shall leave that satisfaction to his destiny. . . . Nevertheless, brethren, he is back among us in his penitent's sackcloth (Melkior remembered Dom Kuzma), ready to drink his full of Giventakian smoke and Parampionic wit! Once again he is our Eustachius the Lampion . . ."

"Imbecile and ass!"

This was interjected by Freddie, who followed it up with a provocative leer. He then leaned toward Viviana's ear. Melkior watched her at that moment: first she had a surprised face as she listened to Freddie's whispers, then she burst out laughing. The overripe hollow-eyed actress sitting with them was enjoying the slur.

And all because of the "five, six female fans," thought Melkior.

In a review during the previous season he had described Freddie as acting like a hairdresser for five or six female fans, and lisping through his lines. If I'd let him have twelve hundred would that have made it right? Ah, five or six was far too few for this head of Hermes.

But Melkior had put the *five or six* there on purpose, using the measly number to slam him in passing. Which was ridiculous. Freddie was why women drank poison, slit their wrists, leaped from windows, dyed their hair, left their husbands—all for Freddie's love. For his love?—oh, that would have been too much joy—for a promise over the phone: tonight, Madam, I play for you alone. And indeed he played *for her alone*, she believed he was playing *for her alone* and inside her she said "my darling."

Freddie, the ideal young lover. The physique, the head, the shoulders, the arms, the legs, everything, everything about him was simply marvelous! The way he walked, sat down, crossed his legs, tapped his cigarette on his silver cigarette case, the way he lit it . . . he definitely oozes charm, they said, already melting in his imaginary embrace.

Freddie's acting style is certainly worthy of a better-class hairdresser. . . . Also, he has a coy lisp . . . he couldn't even deliver the "imbecile and ass" line properly. . . . But Melkior was hunting for her gaze, seeking a wise *objective* state, wishing to rise above his suffering, to be pure, to be pure . . .

She laughed at Ugo's quips and her moist eyes immediately pasted his derisive words all over Melkior. Damn the Parampion, can't he give it a rest?

His rhetorical raptures cut short by Freddie's taunt, Ugo sliced through his formal speech as if with a sword. He turned to face the actor's table and clicked his heels military style, his expression solemn and stern:

"I'm sure I needn't slap you or toss a glove in your face. Accept my formal challenge: at seven o'clock tomorrow morning I shall be expecting you at the upper Maksimir Lake with witnesses at my side. Bring the sword from *Henry IV*, you episodic nobody. I shall bring a fork upon which I will impale you at five past seven, on the dot."

The bar echoed to an explosion of guffaws.

The bartender at the bar burst into a titter and dropped a bottle of a costly beverage; he was in for two months' work without pay.

Melkior sought her: . . . she was laughing, her shoulders were shaking. Freddie seemed to give her a warning kick under the table, she went serious all of a sudden: why, it's "us" they're . . . oh my, well, it was funny all the same. She was embarrassed, caught out.

After delivering his challenge to duel, Ugo spun on his heel and marched back to his table. They poured him a rewarding glass, which he drained and then burst out laughing himself. Somebody exclaimed in admiration, Now there's an actor and no mistake!

Perhaps it was the exclamation that revealed the extent of the insult to Freddie. He stood up, his face pale, and adjusted his tie. He was prepared to take Ugo on.

She intervened. Suddenly afraid of something, she tugged at his sleeve, "No, Freddie, can't you see he's drunk." He had in fact been counting on someone tugging his sleeve (he had a new suit on, white shirt, and tie); he bent down and kissed her hand. He gave his chair an unnecessary little jerk and sat down again. He even smiled like a better sort of gentleman who was not having anything to do with lowlifes.

"There, there, everything's all right again," she purred, stroking his hand.

"All the same, Fred, you should have knocked him a proper one across the snout," said the hollow-eyed actress in her dark voice. "Clobber the brutes, that's the only way." She was very dissatisfied at the outcome of the incident.

"Come off it!" countered *she*. "Do you want him to brawl with the gutter?"—and the "gutter" was loosed straight at Melkior.

His ears felt hot, he knew they were crimson as well. He deemed himself innocent in the face of her insult. He got flustered and failed to answer the host of ritual questions put to him by Ugo. Justifying himself in his mind, explaining to *her* . . . no, this is nothing but the truth: Freddie is a shallow, talentless fop, his delivery's off, he lisps and mumbles . . . spreads his words like butter . . . in a word: a fool.

It was as if she were reading his mind: she bore down on him with all her beauty. He felt a mighty fear in his body. . . . While everyone was calm around him, everyone protected by indifferent laughter. . . . And there: his hand resting on the table was not lying still, it was trembling, frightened . . .

"Are you scared of him?" asked Maestro in a whisper, one eye squinting in the smoke from the sodden butt in the corner of his mouth, giving him a derisive air.

"Scared of whom?"

"That Freddie character."

"What makes you think I'm scared?"

"You keep glancing his way. Move the hand off the table, it's trembling very convincingly. That might encourage him," said Maestro paternally. "And be careful. In nineteen twenty an actor whupped our drama critic. Thrashed him in broad daylight, in front of the Theater Café with a dog whip. I saw it with my own eyes."

"Why did he whip him? Did he get a bad review?" Melkior felt his voice quaver.

"Rumor had it that . . . well, it may have had something to do with a review, the man wrote that the actor spoke with a squeak or something, I don't know, it has been ages since I last went to the theater. He might well have spoken with a squeak for all I know. But it wasn't over the squeak, it was over a blonde."

"A blonde?" smiled Melkior, and there was an agitated twinkle in his eyes.

"Oh yes, a plump one, with all-around curvaceous qualities. I knew her personally. Pulp novels were the total extent of her interest in the written word. She sat around in bars like this one here. . . . Her stock reply to compliments was 'You don't say' and whatever she talked about invariably contained the attribute 'awfully.' So much for charm and coquetry."

Maestro spat out the butt, took a sip of the local brandy, and lit a fresh cigarette, which he immediately maneuvered with his tongue to the corner of his mouth to keep his speech unimpeded.

"But it seems that both artists were smitten with her curves, wherefore the performing artist trounced the pen-wielding artist. Mind your step."

"Why? It's not as if I . . ." Melkior felt the need to hide.

"I'm not saying that you . . ." and Maestro raised his eyebrows in the direction of *her*. "No, that would be a foolishness unworthy of you, great Eustachius. After all, you are different. . . . Come on, no blushing, I'm old enough to be your father. Ahh," sighed Maestro with profound sadness, "I have seen Fijan act! That's why I don't go to the theater any more. When the late Fijan walked down the street, it was as if King Lear himself was passing by. While nowadays, as you can see for yourself, it's Freddie! And as for the thrashing, I told you the story for comparative reasons, to draw the distinction between God and a milliner. Fijan was God! Or at least a demigod . . . a magnificent presence at any rate. People stepped aside out of respect, they made room for him on the street to clear the way for his greatness. And when he shouted, with dead Cordelia in his arms, 'Howl, howl, howl, howl!' our very souls shook. Only a jackass could respond to Freddie's braying, out of brotherly solidarity. I really don't know what he baits his hook with to catch those eels. Because his sinker has indeed sunk. The man's impotent. That's a known fact."

Within Melkior there shone up a feeling brimming with embarrassment and hope. But it's all Maestro's hair-brained malarkey . . . and everything went dark again.

"I used to have artistic ambitions myself in my younger days," stated Maestro all of a sudden.

"Thespian?"

"Literary. Poetic. But that was at a time when we drank wine, pagan style, and sang 'sunny dithyrambs.' We were all of us phallic instrumentalists, the crazed brethren of Eros. And Zeus was a wonderful god. There was never a poem without something 'gasping' in it, the better-class girls were nymphs and our ladies of the night, hetaerae. Vineyards, autumn, the leather flask and Pan. We drank the blazing sun. Bearded satyrs to a man, lustful centaurs, Bacchus's drunken little apes. Anacreon, little Arinoë, the Argonauts . . . all from Volume One of the encyclopaedia, under 'A' . . ." He sneered bitterly and poured brandy down his gullet. "And now it's brandy," he said, giving a shudder of some brand of disgust. "The alembic. Chemistry. We guzzle formulas. C-H-O-H, Paracelsus's hell brews. Brandy is a whorish drink, the seducing tart, the vamp with a hoarse alto voice and blue shadows under her eyes, luscious like our Zara— am I right, Chicory Hasdrubalson?"

"Sorry, Maestro?" and a wan young man with a nervous face, slicked-down blonde hair, and red eyes with puffy lids started with a spasm of laughter.

"Zara, our love, I said, isn't she luscious?" Maestro closed his eyes in admiration.

"Ahh, Maestro, you are so cruel!" Chicory cried out in mock exasperation and burst into laughter, his face twitching nervously.

"Perhaps," Maestro parried, "but such a cinematographic love does bring a new sacrament to our biography. Chicory met her personally, last year, when she was here on a visit. Well, it turned out she was no monstrance, he was disappointed. Fat and stupid, with a pimp or something in tow, heh-heh. . . . Ergo, we're sunk, Chicory Hasdrubalson!"

"Sunk well and truly, my great Master. But Eustachius recommends Viviana, the delectable little fig."

Melkior felt onanistic shame at the mention of the name.

"I don't look between the sheets," said Maestro in an offended tone, "I know none of those Platonic shadows. Explain, Chicory. To what tongue does the fig respond?"

"This fig is Latin. *Figue Romance*. Her little mug drips with nectar for lecherous admirers."

"Ahh, ahh," Maestro sighed quite indifferent and averted his eyes in vexation. "All that is just 'Come out to play, it's a lovely day' . . . while what I need is peace and serenity," he suddenly addressed Melkior, soberly, as if he had said to himself, "All right, enough of this nonsense.

"A cozy little house with flowers all around (so let it be 'idyllic,' never you mind it, I *want* it that way!), a table under the green arbor, a glass of wholesome wine on the table. Inside the little house, the devoted housewife with white arms (that business with the elbow just like in *Oblomov*, remember?), the smells of cooking wafting from the kitchen, whetting the imagination and the appetite, and me all pure and solemn. There, that's the dream I had and still have. And still have, that's the nasty part. And it will be found inside my head when those professors up in Anatomy open it up. The dream that never came true. How on earth can you make a dream come true here and still remain pure and solemn? Where can I lose myself, disappear, when everybody knows me? There I am, walking down the street, daydreaming, polishing a line or two, all I need is to get it down on paper, when somebody or other jumps out at me, 'Well, hello there, how are you?' and it all goes down the drain. If only he cared about how I was! Like hell he does! He's only being a nuisance. . . . Or perhaps he wants to show that he, too, knows me, Yorick the fool, the highbrow drunkard. All right, I know," Maestro went on after a swig, "I can't very well write another *Crime and Punishment*. Where could I find a Raskolnikov here? Are you Raskolnikov? Is anyone in this lot? Well, all right, I suppose you might do, but this one," he indicated with his eyes a skinny student at their table, "is he Rodion Romanych Raskolnikov, the redeemer of mankind? The little bastard, they say he robbed his father and set up house with a little tart (a pro) whom he chooses to call *Sonya*, can you see the presumption of the cur? I would kick him out with the tip of my shoe if I didn't respect Chicory who brought him here. He needs just such a ministrant at the table, *ad Deum qui laetificat juventutem meam*, to pour the wine for him (there, look!) and tuck him into bed. The little deer tick. What can there be inside the head of such a louse—what am I saying? A nit!—but then a nit hasn't got a head at all. Ideas? Ideas, hell! The nit lives snugly on top of your head, keeping warm, the little bastard, having not the haziest notion about what goes on inside. And finally, why am I cooking and kneading all that stuff in my mind—that is to say, for whom? That's what halts my hand over the blank page, leaving me with nothing to show for my pains. Nothing. Nothing ever."

Yes, that was it: nothing. At first Melkior had listened to him with naïve interest, seeing him as a failed genius. But now, after the "nits," he saw a repulsive brandy lush with a permanently frozen snuffling nose and swollen bluish hands, and regarded him with disbelieving wariness. There could well be a tiny animal with horrible instincts hiding in the flowery idyll like a spider. The lecherous libertine, with a penchant for fat, sweaty women, his entire flesh already poisoned with syphilis, they say. . . . Melkior moved away from him and lit a cigarette, disinfecting the air around him.

Maestro was sensitive to such behavior: in retribution, he moved his chair closer and whispered into Melkior's mouth, poisoning him with his breath:

"I could introduce you to that one," he nodded in *her* direction with offensive intimacy. "I know her. This business with Freddie is of no consequence, it's just mutual ornamentation. Their use of each other is a matter of taste: both are in vogue at the moment and are wearing each other like the latest fashion. So if you like . . . ?"

"I wouldn't want the history of my colleague to repeat itself on my back," quipped Melkior and felt pleased at his success. "So he really beat him in earnest?"

"Like a madman. Slamming him right and left. The poor critic didn't even run, no, he just stood there and took it like a martyr. He covered his eyes, for shame I suppose, and never moved an inch. I happened to be standing by the newsroom window and yelled, 'Run, man, run!' But he did nothing, he just stood there in a cloud of dust. I tell you, there's nothing like a dog whip for beating the dust out of clothing!"

"There he goes again: on and on about dogs!" chimed in Ugo from the other end of the table. "If I may ask, is it Zhuchka or Perezvon?"

"I'm not on about dogs, I'm on about dog whips," replied Maestro with a patient smile. "And you, Par-ara-rampion," he stammered with anger, "you really should remember that Zhuchka and Perezvon are one and the same person—I mean, dog; it was only that Kolya Krasotkin called Zhuchka Perezvon in a moment of surprise, in a moment of compassionate surprise."

"You ought to know, gentlemen," said Ugo to the house at large, "that he is by way of being a specialist in Dostoyevsky's beasts. If you please, Maestro, what's the name of the dog in *The Insulted and Injured?*"

"Azorka. It was Azorka," Maestro replied nonchalantly.

"Why 'was'?" asked someone at the table.

" 'Was,' " Maestro retorted punctiliously, "because Azorka died early on in the novel, Chapter One."

"See? He knows it all!" exclaimed Ugo in buffoonish rapture, as if he were offering a parrot for sale. "Please, Maestro, what's the title of that poem by Captain Lebyakin? You'll see, he knows that, too."

"I can't say," Maestro smiled slyly. The unexpected reply left a palpable impression on his party. Ugo was stumped.

"I can't say," Maestro went on after an effective pause, "because Lebyakin has several poems. I'm sure you mean 'The Cockroach.' "

"But of course, 'The Cockroach'!" cried Ugo delightedly. "The Cockroach, the cockroach, ha-ha, I told you he knew! How could he not know about the cockroach, he, the Mad Bug—"

"Inspired!" Maestro corrected him.

"Ah yes, inspired, the Inspired Bug! Of course he knew, the cockroach is an animal, is it not? I would also have you know, gentlemen, that he, too, has written a number of poems. They are not about animals, they're sort of inspired, melancholico-anatomical, 'snip-snap.' May we have *Snap*, Maestro, please? There may be a few disbelievers in our midst, so let them hear it! Here, Don

Fernando's smiling skeptically as if to say, 'He a poet?' Why, it's something right up your alley, Don Fernando, it's humane and all that. . . . So, Maestro: *Snap*, if you please."

"I am not smiling," muttered Don Fernando, blushing horribly, because everyone was looking at him as if he were to blame.

Indeed, he was not smiling. He had hardly been listening to Ugo's silly patter (or at least so it seemed), but nevertheless his expression smiled all the while, and it seemed to be smiling all on its own while he, preoccupied with his thoughts, was unaware of what it was up to.

He had sat there all evening with that derisive smile on, never deigning to say a word; he was watching everything from some distracted, wise height.

Moreover, the self-important smile never left Don Fernando's face. It was, in a way, central to his physiognomy. Ugo said he put the smile on in the morning, in front of the mirror, and then went out, wearing it all day and taking it off only in bed to put it under his pillow before going to sleep. Who knew what lay hidden behind the mask? Revenge against mankind perhaps . . . or some small advance on a great future triumph?

Don Fernando wrote in the same way, wearing his inscrutable smile. A critic had written that he flogged his characters with nettles and tickled them to insanity. There truly was a sadistic side to his writing: he invented people to torture them. But the torture was by no means cruel or painful. On the contrary, the characters laughed and rejoiced, but they laughed like madmen and were bathed in the cold sweat of dismay, as if the author were flogging them into merriment.

"No, I'm really not smiling," said Don Fernando almost angrily, feeling the reproachful glances of the entire company on his person. "What have you gone silent for? Please proceed, Maestro."

"Oh no, no way," grumbled Maestro in a hurt voice, "I can't do this in front of Europe. The scornful face of the most exquisite taste is standing over my piggish talent and smirking. The talent may be piggish, but the pride is not, *Monsieur le Goût!*" He gave Don Fernando a sharp, almost menacing look.

"No, Maestro," interceded Melkior, in a placating tone, "he really is not smiling. It's just his face."

Don Fernando lashed Melkior with a quick scornful glance, but, as if afraid of being caught out, he immediately diluted it with the saintly mercy that he had gushed tonight from his bright eyes all over the Give'nTake.

The Give'nTake did not very often have the honor of being caressed by Don Fernando's eyes. It was a house of drink-sodden madcap living, of devil-may-care and mindless time-wasting, whereas he was a serious and responsible man. He worked, he wrote, he thought. No, by no means did he belong here, and it was a mystery why he came at all. It was where the Parampions performed their lunatic "shows," while he, sensible and sober like a gracious Sun, would spare a ray of attention to throw some light on the silly muddle, and then put its lights out again and, in full blackout, sail away into unreachability.

Don Fernando was simply impregnable. How hard had Ugo tried to disarm the man and subject him to the power of his "eloquence," to topple him from the throne of indifferent and silent derision, to bring him into line and make him one of "the boys"! Don Fernando would immediately surrender, lay down his arms, put his hands up, even insist that there was nothing special about him, nothing unusual, he was an ordinary man, perhaps even . . . well, an inferior man; all the same he remained alien and aloof which was after all what he wanted to be and seemed to relish.

The silence had become oppressive, as though everyone were waiting for something to happen. Even Ugo was wordless. Or was he purposely letting seriousness kill the fun, rob the jollity, so that he might come on in "grand style" to save the day.

He was a past master at handling such situations.

Melkior felt the worst. Whence the guilty feeling? It seemed to him that all eyes were trained on him in a kind of expectation as if he could come up with a solution. What had he gone and tampered with Don Fernando's ineffable divinity for? It had soared frighteningly high above his pedestrian powers, and he had long been cultivating the patient policy of the believer who envies the omnipotence of his God. But into the envy crept some insidious antipathy that he unconsciously sought to disperse with a strange readiness to sacrifice himself. And every time he caught himself preparing for the sacrifice, even as the inferior feeling of fulsome humility was hatching, there also emerged anger and disgust along the way, with himself along with everything else. Whence the slimy feeling of crawling mendacity which clung faithfully to the superior and hated person? Step forward, any who are immune to that particular brand of perfidy! Oh, human nature! sighed Melkior "from deep down inside," cleverly impersonating his conscience, as if he had deftly used "human nature" to plug a stench-spewing bottle.

"I suggest," Chicory Hasdrubalson spoke up mournfully, mid-silence, "that the entire Parampionic Fraternity humbly ask the great Don Fernando to adopt a sad mask suitable for a *pompe funèbres director*, following which we should equally humbly ask the immortal Maestro to carry the remains of the dear departed out of the house of sorrow so that we might fittingly mourn it as one."

They interrupted him with a chorus of laughter (which included Maestro's angry grunts). Ugo amply rewarded Chicory with kisses on behalf of the entire fraternity . . . and things got going nicely again after the standstill. But silence descended suddenly again like darkness and choked the barely revived merriment.

Something was happening on Don Fernando's face and it instantly affected everyone, as if sunspots had appeared and brought about an abrupt climate change. Indeed, dark spots had appeared on both Don Fernando's ruddy cheeks and a grim cloud of anger flew across his eyes. True, he whisked the cloud right away so that no lightning flashed in his eyes, but the spots spread on his cheeks, covering them to the ears.

There was a solar eclipse. A devout silence fell upon the party at the table and mystic anxiety swept through the entire Give'nTake. Doomsday was expected. But in the midst of expectation Maestro finished his glass while Ugo grinned derisively at the darkened sun —Don Fernando's face—intrepidly displaying his black fillings.

Was it the fillings themselves or the heretic defiance of the two chief Parampions that upset the exalted balance of Don Fernando's divine serenity? He snatched his glass greedily as if about to drain it, held it tightly gripped in his hand for a moment (he was trying against all odds to resist temptation), and then with an easy swing, but producing an extremely telling effect, dashed the wine across the table smack into Ugo's teeth. He then stood up without looking at anyone and strode unhurriedly out of the Give'nTake.

Freddie was triumphant, of course. Such unexpected revenge at another's hand! Hurrah! Bravo! He applauded, shouted, chortled with glee, loudly, too loudly. Even *she* tried to tame him, stroking his hand, pleading with him to restrain himself. She saw nothing funny in the excess, her sympathy was apparently with Ugo. (Oh how Melkior was grateful!) At length she let go of Freddie's hand, stood up and approached Ugo with tender concern.

"Did he get you in the eyes?" she asked, pulling Ugo's hands away from his eyes.

Melkior felt a sweet, unmanly ache of tenderness clutch his throat. How kind she is. How dear.

Ugo was rubbing his eyes to gain time (Don Fernando *had* caught him by surprise), whereas she thought he was . . .

"Did it get into your eyes?"

"No, love," he said in a seductively tender voice, suddenly embracing her and kissing her on the mouth.

What a cad! Melkior thought jealously, while the other end of his thought rejoiced. Desecration of compassion, rape of the angel! he added derisively and watched her eyes filling with tears of surprise. She covered her face with her hands and blindly staggered back to Freddie. He took hold of her protectively and sat her down in a chair. He then made toward Ugo, rolling his hips as he had seen in the cinema: here comes the terrible avenger. But he adjusted his tie in passing and halted at a reasonable distance.

"Listen here, you ape! Come outside if you are the man you pretend to be."

"No I won't come out, fair knight!" Ugo bowed like Sganarel.

"You would joust like an errant knight for your lady's honor, but I'd rather not fight you just now. For some reason or other I'm not in the mood really—I had a bad dream last night . . . as I said, seven o'clock tomorrow at the upper Maksimir lake. This is still on. Tomorrow I shall spear you with a silver fork as stated, with all the honors due to your exceptional person. And now please leave alone the man whom Destiny has chosen to be splashed with the Dionysian drink by the hand of her great son. A moment ago I entered the biography of a great man! Future Ph.D.s will be quoting me in their doctoral theses, students will be flunking their exams because of me, learned thinkers will be referring to me in footnotes. Thanks to Don Fernando's sublime gesture you now stand before a historical person, you miserable wretch!"

"I spit on your historical person, you ape!" and Freddie indeed spat into Ugo's eyes.

"That will be totted up to the same account," said Ugo, wiping his face without haste or perturbation. "Your bill is growing fast, Twenty-seventh Citizen in *Coriolanus*. My only regret is that you will not be able to remember how I collected all my debts, because you will no longer be there. The very thought brings tears to my eyes. Oh Destiny, be thou not cruel to this thimbleful of unsalted brains, there is so much he could not help. Now then," he addressed his party, carelessly turning away from Freddie, "over with the nasty digressions and back to the agenda. All right, Maestro, what is it that two shot glasses of the hard stuff say?"

Freddie was left in the middle of the Give'nTake, surrounded by laughter, alone and abandoned. Ugo's great triumph, which Ugo would not even acknowledge!

The overripe hollow-eyed actress shook Freddie's hand, congratulated him for spitting. She kissed him under the nose (long had she yearned to!), leaving behind the victorious imprint of her lips.

Viviana never looked at him. He had sat back at the table, offered her his hand to stroke (as usual), but she fell to rummaging in her handbag, without noticing the hand. That hand was no longer in her good graces, Freddie's Vivianic empire was dwindling.

Oh how favorable things were for the Parampion, the damned jabberer!

Melkior was not missing a trick. I'm monitoring your movements, you fickle cat! He was almost prepared to root for Freddie. And inside he was lamenting, "I'm done for, oh God I'm done for!" and his heart was clenching hopelessly, his eyes wandering in search of a sanctuary. To hide his misery that was weeping in his gaze, sobbing in his naked eyes. How free everybody was, how confident in their gestures, in their stride! While I dare not so much as walk toward that door with the man's shoe drawn on it . . . although it has been a whole hour since I first felt . . . er, yes. The shoe! As if there were a cobbler inside! A misleading sign! The Cobblers' Union ought to protest. Permit us that association of ideas, the sanitary technicians plead. What refinement in Thénardier, the vile condor! With a mere shoe he lifts his establishment to considerable renown, to the level of international urinary language. The Micturition Code. Now, *there's* a European for you!

Melkior was ill at ease with their daring throughout. To have dashed wine in Ugo's face! And with what a regal gesture! To have kissed *her* like that! He proceeded to examine his bitter yearning in detail; the fantasies struck him as terribly forward and he blushed.

"So, Maestro," the invincible Ugo spoke up with a chairmanlike efficiency, "I think this is just the moment for *Snap*. Europe has left through a door that could hardly be called a triumphal arch, and spitting in people's faces, since civilization forbids spitting on the floor, makes perfect sense. And it's forceful in a virile way. Virile in particular. It's not easy getting cast for a spitting role, that sort of thing is reserved for the big players. Roscius himself, in Rome, used to spit in key scenes. But let us leave those sputalitious matters to the spitters, what comes out of their mouths is spittle, not words. Goodbye, snot-dribblers, and hoard your precious ammunition like those besieged in a fortress, your mouths will go dry with excitement. My apologies, Maestro, for keeping you waiting until I finished delivering the war message to those on the other bank, over there where culture leaves off. I was speaking like Caesar to Vercingetorix. So, if you please, what is it that two shot glasses of the hard stuff say? Then again . . . perhaps they whisper, do they whisper?"

"No they do not," Maestro growled angrily, "they damned well bellow! But I will be moderate in playing my *marche funèbre,— moderato*, as they put it in the scores. Parampion, the question!" he said sternly, like a champion demanding his gong.

"What is it that two shot glasses of the hard stuff say?" Ugo asked ceremonially.

"Two shot glasses of the hard stuff say *Snap*," Maestro pronounced solemnly.

He then spat out his cigarette butt, cleared his throat thoroughly and sluiced it with a sip of brandy (which was equally part of the ritual), and, closing his eyes, began to recite, craning his neck awkwardly: *Anatomy, Or My Person on Sale:*

> "Put your money down
> Snip me—I'm a snap."

"That's the introduction, gentlemen," Ugo chimed in, "and a refrain of sorts . . ." But everyone shushed him and Maestro went on:

> "For sale, cheap and mortgage-free:
> every little piece of me.
> First, my skin—no warts, no rash—
> easy for the scalpel's slash.
> Item, one nose, large, purple like a plum
> (which comes of too much brandy, wine, and rum),
> a first-class sniffer of plots and shady deals . . .
>
> Put your money down
> Snip me—I'm a *snap*.
>
> Item, an organ, ill-bred and misled,
> planted by Nature in my head,
> a little horror, devil, razor, snake—
> my filthy tongue, which truly takes the cake
> for foul, dirty, slanderous talk . . .

> Put your money down
> Snip me—I'm a *snap*.
>
> (Here, innkeeper, pour and bring
> shot to shot—shot glasses twain
> and we will knock 'em back and sing
> and thereupon we'll drink again!)"

"Bring shot glasses twain, shot to shot," whispered Ugo to Thénardier.

"Right," said Maestro when the drinks arrived, "the two shots go on to say as follows:

> Item, one brain-casing bursting at the seams,
> holding a brain with many-colored dreams
> of Her, blue-clad Madonna (devils all around her)
> while I, her suitor, am told I'm a bounder
> who's not to hound her and is left to founder . . .
> Hence those scabs from reality on the brain,
> those scars and pimples, welts, and stabs of pain,
> hence the worms, bugs, slugs crawling in slimy bliss
> all over the filthy picture of the selfsame lovely miss . . .
>
> Put your money down
> Snip me—I'm a *snap*.
>
> What else have I to give, butchering MDs?"

"Nothing," Ugo broke in. "We're going to skip the various delicacies. Because he"—this to the audience—"will now be dissecting each organ in turn, and you can well imagine what's in store for you there."

"There are various salients," said Maestro in prose, "or hemispheres, also crevasses and canyons, ridges, openings and orifices all for functions large and small . . ."

"We'll skip all that, those orifices and what-not, and get straight to the point," Ugo told him.

"The anatomy consists of nine systems. I'll just do the bones and a few extremities then."

"Item, in the end, my weary bones
i.e., my skeleton with its creaks and groans.
Let me mention feet (replete with corns),
my mended heart, my trembling arms,
All, all, I give for the march of science!
Fee-fi-fo-fum, formaldehyde, here I come.
The venue of my final rendezvous
Is the Institute of Anatomy, adieu!

Put your money down
Snip me—I'm a snap.
Snap-a-snip
Snip-a-snap."

"What did I tell you!" Ugo exclaimed delightedly. "Snip-snap!"
and he rolled his eyes contritely in holy awe of Maestro's poetry.

The entire Give'nTake rang with boisterous applause and laughter. Maestro did not let himself get carried away with the intoxication of success: he modestly took from his pocket a shard of a mirror
and winked his eye at that same eye in the mirror (the eye was in fact
all he could see in the small piece of glass): we know . . . what we
know.

Melkior swept the premises in search of an alliance with a lonely
soul suffering as much as he was. He was disgusted with Maestro's
anatomy. But all the souls were noisily rejoicing at the muck that
Maestro had tonight purposely dredged out for some cynical reason
of his own. *Her* soul was not rejoicing! Freddie and the hollow-eyed
actress were participating with gusto, but *she*, Viviana, had shyly
dropped her gaze and, see, she was mashing a piece of tinfoil with
her foot with irritation. Melkior watched for so much as a single
look of hers to donate his distaste to a joint treasury of spiritual
beauty . . . he had pursed his mouth in a grimace of disgust so as to
greet her straight right with kindred openness for a tacit, honorable
accord . . . But she sensed his curious readiness, raised her eyes from
the bit of tinfoil and appeared to spit with her look at his stupid offer.
He immediately sacked the grimace of disgust (the distracted secre-

tary who had copy-typed his physiognomy wrong, causing a fatal misunderstanding!) and slapped on a Giventakian smile, a hedonistic, mischievous grin, for Ugo had already pounced upon him:

"Look, good-looking people, the white soul suffers!" he cried pointing at Melkior who had all but sank under the table. He sat huddled as if shielding himself under fire, and kept muttering miserably, "No, no, I'm not, no . . . I'm having a fine time, I am laughing" . . . and he tried to laugh but felt his face disobeying and his ears burning, burning . . . Everybody watching, everybody laughing . . . She, too. Oh God, she too!—He saw no more.

And Ugo was inconsiderately jubilant.

"Don't believe him, he's suffering!" he shouted and pointed his finger, sending him to a hell of excommunication. "The white dove is suffering alongside the Great Vulture that tears out poetry's entrails! The dove's just about to swoon, somebody get a stretcher!"

He was possessed by a delirium of rambunctiousness, by that mad vein of inspiration of his that knew no courtesy and no bounds. His long black hair was parted in the middle and tumbled down either side of his face, he had his hands raised in a Rasputinian orgiastic frenzy: invoking the descent of some maniacal powers to this smoke-infused spree.

"Maestro, you Olympian Vulture, you've hacked long enough at the liver of Eustachius chained to the Giventakian Rock. Can we now have, as a balm, that dolorous-lyrical *Give Me a Heart for Parade?*"

"No way!" Maestro replied self-importantly, indeed with anger.

"Next on the program is *Nobility.*"

All the Parampions gave delighted cries of "*Nobility, Nobility!*" Ugo alone disapproved of the choice:

"Oh no! Not your ancestors. That's his zoological genealogy, you see," Ugo explained to the Give'nTake at large. "But enough of personal family trees . . ."

"It's not personal!" Maestro rasped, offended. "It's a treatise on the origin of species of nobility, based on Darwin's theory and broken down by the branches of the tree of life. When Yorick put his skull in the gravedigger's hands and when the man passed the skull on to Hamlet in turn, what did Hamlet say of Alexander the Great, eh? You don't know? Sit down, you dolt, you'll fail the course! You are as witless as the Prussian clay that filled the brilliant skull of Immanuel Kant! Back to your seat!"

"But Maestro . . ." pleaded Ugo.

"I do not want to know!"

"Please, sir, I'll be prepared next time, sir," Ugo lowered his eyes in shame.

"Report to me when you are."

The skinny student, Chicory's ministrant, had taken the matter seriously and was grabbing the chance to distinguish himself:

"I know," he said, his eyes shining in triumph.

"What is it you know, my young friend?"

"What Hamlet said about Alexander."

"Oh, really? Read about it in *Ali Baba and the Forty Thieves*, did you? You shouted *Open Sesame* and the gate of entire human knowledge opened before you? Or is it that you have moved beyond human knowledge? Is it that you possess centipedal knowledge as well? Think I'm being insulting? That the centipede is mindless? And I say unto you, verily, verily I say unto you, that nobody knows how the centipede walks using a hundred legs all at once. Not even Lunacharsky could do that. Whereas the centipede does, you see. If it didn't, it wouldn't be able to walk at all. Or do you think yourself cleverer than Lunacharsky?"

Chicory Hasdrubalson pled mercy for his ministrant. But Maestro was fully sozzled and denied the plea for pardon.

"You think mec-ha-nisms and objects are the answer? Elec-tri-cities, high voltage . . . Well, did Montezuma have mechanisms? The hell he did, and yet he made chocolate! Licking your chops are you now? Loving Montezuma like Saint Nick now? For his choco-late? But what's the point of me telling you about ancient civiliza-tions, you dense . . . I don't know what. You can tell your father you're a completely failed product."

"I forbid you to insult me!" flared the student and stood up . . . but could not think of a reason for standing and sat down again.

"There you are, Chicory, he forbids. Therefore we shall never insult him again. Never ever shall we insult him again!"

"Damn right you won't!" said the student in a voice collapsing with anger. "I'll never sit with you again!"

"And you say this to me who has loved you like a father?" cried Maestro nearly in tears. "You ungrateful brat!"

Melkior liked the show of Maestro's noble nature, he nudged the student in a plea to relent, to make up. . . . Maestro didn't mean it *like that*, he's a good man at heart. . . . In the end the student flashed a conciliatory smile; he thought he had got his satisfaction. All the same he would not look at Maestro; he kept glancing at his mentor Hasdrubalson, seeking advice or possibly refuge.

"Well, what are you waiting for, mediate, Chicory the Inexorable!" cried Ugo from the other end of the table. "Can't you see your help is expected?"

Chicory blinked undecidedly, his cheeks twitching in nervousness, while all the others smiled slyly into their hands.

"Well, Maestro is no Turkish potentate," said Chicory, "you can always speak to him directly."

"As far as I'm concerned . . ." said the student like a young lover in a Renaissance comedy, in the reconciliation scene.

"There, my boy: peace." Maestro offered his index finger and the student eagerly took the entire hand. "You give him a finger and he takes the whole . . ." Maestro quipped. "No, not like that: you put your index finger on top of mine and it's peace, peace everlasting . . ."

And so they did: index finger to index finger, and their two hands flew off like birds linked by a kiss. And Maestro kissed him on the cheek, paternally.

And the student returned the kiss.

"And now, my boy, tell us what you were going to say," Maestro said with much kindness. "What did Hamlet say of Alexander the Great?"

The cheeks of everyone at the table were bulging; Ugo was on the point of bursting, but the student noticed nothing, he was intent on airing his knowledge:

"He said we could trace in our imagination the dust of Alexander and finally find it corking a beer barrel."

There was a blast of long-brewing laughter. The student had walked straight into it . . .

"What are you laughing at, you morons?" said Maestro in mock anger. "He got it right, didn't he? Plugging a beer barrel, right? Alexander the Great as the great plugger, that's the point, isn't it, my boy?"

But the student had already jumped to his feet and fled. They shouted after him, "Come back, it was only a joke!" Chicory actually ran after him, but it was no use, the insult had been too great.

From all around came loud applause and shouts of "Bravo!"; at the bar, Thénardier's two assistants gave Maestro ovations, banging on glass, crazed with mirth. Ugo leaned across the table and showered Maestro with congratulations and even kisses on his greasy and moldy head.

"What a show!" marveled Ugo. "The *doctor subtilis!* Not even Saint Thomas Aquinas could have played it in so refined a . . ."

"Thomas Aquinas was *doctor angelicus*," Maestro pontificated, "*sed tu es doctor asinus!* You ignorant ass! All of you have driven that bright child away, and he had so much more to tell us! Now you're driving away my dear Eustachius. You're right, blessed Eustachius, this is insufferable, they are behaving like high school youngsters at a school dance. Go if you like, I will not take it amiss."

Melkior had indeed begun to fidget on his chair: he was about to leave.

He, too, had been hoodwinked. He had been taken in by Maestro's "show of benevolence," he'd helped to "set up" the student. . . . The boy is now roaming the streets, bitterly regretting his gullibility. Why didn't I belt the man one right away? No, I had to swallow his "peace-peace everlasting" rubbish, ha, ha . . . He mocked himself and loathed the world. The poison had taken effect . . .

Before Melkior could so much as come unstuck from his chair, Ugo grabbed him by the neck. "Ah, *sacré bleu!*" he cried, as if he had nabbed a spy behind a door.

"Let go of me! What the hell do you think you're doing?"

"Doing?" Ugo smirked, not letting go. "Nothing, this is expressing my will by the use of force. Violence! You've been studying us all night like a shrink with a pack of pickled peckers! Well, that doesn't fly! Sit right back down and ask forgiveness from the magistral personage of this symposium of Concretist poetry! You'd ignore creativity, would you?"

"I've been listening attentively," stammered Melkior. "But now I must be off, I've got work to do."

"Work!" Ugo pulled a pious face. "Did you hear, Oh ye faithful, that most sacred of words? Approach and prostrate yourselves! The Lord our God Himself invented it and said to Adam (after that ploy with the apple), 'In the sweat of thy face shalt thou eat bread.' He stuck a fig leaf on him and booted him from Paradise. That was the end of easy living in the bosom of the Earth. Time to work. And then our forefather, whom this did irk, invented the famous ode to work: cabbages are tasty cabbages are yummy, grow ye cabbages and never go ye hungry. Therefore, brethren, grow ye cabbages and fear not."

"As did your esteemed father—he raised a genuinely exemplary head of cabbage!" Maestro put in.

"Thank you for the compliment," Ugo bowed. But he was taken aback by Maestro's interjection; he therefore went after Melkior again.

"It's a shame, oh sociable Eustachius," he turned him around and spoke into his face. "It's a shame for a Parampionic veteran such as yourself to shut himself in his secret little lab and day and night distill the extract of a most corrosive antimilitarist outlook, one which in further chemical processing might even be described as seditious."

"Ugo!" Melkior pleaded in a hot whisper.

"He can be seen in broad daylight," Ugo went on cruelly, "stepping onto the invalid's weighing machine on the street corner with the secret mission of controlling the weight of his irreplaceable body, with particular attention to certain famous military regulations. For seven years, in his head, he has been nurturing, fertilizing, watering, weeding his sweet little cabbage patch: how to render inaccessible to the Kingdom his body, which in view of its glory is fully entitled to it, as is borne out by all of history. He has, among other things, a poem which sets it all out in a poetic manner. I must confess I don't know its title, but it does not really need a title—if it has one at all, am I right, Eustachius?"

"Ugo, please," whispered Melkior, trembling, "for God's sake stop acting like a fool!"

"What's the matter?" Ugo mused. "Why, the poem's quite good. A bit old-fashioned, perhaps. Listen:

> Begone now, leave me be, 'tis solitude I need
> softly to approach the grass . . ."

"Stop!" Melkior shrieked in desperation and wrenched free of Ugo's grip. "You're not a man, you're a cur!" he added, fending off Ugo's hands, which were reaching to keep him there. When he closed the door from the outside, Thénardier's bell sobbed after him.

"Pity," said Maestro thoughtfully. "Just when we were set up for a splendid evening. Tell you what, Ugo: why don't U-go and u-be-gone, you goon."

White all around . . . and a tinge of illness. The quiet, roomy terrace of an Alpine sanitarium for the consumptive. He did not want to say "tuberculin." Deep down he feared the word. A view of mountain lakes and glaciers. A glass of milk on a small white table. He, reclining on a chaise longue, the chronicle of some thirty-year, three-hundred-year, three-thousand-year war in his hands. A little farther off down the terrace, also resting, a gold-haired and pale-faced one, a consumptive girl reading. . . . At this point somebody else would write that she was reading *The Sorrows of Young Werther* or *Adolphe* or *The Torrents of Spring;* well, just to show them make it a book by Kumičić, *Jelka's Sprig of Basil,* or even *Chance* by the same author. The sweet banality of a delusion . . . The pretty golden girl brushing away a dainty tear over a passage here and there and coughing demurely. Poor thing. Everything pale, sick, sad . . . Banal! Intentionally banal!

Originality almost frightened Melkior with its literary coyness. With its seductive charm that diverts from real cares and smiles in the distance and holds out a promise of surprises to come. Originality might have lifted his spirits and plucked him out of tethering reality. But it would not have been a lasting liberation, it only meant a sweet hour of forgetfulness: a bit of *Te Deum laudamus* and a whiff of incense, with cares waiting around the next corner to throttle him. Lasting liberation required banality and nothing but banality, sickly sweet, dull banality, white all around and a tinge of illness, the terrace, the glaciers, the milk, and the golden girl.

Replete with Kumičić! With no exaltation, with no literary ambition, with no taste, without affectation, he built for himself a tableau depicting the liberation from the nightmare in a most primitive fashion, almost as a stupidity cult which Ugo would have jeered at with a vengeance if Melkior had been naïve enough to share with him his sanitarium, his *Jelka's Sprig of Basil*, his consumptive delusion with a view of Alpine lakes.

And yet the shabby picture postcard gave him the strength to carry on down the road he had taken, offering a way out of an absurdity that threatened to swallow him whole.

He followed the screaming ambulances hurtling down the streets with their cargo of the diseased, the down-and-out, the victims of traffic accidents, the suicides, with engaged, almost envious eyes, and the hearses he all but cursed. He watched the bodies walking past his and compared those puny, no-account, gnomelike beings with his own health, strength, stamina, with his ability to perform anything that might be called Duty which could lay claim to his body. Give me a body, says Duty, and I will show you its strength.

His life was afraid of the life force within him. Here, look, all these moving, masticating, shouting, laughing organisms may have a fault in them, a crack, a tiny hole down which all the laughter and noise will seep away; there are all manner of stones, blockages, ulcers, caverns, all kinds of rheumatism, sciatica, deafness, disjunction, mutilation, right index finger missing, flat feet. The idiot! Long live the idiot! That is the safest kind of mimicry life can offer a being of its creation. From his vantage point the idiot watches history run its course without the danger of getting caught up in the action, just as we cry as we watch a film playing in the cinema. We mourn fictitious travails, while it's only an idiot who laughs at genuine deaths. He jeers at life from his safe vantage point, taking his revenge for being rejected, smug at being spared. Life has chosen Intelligence for its games, it does not use idiots to make history. It has chosen geniuses for grand words on the cross, at the guillotine, at the gallows, facing the barrels of guns, in front of nations cheering the Brutuses and Caesars alike. An idiot ceded the cup of poison to Socrates. An idiot ceded to Danton the glory of being decapitated by history. (And then made it up to him by producing a marble bust of his head and raising it on a square as an example for future generations.) Whereas the idiot wears his head with a strange grimace of disgust, as if he had long since understood everything, sneered derisively, and stopped time in the rigid folds of his mindless face. Long live the idiot!

Melkior tortured himself with bitter, sardonic thoughts. As if he were ranting at a vast power—a god or a force like the collective mind of all men—he spoke like a lawyer and demagogue, preached with prophetic pathos, in the voice of a supplicant, he sought impact-making figures of speech, paradoxes, drastic examples, he championed "his cause."

And saintlike, mortified his flesh. Tortured it with hunger, wore it down with vigils, never for a moment let it be. Burdened it with fabricated, superfluous worries, invented tasks in bed at night: one grain of wheat on square one, two on square two, four on square three, eight on square four, sixteen on square five, thirty-two on square six, sixty-four on square seven, a hundred and twenty-eight on square eight, two hundred and fifty-six on square nine, five hundred and twelve on square ten, a thousand and twenty-four on square eleven, two thousand and forty-eight on square twelve, four thousand and ninety-six on square thirteen, eight thousand one hundred and ninety-two on square fourteen, sixteen thousand three hundred and eighty-four on square fifteen, thirty-two thousand seven hundred and sixty-eight on square sixteen, sixty-five thousand five hundred and thirty-six on square seventeen, a hundred and thirty-one thousand and seventy-two on square eighteen, two hundred and sixty-two thousand one hundred and forty-four on square nineteen. . . . The number grew at a dizzying rate! He had only wanted to play a little game with arithmetic, and it came out a nightmare! Where was it all leading to, and what was the point? Through a small, innocent act of doubling, through the truly paltry mediation of the so beloved, popular, ordinary, friendly, familial, lovers' number—the number two—grew an endless monster, the inconceivable body of infinity, as terrible as fear, as vast as eternity.

That, too, was a form of torture: infinity and eternity. For we have become accustomed to seeing things tamed by forms, harnessed to our limited needs, cut up into mouthfuls to fit our appetite. Things in costume, clean-shaven, groomed for parade, for show; the humiliation of matter, being reduced to a prop, a camera, a razor, a brush.

And things are weirdly superior and heedless. Undimensional. Infinite. And all the symbols that have grown above things—like clouds condensing into being above endless waters—roam inside our heads in the guise of thoughts, worries, wishes, daydreams. Tortures.

Melkior entered his torture chamber with delight. But there was no joy to his delight, only calculation. He took pleasure in reckoning that in the twists and turns among which he ran, in the labyrinths around which he raced blithely shouting at the top of his lungs, "I've disappeared, I'm not here," he would really and truly disappear from the sight of the absurdity that lay in wait for him. That he would be invisible and elude those huge, hairy, greasy fingers getting closer to him whenever his thought faltered, whenever he forgot himself and surrendered to pleasure.

Over there, around the corner, is where he lives: a room with its own access overlooking the parade ground of the 35th Regiment barracks from across the street. And over here, before the corner, is the Cozy Corner, a small bar or café which Ugo calls a *bistro*. That is where Melkior drops in of an evening on his way home to "have a drink." The Cozy Corner is run by a German family: a small pink pot-bellied father, his face certain of the importance of his existence, a long and lean mother speaking Croatian-German in a good-natured, comical way, a plump pale daughter, Else, who looked as if she recently quit a convent, shielding her femininity from male lust and dropping her gaze when serving the tables (as if she were serving at an altar), and the son, Kurt, narrow-shouldered, broad-hipped, and with a large blonde head. Cozy Corner was the local watering hole for the sergeants from the barracks of the 35th; Melkior often wondered why only sergeants, it may be that the establishment was the right match for their rank, or some such thing.

Melkior entered and was greeted by three members of the German family (the father was seldom seen, he was always off on his business rounds), but the mother's greeting rang out, "Goot eefnink."

The sergeants had taken the four sides of one table; on a corner chair sat demure Else, twiddling her fingers in her lap, her eyes downcast, naturally. Kurt was serving another table: a giant and a little old man in a white linen suit left over from summer. A half-pint each.

Two tables were free. Melkior sat down at the one farther away from the sergeants' table, sensibly, out of reach of the mothball smell of the army. Kurt was a deft waiter; he described himself as a waiter although he was a student of engineering. He served Melkior with one of "their own" special sausages and asked permission to join him.

"Ach, Herr Professor" (he addressed Melkior as Herr Professor to elevate the level of the conversation or, more likely, his own image), "I'm sick and tired of it all, you know. You toil and toil—for what? You work for a living. And why do you live? To work. It's a *circulus vitiosus*, Herr Professor, an absurdity. Did you ever think, Herr Professor, that we all go around and around in an absurd circle, that there is no way out, none at all," and Kurt rested his sizeable hands on the table next to Melkior's plate. Ten fingers, fleshy, sausagelike. Melkior had just made the first incision in his sausage, but now granted it free pardon, gave up the idea of slaughtering it after seeing Kurt's fingers on the table. And again there surfaced an idea of cannibals, of the destroying body which may give rise to appetites in another body and become its food. And all the thoughts harbored by that "food," its ideas, appreciation of a blue-and-yellow color scheme, of the tragedy of King Lear, welling tears, anxiety in the diaphragm, fear across the scalp, daydreams about a certain walk, a certain sway of the hips, "a little smile on dear lips, a bunch of flowers in a water glass" . . . all this is contained in the food, in the destroying body.

"A *circulus*, Herr Professor. I mean: you, I, these two gentlemen, the soldiers over there, we all talk. But what can we accomplish? Can we do something with our bare hands to change the world? We talk. That's all we're good for."

"Tell ya shomp'n, buddy," says the little old man to the giant. "Dey're treshpassherzh, poacherzh. And dere'zh no shatishfaction in dat. Did I tell ya how I shlept? I wazh shound ashleep . . ."

"By God! You can ask Else if you like. Here, Else, did I or didn't I down fifteen brandies last Saturday? And did it show? Hah! Got up, buckled on my belt and: about face, forward march, direction the barracks. The old legs steady as all get-out, sparks flying from the cobblestones, you'd say I was marching in review on the First of December."

"I don't hold with guzzling for the sake of it. Not me. What I drink for is my mood. You knock back a couple and it puts you at ease, like. Take me. When I come in here of an evening I just sit there like some damned plaster saint. Like I had nothing to say. But let me have a shot and whee! I could even kiss Else there and then. Get my drift? That's what a good jolt does for you."

"For example, Herr Professor, suppose we build a dam and then a flood comes along and sweeps it all away. What's the sense of it all, Herr Professor?"

"I wazh shound ashleep when all of a shudden dere wazh tap-a-tapping at the winda. Sho I got up, got out of bed that izh, and what did I shee? Moon shining azh bright azh day and a dove on the winda-shill."

"Rrruh," goes the giant, agreeing or belching, it was difficult to say which.

"What did ya shay, bud? Well, I'm no good at reading the dreamzh. And the dove jusht went on tap-a-tapping at the winda. And if I'd opened it, who knowzh, it might have turned out to be a shoul, eh?"

"Grg, no," replies the giant briefly and assuredly.

"It wazhn't, eh? Yesh, well, I'm no good at dat short of thing. But it wazh funny, how it went tap-a-tapping . . . I shaw a film the other day about the Emperor Mackshimilian and how the Communishtsh murder him in Meckshico, shee. And hizh wife the Empresh wazh at Miramare near Trieshte. When the Emperor gave up the ghosht . . ."

"And what about having children? You're not married, Herr Professor? Sensible. There's no such thing as a friend. When they tell you 'friend' you think, What does he want from me?"

Well, well, thought Melkior, so Kurt's philosophy is expanding! He had heard Kurt out on dams before, but his views on children and friends . . .

"When the Emperor gave up the ghosht hizh shoul went to the Empresh right away like shome dove. Shinging, *Open the window, my shoul izh . . .*" (the little old man sang that part). "And you shay, bud, that it wazhn't a shoul?"

"Nah," rasped the giant. "That's just cinema."

"*Far, far awaaay from us, down by the seeea . . .*" nostalgically wails a Sergeant Second Class, throwing his head back and closing his eyes.

"No, no, please," Else implores him to keep the peace. "We can be fined for this. We have no music license."

"What do you mean, music? This is national, a folk song. It's not dance music or anything."

"No, singing is forbidden as a general rule," says Else meekly, almost abashed, as if someone were trying to kiss her.

"Armies are for war, aren't they, Herr Professor?" Kurt then dropped his voice to a whisper and assumed a somewhat confidential air, so that a thought crossed Melkior's mind, almost alarming him. "See for yourself, Herr Professor: that type of mentality" (he nodded in the direction of the sergeants), "is it fit for waging a war? It's only fit for barroom brawls. Fifteen brand*ies*, that's his brand of heroism. War is a science these days. And his idea of a good soldier is sparks flying underfoot. That's the type of mentality I mean. My poor sister has no choice but to listen to the drivel, because it's good for business. It's what we make our living at. And so it goes . . ."

"What? There ain't no man alive like our major. To see him facing the ranks on the parade ground, you'd think he's going to eat your liver for breakfast—but he's all heart. Word of honor. I went up to him once, sir, says I, you know how it is, a soldier's life, there's this gal waiting in town, 'Any good?' says he and gives me one of his winks, 'Welll . . .' says I, wondering if I should tell him she's crème de la crème, 'Off you go, then,' says he, 'and mind you don't disgrace the battalion,' and he does his spit 'n' snort routine like he was sending me out on a patrol. He's all heart, honest."

"And have you ever sheen canariezh kishing, bud? I have. It'sh a lovely shight, their kishing, and mosht interesting, too. You'd never have thought, they being shuch tiny creaturezh . . ."

"Or take your own case, Herr Professor . . . You're a man of intelligence—it's so stupid!"

"What's stupid?" Melkior understood immediately and was seriously afraid.

"That lowlifes like that should suck the blood of a man like yourself for nine months! Can't you think of a way out?" And Kurt became very confidential again. "Herr Professor, my father knows a trick, you see, but it's nothing dangerous and has no harmful after-effects. He picked it up in the Great War, it's a very simple thing to do and there's no professor of medicine who could suspect a thing. You dip two cigarettes in . . . in I don't know what, you dip them in whatever it is and smoke them before your physical. They'll send you home with tears in their eyes. My *Vater* got hundreds out that way. What is it you dip them in now? . . . He ought to be back any minute. If you would care to wait we'll ask him, all right?"

Melkior was upset by the come-on-we're-partners intimacy with which Kurt was assailing his innocent fear of history. You know, it's something altogether different, Kurt, what you have in mind, Kurt, this thing you . . . in his mind Melkior had started stammering some kind of apology to his conscience.

"Leaving already, Herr Professor? I wanted to ask *Vater*. What on earth do you dip them in, *Christgott*? Never mind, I'll ask *Vater* for you. Herr Professor. A very good night to you."

"G'niiight!" Else automaton-like sang her little tune at Melkior's departure, politely and with a touch of blush in her cheeks.

He climbed to his third floor with difficulty, as though his pockets were filled with stones. That's exhaustion, he thought, brought on by fasting.

Kurt's sausage had been his first meal since noon the previous day. He had not even finished the sausage, in view of Kurt's fingers. "Cannibalism" was the thought he had found in the second half of the sausage. And he had left that half to the surprised, even offended, Kurt. "Horses are more expensive than pigs or cattle," Kurt had said. "There's no horsemeat in it."

There is man-meat, Kurt, in our imagination.

He slipped his hand inside his shirt and grabbed a fistful of his hairy chest.

Man-meat. A useful addition to your vocabulary . . . and to your diet, too, in some parts of the world. Cannibals. Reclining on his bed, in the dark, he sailed out again on the *Menelaus*, a Pacific cargo liner. *Cannibals*. That was to be the title of a play he had been contemplating. Of the grotesque, in fact, with cannibal howls, dances, and native rites to the deafening rumble of drums around a cauldron over a large fire.

The cauldron is offstage, of course, because such high-impact scenes in the theater always take place offstage. Simmering in the cauldron is a white man, a fat cook, the plumpest of the seven survivors from the shipwreck *Menelaus*. You thought of it as a symbolical piece of satire or something. . . . Anyway, it does not matter what it was to have been, seeing that nothing had come of it save the momentary flash of an idea that came to you again at the Cozy Corner when Kurt brought the sausage to your table.

The idea first came to you one night on a train, on the hard bench of a third-class compartment. You had the entire compartment to yourself, a privilege bought from the conductor for a pittance. As you tossed sleepless on the hard slats the idea slowly took shape as the memory of stories you had heard in your childhood by the sea from lying old seamen who had not only been captured by cannibals but had also each of them seen the one-eyed giant whose eye each of them had gouged out. But why on the train that night the sudden return of those boastful geriatric odysseys, on that hard bench, accompanied by the horrible clatter of wheels under your ear? At one moment you found one of your hands on your knee and the other on your shoulder, you felt the hard and knobby bones overlaid with taut, dry skin; you poked your fingers into the joints, the holes in the bones, the gaps between the tendons, you separated one from another, registering each one in turn, unconsciously, by touch, by touch alone, as foreign, alien objects, not even thinking about them, and now, in hindsight, everything had fallen into place. You were dreadfully emaciated at the time from fear of events that had a claim on your body (the journey was in fact undertaken to settle some army-related business) and, touching your knobby bones, you suddenly felt a great instinctive pleasure, or rather a kind of perverse and derisive joy over these bones of yours, over the traveling skeleton, bearing your name, that had cleverly bought from the conductor this separate little compartment where it could lay down its bones and feel them and register: look, the knee bones, the shoulder blade, the clavicle, the ribs . . . in a word, where the skeleton could assert the frightening articulation of a skeleton slyly thinking of itself as such: this is I all the same, I who know my name, I who am smoking here in the dark above the clatter of the wheels and—*entre nous soit dit*—I who hope to wriggle free, to wriggle free . . . Hush, hush, mum's the word!

That scrawny body! That scrawny body of yours had gone underground inside its skeleton, hidden itself, insinuated itself into the bones and there felt the security of a snail, of a mouse in its hole, a hedgehog underneath its prickles. The body had simply proclaimed, I'm not there! And then later on, in the sanctuary, during a moment of respite between two fears, there began to germinate the idea of cannibals and castaways, as a lark, in a sunny and almost wanton way, such as when we indulge in the profligate waste of food after satisfying our hunger.

And tonight at the Cozy Corner, to the accompaniment of Kurt's plangent chant, over the sausage and Kurt's fingers, there resurfaced the wanton largesse of a skeleton which served fresh live man-meat to cannibals while itself feeding moderately and carefully lest some flesh appear on it, lest the body peek out. That was where the notion of cannibals resurfaced. The ship already had its name: the *Menelaus*. It had been sailing, after ten nights or so of its dangerous wartime voyage, through the Tonga archipelago (called the Friendly Islands by the Europeans) between the islands of Wawau and Tongatabu, making for Tutuila—or, more specifically, for the port of Pago-Pago—there to take on a load of copra for oil extraction. The previous night the captain had studied the charts of the archipelago (what a pretty word, archipelago) and that night it's That's all, folks, there's a war on, the *Menelaus* is going down.

Having been hit by a torpedo, the *Menelaus*—husband to Fair Helen (the whore, the whore, of the Trojan war)—goes down. But never mind the ship, it's the people that matter . . . there are only seven survivors. Six, actually, because the seventh, an old seaman with a pipe, is captured by Polynesian cannibals hours after the rest, thus arriving barely in time to see the cooking of the ship's cook. But—as Hamlet would have put it—not where he cooked but where he was being cooked, at a merry cannibal party complete with folk dances that have conquered Europe, via America, and, in the process of the Hellenization of cannibal culture, have become more universal and thrilling than Aeschylus or Sophocles. That is when the ship's cynic, a doctor by profession, declares that the cook had been dispatched to the dark world of cannibal gourmanderie with honors rather too high for his sheep's brains—which, incidentally, he had fixed splendidly aboard the *Menelaus*.

But before being cooked, the castaways are stripped naked and taken before some sort of board just like recruits. (Another twenty-odd days and there would be a fresh summons, the seventh so far: draftee Melkior Tresić is to present himself at the Recruiting Center for a physical examination to determine the degree of his fitness for service. . . . The medical board would be chaired by flat-footed ex-Austro-Hungarian army colonel Pechárek. First the speech: "Bwave soldiers and you gwaduate dwaftees . . . In dese gwave times yo' King and countwy ex-pect in-twepid duty" . . . The naked men shivering with cold, nerves, timidity; some covering their hanging gardens with their hands, the more audacious among the "bwaves" lifting them to tickle the frightened, goose-pimpled backsides of the shy ones in front. For the seventh time draftee Melkior Tresić would have the height-measuring bar insultingly dropped on his head, inhale-exhale, I'll cheat them of a few liters of air again, the captain with the snake of Asclepius on his epaulettes would probe his bicep with two fastidious fingers: serious asthenia, deferred service. . . . But there could no longer be any deferment, either-or time is here! A hushed argument at the other side of the table. Pechárek would not release his morsel. Emaciated, gaunt, nothing but skin and bones, says Asclepius, but no matter, the skin will do for King and countwy, not to mention the bones, for the skin's got thoughts buried inside, skin and bones, well, get them into olive drabs, the skin and bones, top them off with an army cap and let them sizzle quietly underneath as per King's Regulations—all four parts, by Jove!) The cannibal tribe's Pechárek with a ring through his nose, cook or butcher, perhaps even the king himself, expertly appraises the briskets, rumps, sirloins on the naked men and designates the cook to be dinner with a single gesture of his hand. The second fattest, the company agent, faints. The others watch their destiny with horror. Only the ship's doctor (the redheaded, freckled cad!) keeps his intelligent curiosity separate, making his appraisal as if he, too, were on the council, dressed in the naked brown skin that confers upon one the privilege of recruiting meat. With care, almost with tenderness, he sends his anatomical gaze gliding over the broad, brawny back of the chief engineer, crawling down his obese frame, orbiting flylike his arrogantly jutting belly, embracing his thighs with what is nearly loving tenderness and pronounces "number three" inside his head with perfidious certainty.

Poor chief engineer! Feeling the rat's cold snout on his skin, and painfully aware of his place in the terrifying chronology, he is unable to conceal his envy of the doctor's physical repugnance.

That is all the snake of Asclepius needs to corroborate his conclusion. Among these aristocrats of the flesh, the doctor is a miserable, stinking creature which has suddenly sensed its advantage. Out there, in that "other world," his body has had him consigned to a hell of loneliness. In the world of fragrances, where the standard smells are confined to special establishments, there to be flushed by water and battered by concoctions of chemicals and perfumes, he has to carry with him that very establishment with his quite unconventional, nonpatented, somehow original smell, horribly aware that his condition is definitive. He yearns for company, friends, women. Even women he pays for refuse to suffer his presence any longer than the job requires. In Shanghai he was told by a fat Romanian woman, who stank of sweat herself, that he had *such a strange* smell. . . . "Oh God, I smell bad, I stink!" He is convinced that he stinks all over, that his walk stinks, his motions, his gaze, his voice, that his speech spreads an insupportably foul atmosphere in which people choke.

He finds his own smell rank. He has soaped, scrubbed, washed himself, he has doused himself with fragrant fluids and oils, he has bathed in the sea, exposed his body to wind and rain, baked it in the sun, but the treacherous thing only developed a bran-colored rash and vile red spots, living wounds. His kinky red hair, his stubbly, sparse, barely visible eyebrows, everything, has been seared, demolished by hot water, soap, and the most shocking cosmetic hoaxes to which the wretch falls prey only too readily. Like a leper, he is aware of being eternally excluded from anything social and human, enjoyable and beautiful, from anything that is accessible to everyone else.

The poor ship's doctor!

But look: for all that he is a captive of Polynesian cannibals, facing the cauldron of death, draftee Melkior Tresić suddenly envies the doctor! He feels an awful pleasure at the man's repugnant body, at his stench, at his poor outcast physical person! They will smell him out, he will get away—he is inferior man-meat for the gourmands.

Watching the captain's plump, well-rounded curves, the chief engineer's strong, meaty shoulders, and the first mate's delicate, pale dreamer's flesh, the doctor comes to feel a certain cannibalistic pleasure at the tasty tidbits, at the superior flesh which had relished food, renown, respect, and love to the full. He is now certain of holding last place, or at worst of being tied for last with the crusty old seaman.

Meanwhile, heh, heh . . . he has only to wait for the natives to give him back his clothes. He has a miracle-working gadget or two in his pockets.

And indeed he gets his clothes back. He and the crusty old seaman. But the officers' uniforms, decorated with golden anchors, ribbons, and buttons, go to the king and his top two dignitaries, who parade them complete with hats. After dining on the cook, the hosts do a few of the latest cha-cha dances and retire sated and well pleased.

The six castaways are spending their first Polynesian night in a small circular hut made of bamboo stalks interwoven with reeds. After the inevitable petty squabble over the choice of sleeping space (the farther from the doctor and the crusty seaman, the better) in that cramped circle underneath a mud-and-reed dome, the two despised Clotheds and the four distinguished Nakeds settled down at last like so many birds captured under a straw hat.

But sleep will not come. Listening, each with his personal anxiety, to monkeys chattering in the nearby jungle, the castaways remember with indignation their celebrated fellow Westerner who proclaimed them, a hundred or so years before, the great-grandsons of that grotesque parody of humanity which swings from branch to branch and shrieks in hot, tropical nights. They are now disgusted by Tarzan's virginal heroism, and with indignation invite Messrs. Defoe, Burroughs, and Kipling kindly to join them in these Robinsonian and Tarzanian and Rikki-Tikki-Tavian beauty spots and in the pristine idyll of the Polynesian cannibal island!

The wretched cook! As they listen through the endless night to mournful squawks of the cockatoo, it seems to them that the cook's white soul is nostalgically looking for its body and, unable to find it, is wandering in the night, lost and miserable like a frightened bird, pleading for help and salvation. The very souls of the Nakeds go numb at those onomatopoeias inviting them to psittacine eternity.

And up there, at celestial heights, carelessly hang the bright tropical stars, swinging on starlight-spun threads to relieve the boredom of their eternal existence. The stars play their games in the blue space above the cannibal island, slinging meteors which fall in fiery arcs into the dark tropical seas.

Draftee Melkior Tresić has sailed away on his Menelaian bed. *Indonésie. Polynésie. Poésie.* The Dream Archipelago! (there is a novel of that title). Archipelagos. Atolls and lagoons. Hawaii—whence the charm of that word? "You and me and blue Hawaii . . ."

He swears with despair in that lonely night. God who is supposed to see all and know all! And the company agent shivers with fever. He is aware of his place in the series: it can happen tomorrow or the day after. . . . The ship's doctor offers help, massage of the head, of a neck muscle, which can be rendered insensitive. . . . The agent calls him a criminal and a cynic.

"Alas, gone is our good cook," is the doctor's response to his rudeness.

The agent bursts into tears.

Nobody heeds his sobs. Everyone is feeling himself in the dark, examining the state of his body and fuming at it. The findings are weighty, grave, fatal, like accusations of a stupid kind of recklessness which has brought them to ruin.

To end up in a cannibal cauldron. Appalling.

Someone is pummeling himself angrily and cursing his flesh. It is, the doctor knows, "Number Three," the chief engineer. The chief engineer is punishing his disobedient belly with desperate hatred, but also with some hope that he might thus flatten it, diminish it, force it inward and conceal it from the cannibal gourmets. He has moreover arrived at the idea of "an operation" and communicated it to the doctor.

The red-headed cynic laughs out loud. "And what about me? Who's to take the steaks and bacon off of me?"

"But you, er, you don't really need to, do you?"

"No, what I need is a helicopter. Give me a helicopter, or at least a common variety hot-air balloon to lift me up out of this terrestrial paradise and I'll shape you into such a repulsive, skinny piece of misery that you will disgust even the cannibals. I await your reply. Ridiculous."

The chief engineer sighs and abandons all hope.

The captain is cursing his "damned appetite" in a low voice. Reproaching himself for sumptuous meals in his past life. The tempestuous symphonies of delectable delights, largely the fault of that fat idiot whom "they" cooked today. Passing before his eyes are solemn columns of glorious breakfasts, lunches, and dinners marching with thick bacon strips taken off incomparable Yorkshire pigs, echelons of yellow ham-and-eggs, slender slices of bacon, ham and Italian mortadella, thrilling goose liver, rabbit, and partridge pâtés; perfidious shrimps march past and bowlegged frogs in batter leotards, splashing saucily through a delicate whiskey sauce, rice pudding, and the most exquisite creams spread sweetly all over the valley of the elect, while atop the holy lake of gourmanderie float lard halos like the metallic sounds of the angelus of eventide in the hills. Ah, that is all the dead sounds of Yorkshire grunts and Scottish clucks, of hissing, frying, and cooking in the accursed galley of the *Menelaus*, all that is nothing but the late memory of yolks being beaten, plates clanking, glasses clinking, and corks popping! And what has the captain got to show for all the festivities? Ah, if only it were possible to say "Nothing!" with a decadent sigh—what he has to show is his stupidly tight-packed personal can of meat, perfidiously seasoned with all the monstrous spices of gluttonous folly as a splendidly packaged delicacy the sight of which sends saliva trickling down the teeth of the voracious savages.

The poor captain heaves a sigh from the bottom of his heart and utters, without knowing why, an obvious piece of drivel:

"Damn it all, if only we'd remembered to bring a compass!"

"Damn it all, yes!" comes an ironic voice from the dark. "But given our navigational expertise I'm sure we'll be able to plot our course in a cauldron full of water."

It is the first mate, a pale young man with a white, henlike complexion, handsome in a rather effeminate way, delicate and sensitive like a pampered only daughter. The long and boring voyages in the Merchant Marines have pushed his melancholy nature to a gloomy spleen and a certain state of bitter depression and sarcasm. Feeling alone in the world, he finds Nirvana quite early on in a Hong Kong opium den.

Deprived now of his drug, he is naturally irritable. He has gone a whole day without a whiff of his bliss, knows that he will never have any again, and the knowledge is driving him desperate. He keeps smacking his head and mumbling idiotic gibberish.

The red-headed Asclepius knows what this is like and tries to relieve his transient pain by offering him the imminent prospect of eternal peace in genuine and, so to speak, natural nothingness. But nothing, not even the cannibal void, can comfort the pale first mate. All he announces is his simple revulsion with such a death. He can well elaborate in his mind Hamlet's thought about a king passing through the intestines of a beggar and is quite indifferent when imagining himself making his last journey in a state of mastication. He is just revolted, that is all. But this, the idea of "living in infernal reality" and never again, never again having a sniff, even if the "never again" lasts only three days—this he finds unbearable.

"How about betel leaves?" the doctor remembers. "You chew them, they're quite good . . . in a pinch."

"Betel grows in India," the first mate sighs yearningly and cries out in pain like a patient in the first night after his operation.

"It must grow here, too," the doctor comforted him, never saying never. "Betel is a species of tropical pepper and we are in the tropics, glory be to Buddha and Vishnu."

"Well, let me have some, then!" screams the first mate as though he is going to throttle someone if he is not given betel leaves that instant. "You'll get them tomorrow," said the doctor with the assurance of Christ promising the right-handed thief paradise on the morrow.

Paradise on the morrow. And something akin to joy welled inside Melkior the traveler, he felt the foretaste of an emotion. But the emotion itself was not forthcoming. First there was the necessary question: where did it come from all of a sudden, this affectation of the heart, this fantastic light shed on his nerves, this ever so soft caress of The Future? As if he had downed a shot of the hard stuff à la Maestro . . . at the Give'nTake . . . In the fog of his fear, in spite of everything, Beauty had smiled—at Ugo . . . It was at Ugo she smiled!

He swallowed Ugo with a dry mouth, forcibly, without faith. Without empathy, with envy. Titania had fallen in love with the ass. She was going to fall in love with Ugo. Titania will abandon Freddie for Ugo. She'll be with us, with the masters. He had entered into partnership with "the boys." The boys were going to have a queen. He would play Pyramus and Ugo, the lion. Maestro would be the wall and Chicory Hasdrubalson the moon. A midsummer night's dream . . .

At the border of the dream he was stopped short by a rough voice—

"Halt!" It was the changing of the guard downstairs, in front of the 35th Regiment barracks. In the light of a gas lamp, the two sentries were touching heads and whispering mysterious words like ants. The new sentry now had the watch. Crunch! went his boots. The boredom had begun . . .

Somebody was going upstairs, making for the third floor. But there were four feet on the staircase. Melkior had a closer listen. Four. Two were treading softly, trying to be soundless, and the other two were pointedly loud, at home there, seeking to cover for the two stealthy ones. The feet came to a stop outside Melkior's door. They knocked. The door was not locked. Without waiting for an answer, there appeared a black goatee with a grin, apologizing for the disturbance. Into the room stepped Mr. Adam, or ATMAN, a palmist of renown. He was wearing a black housecoat with a white scarf around his neck and a golden spider under his chin. He lived in a rented room directly below Melkior's. Melkior came up with his stage name, ATMAN, two or three years previously when Mr. Adam moved in as a totally unknown beginner who, as a sideline, transferred the photographic images of the dead onto porcelain. He now had women clients from all over town, including names from posh society. In the house he was respected more than the Court of Appeals judge who lived on the third floor; he was even a little feared. Passing his door they spoke in whispers and walked on tiptoe.

"Good evening, Mr. Melkior. Sorry to barge in like this. I heard you pacing above my head and I said to myself, Why do we not go upstairs and keep him company? That's my little habit, speaking to myself in the plural. After all, when you're talking to yourself, there are in fact two of you, are there not?"

"Yes, well, there were also four feet on the stairs," Melkior said rather rudely. He was finding this presence disturbing.

"Don't tell me you meant that as a slight," the palmist gave an ingratiating smile. "You didn't mean to describe me as an animal, a quadruped, did you?"

"No. I meant it sounded like two people walking up . . ."

"Double impressions of that kind are not unusual at night. It's an effect of nocturnal fantasy. The night multiplies things, particularly acoustical phenomena. So does solitude. You are alone a great deal of the time. Thinking about things. Thinking up things."

"I expect you are far more alone than I."

"Not at all!" protested Mr. Adam vigorously and sat down, feeling quite at home, settling in for a lengthy conversation. "I am never alone. Why do I talk to myself in plural? There are two of us: me and 'myself.' Like in a play. You don't think in such dramatic terms. You are independent in your thinking. Personal. You simply won't let people disturb you. Whereas they do disturb me. They keep badgering me with their traps and catches and all kinds of silly questions: 'what if' and 'suppose' and so on and so forth. Like, for instance, what if people could carry their homes on their backs, like snails? Silly stuff like that, you wouldn't believe it. Telling me jokes, mostly about dogs. For the barking, disturbance of the peace. That's what my life is like. Teasing."

And Mr. Adam kept smiling, stroking his pointed goatee with the tips of his white fingers.

"We talk about strange feelings as well, the two of us. We stretch, in solitude, and something goes click in the neck, right below the skull. And a door opens to admit curious thoughts. They enter the head, via the spine, from all over the body. Everything we collected during the day by touching, listening, watching. This includes garbage, actual garbage, and all kinds of filth. We touch this and that with our attention, as with a dog's nose. Everything sticks to us, all manner of observations. We sniff with the finger, the ear, the eye. We watch each other and we think, Nothing's out of the ordinary. But at night, when there's this click inside the head—presto, everything seems strange. That's when the teasing starts."

"Was there something you wished to speak to me about?" Melkior asked impatiently. "Something specific?"

"Specific? No, not really. Nothing specific. The *indéfinissable*— is that the right word?—is what excites me much more passionately. God, the amount of muck I've filtered through to get at a grain, a single grain of truth! After all, it's my job: to filter, to sift. A beautiful lady comes to me to have her future told. On what basis? On the basis of the silt she pours over me? She has me drenched with her lies, there's muck trickling from her pretty mouth, a lot of charming drivel. So go ahead, fish for her 'future' in that swill! No way, Madam! I go on screening and straining the stuff if it's an engaging case, I might take a whole afternoon running the muck through the filter. I don't care if others are kept waiting, I decant and precipitate this one over and over again . . . until the lady is frightened. They're all afraid. That's how I get them. It's not the future they fear, oh no!

We are afraid of the future, you and I, people of intelligence. Your fear, of course, is far greater, you being the more intelligent. But they, the society ladies, are afraid of the grain of truth in the silt, the pearl in their little shells, heh, heh, that has come about through them leading *a certain* kind of life. And when I reach for the grain, they quake. They will even swoon if the grain of truth is big enough, heh, heh . . . Do you imagine this repels them? No, sir, it draws them. They are intoxicated by fear, they become aroused—literally, that is to say sexually, aroused. We flee, we who know why the cock crows. We don't want to know. Our past is clean. Our present is . . . hah, that's the question; what about our present? I almost rushed into saying something imprudent, and the fact is that our present, I'm afraid, is none too clear. Fear of the future, that's what disturbs it. In consequence, we don't want to peer into it. We're clever, we know we'd better not, do we not? We'd rather live like this, in uncertainty . . ."

"Well, you mean you live in certainty?" Melkior gave a bored smile. "You know for certain?"

"Nobody knows for certain—not even God, because He can always change His mind. He may fancy 'something else' at any moment. Divine whim."

"You, too, seem to be given to whims. It was a whim that brought you here."

"A whim? And what if it was a sense of gratitude? But if I'm wasting your time . . ."

Mr. Adam had taken offense and was about to get up. But he stayed in his seat and even made himself more comfortable.

"Here I go jabbering away and I've got two horoscopes to cast. One of them for a prominent personality. A politician."

"So what are you going to predict for the prominent personality?"

"I'm worried. Don't mock me. I no longer even know what AT-MAN means. I've forgotten everything you explained to me. I didn't understand it at the time either. ATMAN, Karma, Veda, it's all Greek to me. You wormed it out from . . . India, just to make me look silly. Or you didn't even bother to worm it out, you just told me what first came to mind. Like when I now say MADA. Which does mean something—it's my name spelled backward. Perhaps even ATMAN is something spelled backward, just for fun. I was very suspicious at first. Now I no longer care. Your mockery . . ."

"I do not mock you," Melkior said unconvincingly.

"Oh yes you do. You laugh. Inside. 'This fellow would tell the future,' you say. 'Well, why doesn't he tell his own?' As a matter of fact I do, only I don't speak of it. What's the use of speaking? That's why I say I'm worried, because I know. 'And I looked, and behold a pale horse: and his name that sat on him was Death and Hell followed with him. And power was given unto them over the fourth part of the Earth, to kill with sword, and with hunger, and with death, and with the beasts of the Earth.' Read and memorized. The Apocalypse. And yet I don't mock your fear," ATMAN added suddenly, with a strange smile that made Melkior rather uneasy.

What's he latched onto me for? he thought. What is he after?

"What's this fear you're talking about?" he all but shouted at ATMAN. "I am not afraid!"

"Then why so defensive?" Mr. Adam gave a cordial laugh.

"When a man thinks, his fear is proportional to the power of his thought. Why should I underrate you? Coming ever closer, as you know, is the pale horse with its rider . . . In one of the books I borrowed from you I saw a picture by an artist. It's called *The Mouse*. Women standing on chairs, pressing their legs together, gathering their skirts in mortal terror—there's a mouse on the floor! But bombs they're not afraid of. What about you—are you afraid of mice?"

ATMAN was now looking at him with provocative derision. But this was all still unclear; why had he come up here? What was the point of the entire conversation?

Melkior was simply at a loss for words—and for ideas as well. It had been stupid of him to try to defend himself. From what? From fear. Fear of fear! A new power in the mathematics of fear. Now he was going to have the damned palmist under his ear at night and be forced to think about him, too. He was furious with himself for letting the mysterious vagabond near him.

"Look here, Mr. Adam . . ." he initiated the ceremonial ejection procedure.

But ATMAN had a good ear for that kind of tone, and immediately interrupted the ceremony with a gesture that wiped the slate clean and announced a fresh start.

"All right, let's put it all on the scales. Let's weigh things seriously, Mr. Melkior. A weighing machine is a precise instrument, no tricks, no teasing. 'True weight whatever the freight,' says the peg-legged invalid. I share your respect for it.

"After all, we do check our condition on it, even literally, do we not? How much do we weigh? Because this can be decisive at times, of course. There are such things as the official criteria of fitness."

"I must tell you, Mr. Adam . . ." Melkior made another attempt at ejection.

"Yes, Mr. Melkior. You have my undivided attention. I'm always ready to learn something new. Always!"

Melkior was losing patience. He was on the frightening verge of jumping up and yanking ATMAN's goatee. And booting him in the backside!

"I have an article to write for tomorrow. I'm sorry but I have work to do tonight!"

"I, too, as I've said, have work to do tonight. But what kind of future shall I draw for them?" ATMAN rested his brow on his open palm, worried. "If I were a magician, I'd turn the politician into a bird and let him fly where his wings would take him. That's his future after all: to fly . . ." Then, quite close to Melkior's face, so that Melkior felt the noxious breath from his mouth, something reminiscent of dirty socks, "To fly away, eh, Mr. Melkior? Far away from these people," he nodded in the direction of the barracks across the road. "To safety. But they will not let you go. They bite into your flesh and will not let go. And we, heh, heh . . . we deprive them of the flesh. No meat, sorry! Skin and bones you can bite if you like. But what if they bite into the skin and bones, what if they do after all? Vicious dogs they are . . ."

"Let them bite what they like!" Melkior cried out in desperation.

"What's all this nonsense? Please leave me alone, sir! I want to work, to work!"

"Oh, to work, quite so . . . I forgot we have work to do . . . the both of us."

The palmist stood up, tightening the belt of his housecoat as if really about to leave. Melkior felt a surge of hope, even adjusted a fold on ATMAN's housecoat, in the servile manner of a lackey.

But ATMAN noticed Melkior's freshly laundered linen laid out in neat stacks on the bed.

"Ah. Fine linen you have there. White shirts. I, too, prefer my shirts white. Buy them yourself?"

"Of course I buy them myself. Who else would buy them for me?"

"Oh, I didn't mean who does the *monetary* buying. That would obviously be a bit, er . . . What I meant was have you got an adviser, an advisoress, heh, heh . . . in matters of taste. Because they are in very good taste indeed. The finest poplin. Also two-button cuffs. Not one; two. Most fashionable."

Melkior, as it happened, had not wanted ATMAN's departure to take the form of ejection. He therefore mustered all of his utterly battered patience to build him a golden bridge for an honorable retreat. But no! ATMAN was not even thinking of retreating. He crossed his arms on his chest and began pacing about, indulging in meditation, "We criticize their superficiality, but look how their little hands make themselves felt on our things. On shirts, for example. *That's* their world, those two buttons—indeed their general outlook, their worldview." He put a strong emphasis on the word "worldview," as if everything depended on it. "While we chuckle in our wise, masculine way; we are taken up with important concerns. They laugh at our important concerns and go on doing our linen, always after us to change our clothes and take our baths and cut our nails. Being boring. We give martyred sighs, because it is a kind of terror. We long for any form of *liberation*. You don't know about these things, Mr. Melkior, you haven't been married; I have. Well, there comes at long last that blessed *liberation*. Quite unexpectedly, like drawing a prize at the lottery. So one evening you're preparing for an adventure. Showered and shaved (voluntarily, not under duress), donning a fresh shirt, humming a little tune, pandering to your freelance-lover style—and all that in front of a mirror, to double the joy, as it were; in a word, you're a marvelous specimen, you admire yourself no end . . . and then: hello, what's this? There's a shirt button missing! All you find in its place are those broken little whiskers of thread. There was nobody to take care of it, you see . . . There's the feeling of loneliness for you! Do you think she would have left a different mark? What if she had been there above the buttons?" ATMAN asked suddenly of Melkior, pushing his derisive smile quite close to his face.

"Who's 'she'?" Melkior was gripped by something like fear. "You really are talking nonsense . . ."

"The one you saw tonight . . . at the Give'nTake? Heh-heh! Viviana! But her name is not Viviana. That's your first mistake."

Melkior was speechless. How on earth . . . ? Why, it was sheer telepathy! He hadn't said a word to anyone. . . . As for Viviana, he would have called her that himself . . . No, he simply stared at ATMAN, his flesh creeping with terror: My God, this man knows everything!

"I know everything, Mr. Melkior," the palmist stated, interrogator-like.

"Including your suffering over 'being last.' That, too, is a mistake. You think that even Ugo is ahead of you. As for the actor, he's simply a hairpin, a garter, a comb, if you like. Perhaps you're offended by such comparisons, but take them as figures of speech, in the sense that he's a toilet article . . . Perhaps it's you that she sees as . . . Mr. Right."

"You know her?" Melkior blurted out the very unfortunate question, but impatiently, impatiently!

"Do I know her? She comes to me looking for a husband! As if I had one in my pocket and had only to reach inside. What about personal initiative, I told her. You've got to seek, and knock, and ye shall find, and it shall be opened unto you. What are those two irresistible eyes for, those two legs above the knee, not forgetting the idea of the pair of breasts that tugs at your heart? That was how I put it to her, almost in verse. You laugh at verse? Well, never mind, I told her that as poetically as I could, in rapture."

"And she turned you down!" Melkior rejoiced. He was gaining ascendancy over ATMAN, had almost got him confused.

"Turned me down . . . but not quite." The palmist was already regaining some of his composure. He was visibly dejected. Perhaps he had come up only to talk about her. "That is to say, she turned me down halfway. In fact, she turned me down two-thirds of the way, but I've kept the remaining third—for contact, you see. We are in touch. Was that a frown I saw at 'touch'? All right then: we maintain diplomatic relations. Mutual interests. She is—I take it you've gathered—a parasite."

"You support her?" and a pain kicked at Melkior's diaphragm.

"Never. Why should I? There's another plant that she lives on. Don't worry, it's a female plant. Flora. That's her name. Her aunt. Runs a dressmaker's salon. 'Flora's Fashions,' perhaps you've heard of it. I refer my clients to her. And vice versa."

"That's how it is?"

"That's how it is."

The sun smiled down on Melkior. He smelled the fragrance of roses from the long ago May festivities of his boyhood. He went to church in his short pants to hear a little girl Ana sing in the choir. He wanted to become an organ player, that was how May-like was his love for Ana. Then a cloud covered the sun for an instant and there was darkness in church and Ana's voice sang a sibylline death chant. But the sun shook the clouds off and Ana shone again. . . .

"Is her name Ana?"

"You don't even know her name! No, it isn't Ana. What made you think of that particular name? You'd better stick with Viviana, names make no difference anyway."

"Look," Melkior suddenly remembered to ask, "how did you know what happened at the Give'nTake tonight?"

"How? What a strange question. I was there."

"I didn't see you."

"But I saw you. Thénardier has a small room in the back, an office. He even sleeps there when there's a wild binge. He's got a couch in there. I use the room at times . . . when necessary."

"You follow her?"

"Now and then. I play the waiting game."

"Waiting there? At Thénardier's, on the couch?"

"Not that literally I don't. Freddie will soon change her for a fresh princess regent. That's what I'm waiting for."

"How will *he* change her when you said just now that it was she who . . ."

". . . kept him as part of her toiletry? Yes. No contradiction there. He keeps her—beautified by his presence—to sit with in cafés. As soon as they start whispering 'Freddie's in love' in the Theater Café, the princess regent will be replaced."

"So he doesn't really care for her?" Melkior's interest was keen.

"Well . . . he does all right, but not in *that* sense. He's rather a wimp."

"A wimp? In what sense?"

"It's 'I'm not in the mood today.' It's 'I can't guarantee, I'm playing tonight.' And so on. A male deferred."

How interesting!" Melkior laughed pleasurably. "So Freddie will soon . . ."

"He will. Word's got around the Theater Café. It'll be before the leaves have turned yellow. She was born on December 24, the day before Christmas. She won't be celebrating her birthday with him. She may celebrate it with me, or even with you, but definitely not with Freddie."

"Why me?" Melkior tried a laugh, without any convincing success. He was growing fond of ATMAN.

"You're a serious candidate." Adding, as if worried, "She has asked about you."

"You've just made that up!" and his heart beat a crazy tattoo. This is the beginning of love, he thought.

"By no means. She asked. Freddie had warned her, because of your reviews. He hates you. With a passion."

"I know. He tried to provoke me tonight at the Give'n Take."

"I know. He wanted to have it out with you as well. She was egging him on. Ugo threw a wrench in the works. She wanted to see the two of you fight."

The cloud had covered the sun again. Or is ATMAN pulling my leg? He would have loved to press him with questions, but restrained himself, with a scowl. The palmist was studying him seriously, compassionately even, as one who shared his fate. At length he cracked his long fine fingers and spread his arms like a priest at Mass, with resignation, "*Oremus.*"

"Oh, well, there's no understanding them. Apparently they like that sort of thing. They like watching people run over by trams, too. The gore. The torn limbs. Whereas they sob in the cinema over the lost doggy looking for its master."

"How did you know she was egging him on?" Melkior succumbed after all.

"She said so herself. I joined them, later on, after you left. 'I so wanted to see a good bash.' *Bash*, that's her word. You ought to know her education is minimal. When you meet, she may well ask you what *exemplar* means. She's ignorant."

Melkior was disturbed by the information. He felt a stupid need to ask questions. "So what does she do?"

"Reads love stories. Looks for a husband. Perhaps you could . . . No, you couldn't. Too ordinary. Her idea of a husband is somebody who'd stir things up. If she marries again it will have to be a scandal, in one way or another. My chances are better than yours. ATMAN the palmist. Now that's shocking!"

"Oh, she has been married then?"

"Once. An ordinary sort of thing. To a nice, young, hard-working man. Ordinary. Her aunt Flora says she could not 'look up to him.' The aunt is an old maid with an Angora cat. They don't live together."

Better and better. But why, why was ATMAN saying all this? Was he in love with her? And what was the point of the nocturnal visit? What kind of game was this?

"What did she ask you about me?" said Melkior with a touch of the stern.

"Well, certainly not your mother's maiden name . . ."

"Then what?"

"Well . . . there are all kinds of questions, are there not?"

"Such as?"

"Can't a young man like you be broadly interesting to a woman like her?"

"What's 'broadly interesting' supposed to mean?"

"Perhaps it's 'just you wait, you night owl of a hermit, you're the absolute opposite . . . but I want you all the same' . . . or something. And anyway, who can ever tell what intrigues a woman in a man? It's a good job *something* does. I'll introduce you to her."

"Why? If you've staked your own claim . . . including marriage?"

"I didn't mention marriage explicitly. But it is a possibility, as they say in the classified ads. Thing is, I am patient. And patience is a virtue. I'm letting her have her little fling first. Until she reaches the I-can-always-find-an-old-man-to-darn-socks-for stage. And I won't be an old man all that soon; I consequently offer greater mercy. I'm gaining the edge. And you must admit she is a beauty."

"Sure, she's beautiful all right," said Melkior in the tone of someone who has added a silent curse.

"Very beautiful. I'll introduce you to her so you can see close up. Seeing tears in her eyes would make you write poetry! I myself have moments when . . . But hell, I don't know how to do it, I have no talent, words elude me. I generally employ 'heart' and 'sorrow,' but it's hardly poetry, heart and sorrow, is it? Ugo will be writing sonnets for her. He's made a date."

The news slashed him like a saber. Had he not sensed that she would fall for the ass?

"A date . . . with her?"

"Or on her, as they say in a play. Do you imagine it's any easier for me? Only I'm armored. Patience is my armor, as I have said."

"You really love her?"

"What's 'really'? I love her *with all my heart*, not *really*. To the death!"

"And yet you joke about it?"

"Perhaps it's just my turn of speech. But I have in me a deliberate realism: I wait. After the lot of you, I want to have her *finally*. Do you understand—*finally!* After me, the flood! Is that a joke? Can't you see I'm letting myself be crucified?"

"What about jealousy? Aren't you jealous?"

"Of course I am. But what am I to do? Murder, strangle, poison all those whom she temporarily fancies? *Temporarily*, I say. It's her I want, not your death. It's Ugo's turn now, or perhaps yours, I don't care. That's exactly why I want to introduce you to her—to accelerate the course of history. To have you finish your reign as soon as possible. I'm not saying I'm in a rush. Anyway the war's coming closer. It will drag you all into armies, into battles for someone's complicated Futures. I'm staying behind. It's simple—Unfit For Service. I have a certificate signed by a general, heh heh. Perhaps you will all get killed. She doesn't need dead men."

The account was about to be closed. Melkior felt his skeleton inside him moving comically in front of ATMAN's grin that was eyeing him from beyond, from life. Like in a grotesque parade, Melkior found himself in a column of history's dead marching past life into oblivion, while up there on the stand sat the timeless, eternal ATMAN the palmist, the charmingly grinning and kindly connoisseur of the future.

ATMAN smiled politely standing in front of Melkior and offered him his fine white hand for a "good night." Melkior did not register ATMAN's hand, he was feeling his body as if this were an outspread, undeniable, indestructible fear of everything that moved, that breathed, that lived.

"Well, good night, Mr. Melkior." Mr. Adam accepted Melkior's hand and pressed it hard, in cordial friendship. "I'm sorry to have kept you so long. I badly needed to lay bare my soul to someone. I'm in pain. Good night."

And ATMAN trudged out dejectedly like a wretch who had just

confessed all his weaknesses. He closed the door behind him softly as if it were his very soul that had left.

Loneliness welled inside Melkior as a painful physical condition, as an infinitely sad sense of being lost.

Begone now, leave me be, 'tis solitude I need
softly to approach the grass, my mistress wild,
to tell the nettles, thorns, and prickly weed
of love for Earth in a picture green.

In the picture: dead men, with no arm or eye,
heads in helmets floating down a stream,
a headless eye watching from a tree
the dagger duels of men soon dead to be.

With mortal fear my body has grown numb
—this body of sob, of ache, of grieving herd.
Glory for country, my skin for a drum,
and my bones . . .

He could not remember the rest. ". . . will be broken by sticks and stones," he added mechanically. Oh Lord, forgive me, Lord, forgive me. She doesn't need dead men.

He blew through pursed lips and the air came out as a whistle. It sounded like stage wind in a Shakespearean tragedy. Quiet, you fool, you'll have the Weird Sisters upon us! After he had clammed up there came the voice of Dom Kuzma: "Forgive me for those slaps, my son, I only meant to raise you with the fear of God." A feeling of goodness came over him. He had been moved today by the sight of Dom Kuzma with his scrawny neck quarrelling with death on the weighing machine. He wanted to find an excuse for him. Perhaps God dislikes me and Dom Kuzma is merely here as the executor of the dislike? The entire fault lay up there. Then. Today Dom Kuzma's hands were a discarded, condemned tool. The tyrant had rejected his faithful servant. Sent him wandering from one weighing machine to another to weigh his poor body and de-fraud his death gram by gram.

The death of all. There is but one death. For the crocodiles and the bumblebees, there is but one death. ATMAN knows it, the Great Spirit ATMAN the Enamored who can see the Future, even accelerate it.

In what way does the Future exist? Does there exist something that has yet to happen? If not, how can something take place that does not exist? Does there already exist the bullet which will bore through my head? That very bullet, fitted into rifle cartridge number such and such, manufactured this afternoon at a Krupp factory in Essen, which will pierce my brain in a single second selected out of all of Time for this very purpose? In my mind I follow the bullet from its birth all the way to my head: manufacture, sorting, packaging, delivery. The large ammunition convoys. With the little bastard traveling in a crate just for me. And they have determined exactly where it will arrive, to whom it is to be issued, when it will be inserted into the rifle and then . . . and then, in *my* second, *bang!* and I stop writing its biography. It has spat into my inkwell itself. *Finito*, I follow it no more. It was alive in my thought. It has killed my thought and itself. It, too, is dead. There is but one death. It exists and it shall happen, Oh Immortal ATMAN. "Divinity of hell." A good thought before sleep, Iago, a good thought indeed . . .

He threw himself down on his bed and closed his eyes. To rein in his thoughts.

The seminarian in his seminary is now dreaming of his beloved St. Margaret. Naked. But holy. And all is as God ordains. All is like Holy Communion, the sacrifice of body and blood. What is the name of the beautiful Viviana from the Give'nTake? He had not remembered to ask Maestro, and ATMAN would not tell him. From now until further notice her name is Viviana . . . "For we are doomed, you and I," sings Melkior in his mind to keep awake. Sleep fortifies the body, nourishing, rounding, lining with fat the prime cut, the steaks, the hams. A fine cut of man-meat. Pechárek'sh going to gobble ush up, *bud*, and make no mishtake. And our shoul, the pshittashine dove, will hover over tropical sheazh and warble like the Leopardian lonely shparrow.—Gr, says the giant with the ring in his nose, gr. . . . And at that point a gigantic snoring starts up in the still of the night.

From somewhere up above, from the staircase, in between the sentry's boots on gravel—crunch!—there comes the snoring of a colossus, legendary, dragonlike, a sheep a day, a girl a night. Gargantua has stretched out between two stories and is shaking the entire building. Whooshing the huge bellows pressed in his armpit, blowing and playing his monstrous bagpipes harr-harr, oooh-hah, plhh-phoo, oooh prlhh, pweehh-pliouff . . . Sweeping, rich, luxurious snoring. Careless, cannibalistic. Optimistic.

Mrs. Ema does not snore like that. Mrs. Ema, a widow, Melkior's landlady, snores in a complex, climacterial way, afflicted by dreams of fat snakes and robbers thrusting knives into her navel. She tells Melkior about it all the next day over coffee. She neighs, squeals, meows, brays with dream-felt pains. She is a martyr. Whereas this relisher is a man, brother, snoring for all the five continents of the world, hugely, outstandingly, provocatively.

Here we are, with some damp autumn air we've stored in our nests for the night, and look what's happening—this chap is going to suck it all, gobble it all up, guzzle it all. The voracious sleeper. He'zh going to shuffocate ush all, *bud*, make no mishtake.

The hours pass and the harrr-harrr rolls unstoppably down the stairs, shoots back up from the cellar with the sound and the fury, reaching the attic and tumbling back down again, and splashing and sploshing and hewling and shloofing, craffing, roaring, whistling, dropping—pluff—and rising again, flying, a missile zooming past, whooosh, and piercing, burrowing, drilling, boring—rrrrrr—smashing, cutting, sawing iron bars, sawing the staircase lengthwise, the staircase across, he will bring down the house, the one-eyed terrible cyclops Polyphemus.

What an odyssey! Melkior enjoys the event like a child relishing a catastrophe. Everything is upside down. There is no sleeping. Everybody is getting up. The house is on fire.

There is a stirring in the next flat, that of the Court of Appeals judge. Slippers on the floor, fumblings in the dark. Voices.

Excitement. Muffled calls of "Daddy, Daddy" from his daughters. The judge grumbles angrily. He can hear it himself: a supernatural snore. He sends the maid to reconnoiter the snore and report back.

The door of the judge's flat opens slowly, cautiously, to prevent the snore from sneaking in. The maid's hands tremble, the door gives irresolute creaks. She has thrust the oil lamp through the door into the staircase, better let the oil lamp have a look first. . . . But the door suddenly slams shut and smash!—the lamp has of course crashed to the floor, and the maid shouts fire. Confusion, slamming of doors, great commotion. It seems that the maid is indeed on fire. Mistress shouts "Water!" the judge shouts "Not water! An overcoat. An old one!" They put the fire out. The maid is not on fire at all, it is the anteroom rug. Mistress wails, "Oh my God, the carpet! It's only fit for the rubbish heap now!"

"Who cares about the carpet!" the judge exclaims in anger. Turning to the maid:

"You. How did this happen?"

"There was a draft," stammers the maid. "Something blew and put it out . . ."

"Put what out? The lamp, you mean?" the judge questions her expertly. "But how could the fire start if the lamp was out?"

"I dropped it . . . There was a draft when I opened the door, all suddenlike, and it came on . . ."

"Came alight? The lamp came alight?" The judge is losing his patience.

"It was burning . . ." The maid is already in tears.

"Was the lamp burning or was it not when you dropped it, that's what I want to know!" The judge insists, he wants pure facts, the truth and nothing but the truth!

"I don't know," weeps the girl. "There was a draft . . ."

"A draft? Yes, you've got a draft in your head! Come on, go back to sleep. No, wait. Hold the door and mind it doesn't close . . . in case of a draft . . ."

"Draft, my foot," the judge thinks in a masculine way. He goes out onto the staircase to reconnoiter for himself. But mistress opposes him, his daughters beseech him, "Daddy, Daddy." They will not let him go into the darkness. "What blasted darkness? I'll turn the staircase light on!"

The snoring bursts in through the open door, forceful, mustachioed.

Threatening.

"Can't you hear it, you mad, mad man?" Mistress will not let her husband rush into adventure.

"Daddy, Daddy," weep his daughters. They are losing their father.

"Doctor, sir!" agrees the maid.

"What the hell's got into all of you? What're you blubbering for? Will you let go of me, damn it! Here, you've torn my pajamas, you fools!"

He has broken free of the womenfolk and steps out, bravely. "You hold the door. Watch out."

He has turned the staircase light on and is listening. He is now at a loss for what to do.

"Mr. Tresić! Mr. Tresić!" the mistress bangs on his door. Calling for help.

He does not like his name being shouted. "They know my name, even. Keeping tabs, discussing me . . ." That was what he thinks before he comes to the door.

"Yes?"

"Mr. Tresić, please." Mistress is trembling at his door. "Did you hear?"

(She gathers her housecoat on her breast under Melkior's random look.) "Do you hear what's going on here?"

"No, Madam. What?"

"Can't you hear it, for God's sake?"

The snoring is still "going on." It is serene now, almost sage. Exalted.

"Oh, that? Someone's sleeping." Melkior was enjoying himself.

On the staircase he comes upon a tableau. The judge in the middle, gray-haired, tall, lean, peering up toward the attic, both palms behind the ears, like a priest of a sect at prayer. On either side of him, his daughters in long nightgowns (angel-like), ministering. The maid gripping the door firmly, with both hands, according to instructions, the wife ringing at all the doors, summoning the faithful . . .

When Melkior appears, the daughters squeal and leave the scene of the ritual. "Fled. The foolish virgins." He sees the first florescence of breasts—"buds"—and the two other curves, smooth, sprightly, in flight. And the silhouetted legs, long, swift,—"wild animals"—joined by a shy acute angle. Heretical, blasphemous thoughts smile at Melkior. He forgets the sanctity of fear and gives the angels a parting glance—a lustful one.

"We ought to wake him up," the judge says to him.

"Why bother? Let him sleep."

"Sleep? The man's a cannibal!"

"Polyphemus the Cyclops, the beast, will eat us all, one-eyed . . ."

"What did you say?"

"I said, what magnificent snoring! Homeric!"

The judge turns away from him with an I'm-not-in-the-mood-for-joking grimace.

His wife has woken up two floors, the second and the third. Everyone comes out onto the stairs, like characters in a French film. Everyone is talking at once, pointlessly, without direction. The judge calms them down before explaining the matter. The sleeper is a giant of a man, he could batter them all to death, the situation calls for circumspect and concerted action. They propose getting brooms and umbrellas. Calling the fire brigade (by all means!), alerting the troops in the barracks across the way. Mrs. Ema, still under the sway of a dream, feels it is "quite simple": shear the man's hair while he is asleep and he will be left helpless. Just as Delilah sheared Samson's . . .

At last there appears on the staircase ATMAN himself. The black dressing gown, white scarf and golden spider, the black goatee, and the grin put an end to all the chatter. Reverence reigns on the stairs. Even the judge is relegated to the ranks. ATMAN ascends like the Savior. He takes his right elbow in his left palm, formally, and, stroking his goatee, waits patiently until there is complete silence. Then he says, "I'm going to hypnotize him!"

That is a catharsis. There are even handclaps. With a "shh" and a finger to his lips ATMAN cuts the ovations short and bows to the audience on all three sides with an almost painful grin. "Please don't." Whereupon begins the ascension, for he is ascending to the attic like God to Heaven. And he disappears in the darkness. He leaves behind upturned heads like in a Renaissance painting.

Melkior, too, turns his head atticward. Like a hen catching a drop of water. He swallows with impatience. He listens. Something appears to have got between the cogs of the snoring: it had now become irregular, like an engine winding down. And it stops with a powerful exhalation. And something like an oath is thrown in. Melkior hears angry whispers: the incautious, sleepy raising of a voice being hushed by another, threatening one. Everyone takes it for the sound of Hypnosis, for the voice of a mysterious force lulling the snorer's senses. Now they all await the descent.

The way he'd said, "I'm going to hypnotize him!" No, really, what *is* going on up there? Four feet on the staircase, Melkior remembers, four feet when ATMAN was climbing to my door! An advertising stunt of the palmist's, Melkior decides. It is only curiosity that keeps him out there.

The lights in the stairwell suddenly go out. Fear of darkness grips everyone. Body pressing against body, protection. Something curving, female, half-dressed, cuddles against Melkior. In response he gives it a protective embrace. The curved thing surrenders limply, caressingly. His hands greedily explore the relief of the hemispheres, entering gorges, running down gorges; the mouth enters the jungle of hair, discovering the tiny shell of an ear, "Darling, darling, let's retire" says the mouth of its own accord, inaudibly.

Tens of panicky fingers grope for the switch on the wall. They interweave like languages unintelligible to each other. "It must be hereabouts. Move away, everyone," commands the judge, his voice on the wrong wavelength, quavering. "Matches!" There are none to be found. The switch is not to be found either. "Now where in the dickens . . . ?"

"Darling," whispers Melkior's lips in the jungle, and the *curvy warm* says to the palms of his hands, "yours, yours." Everything is there in his arms, given as gift, as if in a dream. "Darling," whisper the lips to the tiny ear, "my room is right here." Suddenly the sleek slim fish comes to life, gives a frightened start, slides out of his arms and dives into the dark. Damn it, I could have . . . The curse of that masculine "now." That canine "right here and right now" lust. I could have arranged it with her. Now I don't even know who she was. They go for contrivance, for secrecy. Ugo has made a date with her. Or was ATMAN lying? What's going on up there now? Can't hear a thing.

Finally someone stumbles upon the switch. The light snaps on. Which one was it? He searches not by exclusion but the other way around: by choice, following his wishes. "Buttons," Mr. Adam had said. Well, which button? The judge has two girls: the "foolish virgins." Then there is the young wife from the second floor. He selects the young wife from the second floor. She is standing a little way off, next to her husband. Skier, the athletic type, broadshouldered. Melkior feels inferior. He looks at her. Nothing. Another look, a long one, accomplice-like, with an invisible wink. Nothing. Sheer innocence. Her response is an absolutely conjugal, good-neighborly smile. No, not her. The "foolish virgins" then? But they are not even turning around. They are looking up, in the direction of the attic. Everyone is looking in the direction of the attic. "Coming down now," somebody whispers piously.

"Coming down now." The sentence reverberates inside Melkior in strange acoustics, refracted through a sound prism, with multiple echoes. ATMAN is bringing up the rear like a controlling power. Something is radiating from his eyes.

Everyone sees it. In front of him walks the hypnotized medium, his arms dutifully outstretched, like those of a blind man. His eyes are open but unseeing. He is controlled by the power residing in ATMAN.

Why, it's Four Eyes, the lush! The palmist has arranged it all. Four feet on the staircase: that's what had been coming up. A con job.

General disappointment on the stairs. They had expected a man-eating giant tamed by hypnosis. What they get is a rumpled runt, unshaven, dirty. It is amusing all the same. A hypnotized man. Arms outstretched, red, cold-bitten, trembling uncertain, tired, freshly awoken, shaken awake.

The ape's acting well, thought Melkior. This can't be their first show.

On reaching the last step ATMAN halts. But he does not loosen the hold his almighty gaze has on the unconscious subject. Four Eyes's glazed eyes look for someone among those present. Melkior goes numb with fear: he has been found out! The two outstretched dirty hands are coming closer. The brute is indeed a good actor. Before he can collect his wits, the subject falls into his arms sobbing, "*Mon ami, Mon ami.*" At last, at long last, he has found the long-lost one!

"So that's what the 'Let him sleep' was for?" said the judge. He now sees everything clearly. "You knew."

"I did not!" Melkior barely manages to scream from the grimy embrace. Four Eyes has his smelly shoulder against Melkior's mouth, sobbing "*Mon ami, mon ami*" into his ear.

"Ah-ha, '*Mon ami*'! And yet he says he didn't know!" the judge laughs sourly. "This is a hoax, all right, gentlemen. Let's go back to sleep. Good night. As for you, Mr. Tresić, kindly save this kind of buffoonery for your drinking binges and let us get some sleep. Some of us are early risers."

And the judge leaves. He pulls behind him his wife and his virgins, who are reluctant to go: they are held back by curiosity. How *is* it going to end? "Tell me, my friend: who is the sleep-murderer?" Four Eyes asks of Melkior soberly, worriedly even, having dropped his embrace. A blast of brandy shoots out of his mouth.

Melkior steps aside in disgust. He is shaking with rage.

"Mr. Adam, if you don't lead your ape away instantly, I will thrash him!"

"Ladies and gentlemen," ATMAN speaks up with dignity, "do you see an ape here? Pull yourself together, Mr. Melkior, if you please. We have all been roused in the middle of the night. We are all finding things a bit out of the ordinary."

The audience is on ATMAN's side. But Melkior is not aware of his own failure.

"This is the second time this drunkard has insulted me today. I don't even know him."

"Perhaps, Mr. Melkior, in a previous life?" ATMAN is being kind like a psychiatrist with a madman patient. "Never mind, eventually you will remember . . ." Then to the audience, "Under hypnosis, ladies and gentlemen, the soul acquires what is known as metempsychic memory. Here you have a typical example. You have just seen a hypnotized subject find the man he was searching for. In a previous life, as I said, they may well have grazed on the same meadow or, apologies to the ladies present, chased the same bitch. And now, having been reincarnated . . ."

"Will you stop the drivel, you ass? You read about that in the paperback you borrowed from me the other day!"

Even Melkior himself now sees he is losing. If only the judge had stayed behind: he might have been able to grasp a point or two. But these people just stare with fascination at ATMAN, the man in the know.

"There you are, gentlemen, 'in the paperback.' Paperbacks are just about at our level. Whereas they read about things in thick volumes. The secrets of the occult, Mr. Melkior, are to be found not in paperbacks but in here," and the palmist tapped his forehead. "If you wish, I can lead you, too, as a medium, up and down these steps, for all your libraries. In the paperback, indeed!"

ATMAN is offended. But he is immediately rewarded by the sympathies of all those present, which after all is what he was after. The effect is complete: everyone despises Melkior and takes no pains to hide it.

But nobody notices the disappearance of the subject. Four Eyes, possibly at some secret sign from the palmist, has lost himself—simply melted away like a specter. And later on, when his disappearance *is* noticed, nobody believes any longer that he was there at all. They even believe that the snoring was produced by ATMAN and that the entire incident at the staircase was merely a nocturnal magic trick to surprise them, and they are grateful to him for it. They disperse with smiles, marveling at the artifice.

ATMAN, too, has made for his room downstairs, but Melkior stops him. "Just a moment, Mr. Adam."

Turning toward Melkior, ATMAN smiles innocently.

"What was the idea of all this business with Four Eyes tonight?"

"Four Eyes? *What* Four Eyes?"

"Four Eyes the drunkard. You brought him here and arranged this monkey business with him. We're alone, you can speak freely."

"Hypnosis is monkey business? Is that the way for a psychologist to talk? You saw that nobody else understood anything. They just marveled. But you, Mr. Melkior . . . !"

"Flattery will get you nowhere," says Melkior almost threateningly. "Why did you bring Four Eyes here?"

"Here, you even know his name! Yet you pretended not to know him."

"Just tell me why you brought him here."

"Why ask me? He's your friend, '*Votre ami*,' am I right?"

"I heard four feet when you were going up the stairs . . ."

"Well, well, you are good at colorful insults! What a clever way of calling me a jackass! Four legs, huh? There, there, don't be afraid. You don't have to be literary about it—insult me directly. I won't sue you."

"I'm . . . I'm going to . . ."

"Kill me?" the palmist whispers sensuously, squinching an eye. He is offering his cheek to Melkior's blow wholeheartedly, almost politely. It is as if he asks for nothing but being strangled by Melkior forthwith.

He is standing dreadfully close. Melkior feels some maddened cat move inside him because of that nose, those ears, those cheeks . . . But the eyes, the palmist's eyes, set so close to each other under the straight line of the eyebrows, watch him from under a mask, as if through slits, with a different look, one that does not go with his words. With a distant, threatening look that "knows all" and means business.

His beast takes fright, bends its spine, curls into a cuddly ball, meows ingratiatingly.

"Why do you follow me around?" he asks of the palmist in an almost supplicating whisper, despondently.

The palmist's eyes go mellow again, come closer, amicably, intimately touching Melkior's with a sort of kindness.

"Tut, tut, Mr. Melkior," ATMAN was shaking his head, "what an idea! Follow? Me follow you? Isn't it in fact you who are the follower of certain interesting persons?"

"Follower? Of what persons?"

"*Follower* is a deliberately chosen word to underline a certain little idea. Follower of interesting, truly interesting persons, Mr. Melkior. I repeat—interesting."

"You remind me of a fishmonger in my hometown. He would invent things all day long at the fish market and confound people. He 'knew all.' "

"The fishmonger may have invented things; I do not. Try to remember, Mr. Melkior . . . today, this afternoon . . ." The palmist squinches an eye again, derisively. Then Melkior remembers. Prompted by the squinch, perhaps. He had indeed followed Dom Kuzma. So . . .

"So you were following me this afternoon as well?"

"Hah, you think I have nothing better to do? You've lost a great deal of weight lately. Do you weigh yourself every day or just now and then?"

"What concern is that of yours, damn you?" shouts Melkior, quite furious now.

"I wonder myself. What concern is it of mine? Well, I am concerned—not so much with your person as with your error. Your erroneous reckoning, that is. *Circulus vitiosus*, is that right? Because what's the use of a life that you are bound to lose in another way—to disease, I mean? You saw the catechist. But he had been mortifying his body for different reasons. And even he changed his mind. He would now like to live. Too late. He had been renouncing life through penitence, whereas you, contrariwise, want to live. Which is why you're killing yourself. I perceive the absurdity of it, that is what I have long meant to tell you."

"I'm not killing myself in any way. This is just another of your ridiculous conjectures."

But Melkior suddenly realizes he is defending himself, retreating. Why on earth is he letting the cad meddle in his affairs in the first place?

"And stop speculating about my private life!" he says vigorously and somehow definitively.

"Why, Mr. Melkior, it's not your private life I'm speculating about. It's the problem itself, the very interesting problem of saving one's life from one peril—a grave and dreadful peril, granted—at the price of bringing on another peril which is no less grave or dreadful. You are not aware of the latter peril now—you are overpossessed by the fear of the former. I can understand a prisoner mortifying and thinning his body in order to fit it through a hole. His object is right there: getting through, and after the hole come recuperation and fattening. But what's your hole? Where's the hole you wish to fit through?"

"Leave me alone!" cries Melkior in desperation. "Anyway, good night." He turned around and was about to leave, but ATMAN stabs his back with a pointing finger.

"Are you quite sure it will be a good night, Mr. Melkior?" and gives him an insolent grin.

Melkior looks at him with impotent scorn. He is on the verge of riposting, but the staircase lights go off. What can he say to him now in the dark?

The palmist's nearness makes him shudder. Instinctively he stretches out his arms and touches ATMAN, who is coming near step by tiny step with an accelerating hiss of "kill . . . kill . . . kill . . ." He pushed him back hard, in terror, and begins a panicky grope for a wall to cover his back. And fumbles for the switch with all ten fingers to turn on the lights. But the switch is gone. The wall is gone, too. Nowhere around him is there a single solid object to protect him, anything firm, secure, anything but emptiness and dark. And

ATMAN is gone, too. There is only his laughter from some strange, sobbing distance ha-ha-ha. And repeated striking sounds, a bang, shouts. As if someone is calling out to him in French. And the light suddenly comes on.

He opened his eyes. The light was on in his room. How long had he been asleep? Snoring? What snoring? He had been hearing himself snore. Something struck his window again. A pebble. And someone shouting in the street, *"Mon ami, mon ami!"*

He went over to the window. Ugo was gesticulating in the middle of the street. Drunk, of course. Melkior opened the window.

"Elle m'aime, elle m'aime!" Ugo was shouting from down there, sending him kisses blown with both hands. *"Elle m'aime, mon cher, elle m'aime, Melchior!"*

Melkior's heart sank. *Elle l'aime!* Well, let ATMAN hear it, too.

"But who? *Qui est celle qui vous aime?"* Let it be all spelled out to "him below."

"She, *la Grande!"* Ugo shouted dementedly. "Tell you all about it tomorrow. Ah, *l'amour! À demain, mon cher.* Good night, Oh noble and wise one. Ah, *l'amour!"*

And off went Ugo, declaiming Baudelaire in some version of his own, with much pathos, assuredly with tears in his eyes: *à la très belle, à la très bonne, à la très chère . . . qui remplit tout mon coeur, tout mon coeur . . . salut à l'immortalité . . .*

Melkior closed the window. Lost in thought. So they did it straight away, the same evening. No sooner had she met him than . . . The harlot. That's their taste in men—talkers and drunks. Didn't I tell you she'd . . . said he to himself. This is how ATMAN talks to himself. Me and "myself."

Hang it all, am I in love? Or is this envy? The thing, I think, is to drink (hey, a rhyme!), to be a lush, a swooze. The floozy! He even felt sorry for Freddie. Sparing but a single thought for it. Hypocritically. How easily this comes to women! And then Ugo walks about shouting *L'amour*. This is all a brothel.

He threw himself onto the bed. He bit a corner of his pillow and began tugging at it furiously. He felt a chicken feather in his mouth.

There you are. *L'amour.* The hen. She will lie down under any rooster. *La cocotte.* In any backyard. She will even lie down under a parrot, multicolored, chattering.—Sorry, I thought you were the new rooster.—Not at all, *Madame.* I'm a general. Nice uniform, eh?—Divine!—I'm a hundred and twenty. A young parrot.—And a general already, eh?—Yes. That is why, *Madame,* I suggest *un peu d'amour* before the war.—So there will be one?—Certainly.—And you will kill me.—Yes, and eat you, too. I can already see you, *Madame,* in soup. Two drumsticks . . .—Enough of your lasciviousness, *monsieur le Perroquet!*—Oh no, I'm only a gourmet. Troop movements. We have no time for the finer points. Be mine.—Just like that?—Yes. But with love!—Oh, you're not to be trusted. All you males are the same. You want everything straight away.—Oh no, not straight away. Half of you boiled today, the other half roasted tomorrow, *Madame la Poule.* Orderly! See to it that Mrs. Cocotte does not suffer. Use a sharp knife. Give her the Marie Antoinette treatment. Boil the rump.—How tenderhearted you are.—That's what I am like. My profession is something else altogether. I hate cruelty. Do you like my beak?—It's divine!—It's terrific in lovemaking. *Il est formidable.* You will see. I could tell you my memories. We live long. We, crocodiles, elephants, and porpoises. Pity you're not a porpoise. You will grow old soon.—I can't help it, can I?—No, indeed you cannot. Do you lay eggs every day?—How indiscreet you are! I do only when I'm pregnant.—By cocks?—By *a* cock, by a rooster. By my Coco.—All he does is make noise, the fool. Cock-a-doodle-dooo . . . What does that mean? Nothing. Rubbish.—You're jealous of him. It means "the dawn is breaking . . ."—". . . a new day's in the making." So much for "cock-a-doodle-doo." For all that he was a colleague of mine, truth be told. Anyway, they will screech in the middle of the night, too, the fools. And you admire them for it. Women love noise. Women generally love dunderheads.—Not all of them do.—I know. You don't love them. Those who love us are always the exception.—I did not say I love you.—Never mind. You will. It's my charm. We parrot-generals are a charming lot. Shall we have a drink?—Heavens, you'll get me drunk.—Stewed hen. I have seen it before. Not bad.—You are trying to seduce me.—I admit a glass of cognac makes it easier for a woman to understand love.—Is this what you call love?—Well, what do *you* think love is? Clucking? At least I'm a realist.—You are a seducer of poor helpless women. You are low.—And you are marvelous when angry, *Madame la Poule!* I'm going to kiss you.—No! Oh, no. For God's sake, no. Oh, what are you doing? What are you doing to me?—Loving you, my darling. My one and only love.—But I, I love only Coco, my Coco. Him, only . . . Oh you are terrible, you are!—I am, darling, I am. I'm crazy, my sweet little *Poulette!*—My little *Pappagallo!*—I'll devour you, my sweet little *Poupoulette!* I'll devour you!—Eat me, my little one. Eat me, eat me, eat me . . . ohh . . .

Tomorrow I'll give Enka a buzz.

He was tired and out of sorts. He remembered Enka's furious lovemaking and felt a fierce desire for her. Perhaps Coco was on night duty at the clinic? Should he go down to the pay phone and call her right now? How delighted she would be, now, in the middle of the night. She would say, *Quelle surprise!* She liked to clothe her adultery in French phrases. For the sake of the décor. Costume muck. À la Pompadour. She was with him, that is to say under him (as Iago would have put it) on the broad canopied bed. The telephone on the night table rang. He tried to prevent her from lifting the handset. No, she wanted to take the call. Precisely because of the situation! She winked at him. It was Coco. Ringing from the university, between two lectures. "How are you, *ma poulette?*" He was bored stiff. She answered him in French. *Mon bichon, mon chéri.* She was reading the book he had recommended. She did not like it. Boring. When are you coming home? Two more hours of lectures. Come back as soon as you can, *on fera des* chikki-chikki. Coco was chuckling into the receiver. Happy. She rang off. She was laughing. "Now then, where were we?"

"What a harlot you are!" he told her with awe. He, too, was laughing. Everyone was laughing.

"And you're a stupid little burglar. What did you expect me to tell him? That you were here?"

"You could have let it ring."

"Oh, shut up. You're so stupid. He would have rushed over in a taxi to see if anything had happened to me."

"Poor Coco."

"He's happy because he knows nothing. He's wonderful. So clever."

"You love him?"

"Very much. In a different way."

"And you have a good time with him?"

"Marvelous. In a different way. You wouldn't understand."

"Indeed I would not. Perfidious creatures. We love you, trust you . . ."

"Why shouldn't you trust me? Come to me, my skinny one . . ."

Not tonight. He would have probably slapped her cheeks. He would ring her tomorrow. The petite, perfidious, laughing Enka.

"The tormentor" was jangling eagerly. But its clangor burst into the sleeper's slumber like a bully and a heedless drunk. What a mess! Sleep sprang into action, slamming windows and doors, putting out lights, letting night flood in and restore peace. Telling a story about sailing the seas on a big white ship. "The tormentor" is now clanging deep down in the bowels of the ship, signaling the engine men to change speed: go slow, go quiet . . .

Smooth sailing. Stars. Lighthouses winking in the distance: hello, skipper, old chum. He, up there on the bridge, in the dark, smiling: hello, boys, you old night owls. His cigarette pushed to a corner of his mouth, to keep the smoke away. Sea wolf. To the helmsman: fifteen to starboard. Fifteen to starboard, echoes the helmsman as though chanting a litany: pray for me. He harkens to everything. Leading the ship as a general leads an army. She, Viviana, wrapped in a plaid blanket, peers at the compass and trembles like the night. He offers her his hand, she does not take it. He grabs her hand, she pulls it away timidly and tucks it under the plaid. He pushes the cigarette over to the other corner of the mouth with his tongue, squinches the other eye, and says to the helmsman: steady on. To her: let's go. She (docilely): Where? He (resolutely): To die. She (worriedly): What about the ship?—It's sailing on.—And the passengers?—They're asleep.—What about the lighthouses?—Ahoy!—She: I can't do it.—Why not?—I'll show you something. Opening the plaid: look. And shows him a tiny penis and tiny, dovelike testicles. He slaps her lightly using only his fingertips, painless, symbolic. She: Does that mean you love me?—Yes. Pointing his

cigarette at her miniatures: is this for fidelity?—Yes.—Penelope!—
How dare you?—You aren't familiar with the word?—No, I am not.
It must be insulting.—It is not insulting. He's no Ulysses. He's a
drunk.—It's insulting anyway.—Helmsman, stuff the ears with wax.
Lash me to the mast. One-eighty to port.—One-eighty to port.—
Back to Polyphemus.—Back to Polyphemus.—Let the Cyclops, one-
eyed beast, eat us all.—Let the Cyclops, one-eyed beast, eat us all.—
There is no Ithaca.—There is no Ithaca.—Penelope has a penis.—
Penelope has a penis.—Let's toss her to the sharks . . .

"Skipper! The sirens, the sirens!" shouts the helmsman all of a
sudden.

"Wax! Stuff the ears! Lash yourselves to the mast!"

A siren was already screaming over the city. Melkior leaped out
of bed. Is this it? Or is it just an exercise? People were walking
calmly down the street. The sentry was gazing at the passing women
with a lustful gaze. No, this is not it, not yet. An exercise. Let's
phone Enka.

He was possessed by urgency, like someone completing a task
against the clock. He rushed downstairs acknowledging no one to
avoid being stopped for the ridiculous questions about his health,
the war, politics. Many dreams, gentlemen, many dreams lately.
Erotic ones. We haven't the time.

Dial Ambulance Service, but make the last digit 4 instead of 3.
That was how Enka had instructed him to call her. Busy signal. The
coin dropped down. Again. He was dialing with furious intensity.
He used to dial numbers on Enka's breast, for a joke, after lovemaking, as they relaxed, naked, next to each other.

"Hullooo?" Her crooning voice over the telephone had always
excited him.

"Hullo, Ambulance Service?" in a shaky voice, as if this really
was an urgent matter. Grave emergency.

"Wrong number," she answered in a convincingly cold, even
bored voice. And, without replacing the receiver, she said over there,
to *him*, "That was the fourth ape this morning." And there was
laughter, somehow insulting, over there, between *them*.

Even though this was not the first time, he felt like a stranger, an outsider. Ape! She allotted him the same treatment as the three who had dialed the wrong number that morning, as the people who were a nuisance. She did it on purpose, for him to hear. She knew his voice, oh yes, she knew! Why did she choose today to let him overhear that he was that morning's fourth annoying ape who didn't know how to dial a number properly? Something like a trace of jealousy surfaced . . . No, not jealousy! He was fending off the feeling. She had slammed the door before his outstretched beggarly hand. Beggar? No: burglar! He was giving himself cynical airs. I'm plainly not up to the harlot's clever tricks. After two years he still had not learned to adapt his sensitivity to her complicated conjugal situations which she breezed through using her innate low cunning. No amount of experience had protected him from being easily stung. She would laugh at his naïveté, later on, advance sensible reasons, bring him around. But she was not taking the smallest of risks. Moreover, she acquired security, she fortified her marital fidelity at the expense of his pride, his honor, his courtesy as her lover. With her cynicism she was far above his sensitivity, laughing her superior, her wanton laugh, being dreadfully distant, opaque, elusive, disgusting. How many times had he gone to her intending to have it out? To smack her right in her lying mouth, to yank out her tongue, to leave her, forever. And then he had again kissed the mouth, held the satanic little tongue between his teeth and felt its morbid softness as the truest truth in the world.

Someone grabbed him by the neck and spun him around. He saw Maestro's unshaven face. They were standing in front of the newspaper building. "If you were going upstairs, don't." Maestro's words were consecrated by matutinal brandy breath.

"I've got a review to . . ."

"Later. After it's blown over. There's one hell of a kerfuffle going on up there. The Old Man's tearing jumbo-sized strips off the music guy."

"What for?"

"I should hardly think it's over Beethoven. They're raging about technology and politics and what not . . . 'Who cares about the music!' I didn't quite get it. Anyway, you know well enough what kind of a fix we're in."

"I don't understand. Why should he shout at the . . ."

"He's not shouting out of conviction. He's shouting to be heard by the boss behind the upholstered door. You can barely be heard behind that door. You've really got to raise your voice. After all, it's that kind of job and that kind of salary. It pays to shout, even against your convictions."

"But what's the reason? Why? Do you know?" Maestro's obfuscations were irritating him.

"The reason is Beethoven, of all people."

"So?"

"So . . . there was a gala production of *Fidelio* last night and the music guy reviewed it."

"Well, what of it? He likes Beethoven!"

"He likes German music in general." Maestro followed his broad hint with a grin.

"And the music guy didn't praise Beethoven enough?"

"Oh, he did, he did. But the Old Man yelled at him, 'What about the chronicler's duty?' 'We're a political paper'—or rather a 'paper with a political profile,' these were his exact words. And it was a gala production, get it? Personalities. He was supposed to mention the personalities in attendance."

"Which of course he failed to do?"

"Yes. The hell with them! Let's go have a snort of rotgut."

"What's a critic got to do with personalities? That's something for you, for your City Desk."

"Yes, for my Dustbin Desk. We get the rubbish, you get the cream. But it looks like things are changing—now everyone is getting rubbish. The great equalizer. Don't let it get to you. Sooner or later we'll all end on the rubbish heap. Such is the march of history. Let's go have a snort. On me . . . 'on the eve of historic times,' as the boss put it in today's editorial. Here you are—'On The Eve Of Historic Times' . . ."

"No, I've got to go upstairs!" and he started off with Quixote-like I'll-show-'em steps, but Maestro held him back using both hands and muttering incomprehensibly.

"Beg pardon?"

"Did you know that last night Freddie gave Ugo a beating after all? After you left. Lucky thing you did—it was meant for you."

"What was meant for me?" said Melkior absentmindedly, looking up at the editorial office windows.

"What? Come back down to Earth and I'll tell you what: Freddie's . . . got welts. Ugo plastered a few across his physiognomy. Here and there. Gave him a bloody nose. She wiped his blood off with her own little hand and her own little handkerchief. Tenderly. Which cost Ugo a kick, up his Krakatoa, I think."

"Krakatoa?" Melkior was laughing.

"Yes, right up the crater, for the air pressure caused him to mumble 'Umm,' rather umbrageously."

"And Viviana wiped away his blood?" Melkior was enjoying himself maliciously, avenged by Freddie's foot.

"Viviana who?"

"Er . . . The beauty."

"Her name is not Viviana, it's . . ."

"That's what I call her," Melkior hastened to interrupt Maestro. He did not want to first hear her name from this drunk.

"Viviana—sure—crouches like a Samaritan by his head, and he, the aching wounded gentle knight, grunts and peeps up her skirt, ha-ha. . . . God, what shapes! I envied him his wounds."

"What did Freddie do? Keep out of it?" Melkior was attempting to cover up his loser's misery by making a show of curiosity. ATMAN was right—Ugo's next.

"Keep out, hell! He called her back, tried to drag her away, 'Leave the ape, let's go.' 'You're an ape. Get lost!' And he actually went off with that Lady Macbeth. While She stayed with us—with Ugo, to be precise—and we proceeded to put on The Grand Show. The Fall of the Bastille, no less! We almost tore Thénardier's ear off in revolutionary ardor. Ugo was great. What am I saying? Magnificent! She kept kissing his lip where it was swollen from Freddie's blow, and every time she did he put his hand down her dress. Once he even brought the matter out into the open. God, what a Pompeian scene!"

"Was she drunk?" Melkior was seeking an excuse for her. He remembered Enka. I'll call her.

"Drunk, infatuated, the lot. She asked him to take her home. He spent the night."

"He did not!" the joyful truth flew out of Melkior, chirping like a bird.

"Are you sure?"

"Positive. And another thing, I think very little of it is true. Ugo slept at home last night. I saw him."

"Yes, well, whether you saw him or not, don't be jealous, my dear Eustachius. Your turn will come. Mine won't. Fate has made me the gift of The Great Solitude. A large cloak in which I don't even have a flea for company. The hermit. Leone Eremita. The purist. *Vox clamantis.* Leopold by name, called Poldy. Even Polda, by the closer among my drunkard friends. And thus we arrive at the stable of the mammal Thénardier. Let us take a seat, Eustachius old son. Mammal Thénardier, two shots, shot to shot. As for the rest, let's leave it to technology. To the various telegraph wires and high voltage. Known under the important name of cables. Especially electrical cables!" Maestro gave a derisive laugh. "What do you think, Eustachius, is there a telegraph line between the Vatican and the Kremlin? A secret line. Underground. Collusions, eh? If I could manage to dig it out somewhere, what a message I'd have, for them both! From the Carpathians."

"Why the Carpathians, of all places?" But Melkior was thinking of Enka, defiantly, I'll ring her just to spite the bitch . . .

"The word is historical. Also, the Carpathians are halfway between. I looked them up on the map. But it was the word itself that took my fancy to begin with. 'This is Leone Eremita, speaking from the Carpathians with the following message for the Vatican and the Kremlin,' eh? Then I would snap the wire in half and tie a cat to each end and let them yowl in the bastards' ears! Animal Thénardier, two shots, shot to shot." Then he whispered to Melkior, confidentially, like someone revealing a secret, "This Thénardier fellow is a new species of mammal, they don't study him in school, but they will. By the way, look how we stretched his left ear for him last night. You can tell the difference at a glance. Did you measure it, Thénardier? It's as red as a ship's portside light. For nighttime navigation."

"Well, you got one across the snout, too." Thénardier parried with a nervous grimace.

"The Batrachomyomachy. God, how we croaked!"

The sodden, slimy cigarette in his mouth had gone out. He sucked at it in vain. No go.

"Thénardier! Match!"

"At your service, dreaded Pharaoh!" and he lit Maestro's cigarette with a chamberlain's submissive gesture. A ritual.

"After 'Pharaoh' say, 'life—health—power,' you beast! It's what people said to pharaohs, '*onkhu—uza—sonbu.*' That's ancient Egyptian," he explained to Melkior. "And now begone!" Maestro dismissed Thénardier with a pharaonic gesture.

"Ancient Egyptian! Not surprised, Eustachius? Think I faked it?"

"No, I really wonder how . . ."

"I used to study it," Maestro announced boastfully and poured some brandy down his gullet. Opening the gap-toothed mouth, cooling the heated gorge. "They had social poetry, too. The ancient Egyptians, long before the Kharkov school! 'I saw a smith toiling with hammer at his forge by the fire; his fingers like a crocodile's, filthy as fish from the Nile.' Then there's the one about the cobbler: 'The cobbler, a wretched fellow, is in truly poor condition,—if he didn't gnaw his leather he would die of malnutrition.' I am quoting from memory, in rough translation. And the machinists today, they think they invented everything. The cult of the machine! The preposterousness of it! The petrol-fumed inspiration! Their Pegasus a Ford, their Muse, Miss Sonja Henie, the most ridiculous nose in the world! What poetry was ever conceived in an automobile or on-board an aeroplane, that's what I'd like to know! The mollycoddling of one's behind! Where were the power shovel and the bulldozer when Cheops was erecting his pyramid, when Pericles was building the Acropolis? When Socrates was making fools of people all over Athens? Tell me, am I overstating it?"

"Not at all. Only—"

"All right, say it: Progress! Well, Progress is welcome to pass me by. I'm staying put! Let it rush, let it fly! I, a common biped, walk on my two legs, pleased to feel the Earth beneath my feet, happy to be treading on it, treading on it, treading on it!" and he fell to pounding the floor with his feet, enraged, even hateful, "the damned old bitch that birthed me only to swallow me up again! Using my material to make a pig, a hedgehog, or simply a head of lettuce to be eaten by an overweight woman on a diet. It's enough to drive you mad! While they fly, they flutter, they are in such a rush. To reach where? Whereto, engineers, locksmiths, mechanics, drivers?"

Maestro spread his arms wide, asking his question around the empty bar room in a kind of despair.

Thénardier, arranging bottles along his altar aided by his two ministrants, tittered hee-hee-hee, savoring his morning fun with pleasure.

"Let's have the poison, you bloody sophist! And stop smirking! *Margaritas ante porcos*," he communicated to Melkior, shaking his head resignedly. "It was the likes of him who gave the hemlock to Socrates. And what will they give me? The juice. Electricity. Ho, ho, ho," Maestro launched into a fit of mad, frenetic laughter. "Power transmission line . . . ho, ho, ho . . . at high voltage . . . ho, ho, ho. Oh yes, at high voltage, right enough. Attention! Mortal danger! And on the pylons, ever see it? They've painted the old skull and crossbones, as on a bottle of poison. As at a chemist's: I would like a pylonful of high voltage please. I have a mind to kill, ho, ho, ho . . ."

"Nevertheless, mankind has greatly benefited from electricity," said Melkior mechanically, just to assert his presence. So she did let Ugo . . . He may have been going home to sleep afterward. He was late going back, he had been with her.

"Mankind? What mankind?" Maestro was aroused in earnest. "There are lots of different mankinds. Were not the ancient Greeks mankind? In what way did Aristotle suffer by having no electricity? He did know about rubbing amber, but he held that in utter contempt. Rubbing indeed. He had more important things to think about than rubbing. Would Dante have written better poetry under a frosted-glass bulb? If Leonardo had needed any electricity he certainly would have set some wheels spinning to get the sparks flying. He built all kinds of machinery, his designs have survived, he'd have found it a cinch to . . . And yet he painted that perfidious smiling *femina*, heh-heh . . . Smiling there, the little beast of a female . . . I have her back at home, a first-class reproduction, you'll see it when you come by. Ah, you've never been to my place, now have you? You've definitely got to come by one day . . . What am I saying, one day? You've simply got to come for a bit of peaceful conversation. It's essential. Only I think you ought to know I have no electricity. High voltage runs outside past my house, a long-distance trans-mis-sion line even, right under my window, with the old oil lamp guttering inside! Ha-ha, how do you like that? I ignore the terrible force coursing past. Be on your way, you potent nonsense, and leave me be, I have no use for you!"

"So, Maestro, do you hate all forms of energy or just electricity?" Maestro seemed to have sensed the irony in the question: he gave Melkior a suspicious look with one eye—the other being filled with a smoke-induced tear—and replied disdainfully:

"I hate nothing. I merely reject the superfluous."

"And yet you use the electric tram!"

"Never!" flared Maestro, hurt. "I walk a full hour to the office. I walk and think. After all, human thought came into being on the foot. The ancient Greeks thought in the street. The peripatetics walked. As people talk, so they walk—that's my theory, if you don't find it off-putting. Let the linguists and . . . whatever those *experts* are called, hang themselves if they haven't perceived such a glaring fact. What is speech if not thought? The man whose clogs sink into mud with his every step speaks differently from a man who walks on blacktop. The highlander's words are as hard as the stone he treads on. Fast walkers are fast speakers; those who drag their feet drag their words as well. The quantities of certain lowlands, the accents of hard, uneven surfaces. Speech has all the relief of the ground underfoot, the tempo of motion in space. The rhythm and the melody of walking. People walk in major or minor key. That's how they speak, too: brightly or glumly."

"What about you? Do you walk in major or minor?"

"Minor. Some speeches are gloomy even if they're about a cheerful subject. I know how I speak. If it were written down you would call it banter. But you've got to hear me say it. Which is why I prefer speech to writing. Oral literature."

"You are a speaker. That, too, is an art form."

"Because I'm an infantryman. Not in the military sense, of course. Professional soldiers march even as they speak. As for military commands, are they still human speech? You haven't done your National Service yet, have you? A command consists, my dear sir, of two parts: the preparatory and the executive. Such as 'Forwarrr . . . dmarch!' 'Dmarch!' is the executive part. And what is 'dmarch'? Eh? 'Forwarrr' is supposed to stir a special spirit in your bottom; next, 'dmarch' gives each soldier a kick in the backside as an initial impulse for getting a move on. Your illustrious behind will go through it in the fullness of time and you'll remember me then, if for no other reason."

"Octopus, polyp, cephalopod, vacuum cleaner," he went on in a kind tone to address Thénardier, who was doing some accounts at the bar, scratching his pelican chin worriedly with a pencil.

"Yes, philosopher Ugly Nose?" responded Thénardier without raising his head from his accounts.

"Listen, you headless cod, raise what you haven't got when speaking to me. Serve your customers. Shot to shot . . ."

"No, Maestro. That's enough for me," parried Melkior. He had long resolved to get up and was only waiting for a convenient break to flee from Maestro's thrall. He had to find a phone now, he had to ring Enka. She knows I'm going to ring her. She's waiting.

"Eustachius the Kind, drop them," said Maestro all of a sudden, sounding conspiratorial. "You are a man apart."

"Drop whom?" Melkior pulled free of Enka's close embrace.

"Them. Ugo and the others. Superficial cads, clowns." And he went on in a whisper, "As for her, she'll come crawling to you. She'll be asking you to mount her, she'll get down humbly like a hen. I know her. Be a rooster. Head high. Proud."

"She doesn't interest me, Maestro. What makes you think I'd . . . ?"

"Come off it, Eustachius! You are consumed by vanity. You keep making comparisons: 'what's Ugo got that I . . .' And she *is* beautiful."

"Yes, so she is. But I don't care whose she may be."

"You're lying, Eustachius, but that doesn't matter. The hell with her. We could find a better place to talk, you and I, somewhere quiet. We are people who still have something to say. What else have we got left but to talk to each other? Setting our thoughts flowing from one head to another, as it were, letting our minds fertilize each other . . ."

Maestro's voice quavered with an odd tenderness over the last few words. Melkior did not dare look at his face: it was bound to have on it that humbly pleading look, the painful expression of unrestrained, miserable sincerity as the very words melt in the throat with the pleasure of abasement.

"Don't frown. Forgive me, Eustachius," Maestro all but sobbed. "Did I touch some soft spot of yours? Never mind. I can risk it. I no longer have anything to lose—I no longer *have* anything. Even this body's not mine—I've sold my cadaver to the Faculty of Medicine. And drank up the proceeds long ago. I'm a man who has consumed his own dead body—I cannot be bothered by the fine points."

Then suddenly, as though he had been set aglow by an idea, his eyes took on a weird gleam and a smile—superior, triumphant—spread over his face. There appeared spiteful glee.

"Incidentally, the kind of death that mine will be has not been experienced by anyone, ever! Did you notice my choice of words, Eustachius, 'to experience death'? Ha-ha, nobody can honestly say, 'I have experienced death.' Danton noticed it on the eve of being executed: you can't say, 'I was guillotined.' But forget the guillotine —it's so ordinary."

Maestro fell silent and seemed to be musing about something.

"I chose my death long ago, before I sold myself to the Institute of Anatomy. ('Sold myself' sounds a bit prostitutional, don't you think?) That was precisely why I sold myself: because I had chosen. What a death, Eustachius, my boy!" He was waxing ecstatic. "Nobody has ever died that way! So appropriately! So ironically triumphant. Symbolic! So complete!"

"Don't talk nonsense, Maestro," Melkior was anxious. "You're not thinking of killing yourself, are you?"

"Kill myself, he says . . . Don't drag me through the mud, Eustachius!" Maestro was seriously offended. "Killing oneself is for abandoned pregnant dames and spotty boys crossed in love. Also, you need equipment to kill yourself. I despise it. Maiming your body is undignified and hideous! And that's precisely what all the suicides do: they shoot themselves in the head, slash their wrists, throats, bellies, drive knives into their hearts (even nails into their brains!), destroy internal organs using all manner of poisonous slops, drown themselves, fling their bodies from great heights, have them mangled and massacred under the wheels of an engine . . . Horrifying and disgusting. The vicious criminals! The perverted scum! If they didn't do it themselves it would be necessary to put them to death for it. And rid life of those damned slaughterers and lunatics.

"No, Eustachius," Maestro went on in a sentimental tone, "my death is going to be brand-new, medicinally pure, so to speak. No blood, no shit. You'll see. Only I must start urinating more. Urinating harder, that is. I must switch to beer—it promotes micturition. I must begin exercising right away, ha-ha . . . Don't ask questions, Eustachius the Merciful. One day this will all make sense."

It's revolting all the same, your medicinal purity, thought Melkior, getting up. He was disgusted by poor Maestro. Unless the man was merely dramatizing some rotten affair of his in which he would like to play a major role? A hoax. He had very nearly fallen for it. Or was it all an exercise in purposely fouling some very intimate purity? No telling what all you can find in a dustbin.

"Are you leaving me, merciful Eustachius?" and Maestro stretched out his arms after him, desperately.

"I must," Melkior replied briefly, to break free as quickly as possible. "You're not going upstairs, I hope?" Maestro warned him. "I don't think the time is yet ripe."

"No, I'm not. By the way, would you mind passing this review on to the Arts Editor? I've got some business to attend to elsewhere, it's . . ."

"Sexual?" Maestro chortled with libertine envy. "In thy orisons be all my sins remember'd. Remember thee! Ay, thou poor ghost, while memory holds a seat in this distracted globe!"

Melkior almost ran toward the phone booth. It's nearly ten! God, what if she's out? He could not allow being rejected today. The digits were wheeling too slowly on the dial. His impatience was in a hurry to hear her voice, to expunge "the fourth ape this morning" together with that laugh of hers . . .

"Ambulance Service?" his voice quavered with male excitement.

"Yes, what can I do for you?" It was a man's voice.

Of course, he'd made a mistake, he'd actually dialed the Ambulance Service, 3 instead of 4. Make the last digit 4, 4, 4!

"Hullo, Ambulance Service?"

"Yes, yesss . . ." Enka was laughing her familiar laugh, the beckoning one. "How serious is it?"

"Very, Enkie, very serious." What a relief! He pounced on her voice, he sensed she was naked beneath her housecoat. "Can I come over, Enkie?" He was barely able to say the words.

"When, Kior, when can you come?" She was offering herself to him. "Can you come right now?"

"Right now, Enkie, right now!"

"Come over, Kior. I'm still in bed. I'm waiting for you, you know . . ."

I know, oh yes I know! Naked, warm . . . And the tram arrived at just the right moment. The conductor tore off his ticket with a smile. "You're off then, eh?" his thin moustache was saying.

He let his body hang slackly, holding on to two straps, careless, sailorlike. He had surrendered to the ride. MEN'S WEAR gave him MEN SWEAR. BOOKING OFFICE: BOO KING OFF ICE. The booking office hours were part of a poster for SWAN LAKE: ENKA'S LAW, anagrammatically. And what would yield ENKA'S BODY? O'DYE'S BANK? No, there was no such name as O'Dye. Let's see. EBONY KADS? No, it's c-a-d-s, not k-a-d-s, and she's Enka, not Enca. Anyway, *kads* or *cads*, it simply did not make sense.

"And what did *you* say?"

"I told him he was an idiot. The one Tolstoy wrote!"

The two girls exploded into laughter, enjoying themselves. The idiot. They were in love with him, both of them. Pretty, scented, dressed for town.

"I'll go and see it in the theater next week. With him. I told him so."

"See what?"

"*The Idiot*. It's on this season."

"I don't really like Russian plays. They're all about tramps waxing philosophical . . ."

"Did you know there's this play where they say 'hooker' on stage?"

"No, actually they say 'whore,'" she replied in a whisper.

"You don't say. . . ." They laughed. Saying "whore" on stage was funny. Melkior jumped out before the tram had come to a stop. I expect they like the word. They use it more often than we men. They feel it more intimately. In the second act Leone says, "a common, anonymous whore." *La grande putana.* Boucher's azure-and-pink bare-bottoms. Not forgetting Dante—"*donne, ch'avete inteletto d'amore!*" or something—the Aristotelian quintessence of the brothel. The grain of salt in the brain of the animal designated to give pleasure. A modest dose, just enough to avoid insipidity. They then use it to produce—pohoetry! Oho-etryoho-oho-et . . . oho-oho et . . .

He bounded up the stairs, two steps, three steps at a time, hurriedly, thieflike.

This was how Raskolnikov had climbed toward Alyona's room, with his axe beneath his coat. No, not like this: Raskolnikov climbed slowly, cautiously, listening for telltale sounds. Incidentally, there were seventy-two steps to climb. Today was the first time he had forgotten to count them. Did this mean something? ATMAN would have been able to spin some little meaning out of it. . . .

The seventy-second step. Coco's brass nameplate gleamed with hospitable welcome to the old acquaintance and . . . household friend, he added hesitatingly. M.D., Professor, surgeon . . . He felt respect before the gravity of the profession. It was she who first called him *Coco*, he hastily said in his own defense at the door. He pressed the bell, long-short-long, a long-arranged Morse K. For Kior, as she called him. But the door had been awaiting him impatiently —ajar.

"Kior," Enka crooned, stretching herself. "Lock it on the inside." He had already done so, automatically, out of habit.

She was lying in the spacious double bed, her hands under her head, her breasts uncovered as far as the teasing border, in refined style. She was smiling a come-to-me smile.

He threw himself on her as he was, fully dressed . . .

"Ugh, you've been drinking," she made a grimace of disgust, "brandy!"

"Never mind now, never mind! Enka, Enka . . ." There was no time for explanations.

"But . . . take your clothes off . . . and come to me. Look what I'm like."

She showed herself to him under the cover, naked. A small, plump, perfect body.

He made an irresistible onslaught. He pushed his way into the bedclothes next to her. He wanted to have her just as he was, fully dressed, out of some sort of spite, because of the morning's laughter over the phone, because of "the fourth ape." He wanted to pass off his insult as "mad desire," as lust's mindless whim. It flattered her.

"All right then . . . the shoes at least, the shoes . . . you madman, you! . . ." she tittered with glee.

Not even the shoes! Nothing! He had taken full control and was delighting in his superiority. Indeed delighting in it more than in her. There was something vengeful in his lovemaking, as if he were killing her. And she was grateful to him with every finger, every joint; with her nerves, breasts, eyes, mouth, teeth. She bit him on the chin.

"Oww, no!" he mumbled from the softness of the pillow where he had buried his face.

"Priapus! . . . Priapus! . . ." she cried out, demented. "It's a miracle, a miracle! Priapus!"

Suddenly, how strange! he remembered Maestro. "All my sins." "Thou poor ghost." And there emerged something disgusting, something slimy. What was that urinating business all about?

And the tempest subsided. All was now reduced to a gentle rhythm of sailing across bobbing waves. Soft rolling in long amplitudes. A marital outing. "Kiooo?!" she called from somewhere inside, below deck, in a panic, as if she were sinking.

He didn't hear her. What kind of death is he up to? Brand new? Medicinally pure? Can beer kill you?

"Kior, what's happened?" She had come up on deck, tussle-haired, sweaty.

"Tell me, can beer kill you?"

"God, what a question!" She lifted her arms to her head in astonishment and her small breasts went flat. "Why do you want to know now?"

"What's wrong with now?" he asked from his pinnacle of power. "Know anything about it? You're a doctor's wife after all."

God, what a life! he complained pleasurably. Why, she's actually nagging! I have my Viviana ("mine"!), so you needn't think you can . . . And her breasts are two buns with a tiny raspberry in the middle. . . .

"Where were we, Kio?" she asked, nestling up to him.

"At beer being a potential killer."

It was no longer Maestro on his mind. This was for her benefit: he wanted to show her she could not disturb his train of thought, that his head was in the right place.

"You're crazy . . . and a bore!" She turned away from him and furiously lit a cigarette.

He got up. She gasped in horror, the smoke billowing out of her mouth as from a miniature hell. But when she saw him undressing, she put out her cigarette in a conciliatory fashion and clucked in delighted laughter . . . caw-caw-caw-caw-caw . . .

"You're crazy," she repeated with an unmistakable undertone of great admiration. "A man apart," was what it meant. The element of surprise. The strategist.

It flattered him. He pulled his legs out of his trousers with the smile of a general heading for an easy victory. Calm; no haste. His innate neatness nearly made him fold them. He threw them across the chair for all its pull. He might change his mind after all, the enemy will ask to be defeated. She'll be asking me to mount her, she'll get down like a hen, humbly. Viviana? Just another bird . . . in the bush.

"Come here, my little sparrow . . ." he said to her throwing himself carelessly on the bed.

"Small, aren't I? A teeny-weeny sparrow?" But she was acting more like a little bitch. "You like me for being small? Tell me, Kio! Tell me! You like me? Small, yours, all of me . . . yours . . . Kio!"

Desdemona and Cassio . . . Did they have this kind of thing going? Maestro believes they did, with her, on her. The Venetians. Sweet Desdemona, let us be wary, let us hide our loves! Should I ask her for a handkerchief of Coco's? He is even now holding some-body's heart in his hand, up at the clinic. Massaging it, saving a life. "Dear heart," meaning her, this one here, little Enka, dear heart.

That was how Melkior carried on with her, nose above the del-uge. He was able to think, to listen (as he had done recently) to the radio announcing the murder of Trotsky (stabbed in the head with an ice pick), to watch things being quiet in the room. The witnesses.

The trousers across the chair, legs splayed, running; the jacket extending a sleeve to reach for a silver fifty-dinar piece lying on the floor, having dropped from a pocket. He had been hurrying after all. He laughed at the sleeve's fussy-miserly gesture: it would finish by sucking the coin up. A little something for Four Eyes.

"Stop laughing, you tormentor!" Enka managed to surface for an instant and sank into the silt again, as Maestro would have put it.

Villain, be sure thou prove my love a whore! But who can ever prove it? Extract a grain of truth from the silt, thou cruel Moor. Would not this one, too, be able to sing the willow tree song tonight? And to die innocent for all the world. And the world is her world. A happy marriage, for all the world, a love match. I love you, you love me . . . A parasitic opera: ivy all over Shakespeare.

He had his "erotic rheostat" turned on. Those were his words for the resistance he offered his pleasure, the search for disturbing thoughts, the toying with the small, small ones. . . .

Steady on, children, the world is too small for the lot of you. All right, I expect some room could be found for the little girls . . . but the little boys? Not so fast, youngsters! Where do you think you're going? To the barracks? To the wars? Here, look at that eager-beaver little general! Carlo Buonaparte inadvertently sired Napoleon at twenty-three, he was four years my junior. Who knows what hydrocephalic essayist could now be conceived if I were not at the helm? And he laughed dryly: heh, heh.

"You are definitely crazy today!" said Enka crisply, soberly, firmly down on earth.

This third "you're crazy" was final. She sat up and spitefully began to smooth her hair. He turned on his back without a word. He wore a cold, distant smile. He fell to fingering her vertebrae one by one. She felt it on the tips of his fingers—they were indifferent through satiety. She shook them off with hostility, let go of me. He then suddenly hugged her tight and pressed her down on her back. And took her furiously and candidly, no longer thinking about anything.

They were lying on their backs and sharing a cigarette. She had her head on his bicep, he was toying with her breast: the tiny raspberry had swollen angrily under his teasing. A trivial conversation.

"And why did you laugh that silly laugh?"

"Offended are we? It's how I always act . . . when he's in."

"Not to mention 'the fourth ape this morning' . . . *I'm* that fourth ape! You purposely said it with the phone still on, you wanted me to hear I was the fourth ape."

"I wanted *him* to see . . ."

"To see what? That I'm an ape? I can see that myself."

"To see that I was speaking without hanging up first, that I didn't care if he heard what I said . . ."

"That you didn't care if he heard, or rather if I heard, that I was an ape?"

"Not you, he."

"The 'he' is me."

"Not at all. I wanted *him*, Coco, to hear . . ."

"That I'm an ape? You could have hung up, he would've heard you anyway. But then *I* wouldn't have!"

"Oh, you're horrible! You've got me all confused . . . You *are* an ape!" She was angry. "He's my husband! He's a man doing a serious job and I don't propose to torment him with suspicions. Human lives depend on him, he must have inner peace. I love him and respect him. Don't laugh, you demon, I do love him. He's a nice man, hard-working and intelligent."

"And you love and respect him. My God, what a lucky man he is!"

"He is indeed! And you can shove your cynicism. Ours is a happy marriage."

"A love match."

"It's too much for your piggy little mind to grasp, isn't it? I wouldn't give up this happiness for anything in the world! His happiness! And his contentment, his peace of mind. If for no other reason than because—and I know you'll give another of your ape grins at this—because I like people and you despise them. One twitch of his hand could mean the end of someone's life. And what harm could your scribbling do? Getting a beating, like the one that . . . that actor was going to give you. Everyone respects him. I'm honored to be his wife."

Hell and damnation, she means it! She does believe it all, this Iagoan Desdemona! Now what do you make of it? Come on, psychologists, psychoanalysts, psychiatrists, endocrinologists, criminologists, sophists, sadists, casuists, Jesuits, diplomats, gnostics, mystics, dialecticians, occultists, moralists, veterinarians, dustmen, firemen . . . what do you make of it? Oh great ATMAN, you know what to make of it. You . . . and Shakespeare! Of that mental ileus, that Luciferian theology, that whorish moral science, that garbage salad, that sweetmeat made from one's own intestinal content. "Her honor is an essence that's not seen; they have it very oft that have it not."

He repeated the quotation aloud.

"What was that?" she said suspiciously.

"Shakespeare. Iago talking to Othello about Desdemona."

"I get it," she said angrily. "It means I have no honor. You could have been a bit more decent about it."

He laughed from deep inside his lungs, a forced, nervous laugh. This was the moment to slap her face and put an end to the whole affair. But he knew he would regret it the very next day. Not on her account; on his own. He needed her just as she was, paradoxical, mendacious, gifted for corruption of any kind. She provided him with an excuse for his lost state, with a kind of dirty bath for his leprous feeling. The leper. Pile on the filth all around! Oh, to get lost in dirt like a revolting insect living in dung. Maestro: the Crazy Bug.

And yet he was disgusted with Maestro the Bug.

He knew he was lying. It was all an exercise in mimicry performed by a mind horrified at the quicksands into which it was about to be pushed. And the mind was unable to flee, still believing this was a dream, a bad, terrible, infantile dream involving monsters with two pincerlike fingers for hands approaching to embrace you—"I'm your Daddy, my boy." And when his mind awoke to a new day it found it simply unbelievable that people might not walk the streets so privately, that the crippled weighing-machine man might not slurp soup from his lunch bucket in the doorway at noon, that news vendors might not shout "War's Worst Raid On London." That someone down in the street might say in dead earnest, "This is no exercise, this is the real thing. I heard it with my own ears over the wireless." And what of that mountain whiteness of the sanitarium for innocent diseases then, what of the dreams under the shelter of the melancholy white flag with the magic red cross on it, above which, high up among the clouds, pilots smiled like angels? Milk brothers and sisters, reclining on the terrace under the glaciers, thermometer under tongue, leafing through breviaries of love in postprandial contemplations. She is now Viviana. Not Francesca, not Beatrice or Laura or Isolde or Héloïse or Virginie; she is Viviana, a name which . . .

"What have you gone all quiet for?" called Enka in a conciliatory voice.

"What are you thinking about?"

"Abélard. A castrated man in the Middle Ages."

"Did he do it out of piety?"

"No, they did it to him. The Church. For being in love with young Héloïse."

"Would you go through that for me? Like hell you would!" She was actually seriously offended at the conclusion.

"I don't love you," he said, blowing away a strand of her hair that was tickling his nose.

"No?"

"No."

She shooed his hand from her breast and got up irresolutely. She put her housecoat back on and went wordlessly to the bathroom.

That was how their encounters usually ended, to his satisfaction. He actually stage-managed such endings, closing the door behind him with no wish ever to return. And walking downstairs happy to be leaving. As if he were redeeming himself for some piece of perfidy.

He felt the wish to flee. To profit from her absence and go.

He dressed hastily. Prowling about on tiptoe, he tried to walk soundlessly, burglar style. But the parquet creaked. Suddenly she opened the door and gave him a frightened stare, as if about to shout for help. He stopped in his tracks, taken aback. He bent down like someone looking for something he'd mislaid.

"What is it you lost—your honor?" she collected her wits. Rage poured from her eyes.

"Yes. But I expect it must be somewhere in your marital bed," he leered cynically. "Never mind, I'll take yours. It'll come in handy— I'm seeing some scoundrels later on today."

"Kior!" she screamed and flew at him, but her arms threw themselves around his neck instead of pelting him. "Kio, why will you insult me?" She was being cuddly Enka again.

"It's not my fault that all the facts around you are insulting."

"All right. Fine. What would you have me do then? Do you want me to ring him up now, 'Darling, Melkior Tresić is my lover'? Is that what you want?"

He produced a contemptuous smile.

"I may be, well . . . a whore, as you like to say, but I would never wish to hurt that man. That's my morality. Now laugh all you want."

He was not laughing. All of a sudden he said, so dejected that he wondered at the overtone himself: "It hurts me that you should be like that."

He was lying. He liked her being like that, her, Enka's, being like that. But he was thinking about the other one, about Viviana . . . and the thought hurt him. Ugo looking up her skirt while she, the Samaritan, bent over him . . . She knew he was looking . . . Oh Lord, must they all be like that?

And the Lord inside him replied cruelly: Every single one!

His face contorted at the Lord's truth.

Enka started to make a commiserating gesture to him but gave up. She had remembered her own case.

"Yes, well, that's the way I am. There's nothing to be done," and she shrugged.

Do they all shrug like that? Every single one, repeated the Lord inside him. He turned to leave. Enka blocked his way with a sheepish smile.

"Shall we listen to *Bolero*? It has been a long time."

She was being small, humble. Ravel's *Bolero* had worked in the past . . .

"No," he said resolutely. "It's past twelve. I've got to stop by the office . . ."

"When are you coming next?"

"Probably never."

He caught a glimpse of fear flitting through her eyes. There, that was what he had wanted: to run a snap check. She never learns anything from experience. How many times did I tell her "never" only to come back again, and every time there was that flicker in her eyes! Yes, true, but I really believed I wasn't coming back anymore. Could it be that she's tuned in to that very thought on some wavelength of hers? This time, too, I think this "never" to be the last. Perhaps it really is? He now wished with all his heart it would be.

"Kio, please, can't you stay for just a little while?" She was begging.

"What for?" She was quiet. "Come on—what for?"

"Now you're shouting at me." A sob constricted her throat. "Is it something I did?"

"No."

"Why are you angry then?"

"I'm not angry."

"Listen, Kio. Please wait, just a moment longer, please, and then you can go . . . if you like. I don't know what it was I did. But . . . listen, please, if I ever hurt you in any way, please forgive me. I promise I'll never do it again, Kio."

"Never do what again?" he asked with supercilious scorn.

"Give you cause to be angry with me."

"Why, you're the cause yourself, all of you . . . ha-ha-ha . . ." His laugh was bitter and desperate.

Enka laughed, too. She thought, It's better that he laughs.

"Take me, Kio, take me as I am. Don't you think we could have lovely times together, after all?"

"Lovely indeed . . . Wonderful!" he leered all of a sudden. "Your husband has it lovely, too!"

"Yes he has!" she stepped out with proud disdain.

"He doesn't know his happiness."

"He knows it perfectly well! *And* he appreciates it. Whereas you . . ." She began to sob and tears ran down her cheeks. She felt innocent and righteous. There she was, torn between the two men in her life . . . the victim of her own generosity.

"You'll regret all this, Kior, you'll be sorry one day, mark my words . . ."

She wept bitterly and sincerely. And again Melkior invoked the spirits of the occult world, the mediums of tricks and deceptions, the grand masters of murky enigmas, to explain this strange creature here. So when everything's said and done, *I'm* evil? I am Satan, a tormentor, sucking this poor woman's life's blood!

She was standing in the middle of the room, her face buried in her hands, weeping. A symbol of woe.

The phone rang.

In full self-control, she wiped her tears, even patted her hair (the instinct of the coquette, said Melkior to himself), without failing to signal him to stand still.

She lifted the receiver.

"Yes, darlingest," she said into the phone sweetly, smilingly. Another face, a new creature. The metamorphosis of the jellyfish in a summer's shallow. Multiplying by parthenogenesis, becoming countless, endless. Ubiquitous. Eternal.

Indestructible and omnipotent. Look, she can do anything! Oh God, You who assembled her, disassemble, dismember, dismantle her, display to me your Swiss precision handiwork in this priceless mechanism which works without a hitch! Or turn it back into Adam's rib! Oh Zeus, give back to Mother Earth the bones that Pyrrha threw over her stupid head! Give us mute stones along our life's paths to hurt our feet, but save our dignity now that, after the all-consuming destruction, you permitted Deucalion to become a man!

"You're tired, sweets, you can barely speak." She was melting with sincere worry. She was no longer aware of Melkior standing there beside her. "Oh what a shame, what a shame, I don't know what to think. Died how? On the table? Heart? You don't say! But why should you? You did your best, I'm sure. I trust you, my love. Come to me, sweets, come to me now. And hurry." And she sent him two kisses before hanging up.

"A man died on him, under his scalpel, he's in a terrible state." She was speaking sorrowfully, coming up to Melkior, and again tears welled in her eyes. She lifted her arms to embrace him: "Poor man."

He brushed her arms off, rudely, spun on his heel and slammed the door shut behind him. He could hear the scream of "Kior!" and the sound of despondent weeping. There was nothing that could make him turn back now.

Whence the sudden hope of running into Viviana? It was past twelve, her going-to-café time. Presumably she would not be going out that day if she had had a tiff with Freddie the previous night. What would he do if he ran into her? Would he say hello? Funny how he instantly forgot everything that had happened back up there with Enka. Not a trace! So what should I do, fret about it? Poor surgeon, his patient died. Poor bloody patient! What about Coco? . . . poor him, too, in a different way. Oh Lord, he loves her for all that! Yes he does, replied the Lord glumly, with a twinge of guilt.

And the day a fine autumn one, without a wisp of a cloud. And the noonday sun still high. Everywhere it was warm, pleasant. He felt light. He felt like running. The shops had been open until just a little earlier, the scents from perfumeries were still wafting down the streets . . . No, that was the scent of the woman in the close-fitting mouse-gray two-piece suit. *Quelle souris, mon Dieu!* Those legs, those legs, bearing a body well worth bearing. Left-right, one-two . . .

Colonel Pechárek will shertainly have shigned the shummonsh by now, *bud*. Dwaftees, one-two . . .

The day turned dark for Melkior. He became aware of his body with near loathing.

You'll get me consigned to that accursed shambles, he told it with hostility. You and the likes of you. Rifle slingers for Shoulder Arms, hand on trigger, a head to put an army cap on. As for the legs, it'll be left-right, the sole purpose of the legs; direction: the tree over there, forward march! On the double!

A moment before he had felt like running through the bright day, just like that, with no tree in front of him, light, transparent. Now he felt a solid heaviness in him as the dreadful presence of his body. Here it is. You'll get me thrown into the cauldron, to the cannibal warriors, where History is being stewed. Everyone will get their portion on the plate, for the sake of national pride. As for the neutrals . . . they will get smoke in the eyes for punishment. They have no pride, therefore they shall have no portion of history. What is History? It is: Aristotle, tutor to Alexander the Great . . . Seneca, tutor to Emperor Nero . . . Shakespeare, the Elizabethan writer . . . It is not Aristotle the Great, but Alexander; it is not Seneca the Stoic wasting his time in vain with a criminal; it is not Elizabeth, Queen of England in the Age of Shakespeare; that's History. Tell me, dwaftee, asks Pechárek, with whom did Napoleon converse in Germany? With what famous man?—I don't know. I do know that Goethe spoke with Napoleon, but I fear you may mean someone different. I know Beethoven removed his dedication of the *Eroica* . . . But that's not History. History is: the Great, the Small, the Tall, the Short, the Meek, the Fat, the Fair, the Good, the Wise, the Beloved, the Just, the Brave, the Pious, the Posthumous, the Quarrelsome, the Bald, the Stuttering, the Lame, the Hunchbacked, the Stern, the Fearsome, the Terrible, the Red-Bearded, the Landless, the Lion-Hearted, the Father of the People, Born in Porphyry (Porphyrogenitos), the Magnificent . . . Drunks, murderers, poisoners, cutthroats, arsonists, libertines, madmen . . . History, the Teacher of Life. A spinster with glasses on her pointy nose, hysterical, unfulfilled, cane-wielding: we never can guess what she wants, we are always guilty of something or other, kneeling in the corner for punishment, face to the wall, freezing, trembling, we pray to the God above the lectern (above the young King): give us rest, let us live, free us from the fear and death our dear teacher visits upon us only too often! We don't want History, we want Life, oh Lord! But what's the use of our prayers to You? She has taken good care of You, too! She drove nails through Your hands and legs, nailed You to two crossed planks, elevated You to the level of historical scandal and entered You into her ledger under the adjective Crucified. Oh Lord, is there any protection from that madwoman? And the Lord said to Melkior in a low, shy voice, None.

Feeling the pressure of his rising waters, Melkior suddenly found himself at the entrance to the underworld on Governor Square. Ladies descend to the right, gents descend to the left. What chivalry! This makes me a gent. Well, it says so up overhead in green tiles, it says GENTS. And the gents go downstairs to the left . . .

"Behold the gent! . . . Never mind, we'll talk when you come back out." Melkior raised his head following the voice. Over the wrought-iron railing he saw Ugo's leering face with the dark fillings in the front teeth.

"It's all right, finish your prayers first. I'll be waiting here."

Melkior went down. All four corners were taken. Everyone prefers corner positions, to avoid the curiosity of the ministrants impudently peering into secrets from either side. He looked for a free stall and approached the Wall of Sighs. *Il muro dei sospiri.* He gave a satisfied sigh.

"*Sospiri?*" asked the ministrant on his left. The voice instantly stopped his flow. Mr. Kalisto, a papal name, retired postal supervisor, Ugo's father.

"Sighing, sighing, you and that son of miiiine," remonstrated Mr. Kalisto over the marble slab that endeavored to divide the private lives of two neighbors in these private moments when one wishes for total solitude.

"But every niiiight, every niiiight, Melko my boooy!"

"Every night what?" although he knew what "every night" meant; this was how every encounter with Mr. Kalisto went.

"Every nnniiiight with those giiiirlsssss . . ." complained Mr. Kalisto with envy (naturally enough) in his voice. "Wherever do you fiiiiind the monnneeey for it, in the nnname of Gaaawwd? It costs monnney, monnneeey, it's amazing how much monnneey you nnneeeed! Ohh, those girlsss, those girlsss!"

"What girls?"

"The girlsss who call you 'baby' out of looove," leered Mr. Kalisto across the marble partition and Melkior saw a set of lovely pink gums with no teeth in them. Mr. Kalisto hissed across his denuded gums and smacked his words with nasal gusto. "The girlsss who show you their legsss up to their chin, heh-heh. I know it all right, I've sssown wild oatsss in my timmme, too. But alwaysss in modera-tionnn, alwaysss in itsss proper time, but sssleep is sssleep, it's a nnnecessity for the younnng and old alike. You wasssste nnight after nnight. Drinking, carousssing, I knnnow it all too well. I've been through it, thank you very mmmuch, I don't nnneeed you telling me about it!"

The clients at their stalls were turning their heads toward them. Melkior's visit to the white institution had fallen flat.

"I'm *not* telling you," he tried to get Mr. Kalisto to lower the volume.

"Don't even try! What could you tell me? Artisssts? Ugo is no artisssst. Ugo's got to do hisss Nnnational Service, get a teaching job and get mmmarried. I cannnot sssupport him any lonnger. You do assss you like." And winding up sternly, index finger raised above the marble slab, "You leave my ssson alonnne! Go your ownnnn waay. You're an artist, you ssstay with the arty crowd. You have no home and no family, you recognizzze no God and no law. You think we decsssent citizensss are ridiculousss. Well, goooo ahead and laugh. Good-bye."

And performing a final shakeout, Mr. Kalisto buttoned himself and straightened up with remarkable pride. Melkior took a look at him leaving soundlessly on his rubber soles. The father of the son who was waiting upstairs . . . He's got corns on the soles of his feet, Ugo says. He walks on his heels. That's how soldiers walk in boots too big for them—chafed by their destiny.

Melkior let off his jet with pleasure. He watched his parabola like a gunner and fell to conscientiously shelling a cigarette butt until it was completely destroyed. He became aware of a pretender to his stall standing behind and ceded it to him with a fraternal grin.

"You seem to take longer than normal to perform that rite. What is it, prostate?" Ugo greeted him impatiently at the exit from the underworld. "Or has my Dad been knocking again at the door of your rotten conscience?"

"Yes, he's trying to save you from my influence."

"Before it's too late. Dear old parent. After him!" and he waved a hand in which he was carrying something wrapped in a sheet of newspaper.

"I know where my Polonius is off to. That's why he's so generous with his advice," muttered Ugo lifting his knees with effort, like someone treading deep waters. He hurried Melkior along so as to keep his father in sight.

"You are now about to witness the tactics of losing potential pursuers. He's going to the Main Post Office, you'll see. The crowd is worst there at this time of day. He is a circumspect man, is my Prostate Pa. Pro-state-Pa, Pro-state-Pa, the three-quarter-time two-timer. Whereas I'm having to pawn an old hat—mine!—to buy cigarettes!"

Melkior understood none of this.

"Where's he going?" he asked, all but running after Ugo.

"I told you—the Main Post Office."

"Well, what of it? Leave him alone."

"Leave him alone? Do you know what he's like, a man who tells you you're an artist and a libertine? A man who sucks a spoonful of my blood a day telling me I lavish my money on loose women? Don't infuriate me. There, I've lost him!"

Indeed, Mr. Kalisto had disappeared into a crowd that suddenly spilled from a side street. Ugo stood on tiptoe and craned his neck trying to isolate that dignified head of his progenitor's, but he eventually reported from up there: "It's no go! All's lost."

"I really don't see why you're following him!"

"I'm following my star! My paragon! In the footsteps of my ancestor!" Ugo spat out with despairing pungency. "What am I to do now? I've lost a unique chance! Who knows when I'll be able to nab him again?"

They walked idly, in silence. Ugo stole glances at passing women: he was angry and mournful and thought it improper to watch women when he was in mourning.

"To think that he solemnly signed the convention, *tête-à-tête*! Don't laugh. You've met my mother, haven't you? Well, he assured that deaf mistress of his that his wife was on her deathbed—expected to die within the week. And Deaf Daisy came by to see for herself. Mother received her with an open heart, in complete good faith, you know what she's like. Deaf Daisy started grunting like a damned bear when she saw Mother alive and well. You should've heard the conversation in the anteroom: Deaf Daisy cooing in disappointment, in desperation, seeing her hopes blighted, Mother understanding nothing, offering her coffee, tea, cold compresses for her head, aspirin. . . . I'm howling with laughter in my room. Mother's afraid for me, rushes in, Deaf Daisy hot on her heels, grunting away, wanting to see everything for herself. Mother introduces me, politely, hoping it would help. 'This is my son,' says she. She's totally in the dark.

" 'Dat's de son?' grunts Deaf Daisy, even more desperately. 'But he said he'd no chidden!' and down she falls on my bed in a dead faint. I enjoyed slapping her face to bring her to. Mother grabs my hands, won't let me slap her, goes off to fetch water, vinegar, but by the time she's back Deaf Daisy's on her feet again, ready to fight. I had the devil's own job pushing her out. Mother never mentioned it to him on account of my making a shocking exhibition of myself, and she refused to speak to me for a month for being so cruel to the poor bitch. To this day she believes Daisy was just a nut who wandered into the wrong house.

"Following this, the sinful parent was delighted to accept my conditions for keeping the secret. But he's recently taken to complaining quietly, indeed with tears in his eyes: even the worst criminals, says he, know the length of their sentence while he doesn't know whether it's only for life or what. Also, the cost of living keeps going up, and seeing that he, too, is a smoker, that he, too, likes a cup of coffee now and then but is reduced to drinking espresso at a stand-up bar. . . . He pleaded for mercy and I pardoned him. Then he became aggressive again, the dear old moralist, the advising Polonius. Now he's off to see Deaf Daisy again."

"How can you tell?"

"Aah, he's one dirty old man, is Mr. Kalisto! I'm ashamed even to tell you how I know. Can you imagine what it must be, to make *me* ashamed?" Melkior was laughing. He was amused by the naughtiness of Mr. Kalisto-the-moralisto.

"Do you know what he does down there?" Ugo was clearly troubled by his father's sexual roguery. "He listens for sounds from the Ladies! The walls are thin, you can pick up an auditory signal or two from a female organism. Pathetic. But that's what he goes down there for: an aphrodisiac for a spot of how's your father with Deaf Daisy. That's how I know he's off to meet her. Ptui!" and Ugo spat in genuine disgust.

Melkior remembered Maestro: the whole business was nothing more than old men urinating. Tepid waters gurgling, false signals sent.

"Are you sure you didn't make any of this up?"

"Make it up? He told me himself, in a state of cruel bliss, how you could hear it aaall through that waaall . . ." Ugo imitated him with disgusted hatred.

"Now then, this hat . . . What can I expect from Kikinis for it? Not even ten bucks. And not a single hole in it, as you'll see."

He unwrapped the hat from the newspaper and turned it to the sun.

Both their gazes dipped under the brim encountering the sight of a dark night sky thickly strewn with first, second, and third-magnitude stars.

"You can clearly see the Big Dipper, Andromeda, and Betelgeuse Alpha. Happy viewing!" Ugo was watching the constellations with an astronomer's concern, in dead earnest. "Moth-made galaxies, soup-strainer constellations. A miniature astronomy overhead. Oh well. At least we discovered the starry sky above us and the moral law within us, like old Immanuel of Königsberg. Let us therefore follow our Polar Star like the Argonauts, let us harken to the voice of the categorical imperative within us!"

So speaking, in a kind of rapture, he entered the spacious hall of the Main Post Office, with Melkior hurrying along at his heels.

"What are we doing here?" he tried to pull him back. There were a lot of people about, businesslike, patient, as well as short-tempered, addressers. He feared Ugo's excesses.

"I'm looking for a dome to present with the sky," said Ugo, burning with the urge to do a good deed. "Not to worry, it's all according to Kant: Act only on that maxim whereby thou canst at the same time will . . . how does it go on? Give me a clue—you're a Kantian, aren't you? Categorically, imperatively! Caution, the Earth is about to quake, consider lines of retreat."

He selected an exemplary yellowish bald pate of a hurried-looking addresser and placed his old riddled hat on it with a quick, imperceptible motion. He then casually spoke to Melkior as if asking for a point of information.

"*Alea jacta est!*" he whispered hurriedly. "The Earth is already quaking with injured pride. This means war. Flee to Switzerland, quick!" Melkior did not hesitate: he almost ran for the exit. This is sheer madness, those people in there are going to kill him . . .

He just had the time to hear a "Who put this thing on my head?" coming from behind him and then it was, Run for it, run, run! The fear down his back. Knifed in the back, just like that, on account of such a rascal. Death At Main Post Office. Innocent Victim Of Misunderstanding. All over, before the war even broke out. A farewell to arms.

Yes, somebody could really take me for a . . . seeing that I'm . . . er, running away . . . He only calmed down outside, on the opposite pavement.

Ugo's *acte gratuit*. Been reading Gide recently, imitating Lafcadio. He always imitates people. Characters in novels. The ape.

He's going to tell about it tonight (to Her). The thought hurts.

Still, must admit it takes guts. Takes brass nerve to cut such silly capers. Daring. For example:

An old man, dignified, rugged, a rock, features showing the greatest greatness—a Goethe, in a word—coughs in the street (such things do happen) and spits into his handkerchief, forcefully, quite in keeping with his station, and peers—with scientific interest, as it were—into his all-important gob of phlegm.

"Well? Looks lovely, doesn't it?" Melkior loosed his *acte gratuit* and went momentarily deaf, like someone whose rifle had gone off by accident in his hands.

"Im-pertinent cad!" gurgled the rock through his catarrhs, and passersby agreed with him, silently.

"*Gratuit,*" ejaculated Melkior mechanically, by way of explanation to those who had turned around after him. And he blushed, miserably.

No, I'm no good at that sort of thing. No good at all, really . . .

". . . that it should become a universal law. I remembered it looking at the ungrateful sky-carrier. I'm thinking of the tiny suns that will shine on his bald pate when he goes out again. The bastard. That very hat would have cost him thirty dinars at Kikinis. But he still wanted to fight me."

Ugo was regretting the gift.

"We should have looked at it not against the sun but in the dark. And then gone to Kikinis the astrologer. He would have shelled out ten dinars for it, at the very least. We played at being anonymous benefactors and eccentrics, Kantian philistines, victims of the categorical imperative—phooey! When we could have used the ten dindin-din to giventake till lunchtime. A fatal mistake!"

They walked in silence. Melkior was deliberately steering the stroll toward the Theater Café. Toward Viviana. But how is it, if he was with her last night, how is it that they have arranged nothing? Oh but they have. For tonight.

Under cover of darkness. He's avoiding his fiancée. Let us hide our loves. They'll get married after he's done his National Service. And a war. They'll have children. War orphans: enormous heads, large eyes, tiny skeletons, ribs, kneecaps . . . "Have you made your last wish, Eustache? Here comes Scarpia."

Melkior said nothing: his jaw had gone stiff. He had a dreadful fear of the police. The Platonic *Politeia*.

The man was limping toward them on uneven legs, but with a "Make way!" face. Uniformed, gilded . . .

"*E lucevan' le stele . . .*" Ugo burst into song while the man was still quite some way off, following his progress. But just as the man came in line with them he elocuted in the manner of the ancient, pathos-ridden school of acting: "There is something rotten in the state of Denmark."

Scarpia paused in the arsis (on the longer leg) with the thought "Should I take this as . . . ?" and while he was making up his mind Ugo pulled Melkior around the corner. Any port in a storm.

"It would have been an uneven struggle. Don't be ashamed of the retreat. The day of reckoning is at hand. The exact date is known to don Fernando, they told it to him at the Corso."

"Don Fernando" rang inside Melkior like an alarm bell, like the fear of being seen with Ugo in street excesses. Don Fernando was a profound mystery, a myth, a "something else." The approach to problems. The responsible care for mankind. No less.

"Who told him?" The mood for joking fizzled out in Melkior.

"The bearded bods. The sternfaces. At least, not bearded, these days they're clean-shaven; let's say the morose, the men with the furrowed brows. All in the name of mankind."

"While you . . . you don't give a tinker's for mankind?" asked Melkior, suspiciously, even with a shade of moral contempt.

"Frankly . . . no!" whispered Ugo repentantly, while at the same time swelling with incipient laughter. "Somehow I don't seem to care for it at all. While mankind, I know, suffers horribly because of me. Heh, heh . . . I'm an ingrate, *mon ami*, and a bad one at that."

"That you are indeed," said Melkior from his sudden solitude. What's to be said now? Mankind? Well, that's everybody. Including Enka. Including Freddie. Including Maestro. There are various mankinds. The Enka mankind, the Freddie mankind, the Mr.

Kalisto mankind . . . don Fernando's MANKIND? The word and the pathos. You can say anything in a solemn tone—"the Dardanelles," for instance. So what do I care? Rot the Dardanelles.

"Did he smite you hard, good my friend?" he suddenly asked Ugo with ardent sarcasm. "Show me."

"What? Oh, you mean last night, in the battles with Fredegarius? Who told you—Chicory? Yes, it was a nasty altercation, my good friend. Blood flowed in streams. And I got my share of the wounds— a bludgeon in the face. He swings a heavy punch, does that Roscius-Rostratus. I was being your outer wall, *antemurale Melkioritatis!* My physical person stopped the *cabotin*'s creative force, as shown by the upper lip enclosed herewith. Here, look at the left corner, that's where the celebrated protagonist's front hoof landed."

Yes, that part of the lip was still swollen. Melkior eyed the wound with sympathy.

"But we won the war, *pardieu!* Fredegonde has been won and is standing firmly by us. No problems there."

"Standing by you," and a sigh uprooted itself from Melkior.

"No need to sigh, is there? By me, by you . . . *Insomma*, she's with us! And for my sacrifices and bravery in combat, I took my slice of the spoils of war, you understand."

"You were with her, afterward?"—bandaging his wound with a smile.

"*Naturellement, mon petit!*"

"At her place?"

"A studio flat, couch, (two couches!), bathroom, hot water. *Et, ce qui est le plus important, elle m'aime.*"

"What about you?"

"*Fou d'amour!*"

Peeking up her skirt while she wiped the blood from his snout— that was "*amour*"? No, he couldn't take any more. Tension had reached a high point and suddenly he blew a synaptic fuse. Flash!

"You're such an asshole!"—and then darkness . . . and peace.

"Oh?" Ugo was surprised. "And you're some kind of hysteric,

Eustachius the Most Pure? That's what comes of abstinence. I practice sexual congress. Why not follow my example?"

Melkior chuckled inside. Enka. What was she doing now? He
felt the tug of desire to call her. No, Coco was back from the clinic.
They were now mourning his failure with the heart. Well, who ever
had any success in matters of the heart, *mon Coco?*

"Date tonight?" he asked ingratiatingly, begging.

"No." Ugo was being appreciative of his own importance.

"What, the brush so soon?"

"No—at ease. For today." And Ugo smacked his lips, with gusto.

Suddenly he gripped Melkior's shoulders and turned him so that
they were face to face. He looked into Melkior's face roguishly,
derisively.

"Hurts you, Eustachius, doesn't it?" and he burst into laughter.
"Well, in that case none of it is true. Not a thing." He gave Melkior a
protective hug. "Not a thing, get me? She's as pure as Ophelia. She
can go to a nunnery if she likes. But . . . but perhaps she won't, eh?
The fair Fredegonde. Perhaps she prefers this sinful Giventakian
life? Ha-haaa, my good prince!"

And I still don't know her . . . Viviana's . . . name. Now she's
Fredegonde on top of all else! Oh Lord, what *is* the matter with me?

You're in a bad way all right, replied the Lord.

"Hey, Parampion, tell me," he asked hesitatingly, "who is that
woman?"

"A mystery woman!" said Ugo seriously. "Like any other. Perhaps
even . . ." He did not want to finish. "Here comes my tram. Kalisto
ringing for lunch. Tired. See you at the Give'nTake tonight," he
added from the tram step.

"Perhaps even" what? A mystery woman. He seems to have a way
with these mystery women. All sorts of thing can lurk there. Various possibilities. Anything is possible. Nothing is ruled out. Not
under the rules. Under rule. Under their rule. Like the fragrance of
spring's breath they pass by; that is how it all begins. Like a bolt of
lightning they strike our nerves, batter us, roll us, cut us up, cook us,

soften us. We spread ourselves docilely, mushlike, jamlike, over their whims. As long as the whims last. Then they get us unstuck, scrape us off, clean it all out, every last bit, so as not to leave behind a single crumb of "the past," so as to consign all to utter and eternal oblivion.

They course through our veins like poison—a melancholy, moody flow. We yearn for an ending, any ending, for a finality, any finality, for somewhere to stop, to lie down peacefully, on our backs, to watch the branches sway with the wind, to help the ants in their small lives. We shamble like sick dogs along the fences of the happiness of other people, other people's laughter. We give an occasional bark alone in the night. We watch warily, cross-eyed, both sides of life, we are careful. Poisoned. Crippled by missing the warmth of touch, the fragrance of flowers, by missing springtimes, mornings, awakenings, the meaning of walking, of motion . . .

Where to? Poisoned. Poisoned. Poisoned.

And then . . . we take them like a shot of cognac at the bar, hastily, in from the cold, strangers, aloof, accidental passengers through all those distant, random, other people's lives. Indifferent. Locked. Cynical. That is the end.

Oh Maestro, you rhapsody of filth!

And yet he is making for the café, hoping unconsciously . . . No! Hoping consciously, indeed aspiring, to meet her. To find out, somehow to read in her person "the night before" . . . and all the rest of love's hieroglyphs inscribed on her by all the various pharaohs in all the nights of her dirty history. Damned Sphinx!

"Perhaps even . . ." Perhaps even a whore, is what he wanted to say? Ugo knows something about her, something nasty, something you don't tell about the woman whom you . . . whom you . . . whom you . . . he kept repeating in his mind while his thoughts floundered elsewhere, enraged, mad. Is she . . . that kind of woman? Or did he mean something else? She doesn't work for a living, what does she live on? Gentlemen friends? But if she's not *that* kind of woman, if she isn't a . . . Oh, Manon! Yet another name for her.

He was approaching the café. There were guests on the terrace, loud, vivacious. Having preprandial cognacs. Journalists. Waiting for proofs of their papers. In one of the groups, Maestro, mind-blowingly drunk, reciting "I have been on a cloud o'er the sea . . ."

She's not there. She's not inside either. Now then . . . Now then, the thing to do is abandon my self. Leave it here in the café to wait for her. While I go to . . . go to . . . Go where, miserable, alone, without my self? But I'll find her! I've got to see her today, have to think of a way . . .

He realized he was singing nonsense in his head. What sorrow! To sing my sorrow. Or to have lunch? He felt hunger in his entire body. It was Enka's doing. All your doing, baby, billing and cooing, baby. Maybe. Then, to his body: No way. You're not getting anything to eat, not as long as the reason's valid, and I want you to remember it. Be patient and . . . disintegrate, melt into air, into thin air. I let you have a sausage at Kurt's last night, didn't I? I'm speaking to you as if you were a dog. Forgive me, poor body. The fault is not thine. The fault is not mine. You know, *bud*, Pechárek'sh going to eat ush up if we gain weight. Off to the barracksh with you, he'll shay. And den to Hishtory'zh cauldron where the fate of dish faderland izh being cooked.

Those words aroused reflexes in the stomach. It gave an angry rumble. Don't be a fool, stomach, we're in danger! What if someone heard you? They would say, Poor father, such a willful child! Did Pestalozzi live in vain? Moderation, moderation, as the Greeks taught. Epicurus, you say? He was not referring to food only! And you do get "the rest," according to your just desserts. Be a Stoic. Renunciation, my boy, that's the yardstick of true greatness. Dom Kuzma was a giant of a man, sobbed Melkior-the-body, and look at him now! What do you think you're doing? Taking you to be weighed, that's what I'm doing, you greedy bastard! You'll be the death of me yet! replied Melkior-the-mind and resolutely led his beast to the invalid's weighing machine.

The man was holding a pot between his knees and using his spoon to dunk the bits of bread he had dropped into his soup. Sitting beside him on the small bench was an old woman with a basket: the other pot contained meat and potatoes fried with onions. There was a smell of food. Melkior's stomach reared in anger, only to subside into hopeless whimpers like a puppy being punished.

When Melkior stepped onto the machine the old woman stood up to attend to him. The invalid didn't even look up. *Tant mieux*. He was slurping his soup with gusto and . . . leave me be.

"Sixty-two," pronounced the old woman in a businesslike, even mildly unpleasant tone, having cursorily read Melkior's weight from the calibrating bar.

"You didn't round it off, did you? That was a bit quick."

"No haste, no rounding off!" said the old woman sharply, so much so that the invalid looked up, ready to defend the quality of his service. "That's what it showed, no two ways about it!"

The invalid nodded with satisfaction and went back to his meal. Approving of his wife's resoluteness.

"But I couldn't have gained that much overnight, could I?" I'm turning into a Dom Kuzma, noted Melkior, and he felt something akin to shame.

"You can put on up to eight hundred grams, you know," said the invalid with professional patience through a sizeable bite he was pleasurably preparing in his filled-to-capacity mouth. "You're forgetting the eating, sir. You have dinner, you have lunch, well, it all adds up, and the machine only shows your weight, whatever the freight."

There it was, the "freight-weight" again. The firm's slogan.

He paid and went down the street, worrying. Say what you like, I would have to weigh less following the simplest bookkeeping logic. There have been outlays, damn it! fumed the unhappy proprietor of a fresh two hundred and forty grams. And no receipts at all, no dinner or lunch, no food or drink.

Lunch, dinner: what pedestrian explanations. No, no, there is definitely a mystery to this weight business, a whim of physics. Exactitude? Exactitude my foot! There are deviations, exceptions, paradoxes, in the laws of physics. Water gains volume by freezing, said Melkior, triumphing over physics. He tried to recall another example. In vain. Perhaps there *is* no other. After all, weight is gravity. Newton's law: mass attraction. Does the Earth attract me more strongly today as a result? The mass of Melkior Tresić is today drawn more strongly to the mass of the Earth, if you please. By two hundred and forty grams. Exactly. On the other hand, mightn't the Earth have gained weight from some sort of cosmic nourishment and consequently exerted a greater pull? Who knows what stellar spaces Mother Earth traipses about in, what galactic feasts she fattens at. Finally to descend, having eaten and drunk her fill, to attract my underfed self. Will you just look at her? Metamorphoses!

A new law on the invalid's machine: Earth attracts the starving body of Melkior Tresić with a force that is directly proportional to his army weight and inversely proportional to his resistance. The war being W, a constant. Constantina.

Constance! Could that be Viviana's true name? He subsequently found he liked the meaning of the word very much. More so than the word itself. An ugly name, really, but its heart was in the right place . . .

He walked with a queer feeling of weight inside. This was a disruption to his ever-scrupulously-tidy mind. It was as if someone had brought a foreign piece of furniture into his familiar, private domestic realm of peace. Apparently he couldn't accommodate, he couldn't accept the change without frowning and resisting. Normally, when he was left alone with himself he was able to resume his train of thought as if it were an interrupted game of chess, with the situation precisely defined; but now somebody had been tampering with the chess pieces, changing their positions, leaving a muddle behind. . . . He could not abide disorder. Everything inside and around him had to be in its place. Defined, arranged to a certain logic, a system of his for classifying things by value, importance— a subjective, ridiculous hierarchy that made no crucial, objective sense. But it was so important to him that he was apt to climb back up to his third floor just to take out a book and put it "in its proper place" because . . . There was no because, it simply had to be that way for some reason he couldn't explain.

This is a stain of some sort of poison spreading inside me. It's a stain . . . I wasn't wary enough to take care, to take care. It's Enka's lust that has overflowed over, over . . . what? He was climbing the stairs to his room to the accompaniment of such faux musings. Everything was unclean, everything insincere! Including the autumn with its faux sky, faux heat, with its greenery tired and withered like the face of old age done up with cosmetics. There were supposed to be rains, sad, autumnal, and yellow leaves in the parks and the sound of wind in the trees, the days gray and gloomy, the nights long and wet and monotonous. Verlaine. *Les sanglots longs des violons de l'automne* . . . A surrender to sorrows, a relaxation, ease. Instead, this is all tense expectation outside the operating theater. Inside, the mystery of the to-be-or-not-to-be alternatives is under way. It's no longer a question, my good prince, it's a matter of waiting. The only question is: When? When will the blood-stained surgeon slice into my navel and reconnect me to Mother Earth who exerts this gravitational pull on me out of love? But I take away her force. I foster my antigravity using ascetic, saintly, angelical means. Wings will sprout out of my anti-Earth and I will take off for the disinterested, neutral, suprapatriotic, suprahuman skies. I shall hitch myself to a cloud and swing above you, *Mère-Folle*, I, your crazy son, Melkior Tresić the spider.

"Ah! Hail-fellow-well-met!" ATMAN surprised him on the stairs. "I've been waiting for you."

"What can I do for you, Mr. Adam?" Melkior spoke like someone ambushed by a loan shark.

"She's here," whispered Mr. Adam straight into his ear, so that the vowels tickled him deep inside his Eustachian tube.

"She's in here, in my room," whispered ATMAN confidentially, as if making preparations for a murder.

"Yes? What have I got to do with . . . ?" But these were not words turned over in the mind in advance, it was just the tongue knitting a small mask for the palmist's benefit.

"I promised to invite you when she came by, did I not? Well, she has come. Unexpectedly. I've already been upstairs looking for you, in your room."

The palmist spoke with elation, as one speaks of an extraordinarily joyous event. He had the air of a man exalted and aquiver. Nervously interlacing his long white fingers, he was making small bows to Melkior like a shop assistant enjoining a window-shopper to step in and have a closer look at the merchandise.

"Won't you come in, Mr. Melkior? We have been waiting for you."

"But why? She's *your* guest, isn't she?" In fact, he was afraid. Trembling at the very thought that he did wish to go in and was actually going to go in at any moment now. Oedipus facing the Sphinx! But he knew the answer to the riddle, "What animal walks on four feet . . . on two feet . . . on three feet . . ."

"I don't think we ought to put this off any longer." ATMAN was already nudging him toward the door. "Whatever will she think we're doing out here?"

The room was spacious. ATMAN had divided it, using a plush double curtain, into a dark anteroom-cum-waiting-room and a studio, which doubled as his bedroom. Melkior stepped into the dark and put out his arms like a blind man. ATMAN was still guiding him by the arm—or rather holding him captive.

"Would you believe he's afraid of you?" he called through the curtain to her over there in the well-lit part of the room. She shrieked a little laugh, which meant nothing, or merely, "How amusing."

The palmist pushed the curtain aside and ushered Melkior into the room. She had clearly taken up a pose for the encounter: she was sitting crossways on the sofa, her legs out in front of her, a thick volume on her knees. Melkior recognized it as a book of his—a translation of Alfred Adler's *Individual Psychology*; ATMAN used its size to impress his customers.

"Here he is," the palmist said as he set Melkior before her like a wooden dummy. "Introduce yourselves."

In reply to his *Tresić* she mumbled out some name or other and immediately said with genuine modesty:

"I should be afraid of you—you're a critic."

"You have nothing to be afraid of," Melkior replied with conviction.

"That's right, is it not? Nothing!" ATMAN jumped with delight. "And let me tell you he's not just being flattering!"

The corners of her lips curled upward with pleasure. Beautiful,

beautiful, beautiful . . . the words were dripping sweetly inside Melkior like honey being poured out golden-transparent, slowly, long, lazily. She had spread her skirt peacocklike about herself on the sofa so that her waist in the high-necked tight pullover showed itself slim, narrow, and the breasts, large, round, jutted out proudly, self-confident. The hair light brown, slick, drawn into a chignon, two thin laughter lines—that's what makes her look older. But the eyes, the mouth, the chin . . . no, I'll never be kissing them, concluded Melkior and this gave him a sense of inner peace, a resigned satisfaction.

"This is your book, isn't it?" She raised her pretty, bright eyes toward him. "And you've read all of it?"

"Yes," said Melkior with a shade of embarrassment.

"What about you, MacAdam? Have you read all of it, too?" she asked scornfully of ATMAN.

"Of course I have. That is, I haven't finished it yet. But I *am* in the middle of reading it . . ."

"But what do you need it for? Those old hags of yours? Mr. Trešèec is a teacher . . . You are a teacher, aren't you?"

"Bachelor's degree in philosophy," answered Melkior, aware that his ears had gone red, and added for good measure, "And my name is Tresić."

"Yes, well, Professor Tresić. I heard it the first time. Sorry." She blushed slightly, which Melkior took as small change for his fiery ears and felt good.

"I don't understand a word of this. I tried to read it. What's com-pen-sa-tion?"

"There you are—*exemplar*. What did I tell you?" ATMAN gave a happy jump and snapped his fingers with satisfaction.

"You shut up, I wasn't asking you!" she snapped. The palmist hung his head in shame, ingratiatingly, like a child who has intruded on a grownup conversation. But he was smiling with a corner of his eye, slyly.

What kind of relationship did they have then? Melkior was saddened by her authoritative intimacy with the palmist. Why was she free to use such a tone? But he noticed immediately, with doubled sadness, the way ATMAN took pride in showing Melkior her behavior. As if it was his right not to be offended by it, to take it as something familiar, domestic. He even grinned at Melkior—"This is the kind of terms we're on, get it?"

He felt dreadfully lonely in their company. He thought it best to leave while he still stood a minimal chance of having got it all wrong. But he found it hard to relinquish her presence. Better to risk a horrible revelation than interrupt this happy moment . . . Rubbish! they're acting out a charade for my benefit. This is a trap! He realized it in a flash. ATMAN had set up this ambush: they had been lying in wait with that book on her knees. With *com-pen-sa-tion.*

"Do sit down, please, Mr. Melkior," the palmist got suddenly fussy and flashed him a servile grin. "You've frightened him, kitten. Won't you sit down here, on the sofa? You won't mind him sitting next to you, will you? But why do you hesitate, Mr. Melkior? Don't be afraid, she's only arrogant with me. Am I right, kitten—he's not to be afraid of you? There, the kettle's boiling."

"You're talking nonsense, Mac. You're making me look the monster," she said flirtatiously. "Please sit down, Mr. Tresić, I should be truly glad to learn something from you. All these characters ever do is talk nonsense."

"These characters are mostly me," explained the palmist with a pride of sorts. "You are so kind, kitten, thank you very much. But at least I know what *compensation* is—which Freddie for one does not, I'll stake my life on that."

"Freddie's a dolt," she said in irritation. "And so are you. You only differ from him as much as a melon differs from a pumpkin."

"Well, at least that makes me the melon. Admit it—I'm the melon, right?"

"No, you are not!" She showed her beautiful teeth, spitefully. "Melons are sweet."

"There you are, I'm not even a melon. Did you hear her, Mr. Melkior—not even a melon."

ATMAN placed a small coffee table near the sofa, laughing brightly.

Melkior noticed the table had already been set with three teacups. So everything had been planned ahead, premeditated. This actually alarmed him: what are they up to with me?

"So Freddie's the sweet one, then," prattled the palmist brightly, laughing, fetching butter, liver paste, sliced sausage, cheese, bread, doing it all with hostlike, familiar alacrity, with measured, feminine motions. "Whereas I'm the pumpkin, ha-ha. A squash." He poured out the fine fragrant dark amber tea, smiling at some unspoken thought of his. "Shall I spread some pâté for you, kitten? It's genuine liver paste, fat-free. Do help yourself, Mr. Melkior. I recommend the sausage, it's very good indeed. A bit on the spicy side, just the thing for us men."

Melkior's beast gave a start and trembled with hunger. It fell to voraciously gobbling the food with its eyes. But Reason gave the beast a bash on the maddened snout and calmly proclaimed:

"No, thank you very much, Mr. Adam, I'm straight from lunch . . . Just a cup of tea will be fine. Thank you."

"Straight from lunch? You've given up then? A wise thing, if you ask me. I mean, what's the use? I keep asking myself if it really made sense. That treatment you're in for, as it were. Women go through it for their figure, which is also . . ." he gave a hopeless gesture and a benevolent smile.

"Yes, I heard that, too, about you undergoing a treatment. But I don't think you should really, you're far too thin." Her teeth sank into a thick layer of pâté. She bit off a mouthful and fell to chewing daintily.

"Who told you that?" Melkior asked fearfully. "Ugo? He's made up some sort of cock-and-bull story about me and is peddling it about in the cafés. He's mad."

"Ugo? Ugo who?"

The one you slept with last night, you bitch! She read some such thought in Melkior's look and her eyes flashed with malice for an instant, but she drove it all away with a very surprised smile.

"Mac, do I know this Ugo character?"

"By my method of reckoning time you've known him since last night," mumbled ATMAN through a mouthful of food, vengefully. "The wounded guy last night at the Give'nTake, the one you ministered to."

"Oh, the one Freddie clouted?" she remembered very convincingly. "The poor man, he had blood all over his mouth. That brute packs a punch." She laughed aloud, throwing back her head on the sofa backboard. "But he was absolutely brilliant, poor Ugo. I had no idea what his name was."

So much the worse. An unknown with an unknown. Perhaps even . . . Ugo's meaning was now clear. An unknown physiognomy steps into our lives, out of nowhere. Our smooth (smooth, eh?) sailing is boarded by a mysterious passenger who instantly steals our entire sense of reality. Sucks our willpower dry, and our secret wanderings begin. Through a terrain of illusions.

Melkior was already feeling helplessly drawn into this woman's magnetic field. He did not even know her name yet. The damnation —the sense of letting go, the senseless fattening of one's vanity. The words which issued from the charming mouth to sail through space following the most pedestrian auditory patterns assumed higher significance in our intricately distorted mind. We readily spread underneath them our ridiculous expectations, our hopes, for each word to drop where we chose. To cover, cleanse, comfort, delight, stroke, caress, to bite, cut, to draw blood and inflict pain, for that, too, now and then, is something our vanity needs.

Do I love her? And he glanced at her in step with the question . . . as if to make a snap check. Don't speak to me of love! Here, if she were to fall on her back right now in death throes, mouth frothing and body in torment, if I were to see death in her eyes—would I go out of my mind with fear, with despair at the loss? And there surfaced, by way of reply, an entirely cold, cynically grinning wish that this should actually happen, that she should die right here and now, in agony. There's love for you!

He hated her. He hated her with a motivated, cruel hatred,

which was taking its revenge in advance for the future. His future. For there had already sprouted a shoot of pain inside him, he knew it had, and he was watching his tender stalk sway its bitter fruits.

"He's a poet as well, isn't he?" she asked, but didn't wait for an answer. "He recited me some poetry. I don't remember any of it, but it was very beautiful. I mean, soulful," she corrected herself, noticing an ironic twitch of Melkior's lips. "I believe Ugo's an excellent actor. Better than Freddie anyway." ATMAN gave Melkior a look: what did I tell you? His face shone with professional triumph.

"Better as an actor, too, did you hear that, Mr. Melkior?" ATMAN's face dissolved into ambiguity: two conflicting expressions were mingling there like two opposing winds on a water surface; his face was slightly shivering both with hatred and a genteel smile. "So Freddie's quite without talent, is he?"

"Do you know what he did to him?" she turned to Melkior for help. "It was the opening night of I forget which play and Freddie was having this wonderful scene all to himself, and this Othello here . . ."

"That's not true!" the palmist interrupted her, alarmed. "It wasn't me, it wasn't me."

"It *was* you, yourself!" she outshouted him. "You eat pigeons."

"What's this got to do with me eating pigeons? I ask you, Mr. Melkior! She's crazy, is she not?"

"Crazy, eh? You know what he did? Freddie was just into his big scene, dramatic pause and all, you know how it goes. Everyone was dead silent, you could have heard a feather drop, and at that very moment this man . . ."

"I told you it wasn't me. It was his fellow actors who did it, out of spite."

"And this man, would you believe it, lets loose a pigeon from the box where he is sitting! You must have been there, surely you remember?"

Yes, Melkior did remember the pigeon. Freddie's soliloquy had indeed fallen flat. The women protected their hairdos, believing the assailant to be a giant bat. The pigeon kept hurtling into the darkness of the box, into the galleries, terrified, miserable, panicking for its columbine life. There was a pigeon hunt on all over the place, nobody took any further interest in the play. The hunting interlude went on for a long time before it occurred to the pigeon to make for the stage and up to the dome where at last it settled down.

"There you are, Mr. Melkior, is she possessed by the devil or is she not? Even the devil himself wouldn't have . . ."

". . . could have come up such a nasty prank," she completed his sentence with malicious glee.

"But I tell you it wasn't me. I would have owned up, now. I might have done it if I'd been able to think of such a thing, but I'm afraid I'm not as clever as you. I'm just not. The pigeon must have flown in on his own through a hole in the roof—they have their nests up there . . ."

"Oh my pigeon!" she sang derisively. "You did think of it, it came to you as you were going after pigeons up in the attic. He eats pigeons, you know. And how does he kill them? He drowns them. Imagine those darling little heads that look at you so coquettishly, well he pushes them under water till they drown! Oh, Mac, you *are* a butcher."

"Oh, for God's sake, kitten, you eat pigeons—right, Mr. Melkior? You must drown them to keep the blood in the flesh."

"Do you hear what this cannibal is saying about blood and flesh? Shut up, you horrible man!" and she turned away from him capriciously. "All right, sir, I know you don't like Fred, you've never given him a good review, but I'm sure you would never do such a beastly thing to him. While Mac here . . . He pretends to be his bosom pal, mind you. Fred was marvelous, if it hadn't been for the stupid prank with the pigeon he would have got a round of applause on stage, but he loosed the pigeon himself! No, you're a terrible Jesuit! Don't believe a word he says, Mr., Mr. Trecić."

"Better use my first name," said Melkior, offended, "you seem to have difficulty remembering my last. My name is Melkior."

"That's even worse. Did I make a mistake?" she said coyly. "Why do you dislike Fred?"

"Well, you don't have to love everyone, do you?"

"But Fred isn't everyone. He's a prominent artist. A protagonist. What are you smirking for, you sadist, isn't *protagonist* the right word?"

"Oh, definitely, kitten, definitely. Exemplar!" and ATMAN gave Melkior a wink.

"You're an exemplar yourself!" she flared. "An exemplar of a dolt. No, honestly, Mr. Melkior, why don't you like Fred?"

"Why don't *you* like him anymore?" Melkior dared to ask, his face very visibly red.

"That's different. I know him, I know him very well. You hardly know him at all, so to speak, except on stage . . . Anyway, how can you speak of actors if you're not in close contact with them?"

"An astronomer is not in close contact with the stars, but that doesn't prevent him from speaking of them," said Melkior. "And Freddie is not such a star that I should not speak of him."

The retort pleased her hugely. She gave a contented laugh.

"That's good. Freddie's not such a star that . . . Very good indeed. You're a witty crew, you from Ugo's crowd. And each of you is called something funny. What do they call you?"

"Eustachius."

"Why?"

"Who knows. There was a Roman soldier in the army of Emperor Trajan . . ."

". . . the Goat Ears? And what do they call Ugo?"

"Parampion."

"Why?"

"He chose it himself."

"Why?" she asked with childlike insistence, but her mind was already elsewhere.

That elsewhere offended Melkior. But he no longer hated her. He thought, Sure, she's superficial, fickle, and—if it came to that— definitely unfaithful. But he loved the artlessness which seemed to him incapable of being false. She was singing in an angelic choir amid a scent of roses. This is it—I'm in love. And he was in high spirits.

He had found a nest among the branches. Chirping. Baby, he said to her in his mind.

"As for you, Mac, don't you think it's time you stopped that chewing?" She gave a laugh tinged with disgust.

Well, perhaps she, too, was relishing an inner celebration that was being interrupted by Mac's smacking lips.

"Sorry, Mic, I'll be finished in a moment." He began to tidy the table. "That was my lunch. I completed a major commission today. Two horoscopes of historic importance. They took me nearly two years to work out. Well, they are done. Both will end up on the bottom. I finished this morning."

"Oh, it's those ships, Mac?"

"The steel behemoths will be sunk next year. Here, have a look, Mr. Melkior"—he spread some sheets of paper out on the table with constellations, figures, and names on them. "On February the thirteenth last year, at one-fifteen p.m., the battleship *Bismarck* was launched in Hamburg, while on February the twenty-first of the same year, at three-forty-two p.m., the battleship *George V* was launched in Newcastle. Both are going to be smashed like a couple of tin buckets. The greatnesses." He gave a mordant laugh, evidently with something else on his mind.

"Why do you do such things? Who commissioned you? See what he fritters away his time on."

"It's for the papers. For your own paper's Sunday edition, Mr. Melkior. Both horoscopes to appear under the title *Veritas*. This will be a sensation. I've already spoken to Maestro. He was delighted."

"That I believe. He would sink all ships," said Melkior.

"And all humans," she muttered and went red with a great hatred of some sort.

"You know him?"

"Everyone in town knows the fiend. He was telling you rude things about me last night—I saw him. Take care, he's syphilitic." She was speaking fast and breathlessly.

"Come now, kitten, how can you claim something like that?" the palmist protested mildly. "He's simply an unhappy man. You of all people should know."

"Mac, I wish you'd stop throwing me in with that beast!" she cried and stood up. Her breasts were heaving rapidly with some very tempestuous breathing. That was Melkior's first exciting observation; another one, also exciting, was her hatred of Maestro. What was it that Tersitus had done to her? The hatred had a very cruel past. It was still untouched, untapped, full to the brim. What had grubby Tersitus done?

She sat down again and turned her back to them both. She was angry. You're all the same, you're all against me. Her shoulders shook. She covered her face with her hands. Now we're going to see those famous tears in her eyes. ATMAN gave him a phenomenon-announcing look. In for a bit of waiting for her to turn around, still in tears. Perhaps he had insulted her on purpose, with the pretty eyes in mind. He was a real creep, was Mr. Adam. Smiling, patiently. Waiting.

"And I was having such a good time here," she said sobbing. "You always have to go and spoil it."

"Now we're going to make coffee and when we've had our coffee we'll turn the cup upside down. All right?" He was speaking like someone in a kindergarten.

"I won't. I don't want anything from you anymore. And I'll never come back here again, not ever," she was saying through her hands. "And there I was going to stay the whole afternoon. I was having such a nice time." And she fell to sobbing again.

"He's now perhaps in a war chariot, the young warrior," crooned Mr. Adam. "Perhaps he's no longer on his horse, the fearsome knight . . ."

"You're lying now, you're lying! I'll marry the shoeshine man on the square . . ." She started another round of weeping, her gaze on a black tin of shoe polish. Despairingly.

He went up to her and lightly stroked her hair with a trembling, avid hand. She gave a queasy shudder. He grinned forlornly in Melkior's direction and shrugged. It's going to be a long wait, this meant.

The water started grumbling on the hotplate. Mr. Adam opened a tin, the smell of coffee filled the room. This worked on her like a whispered summons: come and see a marvelous scene, darling. A box with a new, hitherto unseen toy inside has been opened. We shall now take a peek at the future's kaleidoscope: bits of colored glass will paint our dreams. Colored geometry, the lunatic's landscape, the innocent girl clad in white walking above the flaming tongues of horrible serpents (symbolizing human malice), a big light in the distance. And he. The cavalryman. Waiting. Ah, I'm coming, darling, leaving all else behind me. Cursed be this world. I was born for you. Far, far away.

The yearnings. They are all far away. Linear. Unidimensional metaphors. *Long ago and far away* . . . The sea, the mountains, the sky and He, the beloved. Distant, exotic lands, the call of the wild. East: the eighteenth century; the twentieth: far-away cities, jungles of light, wet asphalt, the Negro with the saxophone, cognac, the West. What do you expect from life? Give me some yearning, my love, my lover man. That I may yearn for you. A letter. Heads (of state). Tails. Black tie. He's sent me two sets of undergarments (teddies), six (6) handkerchiefs, a silk shawl, and a negligee. It must mean something, the negligee. He's inviting me. I can't make up my mind, here—to leave—everything. Auntie told me, I don't know, love, you'll have to decide for yourself. *Yearning, yearning for you* . . .

She stopped crying. Wiped her eyes. Nose, too. Ruined everything. Snuffle snuffle. The nose had contributed copiously to the grieving, a handkerchief full of grief. And the eyes, the pretty eyes—red-rimmed, inflamed, rubbed raw—looked out with cold disdain, still gnawing the bone of sorrow, sucking the marrow. The boundless appetite of Miss, Mrs. Viviana. Soul feed. She licked her dry lips, cat style.

ATMAN knelt to serve her coffee. His face was grave, almost disappointed: she had not shone in tears. Nevertheless he managed to stretch his face into a now-now smile.

"I could kill you." Her eyes smiled restrainedly. Beautifully. "You antediluvian creature!"

Antediluvian? Melkior snap-checked *exemplar:* Nothing in it. A gas mask, most likely. And even that with the wholehearted aid of the imagination.

She drank her coffee in large gulps. She was in a hurry to reach the dregs: that was where Destiny smiled sweetly at her. She turned the cup upside down and fell to waiting impatiently. Happiness is being born. Extending tentacles, moving in the dark, clearing roads, removing snags, downing obstacles. How powerful, how terrible Happiness is, there is no holding it back.

"I see a long road," ATMAN read in the dregs. "A man standing alone at the far end. Waiting. Behind him, a splendid castle, a green park, a lake, white swans. Above the roof, wild geese flying away. Here, Mr. Melkior, can you see the geese?" ATMAN pointed his little finger at an orderly flock of dots. "These are geese. Meaning it's autumn. It is in autumn that you will arrive by this road to the glittering castle, one, two, three, four, four years from now. But I see terrible obstacles on your way: destruction, fire, explosions. See the explosion, Mr. Melkior?" He was now pointing at a scattered spurt of dregs, the spot where the bomb had hit. "And many people around you, false lifesavers, reaching out, grabbing hold of you in turn, each one for himself, for a time. And now you're on the road again, on your way to the waiting man's castle . . ."

"And then?" She was listening to him with a patient's eager concentration. In her eyes was fear of the unknown, with a humble, flattering plea for a happy ending. If at all possible.

"Then there will be an onslaught of malice and envy. I see a mean dragon with three heads, a flaming tongue in each. Envy, malice, and slander—the three-headed dragon blocking your way to happiness. You will get past the first head thanks to your beauty, you will get past the second head thanks to your kindness, but the third, the third head you will not get past."

"Oh my God," she cried, "not ever?" and covered her eyes with trembling hands, horrified.

Good. That was where her umbilical cord was fused to his, around the twinge of her Happiness. How he kept her chained to the frisson of Destiny! But we who know why the cock crows . . . Melkior laughed inside, but ATMAN's phrase still lay flatteringly in his ear. We who know . . .

"The third you will not get past," repeated the palmist in sibylline tones. "I see snowy whiteness all around. This is the passion of true love . . . to combat slander, and you are nowhere to be seen. I see you no more."

"But you did say, Mac, you did say I was going to reach the castle in the autumn, four years from now? Try starting over again—you forgot that bit, Mac."

"I forgot nothing," ATMAN replied sternly. He put the cup away, closed his eyes and tilting his face ceilingward. "I see you no more . . . do not interrupt, I'm not finished yet . . . I see you no more with my human eyes. Wait, I'm looking inside in another mode. Milk, boiling milk, is what I see. Black milk from hellish feed, an egg hatched by a viper, the accursed generation. Rising, all rising . . . Oh-ho, oh-ho. Ohhho, here comes a dark army, warriors with teeth from ear to ear, tooth by tooth. Blood and knife, blood and knife . . ."

"What about him, what about him?" she cried out dementedly.

"Knife and blood," said ATMAN in a trance, his face contorting with prophetic pain.

"Is he still standing there in front of the castle? Is he standing there alone?" she shivered miserably, deeply in love.

"Standing, standing . . . Falling! Tooth to neck, knife to throat." She screamed. "I see a honeycomb, a honeycomb, an endless honeycomb. Heads protruding from the honeycomb, eyes mournful, ears dry. Heads, heads, a thick cluster of grapes. A bloody vintage. Thump and thump, and thump and thump . . . sledgehammer, blow after blow. Reapers advancing. Murderers. Oh Mel-kiooor, Mel-kiooorrr . . ."

"What?" blurted Melkior.

"Don't ask," she whispered, "you'll wake him. He's not finished yet."

"Very well," said Melkior, offended. "I can leave if you like."

"No." She gave his hand a fierce squeeze. He felt the squeeze with all his body, it was like the touch of a thunderbolt. "He sees you, too. Listen." She left her hand on his. He felt nothing but that hand.

"What happens next, Mac, what happens next?" She wished the dream to go on. Perhaps there was a nice ending. Perhaps even a happy, a happy one!

"He lifts him bodily, does Melkior," ATMAN whispered ceiling-ward, his face clearing up, diluted. "Lifting, lifting. He's heavy, limp, half-dead. There's hope yet, says Melkior. I'll do it for her sake. That and anything else, I'll do anything for her sake, says Melkior. I love her, I love Viviana, says Melkior."

"You love her?" she asked, in near-consternation. "Who is she, Mac? Whom does he love?"

"Vi-vi-a-na," said ATMAN, his Adam's apple bobbing in his throat with suppressed laughter. Adam's apple. Melkior noticed this and blushed. I'll smash him, he thought, right on the Adam's apple bobbing on Adam's throat. I'll smash him . . .

"But who's Viviana, Mac?" She had noticed nothing. "Why's he lifting him up for her sake? Who is she?"

"Your mother's daughter but not your sister," he replied Pythian style, and his Adam's apple bobbed again.

"My mother's daughter but not my . . . Why, that's nobody, Mac! It's nobody, isn't it?" she spoke to Melkior. "Meaning you're not in love at all."

"That's what it means," Melkior readily took the proffered chance.

"So what's the idea of the teasing, MacAdam?" she cried in disap-pointment. "You are all confused. You're spouting nonsense. You can't see anything further, right? You can't see anything further."

"Oh but I can. Melkior is carrying him on his back to the glass castle. I'm doing it for her sake, says Melkior, and gives him his heart's blood. Melkior donates his own blood for her happiness. He comes around, opens his large eyes. (Beautiful eyes, she corrects him.) If I'm dead, he says, then it's all over and done with (as they say); if I'm alive then let me wait, let me wait for her to arrive. They cut your throat a bit, says Melkior, opened your veins and went on. You've lost your blood. But I've given you some of mine, there's plenty more where it came from, says Melkior, enjoy it in good health. I'll give it back to you, he says, when my own is restored, I'll give it back twice over. Please don't bother, says Melkior, and refuses with disgust. I gave it to you as a present because . . . but he won't say why; and the truth is that he did it for her happiness. But I'm going to get you a tutor, says Melkior, because you're artless like a stork—you're waiting on one leg. You need to be taught a thing or two. Oh no, I want to wait for her alone, he says. Anyway, I do know how to stand on two legs. Not at all, says Melkior, you'll need to have a tutor before I fetch her. You're standing on one leg, one and a half at best, and what she needs is an eagle, indeed two eagles for round-the-clock shifts, and a couple of parrots as well, for agreeable chats.—I'll give her everything, everything from inside myself, eagles and parrots included, only please go and bring her to me."

"Is that me, Mac, is that me?" she bleated ingratiatingly, full of hope.

"I said Viviana."

"Who is that? It's nobody!"

"Your mother's daughter . . ."

"We've figured that one out already. It's nobody. You can't say that! Who is she?" she whispered to Melkior. He shrugged: search me.

"There, you made it all up."

"I did not," said ATMAN in an earthly voice and squinted at Melkior. "He did."

"Who?"

"Melkior . . . made it up, Melkior . . ."

"Mr. Adam . . ." but he could think of nothing to say next, like someone caught out lying. He felt the need to wash his hands, which were sweaty. "Mr. Adam," he repeated senselessly and stopped dead, not being wound up. The mainspring had snapped, he felt it all of a sudden when she looked at him with her large eyes: You?

He crossed his legs in order to place a sharp kick with the tip of his shoe just below Mr. Adam's knee. Accidentally, with many apologies, sincere as all get-out.

"Ahh!" groaned Mr. Adam and turned on his small close-set eyes, training them on Melkior with the big threat of an all-encircling octopus, the dreadful lord of the deep. But he sent his tentacles twisting upward, into an after-sleep stretch, into sensible awakening. "What? Was I asleep?"

"No, your father's son was!" she said angrily. All was lost for her.

"But not my brother?" he took it up delightedly. "So it was I who slept, after all."

The penny dropped.

"Why, it's me! It's me!" she clapped her hands and embraced ATMAN the Great.

"What about you?" ATMAN wondered very convincingly. Melkior recrossed his legs and gave him another shoe-to-shin warning. Mildly this time, with a you-cheeky-beggar smile.

"Viviana! I am Viviana!" she cried out her destiny-making discovery.

"Who told you so? Did you tell her?"

Melkior blew through his nose and turned his head away.

"You said so yourself, you crazy Mac! Don't you remember? Viviana? I like it. Did you think of it, Mac?"

"No, it was Mr. Melkior."

She looked at him like a hen, inclining her head toward each shoulder in turn, with each eye—each of two delights—in turn. He went pale. A lump formed instantly beneath his diaphragm, he felt his tea in his gullet, sweet-tasting.

"A pretty name. Thank you so much," she said to Melkior, touching her face to his shoulder in fetching gratitude. ATMAN gave him a deserving look. "And you, Mac, you are truly a pig! You and your eagles! I'm not as stupid as you think. What does that make me, a . . . The parrots, too! No, honestly, you *are* a pig, MacAdam!"

She was angry, a justifiable and dainty anger, at Mr. Adam's peculiar insinuation. She was but an unhappy woman in search of love (pure and true) for her youth and, well, beauty, such as it was . . . and look at him going on about round-the-clock shifts . . . it was clear what he meant by the eagles. No, honestly, what was Mr.

Melkior to think of her? And Mr. Melkior was already thinking, Yes, it's all clear now, she's a . . . Two big-beaked eagles, around the clock, around the clock . . . And parrots to boot, ridiculous, yacking birds.

By now this had turned into a passion for discovery, for augmenting the sorrow. Which was why Melkior had stayed, waiting.

But she got up, sweeping her bric-a-brac into her handbag. The session had yielded some prospects after all: there was still the castle, also *him* in the distance. As for the adversity, well, you had to expect some, haven't you? She was used to them all right.

"Would you be a dear and walk me part of the way, Mr. Melkior?" The idea was to crush Mr. Adam. One, she had no further use for him that day; and two, he had been behaving maliciously. She was teaching him a lesson.

"All right, Mic," he jumped up cracking his knuckles, "would you like me to tell you the whole truth?" There was a momentary flicker in his close-set eyes, something like a wish for tremendous revenge. But a smile broke over his features and showed large spaced-out teeth—Chinese, thought Melkior.

This brought her back to the sofa with a bump. Her eyes were fixed on the cloud above her. She was expecting a stroke of lightning. But the cloud acquired a golden rim as the sun and the skies smiled.

"You interrupted me," he said sweetly, his mouth full of foaming kindness. "Somebody gave me a . . . a nudge under the table and I woke up too early. I haven't finished, Mic."

He had instantly cut short her wedding feast in the far-off glass castle. Horrified, she watched the Demiurge's skittish teeth with which he was about to slash the throat of the promised happiness. She was imploring No with all her body, No, Mac, have mercy. She saw breakdown, loss, finito. Oh how hard it was to find this damned Happiness!

"Because I still have a few things to tell you about what I saw . . ."

"No, Mac, please! Don't spoil it for me . . . don't spoil . . ." She burst into sobs before ATMAN the Terrible, looking at him eagerly, tearfully, with those very eyes he had intended to display for Melkior's benefit. Indeed he signaled Melkior to have a look.

The poor girl. Melkior was about to give her a protecting hug but her eyes sent him back to the position of the defeated. Her eyes! How right was ATMAN-Nero, the poet of those tears. He marveled at ATMAN's cruelty.

"How about a read from your palm? . . . So I can tell you how it all will turn out in the end?" He reached for her hand. She hid both behind her back. "Come on, it's not so bad." He was smiling up there, ATMAN the savage god, all-powerful. Flickering in his hands was a wretched little longing for Happiness.

Melkior stood. She gave him an imploring look; she was about to stop him, but the words died on her lips. ATMAN paid him no heed—he was alone with her, he had simply excluded Melkior. He'd invited me in to take part in the maneuvers, Melkior concluded, and muttered some sort of goodbye as a brief prayer to ward off a spell. Out on the stairs, taking two steps at a time, he fled, wounded, to his room.

You'll get them tomorrow, your betel leaves, the redheaded devil promises the first mate, the Nirvana angel. Tomorrow, opium paradise. He will be content with betel limbo, anything to avoid being cut to pieces with the crystal-sharp geometry of certainty wielded by the night's logic. He who has walked all the way down the Master's Eightfold Path is now offered a betel leaf by the redheaded Asclepian scoundrel to cover his shameful fear of oblivion. Oh Purna, why don't I have your spiritual strength in this wilderness? You, too, are leaving for wild parts inhabited by what might be cannibals, like this savage archipelago of mine. The Master warned you:

> Purna, those are a fierce people, cruel, hasty in anger, wild, violent. If they hurl evil and abusive words in your face, if they oppose you in anger, what will you think?
> If they hurl evil and abusive words in my face, I shall think, Those must be good people, for they hurl bad words at me but do not strike me or throw stones at me.
> But if they strike you and throw stones at you, what will you think then?
> I shall think, Those must be good people, lovable people, for they are not thrashing me with rods or swords.
> But if they thrash you with a rod and a sword?
> Those are good people, I shall think, lovable people, who thrash me with a rod and a sword but do not take my life.
> But what if they do take your life?

Those are good people, I shall think, lovable people, who with so little pain rid me of a body full of filth.

Good, Purna, said Master Gautama, then you can go to those barbarians. Go, Purna, and, being liberated, liberate them; in being comforted, comfort them. When you reach Nirvana, help others reach it, too.

Oh Great Gautama, how am I to break free of the accursed wish for existence? I know the sacred truth about pain, but I love my pain. Pain tells me, "I exist, and as long as I exist so shall you. I am your eye, your hand, your bowels, your umbilical cord that mother bound you with to life. When I am not there, you live only to await me with your body, your thought, your destiny. I am your being, I am your self-awareness, I am you. Do you want joy, laughter, pleasure? I shall give them to you. I give the day, for I am the night, I give the light, for I am the darkness, I give love, for I am death. I am everything." Give me pain, Oh Great Gautama!

For everything is so clearly meant to torment existence. The causality chains, the conceptual crosswords, the syllogistic snares. The Ars Magna, Lulus's mind-dimming invention, the idiotic code of reason. The Ars Combinatoria, a cardsharper's trick. The conniver, the broker, the fence, the pimp *Terminus Medius*, the con man with a fake identity, with a twofold role—now subject S, now predicate P, now you see me, now you don't—the magician, the charlatan, the lover of the two notorious whores—the Premises—the mysterious character M, the anonymous father of the imbecilic son known as *Conclusio*. Not to mention the grandfathers—Principles and the aunts—the Categories! Ten aunts all told!

Oh, Aristotle, Aristotle! sighs the first mate. He feels horribly the identity of his body through the advance on the pain of his soon-to-come transsubstantiation into cannibal meal and muck while the Stagirite invites him to kiss the Identity Principle before the transmutation mystery, so as not to pass into a new substance in mere terms of bodily pain, by way only of the senses, the way cattle do. Consciousness ought to know that a body dumped into the cauldron by the cannibals is not just a sum of sensations, a chaos of pains, a slimy lump of fear; this is the very *it* itself—*it* the theoretical Consciousness, ever present in its continuity, *it* the logical self which may, if it so chooses, deduce a syllogism according to the immaculate BARBARA the scholastic virgin: *Every man is mortal—I am a man—I am mortal.*

This charlatan-magician-mystifier is called Man. What, then, is Man? Man is Terminus M, the middle term in the syllogism of death. I am the Subject, my Predicate is the boiling cauldron, my flesh, the cannibals' teeth, and, under a banana tree, a freshly hatched, still steaming banana. That is my Nirvana, Oh Gautama!

He felt his body in his stomach with a Puritan wish to vomit. Autophagy: quite a good word, he thought, you can enjoy it cooked or raw.

Who wants to go on living here? Everyone. Everyone who tonight would suck up their own blubber, gnaw off their own flesh, swallow up all that is bodily and phenomenal about their persons, leaving only the pure being *an sich*, mouthless and gulletless (they will have eaten up their own selves beforehand), an elusive, inedible, conscious Monad provided with Arielian powers of revenge: all-seeing, all-knowing, all-powerful. All this, of course, only for the duration, until the danger passes. Whereupon kindly restore my body, my mouth and gullet and bowels and all the rest of things bowelly, bowel-conduitly and bowel-pleasing; kindly restore all the blisses, all the treasures and pleasures of Myself the Phenomenon. That was the deal. Oh yes, that was how it stood! Here, I just thought of something—how about being reincarnated as a reptile, a crocodile, eh? Yum-yum, eating cannibals on the phenomenal level, your mind *an sich* living in ideas all the while? What a samsara!

Now to extend the circle of pleasures to include snoring. The old seaman is releasing what you might call historical fatigue. Sucking in strength from the tropical night, sleep, peace, charging his batteries for the morrow. Who knows what tomorrow may bring?

"Give him a nudge, Doctor, wake him up!" comes the captain's imperious voice.

"First of all, why me?" hisses the Asclepian through a malicious snicker.

"Secondly, why wake up someone who may be enjoying a peaceful night's sleep for the first time in his life? And thirdly, the bridge went down with the good ship *Menelaus*. We are but different dishes on the local menu depending on which way our hosts' tastes run and that is all the difference between us."

"Don't forget you're still under my command. In a time of war, I might add. This means I have additional authority. You know the penalty for insubordination in wartime, do you not?"

"In wartime? Whom are *we* at war with?"

"Out here, we are a part of our country under wartime mobilization. We have been captured by the enemy and have POW status."

"Out here we are a part of nature in nature, sir—if I can still call you sir. What enemy do you have in mind? These are the Friendly Islands and we are the food for our friends, Mr. Morsel. We are the provisions."

The first mate laughed mordantly in his part of the dark. The agent and the chief engineer fell to lashing at the doctor with unrestrained hatred. Your very skin shows you're not one of us, God Himself has excluded you, marked you with your bedbug stench, they spoke into the darkness to the doctor and only regretted being unable to see his face. But it was just as well for them not to have seen it. His face was awash with satisfaction: keep talking, keep talking, you chosen lot, you clean lot, you beautiful lot! You tasty, fragrant, aromatic gourmet meals. You tasty treats! Blessed be thou, my primordial Stench! To me art thou like to the turtle's armor, the hedgehog's spine, the snail's shell, the hare's speed, the bear's paw, the buffalo's horn, the lion's strength, the snake's venom, the fox's cunning, the bird's wing, the cuttlefish's ink, the salamander's hideousness. There are anteaters, fly-eating swallows, chameleons, spiders, all kinds of insectivores, but there are no eaters of bedbugs. I am a bedbug among humans! A foul bedbug, the nocturnal prowler of your vigils, the vampire of your fevers, the tormentor of your insomnias. I crawl all over your pretty dreams and suck your pure, wholesome, sweet blood. Oh you archbishops of beauty, the hour of revenge is upon us!

"Wake him!" bellows the captain in the end, for the old seaman's snoring is nearly furious.

"How on earth can you sleep like that, man?" the chief engineer reproaches him gently after giving him a good shake.

"What else am I to do, sir? It's night . . ." the seaman says innocently.

"Yes, but you are snoring!" yells the captain.

"Oh really? Sorry, skipper, I wasn't aware," the seaman apologizes in earnest. "I must be keeping you up. People do tell me I make an unholy ruckus. Never heard it myself, but the boys in the crew, they often told me I roared. I've been stuck with it since my youth. Even had my nose operated on, they cut out half a pound of flesh, broadened the nostrils and all—well, it was for naught, I went on roaring like before. I always snore, gentlemen, when I sleep on my back. There's nothing for it. All you can do is turn me on my side."

"That's not the point, blast it!" flares the captain. "What I mean is, how can you snore like that, do you understand me, as if you haven't a care in the world?"

"I don't rightly know, sir. I expect it comes to me natural. At any rate, it's not on purpose, I swear on my . . ."

"Oh, the blessed fool," sighs the captain.

"Could be, sir," the seaman sighs, too, sincerely. "As for my snoring, you just flip me on my side, if you don't mind, and it'll stop right there. If I could hear it I'd stop it myself. Thing is, you can't hear yourself. Funny, isn't it? Everyone can hear it, everybody gets woken up—except your man. Funny." And the old fellow laughs artlessly at his discovery. "Everyone but the damned snore artist," he repeats to himself, finding it amusing. And he drops off to sleep again. With a chuckle.

"God, he's laughing again!" rages the captain. "Can't you get it through your thick skull, idiot, that those blacks are going to boil you and devour you just as the devils boil and devour sinners in Hell?

That it may well happen tomorrow? And you are chuckling away instead of giving it a thought!"

"What's the use of my thinking, sir? I know I'm a great sinner, so if these devils over here eat me up, at least those devils down there won't. Shame about the head cook though. He was a good man. He would've gone to heaven if these fellows here hadn't eaten him. No, honestly—it was bloody unfair, eating such a man. Such a nice man. Many's the time—I'll say it now—many's the time he let me have leftovers from the officers' mess. Have a nibble, old-timer, tasty stuff. Very tasty indeed, sir, very tasty indeed, thank you very much, sir, for being so kind. Not to mention where he was quite the joker, sir, our Mr. Head Cook! One day I was standing at . . ."

"Look at him—wants to tell anecdotes to pass the time," mutters the captain.

The old seaman sees that nobody is listening, turns over on his side, and falls contentedly asleep in an instant.

The next day a feeble hope is timidly born inside the castaways that things might take a proverbial turn for the better. No cannibal lunch is in the offing. What was the cook's stake the day before is now covered with smoking green branches—to repel poisonous insects, thinks the Asclepian, a wise measure. If only the cook remembered to make a religious speech in front of the cauldron, he would be proclaimed a saint, or at least a martyr in a hundred years' time; his name would be mentioned in all the cathedrals in Christendom. As it turns out, all that is left behind him are the swollen bellies from the *Menelaus* earnestly cursing him for having so painstakingly fattened them with death. No preparations for anything like a feast are under way in the village. The natives dawdle idly around the huts, stepping out of the way of naked women who slap them jokingly on their shiny black behinds. Mothers suckle their young with dull indifference, some of them catering to two at a time, one at each breast. The bigger children enviously watch the feeding of the tiny sucklings and divert milk drops with a finger from the greedy little mugs, licking their sticky sweetened fingers with gusto. A monkey whom a boy has singed with a flaming twig screams piteously in the forest. Presently his entire tribe joins him in a screeching show of solidarity, protesting in an angry chorus. Then the whole forest puts up a horrible howl. The offended monkey folk. The cannibals scoff at the impotent simian rage, hurling provocative counterhowls back. At this the monkeys' screeching turns into a kind of general weeping in recognition of their impotence and defeat. And once again peace reigns in the jungle.

Several natives armed with blowpipes take the castaways out of the hut and into the forest. The four naked swells from the *Menelaus*, using their hands as fig leaves, go through the village past the naked women with their eyes downcast in a gentlemanly manner, dying of shame. Only the first mate holds his uncaring favorite in the pedagogical embrace of his long white fingers as if teaching it elementary skills. A poor pupil, certain to flunk the easiest of tests. But that is not the point: it is just that the first mate is defying the elements. He is making humor of his misery, i.e., of the best raw material of all. But the product remains limited to personal use only as nobody else partakes of it or indeed notices it at all. Not that he minds: he keeps holding his rudder for his own account, grinning squeamishly.

Alongside the naked men walk the two clothed (inedible) oldsters. The old seaman displayed a most brachiate curiosity, casting quick glances at the sky and his surroundings, the trees, the huts, the men, women, and children, harkening to the birdsong, the roar of the wild beasts, the sound of the wind in the treetops, and suddenly says with satisfaction, "By gum, this place don't look half bad." The doctor walks slightly apart from the group, as he has walked all his life. But with a difference! This time it is he who stands out, fully dressed, dandified even, aware of his terrible superiority, which he patiently flaunts to the shitty Nakeds. To that herd of stupid cattle which is shyly covering their genitals with the sorry dignity of former human convention. Stuff and nonsense! As if they've discovered a milder version of this damned mess! As if their sadly pendulous noses are going to shock anyone! Cause a revolt of public decency? Impinge on the moral sensitivity of those ladies walking about naked themselves who pay no attention whatsoever to the presence here of this naked, exciting masculinity?

But as soon as they set foot in the forest the first mate lets drop his wrinkled saint and starts furiously examining the flora, biting into fruits, nibbling leaves, branches, roots. Then, half out of his mind, he suddenly swings around to the doctor.

"Well?"

"Well what?"

"Show me the tree of knowledge!"

"Ah," the doctor remembers, "yes, you're after your alkaloids. I hope we'll be able to find something for you. *Piper Bette* leaves, for instance. Only I don't know what the trunk looks like. But I do know the *Areca Catechu* palm. I've seen it before. Its nuts contain a high percentage of alkaloids as well. The thing's quite tall though, and betel nuts grow at the top, you'll have to climb."

"Trying to scare me?" laughs the first mate. "Climbing is a seaman's skill I still haven't forgotten."

"I daresay. Only will these people allow you to climb that high?"

"Well, where could I possibly flee to? The sky?"

"Don't ask me—ask them. However," the redheaded Asclepian adds slyly, "I happen to know a man whom they would allow to climb."

"You?" said the first mate, looking him up and down with derision. "*You* would climb?"

"I wouldn't know how. I've never been good at the simian skills. But they wouldn't stop the old salt."

"You mean they're not going to . . . to cook him?" says the first mate with envy. "They'll spare you, too," he adds with some hesitation. "I don't resent it, believe me. That is to say, I don't care. Will you just look at our crew scarfing down bananas?"

"Yes, I am looking. Carbohydrates and albumens. They'll be pummeling their bellies mea culpa tonight."

Indeed, the captain, the chief engineer, and the agent are greedily busy peeling bananas. Four-petaled peels fly about them like spent shells. Hunger has pushed aside all their awed nocturnal thoughts; they are feeding mindlessly, almost idiotically, no longer giving any thought to the death that looms so near—worse, so horrible. But all of a sudden, after a young cannibal throws down before them a fresh lot of bananas, coconuts, pineapples, mangoes, sugarcane marrow, and stickily sweet pink Indian figs, the captain seems to have had a brainstorm. He smacks his convex and surely intelligent brow hard:

"You know what, gentlemen? They've taken us out to pasture!"

"Ah, the penny's dropped at last!" mutters the doctor with a pitying smirk.

"They're fattening us!" the first-threatened agent nearly sobs out in horror.

"That's right, gentlemen," the chief engineer states ashamedly, "fattening us like pigs."

Now there ensues a painful awakening in the caring embrace of Mother Nature. The babies immediately release the generous breast. They feel the swellings in their bellies, they feel a dreadful animal slithering and squelching over the mishmash of sweet fruits inside. As if they had been eating live salamanders, rats, crocodiles, their innards rebel at the prospect of sudden catastrophe. Each hugs a tree trunk in an all-out effort to throw up and out their sneakingly greedy and disgusting death.

A disgusting death. A disgusting death you carry about inside you, as you do the image of your home country, the old homestead. My heart's in the highlands. From across the seas I'll come back to thee. And the soul parts from the body. Going hence. But before leaving it dictates the dispositions to be made as hereunder specified: one half of my assets to be left to my legitimate issue, the other half accruing to my lawfully wedded wife to own and manage as she shall see fit for the rest of her natural born life, should she not marry again. In the event of her remarriage, her inheritance shall pass on to my legitimate issue, or my grandchildren if any, upon their coming of age. My widow shall in such a case retain only her personal belongings from her so-called dowry, should any remain. Item, two dresses, one for everyday wear and the other for formal occasions;

item, two changes of underwear, to wit, two slips, two pairs of panties, two brassieres, and two suspender belts, one change being white and the other black (for possible mourning). Items, two pairs of shoes, one of low quality and the other of high quality, the latter to be black for the reason set out hereinabove. Her jewelry shall be sequestered in full, including her wedding ring which through her remarriage will have lost its sacramental value and become an item of personal adornment. Further, there shall be deducted from the estate an appropriate sum of money, at rates currently obtaining, for a Class A funeral (not including a requiem) for my widow. There shall be carried in her funeral procession a wreath of thorns and nettles with a yellow ribbon bearing the inscription COME TO ME, DARLING. My widow shall be buried in a grave separate from mine, with the following inscription to be carved on the headstone: HERE LIES THE WOMAN OF MY LIFE TO THE DEATH. HER LATE HUSBAND #1. While the coffin is being nailed shut there shall—Knock knock knock—violent pounding at the door interrupted The Great Will and Testament. Before he had time to ask who it was, Ugo's leering face appeared in the room.

"Verily, verily, I say unto thee," and in three steps he reached the sofa on which Melkior was lying. "What you're doing to yourself God Himself cannot understand. Been lying long like this? Woolgathering, I gather?"

"Yes, well, I've been doing a bit of thinking," replied Melkior stretching himself as if freshly awake.

"Thinking? Well, I, too, despise the body, Eustachius the Most Kind. 'But God hath tempered the body together, having given more abundant honor to that *member* which lacked.' Saint Paul. I've been feeling spiritual all over today. We had a clergyman to lunch, a certain Dom Kuzma. My mother has the habit of picking up such characters in churches and bringing them home. And he's all spirit, hardly any body left at all."

"With, er, big ears?" Melkior propped himself on an elbow in keen interest.

"Rather like an ex-elephant. You know him?"

"Ahh, poor Dom Kuzma." Melkior could see him on the invalid's machine, miserable, quarrelsome, haggling for each gram of flesh. "We sucked a lot of blood out of him in our boyhood. He was our catechism instructor. But then he had a lot of blood in those days—fierce blood, too."

"You should see him now! *Dies irae.* One of those who come before God's wrathful countenance. Mother kept going out to the kitchen so as not to cry in front of him. Even Kalisto's worm-eaten heart gave a lurch. He vowed, deep inside, to stop seeing Deaf Daisy for a week. But he'll go to her tomorrow, naturally. He hasn't got the least shred of bodily shame, that fundamental paternal virtue."

"Of such a son," added Melkior.

"Why do you believe me so incapable of spiritual elevation? The unholy spirit that proceeds from the father . . ."

". . . proceeds also from the son. *Filioque.* The theologico-sexual problem of every family. That is what the East split from the West over. It preferred to rely on the father, the more experienced of the two. The sexual spirit is the accidental progenitor of the son, the punished libertine paying dearly for his tiny short-lived happiness. The son is his damnation. His conscious sex incarnate, always underfoot when the desire is upon him. A waking ear in carnal nights, a suspicious eye preying on his lust with unjust and cruel disgust. Woe to the parent, having to be ashamed of his own virility because his male descendant has castrated him in his fantasy."

"My view of the issue is more on the financial side. Kalisto's virility is a strain on the family budget."

"Ah, you would like him to have that little item subsidize your virility instead? Because your virility is entitled to financial aid arising from his shameful renouncement? Entitled to your father's sacrifice? But why? What's your honorable Johnson done to deserve more joy than his? Perhaps your father's panicking at the thought of his last twitches? No joy, no poetry, just a poignant overhaul?"

"Don't, don't. You'll have me weeping in a minute!" Ugo made a comically tearful face. "I'll dream about Kalisto in flagrante with Deaf Daisy and cheer him on to beat the band."

"And so you should, were you more of an independent male specimen and less of Daddy's stupid spermatozoon who'd happened upon the notion of the immaculate conception."

"You are hell-bent, aren't you, on depriving me of my little revenue stream. If this transpires, I'm done for. Without sin I cannot peddle indulgences. Mind you, Kalisto is a good-sized sinner as sinners go, and I can tell you he gets off cheap with me. Let him just try his luck in church—they'd give him something to remember. He'd get his sinful knees good and callused like a dromedary's. Not to mention the repentance, the vows, the useful Never Again decisions . . . Whereas I allow ongoing sinning—for a modest consideration, of course. And yet you tell me I have no understanding? I'm kindhearted, I really am. And how does *he* treat his legitimate 'spermatozoon'? Makes him sell old hats, that's how! I have to go off to a date like a consumptive romanticist, with poems in my pockets—I'm too broke to take a girl to a café. I owe money to waiters all over town. Thénardier will sport my guts for suspenders. With all the damp in the parks, I'll catch my death one of these days. But God sees my misery—He's sent us a warm autumn. Ahh!" sighed Ugo in dead earnest. "*And* I've got this rhyme business to worry about! You can't get to first base with blank verse. They look right through you like cows and carry on with their own train of thought: two yards of fabric will do for a close-fitting dress, but you need more for a pleated skirt. Plus a matching striped silk blouse (black and yellow), yes, that would do nicely. . . . No, rhymes are an absolute must. The only thing they understand; *June–moon*. The old tune. It gets their attention. They swoon. My goodness, the way those words go with each other, isn't this marvelous?" he imitated a marveling dumb blonde.

Melkior was chuckling on the sofa. "Well then, my dear Parampion, all you have to do is write rhyming verse."

"Aah, don't laugh at the pragmatic poet, Eustachius the All-Wise. Why not help me instead, you're a ready hand at making those treats which our birds peck at so readily. Listen to this:

The old hope has died the death
Restless is the autumn air
October . . .

and here I need something to happen in her hair, but I haven't got anything to rhyme with the *death* in the first line. *October's gentle . . . breath/Ruffles your hair.* But it doesn't quite click, don't you agree, Eustachius the Gentle?"

"Yes, you've upset the meter in the last two lines," said Melkior. "They need to be heptasyllabic like the first two. Perhaps you'd better put *And October's gentle breath/Permeates your golden hair.*"

Ugo gave him a delighted kiss. "God, what talent! The way you come right out with it, off the cuff!"

U-go and chew bricks, simpleton. Then it came to him in a flash: it's for Viviana! He's got a date with her tonight after all! *And October's gentle breath permeates your golden hair.* She'll ask him to write it down in her album, permeates your golden hair. *What's per-mee-ate, pet? I bet it's something risqué. Just like you!* "You could have thought of something finer for her," he said, with a mouth on which the smile had dried.

"What, isn't it all right now?" Ugo was anxious. "Well, you *are* cruel! Telling me to put *gentle breath!* You conned me, Eustachius, didn't you? Of course you did, it's so pedestrian: *death/breath.* Vacuous. Just like you."

"Don't worry, she'll love it. Ah-ha, she'll say, I've made poetry! If she's heard of Laura, you're Petrarch."

"Wait a minute, Eustachius the Suspicious!" gaped Ugo in mock surprise, showing his large fillings, "who do you think I'm writing this for? You who keep boasting, 'I know him—I'm a judge of character.' Oh no, you don't know me at all. Today's my fiancée's birthday and I can't afford a gift—I'm broke. I'm giving her a poem instead—a sonnet, if you wish to humiliate me to the fullest!"

"*The old hope has died the death* is your fiancée, and the *gentle breath* is in Viviana's hair," said Melkior, and he got up restlessly.

"Oh what a libidologist you are, Eustachius the Unerring!"

"Is this an admission then?"

"Yes." Ugo dropped his eyes like a young sinning girl. "But . . . but it's all innocent, pure, like being at First Communion. On an ideal plane. That's the whole point. Poor fiancée."

Melkior had seen her with him now and again in the evening hours, the time set aside for her. The café, Gita's, mainly a student hangout, fruit salad and coffee, very cheap. Or the cinema, Nelson Eddy and Jeannette MacDonald. *Rose Marie.* Touching. She liked a good cry at the film. A super film. His senior by at least four or five years, fashion dressmaker, skinny, long thin legs, square-hips-flat-behind, breasts gathered into two modest handfuls underneath a virginal blouse, mole on chin with three resilient hairs growing from it. Three palm trees on Happiness Island. She was not fond of Melkior. She did like having a romp, though, in his room with her fiancé.

But the fiancé was getting acute attacks of other loves. Fellow undergraduate, co-ed Cica, springtime, walks, sonnets. *The old hope has died the death.* He would park his fiancée for the night (a bit of student slang, that) as early as nine o'clock and go on to make a night of it with Cica. Hey, why didn't the fiancée fall in love with someone else, too? Idea for breakup, it's all your fault, to think I trusted you so blindly, you sly minx. Worse. He took her to the zoo. Animals mate in springtime, women love to watch, it excites them. In front of the monkey cage—he told Melkior so himself—at the exact moment of simian joy. A young man was standing on the other side of her, watching edgily. Her face changed colors, jealousy. Let's move on, pet. Her voice was uneven, as if she had been running hard. He kept giving her little nudges toward the young man hoping the man would see her, that she would see him, that there would flare up between them a great, irresistible love, monkey-inspired, leaving him free with Cica, in vernal sonnets. A mad hope, a futile one. That hope, too, died the death. The young man, taken onanistically unawares, walked off. Sorry, ma'am. She gave him a parting look after all (or so it seemed to him) in *that* way, the monkey way. Something must have sparked. And he was jealous. And he quarreled with her. You're just a she-ape in rut! You're now ready to do it with anyone. And she cried. *I love you.* He then stroked her thinning hair and took her to the woods behind the zoo and they romped like monkeys.

"If it's so *pure*, you could have written something better for her." Melkior was pacing the room with a vengeful grin. Inside him flourished a sadness in the temperate climate of small despair. A mood of mild poisoning. Fatigue. Yawning. Humor.

"I'm sure you could have!" retorted Ugo in angry frustration. "There was no time, for one thing. I was waiting there to collect the whoring tax from Kalisto after lunch, but that man Dom . . . your catechism instructor . . . went on and on about his red corpuscles. There was no end to it. Mother shed a tear for each corpuscle, and Kalisto went pale with fear—white corpuscles all over the place. It was all I could do to lure him away and into my room for a some-what more spirited tête-à-tête. I cited you as witness to his move-ments around the post office this morning. Well, what do you care—he can't stand you anyway. But it worked, I can tell you that. I also mentioned buying a birthday present for the fiancée. I'm short of cash, he said, I've put money down in advance for coal. Not to mention where she (the fiancée, that is) seems to have birthdays more than once a year. Oh, my son, my son, when are you going to stand on your own two feet? Oh, Daddy, Daddy, I've been standing on my own two feet in front of you for at least half an hour. Oh, my son, you're good for nothing. Oh, Daddy, you're good for every-thing. Following the exchange of diplomatic notes we proceeded to implement a reparation treaty. And, lo and behold, Kalisto coughed up a shiny Protect Yugoslavia." Ugo flipped a silver fifty-dinar piece and caught it in his palm. "Alley oop!"

"Enough for a high-style Give'nTake session tonight, I expect."

"Not at all. It's Give'n *Make* tonight, as a matter of fact," said Ugo triumphantly. "A quiet place with well-behaved waiters. There'll have to be poetry whispered into a shell-like ear. If only there could be a bit of Petrarch, *dolci ire, dolci sdegni et dolci paci. October's gentle breath, oh, quelle différence!* Apart from *permeates*, it's all at a

Kalisto love level. Wouldn't you happen, Eustachius the Generous, to have among your remaindered stock a line or two to spare? Spare Christian, Oh Cyrano the great, a spark of your wit so that with Roxanne he can be a big hit!"

"I haven't got any, poor Christian, the mind's gone dry, my dear. Not that it could help you, with your mouth from ear to ear."

"And the fillings, don't forget, stomp me right into the ground, kind Eustachius, why don't you. Is that the way to speak to a man all atremble before a date with his beloved? With nothing in his pocket but your *October!*"

"All right then, toss it." Melkior flung himself on the sofa back-first. The springs let out a painful sob.

"Toss it? And recite what instead? Damned *Brumaire?* Where's that one with *Little one, I am but a painted clown?* Remember? You penned it for Mina. That time you nearly got crowned with a siphon bottle for your pains. Be honest—who was it who saved you? That's the one I need. It would suit me for other reasons, too; I mean suit my mood and my state of mind in general."

"God knows where it might beee . . ." Melkior yawned fit to bring on tears. He was painfully hungry.

"Well, what do you know, I'm a bore. You're yawning. Don't be a beast, Eustachius, lend us the poem."

"I told you I don't know where it is, didn't I?" and all the while he was thinking, Where else could it be? In the yellow folder along with Mina's only letter, the one saying she was going back to her fiancé, farewell. Fare thee well Mina. Eyes like yours I shall never again . . . Give him that to conquer Viviana with? *Farewell my love. The sun goes slowly down, Preparing my vigil in the endless night, My bittersweet dreams and my thorned crown. May your tomorrow be bracing and bright, While I . . .*

"Well, recite it for me then, Eustachius the Most Lovable—I'll take it down. I still have time to learn it by heart."

"I've forgotten it. *What will it matter if some day I drown in drunken jeers my sorrowful plight? Little one, I am but a painted clown . . .*"

"Oh God, don't tell me you can't remember a single stanza? Eustachius the Sharp-Eyed, just one little stanza, please . . ." Ugo knelt by the sofa and kissed Melkior on the temple.

"*I'll be going now. You close the flower*, I remember that much."

"Go on, go on."

"*When the sun sets* I think it was. Or not. I don't know. I really cannot remember another word. Your kiss was in vain."

"Well, what about that bit?"

"What bit?"

"*Your kiss was in vain.*"

"That bit meant Go to hell!" Melkior got up. He was now afraid that Ugo might remember those artless lines for Mina. He could not bear to hear them from Ugo's lips.

"*I'll be going now. You close the flower*," Ugo was reciting in a soulful whisper.

"Suits me. Be on your way."

"But it's useless, Eustachius the Mindless. What can I do with it? *When the sun sets* . . . What am I to do?"

"Have a pee and off to bed. And when the sun rises again there'll be a war on! War! Understand me, Parampion the Cretinous? War!" he shouted in irritation. Hunger was developing in him a beastly instinct to roar. He felt his entire miserable harassed body present in his mindless voice.

"Fine, Eustachius the Terrible, fine. Forget the poem. I'm off to fight the dragon empty-handed like that biblical hero . . . I forget which." Ugo was put off by the shouting. But when Melkior lit a cigarette he took one out himself and asked for a light. Melkior's hand trembled as he lit it for him. In the match light he saw an ill-shaven face, thick lecherous lips, gaping equine nostrils, and that forehead, low, idiotic, half overgrown with an almost straight band of thick black eyebrows—an ape. That was the conclusion in which his rage was being dissolved, to flow away calmly, even with a smile.

"There, there, Eustachius the Good." Ugo was smiling, too, with his black fillings. "No need to shout: War! on account of my wee bit of courtship. Let the war go on percolating over there across the

Channel. Our uncles will give it a smack or two across the snout for frightening us. We're good little children." Ugo was glad of Melkior's smiling face. "What's the time? I'm off, bound for the electric chair, brrr . . ." he shuddered and took on an ingratiating look. "Mercy, Eustachius the Cruel. Let me have at least that *tired gait* of yours, you read it out to me only the other day. *Here I come, the dark hermit* . . . How does it go? Do let me have it, I cannot go like this."

He spread his empty hands helplessly.

"Stop being a bore, Parampion!" Melkior was morose again. Down at ATMAN's this afternoon, fine. Had she wanted to meet me? Ask ATMAN. "What makes you think she likes verse, anyway? Why don't you treat her to a beef goulash instead? At least she'll know what that is." At "beef goulash" his stomach gave a martyred howl. He'd love some goulash.

"You know her, then?" Ugo's eyebrows merged with his hairline in astonishment.

"To some extent," replied Melkior, being purposely casual. "She's shallow."

"Ah, that would be the hooves of the Mandrake downstairs!" Ugo stamped hard on the floor. "She told me he was keen on introducing her to you. So: she's shallow?"

Melkior did not reply. She hadn't wanted to meet me? Good thing I went off as I did then. Very good thing indeed.

"And what would you think," said Ugo out of the blue, "if I told you that what she wants from me is, how shall I put it . . . well, support—that is, intellectual companionship at the loftiest spiritual level?" His face was inflating, an outburst of laughter was only moments away. Ugo was relishing this. "Beef goulash, eh?" and the laughter did indeed erupt.

Melkior laughed, too, sourly, with a moral revulsion. She thinks she's netted him "at the loftiest level," he mocks her. She's building her sticky-sweet relationship with him on a "soulful" foundation, he's keeping her in that confiture to make her taste sweeter. But they love his kind, they love precisely the rascals like him who tease them. They'll all let him have his way, all the way, right away. I know you're only trifling with me, you bad boy. Yet I do love you. And tear slides down cheeks out of genuine yet spurned love. My love for you was deep and true. First you took me, then forsook me, now you're off to pastures new. Please do not do it, soon you will rue it, no other girl will be so true.—You did love me and adore me, but you've rather come to bore me.

Other Women or *Don Juan on Horseback*, a handy novel for artless girls who, being gentle by nature and shy through family upbringing, find it difficult in liaisons of the heart to withstand men's shamelessly rough ways but nevertheless come to believe their false declarations of love. Hence they experience wrenching disappointments which haunt them later in life in the form of soul-destroying memories. When they marry they do not reveal even to their husband, their Savior and Redeemer from all evils, all the painful sorrow over their youth. They were so inexperienced that they were deceived countless times by countless men who smothered their virginal sobs under bearlike chests and forced them to do things so abominable and horrible that they still have dreadful nightmares and while sleeping in the sanctified marital bed call to their kind and patient spouse for a man's help so that they can find at least temporary respite from their troublesome past and exorcise their unmentionable desires and achieve true feminine purity and live out their lives in marital harmony and love until the day of their death. Amen.

Ugo was grinning in the middle of the room, watching Melkior with a kind of anticipation. He had become impatient: he was wasting his precious time waiting for this fellow here to sort out his Deep Thoughts.

"All right, have you worked out how far it is to eternity and back? You've left me waiting like a coach horse outside a temple until you've performed your intellectual rite inside."

"Well, what's keeping you if you're in such a rush?" Melkior snapped with impatience. He wished to be left alone to lick his singed paw in solitude. I walked into it today like a tomcat after a goldfish. ATMAN the Demiurge. Is he really "speeding up history" using me? A weird sister out of *Macbeth*. Thou shalt be King of Viviana, Melkior! Thou shalt be king, Melkior, thou shalt be king! And thou shalt never vanquish'd be until Great Birnam wood to high Dunsinane hill shall come against thee. Who can impress the forest, bid the tree unfix his earthbound root? Sweet bodements! Good! I shall be King of Viviana, Thane of Thanatos, Thane of Methane, Thane of Drum-and-Fife, Cadaver of the Balkans. Huzza!

"Hail to thee, Thane of Give'nTake!" he spoke to Ugo with a low bow and a manic laugh. "And farewell. We shall meet again to-night upon the heath of Give'nTake. Thrice to thine, and thrice to mine, and thrice again, to make up nine. Farewell!" and he turned away from Ugo, lay down on his stomach, buried his face in the pillow and said not a word more.

The wounded tomcat purrs away. Having been left alone (Ugo had tiptoed out, terrified. And crossed himself at the door: he had this from his mother), he is busy spinning wounded thoughts. Such as: a town built of empty bottles. A crowd of drunkards have guzzled the bottles empty and built the town. A transparent town, chock-a-block with bottles. Glasstown. Soundville. Wind has strayed inside making the glass throats sing to the townspeople, asleep in their drunken stupor. And in each bottle, each transparent dwelling, there is either a wide-awake Lar or an angry Penate. Are you asleep, Lar? asks the angry Penate. How can I sleep when I am duty-bound to watch over the slumbering home? Call this a home? says the angry Penate angrily. There was a time when we stood in patrician atria on pedestals of marble, side by side with Jupiter and beauteous Venus. Look at us now. Here I choke with Bacchus's sour smell. That rancid reek, that sour stench! To live in a glass bottle, Oh almighty Jupiter, and to be called a Penate! This is habitation for dead lizards and frogs, for porcine embryos and fetuses and premature aborted babies in university collections and Institutes of Pathology, not an abode for what is, after all, a god. For God's sake, Penate, retorts in anger the patient Lar. We are not drenched by rain or stricken by frost; we are bathed in light and warmed by the sun and comforted by the wind's sweet strains that are like music issuing from the sublime lyre of Orpheus. I think it was a very good idea these people had to build Glasstown. Oh kindly Lar, those drunkards are now steeped in foul dreams, but when they wake they will fall to barking at each other like dogs and fighting like wild elephants and will smash and break this laughable, transparent Bottletown of theirs for it has the wild spirit of Bacchus dwelling herein.

The patient Lar is unconvinced. But one fine day, just as Glasstown is glittering prettily in the sun, white and green and greenish-blue, the accursed drunkards wake and stretch their limbs and rub their eyes and by dint of loud dumb yawns break into a fight and go after each other in a most savagely cruel manner and raze to the very foundations their greenish-blue Glasstown that had glittered so prettily in the sun. Not a bottle is left intact.

And the homeless Lar and Penate join forces and resolve to seek other, better towns. And they find fresh, indestructible towns and take up honorable employment therein, working as caretakers, directors of old peoples' homes, and doormen in three-star hotels, for the uniforms are very nearly like those of admirals.

The pillow under him was all slimy, from envy. Is she Ugo's? Why flee from the bitter thought? Ugo's she is, (his own) Viviana. Ugo's. I have been preserving the thought in order to say it at this precise moment, inside. To exist is to keep shaking off the sadness. In there, in the bowels, it wells from a secret source, to spread all over the body, bitterly. Sad skin, sad eyes, nose hanging down, dejected. To batten up the source?—*Here, I am no more. Would I were no more! Would I were the shimmering air which makes her lips . . .* Poem for Viviana. Poem One . . . *which makes her lips smile so prettily. Why am I not a demon spreading darkness around her* (an adjective here) *room?*—Wait: her what room? Lustful. *Her lustful room.* But keep this out of the poem for the moment.—*At night I keep a tremulous vigil over her and the dawn finds me between the curtains with the song of her dreams and sighs.*—Song of dreams, no less . . . with sighs to boot. But let the poem sing the cold pane trembling with her breath at night. . . . Right. *If I were no more, I would be with you everywhere forevermore—a perfect pair, my heart in yours and yours (of course) in mine. Your arms have no notion that, moving, they've set me in motion . . .*

As if he did not have enough troubles, the damned fool had turned to poetry. Unrequited love. There is something rotten at the root of poetry. Even flowers grow from manure. Soul fertilized by Viviana, the best-known natural fertilizer in town. Nitrogen and phosphorus. The exact formula known to Maestro. Ask Justus von Liebig if you want the secret revealed. The mysterious generative force, the spiritual impregnation, the poetic florescence: Ugo, AT-MAN, Maestro, myself, Freddie as a possibility—the Pleiad of passionate Vivianic poets. Plus God knows how many besides, onanistically fainthearted, anonymous, hidden in their gloomy rooms and behind their desperate beards, whimsical troubadours, inspired nocturnal rodents who by day collect the bliss of her movements and ruminate by night filled with her, a random, passing figure, *oh girl from my neighborhood whom I saw as she . . . un éclair . . . puis la nuit!—Fugitive beauté . . . ne te verrai-je plus que dans l'éternité?* Eternities germinating from her phosphates and sulphates and nitrates.

Troooo-toot-toot, trooo-toot-toot, toorootoo, toorootoo, tooroo-too . . . The bugle in the barracks opposite playing taps. Eight o'clock. Head tucked under wing, the soldiers, like hens, and off toooSLEEP! Without a care in the world. Watching over you are the sentries, the Orderly Officer, the picquets, and your uncle the Minister of Defense, and your father the King and your Mother Country.

The bugle summoned Melkior to rise, to be alert to his fear of the morrow. He rose with a nervous yawn. The word *morrow* in the mouth, well shaped for a yawn. Another yawn, a deaf-and-dumb's mute song. Standing in the middle of the room, idle. What now? The worm of solitude started drilling, insupportably. And the stomach gave a sorrowful whine, like a dog locked out.

The little old white man was sitting with the giant. The sergeants were there, too, *At Ease*, with Else at her corner of the table. At a third table: a party of veterinary students, large specimens all, using the heavy gestures of the Heavy Drinker variety. Make no mistake, those boys are having one hell of a carouse. Kurt was dissolving them, drunkenly tamed as they were, with his nihilism. This was in progress.

"Got a girlfriend then, Kurt?"

"What's the use?" said Kurt with a hopeless shrug.

"Well, *I've* got one, and I do know what *use* a girl is."

The future physicians to domestic and tamed animals were chortling, seeing the matter from a medical standpoint. They had vivid imaginations. Kurt sat in solemn silence, his face gilded with very refined contempt.

"If you'd ever had your hand up inside a mare . . . ?"

The vets had taken the initiative, Kurt was lost in their laughter.

"But . . ." he tried to say, but nothing was heard.

"Think I'm cracked or something, do you?" shouts an offended sergeant. "Why shouldn't she marry me? Tell 'em yourself, Else, I want them to hear it loud and clear."

"What are you so riled up about it?" Else had her white arms crossed over her chest as if hiding something. "You *are* a strange one."

"There, did you hear that, you garrison dolts? Just you wait and see. I'm going to have her dressed in white from head to toe, like a real lady-in-waiting. Cheers, Else, here's to looking at you!"

"Sheemsh to me dey're weak, *bud*," slurs the little old white man.

"No," bellows the giant.

"No? What about the bombingzh den? Dere'zh bombingzh every day. Dey say London'sh gone for good."

"Rubbish."

"Rubbish? But have Dey got anyting like the *Bizhmarck?* Dey shay it'sh sho shtrong it hazh no match but God Himshelf. Dere'zh no gun in the world can shink it."

"Can, too."

"Can? I shaw the *Viribush Unitish*, you know, *bud*, back in nineteen-fifteen, in the Bay of Kotor. A dreadful shight it wazh, too. And the *Bizhmarck*'sh even shtronger. It'sh dreadful."

"No."

"No?"

"No. The English have the *George V.*"

"Fifth? Izh it shtrong enough?"

"Yes."

"Azh shtrong azh the *Bizhmarck?*"

"Stronger."

"Twishe azh shtrong?"

"Three times."

"Timezh?"

"Yes." The giant made a gesture with his fist, which he then dropped on the table, forcefully, making the glasses jangle.

Melkior settled at the table next to the door, modestly, though he could well have entered the Cozy Corner with a regular's swagger. His entry saved Kurt from the veterinary crowd.

"Ah, Herr Professor! Good evening." Kurt's hand sought Melkior's of its own volition and kept it cordially pressed. "What's your pleasure, Herr Professor?" Melkior asked for a bit of broiled veal or something lean like that.

"Ach, Herr Professor, I'm very much afraid, you know . . . we're a bit short of meat today," spoke Kurt, so unhappy, adjusting the tablecloth. "Meat-free day today, Herr Professor. Armies eat meat," he was saying with emotion.

"War is a big gourmand, eating only the best. Meat . . ."

Preferably man, said Melkior to himself, loudly enough for Kurt to overhear some of it.

"Preferably canned? No, preferably fresh, heh, heh," joked Kurt sweetly. "I'll go and ask Mother if she has something for you."

He presently came back with glad tidings, conspiratorially, a tasty piece of veal, just for you, we can do you a Wiener schnitzel, all right? All right, Kurt, all right. Excellent. Kurt nodded "all right" to Mother and immediately sat back down at Melkior's table, until Mother got the schnitzel ready.

Could be I'm anemic, I've got pale gums. Hence, conceivably, all the defeatism. Liver's good for the blood, they say. Got to have some blood to shed for King and country. Got to fight, boy, got to shed blood! Yes, Your Majesty, that is why I order liver from Kurt, for that very reason: to have the blood to shed. I mean, I would be a poor subject of yours, Your Majesty, would I not, if I were bloodless. What else would there be to shed? Tears? Shut up, you lily-livered ass! Old women shed tears, heroes shed blood. I know. You are right. Blood is the Constitutional essence, the quintessence of my subject-hood, the apotheosis of royalty. So, do you think I could, er . . . siphon half a pint off into a bottle for Your Majesty, and then be left off the hook? Because, truth to tell, I haven't got all that much . . . No way! No cheating! Save that for the bedbugs and the barracks fleas! What do you think I am—a louse? My humble apologies, Your Majesty. I only thought, why not set an amount, that is to say . . . well, yes, an amount, a quota to be met by each of us. Because, the way things are, one never knows how much will be required. And Your Majesty knows full well what the Royal tax people are like, not to mention the generals, the corruption, the friends in high places, the Old Boys' Network. . . . It's only that I should like to see the whole business better regulated, that's all. Also (save your presence), there are other liquids in our subjectful bodies. Why insist so much on blood? Couldn't we shed something else as well? Our Maestro, for instance, has switched to beer precisely because . . .

"A beer, Herr Professor, or perhaps a glass of wine?"

Kurt's reading my lips, blast him—or is he telepathic or something?

"Did I say 'beer,' Kurt?" he asked suspiciously.

"Well you can always have wine if you prefer—at least that's something there's plenty of in this country. But beer goes better with a schnitzel, doesn't it?"

Yes, beer goes better with hmm . . . a schnitzel. Maestro knows this: it goes better with a schnitzel—hence his beer-drinking.

"And they call themselves intellectuals. Heavens!" Kurt launched into his lament. "Vulgarities and nothing else. You can't say a word to them. As if they were from another planet."

"Out on a spree," said Melkior, bored. "Celebrating something, no doubt." He wanted to get rid of Kurt and give some thought in peace to the matter of blood . . . on the thresholds of the institution . . .

"And then I say to her, here, let me whisper something in your mouth, baby, heh, heh . . ."

"And you got one across the snout, right?"

"I did, yessirree. Mind you, I said it dead cool, but I did."

"There you are, Herr Professor, that's their idea of humor," said a scandalized Kurt, rubbing together his moist, pudgy-fingered hands. "Nothing but vulgarities. My sister no longer sits with them. Upon my word, the NCOs are better men. Uncouth but well-behaved. When my sister sits at their table, you don't hear a single coarse word. One of them is in love with her as a matter of fact, he wants to marry her, hm, hm," smiled Kurt, forgiving the man his presumption. "Actually he's not a bad man at all, he's nice. We wouldn't mind him being an NCO—after all Else's not so educated herself—but what kind of future is there in it? An NCO in a weak army, what can you expect? And anyway, how much longer is that going to last? The war's practically here. It's only a question of months . . . if not days," he whispered confidentially.

He knows, he knows, he's got his pudgy fingers in all sorts of pies . . . Melkior had the impression of having felt inside him, in some tangential and accidental way, something like a fear of Kurt. Or . . . how to explain it? A presence of *the fearsome*—and he caught himself developing unconscious cunning designed to keep himself inside the circle of Kurt's goodwill, to retain his confidence, with a view to squeezing that Future a bit more clearly out of Kurt, learning the precise day, *the day* . . . It would be a good move to contradict him just a wee bit, to voice the tiniest doubt . . . to make an ahh-who-knows-there's-no-telling-when-it-will-happen gesture to provoke Kurt's *in-the-know-ness*.

But he did not make the gesture. He merely gave a foolish flattering smile and felt silliness daubed all over his face like a congealed cosmetic mask. And hung his head in shame over the table as if lost in thought, thus to convey himself to Kurt as the picture of indifferent equanimity in the face of destiny. He wanted Kurt to take his behavior for the lofty indifference of a man who simply keeps out of such matters and understands nothing of the whole business.

"After all, who knows, Herr Professor?" said Kurt with a helpless sigh. His mother called him from the kitchen. He was presently back with the food and a glass of foaming beer. Melkior fell to greedily, his stomach thanking him with a low murmur, enjoying itself. Kurt, too, was enjoying himself seeing how well the distinguished guest liked their cooking. A Wiener schnitzel on a meat-free day. It's-a-dream, it's-a-dream, it's-a-dream. Melkior began to dance a Viennese waltz inside: tra-a-lala, tra-a-lala. "By the way, I've asked Father—it's plain old acetic acid," whispered Kurt all of a sudden, leaning over close to Melkior's ear. "You soak a cigarette in it and allow it to dry. And you smoke it, as fast as you can, right before the physical. It'll have your heart pounding like mad, there's not a specialist in the world who can see through this one. . . . And there are no harmful aftereffects, everything's back to normal in twenty minutes. People used it to get out of combat duty in the Great War. Father was an *Einjährig-Freiwilliger*, nobody liked the idea of getting killed . . . for an Austro-Hungarian emperor. The Hapsburgs were a disaster for Germanic thought. It's a good thing the devil took them. The waltz-politics of Vienna 'On the Beautiful Blue Danube' are finished once and for all. It's only today that the Austrian Province has found its true place, within community of the Third Reich. Don't you agree, Herr Professor?"

Melkior muttered something through a mouthful. His body was getting drunk on food, receiving Kurt only on some auxiliary wavelength of consciousness and registering him as a tasty addition to the music of smell and taste and chewing and swallowing. The Wiener schnitzel, Strauss in the mouth. He chewed in three-quarter time and smiled imperially.

"I'm glad you like our food, Herr Professor."

Oh yes, oh yes, I like your sister, too, and your mother as well, and all their chops and steaks and stuffed cabbage and escalloped veal. . . . He felt the cannibal theme approaching and thrust it away in fear. There goes Kurt again, inspiring the meaty cannibal blowout. Oh courteous Kurt!

I left them vomiting nearby in the jungle. The agent is in a very bad way. He lies on his back and howls in pain. His friends are pushing their fingers down his throat, sitting on his stomach, choking him, strangling him, the better to make him spew it all out. They would have preferred to strangle him to death! He has drawn the keepers' attention. One of them has already gone back to the village to report the incident. "They'll kill him," says the doctor in confidence to the first mate.

"Who will? Our . . ."—". . . hosts. That's what all farmers do to sick cattle."—"Why don't you help him?"—"Impossible. It's stress-induced colic. If grazing cattle were suddenly to begin thinking, the same thing would happen. Perhaps he should be told openly that his spasms are taking him straight to the cauldron."—"Well, tell him, then."—"You tell him. He won't believe me. Apart from that, you can break it to him more gently." The first mate measures him contemptuously head to toe. He approaches the group clustered around the agent and stops the entire revive-the-drowned-man exercise with a single gesture. He leans over the patient and says to him solemnly, "Sir, they do not eat the sick, they burn them alive immediately, to prevent contagion. You must therefore be healthy if you mean to survive . . . at least for a time." This does the trick. The agent looks at him, composed, his face pain-free, and stands up right away. He even gives him a polite smile, as a sign of a confused gratitude. "And now when they come to take a look at you, eat as heartily as you can, it is your only hope." But now everyone else throws themselves at the *only way out:* they fall furiously to devouring the fruits (like men just saved from drowning . . .) and the doctor mutters to himself: ptui, the anthropoid apes! and spits in disgust.

"It can't be!" ejaculated a horrified Kurt. "Not a hair, is it?" It was as if he had been present at the feeding of an underage crown prince.

"A hair? What hair?" said Melkior, surprised.

"In your food?" Kurt was apprehensive. "That's impossible."

"Whatever made you think . . . Why a hair?"

"Well, you sort of . . . expectorated a bit," explained Kurt, with tactful hesitation.

"Oh, that?" laughed Melkior. "I spat at something I was thinking about."

Kurt was relieved. "Another beer, Herr Professor? On the house." That was to celebrate the absence of the hair. "No, thank you, Kurt. I've got to go."

Kurt is totting up the bill "one Wiener schnitzel, one salad . . ." and the little old man in white is talking, ". . . and then, my friend, he took after him over the rooftopsh. And you know how shteep London roofsh are. . . . Anyway, there they are: the detective chayshing, the robber running. Jumping like a cat. Getting hold of chimney potsh and lightning rodzh and such. But the cop shtumbled and fell—right acrosh a torn pieshe of tin sheeting, the poor man— and got hish throat shlashed, my friend! Hizh jugular! He shtarted bleeding shomething awful, shtreaming down the roof and into the drainpipe. Raining blood. And the robber—believe it or not, *bud*— the robber ran back to hish purshuer and, let'sh fayshe it, enemy, tore a shtrip off hizh own shirt without a moment'sh hezhitation, and shtopped the bleeding. The cop would've bled to death on that rooftop if the robber hadn't had hizh heart in the right playshe."

Melkior took a long time adjusting his tie, retying the lace on his left shoe, on his right shoe, softening, squeezing, twirling a cigarette between his fingers . . .

"So what happened next? . . . the coppersh caught the robber." So?

"Sho dat'sh my point, *bud*—dere'zh shome goodnesh in everyone. Even in the worsht kind of robber, az dish cayshe showzh. I forgot to shay de man waz a notorioush murderer. And dey shay, Doshtoyevshky!"

Melkior left disappointed, to Kurt's bowing and scraping goodbyes.

Dostoyevsky? Everyone goes to Fyodor Mikhaylovich with their little monsters. Try Dickens, the company for quiet compassion. Don't proclaim every little bastard who can think of an ever so slightly twisted plot to be an Ivan Karamazov, or every lovable idiot, a Prince Mishkin. It's no use our referring to literature—it will provide no excuses here.

He felt satiety like the release after the enjoyment of sin. Now he repented. Once Appetite, satisfied, had dropped off to sleep, Conscience came on with her retinue of Principles. Where had she been when the Great Carnivore was stirring and howling in his empty madhouse? She herself had served at his court as a jester at the well-laden table, regaling him with stories—during the Wiener schnitzel—of the castaways (whom you, following the requirements of your plot, had induced to vomit) eating copiously and discovering a new faith for their existence: "therefore you must be healthy if you want to survive—for a time, at least. Eat as heartily as you can, it is your only hope." Oh, you're too sly by half, Madam! I wouldn't put it past you to search for the more titillating passages in *The Decameron* or drool over pornographic pictures. *Cinémacochon* for the Jesuits. And then it's, My son, you are forgiven for your sins . . . in your soul. On the body, however, the bellies remain. Sins and bellies—noumena and phenomena, *et substratus est appetitus gloriosus,* sang out Melkior like the Credo at High Mass *et incarnatus est* . . . and his belly strutted ahead of him, happily burbling its little song:

Penance awaits the gluttonous twit
Yet for the moment I belch and I sing.
Eating is good as it makes you fit
With wine to boot you feel like a king.

I'll be asking you before long, perhaps as early as tomorrow, about keeping fit, dear Sancho. It may be a question of days, says Kurt. And tomorrow is one of those days it's "a question of." Incidentally, what if it really does all start tomorrow? What's tomorrow, anyway? (If a fool were to hear me he would say Thursday.) *Tomorrow* is the temporal border between two states of wakefulness, two states of awareness of being. Clocks do not determine *tomorrow.* *Tomorrow* is defined only by a visit to Enka, a longed-for encounter with Viviana, a night at the Give'nTake, an uncertain, anxious night in expectation of the day after tomorrow's *tomorrow.* The evening smiles winningly, promising me a lovely day—tomorrow. The meteorological tomorrow: continued clear and warm. (Winter delaying its arrival, most kindly bestowing on us this last autumn.) The pedagogical tomorrow: think about tomorrow, my child. The political tomorrow: Stalin giving Hitler a wink—*khorosho!*—and Hitler winking back—*natürlich*. The historical tomorrow: and when men discovered the divine power of matter, it came to reign over them, confusing their minds, blighting their lives and then swallowing itself and turning into a Force which destroyed all laws and there is now not a single consciousness left that could proclaim it stupid in the name of Hegel. The esthetical tomorrow: when man discovered the ugliness of matter, artists became tradesmen of the ugly. The geographical tomorrow: and the vast peninsula you see here was given the name of Europe. Here lived a biped who composed certain works they called *tragedies*, and whose name was Shakespeare. The original spelling is lost, the name having survived only in a script we now call the Russian alphabet. The philosophical tomorrow: there will be no tomorrow. The Force will drink all of time and swallow all of space and sink into eternal sleep from satiety and boredom. An eternity later, it will stretch, give a hungover yawn like a drunkard after a mad binge in the course of which it smashes everything within reach, and ask: Where are the objects, where are the humans? And will feel the crushing solitude and the emptiness all around it. And it will wretch with despair. And out of the vomit there will come into being a New World and in it sentient worms will hatch which will slither in the mud and revel in its beauty. And they will believe themselves to have been created by the Great Worm in His own image and Himself to cover the entire world with His length, which is so infinite as to be beyond their comprehension. Because they are small worms of finite length, though each believes itself to be longer than any other. And from this will spring their belief in the inequality among them. And a minority will manage to persuade the majority that they, the minority, are actually longer than the rest, hence better able to intuit the length of the Great Worm Himself. And they will become exegeticists and prophets among, and eventually rulers of, their equilongitudinal brother worms. And they will bore for themselves sumptuous worm holes on mud heights where the view of mudscapes is better and danger of flood much less and the population density is lower. And they will regard the valley worms with contempt. They will then quarrel over the ownership of the heights. Each will want to acquire the other's heights for himself—the other heights will seem to each of them to be more attractive and more comfortable—and the heights worms will go saying to the small valley worms: those others have betrayed the Great Worm! They preach that he has no body at all, being of Infinite Length. Or Pure Span. Now, meddling with any of the attributes of His being—and bodily existence is the most essential of them all—would be the first step to disbelief and practically an act of treason. We therefore urge the worms faithful to the Great Worm to fight the infidel unto the death. And so a dreadful war breaks out among the worms, to go on for another eternity. And after that other eternity is done, after the worms have devoured one another in their graves . . .

And so Melkior the worm entered the worm hole called the Give'nTake. But inside he did not find Ugo the worm nor did he find Viviana the she-worm. The absence smote Melkior sorely to his very core and he bent painfully with the ache. So they were together, tied up in a fornicating knot, those accursed worms! He slithered over to the table at which sat bloated worm Maestro and pale worm Chicory, at the very moment when repugnant caterpillar Thénardier was setting down before them two shots, shot to shot.

"Bring a third, you spotted salamander, for our pain-wrenched Eustachius." Thus did Maestro, the bloated worm, welcome the arrival of Melkior the worm. Chicory the worm Hasdrubalson laughed a spasmodic laugh, energetically flicking his fair hair across his handsomely elongated brow.

They had been having a Low Mass colloquy at the altar of St. Giventake's. They stopped their sweet conversation short at the approach of Melkior, the wormy worm, thereby arousing his suspicion at the sudden silence greeting his arrival. He therefore chose not to take a seat but strove to justify his approach to their table by inquiring:

"Look, have you seen Ugo the Wo—" he sliced the worm in two in the nick of time.

"No, we haven't, Wo," said Chicory in jest, his face nervous, and Wo offered him a chair, saying Wo in a worm-eaten tone, being dilapidated.

"Have a seat, kind Eustachius," and Maestro began pushing the chair under Melkior. Using the edge of the seat he bent Melkior's knees so that Melkior sat down automatically. "He'll be along soon enough, to report back. It's the feat that matters . . . though it's not as difficult as he imagines. Be that as it may, don't fret, Eustachius, he'll be lying anyway. Ugo's a born . . . no, better said: an invent-as-U-go liar."

Melkior saw red. It's all so public, so embarrassing. And she's a shameless . . .

"Don't go pale and wan, Eustachius. Ugo's an ugotistical little twit. Quite unlike you. You aspire toward . . . I mean to say, you have noble aspirations. That business between the two of them can't last long. She's after something permanent, matrimonial, and Ugo's no more than an ugreeable evening."

"Why are you trying to draw me into this?" said Melkior in protest and made to get up.

"Don Fernando's just been in, looking for you," Chicory stopped him. "Said he'd be back."

"Looking for me? Why?"

"Cause unknown," responded Maestro, helpfully. "But he was being very important. Got a personal message from Leo Trotsky." Noticing ill will on Melkior's face, he hastened to change the subject. "Now Chicory and I have just been debating a point: how far does *it's written* reach? I mean the sort of thing soothsayers read in your palms, the sort of thing you find in horoscopes under Leo, Virgo, Capricorn, Sagittarius, and whatnot. Because it might be nothing but a mere suggestion, which we then unthinkingly take for a guideline—that is to say, arrange our destiny to fit. I myself, as you know full well, don't give a tinker's damn for all those *futures*, personal and historical alike. But if someone tells me, 'I see complications on your life line.' I become a hypochondriac, I shy away from the least chill of a draft, drink herbal teas, wear amulets around my neck. I even pray. But the *complications* will not stop pecking on my brain, and they keep on pecking until they've got it riddled like a sieve. I then become a perfect madman. I can't eat, I can't sleep, all I do is sit and stare, repeating in desperation: why me, why me? And so I do whatever Fate wills. Actually coaxing death inside me.

"I once heard," Maestro spoke to Melkior, "from that con artist— now that's an understatement—from the practitioner operating in your building, Mr. Adam, how he read a great calamity in a lady's palm. After she'd gone he suddenly remembered seeing something like the presence of death in her eyes. He was overcome by appre- hension, possibly by fear of the responsibility as well, so off he ran after her and arrived just in time to take her down off the noose. The crook had suggested and 'got it right,' see? She had hanged herself on a clothesline in her back yard. He gave her mouth-to-mouth resuscitation and brought her back to life. You can well imagine how sweet those kisses must have been. Anyway, he breathed life into her, like God."

"You believe him?"

"Certainly. Indeed, she later went to bed with him and generally put herself under his powerful (Maestro made a gesture) protection. And she's still in his bed. Crawling after him, as it were, impossible to get rid of. Mr. Adam dabbled at being Fate for a bit and, presto! He has her hanging around his neck."

Melkior had a grin on his face. He was fitting together some of his fragmented observations about ATMAN and getting a much clearer picture of things. And he felt sorry . . . no, he did not feel sorry for ATMAN.

"You're smiling, Eustachius the Noble, but it's you Mr. Adam fears the most. Concerning *the main thing*. Never mind Freddie, never mind Ugo, or all the cohorts and various fraternities of her bedfellows . . . you, you"—Maestro jabbed a finger at him—"you are the worst danger. You have the ability to love . . . don't give me that baleful look, I'm talking about the most exalted of sentiments . . .

and, what matters most, you are capable of marrying for such feelings. And that's exactly who she's after—a Parsifal. She'll nab you in the end, Eustachius, you Lamb of God. Which is why Adam is trying to strike you out."

Melkior was smiling, his heart bathing in bliss. Could it be . . . ? Viviana? This was clearly a plot of theirs. A Giventakian ploy. For all his will to disbelieve, he kept looking for her trap to rush in with all his heart.

"Oh well, that's it then, Adam's going to strike me down," he was already showing off, Fortune's child walking on carpets of strewn flowers.

"I said strike you *out*, didn't I, Chicory? Anyway, you'd do well to help him in the matter if you've got an ounce of brains. Meanwhile may I strongly recommend that you lay the duck on her back, Eustachius the Blessed. Give her a good ride. Join the family, ha, ha . . ."

"You're lying." The words sprayed out of his mouth somehow or other, like excess spittle during an incautious yawn. Idiot style.

"Oh, we're a well-ramified family. I'm sure you wouldn't mind having a more mature relative. Am I right, Cousin Chicory Hasdrubalson?"

"I beg pardon, my lord, my title does not stem from that particular line. My pedigree's a much humbler one, with quite a few bastard elements," replied Chicory with a straight face.

"But what about Princess van den . . . what's her name? That was a trophy for Casanova himself to be proud of!"

"Oh, please don't torment me, Maestro! Mercy! It was but a morganatic mistake for her."

"But did you not, Chicory, once vouchsafe to me in the strictest of confidences that you had exchanged certain sexual instruments after all with our . . . what is it you call her, Eustachius the Chrysostom? with our Bibiana?"

"You overestimate me, I'm sure," replied Chicory meekly, closing his eyes with modesty. Then both burst out laughing.

Melkior stood up, offended. No doubt the pair of them had

arranged it all beforehand. Wordlessly he made for the door, only to bump into Don Fernando, who was just coming in.

"I've been looking for you all over the known world," said Don Fernando with a kindness that understood all and forgave all, in advance.

"The world is large, if you've been looking for me in your world." Don Fernando gave a patient smile. "To what do I owe the honor?" Melkior attempted a laugh.

"Seriously, now . . ." Don Fernando took his smile off, as if putting it away for later, and pulled Melkior outside rather hastily. "Pupo wants a word with you. He's waiting for you at the Corso. That's all. Goodbye." And Don Fernando disappeared around the corner.

Pupo? He hadn't seen the man for years. A chance encounter in the street, in a rush. He was always hurrying somewhere, somebody was waiting for him, he had to get somewhere on time. He would jerk his hand free of the sleeve, glance at his watch, hurriedly. Curly hair, a foppish pencil-thin mustache, his voice a melodious baritone, his dress purposely casual. He bestowed cordial smiles, he liked meeting with his friends but never had time for them. He seemed to be apologizing at every encounter, awfully sorry, old friend . . . He had a long-overdue exam to sit and was almost ridiculous. Pupo at the University, a seaman on dry land. Then he sank somewhere into the unknown.

And surfaced again tonight. Where from? Why? No questions allowed.

The mysterious life of Pupo. Pupo wants a word with you. Pupo's waiting. Melkior was moving in Pupo's magnetic field wrapped up in the force of his relaylike connection with an enigma, with a closed, illegible mystery which showed to the eye only very simple, primitive hieroglyphs. The Christian fish. Melkior knew only that, the fish, and knew he was on his way to see Pupo about something fishy, but he was flattered by the trust, however minuscule. He felt a moral excitement, as if he were off to admit guilt for a deed for which an innocent man had been charged. The diaphragm nervous, the pulse quickened, the breathing deep, serious . . . as if it was Viviana who was asking for him. But he immediately rejected the comparison as . . . inadequate. As a feeling of an intimate, personal danger while the Earth trembled. No, it was beyond comparison, Pupo's trust.

There was no Pupo in the café. Melkior had made three or four sweeps of the entire seating area, but—no mustache, no hair . . . Only to be expected, of course, typical of them to keep us waiting . . . Then a newspaper dipped and he recognized the smile that was looking at him . . . But sans the foppish mustache. The hair very light, long, rather thin above the forehead. Plus glasses—oh yes? clearly a plain-glass mask. Melkior approached in excitement, prepared for a tempestuous encounter, a mashing embrace. But Pupo sensibly reduced it all to a cordial handshake.

"Hello, poet. How are you? It has been a long time." Pupo's baritone sounded somewhat muted, less fresh.

"Long indeed, yes . . ." Melkior noticed he no longer knew how to talk to Pupo. He did not know which questions were permitted, whether even asking after somebody's health was not "forbidden." He wanted to speak *usefully*. But he also wanted to show his joy at seeing Pupo again and to reestablish immediately the old easy familiarity, so he permitted himself a joke: "Long enough for you to get glasses and lose the mustache, not to mention exposing a stretch of forehead . . ."

Pupo kept his grin on, but he was plainly not enjoying the conversation. I've put my foot in it and no mistake. It's camouflage. The . . . people around might've overheard me. He cast a glance around the surrounding tables—the band was playing—and sensed he was making another stupid mistake. Oh Lord, they *are* a hard lot to handle! Yes, aren't they, replied the Lord, leaping at the chance.

"Aren't you going to have a seat?" Well, well, Pupo was not in such a hurry after all.

"Of course I will, I just thought you might be pressed for time and didn't want to . . ." he was saying with a smile, but Pupo did glance at his watch, out of habit.

"There'll always be fifteen minutes to spare for an old . . ." but his mind was elsewhere, and the generosity was a throwaway; Melkior was insulted by it. Fifteen minutes! Why, that's how long you spare for whores. Pupo has always been like that. Melkior now regretted his minutes. Why should his be the more valuable? I could have used them to do some thinking at least . . . or simply to do nothing, to wander about town, look at things. And here I am instead, wasting my time with this . . . Jacobin. The Revolution will be fifteen minutes late. Ah-tchoo!

"Have you got a cold?"

"No. Why?"

"You're sneezing. Still going on binges? What about Ugo—is he still as crazy as he used to be? Or have you fallen out?"

"No. Why? We still see quite a bit of each other."

"In that street-corner dive over there?"

"Yes. The Give'n'Take. We drop in from the office every so often. I'm working for a newspaper—part time."

"On a column-inch basis? What do you cover—literature?"

"Theater and film." He's sounding me out.

"Yes, you always liked those. Is Ugo working for the paper, too?"

"No, he isn't."

"What does he do then?"

"Nothing."

"Nothing? Well, I suppose it's not bad as jobs go. Are you angry with me or something?"

"No. Why? You're asking and I'm replying, that's all."

"Yes, indeed . . ." Pupo laughed again and glanced at his watch.

"So how do you live, writing your column inches?"

"I get by."

"Do you still live like we used to—student digs sort of thing, sharing a room? Remember that time we . . ."

"No, I live alone," Melkior coldly interrupted Pupo's remembrance. He doesn't give a damn anyway—this is just softening me up for something else. He waited for it.

"Got a nice room?"

"Nice. Separate entrance."

"What have you got—a bed?"

"And a sofa." Melkior laughed. "Why didn't you say straight away? Do you need a place to sleep?"

Pupo gave an absent laugh.

"Not I." His face turned into an undecided suspicious mask that studied Melkior long with a worried and sad look. "Listen," said Pupo hesitantly, "you're . . . um . . . a good man, I know. That is why I thought . . . Well, to come to the point: one of our people needs to sleep at your place, see, for . . . well, a couple of nights. I'm responsible for him, see. That's what matters. Anything else to do with this business you'll understand yourself. . . . See? Not a word to Ugo or any of your crowd . . . all right?"

"Right you are." Melkior was feeling grandly emotional, ready to die at the stake. Kill me, you villains! He wondered at his own heroism.

"Whereabouts do you live?"

"Ah. That could be a bit of a snag. Across the road from 35th's barracks."

"On the contrary, it's a good thing. The landlady?"

"Middle-aged widow. But you wouldn't give her more than thirty-six or -seven to look at her."

Pupo laughed: "That's irrelevant to my purpose. Is she the nosy type? Likely to gossip?"

"Oh no, hardly. More the sadly contemplative type. Longing for love pure and tender—eternal, too, it goes without saying—but having nasty dreams all the while. Hence unhappy. Cares for nothing anymore."

"Not even men?"

"Only in her dreams, apparently. However, there is this man friend who comes by twice a week. But it's more of a spiritual liaison sort of thing. Truth to tell, you do hear a carnal sound or two at times . . . but that's all to the good, isn't it?"

"Ye-es, it is indeed," said Pupo distractedly, glancing at his watch.

"Thank you for the flowers, Doctor. Thank you for the flowers, gentlemen."

A horribly emaciated elderly woman was weaving her way among the tables, curtsying and thanking everyone, one and all, most graciously, hand on heart, for the flowers. A thin moth-eaten fox boa had slid and hung on one shoulder only, exposing a thin, white wrinkled neck bending to the left and right: thank you for the flowers.

"Oh, Madame! Thank you so much for the flowers!" she suddenly addressed Pupo, offering him a hand in a badly torn black glove from which her fingers protruded in misery. "How are you, my dear? I haven't seen you for ages. Why, you look years younger! Absolutely radiant. You were at my concert tonight, I'm sure. Wasn't I marvelous?"

Everyone was looking at their table. Pupo was going alternately red and pale. Melkior clearly saw his jaw tremble . . . with rage . . . with fear . . . hell and damnation, all eyes were on him!

"Last Sunday I played at the Mozarteum, my dear. Oh, what a concert! Liszt's Sonata in B minor. You like Liszt, don't you? He's simply marvelous. And how I played! The great Rubinstein was there, too. He said to me, 'Brava, *ma petite!* You have the hands of God who made the world. God give me such hands!' he cried out and melted into tears. The great Rubinstein. Brava!" she exclaimed in ardent exaltation and went on with her demure round of tables: "Thank you for the flowers, gentlemen. I'm most grateful to you, dear Countess, and to you, too, Baron, thank you for the flowers, you are most kind. Oh, what an honor, Monsieur le Comte. Thank you for the flowers. Thank you, thank you, one and all . . ." and with tears in her eyes she blew many kisses to the entire clientele, finally to gather her long silk gown and hurriedly step down from the dais with an enormous bunch of flowers in her arms.

"I think my concert's over, too," said Pupo in a near-whisper, glancing at his watch. "Some in the audience are quite musical. I'll go, you stay. I'll call on you tomorrow. How long will you be in?"

"Until nine, without fail."

Pupo took his hand and gave it two hard squeezes without a word.

Businesslike. He had clinched a deal.

Expeditious, practical, cold. He was left there like a girl deceived. Call you tomorrow—the time-honored telegraphic goodbye after a tryst. That was how he customarily took leave of Enka—I'll call you—and regretted it afterwards, in the street. Some other words were called for, after all, but he would always store them away "for later." Then it would be another *I'll call you*, he would again see the disappointment in her eyes but he was unable to tell her anything else, anything binding, committing, anything with a promise of a closer liaison. Let's make it quite clear: this thing between us has gone as deep as it ever will. No tears, please. So it was with Enka. The polyvalent element, capable of forming many amorous bondings.

As for Pupo . . . Melkior felt he was retreating after a failed attempt at conquest. The conquest of Viviana. He was now accepting a comparison he had rejected as being out of place. As, hah, one unworthy . . . of Pupo. Where am I to spend the rest of this miserable evening? He began rummaging among the options. The Give'nTake he threw the farthest away. Home? . . . and find ATMAN lying in ambush on his landing to see the flower from this afternoon's garden. Ring Enka? Perhaps Coco was on night duty . . . in the morgue, with the heart which had died that morning in hand . . . like a canary. That option he also . . . eliminated, cautiously. He knew he was going to wander off somewhere following his footsteps, pining for Viviana. A quiet place with well-behaved waiters. There'll have to be poetry whispered . . . *October's gentle breath.* He smiled, but sweetened the bitterness using Ugo's tra-la-la-tra-la-la sonnet. With well-behaved waiters? The neon letters of the different café signs lit up in turns. But he kept wrestling with the Give'nTake. Leave me alone, damn you! Like the shadow of a huge vulture the Give'nTake kept flying over the sweet flickering of Viviana's name in a distant darkness. The thing to do would be to explore all the dark recesses of this night, strain the ocean to catch the plankton glowing in those two . . . Vivianic eyes. What was now the use of this entire superfluous night-cloaked space? The thing to do was walk all over the night, from end to end, peer into every dark corner, interrogate every owl, nighthawk, mouse, cat, whore, and thief, walk from bark to bark down to the farthest reaches of the night . . . Oh, where did they hide her? *Gilda! Pietà, signori, prego pietà.* And tomorrow morning Duke Ugo would burst into song *questa o quella per me pari sono* . . . Tears welled in his eyes . . . and he let them flow. In the dense darkness of an old doorway Melkior succumbed to sobs. Oh God how unhappy I am!

"You and I both," responded the darkness with a sigh. Embarrassment lashed Melkior. He turned toward the darkness enraged, irate:

"Who's there?" he bellowed into the dark. "Speak up! Who are you?"

"Go ahead, sir, hit me." Creeping toward him was something four-legged, crawling, down on the ground, on the uneven tiles, rattling huge hooves, armor, fearful machinery. A talking turtle.

"I'm down here, sir, at your feet," grunted the being on the floor.

"What do you want?"

"You could help me without undue trouble to yourself."

"Where are you? Stand up. Who are you?"

"Half a man, that's my name . . . and my entire biography."

"Are you drunk? Rolling on the ground like that?"

"I'm not rolling on the ground. I have no legs," enunciated the man in a low, penitently shamed voice, like someone making a terrible avowal.

Melkior was horrified. He bent over pointlessly with the naïve intention of lifting the man, getting him to stand up straight, restoring his dignity. To stand him up on what? To elevate him to what dignity?

"What can I do for you then?" he asked politely.

"I didn't tell you that to make you change your tone," said the legless man with some arrogance. "You can go on despising me if you like. What I have in mind is nothing to do with that kind of mercy. I need your help in a specific matter, that's all."

"In what matter?"

"The stairs are too high for me to climb—my legs are cut off almost at the hip . . ."

"And you want me to . . . ? But can't you use your arms?"

"I could, but the steps are wooden, there would be the rattle of my hooves and the rest of my harness. She would recognize it. I walk about the house on all fours, she's familiar with the sound. I say she—I mean my wife. I'm sure you'll have guessed it by now, I might as well empty out the sack of my misfortune: she's upstairs in a man's flat. Her lover's," he added in pain.

"Are you sure?" Melkior felt like breaking into a kind of laughter.

"I've been lying in wait for her, here in the dark. She's just walked in."

"So what do you propose to do upstairs? Strangle her?"

"I couldn't reach her neck," the legless man joked grimly. "No, it's nothing of the kind," he went on in a serious tone. "I want you to help me upstairs without making a sound. His door is right at the top of the staircase. You needn't feel any revulsion about touching me, in terms of cleanliness I mean. I'm clean, for all that I crawl along on the ground. She takes care of me, keeps me clean and neat. I'm an intellectual and a man of taste. I'm not poor either. I'm even wearing a new suit—half a suit, that is—complete with white shirt and a tie. You can't see it in the dark, but you can take my word for it."

"I believe you," muttered Melkior. He was already feeling the urge to turn around and run for it. "Why are you going upstairs?"

"To listen in," the legless man said greedily. "I want to hear her love, frank and true. I've never experienced that nor ever will . . . do you get my drift? I fear it's not easy to explain to you people up there, you who are upstanding and whole. But I had a hope when I heard you. . . . Forgive me if it sounds offensive, but I said to myself, This one just might . . ."

"But you'd suffer all the worse when you hear them . . ."

"No, no, not at all!" the legless man interrupted instantly. "Try to put yourself in the position of half a man such as myself who loves a complete and quite shapely woman, a woman neither old nor ugly.

I've no time to explain why she married me—it's a long story. The point is, she's my wife, a girl who married me for love. For my love of course. Because her love is something different, something that will never really blend, combine, commingle with mine. It will never fuse with mine into a single amorous entity which would completely engulf (after all, how could it, with me?) our separate selves, so that you could not tell the one from . . ."

"That, my dear fellow, never happens with any woman's love," muttered Melkior knowledgeably.

"Oh come on now! For an instant at least, for a brief moment of total self oblivion! That's what I'm after. To hear her call to him, say his name . . . see? . . . speak that name with a wild yearning for union, melting, vanishing. That's what I want to hear from her!"

"With another man?"

"What of it—she's mine!" the poor man protested in surprise. "Don't I myself sometimes get carried away by a piece of music, so much so that it's a kind of mental orgasm (I'm very fond of music); well, couldn't I, too, experience orgasm with another? With music, that is, in this case? And am I not then in a more exalted mode of being, a finer one, as it were? I'm talking about qualities, not about a commonplace (indeed a common) activity. It's nothing to do with me, I don't even think about it. When I listen to the violin in a Beethoven concerto (say the one in D major) do I think about a horse's tail scraping upon sheep's gut? I know those are the means, the *indispensable* means, for providing these wonderful harmonies, but it's the harmonies that excite me, not the guts. But let's face it, the guts *are* necessary. The guts of an anonymous sheep, at that. And the tail of some stupid nag—which indeed may not have been stupid at all, but that's beside the point. Why should I be thinking about the horse upstairs (who for all I know may not literally be a horse), about the tails and bowels, about the scrapings and blowings and . . . the dirty business in general, if I want to listen to the love cantilena of a violin that has never sounded properly in my arms? All it has ever done was scrape, scrape, scrape . . . producing no music, that's my stinking lot! I'm not a player, whereas he may even be a virtuoso. It takes an entire body, an entire man—which I am not. There you are, the tail and the guts are a must after all. . . . Am I to hate Menuhin for it?"

The man ardently delivered his entire, long-in-the-making, carefully prepared argument and fell silent. He was tired. This was perhaps the first time he had shared it with someone, with a stranger in a dark doorway, under bizarre circumstances, and was now embarrassed. Perhaps this was the first time he had doubted it, its validity, its viability in the cold world of other people's indifference?

"You're laughing, aren't you?" the man spoke up from the nether darkness. "You think I worked it all out down here like a sapient reptile slithering on the ground? Or evolved a new organ for my miserable existence? Or that this is a whole new, my very own, indeed original brand of generosity? No, I'm as selfish as you, as any *normal* male. (He put a very heavy stress on *normal*). It's out of selfishness that I'm telling you all this."

"No, you're not being selfish," said Melkior without conviction, just to say something.

"Because I'm not snarling at *that business* up there? Why, I pine for that business up there with all my supracanine faith in absolute love. I want love, do you understand what I'm saying, love, not gnaw a bone on the ground in this dark doorway!"

An outcry de profundis. Melkior shuddered. Inside him vibrated muffled affinities with this pathetic ground-bound being who had raised high a huge sky above his head and planted in it a single star in which he had inscribed his destiny. The sky above . . . and Viviana shining in it. Matter of fact, my dear groundling, our love's sky is a common or garden skirt at whose zenith twinkles a stubbornly chosen . . . all right, call it a star . . . That's our destiny.

"You'll help me upstairs then?" the legless man asked uncertainly.

Well, what do you know, the man won't give it up. He wants his cantilena. All right, have it your own way.

"Of course I will. Come on."

"Get hold of me from the back, under the armpits," the man

instructed him briskly, with a kind of joy. He even raised his arms, as if about to take off. Melkior took hold of him like someone teaching a small child to walk and brought him to the staircase. They had just begun to climb, barely clearing the first step or two, when a door upstairs opened and there was the sound of voices. Serious, grave voices.

"It's her! Something's wrong," the man whispered, terrified. "Run for it, run! As far as you can!" He was hurrying Melkior as if some dreadful anger were threatening.

"I can't just leave you on the stairs."

"Then dump me behind the door and run!" the man cried in frightful panic. "All's lost! God, I'm so unhappy!"

Melkior grabbed him hurriedly and carried him back to the doorway. He set him down piously behind the door like a broken saint, whispered "goodbye" and fled outside.

But did not go far. Let's see the violin after all. He positioned himself well, facing a shop window that had a mirror set diagonally in it. He did not have long to wait. Out of the door came an indeed well-built young woman with a very pretty face. But when she stepped onto the pavement Melkior noticed the floating motion of her somehow fetching lameness. With one leg she barely touched the ground in a weightless, fairylike hover; with the other she trod firmly, with all her well-endowed corporeality. As a counterpoint.

Oh, what an instrument! sighed Melkior. Hence the ardent wish for a virtuoso upstairs. He thought of the luckless torso behind the door. Oh poor church-portal saint, not even Johann Sebastian himself could have played your life in a more charming counterpoint.

And now, where to? All the roads are blocked by heavy drifts of uncertainty. The thing to do would be to proceed from some starting point under this nocturnal star-riddled dome. Following what star? Every star is the beginning of some motion . . . Every thought is a star from an undiscovered constellation drowned in the infinity of time. The infinities. The conceptual confidence tricks. The metaphors. The fearful astronomy above the life of a small carnivore rolled up in a ball of yearning under his little sky of a crinoline atop which shines . . . Viviana. This was his destiny. *Stella Viviana.* And he set off, following his lost star, to wander vainly in the night.

Far off in town the cathedral clock tolls the hours. Five o'clock. But night is still strangling the city with damp and cold darkness. The long autumn night. He was freezing in the deserted arbored walk under the tall vaults of withered leaves rustling fearfully on weary trunks. He winced at the roaring of lions. The sound of the zoological tyrant's voice drew responses from other animals, jerked awake from fearful sleep. The emperor was hungering for their flesh.

Melkior smelled the stench of the zoo. The warm furs were unrolling, the beasts were stretching, opening their jaws wide, yawning, roaring into the new day. Zoopolis was waking. And broadcasting the stench of its slavery.

This would be what prisons and barracks stink like. The *katorgas.* The hordes, legions, cohorts, regiments. The glorious armies that gave epochs their peculiar smells. The large-scale collective fumes, the stenches of history. Stenches Persian, stenches Alexandrine, stenches Hannibalic, stenches Caesarean, stenches Avaran, Hunnish, Tartar, Mongolian, Germanic, stenches Turkish, stenches Napoleonic, stenches Samuraic, stenches Prussian, Franz-Josephinian, Benito-Mussolinian, and stenches Adolf-Hitleran . . . Stenches and more stenches, as far as history reaches. Mankind has well and truly made a stink of it in troop and bowel movements. Ptui! Melkior spat on the animal stench with which history had invaded his nostrils from the zoo.

He came out on the long straight road leading back to town. In the distance appeared the lights of an early tram. Here comes Technology, as Maestro would put it. Here comes Power. All right then, let's see what happens. He was suddenly overcome by a strange thought, a spiteful and terrible thought in fact, it gave him goose bumps all over but he was unable and unwilling to resist it. Let it be. . . . He stepped down from the pavement onto the track and set off between the rails to meet the tram. Provocatively, irascibly even, with the comic courage of a cartoon hero—a pint-sized intrepid hunter—thumbing its nose at an approaching rhinoceros. The rhinoceros was clanging his way toward him with an angry grumble. Melkior already felt the ground shake under his feet with the approach of the iron beast. Horror gave him a cold lick down his back. Well, let's see how long we can take it. His imagination began to frighten him with tableaux: limbs torn apart, bowels spilled . . . Flies. He shooed his imagination away from his dead body and calmly fell to gazing straight ahead. And what's that?—*it's* no longer moving, *it's* merely getting larger, more visible. Not approaching at all. The trick is to let the eyes take over. Like in the cinema. That's the entire secret to this courage. The trick is to regard everything as an image on a screen, to reflect the light from the object to the world-image in my field of vision. And the objects become weak and powerless, under my full control. Symbolic of a world I have created and can banish immediately by closing my eyes. A silent film. He closed his eyes. Fiction. There, the celluloid has snapped, interrupting the projection. But the tram grunted on the uneven rails and the projector came back on in an instant. The addition of sound to the picture alarmed his entire body, exposed in space. This may be the critical moment when the body must be mastered, its fear dispelled by an idea. Well, why shouldn't my idea, *Hold on*, be strong enough to bear a courage that is equal to any other great courage? The courage of a captain going down with his ship? A totally useless death. The idée fixe of honor. Which essentially means overcoming one's fear. Bearing the idea of death—to the death. Spitefully. Stubbornly. But this is where you face a spate of individual variations, mixtures, confusions, with flashes of madness. My idea is mad, too. *Hold on.* Quite near now. Two hundred meters. If that.

You can see the driver. Not slowing down. Thinking, The fellow will move off on his own . . . Sitting there calmly. Not yet upset . . . Having no idea that what he's up against is a *thought* on the rails, one stronger than fear of his hardware. Maestro would congratulate me. The tram. The stupid banal machine. The imagination again: arms severed, legs, skull crushed, a mess of brains and blood, the flesh, the bones . . . The Witnesses Of Horror. He did it on purpose, he meant to kill himself. Nah, he was a nut-case, is all. Drunk. Who is he, anyway? Can you gather anything from his papers? His pockets! Enka's photo in the wallet. Enka on the beach: an erotic phenomenon! Everything that is feminine and nubile, soft, cuddly, beckoning . . . He had a flash of desire for the Enka in the photo . . .

The driver stepped hard on his bell-pedal. Melkior's innards quaked inside him. Red alert in the entire body, "attention, danger!" in every cell. His blood shot down from the head into the legs (for they were now more important than the head). At any rate there was nothing left inside the head except: something huge and blue growing ever larger and advancing with a bellow. He closed all his sphincters tight, clamped shut the valves, passages, seams, tensed his will to painful rigidity—he was one superpotent, all-powerful, tearing erection. Come on, you stupid tram! The tram was indeed coming on, stupidly. Well, if that's what you want . . . Twenty, ten, five meters! Clanging his bell in panic, appealing to him, pleading with him: step aside, man! Man! All right, you're clever and I'm stupid, but get out of my way! See how big I am—I'll crush you!

You big stupid hulk, my resolve's greater than you are! I'm not committing suicide, you iron dolt! I've put my thought down in front of you, run it over if you can!

The tram gave a sudden sensible lurch. It let out a fearsome grunt (some dust flew up under its feet) and stopped short as though a huge force had struck it on the snout.

Ha-ha! leered Melkior in mad triumph upward, at the tram. Which was standing still before him, quiet, tired, sheepish. Defeated. Ha-ha, I've stopped you, you mammoth!

The driver had already dismounted and was swearing his way toward him.

"Listen, you . . . Are you off your damned . . . ?" he swung an arm but stopped it in front of his forehead.

". . . rocker? No. Why?" said Melkior in surprise. "I'm no suicide. I'm fine."

"Oh, it's all right to stop a tram like this, eh? What about my timetable? What do you think you're doing?"

"All right, carry on then . . ." muttered Melkior. He now saw revealed the other, banal, city-transport side of the incident.

"I'll give you carry on!" and the driver would have assaulted him, but the conductor spoke up with greater objectivity:

"Leave him alone, will you? Can't you see he's a bit . . ."

"A bit what? A bit nothing. The silly creep thinks he's being funny." The driver was already giving up on the idea of revenge. He was climbing back into the tram. "What about my nerves, damn it?" and he slammed angrily at his bell-pedal and set the car in motion.

Melkior was taken aback by the unexpected victory. How could I explain it to those tram men? I held my own! Eureka! He was crowing with Archimedean madness. I have discovered the biological law of upthrust! A body immersed in fear will lose as much of its mortality as the weight of the fear displaced. Eureka!

Noli turbare circulos meos! is what I should have said to the tram's arrogant captain. Well, it's too late now. *Vivere . . .*

Vivere senzaa malinconiiaaa . . . he broke into song hurrying back to town, and the black sky sprinkled him with a fine melancholy rain to make the song all the more absurd.

Could there be a price out on your head? An underground political conspiracy in a dark cellar dimly lit by an oil lamp. Three unshaven thugs discussing the ways and means of taking your life. Knives stuck into the table, sharp, shiny, with *Rostfrei-Solingen* inscribed on them. Running down the blades is a groove, like the kind on butcher's knives. (First chance you get, ask a butcher what the groove on butcher's knives is for.)

They will surprise you in a dark street, at night, as you walk by, tapping your fingers absentmindedly on a wall. . . . But why do they want your head in the first place? For reasons of politics, no less? It's true, you do have convictions, but they are . . . well . . . convictions, nothing more.

"Look, gentlemen (what kind of gentlemen are these?), am I not allowed to have convictions of my own?" and already you fear that *these people* know all about your pathetic little convictions, that they have furthermore measured the strength of what you believe in using some sort of special device and that you're done for. Because the dreams, these dreams that torment you . . . ! No, you must have been spotted *over there*, your name must have been mentioned and indeed added to lists, to printed forms.

He stood with Ugo by the invalid's weighing machine, waved his hands and insisted: "Mankind, my dear Parampion, mankind!"

An elegant gentleman in a raincoat who apparently had been waiting until then for his tram approached them and, pointing at Melkior with a pipe he had taken from his pocket, asked with terrible authority:

"You were shouting *Mankind?*"

"No, I said *Mankind, my dear brother,* quite discreetly for no particular reason. Just like that, for the sake of humanity . . . and brotherhood."

"Humanity? Brotherhood? Are you some sort of internationalist?"

"Oh no, not at all! I believe we must defend ourselves, resist as a nation, to the last drop!"

"Resist?"

"Yes, take a firm stand, mustn't we, my friend?"

But the *friend* had already made himself scarce, and the gentleman who had been waiting for the tram took Melkior's arm amicably and took him for a stroll . . .

A knife fight, gun play in the dark, dashing to escape, a fall from great heights—this was the program on during a brief morning nap. After *Vivere.*

Wielding gleaming butcher's knives they chase him around the University Library building. He climbs up to the green copper roof and ducks behind one of the four bronze owls, each perched on a book. But they now resort to flinging safety blades at him of all sizes and weights. The gleaming swarms drone and buzz in dense assault formations and swoop down on the bronze owl. They screech and sparkle on the owl's pate, and the owl has its wings outstretched maternally to shield Melkior the fugitive from the lethal flying blades. Across the roof, behind another owl, appears Ugo's derisive face: "Give up, ATMAN is in charge. Four Eyes is at HQ. Maestro has committed suicide and Viviana has taken the veil."

He looks down, but out of their sockets drop his eyes, and, fraternally connected by a nerve as if holding hands, the two eyes float to the ground like twin soap bubbles, look at each other, each shedding a tear.

Dissolve to:

He is sitting on the barrel of a gun. Next to him sits a man-soldier, García (by rank), who speaks none of the known languages. Over there, behind some large crates, are the enemy positions. There is a lull at the front. García takes words out of his tunic pockets and arranges them on the palm of his hand. He then stuffs them into his rifle. He learns languages. Suddenly García is no longer there by the gun. García's head shouts from the gun barrel: *The Maccharones! The Maccharones!* And the gun goes off with a frightening report. The words fly about, shouting and screaming: "*Murderers!*" Gunshots. Words die. Silence. Darkness. The sky is not visible.

You flee. You walk over dead things and dead men. Helmets, pots, broken lavatory porcelain. You expect a stab in the back at any moment. *Merhum* Melkior.

Merhaba! Somebody has caught up with you and prodded you in the back with his finger and your first thought is *merhum.* . . . But the skinny, toothless, and generally comical-looking man who has caught up with you immediately asks: "We're retreating, *n'est-ce pas?*" Obviously an intellectual.

"Yes, Professor, a tactical move. García said so. But our side is putting up a damned fine show."

"Histrionics?"—and the toothless man smiles with calm contentment.

In the next sequence the two of you find yourselves in a cramped school lavatory (the teachers') papered over with old newspapers with pictures of many living kings. There ensues a horrible bellowing, horse hooves, broken glass, a great hullabaloo. Then victorious drums, brass bands, shouts of *Mamma! Cara mamma!* and *Sieg Heil!* Finally the song *Vento, vento, porta mi via con te* . . .

The old professor, for all that he appears to be a military person, is unable to control his knees, which knock as though they are carrying an unimaginably heavy load. In the end he sits down on the toilet seat and, having made a stink, sighs, "Oh, my career, my career!"

"So, Professor, have you any pesetas on you?"

"Seven hundred . . . and forty centimos, here. You're not going to confiscate them, are you?"

"Yes. To throw them out the window to people downstairs."

"Then what?"

"Then you wipe that career of yours and we run for it!"

And while the victors downstairs are squabbling over the handful of change, you make your way through a tangle of dark corridors with changing luck and you would certainly have gotten away were you able to run. . . . But the cannibals are already there, converging on all sides. Surrounded! Trapped! Maestro (for it is he) (as they say in the kind of novel where a character's identity is held back for a time) is immediately rejected as unfit for human consumption (they cut into him a little, the knife tarnishes—*morbus lues*, poisonous, says the red-haired Asclepian), and you are thrown into the cauldron for their breakfast. Making a fire under the cauldron (as a slave, of course, with a certain right to be resentful) is Foma Fomich Opiskin, who mutters: "I'm being persecuted. I work for a living!"

The red-haired Asclepian is there, too, disguised as Sartorius the Critic, smirking smugly: "Look who's claiming to be free of the influence of Dostoyevsky! Rotten lies, lies, lies . . ."

Cut to:

The wharf of a small seaside town. Barges and fishing boats alongside. On the shore, wine barrels and drying fishing nets. And no one in sight. An indefinite time of day, morning or noon, there is no way of telling which, the hands are missing from the church spire clock. Its face is rusty.

You are alone (. . . alone, alone, all, all alone, comes the echo of the ancient Mariner's voice). You have an empty ink bottle in hand and it suddenly occurs to you to rinse it in the sea. You descend two steps, nearer to the water, you kneel . . . but the ink bottle no longer matters. You take out a knife, a big pocket knife, you open it and, grabbing your hair with your left hand, you slice your head off with a natural and easy stroke. A simple business, like killing a chicken. Next you rinse your head instead of the ink bottle: up-down, splash-splash. A clear picture of decapitation: a body minus a head, the head in your hands, its eyes open and indifferent. Suddenly your head slips out of your hands and floats away in the water. You cannot reach it. You call out to it, entreating it to come back, but it only looks at you—a long, hurt look—then smiles sadly and closes its eyes as if in sudden pain. You try to draw it near using a stick; it only spins like a pumpkin and will not come nearer to you. It then gives you a desperately painful, farewell look and says sorrowfully (but seeming to blame you for its sorrow): "Goodbye, I'm off," and you hear it sob. Then it takes a deep dive and disappears.

A feeble-minded man is standing behind you on the shore, grinning idiotically as he watches you. When the head dives he said, "You could've given it to me. My old lady's sister, the deaf one, is dead."

"The deaf one" was what Melkior heard when he opened his eyes. What's this? he said aloud.

The light is on in the room. "Who's there?" he asks the room.

The room is silent. It diverts his gaze from itself, directing it downward, at the bed, at himself, his legs, his belly, his chest, and closer and closer still . . . it would show him his head, too.

The Gaze is frightened. It has discovered you on the bed, fully dressed and with your shoes on, and is now watching you in amazement, as it would watch a stranger, a discovery.

You show it your arms, by turns. The Gaze watches them, unmoved, "The arms" being its sole, indifferent comment. It has no interest in arms. It shortens its range, searching for a target closer to. It closes and crosses, peering at the nose from both sides at once, like Picasso. That is the closest object it can see—the nose. It defines the nose in passing: *a bilateral something jutting out into space and dividing the visible world in two, into the left and the right.* But the Gaze wants the head, the solution to the conundrum, the answer to this night, to his dream of decapitation.

The Gaze wants itself, its very self, it wants to see its own self. And to admire itself, a narcissist, stupid, shortsighted, blind to anything that is not It, a Sharp Gaze, *a pure, eighteen-carat Gaze.*

The Gaze would look at itself, full face and profile, to examine its breadth of field, its acuity, to discover its face from a novel, as yet unfamiliar vantage point. It would penetrate its self, dive into its past, into its ancient, Proterozoic origin, into times when it still touched the world warily, with pseudopods and tendrils.

The Gaze has an intrepid desire to see itself.

But you are put off by the audacity. Who knows what may lurk inside? Perhaps an entrance to an entirely new, undiscovered hell from which there is no return? The disappearance into one's own eyes and entry into an endless ordeal?

You are afraid of your own self lying on the bed. Fully dressed, with your shoes on. (They say sleeping with your shoes on gives you bad dreams.) But who turned the light on? He could have sworn that, this morning, when he'd gone up to his room, he'd taken off the sodden clothes and muddy shoes, put on his pajamas, slid under the blanket, and turned off the light! And proceeded to reflect in bed: Love? how unexplained it all still is! Is it the Song of Songs, Cleopatra, Beatrice, Laura, Phaedra, Don Juan, Werther, Stendhal, or Casanova? What is love?

He remembers quite clearly: first he threw himself on the sofa, rain-soaked and tired as he was, and browsed through Stendhal's *On Love* and then, eyes closed, pondered many inexplicable points about beauty and suffering in love. "*How fair and how pleasant art thou, Oh love, for delights! This thy stature is like to the palm tree, and thy breasts to clusters of grapes. Thou art beautiful, Oh my love, as Tirzah, comely as Jerusalem, terrible as an army with banners. Solomon had the vineyard at Baalhamon . . .*" "*Minus dormit et edit quem amoris cogitatio vexat,*" says *De amore*, by André le Chapelain of Avignon. All those sad, empty days, all those sleepless nights, all the fear, anxiety, pining, misery, folly! All the suffering. All the blood for the sake of love's "delights"! All the hearts aflutter! All the heads cut off!

La douce pensée
Qu'amour souvent me donne!

wrote the poor page Guillaume de Cabstaing of Provence in the twelfth century, moments before his lord, Monseigneur Raymond de Roussillon, cut off his head and pulled the heart out from his chest, had it cooked, and then made his wife, the page's lover, eat it. He then asked her if the heart she had just eaten had been to her taste—and showed her Guillaume's head. It was so delicious, she replied, that no other food or drink would ever erase the taste of Guillaume's heart. Whereupon she leapt from the window to her death, the hapless Madame Marguerite.

He got up and opened the window. Below him was a three-story wet, dark depth.

Well? Should I jump? How do they jump using a parachute?—And he conjured up a breakneck aeronautical grand slalom. The parachute fails to open . . .

But this: lying on the bed fully dressed, with the light on in the room! And dreaming, in the light, of cutting off your own head! In the light, that's the most frightening thing about it!

No, I was attempting to operate on myself last night . . . Perhaps I also got up, turned the light on, dressed, went out, perhaps? The tram? No, the tram happened earlier. It's all hazy, disjointed. Say something, you sightless things! You, too, flaming minister!—he said to the lightbulb. The lightbulb below the ceiling shone indifferently, mute, deaf, it just shone on without a word. The sole witness watching from above, the sole, sighted witness.

Perhaps I was trying to kill myself?

He remembered the paper-knife and began to quake. Where's the knife?

A great deal depends on that. Must be over there, on the desk. To think that people wish you a good night in the evening!

The knife was on the desk, thrust to the hilt in a thick volume that had only half its pages cut. The book lay on its side, helpless, stabbed. This disturbed him even more. Stabbed! Who had plunged the knife so brutally into its gut? (It was Wells's *A Short History of the World*. Poor Short!) He carefully removed the knife from History's belly.

I must have been using the damned thing last night after all! The thought would not go away. Enka's gift, silver-plated, for his birthday the previous year.

He went across to the mirror and was alarmed by *him there on the other side* eyeing him so weirdly. Look how hard he stares! He means to frighten . . . But he noticed that *the other* is also frightened, looking out with mistrust . . . No, honestly, man does not trust man, not even in a mirror!

Well, what about it, friend? What would we look like with no head? He took hold of his head by the hair with his left hand and very cautiously slid the knife across his windpipe with his right. *Glugkhrhhh* . . . went the windpipe, slit. He then held his head in both hands and turned it this way and that as if it had really been severed. What an odd feeling, holding a human head in one's hands!

Then again, it could have been like this: some important, urgent thoughts had swarmed into the anteroom of sleep, knocking, shouting, alerting you, demanding to be immediately received and heard. But kind Sleep, to protect you from the heralds of bad news, simply took away your head and went whispering to your body: you have nothing to think with, you have no head. Sleep on.

Sleep on indeed, with a knife only a few feet away from your sleep, plunged into History's guts!

Your word for KNIFE is NOŽ, pronounced NOZHHH. The *zh* is the terrible bladelike edge of the word. It contains the *zhhhh* needed for the slitting of throats. In other languages the knife could be an instrument used to sharpen pencils, slice apples . . . but *nož* is all about slaughter, murder most foul. The Croatian word for dagger is *bodež*, if you strip the *zh* from *bodež*—you get *bode*, a silly harmless pricking, the paltry sting of a mischievous thorn, a tack sticking up from the seat of a chair. Words like howling—*lavež*, thief—*lupež*, or a house afire—*požar*—all of them are bloodcurdling things of the night and you don't dare lie in bed at night and go to sleep for fear of them.

So you think: what am I to do with the *nož*? You are actually afraid to go to sleep with it near you. So you try to work something out: wrap it up well, in a whole newspaper, tie it up firmly with string, lock it in a drawer, lock the drawer key in the wardrobe, take the wardrobe key to the kitchen and lock it . . . somewhere, go back to the room, lock the room, throw the room key out the window. Too complicated. Foolish, too. It can all be undone by working backward.

What is he to do? He sits on the bed with the paper-knife in his hand, it is night, all sensible people are asleep, and there he is, fearful of dozing off lest he cut his own throat in his sleep. And he thinks with rancor: dogs are muzzled, windows barred, wherever you look there are railings, pillars, locks, red lights, lighthouses, signals, warnings BEWARE OF THE DOG! LEVEL CROSSING! DO NOT LEAN OUT THE WINDOW! HIGH VOLTAGE! (Maestro laughing) POISON! and they alarm you with the skull and crossbones the better to protect you; experts on the railways, on the sea and in the air, experts in police departments protect you and your two shoes from burglars and collectivists, in every capital city there is an expert safeguarding you from sudden attack by means of treaties, alliances, and friendships, and generally protecting your interests abroad. Spiritual leaders protect your soul; statesmen, your body. In fact they vie—nay, quarrel—with each other over who will protect you best, and consequently give you wafts of incense and sprinkles of holy water for the benefit of your soul; and for the benefit of your body they surround you with powerful security measures: the League of Nations, the Non-Aggression and Mutual Assistance Pact, the Maginot Line, the Siegfried Line, guns, tanks, submarines, bombers, rifles, mines, bayonets, pistols—in a word, an impregnable circle of fire and steel, and they tell you: you're safe in here, don't do anything ridiculous like feeling despair. We're here, you can sleep in peace.

Sleep in peace . . . Sorry, gentlemen, a bit of a misunderstanding here. I naturally am safe by your side—I mean, under your wise and powerful aegis. And I'm afraid of no one as long as you are here. But when I go to sleep you're no longer at my side and I'm alone and mindless like an idiot. Can't you see the dreams I have? How can I sleep? Inside your safe circle of fire, treaties, and bayonets—don't be surprised—I'm very poorly protected from myself! I panic like a scorpion.

There's nothing I can do about it—I am a scorpion. And if you don't let me out, I fear I will give myself a lethal injection, just like a scorpion, in despair!

He thought he ought to go back to bed after all. But what was the use, given that van der Lübe would appear immediately, crazed by the terrible death he had experienced, and mutter madly, "Give me back my head, you thieves, give me back my head, my head, my head . . ."

Melkior leaned against the windowpane. The barracks were still asleep. The guard had crawled into the sentry box like a dog and was dozing on his feet inside, troubled by soldierly dreams. In the house next door lived a young woman in the last stage of pregnancy. What is she going to have? A daughter. Then she would be impressing upon the girl, in later years, that the wife holds up three corners of the house and the husband only the fourth. (If a bomb hit a house who held up the corners?) If she had a son, his father would worry about his FUTURE, which might well exceed three months. He would buy him a spring-action toy rifle and some tin soldiers, give the lad something to play with. The boy would guard *their house* all day long, like that soldier was guarding his barracks across the street, and would shoot at the unarmed enemy children on the block. And in the evening, when his father returned from work, he would shoot at him, "Bang! Daddy, I've killed you. Lie down, Daddy, you're dead." Daddy was worried and grave, he didn't even notice the child's game. He had a newspaper in hand, an extra-late addition. The boy was angry at Daddy's refusal to lie down when dead, and shot him again with murderous rage, Bang! but Daddy did not fall. The boy flung himself to the floor in desperation, pounding it with his fists, weeping over the disregard for the rules of his game. "Humor the child a bit, can't you," his mother cut in. "What, and die to please him?" His father was not in the mood for joking. "It's only a game. Don't be a spoilsport." "We'll be playing the game for keeps soon enough," his father said anxiously. The boy had been eavesdropping slyly and redoubled his screams on realizing the failure of his mother's intercession. In the end his father spanked him and sent him to bed. Lying in bed, he sobbed, offended, in the dark. Later on, half asleep, he heard his father and mother talking quietly in bed, his mother crying and his father tossing and turning, saying, "If only it weren't for the boy." And the boy thought: "It's me Daddy's talking about, he's sorry I'm alive. All right then, I'll kill myself in the coal shed first thing in the morning" and envisaged dropping a stone down the gun barrel and shooting himself in the eye.

Leaning on the window, engaged with the little drama, he had not noticed the arrival of the dawn. A gray cloud in the middle of the sky was going faintly pink: from its height it had caught sight of the sun below the horizon.

In the distance, engines whistled, early trains departed.

Melkior greeted the morning from his window. "Good morning, Morning! Welcome! Hey, I'm alive!" But this was only a moment of welcome. "Aah, I'm alive . . . so what?" and he was again gripped by a dull and despairing dread, feeling a strange and repulsive anxiety all over his body.

The landlady was up. He could hear her tottering and tramping in the dawn's half-light, still woozy from sleep. She purposely banged an elbow on his door and muttered, "Up and moving all night . . ."

Melkior felt the cold metal of the knife in his hand and gave a shiver of strange revulsion. He stepped quickly out onto the landing and went into the landlady's flat. He found her in front of the bathroom door, tousled, limp, sodden with sleep.

"Up all night again, were you?" she gathered her housecoat at her chest, concealing her un-maternal and still ambitious breasts.

"Would you please take this knife, Madam?"

Fully dressed, pale, thick blue rings around eyes. She watches him with what is almost fear.

"What's the matter, Mr. Melkior? Why do you want me to take the knife?"

"I have bad dreams when it is near me."

"Ah, I dream of those damned knives myself. Snakes, too." But she took the knife with a kind of passion. Melkior noticed it.

"Why don't you remarry, Madam? It's not too late for you at all."

"What about you? Why don't you get married?" she retorted with fresh matutinal coquetry.

On his way back to his room Melkior thought of Viviana. Of Enka, too, in passing. Her knife. She does not have knives stuck into her belly in her sleep like the poor landlady. Her dreams are like a cat's—nocturnal mouse-hunting.

A bird piped up in a park near by: chee-chee-caw . . . chee-chee-caw . . .

"Chi-chi-kov . . . Chi-chi-kov . . ." replied Melkior with literary sarcasm. *Dead Souls*. And so to bed, with our own soul dead"—this he was barely able to say as he toppled on the bed, dead with exhaustion and lack of sleep.

"They have these binges night after night. He's clearly drunk. He didn't even take off his clothes."

"Never mind, don't wake him. We'll just leave my things and go."

He heard the voices above, but couldn't open his eyes. A tremendous fatigue sat heavy on his eyelids and kept his consciousness in a state of listless floating on the surface of a very shallow sleep. From time to time he felt contact with wakefulness underneath, as if his sleep were bobbing in a shallow and scraping the bottom. He made out "he's drunk"—that was Pupo speaking; "never mind" was someone else, a stranger. But he thought he was dreaming, so he let himself sink into his stupor like a drunkard, using the voices to put together a small sketch:

"Binges for flowers, thank you, thank you," says the old lady pianist over his bed. Pupo tries to drag her away, "He didn't even take his clothes off"; she struggles with him, "Never mind, don't wake him." But there is a third person here, someone invisible, important, "We'll just leave my things and go." And everyone leaves.

Melkior was suddenly frightened at the prospect of being left; he jumped to his feet: "Wait! No, wait! Right away . . . I'll get undressed right away." . . . But his eyes were still closed. "He's dreaming," said a strange voice. But Melkior was awake already, it was just that his eyes were still glued shut by thick, greasy sleep.

Nevertheless he padded with extraordinary certainty over to the glass carafe with water in it, poured some into his cupped palm, and splashed his eyes. Yes, there were Pupo and a stranger, standing next to his bed, beaming at him.

"I'm so sorry, I've . . . I didn't sleep all night." He was making excuses to the stranger. "His kind are early risers," he thought.

"Was it at least a good binge?" Pupo was smiling contemptuously.

"Binge? No. Insomnia. Can't sleep." He smoothed out his rumpled suit, embarrassed. He straightened his tie, too. It was only eight o'clock. "I must have dropped off just a little while ago. Funny, I don't remember." But he was still standing in the same spot, face wet, confused.

"Why don't you put it down on the floor?" said Pupo to the stranger. Indeed, the man was still holding a valise in his hand, undecidedly. A raincoat was draped over his other arm. Tall, fair-haired, lean, fortyish, with a grave, care-ridden face. Melkior finally came out of his trance. He put away the carafe, approached the man, and reached to take his valise. The man put forward his hand. Melkior returned the handshake, cordially. He said his name. The man muttered something unintelligible, looking at Melkior with an apologetic smile. "Right you are, brother," thinks Melkior, the name remains the Stranger.

Accommodatingly, he opened the wardrobe door.

"This is for your things." This time he succeeded in taking the valise away from the Stranger. He put it in the wardrobe. "It's down here. Do sit down. And you, what are you wondering about?" he said to Pupo with erstwhile intimacy. "I haven't been drinking— here, see for yourself," and he puffed into Pupo's face.

The Stranger laughed. "What, does he forbid it?" gesturing at Pupo.

"I educate them. The others are worse," said Pupo asserting his authority.

"You can imagine the educator: carried by us because he's been walking on all fours. He chews drinking glasses, not to mention shouting, 'Down with the monarchy.'"

Melkior instantly realized he had gone too far. Pupo gave him a look of contemptuous rage. He had clearly been playing the saint "here," being in a subordinate position in "those" circles.

The Stranger laughed. But on seeing Pupo's face he abruptly cut his laughter short and erased it completely from his face. The face was now calm and care-ridden again.

"If you'd like to wash up," said Melkior to the Stranger, "the bathroom is across there, in the flat proper." He wished to be alone with Pupo for a moment. He wanted to apologize.

"No, thank you."

Melkior offered him a cigarette. "Thank you, no. I don't smoke."

He offered one to Pupo and smiled in a friendly way. Pupo took it and accepted the smile.

"I always have black coffee in the morning. I'll fetch some right away." Melkior was in high spirits.

"Don't bother on my account," said the Stranger. "I would like only to sit down here for a minute. I'm tired." He sat down on the sofa. But he promptly dropped down on an elbow, and then leaned his head back against the cushion. "I'm very tired," he said apologetically.

"Lie down by all means. I've got to go to the office anyway. You can sleep if you like. I'll tell the landlady not to send the maid in."

Melkior went across to the flat proper to fetch the coffee. He explained to the landlady that a relative had unexpectedly arrived. He would be staying for a few days. She offered to do the room herself, to make the sofa for the guest, out of curiosity, of course. Melkior put that all off for later. He brought the coffee back. The two of them cut their conversation short. He felt extraneous there between them. He slurped his coffee hastily, explained to the Stranger the technique of living in the room, handed over all the necessary keys, and, with a most courteous *Bye for now* to both of them, fled.

He may be a future Marat for all I know, he thought, hurrying down the stairs, even though he had no reason to hurry at all. But why Marat, of all men? The man was killed in his bath—the whore Charlotte cut his throat. Danton, Saint-Just, Robespierre? . . . snick-snick-snick . . . all three heads—snick!—rolling into a basket. None of the examples is good enough. Not Zinoviev, not Kamenev, not Bukharin, not even Leo Bronstein, it was again snick-snick-snick and crash! The ice pick striking Leo's head, whereas I wish my guest the Stranger to live. Long live my guest the Stranger!—Hip, hip, hoorayyy! He was rallying in the street, semiaudible even, making people turn around after him. He would have dearly loved to rush into the Give'nTake and tell everyone, like Bobchinsky-Dobchinsky, what kind of a guest had arrived. Mysterious, secretive, yet quite straightforward and likable, tall and fair-haired and lean and decidedly on the shy side, "No, thank you, don't bother on my account."

No, I must give Enka a buzz. Poor Enka. I'm really a . . . He nevertheless went by the Theater Café and the Give'nTake, just in case. Perhaps Viviana had decided to parade her pretty self there. But the score was zero and . . . zero. Making a total of zero. Too early. A rest after last night's *gentle breath*. He did not telephone Enka either. He mounted the stairs to the office, tired already. Wilted enthusiasm. See proof of review, it's to go to print today. The day's copy was no longer with the arts editor, it was already in the composing room.

"The Old Man crossed out a paragraph."

"Censorship, eh?"—ready for a big showdown.

"Nonsense. Too much copy. Had to trim all around."

"Which paragraph?"

"Do me a favor. What do you care anyway—it was only ten lines or so."

"You could've asked me—I would've done it myself."

"I looked for you at the Give'nTake last night. 'He's just gone out with Don Fernando,' and you haven't got a phone at your digs. How was I to ask?"

"It's wrong all the same."

"Don Fernando's with the editor now. He's brought some article or other, but it's a no-go. They're having a discussion . . . matters of principle." The arts editor was sneering with mild derision.

That was precisely what Melkior had long wanted—coming to a "matter-of-principle" grips with the editor. But when he entered the editor's "Black Room" (so-called because everything in it was black, himself included) the two of them were heartily laughing at something. Don Fernando was sunk in a black leather armchair, his long legs crossed so high that one of his knees touched his chin and his glass of cognac, but he couldn't drink for laughing. The editor seemed to have just finished telling him something and was laughing himself, but his laughter had pauses and long intervals in it, during which he was making it known to his silliness that he could stop this nonsense at any moment if necessary. But he was not stopping it, which meant that *this*—the nonsense, the laughter—was necessary.

So this was what the "matter-of-principle" discussion was all about. The embittered realization could have been read in his face, had there been somebody to read it. They went on laughing. The editor only spared a hand to gesture toward a seat. In a little while Melkior, too, touched his chin to his knee and poured himself a cognac, only he didn't hold it to his nose—he downed it; he did not laugh. Must be something silly to make them chortle like this. A "matter-of-principle" laugh. He was irritated by the laughter. Late for the show everyone else was enjoying, he was the only one without a clue. Damned silly business! He was hurt. For we are hurt by any laughter we can't understand.

"I thought there were big issues being discussed here, I thought I would learn a thing or two . . ." and he knocked back another brandy, miffed.

"Oh, so you think . . . what is it that Maestro calls you—Eustachius? . . ." (the two of them burst out laughing again) ". . . that *big issues* can't sometimes be handled with laughter?" Don Fernando dropped the question from on high, adding the necessary breezy tone to accentuate his condescension.

"They can," Melkior swatted at the question as if it were a moth flying across the room, "if it's a Molière doing it."

"You wouldn't settle for a lesser authority then?" The moth was losing altitude.

"It's the nature of laughter that doesn't settle—it's choosy."

Don Fernando didn't reply. He tried to catch the editor's eye, to assert their spiritual bond. But the editor paid no attention. He got up and sat down at his black mahogany desk. This meant, "We've had our fun, now back to business."

"We've trimmed your review a bit," he said to Melkior with a considerate smile. No more than ten lines or so. Had to trim everything today. A lot of small news items."

"Sorry I was unable to mention personalities . . ." Melkior was trying to provoke *the thing*, the "matter of principle."

The editor flashed a wry smile.

"I wouldn't expect that from you anyway," he said with a pleasant look at Melkior. "The fellow yesterday was a different case altogether. He himself regretted that he hadn't remembered to look around the stalls. That's why I gave him a piece of my mind. He was all excuses and sweet talk, where you would have stalked out and slammed the door on me."

Melkior was overjoyed that this was said in front of Don Fernando. He actually mumbled a *thank you*, which mercifully went unheard.

"Here you are, then," the editor handed a manuscript to Don Fernando. "Regretfully. All right?" They smiled at each other with an already hammered-out understanding.

Melkior caught up with Don Fernando on the stairs. They descended in silence. Don Fernando was trying to slide the manuscript into his inside pocket, but something was in the way, blocking passage, so much so that Don Fernando's small eyes flickered a bit in irritation.

"What, it won't fit in the pocket either?"

"Sorry?" said Don Fernando unpleasantly and rather sharply.

"I said, the article won't fit. Why did he reject it?"

"What makes you think he did?" Don Fernando had flushed a virginal pink.

"I know he did. Do you expect to keep a secret in a newspaper office? I don't have it from the editor—there are at least three people upstairs who are delighted."

"I don't know the other two," said Don Fernando, trying to muster a smile.

"But you know one? And that's me?" Melkior paused for a moment on the stairs. He suddenly felt a kind of painful sadness at the insinuation and asked Don Fernando, looking bemusedly down the stairs, "Why are you so evil-minded?"

"Who, me personally?" Don Fernando had regained ascendancy over Melkior.

"Both you personally and . . . people in general," and Melkior gestured hopelessly.

"My dear Eustachius, whatever's come over you? Ha, why does Maestro call you Eustachius, anyway? The editor told me a couple of first-class stories about him. That's what we were laughing at. Maestro is a splendid variety of madman."

"Splendid? I wouldn't say so. He's more of an uncorrupted cynic. A Thersites among all the shining heroes up there."

"So he is, up to a point . . ." Don Fernando was clearly trying to be *nice*. "As a matter of fact he ought to live in a tub, ha . . ."

"With a mind like his, an unwashed bottle would do every bit as well. He guzzles brandy. The tub is for the Dionysian liquid . . . or Diogenes, if that's what you meant."

"Yes, well . . . sure . . . But the way he does that job of his! I mean, the way he runs his city desk! The way he pecks passionately like a sparrow among the trash brought in by his garbage collectors (that's what he calls his reporters), as if he would use all that fecal waste matter, like a crazy alchemist, to distill at least a drop of some 'genuine' essence or other, be it somewhat dirty and poisonous—it would nevertheless be the *genuine* truth about people, a truth more authentic and real than all those majestic and authoritative politi-cal, and even so-called cultural, scribblings."

"He enjoys his mucky alchemy!"

"Well . . . I wouldn't rule out the personal experience."

"But he simply bathes in feces! He identifies with garbage be-cause he's a piece of garbage himself, and there are no libations there apart from the libation of filth dripping from his . . ."

"Why the sudden loathing, dear Eustachius—if you'll allow me to call you that?"

"Why the sudden love? I don't hate him—I feel pity for him if you must know, because I have a fair idea of where his *reveling in stench* comes from. But you, you'll never understand it. You're too busy tinkering with the model of your proto-Man to be able to perceive the dirty and swinish, semisuccessful and quite unsuccess-ful versions of him in the phenomenological world. You cannot love Maestro, you can't even see him. What you said about him isn't true. Anyway, you were not speaking because of him—you had something else on your mind."

"Your thought is far-reaching . . . and dangerous. You reveal . . . No, seriously now, the editor may have suggested such an affinity to me in the kind of laughter (and here I'm quoting you) Molière uses to deal with big issues. All I wanted to say was that even such a man—while being, as you put it, swinish, and while reveling in stench (which is, among other things, a well-turned phrase indeed) —even such a man has in him an integral, essential something, a nondegradable form that always manifests itself in some way, even as it revels in stench. This is what defines the personality after all. You yourself call him Thersites. So, what makes the parallel doable for you? Were nothing to him but the . . . fecal bath, how would he rise to the level of Thersites?"

Why's he saying all this? It's certainly not about Maestro. But what *is* it about?

"The editor, for one, thinks very highly of him—in a certain way, of course."

"He thinks very highly of anyone who can be useful to him."

"You're wrong. The editor is useful himself; I daresay he's very useful."

Don Fernando stressed the last words with a certainty stemming from a *distinct* way of looking at things. "You seem to buzz around petty details and get snared by them."

"What about his refusal to print your stuff in his paper? Do you find that useful, too?" Melkior tried to draw him out through vanity. Don Fernando smiled.

"Refusal to print my stuff? Only this one article . . . which is truly not suited to his paper. Or any other paper . . . for the time being."

Such an air of the clandestine!

"Tell me one thing . . ."

"You're sounding like Hamlet," Don Fernando gave an almost offended smile. "Never mind—I'll tell you everything I'm able to tell."

"What did you write about?"

"Oh, that?" Don Fernando reflected for a moment. "About the need for preventive dehumanization . . . or, shedding tragedy through skepticism."

Melkior made a stupid face.

"Is this something I could understand?"

"Maybe, if you try. You're a theater critic, after all."

"Then help me, for God's sake!" cried Melkior.

They were strolling around the square by the National Theater.

Don Fernando had dropped his arms to his sides and was staring straight ahead as he elaborated on his thoughts. Melkior watched him, tensely awaiting the results of the process.

"In buildings of this kind," Don Fernando pointed at the theater building, "people force themselves to be naïve for a few hours. Most tragedies, if not all, are founded on false assumptions. Take Hamlet: how is it that it never occurred to him, so intelligent and consequently so full of doubts, way back in the beginning—before the play begins—that Uncle Claudius might be capable of killing his father? I mean, wasn't the uncle a cad, a drunkard, and a lecher the whole time? Hamlet was bound to have noticed. How is it that he was not wary of the bastard rather than wondering after the fact how someone could be such a scoundrel? All right, granted, Othello is naïve (though again you feel there must be a limit to his naïveté), he could not imagine Iago to be such a beast. But whence the naïveté in Hamlet?"

"It's his youth, his faith in life, in people, in love." Melkior didn't think so.

"And all of a sudden, as the tragedy begins, he ages, he no longer has faith in life, in people, in love? Isn't this a false assumption? Is this not a false assumption that Hamlet fails to realize that his mother is a woman capable of going to bed with another man, or that Polonius is a professional Lord Chamberlain who will 'loyally' serve any king, or that Ophelia is a woman whom he might as well have dispatched to a nunnery long before using the same arguments, or that his school friends are young careerists who stand by their royal pal only as long as he is Crown Prince . . . and so on. It took his father getting murdered, his mother marrying his father's murderer, Polonius setting a trap that Ophelia walked knowingly into as bait, his own friends sending him to his death, for him to realize finally he'd been living among scoundrels. Too late. Too late for a Hamlet, and too naïve.

"Or imagine, for instance, just how idiotic Andromache is. She thinks she's being sly, but hers is a naïve and not at all feminine wile. To save her son she marries Pyrrhus formally, the Hyrcan beast as Hamlet described him, and immediately after the 'cunning' wedding she kills herself to remain faithful to Hector. How very clever! She's met Pyrrhus's condition for sparing her son's life: she has 'become his wife,' ha, and killed herself directly afterward, double ha-ha! Tragic indeed! And what, pray, is this terrible tragedy rooted in? A goose's logic: Pyrrhus must not kill my son now because I have done what he asked me to do. He is bound by his word. My dear fellow, don't you see that this is a piece of nonsense, though we are asked to see it as sublimely moving? I'm asked to believe, together with the tragic hen, that Pyrrhus is a gentleman. That he won't go berserk when he catches on to how he's been manipulated by a birdbrain and slay her entire household, all the way down to her cat, to take his revenge. No, I'm asked to believe in human greatness. *Merde!*"

What's Andromache to him or he to Andromache that he should be so wound up about her? For these were merely the advance troops, Melkior was waiting for the main body of Don Fernando's thoughts.

Don Fernando sensed the question with the instinct of a passionate analytical thinker.

"Odd, isn't it, that I should be talking about this?" He halted for an instant, looking Melkior in the eye in an almost provocative way. "I mean, what is Andromache to me? Or Hamlet for that matter? Or all that tragic affectation? And yet you didn't think to bring up Horatio. That would have been an objection worth making. Tragedy presupposes faith in goodness. Horatio is pure goodness, a naïve, magnanimous fellow, and yet he's merely a supporting character. That is why the existence of such a Horatio is not subject to doubt. He is an assumption outside the sum and substance of the tragedy, an almost accidental phenomenon. A satellite, which hasn't quite grasped the ins and outs of the dark constellation of tragedy. That is why I permit him to be good, because he doesn't matter."

"So he who *matters* must not be good?"

"He shouldn't . . . that is, he can't. He's responsible. He must build up his malice inside himself lest he begin believing in goodness. He must doubt. This means he must look out, watch, listen (even eavesdrop), catch words, turn them this way and that to discover their secret meaning, the menacing and dangerous idea. He will thus determine his own thinking, his attitude, his course of action. If I know there's a scoundrel who intends to set fire to my home (and there actually is such a scoundrel), I won't just sit by the fireside reciting 'To be or not to be' with tears in my eyes. I won't sit there believing that he might not set fire to it after all . . . won't wait to become a tragic character. You can be sure that I will load my rifle and sit in wait behind my window to pick the scoundrel off before he sets my home ablaze."

"But what if the scoundrel says to himself: if I don't torch the scoundrel's house he'll torch mine?"

"Never mind what the scoundrel thinks (I know anyway), the point is what he does. The point is that I must be stronger than he is, or at least more deft."

"So if I've got it right, 'preventive dehumanization' means ruling out the possibility of there being any goodness at all, it is the theoretical destruction of goodness?"

"Yes—temporarily destroying it, until conditions arise for it to exist in a genuine sense. Being good *in this world* is naïve and stupid. Anyhow it is a false goodness and consequently a false tragedy. We don't need tragedy to discover the dreadful truth. Indeed tragedy cloaks truth with the charm of art, it seduces us into enjoyment by lifting its soiled theatrical skirt coquettishly before us and showing the seamy sides of life with a fetching grin. Not even death itself is serious here. Nothing is serious, all is simply *beautiful* and desirable. But I want to see the truth naked, without its tragic rags. Because I *know* that underneath those rags lies something else tragic, a profound and genuine and terrible tragedy, one that no Racine or Shakespeare can help me with. I'm no Hamlet, I know straight from the start that my uncle means to murder my father and marry my mother, so in order to prevent it . . ."

"You kill him?"

"Of course, if only in theory."

"But how can you be sure that your uncle's going to murder?"

"How? Let's reply with a question: why shouldn't he murder—what's to stop him? Why shouldn't he, if it will get him all the pleasures he has dreamed of his whole life? You of course would not commit murder, but don't reason in terms of yourself. Our mistake and . . . our irreparable oversight is precisely that—reasoning in terms of ourselves. Which the scoundrel counts on—that we'll reason in terms of ourselves, that we won't smell a rat. But we should reason *on his terms*; that is why I say we ought to watch with doubt and distrust, we ought to *know* beforehand. But we're too deeply caught up with ourselves, we explore our weaknesses, believing ourselves to be some brand of terrible sinner. Meanwhile he prepares, he plots eluding notice, in perfect safety. It's too late *afterward* to smack your forehead: oh if only I had known, if only I'd had an inkling! Why is it that I never saw it, never thought, never paid attention before this? Too late—the deed is done. And now we ought to take our revenge, but we're not up to it. So we reflect: what's the use, what is the point of revenge when our father's gone and our mother's sharing the murderer's bed? We reason. 'Thus conscience does make cowards of us all.' We anguish. Which is exactly what the evil uncle wants—our anguish, our physical inaction; it spells safety for him. We make tragedies for people to weep, but he chortles and enjoys being used for the making of art. Art does kill him in the tragedy (or not, as the case may be), but it kills him in an *artistic*, symbolic way—and he doesn't give a fig for its symbols when he knows he's alive. And exults in being alive. He even enjoys the symbols, in which he sees someone else rather than himself, so that he will actually shed a tear over that Someone Else's fate, for the pleasure. Oh, we pay the scoundrel a tremendous tribute in tragedies! And in real life we leave him alone to savor his criminal plunder. We also leave him his life, which is not only undeserved but actually a threat to other lives. The scoundrel ought to be gotten rid of in time. Physically and simply, not symbolically; without ceremony and catharsis and tragi-pathos mumbo jumbo à la Aristotle."

"So we should kill preventively so as not to be killed?" concluded Melkior with a smile freezing on his lips. "But kill whom? By what criterion?"

"By a simple criterion, medical. There are symptoms. How does a surgeon know where to cut? Does he need a criterion? He simply pins down where the illness is hidden and what it is that is endangering the organism. This is largely a matter of talent, knowledge, intuition—but very often of simple cunning. The killer is lying in wait and the thing to do is provoke him. You've got to tease him out of the armor of his quiescence, to prod his murderous wishes awake. You will of course have observed such a character on the tram: sitting there with his legs stretched across the aisle, blocking the passage of others, everything there is his. Not that he does this purposely—he just feels like it. He doesn't think of his legs as an obstacle, for people to step over, around, grumbling at having to adapt to him. So you trod on his foot on purpose. Step on it good and hard, with all your weight! But you apologize right away, awfully sorry, didn't mean to, an accident, and so on . . . and then look at his face, look into his eyes: if you know how to look you'll discover a murderer. What a pleasure it would be for him to kill you, given half the chance! There's your 'criterion' for you!"

Don Fernando fell silent, wearing a sort of quiet sadness on his face, like someone who has had a good cry.

"Wait a minute," said Melkior without irony, indeed with concern, "who could possibly catch them all?"

"You're talking like a policeman!" frowned Don Fernando. "Then again, why not? That's what the job should be of any intelligent police force which genuinely protects people's safety—to catch murderers before they've committed the crime, instead of producing detective stories after the murder and inventing police geniuses and criminal heroes to tickle the fancy of small-time delinquents and romantic onanists."

"So what you're saying is . . . tread on people's feet in trams and then peer into their eyes? But isn't that a rather unreliable method, telling potential criminals by their eyes? There used to be this thing about low foreheads and beetle brows and skull shape . . . the so-called Lombrosian type . . ."

"There's something in that, too. But a man with a nasty look in his eyes is undoubtedly a potential murderer," said Don Fernando with certainty. "Just give him a chance, take a bit of a risk. Step on his foot—not literally, of course, not on a tram—I mean in a metaphorical sense . . . Incidentally, there's a way that is more reliable still. You mentioned low foreheads and beetle brows . . . and I say:

whoever's been physically *marked* by Nature in any way ought to be put under surveillance. All those ill-matched arms, uneven legs, floppy ears, enormous noses (puny ones as well, mind), hunched backs, squinting eyes, and particularly—and I say *particularly*—anyone under five foot five. I can well understand the suffering of midgets and I believe it was one of them who invented crime. Just look at them in their platform shoes, their craning necks, their broadly inclusive sweeping gestures, settling issues in a 'manly' way; even their voices sound stentorian and heroic. But that's not enough. They're after other deeds, the real, acknowledged kind, the ones that inspire fear and awe. They aspire to *greatness* rather than to being *normal*; they would rule us, whatever the cost. They gave us Napoleon and, so it seems, Caesar the epileptic, too. Therefore beware *the marked*, particularly *the diminutive*. They are haters and will stop at nothing."

"You'd end up with a large chunk of mankind 'under surveillance,'" remarked Melkior acidly. "But who would be doing the job? By what right?"

"By the right of the majority . . ." said Don Fernando vaguely, as if he himself didn't entirely believe this.

"But what makes you think the majority of people look 'nice'?"

"History, that's what!" Don Fernando sprang back to life, fortified by a fresh idea. "Every historical blackguard eventually paid his debt to mankind! But always too late, only after he'd been up to his eyes in human blood. Danton, Robespierre, Marat, and Saint-Just were too busy going after one another to notice the ambitious pint-sized general, and out he slipped between their legs to slaughter half of mankind for his greatness. Hitler should have been bumped off ten years ago (if not before) and Mussolini should have been given a resounding thrashing ten years before that until he cried and begged for mercy. He would have, too. As things stand, it will take a war and a victory at God knows what price (if we even win!) to finally strangle those two historical apes. It will be too late again, too late . . . because of that very same Hamlet-like inertia and naïveté."

"Do you think, then, that anything can be achieved, on a large scale, through personal terrorism and assassination?"

"Assassination, assassination, yes of course!" Don Fernando agreed with a curious kind of rage. "Give the scoundrel a taste of fear on his own hide! It's always educational! This seems to be the only kind of pedagogy these villains understand. Fear. Your fear and mine, that's what the scoundrel should be made to feel! If nothing else, it would give me satisfaction—'tremble, tremble, scoundrel,' as they sing in the opera."

Don Fernando took a breath. He was profoundly agitated, his face flushed bright red, the corners of his lips flecked with foam. He used a handkerchief to wipe his mouth, forehead, and cheeks, as if wiping a mask from his face. His features did in fact regain the exalted expression of his serene internal glow. He was now embarrassed by his excitement, letting the breeze of a kindly smile play over his face and conceal the shame.

"You seem, however, to prefer fairy tales of one sort and another," he said superciliously.

"What fairy tales?" said Melkior in surprise.

"Oh, Russian fairy tales about various forms of goodness . . . Such as the one about Alyosha Karamazov, the little monk. You even gauge that drunken cynic Maestro using the little monk as a standard. But he doesn't fit the standard, it's too narrow for him. Your standards are too strict, my dear Eustachius—and too regular. People are like stones: irregular in shape, heavy, scattered. It's the devil's own job bringing order to the lot, assembling them in one place and arranging them by this or that rule—and it's even worse hewing each individual stone. Indeed it's impossible to carve out what people like to call a 'moral profile.' Illusory is what it is."

This is something he has going on with himself, thought Melkior. I've never spoken to him about "goodness" or "standards." He must be struggling with some "little monk" of his own.

"Incidentally, you haven't asked me how all this fits in with my actual political convictions," asked Don Fernando suddenly, giving a dry and somehow malicious laugh.

"Now that you mention it, did you ever discuss this with Pupo?"

"With Pupo? Discuss what with him?" said Don Fernando in surprise.

"Why, this business of . . . of individual terror . . . and assassinations."

"Why with Pupo? Is he an expert on such things? He believes the man who bashed Trotsky's head in with an ice pick was a Mexican anarchist acting on his own initiative, that Tukhachevsky was spying for the Nazis, and so on . . . he believes a lot of things. He is of course against 'individual terror.' 'That's anarcho-individualism,' and he immediately reaches for the corresponding pigeonhole. Pupo's a sort of monk himself, but one who keeps an eye on his career—in fact, a defrocked priest who goes on believing through inertia, but in rather a Jesuit way. I've nothing to discuss with him."

"So I'm honored with this discussion?" smiled Melkior.

"You are a sensitive individual capable of *feeling* a thought. Not merely thinking (perhaps thinking even less), but also feeling a thought, which means keeping it constantly *in your mind* like private torment. The *Heautontimoroumenos*, murderer and victim in one and the same person, knife and wound, a vampire of your own heart, as Baudelaire put it. Your thought torments you with fear, I know it and appreciate it, because few people are capable of it, particularly in the way you are—and those drunken imbeciles at the Give'nTake mock you for it. I don't mock you, because fear is thought (and vice versa), and I should like to join you at this point, if I may. Our fear is the sensitivity of the thought with which we perceive the terrible future of our existence. (Not that the human future has ever been anything but dreadful.) Your fear is not insane, your quaking is not inane as a Quaker's, and yet there is in you (and this is where I leave you) a maniacal need to study the fear, to explore all its tonalities and tastes, from bitter to sweet. Sweet in particular. For there is a kind of pleasure in the sensation of fear (I remember it from childhood), a possibility of some obscure inner florescence taking place, of some strange solitary ripening going on to produce the black fruit of a particularly bitter wisdom. You have made yourself a home in there and you no longer search for a way out of the mousetrap—you have found your 'accursed' freedom inside. 'Accursed' because you exercise it in the pathetic manner of a prisoner for life who has found a 'great' pastime: drying his straw mattress straw by straw on the single ray of sun that falls into his cell . . ."

"Straw is, as we know, hollow. Are you sure it's in my mattress and not your head?" Melkior took offense and rejoindered rudely, which made Don Fernando flush pink.

"I'm sorry, I didn't mean it so offensively. I meant to say that fear has tricked your imagination, but it came out all wrong. That bit about the prisoner was particularly bad. Fear has hidden its hideous face, which the wise man finds is beneath him to contemplate and generally beneath the accomplished man to address. That is why I meant to say that your fear was highly refined, all the richer for the beauties of your unconventional character, brought to virtuoso level, as it were, like the subtlest of *vibratos* on a violin string (this with reference to trembling), elevated to the point of the highest— indeed musical—sensitivity, ceasing to be a miserable human con- dition and becoming a work of some crazed art instead. Your al- chemy has transmuted that filth into gold. That's why I admire . . . Forgive me for calling it crazed—after all, any art is crazed in a certain way . . . that's why I admire your heroism, for you know how to suffer. My fear is different. I don't want to suffer. I'm afraid of *what tomorrow may bring*, as it may well bring it tomorrow, and there's no rhetoric in it. I'm simply afraid for myself, for my pitiful life, like any ant that feels a storm brewing, and I have no particular 'spiritual values' in mind. I don't care what happens to paintings, to books, to arty rocks. I simply fear, henlike, for my unprotected head, which in my hour of fear is my greatest cultural value, for it's the only head that cares for me. To sum up, then: my fear is no violin *vibrato*, no *vibrato* at all, for that matter; there's no subtlety to it, no art, no beauty—it's intolerant, harsh, and aggressive. I don't propose to 'suf- fer for beauty,' I don't propose to cultivate fear like a poisonous flower garden. I'm less of a hero than you. I can't support fear—that's why I want to remove it from my life, like hundreds of millions of like-minded people."

"But how are you going to remove it?" asked Melkior with grave concern. "And who are your like-minded people?"

"Common people, that's who. Perhaps these very passersby

around us. They all want to get where they're going, to eat their lunch or kiss their wife, without the feeling of pressure in their mind, without a nightmare on their soul, with joy and certainty as if they will live forever. And that's reason enough for me to consider them 'my people'; they may not know it, but they belong to the large community of enemies of fear."

"How can you be sure they're 'your people'? They may just as well be on the other side, they may be in favor of fear, which such 'passersby' usually refer to as order. They are in favor of order under the knout, and you offer them your concept of freedom, which is disorder and anarchy in their eyes."

"What? Surely *this* is disorder, this general anxiety and uncertainty?"

"Anxiety and uncertainty for you, 'the enemy.' In their view, it's no more than you deserve: you aim to bring down their ideals, kill off the leaders they worship precisely because they inspire fear. They *want* fear."

"I'm not relying on those trained monkeys!" barked Don Fernando furiously.

"Whom are you relying on, then?"

"On men! On free, proud men who feel their human value, their dignity—"

"Again, this is a question of standards: what is *human value?*"

"Standards . . ." Don Fernando was smiling quaintly, in a "last straw" sort of way, like someone tried to the very limit of his patience. "I know just where to claim my right to the discovery of *new value* and I reject any attempt to drag in standards as a piece of bothersome claptrap! I have no time to waste on procedural ins and outs, the only thing that matters is *value*, and I have a perfectly clear idea of what it is!"

"So let's get on with the shooting, poisoning, setting of time bombs, bashing people's heads in with ice picks? And all that on I-know-who's-worthless grounds. Here take a look at the little man on the corner—that's right, the one selling newspapers."

The news vendor was crying the third edition of the *Morning*

News. He was indeed a little man, as Melkior put it—ageless, scaled down, as if he had been built with an eye to skimping on material, his arms and legs short, his head small and narrow, but with a hunk of trumpety nose protruding from it, along with two large and floppy ears topped by a vendor's cap like an upside-down pot, showing a logo for the *Morning News.* He was trumpeting through his nose, in a snot-ridden and tearful voice, as if begging alms, "Mawnen Ooze! Mawnen Ooze!"

"There, he, too, is a man, the Mawnen fellow. You can hear him braying, struggling for his existence. He, too, to use your words, is capable of feeling. If you were to come up to him and pull his ear (just look at those ears!) he would try to hit you, perhaps even kill you, for offending him. Because he has his pride. In other words, he *feels his value.* He is a value, by his standards, he, *Mr. Mawnen.* A *human value.* While Michelangelo's *David* in Florence, a fine figure of a nude young man (and incidentally, a masterpiece of human anatomy), large, self-assured, and proud, full of strength and daring, is not a man. He's not capable of 'feeling.' He's of stone. He isn't even 'human' enough to be able to utter the nonsense word *Mawnen* which that little freak over there *is* able to say. And yet *David* is a value, an enormous, unique value . . . or perhaps he isn't, perhaps you disagree—you said just now you didn't care for 'arty rocks'?"

"I didn't mean anything in particular, I meant it conditionally . . ."

"And I say, even 'conditionally,' that all the *Mr. Mawnens* in the world, however many there may be, and I'm sure they run into the hundreds of thousands, are not worth *David*'s left leg. And yet, listen to what I'm going to ask you, 'conditionally': supposing that saving *David* from destruction required the life of a single *Mr. Mawnen,* of our *Mr. Mawnen* over there, for instance, would you approve of the sacrifice?"

"That's a typically 'Russian' pointless question. A piece of pure Dostoyevskyism," muttered Don Fernando with intellectual disgust.

"Even granted it's 'Dostoyevskyism,' the question is there, regardless of who posed it or why. Never mind, you needn't answer it yourself, let's ask the others, the 'common people,' 'your' people, the 'passersby.' Hardly anyone would approve. Not even you yourself, in particular view of your disregard for 'arty rocks.' Were we to show them our wretched news vendor sniffling on that corner over there and tell them, We're going to pounce upon him: right, go die for *David* (David who? I don't know him!), all of 'humane' mankind would rise most resolutely against the very idea of *such* a price being payable for the salvation of a 'man of stone.' All of a sudden all of mankind becomes 'uncultured.' Forgetting the unique, irredeemable value of Michelangelo's sculpture and throwing itself with the full force of unbridled philanthropy at the little man of a news vendor. Raising him to the point of being an extraordinary, 'human' value, which of course not even *Mr. Mawnen* himself can properly understand. He becomes an exceptional, indeed legendary person (many a *Mr. Mawnen* has gone down in history that way), a kind of saint and martyr. And why is all that? Only because *Mr. Mawnen* is 'capable of feeling.' The mere elementary sensitivity sets that hideous body above a genius's unique and unrepeatable work. Because *Mr. Mawnen* has an epidermis capable of feeling pain, while *David* is unfeeling stone. Therefore long live the epidermis, death to 'stone'!"

"This is a conclusion in favor of the epidermis and generally in favor of the sensitive-living, stupid, and mindless, 'valueless,' ugly tissue of a freak who has picked up a handful of attributes along the way which under very superficial conventions are granted to man, too. The *David* is also a synthesis of attributes, which, by somewhat more cautious conventions, have turned stone into a 'man.' They both *exist in some way.* Don't you feel that the Siamese concrescence of those two existences, no matter how it might intentionally be arranged to suit my purpose, is a question of existence in general? The question of *who* and *what* should go on living. Chang or Eng? But how is one to decide—that is to say, by what standards?"

"But I can't wait until the standards have been agreed upon—I must live *now*. I must act, I must continually make decisions."

"Well, whom do you find for: *David* or the news vendor?" Melkior slipped the question in with derisive curiosity.

"Sometimes for *David*, sometimes for the news vendor," replied Don Fernando at once, without pausing to think.

"Depending on the circumstances, is that it?"

"Of course. It's easy to find for *David*. What he stands for can never be a threat. But that which can be conceived by the news vendor, the news vendor idea, the freak idea . . ."

"But I'm not talking about an idea, I'm talking about this here flesh-and-blood news vendor, that nose and those ears, do you understand, the man who's selling *Mawnen* . . ."

"That's just what I mean—if those noses and ears, if hundreds of thousands, if millions of those *Mawnens* usurped the right to assess all values, if they established themselves above us as the masters of our lives . . ."

"That's impossible," Melkior interrupted him halfheartedly, merely for the sake of contradiction; he did not believe it impossible himself. He meant to provoke Don Fernando.

"Impossible?" asked Don Fernando in an almost offended tone. "Impossible to find such an idea for freaks (and I'm not talking about only physical deformities here) which will draw everyone like flies to vomit? (After all, haven't they already been drawn in?) Impossible to tell them: you have been chosen to live! Destroy and slaughter anyone who is not like you! In the name of your superiority! You are the chosen species! My dear chap, do you think they won't form an alliance? You bet they'll form one, because they have something in common. Each one of them has an epithet—like those notorious rulers *The Lame, The Stupid, The Beardless*—implanted deep in their flesh and bones, where it humiliates and offends them, and that's what binds them together. And what's going to bind together the so-called normal people? The proud, pure, strong *Davids*? They have nothing in common, no shared trait, no grounds for 'brotherhood.' They have no attributes, they're 'only human.' Each one of them is normal and good and honest and handsome in his own way and knows of none other. Each one of them is a discrete individual, a solitary contemplative monad, and in between them there is an uncommunicative and desperately senseless void. The strength of the freaks is that they are organized and dynamic, because there is something that binds and propels them, and so they bring us down piecemeal, finding us unprepared, in an hour of weakness, in 'prayer,' that is to say in an hour of sensitive poetic contemplation, in hours of wonderment and love's rapture."

"There are other, more robust raptures, more than 'sensitive,' amounting to a force, a mighty force indeed! One capable of standing up to . . ." Melkior was speaking with the conviction of personal experience: he had in mind the Stranger in his room.

"Where are they? Show me!" shouted Don Fernando, irate. "Show me these 'robust raptures'! Haven't they left us high and dry? Have they not 'signed a pact'? They've given the murderers the green light!"

"The question is, for how long?"

"Until you and I bite the dust!" Don Fernando gave a malicious laugh.

"So you really are afraid?" Melkior looked at his face: it was red with anger.

"Have I ever hidden that? I told you just now I'm afraid. Yes, I fear for my hide, and very 'selfishly' at that. More selfishly than even you, because I aim to defend my hide! Not *protect* it—*defend* it, by all and any means, whatever you choose to call them! Who's the 'robust rapture'—somebody at a secret meeting selling me the idea that 'individual terrorism is no solution'? What *is* the solution then —those two 'historical' signatures on that pact of Hitler's? When I've been betrayed and brought to despair, I act desperate, damn it. What do I care now for Michelangelo or your casuistic problems: *David* or the news vendor? to hell with both! I call for terrorism, for extermination of tomorrow's murderers in our midst. That's why I wanted to publish the article. . . ."

Don Fernando had grown tired. He sensed his failure to *convince* his man. I spoke badly, in haste, in rage, helter-skelter . . . he thought angrily.

"I'll make this into a novel one day . . . if I have the chance," he said after a longish silence. "I didn't explain the main thing well enough—what it is like when your teeth really chatter . . ."

He fell silent, somehow sapped and empty. He looked straight ahead in solitary disappointment, gloomy. He kept taking off his hat and waving it strangely about in an unconscious gesture as if shooing away invisible bats: the *bitter thoughts* were still buzzing around him, preventing him from getting his face to resume its small superior smile behind which he normally hid the false divinity of his inaccessibility. But there he was—he had thrown the tabernacle wide open, the divine bird had flown the coop! What was there left to hide? He hated Melkior for his own failure.

Hell, was he being serious about "preventive killing"? Melkior was suddenly offended by a fresh thought: the man wants a Smerdyakov! An executioner! That's why he's been telling me all this! He doesn't want to get his hands dirty. He, the founder of "new values"! The intellectual instigator . . . acting from the rear. He thinks I, a desperate man, would . . .

Melkior shuddered. He looked "up" at Don Fernando's face (for all that they were of an equal height Don Fernando's head had always seemed to him to be "up above") and saw the likable mask, but the eyes . . . the eyes radiated a dark, evil look. Why, he's a murderer, he thought fearfully, a murderer by his own definition. With his personal safety guaranteed. "To provoke the killer . . . to jerk his murderous wishes awake." Is that *having your teeth chatter?* . . . And there I was this morning defying a tram! What a delusion!

Melkior laughed, commiserating.

"Imagine a man on tram tracks . . ." but Don Fernando had left him without a word. He had set off, with his long hurried stride, through an alley lined with trees which had majestically woven their branches into a triumphal arch . . . This is how rulers are saluted, said Melkior with an affronted sneer. That head deserves it, and he turned unconsciously to follow the needle of his love's compass, toward the Theater Café. It's not too early, she might have come out by now . . .

Restless is the autumn air . . . restless is the autumn air . . . he kept repeating stupidly, suddenly saddened to the bone.

Coming from afar was the news vendor's pitiful, nasal voice *Mawnen ooze, Mawnen ooze,* as if the man were begging for mercy. Don Fernando's already grabbed hold of the man's ear, thought Melkior, and is dragging him off to hold him accountable. For Michelangelo's *David.* You're one of the crowd of nasty little men who'll draw together around the heap of vomit! One of the chosen freaks just off the leash. "Kill, slaughter, is that it? You're one of them! You hideous little creep!" The poor man has no inkling of his hide being (theoretically!) at stake.

Mawnen ooze . . .

Quiet, you wretch! Don Fernando Karamazov walks the streets dreaming of his "preventive murder" theory. Looking for a Smerdyakov, an executioner. To murder you—or Hitler, it's not yet clear which. But one of you has got to confirm the theory; that much *is* clear. People of all countries, dehumanize. Preventively. Whatever the cost. Tragedy is no more. It has been abolished by skepticism.

He was parodying Don Fernando's thoughts with malicious glee. Bitter.

The day was absurdly clear and warm; a capricious October scherzo, as if summer were coming back. Melkior walked toward the Theater Café slowing the eagerness of his search: I won't find her. He feared her absence as if it were an attack from ambush. The terrace was lively and noisy—no Viviana.

He poked his head into the café proper: the emptiness grinned at him hopelessly. But from one of the corners cawed Maestro's brandy-inflamed gorge:

"O, Eustachius the Outpoured! You're like water for watering flowers. But in this flower garden there is no Lily, or Ljerka, stemming from *Lilium candidum* or white lily. The lily hasn't opened its petals yet, the white flower's still sleeping. Come closer that I might kiss, or rather lick slick, your feet which brought you here."

He was well and truly drunk. His head was a fit-to-burst red and his eyes had a madman's glaze. Sitting at his table were several junior reporters from the office; among them Freddie, sporting an offended smile. He was not, as even Melkior could see, at the center of attention; this was in fact why he was angry and offended. "Let's have your opinion, Eustachius the Metaphysical, for this is indeed a metaphysical point. I keep saying so to our protagonist but he will only give me a derisive smirk, as you can see there on his physical physiognomy—he doesn't even know what metaphysics is. We're just talking about the fate of various tiny animals, metaphysically. I don't see why people shouldn't talk metaphysically about the fate of tiny animals. A worm in an apple, for instance. Living alone like a curmudgeon, a hypocritical hermit in a solid full universe. Board and lodging, possibly with a bit of light entertainment thrown in— vermicular masturbation, for all we know. Happiness we can't even begin to fathom. Yes, but how long can it last? Until some god or other feels like an apple. Tooth or knife, it makes no difference which, rending and laying waste to the vermicular world like dreadful inexorable fate. Reaching the worm, tearing it in half . . . Or not reaching it, huh? *That* is the question. To be or not to be—for a worm. That is beneath a Hamlet—am I right, oh Exalted One?" and Maestro squinted derisively at Freddie. He then spoke to Melkior, pointing his cigarette at the actor: "Pestering them up at the theater to cast him as Hamlet, but he hasn't even read that bit about the worms mediating between king and beggar, or rather the beggar's bowels; he skipped it, it was so yuck! He only reads the soliloquies. You, Frederick, are as hollow as a bamboo stalk."

Freddie swung a fist at Maestro, but the reporters grabbed and held his arm midair. He was pale and trembling. So Maestro's protasis had been going on for some time then, thought Melkior with pleasure. I hated him a minute ago in conversation with Don Fernando; he was now wondering at it, was even ready to defend him from Freddie if necessary.

"Let go of me!" mumbled Freddie, his mouth full of holy anger. But nobody was holding him any more: the reporters were sitting so closely on either side of him (in front of him the table, behind him the wall) that he couldn't get up. To make things worse, the reporters were laughing.

"So Brutus raised his little paw against Caesar? Ho-ho," said Maestro coolly, like a celebrity after a failed attempt on his life. "By the way, speaking of paws, apropos there's an anecdote about a wolf. Shall I tell it? But mark you, children, it's not Little Red Riding Hood."

"Tell us, tell us!" clamored all. Only Freddie was staring sullenly at the floor.

"What about you, Eustachius the Patient?"

"Go ahead."

"Apparently there were some foresters walking through a forest—naturally enough, it being their trade. We walk in various ellipses and spirals, which is *our* trade . . . and a digression in this narrative, isn't it? There were wolves in the forest, and the foresters were afraid, of course. But one of them said, 'Don't be afraid, I've got a handsaw,' and they relaxed again. It did occur to them that a handsaw was hardly of any use with a wolf; then again, they thought, the man surely knew what he was talking about. And so on they went without fear. Suddenly a wolf appeared out of nowhere and went for them. They cried, 'Oh God, we're done for!' But the one with the handsaw said again, 'Don't be afraid, brethren and fellow-citizens,' went right up to the wolf, grabbed hold of one of its legs, and zip, zip, zip, sawed it off. He was, as could have been gathered by now, a cunning and nasty man, was that forester-sawyer: he threw the sawn-off leg into a church, through a window which happened to be open because the sexton was dusting the saints off for the Easter holidays. And the wolf whined and whined, helpless; I ask you, what can a wolf do if he's got only three legs, not to mention the pain. He had no idea where his fourth leg had gone as he hadn't seen where the forester threw it—it never occurred to him, of course, that the leg might have been in the church. Even if it had, he couldn't have gone in, not being baptized . . . Inside, the sexton suddenly saw the freshly sawn-off leg, still bleeding, in front of the altar, and thought one of the Elect had just finished his duel with Satan and sent his trophy to the Lord, throwing it at His most holy feet. Full of the fear of God, the sexton took the leg to the priest as one better at understanding this kind of thing. But the priest only turned the leg this way and that and couldn't understand a thing. It was a miracle all right, but one he could make no sense of. He found no holy mark on the leg except for the blood and the nasty wound, so he sent the leg on to the bishop in town. The bishop, the canons, and all the religious teachers examined it closely for three days, but came up with no acceptable explanation for the miracle, so they had the leg well salted and sent it to Rome to the *Supreme See*. Over there, the cardinals and prelates, the learned Jesuits, and the most excellent of theologians got together and started leafing through the ancient books, patristic and gnostic, Tertullian's, Origena's, and Augustine's —even some Aryan and heretical writings—to explain the missive of the leg one way or another. After many sessions of councils and cardinals' *collegia* and Jesuit secret seminaries and Dominican plots (they wanted to profit from the event by inserting one of their people into a secret congregation), the learned fathers came to the seemingly unanimous conclusion that it was indeed a paw of Satan's, severed in a holy duel with a heavenly saint, most probably Saint George, who had had long-standing accounts to settle with the unregenerate bandit. The way the flesh was fringed around the cut was proof enough that it had been Saint George's work—he wielded a truly vicious battle-ax. Our poor wolf's leg was added to the collection of dogmatic evidence of Satan's existence and the Lord's power over him. As for the wolf itself, it's probably even now hobbling about the forest cursing its short temper, as this happened quite recently, only three years ago, in the mountains of Guadarama, in Spain."

"Nonsense!" Freddie forced the word through his teeth in unrestrained intellectual disgust as the reporters' cheeks puffed up with choked back laughter in expectation of Maestro's rejoinder.

"Nonsense, Frederick, that the Jesuits took a leg for a leg?" asked Maestro patiently.

"The whole story's nonsense!" said Freddie with undiminished disgust. "That bit about the sawing is the biggest idiocy of the lot. The church, too . . . How can there be a church in the middle of a forest?" He was trying to show he was nobody's fool.

The reporters exploded with laughter. Melkior laughed, too, but in a private, separate way, because he was only standing by their table and did not seem entitled to full participation. But Freddie chose none other than Melkior's "separate" laughter for venting his anger. In addition this was an opportune occasion, there were old scores to settle . . .

"Look who's laughing!" he looked Melkior up and down from below. "Plucked a feather from a hen's bum and took it up to scribble, the hack!"

Melkior said nothing, but he was no longer laughing. He felt the color draining from his face and anger raging in his bloodstream, bestial, murderous. Don Fernando flashed for an instant in his memory: I now have an evil look in my eyes. He failed to decide right away to spin on his heel and leave, and made an immediate note of the mistake. Now he had to stay on, even if only a moment longer.

"All our means of expression come from one bum or another, Frederick," said Maestro, coughing hoarsely. "Eustachius's quill, as you have observed, is from a hen's, and your speaking trumpet is from a human's. You're at a higher evolutionary level, no offense meant."

Right. Melkior's side had won and he could now leave. It was another blow dealt to the adversary: departing with a triumphant smile.

Maestro shouted something after him, he required his presence still.

"Frederick, you exude the reek of cretinism," was the last he could hear from behind, as bait for his return.

Where to? Perhaps chance would toss him some small pleasure. To run into Viviana. He had still believed it possible this morning, for love will cultivate just such a religion: that of chance which sometimes transforms the world in an instant, granting the desperate man a rare boon.

He watched the shop windows. He saw nothing but himself. A narcissist projection, he thought. He winked conspiratorially at his reflection in the window, noticing only some instants later that a shop girl who was arranging something in the window had smiled at him from inside. He looked back without breaking his stride: she was still gazing at him, with the same smile on her face. Pretty. There was a chance. The possibility of starting something new. If he now returned and signaled to her: I'll be waiting on the corner at noon. He would gesture at his watch, count to twelve on his fingers, nod toward the corner, she would give a slight nod, coquettishly lowering her eyelids; she'd agree, happily. Or she would stick her tongue out: take that, you creep! What do you take me for? I'm not that kind of girl. *I'm* not for sale. They get better offers. Freddie's hatred is terrible. Murderous. For the sake of twelve female fans. Apostles. Fallen for him. The fallen angels. Is this the region, this the soil, the clime? Everything has its own devil. On top of us and inside us. The patron devil of motion and function. The devil has now set my legs in motion, taking me . . . where? Well, he will have seen to that.

In a shop window, an elegantly dressed mannequin was in a discreetly balletic stance, a sly expression. Embarrassed at being watched by all and sundry. Melkior gave her a long, hard look. She dropped her eyes in shame. She would have fled if she could. Well, Melkior said to her, that's what you're there for, miss—to be looked at. He was trying to imagine her naked. I may have seen you naked, come to that. Many a time had he watched the mannequins at night being changed in shop windows behind carelessly drawn gray curtains. Like in a charmed brothel, those stiff, waxen anemic naked ladies with the faces of virgins. The Pompeiian Lupanar after Vesuvius erupted. He was trying to imagine her naked: the gray fabric flowing down her narrow, curved hips, fitting closely in front over the daintily convex delicate breasts. Tits, he said, because he had stripped her naked. He found himself weirdly lusting after the dainty dead girl. And the painful source of lustful restlessness was surfacing gradually as a fear of the similarity of that waist, those (slender) long legs, the narrow hips, those breasts, that fetching motion frozen in mid-stride, those slim, long fingers which she held slightly splayed like a bather going in for a dip. Look—all of it was actually moving in the window: the legs were beginning to walk, the hips to sway, the arms to swing; all of a sudden Viviana emerged from the mannequin! He thought he had gone mad. But no, it *was* Viviana moving in the window. She was crossing the street. He drew into himself, staring alarmed at her reflection in the glass. The sun was beaming down all over her, she was carrying radiance. He was already blinded by the terrible glare, and his eyes no longer saw anything. But he sensed with his whole body the approach of the fateful star from the mind-numbing skies of chance. He was being demolished inside by a dreadful disorder in his body and mind and thought. He could make nothing of his entire self except for a chaotic sense of awe. Could chance be so cruel as to catch him totally unprepared? He was aware of his long nose and moronically grinning face. And his arms: long, ponderous. He tucked his hands into his pockets. He felt relieved after this little act of tidying up. After achieving a clearer, better defined, more masculine image of a blasé gad about town with his hands in his pockets, an aimless, boredom-driven stroller. The difference that hands in pockets made! It was a great discovery of salvation, as if a comet were approaching. He was ready for a collision of worlds.

The shop window had attracted her attention. But he thought she had spotted him and went immobile like an insect faking death. He got interested in something or other down there in the corner, he even bent down to take a closer look. The eccentric; God knows what he'd discovered. She had flown up to the window like a butterfly, indeed she collided with the glass in her greed of watching; he heard a slight tap, that must have been her forehead. He felt his playacting falling flat and was out of his role again. There were his hands—not in his pockets—and the nose, and the moronic face. And he made an attempt to flee the stage. The movement near her broke off a morsel of precious attention (a male was standing there, after all) and she discovered him like a frightened cricket in the grass. He surrendered. Mercy.

"Well? What do you fancy?" she asked suddenly.

"Her," he said pointing at the mannequin. He was being "bizarre." "She looks like you."

"The mannequin? I don't know whether I ought to take offense." As indeed she didn't. She was smiling irresolutely, fifty-fifty, just in case.

"She's awfully well built." He had his hands in his pockets again by now, and that was how he delivered his line: hands-in-pockets style. He was pleased to be carrying it off.

"Yes, that's all you men care for—the body."

The body disturbed his diaphragm, queasily. Maestro had sold his *body* to the clinic, yes, but the word she had chosen hurt Melkior much more intimately, more sadly, like grief over the loss of a kind of innocence.

"You're frowning? Would you say it wasn't true?"

"What?" He was losing the thread. Chance's festivity had been disturbed.

"That men . . ."

". . . have generally had their way with her? No doubt."

She gave him a surprised and hurt look. "Who are you talking about?"

"Her," and he nodded in the direction of the mannequin. "I've seen her naked at night, being pawed by men. Lustfully, with no tenderness at all. I think they're all harlots, those shop window dolls."

She was laughing. But seeing that he was not, she got serious and anxious. "How strange." And she touched him with her hand like someone touching a sleepwalker to wake him.

He had come to feel at home playing the madman and was loathe to abandon the role so soon. He felt confident and superior in psychological games where she could not follow him while he could say just about anything in lunatic allegories.

"Those shop windows are nothing but small-time brothels. The girls stripping naked at night, receiving customers, mainly shop assistants who behave like impoverished princes of dethroned dynasties. All but dancing with them."

She gave a short, insecure laugh.

"I've no idea what you're talking about, Mr. Tresić. Have you by any chance been celebrating something today?"

"Drinking? No." He was feeling a kind of wretched happiness; fearing that it was going to leave him, he quickly went on in Ugo's manner: " 'No, my lady, no, I'm sober indeed, of intoxication. I have no need when in such a fetching patch of sky, made golden by the sun on high, I behold . . .' and so on. We could have a drink somewhere though. But not at the Theater, if you please. Maestro and Freddie are in there, unless one or the other isn't dead by now."

"They can both be for all I care," she said coldly and maliciously. "I'm afraid I can't have that drink. I've been making a round of the shops all morning, looking for some fabrics for my aunt. Why don't you come along to keep me company—if you have nothing more worthwhile to do, that is."

"More worthwhile—well . . ." he made a sweeping movement with his hand as if to indicate something far away. "But I truly have nothing more pleasant to do," he said with unrestrained delight. "I'll follow you anywhere, even to . . . Cythera, which doesn't exist, Viviana."

"Funny you should say that. I had almost forgotten about my name. I like what you call me very much."

"So do I. But Viviana doesn't exist either. I invented her."

"I thought I was Viviana?"

"You are and you aren't. You are to me. Or not. What you really are I don't want to know. Nonny nonny no—I don't want to know."

"Singing?" She was laughing. His elation flattered her.

"That was the Duke of Mantua's aria. Does my singing bother you?"

"Not at all. Do go on."

"Unfortunately that was the end of the aria."

"You're such an amusing fellow. That time at MacAdam's I thought you were a horrible pessimist."

So much for "exemplar," thought Melkior in passing.

"Indeed I am something of the kind on working days. But today's a holiday. Incidentally, why do you call my friend MacAdam?"

"That's what that stinking, rotten . . ."

"Maestro?"

"Yes. That's what Maestro calls him. There's a language, he says, where it's the word for asphalt. Stupid as asphalt, he meant."

"And you hate him terribly?"

"Mac?"

"No, Maestro."

She halted in front of a shop window. Offended. To avoid replying. But Melkior, too, seemed to have vaporized beside her: she was totally absorbed in observation, taking no further notice of his presence.

He felt miserable and superfluous. He followed her faithfully and dejectedly. She went into shops with the self-important dignity of a grand customer. Rifling, plucking, touching, pinching . . . Pushing away mountains of fabric. He could see the assistants' sweaty armpits: lifting their arms, taking down bolts of cloth from the shelves, stars from the sky, here you are, Miss, rolling out the bolts with easy sweeping gestures, intoning the usual textile lauds. She turning away with the fetching disgust of an overpampered taste, spotting this, that, the other, it can't be, you had it only yesterday, here, let me see that one up there, no, not that, darn!, hands up, armpit sweat, armpit smell, oh for fresh air! Give it a miss, Miss! The mess on the counter tops, the multicolored massacre of merchandise. You don't seem to have anything I need. The grand exit. Dignified. Taste above all.

Melkior felt the shame of shared guilt for torture inflicted. But he went on following her docilely like an Ivan, a servant, a martyr. She gave him only an occasional smile to show that she now acknowledged his presence. The insult of it he felt only later, when considering the small kindness thrown his way. But the kindness began recurring at ever shorter intervals as an apology, as tidbits to a lapdog, as a reward for fidelity. And he followed her with gratitude, aquiver with the pleasure of her nearness. A wealth of curves moving within reach. The up-down-up-down of the two exquisite hemispheres of most holy flesh (kiss left, kiss right), the rustle of tightly stretched stockings, of full legs passionately fondling each other in the skirt's semidarkness, joined to the Mound of Venus, to the Delphian gorge at the foot of Parnassus. Oh Pythian mystery, Oh weird sister, will I ever be the thane of Viviana? Nay, you shall be more, king, you shall be king! screamed the astounded Fool as if seeing the blood of one murdered in his sleep. He hankered for grapes, for the eating of grapes: the crisp globules popping open between the teeth (the cranky worm? it's in the apple), the juice flowing down the throat, the sun's sweet juice that has not matured to the vertigo of fermentation and become wine-the-lad, the alcohol brave. Ugo drinks the must, acidy-sweet, at the Give'nTake, at doctor's orders, he has a spot on his liver. From alcohol. For he's a jolly good fellow. *October's gentle breath . . .*

"He's nowhere to be seen today," he said, glumly contemplating the barrow of the man who bought used bottles and kept shouting at the top of his voice that he did. For Glassville, he thought in passing. "Was he out drinking last night?"

She gave him a cursory interrogative look, but all her attention was directly sucked in by the shop window.

"Because he usually makes a night of it," insisted Melkior, as if he meant to extort an admission from her. "He would still be asleep now." He looked at his watch: "Why, of course, it's not ten yet. He's asleep."

"Who's asleep?" she asked distractedly, absorbed in some fresh textile phenomenon in a display. "What do you think of the yardage over there for a two-piece suit? A nice classical one, close-fitting, eh? Let's go in to have a closer look—it doesn't look bad in the window. Who did you say was asleep? I'll be disappointed again when I see it up close, I know myself. It all looks lovely in the window, but as soon as I take the stuff in my hands it feels like matting, like a horse blanket. Sackcloth, really. I'm awfully unhappy when I have to buy something. I keep thinking there's got to be something better somewhere else. That's the story of my life. I always end up disappointed."

Sure enough, she bought nothing this time either. She had everything taken down from the shelves, turned the lot upside down, and went out again. Disappointed.

"What did I tell you?" she said all hot and bothered, splotches coming out all over her face. Who is she angry at? She's gone a bit ugly even, he smirked to himself with a kind of glee. Look, she's even got tears in her eyes!

"No, no, I tell you," she said, barely managing to hold back the tears. "Nothing ever works for me. Nothing, nothing, ever! Don't laugh at me, it's true."

"I'm not laughing," but inside he was, impudent and vengeful. He was deriding the mannequin-like sorrow that robbed him of the importance of his existence with her, making him a lonely companion: he was trotting along by her side all but unnoticed. He suffered grumpily. Homeomeries, the great-grandmothers to atoms, the seed of the world according to Anaxagoras, I know about them, too. He was reminding himself of his own importance, to prevent himself from sinking. He was clutching at straws. At homeomeries. Embraced by Aristotle, too. How well-shaped and pretty her mouth is, the lower lip slightly swelling—for a *kiss!* But no, it's not only a *kiss.* Oh love, for delights! The subjective derivative of proliferation. The bait. The biblical apple. The warbling. Come to me, darling, we'll have a lovely time. Enka naked. Kior! Oh, Kior . . .

He kept trying to ward off the black fillings in Ugo's wide-open, lustful mouth, which guzzled lechery with kisses. The fleshly feminine existence. If I am then I am what am I. The pride of the body. The breasts making their announcement in advance, trumpeting to the world to tell it who is coming. The fascinating damned holy leg tapping the patient Earth's head with pointed sandal, the elevation of the rump. Here she comes, here comes the proudly exalted empress of the world. Noses jerking after her, eyes staring, tongues dropping. The great drooling of mankind. While NATURE, the old seductress, the Madam of The Great Brothel, murmurs contentedly, Aren't my girls lovely?

"I buy bottles! Bottles! Old newspapers, bottles!" the voice of one crying in the wilderness, issuing a final warning. *Vanitas vanitatum et omnia vanitas.* Repent while ye still have time. The Great Pestilence is upon us. It's ravaging these lands. Say your prayers and sell your bottles. Old newspapers, too. Bottles.

"I just don't see what they want those newspapers for," she spoke up derisively. "Forever whining about things. Now, the bottles I can understand . . . but the old newspapers? What can they possibly need trash for?"

"To cook and recook, and make into new newsprint."

"New newspapers from old? No wonder you can't find anything worth reading in the papers. Just a load of rubbish, nothing but war and bombs. They've nothing better to do."

"While they could be weaving marquisette . . ." Where had he come up with "marquisette"? He wondered himself.

"Why marquisette?" But the penny dropped: "You're making fun of me, aren't you? Well, I did tell you I was looking for cloth . . . for Aunt Flora. But there's no point in boring you. I'll go on alone."

Melkior was afraid she might abandon him mid-street. "No, Viviana, please don't, I'm not bored at all. I only said, wouldn't it be more useful to weave pretty fabrics for pretty women? To make the world a more beautiful place. Then you'd find what you're looking for."

"Ah, if only I knew what I'm looking for!" she admitted with a sincere smile. "I have to find it first to discover what it was I was looking for. I'm over the moon when I finally find it. And I don't mean just the cloth—that's who I am."

That's who I am—did she mean "unfortunately" or "hooray"? For there was neither sad tinge nor boastful triumph in her voice, it was a simple statement of fact: anything goes—I'll see what you have to offer.

Melkior was offering himself. Offering up his person with all his heart and soul, in order to be found, discovered. Here I am, Viviana, with all the devotion of a love which . . . No, they prefer charm boys, euphoric babblers using fetching lies to decorate a night. A wonderful night. The very stars were bursting with laughter. Wow, what a time we had!

She has been sucked dry with kisses, gnawed bare by those black fillings. She has got the "wonderful night" circled around her eyes in a spreading sfumato of carnal blue. The stars of pleasure are even now bursting in her pupils. She is still being drenched with caresses. Viviana! Rattling inside him was a shattered sky, Ugo was stomping on the shards.

They walked down a street thick with special offers and passersby. A warm and idle morning. Elbows, shoulders, legs. Heads turned in salute to shop windows. Noses and one ear each in profiles. Eyes, greedy, snatching in passing at the fetishes behind the thick panes of glass of the sanctuaries. Inside, priests and Pharisees discovering with delight the secrets of the genesis of pleasing shapes, deluxe qualities, the wonders of the most-moster-mostest of sophisticated civilization. Suddenly, among the splendor-lovers' ecstatic profiles, Melkior spotted a heretic *en-face* scornfully erasing the bustling fairground enthusiasm and leaving in its wake grave concern. The Stranger strode in a "superior" manner towering above all the heads, even though he was no taller than they. Melkior spotted him a long way off. Instinctively he ducked his head down, dived into the dancing waves of heads, shoulders, bodies in motion, moving on through, and hung his head like a culprit. He wished to dissolve like an anonymous droplet in the thick stupid sea of senseless motion, to pass unnoticed, invisible. In the company of this pretty, *unnecessary* (ah, Viviana!) female I'm loitering among the props of a superficial, irresponsible life, suspected in *his* mind of being an accomplice, perhaps even a believer.

But the Stranger was moving through the crowd headed directly for him. He was cutting his way through the thick rolling magma like someone wishing to meet a man amid all the frivolity and to offer him his hand. He's spotted me. So . . . Melkior straightened up like a man, stood apart from the throng and made his way toward the Stranger, leaving Viviana agog in front of billows of silk in a shop window. He had his hand ready to proffer, along with a question about a good night's sleep . . . but he noticed that the man was looking over his head, into the distance, with the eyes of a railway inspector, of a man responsible for regular traffic flow. In this way the Stranger passed by Melkior (for it would have been silly to say *over him*) like a mute and hermetic armored train with a vital mysterious destination at some unintelligible distance.

Melkior looked after him, disappointed, cast aside, superfluous at this "historic moment." Now, Danton would have halted, perhaps even offered a hand. But this Dzhugashvilovich . . . He felt embarrassment at his own outstretched hand, at his thoughtful question, "Did you have a good night's sleep?" at his puritanical renouncement of Viviana.

"Nice," she took hold of his elbow, "and me looking all over for you. Trying to give me the slip?"

"I was trying to avoid encountering a man . . ." He felt her fingers and his own embarrassment at the lie.

"Or a woman?"

"No, a man," he mouthed, almost repentant, but he was pleased by her suspicion though he knew it was no more than a stab at a conventional flirtation. Which was true—she followed with no retort to his repeated claim. So that's how it is—she doesn't care, man or a woman. What on earth am I wasting my time here for? He was beginning to feel tired, for one thing. In need of sleep, hungry, tormented by dreams, thoughts, and wakefulness, he wished to sit down somewhere, alone, to rest from the nearness of her. Gloomily to ruminate on a happy love, withdrawn, in solitude, *in the dark . . . I watch your pretty eyes* . . . and offer life a chance to savor the sweet taste of pain. That legless wretch (the man last night) couldn't afford it, so he discovered an even more miserable metaphysics of love. Pure music. With no guts or tails, as he put it in his terrible humility. Or was it that he wanted to spill his Penelope's guts and snip off the tail of her stallion? And him saying he wanted to listen to the cantilena of traitorous love! No, it is undeniably the fate of unhappiness to bite its own fingertips, with pleasure.

"Will you be coming again soon to visit Mr. Adam, Viviana?" he enjoyed using his name for her.

"What, to have him torment me again? No, I won't," she said defiantly. "I'll never go see him again!"

"Why ever not, Viviana? He likes you very much."

"Oh yes he does, in that way . . . what's that word for liking to torture people?"

"Sadistic."

"Yes, that's it. You saw what he did to me yesterday. *And* he keeps insulting me. He's a really nasty piece of work," she added with a smile that attenuated the words. "And generally speaking, all you men are such good-for-nothings."

She laughed, showing her incredibly white teeth.

"All?" asked Melkior rather worriedly, then stammered in fear: "Even Ugo?"

"You mean the one whom Fred . . .? Oh, he's the worst of the lot. . . . And such a liar! He thinks I'm some kind of . . . Apart from that, he's quite a likable rascal—he's so funny," she gave a cryptic smile, "he had me laughing all the time!"

"Last night?" Melkior groaned bitterly.

"Last night?" she said, perplexed. "No, the night before. At the Give'nTake, when he kept teasing Freddie. Why, you were there, too. Weren't you? Frankly, I don't remember."

She doesn't remember. "I am democratic," say the finest ladies. But she doesn't; Maestro may have lied about it.

"Oh, I was, I was," muttered Melkior and heaved a sad sigh. "You were looking at me with such an inexplicable loathing . . ."

"With loathing?" she said with unconcerned wonder. "Why, yes, of course, you are the critic! It was on account of Fred. Anyway, perhaps I wasn't quite wrong to have looked at you that way," and she gave him a birdlike look, coquettishly inclining her head to one side.

"You were wrong, Viviana, you were wrong indeed . . ." Melkior suddenly threw his soul open like a shirt, with unrestrained senti-mentality. "I was looking at you . . . differently. You were awfully unfair to me."

"You were looking at me with . . . you know what kind of interest. That syphilitic pig next to you . . . I saw it. I know the kind of thing he says about me." The dark splotches broke out over her face again and her eyes went moist with suppressed tears.

"It was Freddie we were discussing," he lied, "not you."

"Why should I believe you? Do I know who you are? The first time I ever spoke to you was yesterday, at that crazy Mac's. In fact, we didn't even speak to each other. I scarcely heard you speak at all. You're a curious person. Mac says you're a very clever but curious person."

"What does he mean, a curious person?" Well, at least she did think about me, he thought consolingly.

"*I* don't know. I suppose you're not like everyone else. That's a good thing, isn't it?"

"No, it isn't," he blurted out nervously. "For one thing, I'm not witty like Ugo. I'm a bore. I'm boring you, too."

"You're not boring me at all," she said candidly. "That's where you're wrong . . . and where it shows you don't know me. I am democratic (ah-ha!), I'll talk to anyone . . . if they're interesting. You are curious but interesting, and I'm glad I've met you."

"Are you really, Viviana?" He skipped the "democracy" bit and was pleased. "If only you knew how happy *I* am to have met *you*! I walk alongside you, thinking: if only she had an inkling of . . . and so on. I talk sheer drivel to myself—those are not thoughts really. Any-way, where could I get thoughts from when I'm all confused, I expect you've noticed. I'm happy one minute, the next I'm totally unhappy again, swearing at you inside, being angry with you . . . I was about to leave and go away just now."

"Oh, you mean when you ducked me?" She was laughing.

"No, that was really because of a man."

"Or a woman. Admit it—you didn't want her to see you with me."

"There's nothing to admit, Viviana. It was a man . . ." He really hadn't wanted the Stranger to see him with her . . . and he was now ashamed of that. He was amazed that he should have been ready to abandon her because of . . . What's the matter with me? He knew he could not stop now. And he was giving in to it. I'm snared, I'm snared, he complained to himself, but was unable to pull himself together and so began blurting out a series of "ownings up." I'll own up, Viviana . . . no, I know you're going to laugh, but I'll own up all the same . . . I must own up, Viviana, come what may . . .

This was all very flattering to her. Such a declaration. Including all his suffering, even this morning's business with the tram. (She took the tram to be a suicide attempt abandoned at the last moment. He presented it like that himself, in a confused and muddled fashion, so she was bound to take it as she did.) It was too late to "mend" anything. She carried her smile high, triumphantly, as if following a victory. Flags fluttered over her head, brass bands blasted away, and everyone was shouting, there she is! There she is! The one alongside Melkior Tresić, that's her, Viviana! Long live Viviana! In a gracious moment she actually slipped her arm through his, she was democratic, what of it, she didn't care who knew, let the whole world see, Mr. Adam the palmist himself, Fred, too, and Maestro and Ugo, the entire Give'nTake brigade . . . that she was not ashamed. And he walked at her side like a "secondary personage" in a parade, the royal consort, a self-styled king, cuckoo-king, thin-king, sin-king, sunk in gloom and indignity. She withdrew her arm from the misalliance after ten steps or so, because . . . well, enough was enough. Blackness engulfed his soul again and he covered his eyes for a moment with the sad arm she had abandoned. He walked thus for a few moments like someone blinded by a blaze. All had been lost in an instant. He longed to be alone among the ruins.

"Did something get in your eye?" she asked with concern.

"No. Something just occurred to me," he replied hastily retracting his hand.

"Yes, I've noticed that," she said sarcastically, "some people lay a hand over their eyes when they're thinking. Does it help you to think more clearly?"

"Yes it does . . . I'm sorry, Viviana, I must be off," he said in a sudden rush.

"Just like that? All of a sudden?"

"That's right, all of a sudden, there's something I forgot to do. Goodbye."

"You *are* a curious one. . . . All right then, *au revoir.*"

She held out her hand with a touch of regret. But he didn't notice, he didn't even notice the hand, he was already turning to go.

"Won't you even give me your hand?"

"Oh, right, sorry . . ." He felt her small soft hand in his and wavered for a moment. But then a strange fury swept through him and he said *Goodbye* in a near shout and made for the first corner in a genuine hurry.

For the corner, for the corner, run for cover! She had her gaze trained on his trembling back. He walked at a weirdly uneven pace, ridiculous, shameful, like a petty thief with a stolen book under his arm. He was treading across a miry and accursed world, alone and desperate. His body felt to him like a frightened piglet, a seal, a turtle, cumbersome and sluggish, something which could only roll, stumble, and crawl. Something which never got where it was going, as if in a dream. The treacherous body jeering at its own misery. Would I were no more! Would I were the infectious air . . . I would suffocate the . . . *preventively* . . . But he was around the corner by then and the madness subsided instantly. Moreover, there surfaced Don Fernando's *preventively* as a good sign of mordant humor. Yet he was still striding fast, like someone hurrying to reach an impatient destination. . . .

"Hey, what's the rush, fair knight? Has it already started?"

The grinning fillings and the thick, lust-swollen lips. Melkior barely stopped himself from spitting into it all. How many times had he felt the symbolic impulse in his mouth as the resolution of his strange relationship with Ugo! Missed the opportunity again! An encounter of this particular kind was the last thing he needed. Ugo was blocking his way, his arms open for a vehement embrace.

"I want you to know I'm happy, dear friend!" he cried out loud, trying all the while to hug his friend and shower kisses on him, but Melkior had his arms out and kept retreating. "So exquisitely happy that it's almost beyond your esteemed-accursed (read: wild) imagination. *October* brought a harvest surpassing all expectations. I have picked the fruits—I'm still sticky all over with the sweet dreams."

"Only with the dreams?" smiled Melkior in a provocative way. He wanted to know, to know, be it even . . .

"Oh, with reality as well—and how!" exclaimed Ugo delightedly. "The dreams came later on, as a brief recapitulation. I belong to the genus of ruminants in that respect."

"Meaning what, specifically?" Oh, he knew only too well what it meant, but he wanted to hear it—hear it! Unless this creep is . . .

"Meaning? You want me to . . . go into the details?" baring his fillings in a grin, drool pooling between his lip and his lower teeth. "Now, that would be a bit of . . . No, really, you must admit, we can't violate a lady's privacy, now can we?" and he burst into terrible, provocative, teasing laughter.

The night's dark rings around her eyes had now acquired a very authentic explanation. Oh well, there was nothing for it, might as well get to the bottom . . .

"Which is to say you . . . ?"

"Yes, I did." Ugo was looking "innocently" into his eyes, but his snout was filled full of laughter.

"You're lying, Parampion," Melkior spat out the words with a pained smile, "I was with her until a minute ago."

"Buying the precious fabrics for her aunt? I was supposed to go with her, only I overslept. Heh-heh, does it fit?"

That's right. It fits, damn it! Of course, it *fit in* with her plans, too.

"And where did you . . ." Melkior made an easy-to-imagine gesture.

"First *in a quiet little café*, to quote a pop song from our puberty, if you still remember it. It's actually a great place for 'undercover' people (I mean couples with a skeleton in the cupboard) with well-coached, discreet personnel. Then at her place."

"Her place?"

"Yes. Is that beyond the imagination? But I made with the poetry while still at the café. *Restless is the autumn air* . . . while the hands, of course, went about their business . . . poetically. First the hair, for the sake of the rhyme, and then over the rest of the poetry. But the hardest of all, you know, was the passage across those zones . . . you'd explained it to me, scientifically, the erogenous zones. They are indeed—you were right on that point—highly sensitive points in women. Not to mention that it wasn't quite the thing to do, getting sexually aroused in public. We're not in a cage at the zoo, *perbacco*, the monkeys, remember? I told you about that time when I was nudging *la fiancée* toward the potential liberator . . . Oh, *mon Dieu*, I'm a right bastard, aren't I? But once we got to her flat everything went smoothly, no resistance at all, over all the zones, heh-heh . . . But your eyes are flashing, Eustachius the Envious! Well, it wasn't so hard to predict, eh?"

He may indeed have noticed a glint in Melkior's eyes—he started fussing over him to give comfort in a flash of generosity.

"She likes you, too, you know. Thing is, you think too much in the late Plato's terms. Which is not her cup of tea. Frankly, she doesn't understand that sort of pragmatics. The problem of the transition to the horizontal was invented by male insecurity. We have built poetry upon it. They like being brought down. Their worn-out 'no' is a form of the verb 'keep going.' You don't have to be Caesar to cross that dried-up Rubicon—if indeed anything had ever run there except crocodile tears. There, I've expounded things at your intellectual level. You've got to admit. I've even used oratorical metaphors. Applause."

"Nevertheless you weren't at her place last night," said Melkior with mulish obstinacy. "That I won't believe."

He really did not believe it. He could not bring himself to believe it. She's no Enka . . .

"You don't? Well, have a gander at this, Eustachius," he took out a small latchkey from his pocket, "I can usher you immediately into that heaven, *ecco la chiave del paradiso*. '*L'Amor che muove il sole e l'altre stelle*,'" he declaimed, his face gazing skyward, with a gesture of high pathos. "Do you believe me now, my poor Eustachius? I really can't see why you persist in being so hard on yourself in so determined a way, sipping from the palm of your hand, as it were, all the while surrounded by goblets and chalices brimful with pleasures. Oh you Dio-genius, you ascetic-onanist, you slimy *omnia mea mecum porto* oyster, you quaint plaster saint above the portal of History's brothel, you martyr to martyromania, you self-elected weeper over the fate of Mankind . . . which, incidentally, includes my worthless self! Spit on me and everything else (for you do seem about to spit), make a one-hundred-and-eighty-degree turn around your vertical axis and give those mischievous hormones free rein. Life is no dream. Life is the unity of all the piggish ways known as Man. I don't believe you still agree with the tramp Satin that *man* has a proud ring to it. Don't tell me your soul admires the self-denial of the carrier pigeon or the loyalty of the dog. You are proud yourself—what do you care for loyalty and self-denial? Liberate your pigs, let them root through the pleasures, let them grunt with delight. There you have it. Call me an idiot if you like."

"No. You're a Superpig . . . in the Nietzschean sense," smiled Melkior in bitter disgust. He started to turn around and walk away, but Ugo rushed out in front of him and made a mocking bow.

"Oh Master, teach me to achieve life eternal!" He then puffed out his chest boastfully: "At least I am a Superpig! That *is* something, after all! What matters is being above average. I hate the average, even the porcine average. But where were you dashing off to, Eustachius the Purest? Wait, there's something I have to tell you! It's important. It is about her."

In vain. Melkior had taken off at a brisk trot and hopped aboard a tram that was just pulling away from the stop.

He could not resist looking back. Ugo was not watching the tram move away. He was walking purposefully toward the corner, entering the street where Melkior had left Viviana. He was going to run into her there. He did not need the mercy of Chance; he was guided by the smiles of angels. Black envy darkened Melkior's thoughts. He fumbled, like a blind man, through the previous night's uncertainties—but his tentacles found nothing. Nothing that the imagination could offer as a visual document of Ugo's sortie. The studio flat. A projection of his ex-girlfriend Mina's studio: the shortwave radio always on—the nocturnal green eye of the basilisk lulling the beauty to sleep on the chest of the weary hero, the display panel with its tiny illuminated windows KALUNDBORG—HILVERSUM —MOTALA—NWDR—GLW—SWF—GLW—HÖRBY. . . oops, this was the wrong film. Melkior was booing, I've been swindled, I want my money back! Show aborted. House lights up. Imagination threading in another reel . . . Now presenting GENTLE BREATH, b/w, love story/ pornographic exploit, starring BLACK FILLINGS and VIVIANA PUTTANA —directed by MELKIOR—produced by TRESFILM—stunts by UGO— masks: DON FERNANDO . . . and that's it. The film proper never begins. The same opening credits keep running again and again: starring . . . directed by . . . produced by . . .

"Tickets please?"

But the show hasn't even started! protested Melkior in the dark-ened auditorium. The voice had golden wings on its hat, with the heraldic arms of the city between. A dignitary of the tram line in visitation. Each of the faithful receives a blessing and absolution upon presentation of a ticket. Melkior, too, presented his creden-tials with due contrition and received blessing and absolution. And he felt pure and worthier of continuing his ride on the City Trans-port system. The sheer satisfaction of it! A clean-shaven ticket in-spector in a dark blue uniform, with gold on his hat, a strong, tall man moving from one passenger to the next, distributing indul-gences: May I see your ticket? Thank you. May I see your ticket? Thank you. . . . *Te absolvo in nomine tramcar, amen. Te absolvo in nomine tramcar. Amen* . . . Hallelujah, hallelujah, respond the pas-sengers while wheels under their feet sound Bach fugues. And the sun shines on the honorable tram windows . . . Melkior felt a trav-eler's piety in his weary heart and said contritely to himself: what a joy it is to be alive once you've settled your accounts with the electric tram.

But what about the *iron mammoth*, what about the *big oaf?* It's a sly challenge to the big benefactor who would never—and this deserves repeating—*never* entertain the idea of running someone over. Never trust the scoundrel-automobile. But the Tram . . .

Rolling on, rolling on . . . one *tram*, one *way, tram-tram . . . bus-bus trambus*, the lyre on the roof thrumming *way*, the wheels drumming *tram-tram* . . . But the rhythms shaking his body went for nothing; his thoughts kept stealing back to Viviana. Now that's love. What on earth am I to do? He knew that tonight and tomorrow and the day after and all the days of his brief civilian life until the day Pechárek howled *dwaftees!* he was going to be searching for her . . . *Roaming street after street, just hoping we'll meet, and when at last we do I'll give my heart to you* . . . his thought itself gave forlorn and dejected voice to the banal tune, and a welling of pain rose in his throat. He fought back sobs. He leaned his forehead on the window pane and sought to disperse his thoughts by paying attention to the world around him.

A drunk was speaking loudly:

"I'm taking no orders and that's final!" he gave a formidable hiccup and reared to his full height, driven by the spasm in his stomach, making it all look like the position of attention, clicking his heels and raising his arm in salute:

"Humbly report, I'm taking no orders from anyone! That's first— and most important. Secondly . . . if you want to put me in the cavalry, the answer's yes. Then I'd be a cavalier, right? Make me see the horse's ass. So what. Like the Sergeant used to say—horse's ass. To me. And there I was serving King and country at the fortress in Petrovaradin. And the Sergeant had Mitzi a singer across the river in Novi Sad. Fine, but old Mitzi needed to be kept in her liqueurs . . . So . . . who was chosen to do the honors? Yours truly, of course. With the blue Danube out in front of me. But they never asked *Can you handle it, soldier?* oh no, it was *Forward, march!* (that's what *must* comes from—march or bust, get it?) But who should I get killed for, eh, a horse's ass? Ever seen the Danube?" this to Melkior, his sole listener. "No? Well, it doesn't matter if you haven't. It's water plain and simple. Common or gar-(hic)-den variety water. Flowing all the way from Germany. And I pissed in it at Petrovaradin. Heh heh. But that was before Hitler's time, just to be perfectly . . . I'm not the kind to muddy a Führer's waters. No, it's just I wanted to send something of mine to the Black Sea, get it? If only the Danube ran upstream, eh? Wouldn't that be something, eh? Got your call-up papers yet?" he suddenly asked Melkior, dropping his voice confidentially. "No? I have. So will you. Anyone with two arms and two legs will be served. I'm in a Camouflage Company, camouflage kit to cover your shit. That's the long and the short of it. Reporting tomorrow. Oh what a brave fighting man I am . . ." he sang in a magpie voice, twisting his neck derisively this way and that, as if defying someone in the tram.

Melkior jumped off the tram before it stopped. He was not far from home and hurried along, the sooner to shut himself up in his room . . . unless the Stranger is back, he thought morosely . . . to think about everything in solitude, in the peace and quiet of a horizontal stretch on his back, reading from the white ceiling the invisible letters spelling his idiotic fate.

Approaching the Cozy Corner, he saw Kurt waving to him from afar. As he came closer, Kurt told him in confidence he was going to have a roast heart for him tonight, do come, Herr Professor, and we'll have a nice long chat, it's always a pleasure talking to you. He said yes to Kurt. Courteously. He had no intention of going there. Those cigarettes soaked in the acetic acid, Father's recipe, had him upset again. Isn't that some kind of . . . And the stupid-oaf sergeants coming for the sake of Else the purest of virgins . . . He felt a patriotic rage mounting. Offering me a heart for tonight. A pig's heart. The derisive servility. The symbolic heart. Roasted. With cigarettes in vinegar. All for the heart. My aching heart is torn apart. I don't give a fart, he added to himself and laughed on realizing that he had done so unconsciously, for the sake of the rhyme, having simply been led on by the baa-ing inspiration. Baaa . . . he bleated angrily at the whole world.

All I need now is to find *that fellow* upstairs, he muttered walking up to his room.

"Oh no, he's out," said ATMAN, who was standing there in front of him in his black housecoat and white scarf and bowing. "He went out, oh, about two hours ago."

"Who's out?" What's this—can he read thoughts? Melkior was amazed, he was not aware he had been thinking aloud.

"Why, your friend and dear guest!" exclaimed ATMAN. "A very nice chap, too."

"How do you know?"

"That you have a guest?"

"That he's nice!" shouted Melkior impatiently.

"Oh, you can always tell. We exchanged greetings. Quite cordially, too. Right here, on this very spot."

"What do you mean, 'cordially,' when you don't even know the man?" Melkior was upset. How on earth could he have forgotten about the magician when he spoke to Pupo?

"Does that matter? I wished him a good morning, he returned the greeting in a civil way. What of it?"

"You went out on purpose to see who was coming down?"

"No, quite accidentally—that is to say *pour faire pipi*, which of course is hardly accidental. There, see how low we've let our conversation drop, Mr. Melkior!" ATMAN reproached him.

"You're as curious as an old biddy, Mr. Adam," snarled Melkior.

"Curiosity is the beginning of wisdom, said . . . well, you know who said it. You know so much—I know nothing. Hence the curiosity. You must allow me that much, if only in view of my occupation."

"Allow you to poke your nose into other people's affairs?"

"What affairs, Mr. Melkior? I say good morning to your friend and suddenly I'm poking my nose into things! Whatever's the matter with you?"

"I wish you wouldn't concern yourself with the people who come to visit me!" But even as he spoke he realized he was talking drivel in anger and that the whole business was getting out of hand. What now? ATMAN was standing innocently in front of him. I may have led him on myself, acting so silly . . . Damned Mandrake! Now I'm going to have to mend things. There was nothing for it, he'd have to mend the damage. ATMAN felt it and offered his earnest help.

"Mr. Melkior, you seem to mean . . . No, you're wrong. Discretion is part of our professional code. Doctors and us . . . Incidentally, I can tell you doctors are even less circumspect. My dear sir, I could write novels—novels you wouldn't believe . . . But do come in, won't you, we can have a cup of coffee if you have the time. No point in discussing this kind of topic out here on the landing."

Melkior gave a fairly agreeable nod and followed him. Topic? What kind of thing are we discussing? Did he say that just to have the word heard from his lips? Or did he really have a "topic" in mind? Melkior sat down worriedly and it took him some moments to notice he was sitting in the same place he'd sat the day before—next to her. He stroked the spot next to him, inadvertently. ATMAN seemed to notice that, too.

"She was so sorry yesterday when you left. Me, too, as a matter of fact. You, too, I'm sure. Why did you get up so abruptly? I'd laid it on a bit too thick, had I? Well, you realized it was all for her benefit— I mean, you did give me a soccerlike signal or two under the table. A bit rough, if I may say so, even painful, heh," ATMAN gave an unpleasant smile with his wide-set teeth.

"You had mixed me rather too liberally into that marmalade of yours," Melkior smiled, too.

"Ah, marmalade, that's a good one," laughed ATMAN in his turn for the sake of the friendly, "manly" atmosphere. "Every now and then I smear some over that pretty mug of hers—let her have a lick. When she's licked it clean she comes back again."

"She won't be coming back," said Melkior with a wistful sadness.

"She told you so this morning?"

"Whom were you spying on: me or her?"

"Neither. I knew you'd be looking for her after yesterday."

"Mf, I wasn't looking for her. I ran into her accidentally."

"Well, there you are—you are allowed to run into people 'accidentally' yet you won't grant me the right to do the same. That's fine, don't get angry, I believe you, I do. Never mind, she *will* be back . . . when she's finished with the marmalade, heh-heh . . . They all come back, it's a law of nature. It's what my trade is founded upon. It's more reliable than any doctor's office. The time will come when people will pick up pills at their chemists' on their own . . . but women will keep on coming to our poky rooms and offering us their palms to read and turning their coffee cups over on the saucers, anxious about what we'll say, trembling at our words. They will come back, if only to scoff and say we were 'all wrong,' to parade their contempt, their superiority. Which is, by the way, what they are always doing, especially the intellectuals among them, they put up a fight, heh-heh . . . Then they go away calm and meek like cats newly impregnated, full of joy and hope. Happy about their future happiness. And that's how it is, over and over again. The confessionals will vanish from the churches, but women will keep coming to us for confession, that I guarantee. Novels? What novels! Leo Tolstoy himself couldn't imagine what manner of things they prattle to us about. The secrets of marital and extramarital beds. Especially extramarital. Such salacious details! Maestro offered me a fifty-fifty deal—I'd supply the material, he'd write it up—and I would never have to work again. A *chronicle of scandals*—there's nobody wouldn't go for it, right? Plus Maestro's filthy stuff as dressing on top . . . An all-time winner, I tell you! But I didn't accept, oh no," ATMAN shook his head decisively, as if he had only just decided definitely to reject Maestro's idea. "And you tell me I poke my nose into things. They push the stuff under my nose themselves, of their own free will, so what am I to do? Sniff I must, and sniff I do . . . enjoying it in my own quiet way, I admit. But it's all in total confidence, all between myself and God."

"You think He concerns Himself with such things?" Melkior threw him a derisive look.

"He must, seeing that He made them to be that way. Sowed those charms all over, stuffed them with hormone glands and whatnot—that's why they're like that, spongy."

Melkior was laughing. Maestro had clearly had his fingers in this in a big way.

"And you . . . believe in God?" he asked just for the fun of it.

"Of course I do," replied ATMAN eagerly. "That's the foundation of my belief in Fate. How else would I be able to go on with my work at all?"

"So your faith is 'businesslike,' then, is it?"

"It's practical! I must believe. I need Fate as a kind of down payment. All is risk. On the other hand, you've got to put something down in advance. Everyone, of course, invests according to ability; I invest stupidity for lack of wisdom."

"Well . . . that's not much of a risk, is it?" Melkior took up ATMAN's malicious game. "Win-win."

"You mean that losing stupidity is a win? Because stupidity is not merely a lack of cleverness—intellectual poverty, as it were—it's worse than that, it's something like an endless deficit. . . . But that's only how things look to you wise men. To us, it's everything, all we've got; what do we have left once we lose it?"

"Malice," blurted out Melkior, losing his patience.

"Oh no, that's out of bounds for us. Wise men may be malicious, geniuses may even be criminals, but we . . ."

"You people may be small-time crooks, schemers, writers of anonymous letters, libelers, seducers . . ."

"Oh yes, oh yes," ATMAN took this up with eager pleasure, sporting the smile of a good-natured loser, "it's all according to one's ability. This is easy-peasy to you intellectual moguls! Your capital is inexhaustible. You break off a piece of your intellect, a biggish one if need be, and plunk it down as your stake. You couldn't care less if you lose—the capital is undiminished, while your greatness only grows. Meaning, you become tragic characters. Heroes, victims, exiles, sufferers, generally accepted martyrs, and so on . . . up to and including sainthood. Streets are named after you, towns, factories, even stars and celestial bodies. That's in case of so-called *personal* failure while you're alive . . . But what if your undertaking succeeds, eh? . . . That is to say, what if the sneaking up- and downstairs and clandestine accommodation in other people's rooms and nocturnal meetings in attics should give birth to a great historical act . . ."

"Then what?" asked Melkior with impatient sharpness.

"Then that's a good thing, is it not?" ATMAN bared his teeth in a strange grimace of derision. "Yes, but a good thing how? Because your wise man himself begins to believe in something which is no longer the mind, heh, heh . . ."

"What is it, then?" Melkior was suddenly worried. ATMAN's words were buzzing quite unmistakably around his thoughts, the ones that were now flashing on and off in panic, like an alarm light.

"What?" said ATMAN with an enigmatic Chinese smile. "Sometimes it's an overly powerful organ in the body of the wise man. A good stomach, for instance, complete with ample appetite, a good nose for gauging situations, or a special virility. He's renounced it all for the moment, hermitlike, all for the sake of the mind, but what happens when the machinery starts running, in peacetime, in comfort, eh?"

Melkior stood up at the *eh*, as if at a signal for the last train home. But where am I to find *him* now? He pushed his hands into his pockets in deep thought. You've got to make arrangements in advance when dealing with *them*. If only I could find Pupo . . . but where?

"You're not leaving, are you?" ATMAN looked at him in sham consternation. "And I invited you for coffee only to forget it! I'll have it ready in no time. Look, there's the coffee machine, takes only a minute to do the job. I brought it back from Germany."

"You've been to Germany?" and Melkior gave an incautious start.

"Austria, actually," replied ATMAN nonchalantly. "But it makes no difference after the Anschluss. Yes, funny, that—no more Austria. Vienna with swastikas. Ridiculous."

"Please don't bother, Mr. Adam, I really must be going." The reasons for leaving had grown very serious. But where am I to find them now? Under no circumstances is he to spend the night upstairs . . . under no circumstances . . .

"And what do you propose to do up there? Pace the room and think about things, that's what. What's the point of it all, Mr. Melkior? And why are you looking at me that way, like a sick man staring at a thermometer?" Adam's two curiously close-set eyes had come even closer, almost becoming a single, small and fearsome, threateningly squinting eye in the middle of his forehead.

Polyphemus the one-eyed Cyclops . . . thought Melkior: in a momentary fading of consciousness he had seen in front of him a symbolic hideous specter, and he rubbed his eyes to regain his senses.

"That's the way, Mr. Melkior, do it more often," ATMAN was seeing him to the door with a jeer. But he added right away, solicitously: "You've lost too much weight, my dear fellow, far too much. You're starting to see spots before your eyes."

Yes, it could well be down to hunger. His knees trembled as he went up the stairs, his head lolling as though he were drunk. I'm not doing it for myself, word of honor, I'm doing it for . . . he assured someone as he entered his room, finding nobody there. But what if ATMAN . . . ? No, it's impossible!—Then again . . . I've been left in charge of a small child, and I've just learned something about would-be kidnappers. And the child's gone for a walk, alone, without its nanny, who knows where it might be now? But tonight, when everyone's asleep, here they'll be! . . . like with the Lindbergh infant. This is no time for joking, he reproached himself. The kidnapper's name was Hauptmann . . .

Mechanically, he wrote "Don't come here" on a piece of paper. He crumpled it up instinctively and gave a demented laugh realizing, as he did so, the absurdity of what he'd written. He burned the scrap in his ashtray and blew its black soul away out the window. He felt mild relief at the piece of conspiratorial pedantry, as if it had settled something by itself. But of course nothing was settled and he didn't know what to do. Tell the police a kidnap was brewing?— another joke smuggled its way in and he gave himself an angry blow to the head: you imbecile! If only they'd left a telephone number, just in case! But perhaps even that is forbidden, let alone leaving messages, of course. Nothing in writing! *They* actually swallow messages, he should have swallowed his *Don't come here*.

He locked his room and skipped downstairs into the street. On the pavement in front of the house lay in suspicious solitude a black crumple of burnt paper. He calculated his steps and trod on it with his entire foot without looking back. With any luck there'll be a benevolent wind to scatter the black ashes behind me. And he went off in the direction of uncertainty.

Now to look for that four-leaf clover. To go bleating after his brother the sacrificial ram in the field: run, brother, run, the gods are thirsty!

By the time the veterinary experts arrive from the native village the agent is grazing peacefully, like all the rest of the cattle. Nevertheless down his throat they force several slimy balls made of herbs they have chewed and then kneaded between their fingers, spitting on them copiously. For all that they make the agent gag, he does his best to obey his well-intentioned tormentors: he downs the green pellets, with effort, like a hen. They are treating him. And his spirits immediately rise: if they're treating me it's surely because . . . and he smiles at them with agreeable gratitude.

"What is that stuff they forced down his gullet?" the captain asks of the doctor in a paterfamilial tone.

"Vegetal purgatives, I'd say. The gentleman is in for a good and thorough bowel flush. But this doesn't seem to be the end of the procedure. They'll go on to exorcise the evil spirits from his belly."

And sure enough the patient is laid on his back and while four natives pin down his arms and legs the High Medicine Man thrusts a bamboo pipe into his deeply lard-lined navel, then takes a smoldering brand from his assistant's hands and uses the ember tip to trace circles around the pipe on the agent's swollen belly, uttering ritual words to which his assistants respond with the rhythmic chanting of other words, probably on behalf of demons which apparently are not leaving our friend's innards without resistance. The agent is, naturally, howling in pain, which the High Medicine Man takes with satisfaction as a sign of a successful birth via the navel.

The chief engineer, who appears to be the most humane and

certainly the strongest among the whites, makes a movement that would probably have him strangling the High Medicine Man had the doctor not stopped him in time.

"Have you gone mad, sir?"

"How much longer are they going to torture this man?"

"Until they've forced the last demon in his stomach through that chimney pipe in his navel. Demons are thought to flee from fire . . ."

"And when will that be?" asks the captain artlessly, with a layman's curiosity.

"You'll have to ask them," replies the doctor unpleasantly. "Probably when our friend stops howling—the sign that all the puppies are born. Whelping over."

"Why don't you suggest he keep quiet for a bit then?" asks the first mate, who is dreadfully pale.

"I'd rather not get involved. Anyhow, I'm not sure. It could turn out to be a tricky business—perhaps they'd kill him then and there. I can't assume responsibility. I know what it's like when a human life is at stake—I'm a doctor."

"You're a demon. Burning's too good for you!" hisses the captain hatefully.

"Well, angel . . . you help him then," replies the doctor and turns his back.

"Sir," the first mate addresses the agent, earnestly, "dear sir, try to control yourself if you possibly can. Grit your teeth and try to be quiet for just a moment. Perhaps they'll stop. Pretend you're feeling better and they will definitely stop." The agent, mustering all his forces, obeys, and indeed they "stop."

The High Medicine Man removes the bamboo pipe from the agent's navel, cauterizes both ends on the embers and then tosses it far away, voicing horrible shrieks as he throws it, to which monkeys respond from the jungle. All the natives burst into loud and hearty laughter.

"Gloating at having cooked his goose," says the captain maliciously.

"No, sir. They're glad the demons have passed over to the monkeys," replies the doctor. "They're much kinder than your goodness imagines."

In the evening the agent is separated from them. They don't know where he is taken. Perhaps this is the poor man's last night, the chief engineer voices his terrible suspicion and shakes with dread at the thought of his own place in the accursed hierarchy.

"Oh no, Mr. Doctor is of a different opinion," says the captain, "he believes in the kindness of the cannibals."

"Did you, sir, despise all the cattle you've enjoyed your steaks from?" the doctor asks him. "What malice have you nurtured in your heart for the many animals whose bodies have passed through yours? Just think of the little chicks cheeping for their mother . . . why, they were but young things!"

"But we are not animals!"

"As far as they are concerned we are cattle. If not swine."

"That's what *you* are!"

"Perhaps. Whatever the case, I thank you, sir. I would have considered you a gentleman myself, were that compatible with certain overdeveloped bodily characteristics of yours."

"You truly are a swine!"

"A lean one, to your regret. Inedible, too, I expect."

The captain, his dignity gone in a flash, tackles the doctor and would have knocked him down with his bare belly had he not been stopped.

"Gentlemen! Just think of our friend at this moment!" cries out the chief engineer with much pathos. "Not to mention our own fate."

"Anyhow, gentlemen," speaks up the doctor who has collected himself quickly, "is there really any point in panicking prematurely about our friend? Perhaps he's receiving special treatment as a patient. Perhaps he's even taken the place of a nursing baby at some native woman's breast."

They all spit disgustedly at this. All except the old seaman, who is chuckling as he imagines the scene. He has found many things to be good and amusing. First of all, he is in excellent company.

Previously, he couldn't have dreamed of passing his time with such gentlemen. Or of seeing them up close like this—stark naked, too . . . And while he feels sorry for them, he also finds it all very strange and funny. Somehow he still cannot quite grasp what has happened. And why are the gentlemen so angry at each other all the time? When they all could be living together nice and peaceful . . . like one happy family, so to speak. . . . He even feels ignored and outranked again for being dressed, which makes him regard the doctor as "lower class," too, as his near-equal. It does mean after all, doesn't it, that the two of them are not good enough to go showing their bodies in front of these gentlemen. That must be why their "hosts" have so ordered. No matter, he is used to being lower class and is not bothered by the situation. Apart from that he finds every-thing excellent. He feeds abundantly on the fruits the Earth offered up in this blessed part of the world that knows no hunger or cold or fatigue. Here you eat, sleep, and laze in freedom, in warmth, in nakedness, in God's peace. He doesn't seem to share the white masters' fear, or to grasp just why these blacks take them out to pasture and fatten them up on the tasty fruits. He simply eats and enjoys lying down, his stomach full, in the shade of a thick-crowned araucaria or under a giant eucalyptus and snoring in carefree bliss. The old fellow takes his captive life with the Polynesian cannibals as an overdue kind smile of Fortune that is affording him, at long last and quite unexpectedly, some retirement benefits—and God knows they were well earned. He takes care to eat what he can get and to sleep his fill; as to other needs he has none. He has never spent enough time on dry land to marry; he has made love to girls, as long as he was able to, in all the ports (as was the seamen's wont), he has worked and slaved knocking about the seven seas, and he has noth-ing to show for it but his own old and skinny body, which, on the Polynesian island, he has now suddenly discovered as something truly his, all he has in the world, and has come to like it and care for it so as to keep it as long as possible. The only thing he regrets is not having any of his old mates from the *Menelaus* around for company, because he feels lonely among all the gentlemen.

On top of his other shortcomings (social and intellectual), his body differs so much from the other *Menelavians* (including the doctor!) that they no longer think of him as "one of them," not even to the extent required by the traditional solidarity of seafarers forced to share the common fate of *castaways*. He is already so distant from their fate, so firmly anchored in security by way of his body, that they not only despise his "animal" contentment but actually come to hate him.

For all his excesses of eating and sleeping, for all the unlimited pleasures with which he has surrounded himself, his body stays stringy and bony, in addition to being tanned so dark as soon to become uninteresting to the hosts in *that one certain*, most terrible, *sense*. They note his solitude, which quite probably strengthens their conviction that he is not the same as the others, that he is different from the cattle they are fattening for the slaughter, that the old fellow is not *meat* but . . . well, some kind of human not unlike themselves, and they no longer lead him out to pasture: they let him move about freely, feed as he likes and when he likes, and generally do as he pleases. The captain is enraged at the injustice of it.

"They lead us out to pasture as if we were their cattle, while he . . . I ask you, is that fair?"

"No," says the doctor in sympathy. "But it's much more unfair that a stupid crocodile might outlive Shakespeare. To say nothing of the various insect species . . ."

The gods are thirsty, my friend, but they're not looking for a bedbug, a bloodsucker, to crush—they're looking for you, a man. Possibly a man of significance, I don't know—a Danton, as I've said . . . But where are you, secret man? exclaimed Melkior half-aloud in the middle of a noisy street. It was long past noon. *They, too,* have to eat, be it with angelic moderation, they do have bodies after all . . .

His own body spoke up, presenting its old demands and clenching the stomach like an enraged fist under his nose. He resisted its demands using the ever-ready force of intellectual reasoning and brandished the threat of the invalid's weighing machine. You demented fool, would you like to stand in a doorway yourself one day, minus a leg, minus an arm, minus eyesight . . . next to a weighing machine with a card saying CRIPPLED IN COMBAT and call out beggar-style to the soulless street, "Check your weight—it's never too late"?

He made the rounds of the large and expensive restaurants with delicate aromas (that was where *they* went to allay suspicion), going from table to table, peering into the faces above the plates . . . and, surreptitiously, into the plates themselves. Nothing but mouthfuls, munch-munch and the murmur of prayers, the clink-clink of glasses, *corpus homini*, trans-substantiation, gluttony . . . *Dominus vobiscum!* Melkior turned away in horror at the carefree ways of the "people of his day and age." Stuffing sacks for better targets. While hiding their bellies under tables like something to be ashamed of. No, the cannibals will not eat the agent! You must intercede on his behalf, Melkior Tresić, don't let him be eaten. He could come in handy. He could, for instance, organize a future economy. Exports of pineapples, coconuts, bananas, monkeys, and parrots— a large firm with the name PINACOCOBANAMONPAR-EXPORT, Pago Pago, Polynesia. The others, too . . . The captain . . . why he could set up a merchant fleet (the TUTUILA-LINE); the chief engineer could build workshops and servicing units to provide the basis for a future industry; the doctor might start a public health service, build hospitals and infirmaries; the first mate could come up with a new, more humane religion forbidding the eating of slain enemies and recognizing the prisoner-of-war status of captives in keeping with the Hague Convention, and the seaman . . . he would found trade unions and a Labor opposition . . . Yes, that would be about right. . . . But all this was wishful thinking as long as the war was on. The *status quo ante bellum*, i.e., the castaways might still end up being eaten—it would depend on their personal initiative, as well as, to be sure, on Melkior's imagination, which was today charitably biased in favor of any man in danger.

Again he fell to leafing through the streets, as if they were so many albums with the photographs of strangers. But his untrained attention soon grew tired of a police-style checking of the passersby and he forgot the purpose of his unproductive wandering. He felt the bitter taste of his solitary roaming and all his efforts went into moving his body through bright, sunlit space, which suddenly appeared to him to be terribly large and empty, unnavigable. He therefore utilized every intersection to change direction, hoping for a small discovery. But there always stretched before him again the most merciless of the dimensions—length, with its illusory shortening in perspective. No one, it suddenly occurred to him, had ever built a street which really tapered off at the end. There was no such worldview. It was more dreadful than despair. He imagined two endlessly tall blind gray walls closing in at an acute angle and, between them, a solitary man who was no longer looking back. He went slowly toward the corner, his steps quite short now because he knew this was the end. Everything was now behind him: life and love and trust . . . and what used to be known as happiness. He was sentenced to live until he reached the corner, but he couldn't stop because it was *time* itself that drove him on. He tried zigzagging, discovering the merciful dimension of width. But it, too, grew ever shorter, ever more yielding, ever more inclined to disappear in a mathematical zero. And the zero was the gallows noose, the rifle volley at the wall, the guillotine's blade, and the severed head was the period that rolled along to the end of the sentence. A bloody, protruding, bitten-through tongue—and the end.

He spotted them from afar as they strolled in confidence down the colorless streets surrounding a block of police buildings which sporadic passersby eyed with suspicious and naïve courage, asserting their own innocence. ATMAN held her arm tucked under his with ostentatious intimacy and was speaking quietly to her, his mouth near her ear. He was not telling her funny stories, Viviana was not laughing. Indeed she had her head inclined toward his the better to hear him.

He didn't remember to be surprised by the encounter. He himself was wandering around obeying a strange force of motion. Behind those gray walls of government property with barred windows at night old favorites could be heard played on a gramophone. Noisy music overhead, blaring through the attic windows. Underneath there yawned dark inner courtyards, salvation-bringing chasms of desperate heroism. Down there, on the silent, dull concrete, thudded the last answers to questions that had been plied to the musical accompaniment.

Melkior had his guest on his mind and it was this that brought him, via the peculiar convolutions of his restlessness, to this place. And look, what a catch—the two of them! Which of Hell's gates were the trumpeting angels going to take? He followed them with the black pleasure of despondent disappointment. This of course had to do with Viviana. The mysterious cad he had never trusted or . . . no, that was not quite true . . . he had experienced frequent and fundamental changes of opinion about ATMAN. And he now honestly admitted this to himself. Adding the probability of further surprises. Elusive in his muddy waters, the bizarre ATMAN . . .

There, they were past all the entrances to the institution of torture and walking on, heading due south in the direction of the autumnal migration of birds, whence the trains whistled. But they were now slowing down, halting whimsically every now and then in the manner of a well-established couple with a sweet life of shared love stretching out reliably before them. There was laughter now (her laughter!). To Melkior's ear it sounded like one of the torturer's pop songs . . . blasting up in the attic . . . Which bitterness was the more bitter? He felt a muffled thumping of beats, either his steps or his heart, he could no longer tell, he was confused, in the middle of the street caught up with the job of spying.

"Ah, Mr. Melkior!" ATMAN was patting him on the shoulder, having suddenly materialized next to him (and he had been following the two of them at a distance of over thirty paces); she was approaching in a hesitant sort of way with the most conventional of smiles.

"Why, we seem to be running into each other every few minutes, like people in love!" At which he gave Viviana a wink, or so it appeared to Melkior. Taken unawares, his attention ripped asunder, he stood in front of them staring at the three pairs of shoes on the ground. His own, old and worn shapeless, the dusty shoes of a weary pedestrian; ATMAN's, gleaming and new, pointed like beaks pecking at the ground; and her small-size shoes like two light-winged little blackbirds . . .

"Off to register, is that it?" asked ATMAN, gently tugging at his sleeve.

"Register what?" Melkior cringed at the touch.

"Why, your friend . . . your guest. See, Mic, he didn't even remember. You have a guest, you should register his arrival with the police. There's the Registry Office," he pointed to a sign above Melkior's head, "that's why I asked. They've become very strict about such things lately, on account of the spy scare." ATMAN even gave a caring smile and showed immediate readiness to be of service.

"Oh, the registration . . . Thank you, the landlady took care of it, she went this morning. . . ." Melkior was still standing in front of them, motionless, as if movement hurt.

"But we're holding up the gentleman," she mediated, "perhaps he has . . ."

"No, no, I haven't," Melkior said hastily and looked up at her, the accursed beauty. She wants to get rid of me. "I merely came out for my walk, as convalescents like to say," and he tried to smile at her but barely managed to bring it off.

"Patients on the mend," ATMAN translated for her acidly.

"And you, Mac, you take me for such a fool!" she said in serious anger.

"Come on, Mic, I only meant this was not the best kind of air for a walk such as that," and he peeked confidentially up at the building above. "The atmosphere's rather . . . errr . . ." (he could not seem to find the right word), "wouldn't you say?"

"*The atmosphere* . . . what a load of rubbish. Why don't you come right out and say let's all of us take a nice walk somewhere." She was warming to the idea in the usual feminine way. "The Botanical Gardens, for instance. We'll read the Latin names for the plants. There are ever such lovely names there."

"Yes, that's where many have come up with names for their daughters," laughed ATMAN. "The Botanical Gardens are for pregnant women and jilted students to stroll in. Come to think of it, Mr. Melkior can come up with pretty names, too. *Viviana*, would that be a plant?"

"No, I don't believe it is," snapped Melkior churlishly. He feared ATMAN was springing another of his traps and thought he'd like to get away.

"Going to leave us again, are you?" asked Viviana coquettishly. "Like you left me this morning in the middle of the street . . ."

"Did Ugo find you? I met him afterward, he was very sorry he'd overslept your date." Melkior said this deliberately, but in a completely innocent way, like a small child innocuously prattling cheery information. He was getting his own back at her.

"Date? Hah! The things people make up!"

He saw he had elicited a profound hatred: she was giving him the same look she had given him that night at the Give'n Take when she was with Freddie. The same splotches had broken out on her face, too. Sunspots! A storm is brewing . . . He therefore set his legs in motion, said goodbye and disappeared around the nearest corner without bothering about the direction.

The Quisisana was crowded and the air inside thick and noxious. The smells of fried onions, black coffee, and human fumes. Melkior felt sick from the medley dropping to his stomach via the nose. That's from hunger. He blocked the spasm and hastily inserted some small change in the automat, which congenially offered him a sandwich. He downed it in two bites. The piece of pickle instantly calmed the sickly roiling of his insides. He inserted another coin or two: the miniature lift dropped to the floor below and the open door (here you are, sir!) revealed a sardine's tail between yellow figure eights of mayonnaise, both covered by a disk of salami and a thin triangle of riddled cheese. This "still life" received different treatment: he ground it methodically with his teeth, letting the hungry mouth caress its fill of yearned-for love. And the mouth seemed to whisper its ahhs and ohhs in a vulgarly sentimental way, exactly as in a genuine orgasm. The stomach, for its part, gratefully acknowledged the divine poetry from up above and went about its business humming contentedly. Flooded subsequently by a beer shower it gurgled delightedly, overjoyed. And burped "thanks."

Up above, Lord Melkior was already perched godlike on thick clouds of smoke and, in an Olympian mood, allowing voices into his pampered presence.

"Peculiar, very peculiar indeed," said a tall man gloomily bent over an unfolded sheet of newspaper on which he was eating something. His short interlocutor was standing on tiptoe with an important air, displaying full comprehension of what he was being told.

"Even when contemplating the crucial decision to take their own life, people can be quite peculiar," went on Gloom & Doom, and Shorty raised and lowered himself twice in agreement. "Some have been known to invest remarkable effort in their suicide. The most bizarre suicide of our times was certainly that of a very rich Texan farmer. One day, while flying over his house in an old farming-cum-produce-transport aeroplane, he leaped out, impaling himself upon the pointed stakes that supported the fencing around his farmhouse. The impact drove the stakes straight through him, for he landed flat, back first. Apparently he had settled on the spot in advance.

"But the most romantic of all was the suicide of a certain French-woman. She checked into a hotel, asking for the room in which she had first slept with her lover, who had subsequently left her. For five days she brought armfuls of fragrant flowers to the room, sleeping meanwhile elsewhere. On the sixth night she locked herself in, never to come out again. She was found two days later in her bed, covered with flowers—dead, of course. Suffocated by the flowers. How about that?"

"Yes," said Shorty, self-important. "Some even drive nails into their skulls!" "Right, right, right!" responded Gloom & Doom with curious elation. "They even choose which sort of nail in advance! Not just any nail—it's got to be a particular sort of nail . . . The selection sometimes takes years."

"Right," said Shorty with gusto. He liked the level of the conversation—he obviously enjoyed a discussion of psychology.

"Take for instance the Chinese immigrant somewhere in Australia . . ."

"Where *do* you get it all from?" Shorty was clearly envious.

"I follow it in the papers. I take an interest in these things," replied Gloom & Doom with a modest smile. "The Chinaman spent a year building an extremely elegant, polished gallows replete with ornament and artistic detail. Everyone wondered at the idea of building the curious structure, but his sole reply to all questions was the well-known gentle Chinese smile. Once he had decided the gallows was finished he hanged himself on it."

"Did you ever hear," Shorty barged in, "about the man who opened graves and tied green ribbons around the cadavers' big toes? He was wanted by Scotland Yard," he finished triumphantly.

"I know, I read about it," Gloom & Doom took it up delightedly. "Tell me more."

"Oh, well, seeing that you know already . . ."

"Never mind, I like hearing about it again! Thing is, though, he tied yellow ribbons to some, but the reason for this has remained a mystery. He has evaded arrest to this day."

"Yes," Shorty drew himself up importantly (a man in the know), "it was thought at first there might be something anti-Semitic afoot, but that notion was given up eventually. . . . Very few got the yellow ribbon, only three or four. A mystery." Shorty sank into deep thought.

"Because he can't have done it for no reason—I mean he must have had a purpose," prodded Gloom & Doom to keep the conversation from petering out. "It's no picnic, opening graves, it is hard work, physically speaking."

"Quite so." Shorty was still worriedly absent and far off in his thoughts.

Ugo would have stepped in by now, thought Melkior on his apathetic way out. What little food he had thrown to his beast had sunk him into a kind of limp stupor; he no longer had the stamina to look for his guest and had left everything to fate.

Fate will have her way with the castaways. You don't know what to do with them. And you no longer wish to be involved. They bore you. They will nevertheless try to talk the old seaman into . . .

"If only he had the sense to escape!" pronounces the captain.

"Why should he bother?" smiles the first mate. "They're not going to eat him, he's fine—eating, sleeping, and idling away the hours. Anyway, where would he run?"

"Where? What a silly question!" says the captain angrily. "Seawards, of course, to reach the mainland. There's bound to be a passing ship—he could hail our . . . Come on, man, don't tell me you wouldn't like to be rescued!"

"Aah," says the first mate, waving an indifferent hand and sinking back into his morose thoughts.

"I for one am very keen on getting rescued," joins in the doctor, "but I still can't see why the old fellow should risk anything for our sake. Even supposing no risk were involved, why should he lift a finger? What did we ever do for him? You in particular, Captain. Even if the rescue ship were to sail by, he would simply deny any knowledge of us. And he would be right."

"That sort of idea could spring only from that sort of mind!"

"There are other ideas in *this* sort of mind, Captain. Listen, supposing the old boy rescued us—what could he expect in our civilized world?"

"Our eternal gratitude!" cries the chief engineer. "Here, I pledge . . ."

". . . to find him a place in a home for the elderly?"

". . . that we shall all chip in to provide a decent lifetime pension for him."

"Ahh," the doctor dismisses this with a contemptuous wave, "that's all conjecture as far as he's concerned, that pension of yours. He's got a better one right here. To top it all off, he filled his pipe today with some pungent dried leaves; says they're finer than tobacco. . . ."

"While you still haven't found the leaves you promised me," whispers the first mate in the doctor's ear in a trembling, spent voice seething with reproach. The doctor casts an angry look at the whinger and makes no reply.

"All the same, why do you keep rejecting stubbornly, indeed maliciously, the captain's idea that the old man might try to get out to sea?" asks the chief engineer piteously. "I should think the suggestion ought to be coming from you. He listens to what you say."

"Sure I will," agrees the doctor suddenly. But everyone immediately suspects there is something behind it.

The night appeared to descend all at once, with no dusk. The sun went down behind the dome of the First City Bank, cast a final handful of red around the city's uppermost windowpanes, and instantly wrapped itself up in the black fur coat of a thick cloud rising out of the west.

Melkior looked at the cloud as if at a kind of promise: a change would come from there. Rain, he said in an inspired way like a slightly mad poet fond of precipitation and wet pavements. Melkior disliked wet pavements; he liked the sun overhead and short noonday shadows beneath. But the fickle autumn sun promised a false warmth concealing the icy truth approaching ever faster and ever more inexorably. What's the idea of the sun hammering into my head the beauties of *golden autumn* and feeding my eyes with flashes of false promise? Lulling me to sleep with a hope of happy dawns and days replete with small pleasures and nights of endearing fantasies! Let the clouds gather, let the rain fall, let it be night at once! Melkior protested loudly (inside), shouting against the sun. He shook himself dry like a wet dog, cleansing himself of his illusions.

MAAR suddenly flashed on above his head. The mighty MAAR was pushing back the night, showering the sparks of its promises on all sides. Tungsram, Singer, Bayer, Bata, Flit . . . began their cunning game: they had stretched their spun-light spider's web high above the city and were snaring the eager attention of the onlookers. They sifted out the grains of gold from the huge mass of useless silt . . . and there shone Tungsram, Radion warbled (washes by itself), and Remington the Emperor grew. While down below, in the doorway, the blind veteran of the glorious battles described above mumbled his endless prayer: *shoelaces, black, yellow* . . . the colors for which he had lost his eyesight.

London in Flames! We'll Fight Alone, Says Churchill! London Burning! Latest edition! bellowed the news vendor to outshout MAAR's mighty acoustics.

"That's what they're calling us up for," Melkior heard a voice at his side. "As if we were firemen."

The man was alone. He was watching MAAR's magic tricks sadly, as though bidding farewell to something. An orderly city dweller with modest habits. Judging by his appearance, he needed neither the Singer nor the Remington, but he enjoyed watching the luxury of pretty things in the "free cinema," the guileless play of light, during his evening stroll. This, too, was going to be taken from him by . . . *them over there.*

We'll Fight, Says Churchill!

"So fight," muttered the man cholerically. "You cooked this up yourselves . . . years ago, at Versailles. Now you can eat it—piping hot!" said he with a gloating laugh.

Melkior felt like slapping the man's face. Instead he stepped very convincingly with all his (admittedly modest) weight on one of the "implacable" fellow's big toes. And said "Oh, so sorry" to him with an expression of the most sincere regret. Don Fernando's prescription for "murderers in trams," he thought, and this fellow does have an evil look in his eyes.

"Sorry, hell!" screamed Mr. Trodden Underfoot. "Go back to tending your goats if you haven't learned how to walk in a city!"

"Goats?" The insult shot through Melkior's body with lightning speed. He turned to face the city dweller in confused indecision and, trembling all over, repeated, "Goats?"

"Yes, goats!" said the city dweller definitively, ready to take him on.

A circle of curiosity seekers instantly formed around. "What's this about?" one of them asked his neighbor. The man gave an indifferent shrug. "Any fighting yet?" asked Curious. "Not yet," replied Indifferent. "What did the fellow say to him?"—this from Curious. "Nothing much. Goats or something." "Meaning what? Something political?" "Could be."

Melkior was unhappy . . . and afraid. What the hell had he got involved for? Everyone around was against him, they knew he'd done it on purpose. . . . He had a feeling of miserable solitude . . . and thought of Ugo. How he would have worked wonders in a trice, won over the lot of them, how everyone would take a shine to him. Ugo, Ugo, he cried wistfully, like the captive Croesus of the moralizing legend.

"Leave it to me. Gangway!" he suddenly heard a voice from heaven, the angelic voice of Ugo. "I said gangway!" and there he was within the circle, stern and purposeful. Eyebrows gathered in an awesome frown, he drilled Mr. Trodden Underfoot with a tracer-bullet look.

"So you're the one, eh? . . . Well, well . . ." nodding victoriously.

"I didn't do anything . . ."

". . . worthwhile! Not that you ever did." Ugo appeared to mean business.

". . . but don't tread on me!" the city dweller was offering resistance in retreat.

"Oh, you'd prefer us kissing you on the lips? Judas!"

The last word had the effect of a spreading stench: the circle began breaking up, crumbling, dissipating. Everyone was trying to sink back as soon as possible into the innocent mass of people charmed by MAAR's capers, to camouflage themselves with carefree civic loyalty.

But Ugo was not falling for it. He knew there were at least twenty eyes following the denouement within the abandoned triangle, wishing to read THE END in large capitals at the close of the film. The soccer fans seeing the match through until the referee's last whistle. He therefore went on with his game.

"Follow me," he whispered sternly to the petrified city dweller, plucking one of his overcoat buttons. "You come, too, Eustachius."

"Oh, so you . . ." stammered the fear-frozen prisoner.

". . . know each other? You bet! You're in luck though: I'm feeling a bit indulgent today—it's my mother's birthday. Come along, come along. Follow us!"

The city dweller was making his docile way in the wake of his destiny, following Ugo's restless head of hair, the black star of his undoing. Ugo knew it. He suddenly pulled Melkior into the thickest of the crowd, bent his head down as if his neck had been broken and said to him: "Head down! Turn off the beacon and our prisoner will run aground." And sure enough they presently heard the man's forlorn supplication: "I'm over here, sir. Where are you, sir? I'm over here."

"Search on, you pest, just you search on! Let's play hide and seek, shall we, Eustachius?" They stepped into a doorway and lit cigarettes. "So how did you make contact with the enemy?"

"I stepped on his foot."

"God, don't tell me you did that on purpose!"

"I did," admitted Melkior boastfully: he wanted to show off for Ugo.

"You *are* a piece of work!" Ugo was glad of the feat. Melkior felt a stupid kind of glee.

"He was exulting about London being bombed, the dolt," he hastened to consolidate his merit. "He gloated out loud about London burning."

"Oh, you did it for London?" Ugo was disappointed. "I did have a hunch it wasn't an *acte gratuit*. Aah, if I'd left you to the mercy of the violence lover it would've been no more than you deserved. Will you look at him—he's sniffing the air in the street: looking for his master." Indeed, the city dweller was anxiously peering this way and that, looking into the faces of passersby like a dog that has lost a scent.

"I bet he'll be off on his own to report himself to the police. Conscience? No. All he wants is to sleep in peace tonight, even if it's on straw. I think he's been sufficiently punished. Let's get out of here."

Melkior remembered his guest and felt what is generally described as a stab of conscience. He felt guilty in advance of any possible . . . Perhaps the man was already back there and ATMAN was dialing a number: Hello, have I got a bird for you. Yes, a redwing, I think you'll be interested. . . . He was overcome by an odd kind of anxiety at evil forebodings and suddenly tugged himself free of Ugo's arm.

"Where will you be a bit later? I've got to dash over to my place now."

"To look at the ceiling? Take me along. We'll look at it together."

"No, really I must. I won't be long. Where can I find you?"

"Nowhere. I'm coming with you. Where *can* I go now, on my pitiful own? It's too early for the Give'n'Take . . . or anything else."

"But I might be as long as half an hour . . ."

"No more? And you keep wondering why women shun you. I devote my whole life to them!"

They walked in silence past well-lit shops through the evening throng. Melkior was thinking about Enka. Half an hour? Well, that was precisely how she liked it. Ugo had lifted his moist, runny, funny nose, miming an offended wisdom.

"I could have taken a different approach back there. For example: What, this character? (Pointing at you): I've seen him collect money from *them*. He works for the you-know-who, of course. Or: I know him as well as he knows my pocket. He's robbed me blind, too. How much did he steal from you, sir? Or: hold him, gentlemen, and I'll get the police. (To you): Are you aware she's about to give birth, you scoundrel? She's my sister, gentlemen, a teenager, her whole life ruined. Or: who did he claim to be—Napoleon or Mohammed? It all depends on which way the wind is blowing. (Taking the audience into my confidence): We've been looking for him six days, the Head of Psych's beside himself with worry. Or would you have preferred me to introduce you to the honorable citizenry as a pervert, an escaped convict, a forger, a crazed arsonist, a grave robber, a fratricidal maniac, a paralytic, an epileptic, a phantom ripper, the founder of a sect of cut-off ears collectors, a cannibal . . . ? I could have done any of those things, but I saved you from a certain lynching instead. And how do you thank me? By dumping me in the street, that's how. Got to nip over for half an hour. A half-hour secret? Some damned secret! Ptui!" and Ugo spat forcefully on the window of a gourmet cafeteria famous for its delicate delicacies. But presently, as if regretting the gesture, he went inside following his "mad inspiration," and for Melkior's benefit (who had remained standing at the door in bewilderment) he performed an impromptu pantomime:

He selected the fattest customer, one with a hunting hat atop a fat head who was bent religiously over his plate. Ugo approached him from behind; nobody noticed. Using both hands, he lifted the hat off the man's head, solemnly, like a priest lifting the monstrance at Mass, and gave him a brotherly and very loud kiss on the denuded and shiny pate. He then covered his kiss with the hat, still ritually serene as if concealing a holy secret beneath it, bowed to the bar—the main altar—crossed himself meekly and went out into the street, his face piously upturned, his gaze directed skyward.

The scene had taken no more than half a minute, but everyone was too surprised to utter a sound. Even the "kissee" did not protest: he was taken so much by surprise as to "comply," he even helped Ugo so as not to spoil the performance of the rite. It was only a moment or two later, when Ugo was already outside, that they realized something odd had occurred. Whether it had been a lunatic or a joking rascal was now being loudly discussed. There was laughter, too.

"Now *that's* an *acte gratuit*," said Ugo didactically, "not treading on someone's foot for London."

"I wasn't trying to . . ." Melkior cut his sentence short: he realized he was "explaining himself."

"Yes, yes, you sought to avenge mankind. To squash Hitler on someone's corn." Ugo was poking provocative fun at him. "Petty malice was all it was."

"What about the kiss on the thinker's head then? What was that?"

"Nothing. I kissed Stupidity, through one of its models, if you must have 'meaning.' Kiss thy neighbor rather than tread on him, my dear Eustachius. That's how we reveal our true nature—by those small acts in moments of inspiration. You're inspired to tread on feet: a future dictator. Did you at least tread on him good and proper, Eustachius the Purposeful?"

"Go to hell! I've no time for your shenanigans!" Melkior was terribly irritated; he was wishing he could shake free of Ugo and dash home, but how, how? He was raging. "I've got to go, do you hear me, I've got to go back to my place . . . to see if my papers have come," he lied in the end.

"You have your evening papers delivered?" smirked Ugo. "How nice."

"My call-up papers, blast you! I've been out all day. I wish you would stop hanging on to me like a . . . Leave me alone!"

"Think very carefully, unreasonable Eustachius—do you mean precisely what you say?"

"Yes, I damn well do!" yelled Melkior, now quite beside himself. "I've had enough of your damned romping around, understand? I have *serious* business to attend to. Get lost!"

"Oh, so we've come to damned this and damned that," grinned Ugo, taken aback. "This can only mean things are very serious indeed. Couldn't you grant me pardon all the same, Eustachius? Mercy please!" and he attempted a laugh, his lead-dark fillings managing to elicit a kind of sad sympathy in Melkior. But he would not give in. Indeed his rage flared afresh.

Ugo had felt the new outbreak coming and took care to weather it in the shelter of his resourcefulness.

"All right, Eustachius dear one, all right." He spoke feelingly, his voice drenched with invisible tears. "I shall remove my disgustingly feather-brained self from your sight, perhaps forever. Perhaps indeed in a way that will make you sorry when you have learned all the details. Farewell." He turned and walked off.

"Wait, you crazy Parampion, wait!" Melkior ran after him and spun him around. There were genuine wet tears rolling down Ugo's face. For all that he well knew all the many sources of Ugo's tears, Melkior fell again for the old trick of Ugo's, which after all was not entirely false. Ugo had the knack of instantly imagining himself the most wretched creature in all the world: a down-at-the-mouth, despised, rejected orphan suffering from solitude, hunger, and cold, driven from pillar to post in this cruel world and having no recourse but to "end it all," that is to say take his own life. But the most moving part (and that was where the tears flowed most copiously) was watching "from beyond" the doings of *his set*, who had been "spared." There: it is evening, the Give'nTake has come to jovial and noisy life, but he is no longer there. The girls are pretty (well, females, generally speaking—he preferred the more mature, plumper variety), they think of him and of the times they had while he was . . . But there is nothing to be done—he is gone. As for the fiancée, she already married "the monkey man"—*Mr. Romp*—and thinks of Ugo no more. Only his aged mother, silver-haired and despondent, weeps at dusk . . . and the tears flow on and on . . .

"My dear Parampion. Listen," said Melkior, moved in some silly way himself, "wait for me here, at the Cozy Corner. I'll be back in a flash."

"Wait at the corner . . ." repeated Ugo in a childishly artless voice.

"That's right, sit at a table, have a drink . . ."

"Sit how, dear Eustachius?" sobbed Ugo, his manner quite infantile now.

"On your behind, dear boy, sit on your behind . . . until I'm back."

"Money," stammered Ugo in a paroxysm of sobs, "I've got no money. I was trying to sell my old nappies today . . . the ones I had as a baby . . . Kikinis wouldn't buy them."

"On me," said Melkior on his way off. "Tell Kurt to put it on my account." "He invented this nappy business to make himself cry. His old nappies . . . the ass . . ." he laughed inside with relief.

Strangely enough, he did not run into ATMAN on the landing. He skulked past the palmist's door cautiously, on tiptoe, holding his breath, then hurried up the stairs three at a time and lurched breathlessly into his room. His guest was not there. He locked the door behind him without turning on the light. He sank, exhausted, on the first chair he came to and, propping his elbows on the table, dropped his head between his palms. He felt his face under his palms, finding it a curious sensation: it's as if I were fending off slaps in the face. . . . At school, in Dom Kuzma's class . . . what is love, Seal Penguinsky? . . . Dom Kuzma's slaps burned his cheeks with a new, "adult" shame as though he had just brought them, still fresh, back to his room. He felt the heat of his cheeks on his palms. Slaps. So insignificant the physical pain, so lasting and incurable the burn! A slap is the fault of the victim, that is what makes shame indelible.

There begins *The Great Recapitulation*, but the entire sense of shame clenches itself spasmodically and makes the leap into the present day. Once here, it latches onto Viviana. He notices it latching onto her, notices, too, the phrase *onto her* with which he has zeroed in on his thought, and feels a tickling current down his back. He pounces upon her vengefully (to hell with hesitation!) and falls mindlessly to embracing her (at last!), pawing and kissing her, pressing impatient hands up and down her dress, undressing her . . . preparing her, in the rough masculine way, for "surrender." She puts up a "demure" resistance to the onslaught (oh, what are you doing? Whatever will you think of me?), being refined (for greater triumph), resourcefully fanning his lust. But just at that moment Dom Kuzma enters the field of vision: he is crossing the street; he is headed for the invalid's machine, his black hat pushed way down (to make the ears less conspicuous), his lips moving—talking to himself. And Viviana's marvelous body falls apart, melts into defeated anguish. All that remains is a virginally empty skirt and arms embracing ruined desire. And Dom Kuzma's lackluster eye, full of life's bitter pain, leans paternally over the broken wave of yearning and speaks in a moralizing way in despair: that's right, son, that's right. *To have is not victory. To renounce* is victory. "Sour grapes!" shouts Melkior into Dom Kuzma's large ear, "Sour grapes!" and the Ear falls to caressing his face compassionately, panting with deathbed breath: haughty is the fox, haughty. Let the birds of the air peck the grapes that ripen on high, let them carry the grapes back to their nests; they sow not, nor do they reap . . . so be it! And the son of man . . . let him travel through the vale of gloom that is this earthly existence—continues Melkior in poetic anguish—over thorns and stones, driven from pillar to post . . . And when tears come to his eyes he lets them run down his cheeks and lets the poet's whispered words weep on their own from within:

and his feet are bloody,
and his heart is wounded,
and his bones are weary
and his soul is stricken . . .

. . . and Melkior the son of man holds his head in both hands and shakes it vigorously like an enraged Demiurge shaking the skies in his fury. Galaxies shake, scattering stars and setting up a new order in the universe. But Melkior creates no new order with the shaking: all he does is to bring about a crazy whirl of circles around his weary eyes and a dull ache in his bent head. And when somebody knocks at his door the pain in his temples wakes in a muted throb.

The knocking came again as the voice of inanimate things in the hungover dawning of wakefulness and the word, fully awake by now, found itself in Melkior's mouth. *The Police.* Down beneath his feet he felt the palmist's foul existence (he had himself, for a joke, dubbed him ATMAN the Great Spirit) and some dull indifference set him moving toward the door. He unlocked and opened it without fear, giving himself totally over to his lassitude.

Swaying at the door was Four Eyes. First there issued from him a cellarlike breath, a whiff of barrel and mingled smells, and then the herald spoke, gesturing hurriedly.

"Things have taken an interesting turn *over yonder* . . . that, if I'm not mistaken, is what I was told to say *over here.*"

"Who . . . ? Over where?" asked Melkior, upset by the inklings. He thought of his guest and quaked.

"At the Corner is where things have taken this turn," said Four Eyes with his foul breath; the words were barely audible, "and the message is from Parabrion, is that it? I can remember names even more difficult—Periplectomenos, Batrachomyomachy—from high school. They really force-fed us with the drivel. Your immediate presence is required, everything's up for grabs. May I go back reassured?"

"Yes, you may." Melkior was relieved—it was only Ugo "doing his thing." He leaned against the doorframe in exhaustion.

Four Eyes was still swaying in the doorway.

"All right, what is it?" asked Melkior tiredly.

"What shall I take back *over yonder* as your reply? Because things have taken . . . like I said."

"Tell them I'm coming. I'm coming," said Melkior impatiently.

"Straight away, isn't it? Coming straight away, coming straight away," and Four Eyes went hopping down the stairs with idiotic glee.

Come out, come out,
See the drunken lout
Being thrown out,
On his ear, out of here . . .

the drunkard, was saying, gesturing tragically. He went into the Cozy Corner with his recitation still ongoing, but shortly he came back out—or rather flew out back first and sat down on the pavement. Behind this piece of action were Kurt's strong arms. Melkior saw his silhouette against the yellow curtain: immobile, sleeves rolled back, at the ready.

"As I said, out of here, on his ear . . . correction, on his bum. Well, who cares, it's still the same old fun." The drunkard was not getting up from the pavement or speaking to anyone in particular: he was now explaining an important and very complex point under his nose, using small, myopic gestures like someone doing lacework.

Inside, things seemed to have got out of hand. One of Ugo's favorites, *Spare the Horses, Driver*, could be heard, a number from *The Russian Balalaika*; Ugo's solo passages alternating with a ragged chorus (of the sergeants, probably), destroying the song with drunken disorder.

Out in the street Melkior laughed at Kurt's silhouette, standing at attention guarding unwavering sobriety amid the crazed orgy of Russian song. And when Melkior, after hesitating for quite a while, was finally driven by his sensitive conscience to enter the Cozy Corner, Kurt took this as a ray of sunshine. He immediately abandoned his post at the door and all but licked Melkior's hand, wagging an invisible tail.

"Ach, Herr Professor, Herr Professor! Would you just look at what's going on—this is sheer Bolshevism," whispered Kurt confidentially, as one sober man to another. "Nevertheless I didn't call the police. We got word from you. I was sure you would come . . ."

Ugo was standing on the table among overturned glasses and waving an unsheathed saber like a leader of the insurgents, and the sergeants around him were screeching, insolently, in a mutinous mood, "*iamshchik, ne goni . . .*" a Russian song. Four Eyes was kneeling piously on a bench at Ugo's feet and following, with marveling fear, the swish of the saber above his defenseless head. Else had retreated to her mother behind the bar and the two of them were counting the broken glasses in strictest secrecy.

"Caliban, you sluggish fish, can't you see who's here?" said Ugo to Four Eyes, interrupting his singing for an instant.

"I'm swimming, my Lord and Master, swimming," and Four Eyes swam, his fingers splayed at his hips in imitation of fins.

"Bow low, hideous son of Mistress Barrel, and pour a wassail for my friend Eustachius. Eustachius the Magnanimous, I leave you in the charge of my cup-bearer."

"But there's nothing to pour, oh Lord and Master," whined Four Eyes, holding the bottles up to the light, "the wellsprings have gone dry. Mother's corked the barrel!"

"Crawl, you turtle, over to Mama Cork and knock your useless head on the stone floor until you've softened her heart," said Ugo, sovereign, and was swept up in a fresh song with the sergeants: *Chubchik, chubchik, chubchik kucheriavyi . . .*

"There, you see, Herr Professor," lamented Kurt in a lowered voice. "He's quite mad. He's driven our regulars away and brought in this guttersnipe instead. They've broken a lot of glasses, too. . . . I'm very sorry, Herr Professor, but the bill is going to be rather steep." Kurt noticed Melkior's baffled face and hastened to explain:

"He said it was all to go on your account. Otherwise we wouldn't have served him. I'm sorry, Herr Professor. I hope there won't be a fine to pay as well. We haven't got an entertainment license you see."

"I told him only to have a drink for himself . . ."

". . . and he went and started ordering drinks for everyone, as you can see. *And* breaking things! Tsk-tsk-tsk . . ." said Kurt in dismay at the appalling display.

Melkior watched Ugo savor his madness. God, the sheer amount of energy this madman blows off—into the air, into the smoke of the night! He tried to imagine him old, tired, spent, slouching in a café and playing a one-handed game of dominoes, coughing slightly every now and then. The row of dominoes progressed, but instead of Ugo he found himself, his own shriveled hands, lining up the tiles. And he chuckled at his imagination's deception. He'll die *as he is:* he'll be stupidly, accidentally killed in the drunken euphoria of a night like this . . . or take his own life. The animal setting this force in motion will not be able to languish in the cage of old age.

"Gentlemen centurions," Ugo addressed the sergeants, the saber whistling playfully over their heads, "gentlemen centurions of the 35th Legion, may I now request a song for Fraülein Else of Germany. Enough of the Russian steppe and swirling snow. A song for the Fraülein now, as befits your military dignity. If you please!" and Ugo, dipping the saber in a formal way, launched into song: *Adieu, mein kleiner Gardeoffizier* . . . But the song was unfamiliar to the sergeants and Ugo sang it through on his own, ceremonially facing Else with Junker-like dignity.

Four Eyes was ranging about happily like a drunken dog under the table, where he had been lapping spilt wine off the linoleum and making clicking noises with his tongue in derisive rhythmic accompaniment.

And when the sergeants saw the honorary smile on Else's face (for manners and female vanity required it, let Kurt say what he liked) they, too, unsheathed their sabers and, at the final *adieu, adieu,* crossed them above Ugo's head in an operetta-style apotheosis.

The tableau with the sabers (there *was* some military order to it after all!) managed to move even the angry Kurt: "That was a very good display the rascals made, wasn't it, Herr Professor?" and he gave an admiring smile. But his sober gravity returned presently and his sober worries got hold of him again: "Well, this, I take it, concludes the show. Well done, gentlemen, bravo!" and he applauded artfully.

"And now it's time, gentlemen, please, we're closing, that's it for tonight, gentlemen, if you would be so kind . . ."

How wrong Kurt was. Now was in fact the time to begin the crowning mad revelry in which Ugo was expecting a reward from the Corner owner in the form of further drinks on the house. If only for the sake of the establishment's reputation, sir.

"Sir," he addressed Kurt with the haughtiness of a celebrated virtuoso, "I do not remember when I last visited your highly esteemed establishment. Your name is Kurt, but there is no courtesy in your arrogant nature, sir. We have already performed, bona fide, a part of tonight's show which promises much enjoyment to follow (Caliban, stop smacking your chops like a ravenous beast!) but where, Oh Mr. Kurt, is the due *courtage* for this worthy artistic body, not forgetting our household cur that is in this critical moment sniffing the ground vainly for bones and gnawing at a table leg in desperation? (Four Eyes gave a consensual growl under the table.— "Hush, Caliban!") Very well, take no notice of the cur, or indeed of my humble self, but do take notice, sir, of these intrepid men who may all too soon lay down their lives on the altar of their country. Is that not so, gentlemen centurions of the 35th Legion?"

"So right!" the sergeants shouted in unison, genuinely aroused by Ugo's pathos.

"Indeed I'm right. Fräulein Else, Ophelia had a brother, a nobleman who was killed defending her honor. Your brother would be capable of getting killed defending only the cork of his barrel. . . ."

Kurt had all the while watched him with the patience of a wise yet suffering individual, but now a baleful look flashed in his eye at the insult. Ugo proclaimed the situation to be "highly critical."

"The coward does it with a kiss, the brave man with a sword!" he declaimed with insolent pathos and, in a show of silly threat, pointed the saber at Kurt's chest. Kurt did not flinch. On the contrary, he thrust his chest out valiantly, ready to die. The women screamed. But Ugo, with a peace-loving gesture and a cry of "Farewell to arms!" flung away the saber, which speared the floorboards

with pleasure. He then leaped off the table and hugged Kurt so hard that Kurt could not help but hug him back.

"There, gentlemen warriors, that is how to settle differences! Pass this on up high to your generals!" and Ugo planted a smooch on each of Kurt's perplexed cheeks while winking slyly at the sergeants. "You, Mr. Kurt, are as brave and ungrateful as Cinna, let me shake your hand, let us be friends!"

Kurt was taking it all in good spirits, with nobility. Like a man he took Ugo's hand and shook it vigorously, as one hero to another.

"Right, gentlemen, peace is signed. Now all that's left is to drink to it . . ." Ugo winked at the sergeants, who took it up with the wile of drunkards: "That's right, this calls for a drink." And Kurt indeed signaled Else to bring a bottle of wine, on the house.

After Mother retired there appeared a second bottle, a third, several bottles, and the glass-clinking brought Kurt's drunken declaration that he would go out of the Cozy Corner and into the street on all fours if they would not believe that he was *sincere* and that he *genuinely* loved all of them, his friends. Twice he went down on the floor and started to crawl toward the door; they had to force him up and pledge their trust. Four Eyes alone (pulling his leg) "disbelieved" him and Kurt started crawling again to reassure him. Kurt kept hugging and kissing Ugo, while Ugo, in full abandon as he was, kissed back brother and sister—particularly the sister, who made no effort to conceal her pleasure. Aroused by the wine and the kisses, Else danced with Ugo to a tune played by Four Eyes on his grimy pocket comb. And the sergeant who aspired to Else's love twice grabbed Ugo by the ears and shook him jealously.—Are you a man? —Yes I am, Ugo grinned his fillings bare.—All right then, carry on, selflessly shouted the sergeant, at great pains to conceal his feeling of being ignored.

"You imbecile!" objected the other sergeants. "You nearly spoiled the fun. Why, he's not a *man*, he's a *man and a half.* A he-man!" and they clapped in time to the music Ugo was dancing to. The sergeants were ready to give him their hearts' blood.

"Gentlemen centurions!" exclaimed Ugo in his abandon.

Nobody paid any attention to Melkior. Not even servile Kurt, who had in his drunken bliss totally devoted himself to Ugo. Melkior, too, had had several glasses and his stomach was now clenching in pain: that roast heart wouldn't come amiss, whinged the stomach.

"Hey, Kurt, we'll settle up tomorrow," he whispered into the man's red-hot ear.

"But Herr Professor!" Kurt turned his greasy diluted face to him, "it's my treat, you will allow me, won't you? I'll walk on all fours all the way out to the street corner . . . and I won't have any of . . ." Kurt was ranting, demented, trying to get down on his knees, but he fell over and stayed there lying on the floor, muttering helplessly, "on-on-on all fours, giddyup . . ."

Melkior availed himself of this to sneak undetected out of Cozy Corner.

Autumn rain was drizzling down and the air was clean and fragrant. That's right, Melkior approved of the long-awaited rain and the restorative air. Like a rooster slipping out of a chicken coop he spread his wings easily and felt like crowing.

He sidled quickly into his room, without turning the light on so as not to wake up his guest. The door was not locked. Oh-oh? wondered Melkior.

"Turn it on if you like," said a voice from the dark, "I'm not asleep."

Melkior did so and stammered a hesitant good evening; who knows, perhaps this is frowned on as well. The Stranger muttered something in reply. He had chosen the sofa to sleep on, leaving the bed to his host. On the floor by the sofa lay a huge pile of domestic and foreign newspapers, thrown down in disarray. A thorough briefing . . . before sleep, thought Melkior.

"The bed was meant for you," he said, locking the door with careful precaution full of a certain awe. (At which the guest gave a superior smile.) "You won't sleep well on that."

"I never sleep well . . . anywhere," said the guest with a cautious hesitation, as if revealing a secret. He gave a cordial smile and added: "like a rabbit . . . I see you have many fine books. While I have to read this trash," and he pointed at the papers. "I manage to crack a book now and then on a train. But that's not reading really . . . it's cinematographic, flickering, broken," and he heaved a sigh of resignation. "If you want to work or anything . . . the light doesn't bother me."

Melkior was touched by the consideration. He felt like making a gesture, showing his goodwill, his respect. . . .

"I'm sorry, here we are sharing a room and I haven't even told you who I am," and he made to approach his guest with his hand out, to introduce himself.

"No," his guest stopped him very energetically, "don't tell me your name! No names, please . . . The people I know," he went on with a calm smile, "I generally know by assumed names. I don't know what my own is anymore," laughed the guest cheerfully. "That business this morning . . . when we met on the street . . ." he shrugged helplessly: "there's nothing for it—that's *our* life. I'm sorry."

Melkior was moved by this: there, it's not as if he were . . . ! He remembered ATMAN in a flash and the worm inside got on with its business: I'm duty bound, he thought romantically.

"I was looking for you all over today, on the off chance."

"Did something happen?" the guest asked rather incuriously. "I'm not easy to find . . . especially by those who look for me," he joked. "Why?"

"This man downstairs, the palmist . . ."

"The palmist?" laughed the guest. "That's right, there was some magician who greeted me on the staircase this morning, on the landing below."

"That's him, that's ATMAN," said Melkior apprehensively. "ATMAN is his 'stage' name. I suggested it to him . . ." he couldn't help boasting, derisively.

"ATMAN?" laughed the guest. "Yes, he greeted me in a very distinguished way, asked me if I was staying 'upstairs,' and pointed upward, without mentioning you. 'He's a most honest man. An absolutely great soul, the pride of the house, you can trust him completely,' that's what he blurted out in your honor, quick as a flash."

"There, you see?" shivered Melkior in horror.

"See what? Oh, that," he understood Melkior's fear. "No, no; nothing to worry about, I know *them*," said the guest confidently.

"You don't know ATMAN," Melkior insisted on being suspicious, "he's a mysterious rascal."

"Well, he would be—being mysterious is his stock in trade," the guest was enjoying himself. "What's ATMAN mean, by the way?"

"A great spirit in ancient Brahmin philosophy. But it's also what Schopenhauer called his dog."

"Ah-ha, a point for you. So this 'great spirit' tells the future, does he?"

"You can well imagine his clients. But he's got loftier ambitions: he works out horoscopes. Historical forecasts, too . . . Has them published in a newspaper. He is predicting the sinking of the *Bismarck*."

"Hah, that is an easy one. The English will sink it."

"But he says their *George* V will go down, too."

"Of course it will—the Germans will take it down. You don't have to be ATMAN to see that. Much more valuable things are going to be destroyed in this stupid war along with it," said the guest with a nervous yawn.

"I hope you won't get me wrong," said Melkior cautiously, "do you believe Hitler will be . . ."

"Done in? What does believing have to do with it? I'm working, together with all the other anti-Hitlerites, to bring him down. That is my belief. If I didn't work, I wouldn't believe."

"Or is it the other way around?"

"Well, perhaps . . ." said the guest with vexation. Melkior feared he might have offended him, but he did not intend to conceal his doubt.

"It's only . . ." he began hesitatingly, "that it doesn't look like everybody's at work to bring him down. The firmest believers aren't." They've reached a pact, he thought of Don Fernando.

"Oh yes they are," said the guest unkindly, "and they'll be working harder still. They'll do the hardest work of all. They will have to!" he finished with a fury that went beyond Melkior's evident falter, reaching much further to strike at something big and hard.

This seemed to conclude the conversation. Melkior undressed and got into bed.

"Shall I turn off the light?"

"As you wish," the guest answered harshly, evidently far away in other thoughts.

Melkior switched off the light and said goodnight. He got no reply. Fatigue had him in its close embrace in the bed but was not letting sleep near him. Instead it loosed a pack of weird thoughts to rip apart his exhaustion. Surefooted travelers who know their way. Beyond seven grim mountains and seven cruel crocodile-infested rivers there lies something, something founded on wisdom and justice. And they set off to reach there. Across a trackless, muddy wasteland, bone-weary, they trudge on, never for a moment doubting the point of their march. For ten years, night after night (they hide by day) they have carried iron levers and pipes slogging through mud, inquiring as they go: "Where's the supervisor?"

"What supervisor?"

"The levers and pipes supervisor! We're tired, will the supervisor please speak up?"

"You are gullible. There is no supervisor."

Standing in ankle-deep mud they plead, but they do not put down the levers and pipes. It would be more sensible to drop their load in the mud and get some rest while inquiring about the *supervisor* who is not there.

This saddens me. Then again, I can't very well tell them to lay down their load, can I? After all, who am I? Am I myself the missing supervisor? Does anyone know anything for a fact? There is a moment when it occurs to me to tell them I am the supervisor just to see what will happen. But, but then, there'd be no telling what responsibility I'd have to shoulder. Carrying the levers and pipes through mud for ten years, night after night . . . Who's to tell where this leads to, what purpose it serves, and who is behind it all? Oh no, let them slog on searching for their supervisor—I've turned up only by chance, I'm passing through, and I have no idea whether or not there even is a supervisor. Perhaps there is one after all.

"Then why do you say there isn't?"

"Oh, people say all kinds of things. Would you be better off going back?"

This I say just for the sake of saying something, with a cautious man's uncertainty. I am afraid to interrupt the conversation; who knows what the consequences might be?

"Go back?" they reply in rage. "We've been carrying this stuff for ten years and now you want us to carry it back? Well, that makes it clear—*you are the supervisor!*"

"I? Not a chance!" I begin to tremble. "I'll help you if you like, I'll join you." Oh God, now I've gone and made a mess of it! I know I have even as I say the words.

"All right, if you say so. Prove you are what you claim to be."

But this is not said in an unkind way, perhaps not in so many words as it later seems. They speak gently, in the manner of weary people who have few words to choose from but suit what they say to their mood, so that while the words themselves may be cutting, the tone is soothing.

"Come on, come on, don't let's waste any more time. What's the idea of going all pensive on us? You're studying us, right?"

This is what is terrible: how am I to behave? Is my every thought plainly written on my face? You've got to think as you walk—somehow it shortens the distance and conquers fatigue. And I (oddly enough!) try to do my thinking in my pocket! Don't be surprised—it can be done. As soon as a thought comes to life in the mind, another thought takes it down to your pocket, see, and you can turn it over and over in there . . . for who would think of such a thing? It's like having a handful of coins in your pocket and counting them with your fingertips: sorting them by size or value, adding, subtracting, multiplying, dividing, combining *big* with *small* according to what fits or doesn't fit where, carrying out mathematical operations, building whole phrases with additions, with subordinate clauses even, with metaphors and ornaments, all of it making sense or not . . . in a word, thinking in your pocket. "What have you got inside you that keeps making that jingling sound?"

"Jingling? Am I a gilded plaster-of-Paris piggy bank?" Thinking (in my head): well, what do you know—it's audible. Saying to them: "I've got some small change in my pocket and I'm fiddling with it to pass the time. Why, is that so bad?"

"Don't go all innocent on us. You know what is and what isn't good far better than we do. All we know is that we must carry and *deliver*, but that doesn't mean we're bored."

"Have you still a long way to go?"

"We don't know. There you are playing innocent again. You know we don't know; it is cruel of you to ask. You can see we're on our last legs."

This is true: they have no way of knowing, but I am not asking out of cruelty.

Indeed it seems to me that my conscience demands that I share with them the painfulness of that infinity which even in the imagination cannot be seen as having an end or offering any respite. Well, it turns out I am wrong. What is the point of such a question out of courtesy when there is no answer—and if there is it might well turn out to be pointless. Would the levers and pipes be any less heavy if you knew where and how far they were to be lugged? Of course not. And yet . . . the effort factor is correlated to the distance to be covered while lugging the load. True, neither is the load lighter nor is the distance shorter if you know its length. But there, at least the traveler has something to keep his mind on during the tedium of marching. He can, for instance, divide (if only in his pocket) the vast quantity before him, split it into smaller parts, into halves, the halves into their halves, the resultant halves into halves, and halves into halves again . . . and so forth, until he *reaches* (note the word) such insignificant quantities that it seems to him he no longer has in front of him a magnitude which frightens him. Everything becomes as easy as zero, as a fraction of the insubstantial. Both the distance and the load.

Smiling cheerfully before him is the cunning wisdom of the Greek hair splitter . . . Come to think of it, a hair, too, can be split to insubstantiality, as any bald man will tell you . . .

"What did you say?"

"Nothing. Did I say something?"

"Look here, I lost my hair working, sweating. Don't mock a man for looking like this through no fault of his own."

As if any bald man looked "like this" through any fault of his own? That is what I could have told him, it would have been instructive; but I do not dare—I only think it, in my pocket, too. . . . The man is furious, which is why he reads my thoughts . . .

"Of course there are some who appear as they do through every fault of their own. I refer to libertines, lechers, and all the other drunken scum for which there isn't enough rope out there to hang them with or lead to shoot them. Parasites."

He couldn't be meaning I'm a lecher, given that I . . . But is there any need for me to prove all this when I am so clearly not one of them. Not even with Enka. On the contrary, as a matter of . . . there's Viviana . . . but what's the point of getting into that? He probably only means to insult me with the groundless allusion . . .

"Because some of them act the saint supposedly expiring with chastity while blazing inside with sexual agitation. Then these low-lifes tell me I'm this and I'm that, that all I know to do with my wife is make babies. Well, what am I to do with my wife? Have her put on black stockings, tie a black ribbon around her white neck, and then whisper vulgar nothings in her ear? Yes, I would be somebody to those no-goods if I did that, they would see me as one of them. As if I cared to be. One of them in what, I ask you—in abominations?"

The man is sincere enough in his anger. Moreover he makes no effort to conceal the threat in his tone as an advance on his future high salary. Yes, he does expect the Future to reward him for his present privations, for his righteous agitation, even for his faithful thoughts with moral fasting and Lenten fare. He wishes to enter the Paradise of the Future pure as a saint and torment-stricken as a martyr—not so that he can claim any additional privileges or get a better mark at the future moral assessment of his person, but simply to be able to look back and see the past in himself as a scarecrow, a horror, as something never under any circumstances to be wished for again. In this way he is insuring himself against the diabolical longing to retreat, against any silly curiosity drawing him back, singing the sentimental siren call of the past. He knows the Future to be grand and marvelous, but where is it? At which spot is the entrance to that wonderful place strewn with flowers and justice? Not only does he not know—he is angry at the very existence of such a threshold and at the nagging desire to find out how much more he needs to walk to reach the doorway to the Future.

This is why he dislikes those who think about this, and generally those who think at all. He views them with suspicious caution and alert hostility as if they are terrorists plotting an attempt at taking the precious life of his faith in the Future . . .

The Future? What about you—do you believe in the future?

He could not tell, at first, whether it was his guest asking him or he was still listening to his own insatiable train of thought.

No, the guest was sound asleep. His regular breathing was dividing the night into equal slices of darkness, neatly, justly, like mouthfuls to the hungry.

What can I say, gentlemen of the jury, in reply to your question, as strange as it is vague? (This was the opening sentence of Melkior's grand defense speech.) As a short-lived individual facing the totality of duration, what idea can I form of that which you call the future? Is the Future merely a tomorrow-or-the-day-after I can purchase for cheap (at a discount) downstairs, from my neighbor, ATMAN the palmist? Or is it something distant, very distant, so distant that not only does it dwarf my lifespan (thus allowing me as an individual to say that it has nothing to do with me) but also renders itself elusive to my very thought, no matter how hard I'm trying to imagine future events from my present? True, my thought itself reaches out for that blank, unfilled time before me . . . and gives free rein to my ranging imagination. My imagination fills future time . . . but *with what?* That is the question, gentlemen. This is a test of man's consciousness—moreover, his conscience: this is what reveals who belongs to whom. Your imagination reveals who you are; it also determines whose you are.

Imagination has divided men whether they like it or not . . . But, gentlemen of the jury, do man's imaginings decide his destiny? If future is the next, as yet unwound reel of life, gentlemen, then I ask: what can my imagination ever do to alter a single frame of the film? It has already been developed and printed. It is already out there, it has as yet only to *happen*—that is to say, to be run for our experience, for my eyes and ears.

To the pertinent question: But who did the filming? (Shouts from the gallery: that's right, hear! hear! who did the filming?) I reply: No one! (Excited buzz to the right, among the theologians . . . and to the left, among the causalists.) (To the theologians:) Yes, you find this difficult to grasp. Nothing without a Demiurge. You consider the chair squeaking beneath you: was it not made by someone? It, too, did not at first exist and only came into being in some "future" or another following a cabinetmaker's concept. Oh if only the Future were a chair, gentlemen, mankind would be able to lounge in it without a care! If it could be built following a concept—be it an idiot's—it would at least contain the sense (or nonsense) of an idea, whether it were idiotic, absurd, monstrous, unacceptable. The idiot's whim could be that there would be only female newborns for the next forty years: mankind would thus be deprived of two generations of males. Can you imagine the consequences from the sexual, and particularly from the military, vantage point? God be praised— you theologians would say—the future is in the hands of Providence which maintains the order of things and events (I note your policelike style as regards "keeping the peace"), and that is why the male-to-female birth ratio is kept in balance, therefore. . . . Well, go on, finish your priceless thought . . . therefore mankind is content, even happy in every way, and especially from the military vantage point, right? Hear! Hear! So let's toast mankind for its secure future whenever we happen to get drunk, which we do with great success, particularly on New Year's Eve.

(Speaking to the causalists): You, gentlemen, naturally laugh at such drunken contentment. Being drunk is poetic at first, then later on it comes to resemble idiocy. You still respect the ancient *ex nihilo nihil fit* principle too well to be able to leave the world's destiny to a very doubtful Providence (of which there is no factual proof), still less to an idiot's whim. It having been established through long-term human experience that everything evolves according to the law of causality—from cause to effect—the principle is clear as day and strong as a mountain . . . Until someone "shall doubt in his heart" the mountain will stand and not be cast into the sea. But if ye have faith as a grain of mustard seed, the mountain will fall down. David brought Goliath down by doubting in his strength. I am reminded of David Hume, a good man. But regardless of his grave doubts regarding Causality (which, like ATMAN the con man, passes itself off as a Principle while in fact being no more than ordinary *habit*), I do not propose to offend the deity in question; I would ask only: what if one day we were to push a stone and it didn't fall but instead rolled back to its place? I mean, what if the effects betray the causes? If snakes hatch from hens' eggs? If parrot speech gives rise to a new linguistics, rhetoric, logic, even literature? If crocodile laughter evolves into a new kind of humor? And all that out of habit which through sustained practice could become a Principle?

Allow me, gentlemen, to voice here my thanks to a wise man who discovered in the Principle poetic subtleties that Aristotle himself never dreamed of. I am referring to Sganarel, a servant who was deprived of his wages through the peculiar death of his master, Don Juan, the most brazen of your followers. (Kindly pay causal attention to this: cause, death; effect, loss of wages).

Sganarel's syllogistics are a Dadaist poetry of causality as expressed in the logical inconsequentiality typical of that kind of poetry. Depoetized by causal rigidity and reduced to a pure syllogism it would appear as follows: in this world man is like a bird on a branch;

the branch clings to the trunk; he who clings to the trunk is following good advice; an ape clings to the trunk; therefore an ape follows
good advice . . .

"I'm an ape! Eustachius the Vivianic, I'm an ape!" Ugo was
yelling under the window, loud enough for the whole street to hear.

Let the street hear it: he is following good advice. Even so, Melkior raised an ear from the pillow for Ugo's anguished nocturnal cry:

"All right, Eustachius, I admit it, I'm . . . what am I?" This, now,
was only a spent reflection, which was nevertheless audible in the
still of the night. On its heels came another flicker of hope sent
toward the dark, mute window up on high:

"Eustachius the Cosmic, what am I?"

"An ape," said Melkior and a voice out in the street simultaneously. But Melkior could not follow the street quarrel between
Ugo and the inimical voice—Sganarel had come back on with the
powerful rhetoric of syllogistic chains. What is the future built on?
Promises. What is being promised? Happiness. What is happiness?
No one knows, but everyone would like some. To want is to have
not; to have not leads to penury; penury is poverty; poverty is not
wealth; wealth is power; the powerful rule; he who rules ignores the
law; he who ignores the law commits repression; repression gives
rise to fear; fear leads to hate; to hate is not to love; love should be
cautious; caution is the mother of wisdom; wisdom is not stupidity;
stupidity is often boastful; a boastful man is a braggart; braggarts are
often liars; liars lie through their teeth; teeth are part of the body; the
body will perish; to perish is to give up the ghost; the ghost is
Hamlet's father; the father is the head of the family; the family is a
unit of society; society is a collection of individuals; an individual
amounts to nothing; nothing does not exist; to exist is to think; I
think, therefore I am; I am and I am not; I am not what I was
yesterday; yesterday was a fine day; day comes after night; at night
you go to sleep; sleep is what I seek in vain; in vain do I try to stop;
stop me, please; please stop me; stop me, please; please stop me;
stop me, please . . . Will nobody stop me? Gentlemen of the jury . . .

"Nobody," came a voice from the empty space around Melkior.

"Yes, yes, quite . . . But your revenge is pitiful, gentlemen!" he shouted on surfacing from the whirlpool of logic. "Is it fair to leave a man in that vicious circle of conclusions and let him spin around forever? Let me walk down the straight line of duration and I'll set off with a song on my lips. Neither am I interested in speed (I can crawl if need be) nor am I afraid of the eternity before me. I shall moo in reply to the Sphinx's questions for I do not know the answers, and she will let me pass. On the other side is Oedipus Rex, patricide, the husband of his mother, the brother of his children. His tragedy awaited him in the future and no amount of time could have averted it. Time merely brought it about and ran the tragedy through itself so it would happen. To become looking and listening, the fulfillment of prophecy and apprehension. To stop existing as fear and imagination, to become the reality of a horror. Time is a fearful dimension of existence, gentlemen, wherein our futures are insidiously hidden. I hate time, murderer of all life!

But to return to your question: what can I say in reply to it, gentlemen of the jury? I am no warrior with belief in victory. I am no statesman to believe in force. I am no poet to believe in glory. I am no believer to believe in angelic trumpets at the Last Judgment. I am no penitent to expect mercy. I am no desperate man to wish for death. I am a man, conceived in the blindness of passion, in the dark of the womb, launched into time for a painful duration. By way of provisions I was given joy and pain (more pain than joy) and two eyes to watch torment and two ears to listen to the sobbing of the most anguished among creatures, the one that invented tears and laughter alike. I was also given a mouth to chew my bitter crust. And a tongue to be saying *woe!* I was given arms to build and destroy, to embrace and to kill. And legs to flee when pursued, and to pursue in turn. I have a heart that allows me to suffer worse than any other creature. I have reason so that I can lie to myself and *know* I am lying to myself so that I can go on living. In order to look forward to the next day which may bring joy. And when no joy appears I will hope again and fill my thoughts with lies to bring on sleep. And I shall dream that I am *alive forever.* But then Polyphemus, the one-eyed

Cyclops, will wake and plug the cave of my dream with an enormous rock and there will be no way out.

Something dreadful and huge will snatch me and I'll wake up in the hands of cannibals . . .

How much longer the night lasted is not known, but somebody was trying to smash the rock apart at the entrance, striking it hard. Melkior listened to the rescuing blows. He wanted to call out, "I'm alive in here," but couldn't; he meant to strike from inside, but was unable to move. The blows grew faint, as though the person was giving up. He panicked, oh no, they'll leave, and he bellowed with all his might, "I'm here, I'm alive!"—"Open up then," came a voice from the other side.

The rescuer seemed to have laughed, too, muttering something. Melkior sat up in bed. A gray autumn day, rain-soaked and gloomy, glanced at him morosely through the window.

"Come on, open up!" said the voice, giving the door an open-handed angry slap.

"Coming . . ." The police, he thought and instantly remembered . . . But the sofa was empty. Tidied up, moreover, the bed-clothes neatly folded on the headrest, with a "thank you" look and salutation.

Standing at the door was the city coat of arms on an official hat, wringing wet with rainwater.

"What a sound sleeper! I could've raised the dead," said the coat of arms. "Summons for you."

"From the police?" smiled Melkior, the word giving him a nasty kick to the gut.

"Nothing to do with the police," and an index finger pointed to the coat of arms. "It's from the army. Town Council, Department of National Service. Sign here, please. Goood. Than-kyou!"

Well, well. So it's turned out to be . . ."civilian" business after all. Except for the hat . . . But the coat of arms is civic, historic, tramlike. All nice and peaceable—nothing to do with the police. Heh.

The summons lay on the table, facing the rainy day. (Yes, that was how it had been in his mind's eye: it would arrive on a rainy day.

Service days are rainy, pursuant to olive drab regulations.) The small white square piece of paper exerted its might, exhibiting the power on its brow in bold large type and addressing odds and ends, the particulars, which were, after all, immaterial. . . . Destiny has come under my roof . . .

Melkior stood in the middle of the room like an idiot—barefoot, in striped pajamas (clothing for a lunatic asylum)—and shivered. A frozen grin of surprise clung to his face. This is how they come for you at dawn and take you away for *execution*. He said *whoa* now and again, *whoa*, trying to slow down his frightened mule. But the mule only pricked up its cautious ears . . . Whoa! If only I could stay like this . . . forever!

A discarded cigarette is burning down in the street. A butt flicked out of a high window. A sizeable butt, nearly half the cigarette; as there is only a gentle breeze it might survive for quite a time, fifteen or twenty minutes, under favorable circumstances. Perhaps even longer, as long as an insect would survive crossing the street. A cockroach. No, a cigarette butt is a fallen firefly . . . A woman of sin expelled from a bed where love has come and gone. It flew in a burning arc like a meteor, out the window—into the street. It is now sending up smoke from the ember. Burning, alive . . .

"I could step off the pavement, go out into the middle of the road and kill it, stomp on it."

A murderous thought requiring decision and deliberate action: that of stomping underfoot. Of murder. "For it is stupid for a butt to be alive in the middle of the road while upstairs there is only exhaustion and boredom in bed. The end."

"You don't love me anymore, I know. You would dearly love to flick me now out the window like a cigarette butt, for someone to crush on the street. You're done smoking me . . ."

"I'll be smoking again . . ."

"Yes. Smoking another cigarette. I'm finished. I'm a butt."

"You're a briar . . ."

"That's right, call me a liar!"

"I said briar. A briar pipe."

"Why a pipe? Does that have to do with your desire?"

326

"A pipe is something you don't throw away. The longer you use it the finer it gets."

"Like a violin. The longer you play it . . ."

"Yes, exactly like a violin."

"And you will play?"

"Like a virtuoso!"

"Don't play like a virtuoso. Just plain play."

"*Plain* is how you play the bass. The violin should be played virtuoso. You are a violin. Look at yourself in the mirror over there, full figure, naked—aren't you a violin?"

"Yes I am. Shall we play?"

"No, we'll sleep. I'm a recruit. Hair shorn to the skin. Army cap lying low on my ears. Belt above the half-belt, you horrid little man!"

You've got to get up, you've got to get up . . . screamed the bugle.

"You woke it with your *shall we play!* You're . . . Where are you?"

"Not looking for Greta Garbo, are you, pretty boy?" leered the drill sergeant from his bunk. "They're tarts, all those night birds—flitting away at the crack of dawn. Take it from Nettle, old garrison rat."

The barracks room laughed a dry, flattering laugh in the groggy grayness of the cold, senseless dawn.

. . . *you've got to get up this morning, you* . . . toots the bugle outside to the gray sky. Screeching into Melkior's silly, sleepy ear: Rise and shine! Gotta groom the horses for King and Country! This is no hotel, you spoiled brat. Get your ass out of bed and off to the stables with you!

A penetrating jet of stable stench shot up his nostrils. But the equine ammonia cleared the torpid mind and stirred fresh, unsoldierly thoughts.

Is the King really so keen on horses? Each horse is my senior by a year or two. This ought to be very old age for equine gerontology. Hence the care. (Above each stall there is a board with the occupant's name and year of birth.) So nice and caring. I'm glad to see the horses are well looked after.

"Tennn-shun!" yelled the sergeant, who for some reason called himself Nettle. All the skin-shorn heads under army caps quaked on the spot: through them, down the wire of discipline, had passed a jolt of Nettle. They stood in line along the stable passage stretching all the way down the row of stalls, and waited for Nettle's command to jump to, each to his horse. The pampered animals are angry and hungry in the morning, biting and kicking, neighing wildly, will not let anyone come close. The recruits were trembling.

Melkior was reading the names on the boards: Prince, Caesar, Lisa (a mare), Boy, Ziko . . . He was standing in front of Caesar. Rather, Caesar was standing in front of him, idly flicking his tail left and right. Waiting.

Oh mighty Caesar (spake the wretched Melkior, trembling before the powerful rump), my heart is not the heart of Brutus. I kiss thy mighty hoof, not in flattery but with a plea to spare me, so that I might live on after we have parted ways. Receive my tribute as thou would receive the loyalty of Mark Antony who loved and feared thee and fearing thee respected thee even as I respect thy almighty haunches and thy gnashing teeth which in thy just rage . . .

Caesar gave an impatient neigh—he was bored with the speech. Cut to the chase! But that was a psychological trick of the high and mighty, as Melkior knew, and he clearly saw his plea for mercy had failed; Melkior must not approach the tyrant. He awaited Nettle's command with trepidation: he knew he was not going to budge.

"Now then, crew," Nettle strutted before the men (the entire barracks rested on his shoulders!) and issued instructions, "I don't want none of the you-never-told-us stuff. I want the horses looking like prima donnas! Get it? Hey, new guy over there, whatcha laughin' at, pretty boy?" This referred to Melkior, who had not been laughing at all. "Y'know what a prima donna is, dontcher?"

Melkior was silent, afraid of this being a trap. The boys nudged each other in the ribs, their cheeks bursting with laughter.

"Well, here's a fine kettle o' fish!" Nettle was dejected, omnipotently so. "An in-tel-lec-tual who don't know what a prima donna is? Didya hear that, my sorry lads?" he asked the men.

The men knew the moment has not yet come and they bit their tongues. "What are ya—a civil engineer?" Nettle asked Melkior as if he had known his father.

Melkior knew it was time to step into Nettle's trap—further resistance might only worsen the man's mood . . .

"A teacher," he mumbled.

"Don't say! Teach!" Nettle was overjoyed at the news. "So you oughta know how to turn off a lightbulb, then?"

"Er . . . yes, I do." He could not help but reply; it was the rules. He even mimed the switching off of a light switch, to increase the merriment.

"Oh, like that," Nettle was disappointed (and the men were still keeping a straight face), "well, anyone can do it like that, even Numbskull here," and he pointed at a little soldier with a constantly bewildered face. "Right, Numbskull? Now you know how, dontcher?"

"Know what, Sergeant?" Numbskull was not paying attention, he hadn't been following the exchange . . .

"How to turn off a light."

"Yes I do, Sergeant. By barking!" Numbskull rattled this off like a lesson learned by heart.

"Barking at what?"

"The lightbulb, of course."

The stable echoed with a burst of laughter, which made the very horses neigh—they, too, found this hilarious.

"You're lying!" Nettle was outshouting both men and horses, "you're lying!"

Damned Numbskull had spoiled his fun! That was why the silly idiots were laughing—laughing at him, blast 'em . . .

"You bark at it, eh? All right, Numbskull—go on, get barking. Bark at the one over your head," Nettle was taking his revenge. "Bark at it till it goes out. Now!"

And Numbskull started to bark, sharply and earnestly, like the worst tempered of dogs.

But Nettle was not winning: Numbskull seemed to enjoy it. He barked in all registers and tonalities, interpreting various types of canine character—various scenes, too. He whimpered like a pampered poodle, snarled like a mean flesh-ripping boxer, barked in the formal sluggish manner of a chained guard dog, shrilled in a frenzy like a stupid hysterical dog shunned by bitches, yapped merrily teasing the passersby like a roving ownerless dog, and howled piteously as though his master had died the day before. He really had barking down pat. He had them all admiring him, even emotionally moved, there was muttering in the row.

And Melkior envied him. Why the devil hadn't he known how to turn off a light! (Well, now it was obvious—by barking! Yes, it was obvious, *now*; like Columbus's egg. Nuts to you!) He would now have been standing there under the lightbulb and barking away to his heart's content as if singing under the Christmas tree: "Angels we have heard on high . . ."

He would not have been forced to approach the great Caesar and beg for mercy from his hoof. For Caesar was a horse known in this stable for his imperial whims. Perhaps he would have deigned to accept only someone who matched him for greatness, some horseman of renown, Colleoni, Gattamelata, Napoleon, not you, shorn-to-the-skin recruit Melkior, full of human fear. Bucephalus would let no one come near him but Alexander known as the Great, Bucephalus was afraid of his own shadow . . . What are *you* afraid of, Oh illustrious Caesar? The Ides of March? Shall we ask ATMAN—he will know. Well, it might be later or it might be earlier, dear Caesar, who's to know about all the beastly tricks that you horses and horsemen use to make history? Anyway, your Capitol is definitely on the cards, you'll be neighing the famous *tu quoque* soon enough.

He was hating Caesar and mocking him. And Caesar snorted to placate him "don't worry" and swished his tail hypocritically.

Sure, don't worry . . . and then you'll make with the hoof! You thick-headed envious brute, you'll smash all my ribs yet! Damn you and your entire warrior race!

We didn't want to go to war—they made us do it.

They made you do it? For all your strength? So why didn't you bite and kick them? Why didn't you bristle like a cat and throw them? Instead of tormenting an innocent young man here now. Yes, but those were famous horsemen (you were not ridden by Socrates or Plato). The combat bugling, the charges, the gallops! . . . Monuments in impressive postures! Neither Homer nor Shakespeare nor Dante has such monuments as you, Horse the Great! You've become a major celebrity indeed!

"To the horses!" bellowed Nettle suddenly, fit to shake the stable. And the words gave birth to a weird bedlam: human and equine voices mingling to produce a horrible shrilling (they feared each other), neighing and the screams of those kicked by the hooves. The men rushed in, storming the stalls, and there went up a terrible supplicant shouting:

Prince, stand!
Lisa, stand!
Boy, stand!
Ziko, stand!
. . . .
. . . .
. . . .

in voices full of wretched human despair as if each man were invoking his own saint. Hooves resounded on wooden partitions and the hapless young men leaped back out of the way, dodged kicks, and coaxed the exalted animals with bread and sugar, and some of them, the more daring ones, pacified them (covertly) with open-palm slaps between the eyes. (Raising a hand against sacred equinity! the crime carried a heavy penalty.)

But Caesar's glorious name was not mentioned. He was not asked to please "stand." His groom did not step forward. He did not rush into the stall under Caesar's hooves. He remained standing in the walk with "Numbskull," who was still doggedly barking at the lightbulb.

At Nettle's command Melkior did not move. Perhaps he wanted to move, he hadn't meant to resist, but his feet would not budge. All his fear had gone into his feet and they anchored themselves in security, knees touching lightly, consoling each other. Then a darkness began to descend, Numbskull's lightbulb dimmed, and his barking became distant, distant, barely audible, from somewhere beyond the silent hills . . . "He did it—he managed to turn off the light," thought Melkior pleasurably, sinking into the murk . . .

Rain beating on his eyes, lightning flashing, thunderbolts striking his head . . . He had wisely gone still and was waiting for the storm to blow over. Day was already breaking, he could make out a mournful grayness: his eyes were peering into the fog; he could hear strange voices, up there, above his head, floating in the air, whispering softly, gently, considerately—angels conferring. Never mind, he'd better wait for the sun to come out, to warm him and dry away the rain and the night's horror . . .

But the rain splashed down again . . . Slaps smacking his cheeks . . . Human words near at hand . . . Horses, the stable . . .

He opened his eyes. Faces . . . a lot of funny noses . . . Numbskull's lightbulb shining on above, under the roof beam . . . The barking had stopped. . . .

"All right, Mama's boy, can you see me?" asked Nettle's face from up on high, enormous, round, painted on an inflated balloon. "A shame we haven't got a Perfumery Corps, it would've been just the job for you, eh, doll? Handling scented soap, not horse shit," Nettle was joking crudely up there above Melkior, his hands ready for any further face-slapping. "Sorry, ducks, but that's the army for you—shit and piss. Man's work. Can you stand?"

Melkior stirred. He felt dirty wetness around and on himself (they were pouring water from the horse trough on me) and sank back down, helplessly. He was lying on wet and smelly straw, in mud. Around him were a multitude of boots in a ring, with legs growing upward from them, slim like sickly trees, swaddled in olive drab nappies. And above him faces, curious, derisive, strange, unknown. I have betrayed Caesar—and a kind of smile tickled his lips.

"Get him up," commanded Nettle. "You and you, take him outside, let him get a bit of air . . ."

Day was breaking, gray and desperate. Dreadful birds were cawing from bare black branches. In the distance, the city was waking, stretching its limbs, yawning into the hopeless sky, muttering morosely.

Melkior shivered with the cold: wetness around the neck, wet on his back, on his chest, a wet army cap on his head. Wet wetted, wet living.

Two kind recruits helped him up on either side.

"Well done, man," spoke up the one on the left. "Next stop pneumonia, I shouldn't wonder. That's a month in the hospital, plus at least three weeks' Light Duties Only afterward. With any luck, there might also be a spot on the lungs and a medical discharge."

"I didn't fake any of it. I think I passed out."

"You think, therefore you are—a genuine case, I mean . . ." laughed the left-hand recruit. "Come on, man, don't be afraid—you don't think I'm having it any better than you, do you? We're in the same shit."

"You're shivering—you've got a fever," said Righty with selfless hope.

"You want to report for a medical tomorrow."

"I'm wet through, I'm cold," said Melkior through chattering teeth. "Can't I report today?"

"Too late. You must report to Staff first thing in the morning tomorrow." Then, having glanced at a barrack where lights had just gone on, "Oh look, the hotel guests are waking, the pajama boys are getting up."

"What's that—officers' quarters?" asked Melkior naïvely.

"Pajama boys? Golden chains around their necks. Ministers' offspring!" said Righty, taking off his cap with mocking respect. "Our young Majesty's nursing cousins," he added, whispering in Melkior's ear.

"That, you must know, is the 'exemplary school of rough military life,'" said Lefty. "They get the *exemplary* treatment, and the rest of us get the *rough*. You'll be hearing about it in Theory Classes."

"So they . . . don't groom horses?"

"No, it's the other way about—horses groom them."

"The boys were transferred over here from their regiments to have someone wipe their asses for them," said Righty humorlessly. "Their daddies came up with the idea of setting up a Motor Transport Company to keep the lads occupied. So they drive army vehicles up and down the capital, going to their Mamas on Sundays. They're generally back in the barracks by Monday; some don't come back for days at a time, it all depends on how powerful Daddy is. They're off to the mess now, for cocoa."

"And when the war breaks out they'll be off to Switzerland with their Mamas, to treat their enlarged hila. You and I have to spit blood, my friend, to make it into the hospital. Unless the horses get you first."

Melkior shuddered at the prospect. Nothing had helped: the fasting or the vigils. Pechárek had got him in his clutches after all. He had consigned the fifty-six kilograms' worth of this wretched body (dwaftees . . . Kink and countwy) to Nettle the trainer in the royal reservation fenced with barbed wire. Procrastinating, delaying, passing examinations and medical boards—no go! Right, pal, this is where you'll be preparing to shed blood and lay down your life! And here was Melkior trembling in death's anteroom with cold and fear and a hundred other unspoken pains. He was not made for Nettle's "man's work," the horse urine and the muck . . . his masculinity wasn't adequate, the damned exclamation mark in front of his life!

"There's some dry straw behind the stable, we might as well hide there until it's black-chicory beverage time (Ah, Chicory Hasdrubalson, gentle my friend! sighed Melkior). Why, you're shivering all over, pal! Come along," Lefty dragged him around the corner of the stable and actually buried him in straw, leaving only his face free—to let him watch the birth of the new day.

"You'll have to get out of here by hook or by crook," said Righty seriously, rolling a cigarette from dust he had collected in his pockets. "You're too weak—and you haven't seen half the trouble yet.

First puff of breeze, you'll be blown off your horse. Ever ridden before?"

"I have. On a donkey," smiled Melkior in the straw: he had begun to feel the warmth.

"Yes, well, you wouldn't have horses down in Dalmatia. I'm a country boy myself, I've been riding since I was a boy, but the ones in here have got even me scared. Nasty brutes, every last one of them. And Nettle's assigned you to Caesar, the worst of the lot. Watch your back—he's got it in for you. Get out of this place. Your goose is cooked if you don't."

In the mess hall Numbskull sat next to him for breakfast. Not purposely—it was a quirk of the seating arrangement—but he seemed to take it as a lucky coincidence; he had wanted to talk to Melkior, who had not touched his food. "Don't take it personal," said Numbskull, watching the slice of bread spread with some kind of black jam in front of Melkior. "I did it on purpose, see. After all, you're a high-class intellectual, a teacher, right? You can tell it just looking at you. Now I, well, I enjoy that kind of thing. I always liked barking—bow-wowing, I mean, doing dog imitations. I can rouse all the dogs within hearing distance. I'll show you one of these nights, you'll see."

"I believe you . . . uh . . ."

"Call me Numbskull. Doesn't bother me, let them get used to it, it serves its purpose."

"What do you mean?"

"Getting labeled. Numbskull is a pet name for dimwit. I mean all this business about pride . . . what do we need pride for? A prideful recruit? Pull the other one why don't you! Aren't you eating? No? Can I have it then? Thanks, mate, I do appreciate it. So: say I show my pride in dealing with the old whore Lisa (the mare, I mean) and she up and bops me one with her hoof, maybe smack in the middle of my pride, eh? No darn way! I'd rather bark at the lightbulb!" He chewed the fresh bread and black jam with gusto and spoke in confidence, revealing his secret. "He knows he's a nobody. You think he doesn't? Come on—he's got seven Honors degrees! But I, I have nine! Ever worn trousers with a patch on the seat . . . or not even a patch, just a hole? Well, I'm a graduate of that particular institute of higher learning myself. Nettle isn't—he's had the army keep him in new trousers. But he's got the power and I don't. So when he's pleased to have his fun with you all you've got to do is guess which road he's taking. He needs it, see? What would he be compared to you, for one? A beat-up insect, that's all. A nit. You know about the Pythagorean Theorem, and he knows a horse has four legs. So you want to keep your eyes open . . . or else he'll kick you with all four, damn him!"

"But what have I ever done to him?" Melkior pleaded mournfully, on the brink of tears. "I obey him."

"You obey on the outside, but inside you think this and that . . . I needn't quote you. And he knows, see? That's why he asked you how to turn the light off, to destroy your thinking. Which makes your human dignity protest, doesn't it? Well, forget it. The insects will sooner or later devour mankind, they outnumber us a zillion to one. I look at everything this way and I don't get all hot and bothered about my temporary dignity. I leave that to the greats. Future archeologists won't find a trace of it on their skeletons. A hundred years from now, even sooner perhaps, there'll be Hitler's bones on the market—fake ones, of course. The Yanks will be paying big bucks for a single filled tooth of his, for two hairs off Mussolini's head, never mind that he's bald as an egg. It's all a load of pitiful crap, Yorick's skull, nothing more. The thing to do is stay alive. Make sure your bones survive Nettle's authority, even by barking at electricity if that works. But you seem to have different tactics. All right. Watch out for him. They say Caesar has killed two men so far. When he kills the third, they'll have him put down. What a satisfaction for the third guy, eh?"

There was a command of some kind in the mess hall. Everyone stood up. "All right, get going," said Numbskull giving Melkior a nudge to get him up.

"They're issuing boots and belts—it's fancy leather goods day. We're going to the company store."

Numbskull was waiting faithfully outside the storeroom. When Melkior appeared he gave a skeptical smile.

"I'm not sure this is a good idea," he said looking him over. "You're much too conspicuous, looking like this."

"Why?" asked Melkior suspiciously, indeed with some fear.

"Oh, come on, old boy—you'll have everyone wondering what kind of a scarecrow you are. And now you've got the boots to match."

"What do you mean?" Melkior was still playing it close.

"I mean everything you've got on looks like your little brother's. Except the trousers: it's as if Falstaff lent them to you. Cap plunked down on those ears, right-hand boot big as a bread pan, left-hand boot . . . it'll chafe the dickens out of you, believe me, you'll be cursing the day you were born. It's an awful fix in the army, having boots the wrong size: there's nothing for it if your feet get scraped to the bone, it's Never mind, soldier, forward march, what you've got is not a disease." He went around behind Melkior's back and clapped his hands: "Look where his half-belt is! Just how do you propose to buckle your belt, you mighty warrior? Under your breasts, like Madame Récamier, Empire style? You made a bad job of it, pal— you stick out like a sore thumb."

"It wasn't on purpose . . ." Melkior tried to defend himself. "I took what they gave me."

"Come on, pal, don't give me that nonsense—you took it on purpose," insisted Numbskull. "Do you really believe they're that dense? Do you think they don't know how to make scarecrows? You make a freak of yourself and you think they'll be so disgusted they'll send you packing?"

Numbskull walked alongside him with small steps, but remonstrating with him in a paternally mature tone, knowledgeable, and his manner showed sincere selflessness, worry even. Melkior was wondering: why should he care? I've known him less than two hours, and he did not trust him, he withdrew into himself and kept silent.

"Yes, well, you're wondering why I'm being such a friendly uncle. Well, I can't just stand back and watch a clever man make a fool of himself, can I?"

"What makes you think I'm . . . clever? I'm not."

"Yes you are, don't piss about. It's only that you're a bit of a square peg in a round hole and . . . no clue, above all else. I've been watching you for the past two days: you just sit there, you don't eat, you show contempt. Do you refuse to eat just for the hell of it . . . or is this a plan? But you show your contempt in an awfully holier-than-thou way. And Nettle's got the message. Even dogs can sense dislike in a man—and that kind of instinct is very keen in Nettle, be forewarned. He can read you like a book. You heard him at reveille this morning, that 'looking for Garbo' bit, you must have been dreaming of something or other (a sigh escaped from Melkior, pain-fully, from deep down, over Viviana, in the "dream"). There you are, you're still sighing over it—and I thought right away, oh-oh, you'd better watch it, pal. And sure enough, as soon as we get to the stable, out he comes with 'How do you turn a light off?' And throws you to Caesar, the bastard! I got you out of the 'turning off' and the faint probably saved your life. He's afraid of Caesar himself, he was clearly aiming to drop you in the soup. You should've seen how much fun he had slapping your face as you lay there out cold—anybody would have thought you'd called his mother a whore in public. He hated you at first sight. So tell me—do you want to rub his face in it, with those Falstaff trousers and your cap plunked down over your ears?"

Numbskull was right, and Melkior admitted it. Perhaps there really was in the little guy that curious kind of honesty which searches impatiently for a man so he can offer him both hands in friendship. Looking at the glass pane set in the canteen door, he saw a truly weird scarecrow in it. Two days earlier he had dressed in the company storeroom picking up from the smelly rag pile, without any particular intent, the first thing that came to hand, indifferently, what the hell, it didn't matter what he put on, it was all foul humilia-tion and dirty travesty. The pieces of dismembered bodies, olive drab greasy-soiled, drenched with the sweat and pain of the poor deceased. From the shambles of the army storeroom of massacred clothing emerged Monster (previously known as Melkior), assem-bled from various parts of other people's bodies, himself amazed to be walking on two legs like a man.

The Quartermaster Corps second lieutenant, an effeminately

pretty and dandified young man, gave a giggle when Melkior came in to sign for his kit and asked him in an offhanded tone: wasn't there anything better in there? Melkior replied: no there wasn't, and set off, with a sleepwalker's feeling of absence, across the empty parade ground, as if walking across some strange world invented by a cruel mind.

Encountering an officer there, he nodded and said, "Good morning, sir," his hands dangling from the too short sleeves. The officer, a portly good-natured soul, burst out laughing and returned the greeting: "And a very good morning to you, lad. New boy, eh? My word, do you look elegant!" and gave another burst of laughter.

A father, thought Melkior with emotion. Perhaps he has a son, a gangling galoot like me . . . He didn't realize he was now smiling as he thought back to the officer father. . . .

"Having a quiet chuckle, eh?" spoke Numbskull at his side. "Think I don't know what I'm talking about, is that it? All right, just mark my words when you get yours, that's all."

"Not at all, sorry, it's something I remembered . . ." He's taken me under his wing! thought Melkior, but stifled the smile. "But what if *you* got yours? You keep fussing over me . . . Nettle could 'read' you 'like a book,' too."

"Me? . . . unh-unh," he shook his head with conviction. "I'm in his ledger as Numbskull, he doesn't even waste his time reading me. Not interesting, *tabula rasa*. But you, now you're a book, attractive reading, a chance for self-assertion: 'watch me whup the bejesus out of the teacher.'"

"Well, you're an intellectual, too—you attended the university . . ."

"Three semesters of chemistry, and even that wasn't . . . I don't even know all of the stuff with H-2 . . . But the University of Life, hah, now that's something else again! . . . I had this pal, he was a real character! Lady walking a dog in the park, lets it off the leash, a bit of exercise, so good for iddy bitty's digestion. So the doggie romps about, enjoying itself, and my pal gets to barking, lures it into a bush, tosses it into a sack . . . and sells it in another part of town. It became quite a case in the end, got into the papers, you might've read about it. Well, he taught me to bark. He was an expert at doing impressions, he could do anything: idiots, animals, a squeaking wheel, bedsprings, an oil lamp fizzing out, you name it. We spent a winter in an abandoned barge on the Danube. Ice all around, we're sitting there frozen to the bone, and he starts doing mosquitoes and summer bugs, conjuring up summer, God strike him (and He did) —and sure enough, it got warmer and somehow brighter, cheerier, as if it was a scorcher of a day outside. He could even do impressions of moths eating his 'cold weather apparel.' Will you listen to me: 'cold weather apparel!' Matter of fact, we had only a smelly sheep-skin shepherd's coat, Gosh how the fleece stunk, it had people running away from us, we wore it on an alternating basis, you put it on only when it was your turn to go out and scare up some grub. Grub meaning vittles—well, food."

"So what happened to your pal? He's no longer with us?"

"Probably not. He went over to this towboat—a boatman was giving a party for his saint's day—and I never saw him again. Fell into the Danube drunk, maybe dragged off by the current?" Numbskull was speaking with indifference, as if about a lost bauble.

"But I still think he got out of the country—stowed away in the towboat. He had a fine singing voice—baritone—it was a treat to listen to him sing this Czech song 'Water Flowing, Flowing' . . . I'm thinking he cleared off for Czecholand up the Danube, got rid of me, well, I'd only have been a hindrance to him . . ."

"And you were left alone in the barge?"

"I went respectable. Got a job. Had a paper route, a milk route. Worked in a nightclub later, dress suit and all that, assistant to their magician, learned the tricks, coaxed watches off people's wrists . . . set up in the watch-coaxing business on my lonesome, got locked up. 'Water Flowing, Flowing' . . . I was a circus ticket vendor, spare clown, too, the full understudy bit; I knew the program inside out but generally I was the one who got the pie in the face and the box in the ear—for real, I mean; no tricks. But that doesn't matter. Love, love was my undoing. The prima donna Marie, star acrobat, missing her little finger—hang it all, which hand was it? Funny, I can't remember anymore, a polar bear did it. She thought, What a lovely fur coat! And stroked him, and the fur coat went zap! and bit her pinkie off. But she was so clever at hiding it I can't remember which hand it was. Well, left or right, it doesn't matter, neither ever reached for me, for all that I would've loved to kiss all ten of her fingers. Well, nine."

"The magician in the night club . . . by any chance would his name have been Adam?" asked Melkior, just to ask.

"Where did you pull Adam from? Hang on! Yes, it *was* Adam! How did you know? That's right, his name was Adam, and he had some kind of artiste-style tag to it. Brahmaputra or something, I forget which. Adam, of course, that's why they called his wife Eve."

"Did she also work in the circus?"

"Ticket girl, one heck of a looker, that's why the manager stuck her in the ticket booth. And this character Adam followed her—joined the circus himself. Oh, Eve rolled into everyone's bed like a fragrant ripe quince. The whole troupe had tumbled with her in turns, down to the seal and the monkey, and finally it was my turn. I forgot my (heh, 'my') angel Marie and got going with Eve the ticket girl. Brahmaputra got to suspecting the fidelity of his lady wife, well, it was the talk of the dressing room after all, everyone knew, except himself of course, which was only to be expected, and she, the mega-whore, 'confided' in her husband, which again was only to be expected, told him I kept bugging her, she was at her wits' end how to defend herself and people were starting to talk, if he hadn't heard he'd hear soon enough . . . Of course he couldn't believe such a beauty would fall for me, the failed son of an unknown father and a random mother, looking like they'd made me in a dustbin.

"Well, to cut it short, he gave me a thrashing (poor ATMAN, thought Melkior) in the stable, even the horses were sorry for me, with her singing outside at the top of her lungs, to drown out my cries I suppose. I thought he'd figured it all out and was paying out my just desserts. But I couldn't see why she would be singing. And when he'd finished she rushed in, pretending to be surprised, harping on him for being too jealous, pleading with him for mercy, also forgiveness or something, me being so young, etcetera. He then let me have another round of the same and I was still wondering why he didn't give her a beating, too. Well, he didn't want to light into her in front of me, I thought, he'll settle with her later . . . I stayed lying there, all battered by those dreadful bones in his hands. (Melkior remembered ATMAN's fingers cracking at the joints.) And she came back in the evening, while he was doing his number, started hugging and kissing me, wanted to do it right there in the straw. Somebody must've told him about us, she says, and he, the fool, can't do anything short of murder; come on, she says, take your revenge here and now, at the scene of the crime. I was in no condition to do it though, beat up as I was. But she was such a bitch I could have done it dead. Well, never mind—the thing was, his trouble was yet to come. The next day, just before the show, I mucked up all his props, but I took care to leave them looking all right. I watched his catastrophe from behind the curtain: all his tricks seen through, the audience rolling with laughter—they thought the screw-up was a trick, too, they took it there was going to be a clever high point at the end. High point heck, there was no point at all, everything went like that straight to the end, and in the end, when his downfall was complete he grabbed his head with both hands (and you can imagine the booing in the audience) and staggered back to the plush curtain and roared 'Where is he? I'll kill him!' I was of course well away by then. But how did you know his name was Adam?"

"Oh . . ." said Melkior with hesitation, "I used to know a palmist who was called that."

"Tall, bony? Eyes by Picasso?"

"Yes, just about . . ."

"So he's into palmistry now? Doing old women, ha-ha. Is Eve still with him?"

"He's by himself," though, not quite, Melkior added bitterly to himself, thinking of Viviana.

"So, no more Earthly Paradise." The bugle sounded. "Ah, there it is, Theory Class call. Don't laugh in class, I strongly recommend. There'll be important scientific discoveries to hear."

School. Four shorn heads per bench. Numbskull sitting up front, among the shorter men. A handsome strapping lieutenant walking among the benches. He let his saber clang importantly on the floor (it didn't seem to have any other military purpose anyhow) while running, up high, his long slim fingers over the stormy waves of firm dark hair, checking the wave level of the officer haircut. A symbol of superiority over the shaved heads. A kind of power, Old Testament style, over the shorn Philistines. The lieutenant was moving his jaw; speaking. Melkior didn't understand what he was saying—he was only watching the jaw work and the slim fingers dance on the waves. And Melkior spoke, saying: With the jawbone of an ass, heaps upon heaps, with the jaw of an ass hath he slain a thousand men. With the jawbone of an ass hath he slain us. And Melkior's jaw dropped in wonder at the marvelous wavy hair and the power that lay therein.

"What're you gaping at like an imbecile? Are you listening to me?"

"I am."

"I am, *sir*, you moron!"

"I am, sir."

"All right then, let's hear Guard Mounting Procedure. On your feet!"

Melkior stood up, speaking not about Guard Mounting Procedure but (inside) about how with the jawbone of an ass, heaps upon heaps, with the jaw of an ass hath he slain a thousand . . . warrior tales.

"You don't know? Oh, you're new? Well, make an effort, listen to the others. Sit down." He may have sensed a grin somewhere.

"You, big nose, what're you laughing your silly head off for? C.O.'s report tomorrow! Let's hear about the GMP," using the already familiar acronym, "from you, Numbskull!"

Some powerful spring threw Numbskull to his feet; all aquiver with his tense alertness he ripped off Guard Mounting Procedure like a volley into an enemy's breastbone, in a resolute, soldierlike manner. Nine Honors degrees! thought Melkior.

"Was it Nettle who first called you Numbskull? I must say you seem to be a bright enough boy."

"Don't know about that, sir," reported Numbskull briskly, "I do my best, sir."

"Very good, Numbskull."

"Thank you, *sah!*" yelled Numbskull in the prescribed manner.

"All right, no need to shout, this isn't close order drill. Sit down."

"Yes, sir." Only when he sat down did Numbskull command his body, At Ease, but kept his head high, within the lieutenant's sphere: he was not going to be caught napping or clowning.

"Diplomacy? Balls!" Among the rows of benches strode a large major, a warrior type, a bowlegged horseman in riding boots. Jangling his spurs. Hands clasped on his rear end, shoving the benches with his knees, get out of my way, speaking in a quarrelsome tone: "Lying in their teeth! Dinners, luncheons, grand receptions, champagne, cakes, mayonnaise! Top hatters! Greedy bastards! Going at it in limousines, in damned opera boxes, chignons, lorgnons, white tie and tails, gold, diamonds, buggers, actresses, ballet dancers . . . Distinction! Protocol! Damned whores, the lot, women and men alike! Scum of the Earth! Right, but there comes a time when the whore's feast comes to an end! No more drivel at the green table! They are running for it with their damned lorgnons, scrambling down into miserable rat holes, lily-livered vermin! Well, that's when we soldiers step in and go to war! No more *plizz* and *par-dong*, *Monsewer* and *Modam*, it's get shooting and get pounding and we'll see who ends where! You've shat out plenty of 'diplomatic notes,' well, by God, it's time we rolled out a note or two of our own on our own damned instruments!"

The major stopped pacing about—there was a war on. Over was his cursing, quarrelsome, prewar mood when he had borne the diplomatic toadying and whorish duplicity with humiliation. Now you knew who you were: a soldier, damn it! Now you settled your differences openly, face to face, in plain language, and may the best man win!

Yes, but it didn't follow that any old fool could make war. Resolution and courage were all very well, you couldn't hope to be a soldier without them, but that was not all. You needed a bit of learning —the art of warfare. That's why you were here, basic training.

"Listen up, look at him! Say, getting your bearings. You've been cut off from your unit—or dispatched on assignment—how are you going to find your bearings? You there. What are you—a professor? Shoot, prof."

"By the sun, sir."

"There's no sun. It's night."

"By the stars then, sir."

"No stars either. Sky's overcast."

"Oh, well," the prof remembered, "I'd use my compass."

"Clever son of a bitch, you haven't got a compass, you haven't got a thing except your useless brains."

"Then I don't know, sir."

"Of course you don't. That's why you're here—to learn. Listen up, look at him! How many of you are from the country? Ah, plenty of peasants, good. All right, you, the hick, suppose you tell these city slickers how you'd get your bearings."

"I'd ask, sir."

"Ask who? God the Father?"

"A peasant, sir."

"Oh, you mean a peasant would be hanging about there in the middle of the night, just waiting for you to ask him?"

"He might happen along . . ."

"Happen along indeed. . . . How's your Hungarian?"

"Hungarian, sir?"

"Well, we ought to be good enough to advance the front line to Hungary, should we not? That would make him a Hungarian peasant."

"No, I don't speak a word of Hungarian, sir. I do have a touch of German, but Hungarian . . ."

"Of course you don't! Can anyone do better than him?"

"I can, sir. I'm from Senta."

"Well?"

"I can, sir. I speak Hungarian."

"Now listen here, Mama's boy," the Major brought his face close to his and lowered his voice, and that spelled something truly dreadful, "is this your idea of a joke? A C.O.'s report? no fear! I'll have you pissing blood, I will! 'I speak Hungarian'? You'll be speaking bloody Turkish before I'm done with you—and you'll be free to complain to Father Allah and Saint Mahomet then!"

"I'm sorry, sir, I didn't mean no . . . I thought . . ."

"Silence!" the Major shot the word at him like a bullet from a pistol. "'I thought,' indeed! You're not supposed to think! You can sell your profound thoughts to your no-good buddies over in Senta! You're just a lot of seditious rebels anyway, all of you from over the Danube and the Sava! Over here you think like I tell you to, see?"

"Yes, sir," stammered the boy, but the Major was paying him no attention by then.

"Listen up, you . . . Silence! In a forest, where you can see no sun and no stars . . . and look at him, wants me to give him a compass, like hell I will! . . . you will orient yourself . . . listen up, look at him! . . . by moss. What's so funny, look at him! (Nobody was laughing, of course.) Why moss? Anyone?"

"Sir," spoke up Numbskull.

"Go ahead."

"Moss grows on the shady side of the trunk, because that's where it's damp. . . ."

"Very good," enthused the Major.

"Thank you, *sah!*" yelled Numbskull.

"Never mind thanking me—get on with it!"

". . . and the shadow is, as we know, on the north side."

"That's right, on the north side! Damned good show!"

"Thank you, *sah!*" Numbskull was not forgetting the Royal Regs.

"Right, now establish your bearings. See that dork—thought he'd ask an enemy peasant. So smart he'd try to hitch a ride on a hedgehog."

"Now that I know which way's north, I position myself so as to face due north, where the moss is. Behind my back's south, my right arm is east and my left arm west."

"Damned straight!"

"Thank you, *sah!*"

"Wonder which fool chose to call you Dimwit."

"Numbskull, sir," Numbskull corrected him shyly and modestly. "It was only a joke, sir. . . ."

"This is no joking matter! This is not a circus! I'll get that Nettle yet!"

"Sir, I never said anything about . . ."

"Silence! I know him—this is his brand of shenanigans! That Cossack from the steppe making my finest men a laughingstock! Here, you knew about this orientation by moss business all the time—why didn't you come out with it right away?"

"I hadn't remembered, sir, until you said."

"Good. Sit down."

"Thank you, *sah!*" Numbskull was not letting up. He sat down, broadcasting his pleasure.

The Major was very pleased, too. He was still shouting and swearing, but with a paternal smile—even addressing them as "lads"— "listen up, lads, look at him!" And it was all thanks to Numbskull: he had created a cozy family atmosphere out of nothing, out of a handful of moss, as it were.

"Listen up, lads, look at him! Pay attention to me, slacker! Here, what is it we learned about orientation by moss? Let's hear it from . . . you!" and he suddenly skewered a beanpole in the back row with his finger. The beanpole gave a start, jumped to his feet and said all about shadow, damp, north-south, east-west . . .

And everybody else turned out to have it down pat. Melkior, too, had it down.

"Very good, boys!" exclaimed the Major in delight.

"Thank you, *sah!*" thundered the boys. The Major marched down the aisle between the benches reveling in the tribute from the skin-shorn heads and went out of the triumphal door: with boys like that he had no fear of Hitler's moustache or Mussolini's shaven pate!

Melkior, too, was carried away by mellow thoughts: see how we could live in peace and mutual respect . . . If we took a leaf from Numbskull's book . . . But how did he know which side the moss grew on?

"How? Heh-heh, I told you: nine Honors degrees!" replied

Numbskull in the mess hall at lunch, tapping his nose. "You know the year of Luther's death, not me. You can wipe your butt with all the Schopenhauers. What counts here, as you can see for yourself, is moss!" said Numbskull, eating Melkior's lunch.

Lifemanship. Melkior felt his being trapped, deprived of ingenuity, exposed to Polyphemus the cannibal, defenseless. Oh Lord (why do you invoke Me, said the Lord, if you don't believe in Me?), I will have to surrender. I have no choice but to surrender to the man-eating Cyclops, come what may. There are fifty-seven young men and thousands of young men more and millions of young men beyond them caught in a high-ceilinged cave overgrown with laurels, and Polyphemus the huge Cyclops has lifted a boulder and plugged the entrance to the cave . . . and everyone inside awaits, meek as lambs, for their destiny to be chosen by the Lord. So why should you worry at all about your stunted little body?

Polyphemus does not fancy gnawing scrawny bones. Maybe you will not be chosen at all for his Cyclopean meal? *Maybe, maybe . . . Maybe* is worse than "he will not eat you tomorrow." Oh Lord, I don't want *maybe*; give me certainty: deliver me or destroy me now! Throw me under Caesar's mighty hooves to be trampled in a blaze of glory! Deliver me from Nettle, from fear, from shame, from barking at a lightbulb!

Fear prolongs life, someone had said in honor of Caution, but Numbskull's uncomplicated art made Melkior's pitiful cunning seem ridiculous. The way Numbskull had decoded his "secret device" at first sight! Read through it right off the bat and spotted it as naïve . . . and teased him for it. He was going to make mistakes under the expert's knowing eye, bog down in details while forgetting the bigger picture, show his hand while hiding his nails. He feared Numbskull's ingenuity and the man's taking so damn much interest in him!

He opted for an unpleasant silence, in payment for the friendly care in bread and meat.

"All right, if you really don't want it," Numbskull ate from Melkior's barely touched plate, but kept on musing in a conscientious and friendly manner: "Thing is, do you propose to wither away here from one day to the next? What difference will it make after all's said and done: this way or . . . *that*? I'm afraid you're going about this all wrong—your sum is lose-lose, no matter how you slice it."

But Melkior wouldn't listen to him anymore. He'd had it with that kind of logic in ATMAN's school. Too many dreadful truths were concealed in that line of reasoning. He tossed and turned through another pointless night under the olive drab blanket trimmed with the royal tricolor, hopefully counting the beats of his racing pulse. He had trouble swallowing his saliva in his parched throat: a stab of pain appeared as a yearned-for promise. *Strep*—a warm, indeed seering, medicinal word, beyond the reach of the stable and Nettle, capable of reducing his tense vertical stature to a patient's relaxed helplessness, to a white scene of whispers and obligatory quiet.

Tomorrow there would be fever to boot . . . *sick bay* . . . that was the proper military term. The next day there was nothing to show for *sick bay*. The throat fresh and painless; the pulse ticking shyly and modestly, nearly inaudible; the forehead pale, hunger-spent, cold. There you are: a picture of health! And his animal was already looking forward, with thick-headed relish, to the chicory brew and the black jam on fresh, still-warm black bread.

Oh no you don't, you greedy brute! And the Body, miserable as a starving dog, gave a piteous whine and nearly dropped with exhaustion to the muddy, unfriendly ground. (Well, look at what I've been feeding it these days—not enough to keep a fly alive, admitted Melkior loyally, but launched into a didactic sermon out loud): Here, consider the bodies of ascetics and hermits and whatnot. A jug of water and a crust of stale bread are all they got to sustain them for up to forty days, so what?—they were gaunt yet sturdy and resilient, they could take any climate, hot or cold—*and* they left their Master alone, no dreaming of Enka and similar filthy stuff, they kept themselves to themselves while the Master was meditating and cultivating his soul. You'll be the death of me (of yourself, too, in fact!) with your "got to guzzle," you glutton, you Sancho, you abyss of hunger, you lowly earthbound engine of foolish Pantagruelian life! At least

remember our castaways! It's for your sake that I invented that pedagogical "Telemachiad" (although you're no Duke of Burgundy but
merely a greedy intestine) to show you where your stupid motto *eat,
drink, and* . . . will get you—there, you see, it will only get you into
another intestine, and with you all, damn you, it's nothing but out of
one intestine and into another . . . and so on to infinity, you bloated
guzzlers! Given that I was so fatally placed astride you to ride your
arched and uncomfortable back (if only I'd sat astride a turtle!) at
least be wise as a donkey, mind how you walk through this life of
ours, don't rush and don't race, nothing is worth haste, see to it that
our travel lasts as long as possible, there's no Promised Land out
there. At the end is the Promised Pit, we'll tumble into it together,
you and I, you and I . . .

"Hey you!"

"Me?" echoed Melkior like distance, surprised.

"What're you doing here?"

"Trying to report for sick bay, Sergeant. But there are signs on the
door, Do Not Knock and Enter Only if Invited, so I'm waiting, I
don't know how to get in."

"Come in." The taciturn irascible clerk, a troop sergeant, sat
down at his desk, dunked a rusty pen into an inkwell and held it
poised over a sheet of paper. He waited, looking distractedly through
the window. "All right, shoot!"

"Shoot what, Sergeant?"

"First name, father's name, last name . . . Right. Year of birth?
Village? County? District?" and handed Melkior the paper. Melkior
was still waiting, standing by the desk, this can't be all, it's much too
quick and efficient, no shouting, no swearing . . .

"Well?" bawled the sergeant. "Want *me* to examine you?"

"Y-yes, Sergeant," quavered Melkior, happiness making him attempt to click his heels like the soldiers he had seen in the films
saluting their superiors, but he missed and his boots responded with
a dry, hollow sound.

"OK, OK," the attempt did manage to bring a thin smile of

satisfaction to the sergeant's strict (but fair!) lips. This is Numbskull influencing me already, thought Melkior about heel-clicking on his way out of the company office.

There was a smell, in the infirmary, of hot, undressed bodies, all of them feverish, sweaty, red. The orderly, a private, gave Melkior a thermometer patched with a strip of plaster and explained that you stuck *this* in your armpit. I now ought to tap it on the tip (literally, that is) so the mercury will rise above ninety-eight point six, but how? it's got a hole in its head underneath the strip. All the same, he flicked his index finger from his thumb, knock knock knock and knock, three strong knocks and one weak, then took a cautious peek at the resultant ninety-nine. Was this a reliable enough thread for a Lost One to follow?

The young doctor in the infirmary thought it was. He listened carefully to Melkior's lungs and heart and stated with amicable satisfaction that he had heard nothing of interest. But he did not hide his concern over such an assertive presence of Melkior's skeleton: you're only skin and bones, man, you haven't got an ounce of flesh on you. He drew two semicircles across Melkior's chest with his thumbnail; the nail left a red trail. Of course! nodded the doctor, something was matching his expectations one hundred percent. "Here, this is a note for Pulmonary," and then privately, as if to a younger brother, "you must eat, you must eat a lot. You're dangerously thin." This ended the examination.

So danger lurked in the bones. Melkior was gladdened by the Medical Corps care: it was their business to upholster the skeleton with sound patriotic flesh, to make the King happy by producing an army under whose feet the very Fatherland shook.

"You here for the 'special'?" a sergeant greeted him outside the infirmary.

"C'mon, fall in!" he ordered the seven unwell soldiers in the yard. "By twooos, numbah!"

"One, two, one, two . . ." the garrison rejects numbered off halfheartedly.

"Double file, right!" clack-clack, responded the boots submissively. "Here, you, new guy, look where your belt is! You're not according to regs!"

Of course—Numbskull said so! thought Melkior. But I'm not à la Madame Récamier . . . and he made a surprised face at the sergeant.

"Belt above half-belt, understand?"

"Yes, Sergeant," said Melkior and hoisted his belt; the half-belt was halfway up his back. "Wouldn't this be too high, Sergeant, across the chest?"

"Never mind!" yelled the sergeant. "Look who's complaining—a real scarecrow! Who the hell took you into the army—a blind man? Move to the rear, I don't want to have to look at you!"

Melkior moved to the rear so that the sergeant didn't have to look at him, belt across chest (above the half-belt), well now he was according to regs. Forward march, direction gate!

This is town. Melkior was sniffing the streets like a city dog: he felt like trotting to the corner, roving a bit, stopping to examine the posters, perhaps even cocking a leg . . . with joy. And back there, in the stable, Caesar had by now been served. That, too, was a pleasure: knowing that Caesar had been served for today. Oh illustrious Caesar, I am on my way through town! I am marching down the middle of the road (in the rear, for the sake of the Sergeant) where your less fortunate brethren pull appalling loads; they are whipped and sworn at by drunken carters, their haunches are sweaty and their eyes frightfully sad, but I would rather change places with them than with you. None of them is good enough for a monument—and a monument is a dead horse . . .

Several passersby had stopped on a corner, watching the soldiers and laughing. One of them pointed a finger at him, Melkior, and instantly they all laughed anew.

The sergeant slowed down his pace, dropping to the rear, and spoke through clenched teeth without looking at him: "You're putting me to shame, damn your eyes, I don't know where to hide my damned face! I could kill you here and now, you seditious bastard!"

Numbskull said so, thought Melkior. There was no going back under Nettle's wing, now: the sergeant had supplied him with all the strength he needed. The specialist checkup was sending him benevolent smiles already: there's the hospital, hopefully there would be red crosses there, too . . . white all around and a tinge of illness. The entire tableau was less ambitious now: no need for a terrace at Davos, or glaciers, or pedestrian reading matter. All I need is just to get my head under the sign of the red cross, out of reach of Nettle's and Caesar's world.

"You, over here!" yelled the sergeant after they had entered the hospital grounds. "Wait here." Melkior waited. The others knew their way to wherever they needed to take their maladies. But they envied him, they told him, "Goodbye, you'll be staying here."

The sergeant returned. "Through this door. Assembly point outside the canteen. Over there, see it?"

"Yes."

"Like hell you do! Be the best thing for all of us if you kicked the bucket while you're here!" the sergeant bared his teeth in a canine grin. "Rid the army of the likes of you," and he went off, lighting a cigarette.

True to form it was white all around . . . He was greeted by a white nurse, young, white arms to the elbow, hips, a pleasant smile as she entered Melkior into the large logbook. This was perhaps how you were admitted to Paradise—a heavenly secretary . . .

"Tresić?" smiled the secretary above the book. "Perhaps we're related. My name is Tresić-Pavičić, the poet's my uncle."

"Well, I'm just Tresić," Melkior smiled modestly, his heart fluttering with gratitude.

"But you know Uncle, don't you?" She lifted her heavenly head and looked at him with her pretty eyes. "I mean, you've read his poetry?"

Melkior recited a handful of the poet's pathos-drenched verse.

"Ahh," she marveled. "Tell me, are you from one of the Dalmatian islands, too?"

"No, I'm not." He did not want to afford her even that little pleasure. "I'm from . . ." but he was interrupted by the buzzer: the major wanted her.

"Excuse me." She went through a white door and returned in a moment.

"The Major will see you now. Step in here, please, and strip to the waist, then go through the other door. Don't be afraid, the Major's a very nice man," she added in a confidential whisper, like a cozy secret.

"A very nice man . . ." He undressed in a dark cubicle saturated with the smelly fumes of sweaty bodies. She's in love with him. Common knowledge: doctors and nurses . . . and there's bound to be a couch inside . . . "Such a nice man . . ." Stripped to the waist, a half-peeled banana, a white . . . no, a dried fish in oversized trousers, a cartoon character in boots . . . He hugged his emaciation with a virginal shyness. Actresses and directors, horizontal occupations . . . then go through the other door. He went. The "very nice man," tall, slim, with a touch of gray at the temples . . . they go for that particular type of intellectual. With a slow and weary gesture he was told to approach. He felt respect, bowed with the bare half of his body. The Major gave an amicable smile and put his paternal hands on Melkior's pointy shoulders. Melkior was afraid the man would be disgusted by such a body. . . .

"Would you turn, please?" said the Major in what was almost an imploring tone. Oh look, they use *would you* and *please* here! He felt like kissing the hand on his shoulder!

"Breathe normally, please. Breathe deeply. Cough. Breathe fast. Faster."

Melkior panted like a dog, fast, comically, immodestly. He looked at the white couch . . . the panting . . . that's where they, the poet's niece and . . . but he couldn't believe it. A nice man, really.

"Now please lie down." Melkior hesitated: to lie down on that white couch . . . he feared desecration. *That* tableau: their love . . . he thought like a romantic knight. Well, if they're truly in love . . . "Do lie down—it's clean," the Major pleaded.

He lay down on the clean, cold sheet and begged forgiveness (inside).

The Major tapped all over him, listening carefully, seeking out the hidden enemy. Nothing. The X-ray machine also revealed nothing.

"Nothing," said the Major with a smile of hidden satisfaction. "Serious asthenia. But you'll stay here, you need to convalesce," entering enigmatic words in the Medical Corps form as he spoke. He then pressed the buzzer button.

How do you mean "you'll stay here"—Caesar, the sergeant, and Nettle are waiting for me! It's not as if you had a sun here under which I would be warmer than under the sky of their love and affection. Do you realize the implications of depriving Caesar of such a soldier? The centurion Nettle will be terribly worried about me. Also Major Moss, listen up, look at him . . . Ugo would have made that into a number for his show by now. He's still asleep at this hour, the cur!

They're all still asleep, the curs! It's too early. They've got it made. What about Ugo (his liver is swollen), hasn't he received his call-up papers yet? Mr. Kalisto must have some good connections in the right places, because in these war-threatened times Pechárek will not pass over people so easily, dwaftees, hell no! we're all equal and naked before the King.

She would come in any moment now, and here he was, all gangly in his trousers, all pitiful and naked . . .

"Yes, Major?" she came in, the darling niece, rustling all over with whiteness. She remained motionless at the door, waiting piously for the Major's signal to approach. So this is how it is between them, a formal relationship? Melkior felt relieved. He had his arms crossed on his chest in a manly way, like a naked brave in his Chief's tepee.

"We'll keep the boy here," said the Major taking the stethoscope out of his ears. "Would you take him upstairs to the ward, nurse, Room Seven? Good."

"Thank you, Doctor," Melkior retreated backward, the trouser mouth around his thin waist blooming with pious gratitude. He had his backside misdirected, aiming at the wrong door, and She directed him with her finger, not that one, this one, get dressed again where you undressed then come back to see me, they were both smiling, he caught a lightning-quick exchange of looks, an arrangement for "later."

He dressed with the chagrin of a male ridiculed. But when he reentered her "marble halls" with his greatcoat over his arm he felt like a traveler in a tourist office facing a hostess whose most sacred duty, for all her hidden contempt, was to smile in the kindest way possible, showing her teeth a little. She was going to escort him to his stateroom, here's the bathroom, these are the usual offices, please ring here if you need anything . . . and the transatlantic liner would set sail over the light waves (suitable for a postprandial on-deck snooze and providing an attractive seascape), making for a bright new world beyond the reach of the cannibal reek of Polyphemus the Cyclops, the one-eyed beast.

"The Major's a nice man, isn't he?" she said proudly, as if he were in some way hers. Melkior threw his greatcoat over the other arm in a routine gesture of impatience, and gave an understanding smile. She reddened.

"Yes, an understated and dignified man," he said to confuse her further and possibly make her confide in him. "Rather aloof, I thought."

"He is first and foremost a doctor." The blush was receding from her face, but her white hands trembled, the papers in them rustled. "In his book an unwell soldier is a *patient* to be brought back to health."

". . . and sent back to Caesar when he's fit again. Give unto Caesar . . ." chuckled Melkior dryly.

"Caesar?" she looked at him in surprise; she had put the papers on her desk.

"Oh, that's a horse—a talented one, allegedly—back at the barracks." Melkior was speaking with due respect. "Two sons of grieving mothers has he already dispatched to Hades, unto Aides . . . as your uncle would put it. Men now wait for him to smite the third and thereupon feel Death's bludgeon himself . . ."

She laughed, showing a great deal of her teeth.

"Ah-ha, so that's what sent you over here!" She offered him rubbery green *Eucalyptus* gumdrops from a small tin box: "Go on, take one—I won't poison you. They disinfect the throat—very good for this autumn weather with so much flu around. Ah, isn't that just like men? Heroes, but afraid of horses."

"While you women are not afraid of horses, not even of lions, but you're afraid of mice and, *ha-ha, you're afraid of roaches.* It's common knowledge, of course, that roaches are far more dangerous than lions. . . . A fly is afraid of spiders, not crocodiles. That's instinct—which, as they say, *is never wrong.* Then again, your fearsome enemy the mice know that cats are far more fearsome than lions . . . and that's how those circles of fear work, hobbling anything that lives, anything that moves in one way or another. Did you ever touch a tiny insect crawling on a windowpane? It drops dead on the spot, doesn't it, all dried up and hollow somehow. Dead my foot! It's only faking death, the crafty little creature. It thinks: I'll be unimportant looking like this and my enemies will pass me over. Wise—for all that it's so minuscule! It hasn't even got a brain."

She was now sucking her *Eucalyptus* pensively: "thoughts" like these must require a grave face. Melkior had long since swallowed his, it had only impeded his speech. She's *disinfecting* her breath for kisses. Perhaps there's the smell of rotting tonsils or the matutinal empty stomach, and the Major . . . But this is ingratitude! He remembered and felt ashamed inside. Haven't they both been good to me? If I had my heart in the right place I would bless their love, he went on gibing with a bitter bite.

"Maybe you're a poet," she said, giving him a timid glance.

"No, I'm not. I'm not talented. I know too many poems by heart—anything I might attempt would resemble one of them. But that doesn't mean I have no right to be afraid of horses. Indeed, Byron, one of the greatest poets, was a fine horseman, perhaps because he had a club foot. But he preferred walking—he was a most handsome figure of a man."

She looked at him with curiosity, but the buzzer turned her look off: the Major was wanting her.

"Here, report to the ward with these," she hurriedly handed over some papers. "We'll continue this conversation—we'll be seeing quite a bit of each other from now on." And she disappeared behind the white door.

It was couch time, time for the divan . . . I mean time to talk, in Turkish, he corrected his words; but the thought lingered, filled with bitter, jealous suspicion. "We'll be seeing quite a bit of each other from now on." . . . Well, this was the first encounter and then (he remembered) goodbye, Viviana!

He went out in high spirits to look for the *ward*. Well, where was it? He asked a soldier in white, Medical Corps, where to report with his papers.

"Says right there above your nose," said the soldier in white. He looked like one of those Russian men who was fighting in the snow, on skis. They did in the end lick the Finns. They were first rate, that's for sure, shooting while the ground slid beneath their feet.

He read once again the writing "right there above his nose" on the black sign by the entrance: TUBERCULOSIS WARD. Yellow lettering on black background—an undertaker's. Hats off!

I've been suckered! he whispered, crestfallen, turning to go back to the doctor's office. He'd prefer Caesar and Nettle both to Koch's bacilli. The hygiene teacher had drawn them on the blackboard: rod-shaped, millions upon millions of tiny vermin. She and that "very nice man" had sprung him a handy trap: Caesar and Nettle here, the Koch bacilli there—all right, take your pick. Chortling in there, I bet. "We'll be seeing quite a bit of each other from now on."

She was not out in the waiting room. No sounds came from *in there*. He had a closer listen, putting his ear to the white door. Nothing. They were being cautious. And the couch, loyal, humble, with its teeth clenched, was silent as the grave. They must've locked the door, too. He pressed the knob. The door opened dutifully: at your service, sir. Inertia drove his head into the room.

"Yes?" The Major was sitting at his desk, signing papers; she was ministering to him, blotter in hand, pressing signatures.

"Is something wrong?" she stopped short above a signature.

"It says TUBERCULOSIS WARD on the sign," timidly uttered the head inside the door.

"So what?" said the Major. "Did you find that alarming?"

"I'd rather go back to the barracks . . ." said the head stupidly. "I'm sorry," and it made to withdraw, "I'm disturbing you."

"Wait." The Major stood up, pulled him by the shoulder, drew the whole of Melkior inside. "You're too weak, you must stay here. Don't be afraid of what it says on the panel—the *positive* cases are accommodated separately, those who really have T.B. Room Seven's clean, comfortable, five beds only, intellectuals, malingerers," the Major gave a smile, "a bit on the skinny side, on hi-cal rations, a jolly crew, you won't be bored." The Major encouraged him and thumped him on the shoulder, and Melkior felt himself blush . . . over his it's-a-trap suspicion . . . and over her, the poet's niece. Ugo would now kneel and kiss the ground he walked on, blessed be your every footstep, you kindhearted man! His eyes filled with tears of gratitude, he was afraid he might burst into sobs. The Major intelligently guessed his condition, gave him a "manly" slap on the cheek: "Come on, back to the ward now . . . pay no attention to the sign. Oh well, we're not all born to be soldiers," he muttered to himself sitting back at his desk again.

"Much obliged, Doctor," bowed Melkior as he retreated.

"All right, my lad, all right, goodbye," the Major went on signing the papers. "Scary thing indeed, that T.B. WARD sign . . . Not the first time," was what Melkior heard the Major add as he carefully closed the door behind him.

In hospital dress with thin blue and white stripes, his greatcoat draped beggar style over his shoulders, Melkior entered Room Seven. Hesitant. He stopped at the door, his gaze wandering anxiously from bed to bed, at faces peeking out from the covers and watching him with curiosity and, it would seem, terminal exhaustion. Melkior stood lost before the cold gazes, like someone pleading for mercy.

"Take off the mask, Tartuffe!" shouted one of the faces all of a sudden, sitting up in bed. "Come on in, no need to panic."

"Hello, boys," said Melkior in an undertone, but without moving from where he stood. "Is this my bed?" he indicated with his head a made-up bed next to the door.

"Yes, that's yours," replied a dark-haired young man with a thin moustache à la actor Adolphe Menjou. "So you'd be another of the Major's bad cases, would you?" There were subdued chuckles from under the covers . . . But the eyes outside the covers offered the newcomer their profound sorrow, they had nothing to do with the ripples of laughter. What training! thought Melkior with envy. Let's see you do your stuff *here*, Numbskull! And he suddenly remembered the-assembly-point-outside-the-canteen sergeant. He threw his bundle on the bed and rushed out into the corridor. They called out after him from the room, shouting: where you going—we were only joking! Perhaps he *is* a bad case?

The sergeant was waiting at the assembly point outside the canteen, with four men: they didn't make the cut, thought Melkior, as one of the select of medical fortune.

"How much longer were you expecting me to wait for you, eh?" bawled the sergeant. "What is it then?"

"I'm to stay." The four looked enviously at the hospital wear under his greatcoat. Melkior showed the sergeant his credentials.

"Oh no—you'll have me in tears!" the sergeant leered at him in rage. "How am I to manage without you?" Then, after closer scrutiny of the papers: "Right! Get out of my sight, I don't want to see you ever again!"

Amen, thought Melkior, but out loud he said: "Yes, sir, Sergeant, sir. Understood, Sergeant."

"You'll never understand in a million years!" Melkior heard the sergeants' valedictory blessing behind him.

Now then. Here it is, white all around and a tinge of illness . . . more or less. She's no *Goldilocks*, she's got black curly hair peeking from under the starched white cap, and we call her sister, devoutly, to repress carnality in the quiet, white temples of health. Only the priests take an occasional sip of the wine. "We'll be seeing quite a bit of each other from now on," but when? He was already yearning for the promised meeting. Melkior had got warm in his bed (the man rescued from drowning was coming back to life), the skinny little creature was drinking imagination in deep draughts, beginning to stir in a lively way under the covers in the luxury of greedy solitude. He had let the body devour a whole "hi-cal rations" lunch, a bracing and nutritious meal, and was now afraid of the creature's glee. It was going to get used to the comforts of pampered hospital life, give itself over to stupid, blind fattening, make itself into a succulent tidbit for Polyphemus the cannibal.

The castaways are asleep. A regulation siesta after a good lunch. All for the sake of fattening, you've got to be nursed back to health! Light snoring with the postprandial mute on (full volume being presumably reserved for night). They have had no news of the agent. Days are passing in conjecture. The chief engineer believes the *hosts* put him into a hospital of theirs: he was a sick man after all, they couldn't very well . . . Everyone understands what it was that "they couldn't very well" do and thought: aw, why couldn't they, cannibals, what can you expect? But there would have been some sort of sign (a tuft of Orestes' hair, Odysseus's scar, recognition according to Aristotle) of the agent having been . . . He had a golden chain around his neck with a cross and a four-leaf clover on it (double insurance)—surely the cross and the clover had not left him in the lurch at the crucial moment? This hope is voiced with lack-luster sarcasm by the first mate as in his corner he apathetically chews some "narcotic" leaves the doctor has found for him. The seaman is not there in the cabana. He has built himself a Tarzanian tree house in the branches of a giant baobab and is now living up there, squabbling with the monkeys. He is able, at long last, to snore to his heart's content! The animals understand the kindred sound of

Nature and pay him joyous respect, the parrots laughing in chorus, the songbirds lilting dithyrambs to Slumber.

Slumber has settled on his brow with its soft, heavy bottom: rock-a-bye, baby, burbling about all manner of promises. Lulling him with sweet picturesque stories: the white nurse, the poet's niece . . . then I say to her, then she says to me, and then I say, and then she says: for God's sake, not here, someone will see us! And on we walk, behind the dense-crowned dark tamarisk leaning over the sandy beach. I lead her by the hand, she's not resisting. Only her dainty little hand trembles like a bare birdling in my manly hand: where are you taking me? To show you how clear the sea is over here, you can see every pebble on the bottom.—How can you see them in the dark?—Phosphorescence. The glimmering plankton, a flock of tiny stars, you'll see, it's a wonderful sight . . . I stammer putting my arm around her waist, her supple waist, while up there the ample breasts breathe heavily, now rejecting me, now inviting me. My lips seek hers . . . and find an ear. All right, so an ear. I'll take the ear. But what are lips doing on an ear? The ear is firm, complex, and hollow. To kiss the hollow? But then a polyp, a moist cave-dweller, creeps out of the mouth and fills the entire shell with damp caresses. And I say ugh! (because the ear tastes a little bitter), but now she clings to me and says ah and oh and what are you doing darling? But the imagination will not set anything else in motion. Our heads set a tamarisk branch above us swaying, out sweeps a buzzing swarm of mosquitoes and makes an auditory halo around our heads—*zzzzz*—using the last letter of the alphabet.

Slumber is droning a sleepy song . . . choosing, however, the wrong image, one with angry insects in it. Melkior felt wakefulness on his goose-bump skin. His eyes reject the dream. Another sleepless one is the doctor. He is trying to think of something to do. He is thinking of playing a prank on them by persuading the old seaman to disappear for a few days, to keep hidden, then he will tell the others: there, I did as you said but off he went and sailed away without us. Didn't I tell you so? But he gives up the tasteless joke, his colleague the Major talks him out of it. The doctor has changed since meeting the Major through Melkior. He has become "a different man." Melkior is using all his demagogic skill to put the red-haired Asclepian to shame before the humane and sagacious army phthysiologist. But the conversion is not proceeding smoothly—Red has arguments of his own. In your place the Major would be trying to snatch these unfortunate people from the jaws of the cannibals, while you're relishing their mortal pain. He would at least try to ease their horrible death . . . It's not true that you can do nothing—you didn't even bother to think whether you could. All right, they're haughty and stupid, as you say, but is that alone reason enough to condemn them to such a horrible and repulsive death?

Granted, any death is horrible and repulsive (particularly one that is imminent), but this kind, you must admit, holds a horror all its own. To be cooked and eaten—good God!—We're all "cooked" in a way, smiles the doctor, and eaten, too, for that matter. All kinds of crooks cook us in the cauldrons of hellish plots, poison us with their contempt, drive us to madness and loathing, and when they've goaded us they push into our hands all manner of contraptions so that we can kill each other. Why? To feast on our flesh? Rubbish. They are disgusted by our carcasses. We are meat to hyenas, worms, carrion eaters, fish, beings unworthy of such delicacies. While over here, these "unfortunate people" will be eaten by people, by our hosts who take the bitter joke of Mother Nature a little too seriously. What particular horror is there in it? They'll kill us without hatred, at an evening of cultural manifestations and a popular celebration, and they'll be eating us with gusto as rare game coming from a curious world they cannot even imagine. It's an honor of sorts, after all, to be eaten by people rather than worms.—And if you, too, were destined to experience the honor (please note the verb *experience*), would you speak with equal cynicism?—Not in so many words, but I would be forced to think so.—And you would attempt nothing to be spared the "honor"?—What *could* I do? Mortify my body like *these people* and yourself? Mortify the flesh? Deprive them of a morsel? Well, my skin would be left in any case! They'd make a drum of it! Or should I set about converting them in the name of our God:

Don't eat me—I'm your brother? (Why, they take particular plea-sure in eating missionaries.) Should I pull off a miracle? Stage a putsch overnight, abrogate all laws (go on, living animal, feed on air and stones!), forbid cats to eat mice? Invoke disorder, confusion, and chaos? Of all the known gods, not a single one has managed to abrogate Nature. None of them tried—it never even occurred to them. Each of them is wise in his own way, knowing that Nature is somewhat more powerful than he, that he is unable to change even the destiny of a drop of water. That's why the gods hold on to Nature rather than going on about *helping poor man*. One man actually tried it and they chained him to a rock and let birds peck out his liver. They preferred to confirm the laws. If a volcano is to destroy a town, they're for the destruction; if people are to slaughter each other, they're for the slaughter. They even claim all that to be Their Will. They're always on the side of what men (out of ignorance) call Destiny. They approved of a son killing his father and marrying his own mother, of his mother giving birth to his sons and brothers, daughters and sisters. One of them even left his own son high and dry and let men crucify him so that The Law might be fulfilled. It must follow then that gods also approve of men eating men in compliance with the laws of hunger. Take this up with them, then, and leave me alone.

Yes, that is what the red-haired Asclepian (with unpleasant sub-cutaneous gland exudations, we must never forget this condition of his) says, but not even he quite means it. What he does mean is beyond Melkior's invention. The Major has embroiled himself in the story. What is he to do with the poor Asclepian who, through the Major, is now turning into a Nice Man? As recently as yesterday he was about to play a cruel prank, and now he is trying to think of something to do for *his lot* from the *Menelaus*, who are waiting to be eaten. Possibly out of mercy (if Don Fernando would allow) there is germinating in him a curious ambition to change these people's destiny. But how? That is what Melkior cannot work out.

What is he to do? he asks his imagination in creative despair. In passing he addresses the poor agent's destiny. But the very next day the old seaman tells him that Mr. Agent has become a big wheel. He had been given a palm-leaf skirt and a parrot-feather cap, become the High Medicine Man's chief assistant and a personage close to the Chief himself.—And what about the gold chain? Has he been allowed to keep the chain with the cross and the clover leaf?—But this does not allay the doctor's envy. The merchant fool making such a career! Mercury's porter assuming the place of a child of Asclepius! Well, one thing was clear: something decisive and important must be done immediately! But what, but what?

From the corridor came the holy rustle of a stiff dress and hurrying little footsteps on rubber heels. Melkior's body trembled in fright. He whispered, "She's coming," and set about selecting a welcoming face. He felt repeating on his face the selfsame unprepared surprise with which he had encountered Viviana, and closed his eyes like a child, seeking shelter in mimicked sleep. But when he felt her entry he opened his lashes just wide enough to check, will her gaze search for me?

Darling! Even as she was saying good evening her eyes sought his bed. He closed his eyes happily like a blissful little dog being stroked. Darling! He was choking with a thick feeling of happiness.

"The new man . . . is he asleep?" he heard above him the careful whisper by his cot, in the muddled daze of his childhood fevers, the voice of his young mother. But the happy spasm suddenly receded in an unexpected and mournful recuperation. The cold indifference of the familiar, in-house term "the new man" humiliated him like a number on a prison jacket. That's the extent of my presence here, as *the new man*, the striped anonymity of one of *those*. And Melkior did not open his eyes. He went into a false sleep, with the breath of a weary sleeper, from disappointment and spiteful misery. He felt her vertical proximity touch him with cold aloofness. She was moving, rustling like paper, in the magnetic field of his great amorous yearning, with the insensitivity of a foreign, indifferent body. She is not sensing the presence in me (under this army-issue blanket) of a wonderful world made for her beauty. My heart is tired and I no longer have a body with which to kiss you. I give you, beloved, the clouds floating over my dead eyes. And Melkior pictured himself dying (in revenge) under the gray blanket loyally trimmed with the royal colors. Inside, in the death of his eyes, he saw a strange life of liberated colors, a wondrous hovering of multicolored fancy over the black expanses of his dejected solitude. He felt the need to crawl inside his quaint kaleidoscope, to hide and vanish before the fear of further yearnings.

"All right then, we'd better let him sleep," came her voice from that other, former space where life was dangerous and bitter. And he wished to return from the labyrinth of his forlorn absence following that voice, to wake up among things in the grayness of the rainy afternoon under the tender protection of her benevolence. But he heard no benevolence in the casual plural, which meant only the resolution of a dilemma—should she or should she not wake him in the line of duty. So much the better if he's asleep, that had meant, no need to bother with him, then.

"But he's not asleep at all, Sister . . . atchoo!" sneezed the one who had called him Tartuffe; the others responded with a salvo of sneezes.

It's some kind of salute, that volley, thought Melkior, and he was afraid it might conceal a form of mockery.

"Gesundheit!" she replied with a peal of laughter, apparently honored by it. "The epidemic's still on, is it then?" and she took five thermometers from a breast pocket, one for each to tuck into his armpit.

But the fifth remained in her hand. "This one's still asleep."

"Like hell he is!" spoke up Menjou. "Stop playing the fool, Tartuffe. Reveal the secret of your bodily temperature."

Why couldn't I be asleep? protested Melkior in his fake sleep. This is a bit too much, doubting a man's sleep.

She leaned over the bed studying his face.

"He really is asleep," she whispered (he felt her breath on his eyelids).

"Leave him alone—he's tired, poor boy."

"Tartuffe," said the little fellow in the bed next to his in a harsh whisper, "there's an angel hovering over your head. Reach out, embrace the angel, Tartuffe."

Everybody laughed in an ugly, teasing way. She, too, was smiling, bent over his face. Through his barely open lashes Melkior could see the sun between the black curtains: the beauty of her breasts under the white shield, and the white neck and the smiling eyes. Her breath caressed his face, he felt the fragrance of her nearness, and the Little Mephistopheles whispered on, "Reach out, Tartuffe, embrace the angel . . ." and his arms really reached out on their own (he knew full well he did not mean to do it), embraced the pretty niece, and forcefully drew her angelic head down to his lips.

Her scream shot the two predatorial limbs through, they released the victim and dropped back lifeless onto the royal colors of the army blanket.

Melkior started from an insane dream (and he really felt like a man waking up), propped himself on his elbows, and peered around in surprise—he was understanding nothing. "No, it wasn't an *acte gratuit*, I was dreaming, ahh, I was dreaming . . . Not an *acte gratuit*." Stammering it forth like an explanation to his awakened consciousness.

She had her face covered with her hands and was still shaking all over.

Moustache à la Adolphe Menjou was already there at her side, trying to peel her palms from her face: "But what did he do to you, Nurse, what did he do to you?"

"Nothing, nothing," she replied from inside the palms, fighting back tears. "He didn't do anything to me. He was dreaming . . . God, it gave me such a fright!"

"Thtuff and nonthenth! He wathn't dweaming at all!" lisped a fat, toothy hermaphroditic individual from the bed by the door. "He wath going to kith her, that wath hith dweam."

"Listen you, whatsyourname," Moustache à la Adolphe Menjou said threateningly to Melkior, "what were you trying to do to the nurse?"

She had now moved her hands away from her face and stepped

protectively between Menjou and Melkior: "Leave him alone, it was in his sleep. Go back to your bed."

"Hee-hee, he was prompted by my suggestion," triumphed Little Guy. "I had him hypnotized."

"You what? Don't be ridiculous!" interjected Tartuffe angrily. He wished Menjou would tackle Melkior.

"No, honest! I've worked at it!" protested Little Guy. "We did suggestion and hypnosis at the university. I'm a psychologist."

"You *are* a psycho all right! Don't give us that crap!" Menjou was really angry. He had not succeeded in hitting Melkior. He was jealous. He thought he was entitled to be because he was handsome.

"Tell me, sir," Little Guy pleaded with Melkior, "tell me, please —did you do it at my suggestion?"

"I don't know what I did," replied Melkior worriedly and some-how tired. "I must have done something in my sleep. I'm so sorry, Sister."

"Why, he's insane!" exclaimed Tartuffe delightedly. "Can't you see he's insane? Look at his glassy eyes! I saw right away he was mad as a hatter."

"Why a hatter?" Little Guy the psychologist was being the deri-sive expert.

"That'th how the thaying goeth, thtupid," Hermaphrodite in-formed Little Guy. But Tartuffe didn't feel like talking to Little Guy: "Hey look, he's out of his mind. He's dreaming about something again . . . Look at those eyes!"

Melkior was still sitting motionless in bed, mournfully gazing into an invisible distance. He was muttering the same question over and over again: "Was that an *acte gratuit?*" No, it was not an *acte gratuit*, he replied, seemingly disappointed, but that was not what was on his mind at all. He was only using the words to build a roadblock to another thought struggling to break through to his consciousness, a thought he feared and consequently set a trap for in the form of Ugo's leering black fillings: now that's what I call an *acte gratuit!* Well done, Eustachius! But no, no, it wasn't an *acte gra-*

tuit . . . He was fighting for the truth. And while the fight went on he could hear his thought outside, outside this fog enveloping his consciousness, from a clear world where things could be seen for what they were: why, he's insane! Can't you see he's insane?

This, then, was insanity? Melkior lay down on his back and drew the covers over his head. Such a strange condition: nothing going on in the head, a roar of blood in the ears, and a terrible desire in the arms. I'm insane, then. The thought sounded almost funny in his mind. He was smiling under the blanket. Well, perhaps I'm sly, eh castaways, perhaps I simply *pulled a good one* with that kissing business? She'll be feeling sorry for me yet. So, it wasn't an *acte gratuit* after all, it was simulated madness. Which is much more preferable in my situation. A military situation. A thtwoke of geniuth! he marveled at himself. It'll get about, that kiss. And tomorrow I'll kiss the Major, too, to dispel all thuthpithion. Deprive them of a "sexual" explanation. Never mind an *acte gratuit*, I'm insane! Parampion, I declare myself insane. *Orate, fratres!*

"He's apt to slaughter us all in 'in his sleep,' " said Menjou like a wise man. "We ought to report this to the Major."

Judging by the moustache Menjou could be aiming to be a tour guide in the summer season (the Adriatic coast, with Dubrovnik at the top of the list) or, judging by his chivalry, an actor (growing his moustache to match the uniform). I don't suppose she's gone back to Freddie . . . if Parampion has gone the way of the call-up off to Petrovaradin (bastard!), and Don Fernando . . . By the way—there! I had an idea in my insanity!—if the Maestro has already sold his body, couldn't Don Fernando use him for . . . well, let's call it an experimental preventive murder? So that's why he is so partial to Maestro! God knows what all may have happened back there by now. How many dead, wounded, under investigation, under suspicion . . . ?

"And what would you report to the Major?" he heard her voice. "That this patient reached out to me in his sleep?"

"Not 'weached out'—embwathed you and kithed you!" This from Hermaphrodite.

"That's not true! He didn't kiss me!"

Oh Lord, she's defending me! (Yes she is, you cad! replied the Lord.)

"It's true—I saw it," said Little Guy. "He did kiss you, but he was under my hypnosis at the time. It's not his fault."

A brilliant little ATMAN, thought Melkior, amused.

"Listen, short stuff," said Tartuffe, "don't make me hypnotize you, because if I do I guarantee you'll never come to again! Stop wasting our time with that womanish bilge! This guy's a loony, no doubt about it. I agree this ought to be reported to the Major. I'm not sharing a room with a lunatic! Let them transfer him to Neurology. For observation!"

Well, I *will* kiss the Major! Prove Tartuffe right.

"I tell you, he's apt to slaughter us all in our sleep," said Menjou.

"Are you really so afraid of this emaciated young man?" Speak, Angel, I'm listening! "You ought to be ashamed of yourself. Such a coward—and you a cadet, too! An officer-to-be!"

Not a tour guide then? A future warrior? *Sing, Oh goddess, the wrath of Achilles son of Peleus. . . .* But why did they sneeze at her?

He felt an itch in a nostril and sneezed beneath the covers, a muffled but genuine and forceful sneeze. That's from the water they poured on me, next stop pneumonia, I shouldn't wonder, that's what Lefty said.

"Now, he's sneezing, too," she looked back. She approached with circumspection and uncovered his head. "And I thought you were serious!" She was laughing.

Melkior raised a humble gaze in her direction: "I sneezed in earnest. I'm cold." He was lying, he was in fact hot, but he had a role to play to the end.

"Nervous chills, definitely," murmured Tartuffe implacably.

"Did you hear it—he sneezed in earnest! Hee, hee, hee," chortled Little Guy.

"It was a genuine sneeze," Melkior was playing Prince Mishkin.

"I believe you, I really do," she tugged at his big toe peeking out from under the covers.

"I may have caught a cold. They poured water on me, over at the barracks. I fainted and they dumped water all over me . . ."

"Cold showers, of course. Treatment for schizophrenia," explained Tartuffe.

"Theth he fainted. That would be epilepthy," said Hermaphrodite. "It'th going to be a pwetty pickle when he thtartth having thiezurth in the woom."

"I fainted in the stable, from the smell . . ."

"I've never heard of anyone fainting from smells," said Menjou with superiority. "You can faint from hunger, but . . . You're not telling us they didn't give you anything to eat in the barracks, are you?"

"Of course they did. They gave me good food, meat, even jam. But I fainted before breakfast. You go to the stable before breakfast. But I wasn't hungry, it was just the pungent smell inside . . . 'Next stop pneumonia, I shouldn't wonder,' is what Lefty said. It was cold when they carried me outside, and I was soaked . . . Maybe I've got pneumonia?"

"We'll check that right away," she took out a thermometer and stuck it in his armpit. "Let's take your temperature first." She put her small moist palm on his forehead: "It's not too hot."

"So it was 'Lefty' who told you so?" Menjou had become curious. "What else did old 'Lefty' have to say?"

"Who the hell is 'Lefty,' you loony kook?" laughed Tartuffe.

"The one who was to my left when they took me outside the stable," explained Melkior in detail. "There was also Righty, the one who was to my right. They were detailed by the sergeant."

"This clinches it. Don't anyone tell me he's not mad!" exclaimed Tartuffe angrily. "Why, he's a total idiot!"

That's right, a total idiot, approved Melkior. That's better than a Madman even! For what's a Madman compared to an Idiot? A mere fool, babbling gibberish and inventing nonsense. Such as that there is a people called the Buriaks or some such thing living there under his bed; boasting that he'd seen the largest hole in the world and demanding that they address him as Your Highness. Now that's a lunatic. A boaster. A show-off. Wishing to live in grand style. Playing

King Lear and Prince Hamlet. An Idiot is a refined and modest sort of fellow. Introverted and taciturn. Quiet as a snail. Says only what he knows, responds when asked, and when he doesn't know, says nothing. And everything he says is logical. And quaint, because it's simple; comical, because it's innocent. Cautious and wise as a donkey, always in love, with a heart so big! Melkior showed under the blanket the size of the Idiot's heart. There, that's the Idiot. A distinguished gentleman amid the common folk. Even a bit of a snob. Discriminating. Isolated. Choosy as to company. Taciturn, preoccupied with his thoughts. A wistful, rarefied, refined soul—that's the Idiot. Just take a look at the wrinkled forehead and the gaze floating above everyday things . . .

She had sat down on the edge of his bed. Her skirt had stretched tight across the hips and the two hemispheres, one of which was leaning on his outthrust knee. The knee, sunk in the soft warm cushion, was quietly blissful. Knee-deep in clover . . . He envied his knee. And in the body there sprang up an unexpected desire for Enka, the petite, naughty one . . . "Priapus, Priapus!" She was in a light sweat all over, the small arrogant bum, two brimming handfuls of overjoyed lust.

Enka had made him forget the thermometer. They follow us everywhere, the accursed vixen (putting it Russian style). He knocked the thermometer on the head under the blanket, three hard taps and one weak one, just in case; high fever does not come all that easily if you're a soldier. He sneezed (this time artificially) to corroborate the thermometer's false testimony.

"You're teasing me, too?" she asked with a bit of natural feminine coquetry.

"Teasing you? Why?" He was afraid of the touch of the knee but dared not break it.

"Haven't you noticed they all sneeze in here?" she asked in a conspiratorial whisper.

"Yes, I have. Why is that?" Melkior was whispering too. Our Little Secret was born.

"To tease me. My name is Acika," she reddened, "and it reminds them of the sound 'atchoo' so they sneeze to it. A silly name. You sneezed because of it, too."

"No, Acika," he said loyally. "I'm actually not well, I've got a cold."

"Please don't use my name," she said earnestly. "It makes me feel like you're teasing me. I'm so embarrassed to hear my name spoken. It's as if I were caught off guard at . . . that's how I feel, if you follow me," she was blushing bright red. "And what's your name?"

"You know it—you took it down this morning . . ."

"I'm sorry, I don't remember. I handle so many names . . ."

"It's an odd one . . . Melkior." She's right, it's not pleasant to hear your name spoken, and when you say it yourself you're downright awkward.

"Well, that's a nice name," she said aloud, even with a tone of encouragement, as though it were a matter of their common interest.

"They'we alweady exchanging namth on the bed, hoo-hoo," stage-whispered Hermaphrodite, his gut rumbling with laughter.

"What does that . . . character say his name is?" inquired Menjou, with dignity.

"He's got a nice name—Melkior! Isn't it lovely?" she spoke to them peaceably.

"Nithe. Hoo-hoo," hooted Hermaphrodite mockingly.

"What sort of calendar of saints did your old man find you in?" said Menjou contemptuously.

"Christian," said Melkior. "There were three kings of the Orient. Following a star they came to Bethlehem, to worship baby Jesus. One of them was called Melchior . . ."

"And that'th you," mocked Hermaphrodite.

"Well, there *is* something royal about him, I noticed it right away," said Tartuffe.

"My word, so there is . . . and you clods think it's funny," stated Menjou, encouraging them to laugh on.

They are laughing like warriors, beating their tom-toms around my stake. My lovable missionary Miss Acika is unable to save me. Lord, how pretty she is!—be it said in passing. Yes, pretty indeed, replies the Lord, as indifferent as a eunuch.

They'll burn me at the stake like a heretic. They'll cook me like the cook off the good ship *Menelaus*. But what's the use of these scrawny bones, Oh brave chieftain the Great Menjou? They are a bundle of misery, covered with mangy ascetic skin! Nothing but three drops of blood inside—wouldn't make a proper meal for a domestic flea! Spare me, Oh Great Menjou! Mercy!

"Sister Acika" (Menjou did not sneeze, joking time was over), "the thermometers are boiling in our armpits."

She stood up (Acika surprised . . . on my knee, thinks Melkior) and looked at her watch: "Pipe down, it has only been five minutes. You never give me a moment's respite, I'm on my feet all day."

"Theuw aww other playtheth to thit," Hermaphrodite offered her the edge of his bed.

"Thanks very much. Perhaps tomorrow."

"Tomowow will be too late!" Hermaphro gave an offended grin, spittle spuming through his jutting wide-set teeth.

"There, there, don't be grumpy," she stroked his head.

"Who'th gwumpy? I'm laughing: hoo-hoo-hoo . . ."

"That's better."

She traced their temperature graphs in their lists, felt their pulses, counted the beats, in a well-practiced way, deftly, with her small, pretty hands.

Her fingers were soft and moist. She held Melkior's arm, the hand dangling lifelessly, alongside her hip; her eyes were down on her wristwatch and she was counting off the seconds with her long black lashes. It was as if they were animated by a mute suffering (that's how eyes prepare to shed tears, thought Melkior). He felt like touching the pain, stroking her in a brotherly empathetic way (darling!), and two of his fingers (two mellow eyes, two pure tears gliding down his loving heart) moved eagerly toward the touch. They felt the cold encounter of stiffened fabric (the consecrated armor of cold chastity). And yet there was *she* inside, beautiful and alive . . .

The fingers now huddled miserably at the walls of the ivory tower and fluttered in a desperate plea . . . And lo, the imprisoned body responded, returning the tremor with the trembling of a frightened bird, as though two fears had touched at the border of unexpected happiness.

With a seemingly accidental movement she brushed his hand away from her hip, heaving a deep sigh and closing her eyes. An instant in which Melkior saw the devil with ATMAN's eyes and Ugo's fillings, a leering, mocking face: enter my kingdom, Eustachius.

She was by then slowly lowering her hand to the gray blanket, training a dimmed, distant look at his face. The face of a skin-shorn, desiccated, *total* idiot—those were the terms with which Melkior was now despising himself. While she, on high, above him, was a tower, solid and far too tall! What had happened to the frightened bird? . . . The bird had fluttered away, silent, soundless . . .

She entered his pulse and temperature in his list.

"Come downstairs tomorrow morning for a lung X-ray," she said without raising her head.

"At what time, please?" He wished her to say something more to him, be it no more than the time of their "meeting again."

"Seven," she said on her way out, without a goodbye, in businesslike haste.

Leaving angry gloom in the room—nobody even sneezed after her.

He lay in state: arms down sides, chin above blanket, eyes closed. This is what it will be like one day. Candles, flowers, whispers all around, everything in black. The widow. Acika. An unfitting name for a widow—too coquettish. She "exchanging" glances with "Menthou," with my nose not even cold yet. It's best to beat them while you're still alive, *preventively*. "Why are you beating me? For staining my memory, you bitch! Two strange trees will grow at the head of my grave, your monument to me—the horns of a cuckold!"—and I'll carry on: bam! bop! . . . Or I'll dispense with the explanation and just beat. No, Acika doesn't suit her. Not the right name, Acika. Lucretia.—I would have liked your name to be Lucretia.—Why?—

Lucretia was a legendary woman. She killed herself after being raped.—I'd kill myself too if that happened to me.—I don't believe you.—Why? Just because my name is Acika?—I don't believe in rape any more than I believe in the immaculate conception. I don't believe a woman can be raped.—It has happened to more than one woman, you know.—It may have happened to some, but only partially. I don't propose to go into the details, I'll leave them to your imagination, but the second part of that violent act is no longer violence.—Well, what is it, then? (she, flushed with anger).—A kind of . . . acceptance, and I won't swear there isn't a certain sort of pleasure in it either; a "peculiar" kind of pleasure to be sure; "painful" even, as you might put it. It's only afterward, when it's all over and exists only as a memory, that the "shame" sets in. But the shame stems mostly from disappointment. With the man's savagery and, even more, his lack of consideration, his selfishness and cynicism. If a savage were to convert while on top of her, in a manner of speaking, this could even blossom into love. She would forgive him everything thanks to his subsequent redeeming tenderness. "Ah, I remember how rough you were when you first took me! But I can now confess I liked it so much. What a he-man! A warrior! Then again, perhaps it's the only way to find true love. You know, we women actually prefer to believe we're being raped. We would 'never' have *acquiesced* if we hadn't been 'forced' into it. We say, 'no, no, no,' don't we, but woe to him who believes us: we never forgive him for it. Now I've told you all." And then he beats her for being sincere (there, that's the thanks you get for being sincere with them!) and calls her the worst names he can think of, as you can well imagine.— Ugh! That's a fine opinion to have of women! Since you're like that, you can't really love a single one. It can't be that all women are tarred by the same brush. Do you really think so about all women?— No, Vivi . . . er, Acika. That's what the Parampion—my friend Ugo— thinks, and he fancies all women.—Well, that's the most repugnant thing—fancying all but loving and respecting none.—But they like him, too!—Every one?—Well, most of them. You, too, would find

him appealing if you knew him, precisely because he's like that.—
Then you don't know me at all! (deeply offended).—No, no, I'm
sorry (Melkior took fright), I really don't know you *yet*. Nevertheless . . . (after some timid hesitation) I daresay you, too, are unable to
love someone truly—a man, I mean. You belong to the Major's
Samaritan school (that's why I'm going to give him a kiss tomorrow):
a soldier in hospital is a miserable patient and nothing more. Your
kindness has only sanitary value. Duty. Therapeutic, optimistic, a
cheery atmosphere for the pulmonary patients: the cheerfulness of a
headwaiter in the service of good appetite—have a nice time in our
establishment. The winsome blandishments of an air hostess at
celestial heights. The angelic smiles for sick bodies, for boils, for
wounds, for the reek of rotting lungs, the stale stench of candidates
for death. What's a white swan doing in life's repulsive hellholes? Is
this a climate for love? Swan lake . . .

"You there . . . whatever your name is," spoke up Menjou in the
end.

"Melkior." Of course. Here it comes. He had been expecting it.

"You there, Meteor . . ."

"Melkior!"

"Listen, Meteor," said Menjou with the greatest contempt, "have
you been up to any funny business with her?"

"You won't thcore with her, my boy . . ." Herma was saying in an
almost friendly tone.

"There have been better Toreadors before you, Mon-sewer Mata-
dor, and they've all drawn a blank."

"I was polite with the young lady . . ."

"Listen to this—he was polite!" exclaimed Menjou, stirring them
up.

"She never, never went away like that before, without a goodbye," said Little Guy to him in a low, confidential voice. "You
must've offended her in some way."

"Tho, thee!" jubilated Hermaphrodite maliciously. "You offended the wady!"

"I didn't say anything bad to her . . ."

I'm being defensive, thought Melkior, and that's not good, damn it. The Parampion would have attacked. He would have pulled off a putsch and taken control.

But how do you go about it? (He had long been trying to think of a putsch whereby the red-haired Asclepian would take control of the cannibals.) Perhaps if he opened the window overlooking the courtyard and spoke from there, made a demagogical speech . . . Oh no, friends and countrymen, I come not to the window to denounce, for Menjou is an honorable man; so are they all, all honorable men . . . (muttering in the courtyard—a sign of protest) but only to vindicate my vain heart. You know how weak the human heart is for you are good, kindhearted men; and mine is wounded withal. I would show you my wounded heart, but this dare I not, for I should do Menjou wrong, I should do them all wrong, and they, as you know full well, are honorable men. (Hem, hem—uncertain muttering in the courtyard.) I choose, then, to keep my silence and bear my pain for the sake of peace and for the esteem in which I hold so honorable a man as Menjou. But he says I offended her and was up to, ahem, *funny business* with her . . . and his words are prompted by love, by care of her honor, for he is an honorable man and doth love her honorably. He knows, therefore, what love is and could certainly tell you what offense there be in one man's love that there be not in another's. I know not—alas!—how my sighs can be an impediment to his love. Can sighs infect the air wherein basks a man's bliss? I am not the orator Menjou is; I have not the power of speech to couch in sweet-sounding words that which you yourselves do know. But he is wise and eloquent, and thus bound to tell you wherein my offense lay. (Let us ask him! Let him tell us!) He will no doubt answer you for he is indeed an honorable man.

But what will he be able to tell you? That I did with but one finger touch her dress; that and nothing more. What private griefs they have, alas! I know not, that made them call me impertinent. They know it. But what impertinence be there in that light touch of a finger—a finger which fear had made to tremble withal? (A voice:

Oh woeful day!) Sweet friends and countrymen, a brazen fellow hath not a blushing cheek, as you know full well. Not a trembler he, but a grabber. And I tremble e'en now at the thought of the touch of that sacred dress. Perhaps she expected me to grab her hand and kiss it. What woman does not? As she was counting the beat of my maddened pulse, perhaps she felt the same stirrings in her own blood? And what is it I did? Nothing, or nearly nothing: I touched her dress with a finger. Did this in me seem brazen? (A voice: Never! Another voice: If thou consider rightly of the matter, he has had great wrong. Third voice: Truly spoken! He is a just man, and they are villains! First voice: We see it now—Menjou is a traitor! Second voice: Let not the traitor live! We'll burn the bed of Menjou!)

Stay, gentle friends! You go to do you know not what. Wherein have I thus deserv'd your loves? What am I to you? (Voices: You are our leader! The Admiral!) Other voices: Hear! hear! You are our admiral! Let us board ships and sail away! A voice (poetically): Let us sail away. Gulls and clouds will ask us: who are you? what do you seek? . . . and our sails will reply: Melkior sails! Melkior seeks a barren reef . . . (the poetic voice drowns in tears. All the others begin crying, too).

Blessed be those tears, my people! Away, then! But . . . wait an instant . . . for I wish to be quite clean before you. (Voices: It's all right, you're clean! Let's go!) Not quite I'm not, friends and countrymen. (Yes you are, pure as an angel!) No, no, I have passions and lusts flaming inside me. (All the better—that means you're a man! ha-ha laughter full of admiration.) Yes, but what kind of man? One with low, Priapic passions. Priapus, Priapus, exclaimed . . . I can't tell you who, she's a married woman. As for our chaste, white nurse . . . Acika (indeed a name to sneeze at, he thought in passing), I tried to embrace and kiss her, too, by force, friends and countrymen, because she's a smashing little muffin, is she not? (Wow, Admiral, you do take the cake!—this in admiration and approval down in the courtyard.)

"You're not to trust him, good-looking folk, you're not to trust him!" shouts a voice from above (*deus ex machina*, thinks Melkior).

"You're not to trust him, he's up to his ears in love—I know him! (Goodbye Viviana, mutters the voice in passing.) Lets on he's a cynic—and him an honorable man indeed. Eustachius, be our leader! Our admiral!" and the huge black fillings darkened the sky. Ugo's appealing voice. But what is he doing here? "Exalted Parampion, it's you!" exclaimed Melkior joyously and heard his voice strangely distant from himself as though it had been an echo exclaiming.

Melkior felt his nose being pulled. He woke up instantly and opened his eyes wide in surprise. Sitting on his bed was a bulky young man in white, his mouth stretched into a make-believe smile, looking at him in a sticky-sweet way, "Good morning" fairly flowing from his ocular liquid.

"Name's Mitar. Vampire, they call me. Shh, don't wake 'em up, I got the moniker here in this very room," whispered the man in white. "It's all right—I'm just a lab tech, I came for a drop of your blood."

Melkior thought he was dreaming. "Friends and countrymen," he said mechanically and propped himself on his elbows to clear his head. They come to suck your blood in your sleep, the vampires . . . Old wives' tales. All the same horror slithered up his back.

The others were still asleep, slurping up the last dregs of sleep before morning wake-up. They blew in and out cooperatively at their common task, Hermaphrodite's lusty snore taking the lead. Melkior heaved a sigh of envy.

"What do you need my blood for?" he said, looking hopelessly at the gray wall in front.

"All right, so you refuse," Mitar concluded indifferently. "I'll report that to the Major."

"I only said, 'What do you need my blood for?'" Melkior now fully awake. "I haven't got two thimblefuls in me."

"I can make do with one," smiled Mitar sweetly. "But it doesn't follow that I'm just a lightweight . . . I do have some say in things. Know what blood work is?"

"No."

"Well then."

"Where will you take it from?" Melkior offered him an arm.

"Take it easy. We don't have to do it right away. Just relax and lie back down." He cautiously laid Melkior down on his back and covered him up to the chin. He even pushed Melkior's arms under the covers. "You're a patient, you must take care of yourself. If you want to get well again, you've got to comply. What do you think we're here for?"

Melkior yielded. He couldn't understand what this Mitar fellow wanted.

"Well, there you are, you're saying nothing. Not that you could say anything—it's true what I said. Everything can be read from your blood: health and disease and malingering. It's all written in there as in the Bible, your destiny. That's why it's called blood work, and that's where I'm in charge. What I say goes. And there's no 'let me see' or 'I wonder if' with me. I give it to you plain: sedimentation rate, Wassermann reading, erythro and leuko counts, bilirubin, the whole kit and kaboodle. And if I mark it all 'Negative' and 'NTR,' it's forward march, direction barracks and not even God Himself can get you off."

Mitar the Vampire made a telling pause. He then brought his broad, greasy face over Melkior and ran his gaze over him: searching for a likely spot to grab.

"Then again, there's blood work and there's blood work . . ." he cast a cautious glance around the other beds and whispered with a kind of considerate contempt: "Sleeping, the weary heroes . . . It's like having your picture taken at a photographer's: you can ask for it to be warts-and-all or you can have it retouched. Now retouching's no problem, you just leave that to me."

"Is this expensive?" whispered Melkior conspiratorially.

Mitar seemed not to have heard the question and went on whispering; this time, in what was more like a private lament:

"Oh, oh, what a greedy bastard I am, from head to toe, God strike me! Look at the size of this!" he boastfully displayed his rotund belly with his trouser belt buckled prudently below it, "that's my lord and master! The only one I serve—the rest can go to hell. It's grilled meat, grilled meat makes the world go round, as the poet says—and that's what's going to bankrupt me, too. Braised heart, grilled liver, lamb chops, mincemeat steak, not to mention tripes on the fatty side . . . you've no idea how much I like gourmet food, God help me! Funnily enough, I don't go in much for kebab, not even with sour cream—unless it's tucked into a grilled bread pocket. I'm a big man for young spitted duck, with fat dripping from the tip of its crispy little bum, he, he," tittered Mitar licking his lips and purring hoarsely: "Grrr . . . grr . . . grill grrates, grrill grrates, that's what the Gypsies shout who hawk them. Find my taste amusing, don't you? Your shit's fat-free, right? A piece of boiled fish, an olive or two, that's more the way you like it, eh? Oh, and Swiss chard, I bet. I can just see your gut piping *Take me back to my home by the sea . . .*"

One of the sleepers grunted before waking. Mitar quickly got going with his instruments.

"Let's get this over with, all right?" he whispered in a seemingly casual way, making his preparations.

"Very well, let's do it," Melkior proffered his skinny white arm.

"Retouched, am I right?" Mitar tightened the rubber tube around Melkior's upper arm. "Jeez, not an honest vein in sight. This is going to be tricky," he said out loud, worriedly shaking his head; as his head moved he whispered hastily: "Fifty up front, the rest when you get your ticket, OK?"

"How much is . . . the rest?" muttered Melkior all but unintelligibly.

"Well . . . another hundred fifty. To keep me flush for taking the girlfriend out. She's into the green liqueurs, damn her . . . and they are pricey." He glanced at Melkior's undecided face. "All right, a hundred, because it's you—I can see you suffering. Christ, you are a stingy crowd, you types from Dalmatia, strike you . . . Turds in olive oil! What can you buy for the money? A pair of pajamas, if that . . . *Chic à la française* and look at you—so damned miserable you can't take a decent shit. Look at the state of your veins. Two thimblefuls, you say? Hell, you haven't got enough to give a bedbug a square meal. Things are tough these days, you know," Mitar spoke in a whisper again. "There's a war on, man!" he cried sternly, "and we're in the army, we've got to be prepared!" and he gave Melkior a sly wink: he was saying this for the benefit of "the guys."

"Shall I give you the money now?" whispered Melkior, watching the short deft thievish fingers on his wretched arm where Mitar was poking around for a spot to puncture with the proboscis of his bloodthirsty device.

"Not here. Meet me in the fancy gents after the morning round."

"What's the fancy gents?"

"The better-class bathroom, for you cadet types . . ." He finally found the vein and thrust the needle in quickly, deft, so skillfully that Melkior hardly felt the prick. He saw the thin pink blood follow the cylinder in the syringe, filling the little glass stomach of Mitar the bloodsucker. My blood, Your Majesty . . . but he felt himself go pale, the joke had barely begun before it melted away in a strange laxity; sleep seemed to be settling on his lids . . .

"Hey, look," Mitar gave him a yank, "there's a pigeon at the window!"

Melkior awoke with effort and looked gullibly at the window. No pigeon, just a gray day. Dove at the window, he uttered with effort, barely moving his lips, driven by memory's quaint force as if he'd been obliged to say it, and remained so in a state of apathetic immobility, watching the gray patch of sky above the grim wet roofs. "Taken your fiww of bwood, vampiwe?" Hermaphrodite teased Mitar. "I wouldn't use yours to fertilize my cabbages," Mitar replied, but Melkior received it all from a great astral distance and it seemed to him that he was hearing not human voices but the cawing of irritated parrots.

What about the lung X-ray? he thought with mixed feelings of sudden joy and an uneasiness which demanded that he stir from the sweet laxity to which he had fully succumbed. I might see her downstairs . . . while having my lungs x-rayed. And be alone with her. *Alone together*—so what? The phrase was so promising and exciting—and yet so meaningless. At least in a certain sense. *Alone together* meant trying to approach her using excited, inept words— in fact, false words that could rely only on the hands for help. And everything would be fumbling, with both words and hands: the hands impatient and the words deaf, witless, thrown into echoless empty space. She says, "Talk to me," and what you want at that moment is to seal her mouth with yours, and even if a word or two escapes there is no conversation to it at all. Desire turns you into a stammerer, a quaking imbecile, an epileptic, an impotent lecher, an angry pig, an onanist poet, an abased devotee, a man with no pride. I won't go and have my lungs x-rayed! Defiantly, Melkior set to thinking about Enka: enter my kingdom, Kior, and he entered with regal triumph, as Kior the Great. Mitar appeared in the doorway.

"I forgot to take your urine sample. Had a piss yet?" He had a glass like a champagne glass in his hand.

"No," said Melkior, adding to himself: here's my cup-bearer.

"Come along then, wee-wee for Daddy," he showed him the glass as bait.

"Yes, Meteor, come along—Mitar's just had his snack," spoke up Menjou.

"Is it today your sister's supposed to drop in? It's visitors' day," said Mitar with such an overpolitely fraternal and innocent face that Melkior was greatly surprised to see an object flying toward the spot where the Vampire's head had been a moment ago. "A moment ago," of course, because no sooner had it inquired overpolitely about Menjou's sister's visit than it ducked away.

"Leave my sister out of it, you bastard!" bellowed Menjou suddenly. "I'll tear out his throat with my bare teeth . . . drink his blood!" he was writhing in his bed, waving his arms about in a curious way, as if torn by horrible pain.

The other three hurried over to pacify him, stroking his face, patting his head, slapping his hips, ostler fashion.

"He'th weally cwuizing foww a bwuizing," raged Herma, clenching his hands in fists.

"Next time he comes in we give him the blanket treatment . . . We beat the shit out of him, word of honor!" said the one who had called him Tartuffe the day before in a solemn tone, like someone taking a vow.

"Just let me work him over—his own mother won't recognize him!" Menjou was simmering down already, the thirst for revenge was fading.

"Unleth thomebody betwayth uth!" Hermaphrodite gave Melkior a suspicious look; he was taking the matter very seriously, as a conspiracy.

"The traitors will get their just desserts!" threatened Menjou.

"He won't betray us," said Little Guy confidently. "It's all about a sister's honor! You won't betray us, will you?" Little Guy was applying the power of suggestion on Melkior, ogling him weirdly and circling his open palms over his head: "You will not betray us, you will not, this is about a sister's honor, you will not betray . . ." he was hypnotizing him.

Melkior barely heeded the mumbo-jumbo. With laughter bubbling inside him, he kept thinking about Mitar's glass, which had aroused in his body the urge to urinate. And he felt it as an undeniable imperative, which he was presently to obey. He was going to get up and follow Mitar's glass like a sleepwalker, like a hypnotized fool. Conditioned reflexes, as defined by Pavlov. Thank you for doing me the honor, my dear Little Guy, but I was already in a trance, he thought, getting up. This, I expect, is how poets follow their inspiration. That glass is now my Laura. And Melkior's mournful face cracked a smile.

"He'th waughing at uth," said Hermaphrodite.

"Are you off to snitch to Mitar?" Menjou leapt out of bed, menacingly.

"I'm off to fill his glass."

"You're OK!" he heard behind him their assessment and their laughter in reward of his loyalty.

Oh Lord, my cup shall be full! Knowing you, it will overflow, replied the Lord.

And indeed it overflowed, just as the Lord said. For great was the need in him and he rushed into the better-class bathroom and snatched the cup from Mitar's hand, greedily, like a drunkard, and like an utterly lust-crazed lecher he sought his uncaring member in fumbling haste, so that it slipped away at the first try, listlessly, as though this was not its job (well it isn't either, the conniver knew that all right) but on the second try brought he out, in the manner of a vainglorious man, all his fortune plainly to be seen and then the terrible rain was upon the glass for forty days and forty nights . . .

"Hey! Stop it, will you!" cried Mitar in fright. Say *Enough!* to the raging torrent, stop the mighty wave rolling in from the high seas! . . .

"Look what you've done—there's piss running all over the place," Mitar tittered brightly: he liked abundance. "Pour out a bit over there, damn you . . ."

Ha, Maestro, remembered Melkior, what an outpouring! I would have overshot the rooftops, extinguished the Lilliput royal palace fire like Gulliver! He felt pride at some kind of virility, though it was in fact a feeling of quite pedestrian relief which he was interpreting with arrogance.

"Did you bring the money?" asked Mitar with a full cup in his raised arm, as if proposing a toast to him.

"Yes. Here you are," Melkior was doing everything with delight, in a hurry, full of cheer, which made Mitar watch him with curiosity and feel sorry for not having asked for a higher price. The stupid nut would have coughed it up easy.

"By the way, what did that character say? Is he going to report me?" asked Mitar.

"Why would he? What did you do to him?"

"Well, it's this business with his sister, see. They're very touchy because she's rather . . . free with it . . ." Mitar had lowered his voice and his head, so it wouldn't stick out. "And he really walked into that one. Mind you, it's very, very tricky, his old man's a general in the Guards. Lots of clout. He only has to lift a finger and it's curtains for yours truly, Mitar the lab tech."

"What about the others?"

"Upper crust lads, all of them. That fat hairless bugger, th-th-th-the one, he pocketed an important paper, top secret and all that, from his old man (the pater familias is on the Council of State) and gave it to a spying bitch in exchange for a bit of the other. Luckily enough, the counterespionage blokes caught him at it, sent the bitch to the slammer and himself to his Daddy. Daddy thought it best to have him do his National Service, 'He'll come to his senses in the army,' like, and here he is, coming to his senses. Little Guy's the son of a lady-in-waiting—or ex-lady-in-waiting, that is . . . They called her the Guards' Pompadour. She never said no to anyone from private to major; upward from there, it all depended on how influential you were. They say the lad's father is a hot-shot crazy general . . . well, you saw it—he's some kind of mad psychologist himself. But the fourth, 'The Parisian,' he's got the most clout. His old man's . . . well, nobody even knows what he is; lives abroad; imports weapons, they say. The boy only came back to do his student stint in the service—he'll be going back to Daddy afterward as his assistant, to help with the war effort if things come to a head. Everyone doing their bit, as they say. They've all got their suitcases packed, my old friend, and their passports ready in hand. That's why they call it the Diplomatic Room."

"You seem to know everything," said Melkior diffidently. "So how did I end up there?"

"How?" Mitar raised his head as if about to crow forth some weighty truth, but changed his mind: "You can thank God and the Major . . ."

"But I don't even know the Major!"

"Well, that's it, just because you don't. When you get to know the Colonel, you'll get to know the Major too. The Colonel's Head of Department, a soldier and a patriot."

"Meaning the Major isn't a patriot?"

"Course he is, who says he isn't? You're asking an awful lot of questions," and Mitar gave him a suspicious look. "I've told you too much as it is."

"Well, why did you? Perhaps I, too, am a . . ."

"You?" scoffed Mitar. "I've had a look at your papers, my man. Do you think I'd be talking to you like this if I hadn't?" Mitar slapped the white coat pocket into which he had dropped Melkior's money. "You're exactly the kind the Major has a soft spot for. That's why he put you in here with this lot. He'll never be a success—he's not the army type."

"Why not?"

"Where will it get him, standing up for you?" cried Mitar angrily. "He'd kick all four of them out of here and back to the barracks if he had his way, he'd only keep you in. You think that's the way to build a career?"

"Why doesn't he resign his commission, then?"

"In the old army his father was in command of the entire Medical Corps, a general, he was in the retreat across Albania in World War I. Old King Petar's personal physician. Old school. That's how the doc brought up his son," Mitar gave a pitying smile. "The Medical Corps, sure, fairness and justice, the whole bit. . . . It'll all go to hell one day, see if it . . ." but Mitar suddenly cut it short: he realized he was still holding the glass aloft in a "formal toast" and laughed. "A nice place we've chosen for a . . . And me holding your champagne here . . . Right—take care now; off to bed. There's the morning rounds coming up in a minute. You'll have the honor of meeting the Colonel. He's going to have your hide, of course, because you're 'the Major's boy,' get it? You just grin and bear it, and look at him with respect and fear, as if you've just shit in your bed, get it?"

"Will the nurse be there, too?" Melkior couldn't help himself.

"You mean Acika? Fancy her, eh? Well, you might as well forget about that, you'll find no joy there."

"I'm not expecting any. Just asking."

"I'm not blaming you—she's quite the looker, she is."

"Yes, she sure is pretty," sighed Melkior. "Has she got someone?"

"Search me. She's nice to everyone, you can't tell whether she's really like that or just playing a silly game. An odd sort of girl. Right, see you."

An odd sort of girl, you say, Melkior kept repeating in his bed, covered up to his chin. But he was saying it mechanically, there was no thought behind it at all. His body was hobbled by a tinge of apprehension. Slight tremors had started from his chin downward to his belly and legs, and suddenly developed into uncontrollable feverish shivering. Look, my teeth are chatter-tattering, he attempted a joke, but it only produced nervous spasmodic yawns along with deaf-and-mute mumbles.

"Did you say something, Meteor?" asked Menjou benevolently.

"Nuhhing," he managed to articulate in his wide-open mouth. But the brief contact with the "outside world" greatly relieved his internal tension: the shivering suddenly stopped, his body felt much more secure in the favorable climate of the bed.

The door opened soundlessly, with due respect. A white procession filed into the room solemnly and mutely, as if in a dream ceremony. It was headed by a shortish, lean old man, his goatee white and sternly pointed, his gaze penetrating and sharp, "I'm reading you like a cover page, boy." Under his white coat moved his thin bowed legs (in high boots), the metal claws on the heels jangling, dandy-style, the fashion of a Royal ball. A white polar bird waddling across ice on black feet was how the man looked to Melkior. That of course was the Colonel: a soldier and a patriot.

Behind him walked the Major at a slight distance, thereby emphasizing his subordinate position in the solemn march past. He said, "Good morning, boys," at which the tip of the Colonel's commandant-like beard shot upward in surprise. She was next to the Major, sick lists in hand, with an open fountain pen poised above them. She was wholly dedicated to respect for the exalted proceedings and moved eagerly in the solemn march. There were also several youngish, carefully shaven faces attending the pontifical function with clerical patience as unimportant personages. Bringing up the rear was Mitar, but he remained just inside the door like a poor relation at a funeral; he was well aware of his station.

The Colonel proceeded to do the rounds of "his" quartet, stopping at the foot of each bed in turn and inquiring after their good health.

"Well, how's it going, lad?" he said to Menjou with paternal irony. "Your father's asking after you—what shall I tell him?"

"It's getting boring in here, sir," Menjou replied coyly. "I wish I could go back to the Academy—I'll fall behind with my studies like this."

"Health first, my boy!" the Colonel raised his goatee resolutely. "What's the rush? You'll catch up with them soon enough. How do you rank in your class?"

"First, sir," snapped Menjou and clicked his teeth, his heels coming together by themselves in bed.

"First?" said the Colonel in feigned marvel. "What're you complaining for, then? Not to worry, it'll be a snap for you to catch up. I'll say hello to your father for you," he tossed off before moving to the next bed.

"If you please, sir," and Menjou gave a brisk nod by way of saluting.

"What about you, diplomat?" he asked Tartuffe. "Any news from your father? Did he get safely over to England?"

"Safely indeed, sir . . . at the last moment," added Tartuffe with a confidential smile. "The Germans had already taken Bordeaux . . ."

"You don't say? So he made it after all, did he? Good man. Good man indeed. Where's he now—in London?"

"London and Glasgow, sir, traveling on business. He wrote and told me bombs were dropping like ripe pears in autumn, sir."

"There, you see, he's not bored," he threw the remark at Menjou. "And what are we to do with you, lover boy?" he shook his head reproachfully at Hermaphrodite, the entire suite laughing ingratiatingly at his joke (except the Major: he was still serious). "Do you find this place tedious, too?"

"Yeth indeed, thuh," replied Herma with conviction, "it'th bowwing aww wight. Ethpethially in the evening . . . nothing to do, we jutht thit awound twiddwing our thumth. . . ."

"Twiddling your thumbs, eh? . . . Now, Nurse . . ."

"Sir?" She was putting Herself totally at his disposal.

". . . why are they all bored here?" Everyone burst out laughing. She blushed. The Major was frowning. "I mean to say, why don't you get this Don Juan here some lady friend or other before he dies of boredom?"

Hermaphrodite guffawed merrily. He even exclaimed "Nithe."

"Shut up, you bloody Judas!" thundered the Colonel at him, his goatee quivering with a suppressed smile. "To disgrace such a father! If I were him, I'd . . ."

". . . cathtwate me!" cracked Herma, with a see-if-I-care tone.

"Teach me, would you?" snapped the Colonel in a fit of pique, but he would clearly have preferred to laugh; he was going to tell Herma's father all about it . . . "Yes, that's it exactly, I'd geld you like a boar, give you something to remember me by."

"Thank you, *thuh!*" Herma snapped resolutely.

But the Colonel ignored him. The fellow had gone too far, it was clear to all (nobody was laughing anymore), his authority was being challenged . . . He approached Little Guy.

"What about you, young man? Are you all right?"

"Quite all right, sir, thank you."

"Mama still bringing those cheese pastries?" he asked with avuncular bonhomie. "It's the pastries you like, isn't it?"

"Well, yes, sir, I do . . ." Little Guy was expecting Mama today and felt uneasy at the mention of her.

"There, there, liking pastry is nothing to be shy about," the Colonel stroked his head, "I like a nice piece of fresh baked cheese pastry myself. What about this one?" he gestured at Melkior with his goatee. Melkior was looking at him *with respect and awe, as if he had just . . .* like Mitar said.

"He's new, Colonel."

"I can see that for myself," the Colonel was already losing patience, "but what is he doing here? What unit is he from?"

"Transport Training Course," replied the Major patiently.

"Draftee?" said the Colonel as if disgusted by the question.

"Yes." The Major was restrained and cold.

"So what?" asked the Colonel in a pronouncedly superior-officer tone.

The insult flashed across the Major's face for a moment: a dark cloud flitted over his intelligent calm.

"Seriously enlarged hila," he said in his unruffled way. "The X-ray view of the left lung shows what may be a focus with typical fibrous staining and a shaded area. . . ."

"Any jerk shows enlarged hila!" the Colonel interrupted him rudely.

She fluttered her eyelids in embarrassment. The Four snickered under their covers.

"The patient is a fully mature young man . . ."

"The patient is fully eligible for a court martial! Why, this is tantamount to desertion!" The Colonel was looking at Melkior with loathing (and he looked at the Colonel . . . as instructed by Mitar).

"Additionally . . . would you uncover yourself, please," said the Major to Melkior, "we have here a case of serious asthenia. Would you observe, sir, the rib cage, the arms, the shoulders . . ."

"Sir, the army does have some men who are not like Hercules!" the Colonel raised his voice in rebuke. "In my book, a finger on the trigger is all a soldier needs! That is how I see it."

"If you please, Colonel, here's the patient's chart." She handed him Melkior's record. "Nurse, has he been x-rayed?"

"Yes, Major," she lied readily, her gaze slithering over Melkior (he kissed that expanse of air above him), "but the film has not yet been developed; it will be in twenty minutes."

"Then file it here," said the Major dryly, ceding to the Colonel his place at Melkior's bed.

The Asclepian's giving me up, next to approach is the cannibals' medicine man. Melkior's gaze sought Mitar, a last-minute appeal for help. Mitar offered help by way of an encouraging smile. But Melkior saw Caesar's bared teeth, heard horseshoes on the stone floor . . . The Colonel had stepped closer (his spurs making a ritual jangle). The Medical Corps officer leaned over Melkior showing his large yellowed teeth . . . He'll bite into my head first, thought Melkior . . . But it was a smile, a seemingly benign one, the smile of a saint who comes to children at night and tucks presents into their bed. Meaning he won't bite, Melkior hoped. A grave case of asthenia. Here, Uncle, just look at those arms and shoulders and rib cage . . . skin puckering, bones bulging, ribs rattling . . . Melkior was feeling himself all the while under the covers, thin dry skin stretching in his palm. No, the Colonel's not going to bite, there's nothing here but *a case of serious asthenia*. But he was (just in case) looking at the Colonel with fear as if he had . . . as Mitar had put it.

"What're you looking at me like a shitty dog for?" the superior-officer's voice boomed over him. "An intellectual, eh? Thinking you invented gunpowder all by your lonesome. Let's have it: did you invent gunpowder? Well? Did you or didn't you?"

What do I do now, Numbskull? Would barking help? Presumably it works only when there's electricity involved. When it comes to gunpowder, it's Mitar's advice that applies: don't answer, look at him with respect and fear as if *you've done that thing* in bed; and Melkior went on looking at the Colonel as advised by Mitar: with respect and . . . and all the rest—he only added a bit of the manner of a dog in *that kind of predicament*.

"Not answering, eh? Despising me? You're thinking: what's this? we're both men with University degrees, but he still speaks with me in an informal tone! What a dolt of a soldier! That's what you're thinking, isn't it? What an untutored lout in uniform!"

There was no sound to be heard in the room, not even the squeak of a shoe. There was no ingratiating laughter. The Major was looking at the window, baffled, bright red with shame and, possibly, anger. She never raised her eyes from the charts as if checking something with her pencil. The shaven faces were serious and somehow mournful; the Four, too, were silent in their beds.

The silence was what got the Colonel irritated, fanning the desire *to show them all!* Introducing *certain manners* in here, are they?

He bent over the bed, bringing his face quite close to Melkior's frightened face. Melkior felt the odor of the yellowed teeth, words were spilling all over him but he no longer understood them. He watched the teeth coming closer . . . look, no fillings, all in a regular row, yellow but healthy . . . thanks to cheese pastry . . .

"Now, sir . . . in case you think I have no manners . . ." said the Colonel in a low voice from quite an intimate proximity (Melkior could see the close-grown short hairs in his nostrils), "why is it, sir, that you do not wish to serve in the military? What is it that your esteemed mind dislikes? Is it perhaps that you have a different opinion of the way this country is run? Feel free to tell me what it is you object to! We're hateful, is that it? Rude soldiery, clods, backwoods types? You don't like my face either, I can tell. Very well—go ahead and slap it!" the Colonel placed his cheek provocatively, at exactly arm's length, and stood there, waiting. "Well, what're you waiting for? Why don't you slap it? Oh, I see—you say my cheek isn't worthy of your palm. Tarnation! All right, spit on it then!" and, lowering his cheeks all the way down to Melkior's mouth: "Go on, why aren't you spitting? I'm waiting!" shouted the Colonel, quite beside himself by now, at Melkior's calm. Perhaps it was his shout that jerked Melkior out of his lethargy. His head, like that of a dead man come back to life, moved, went up, and before the Colonel could pull back, he hit his cheek with his lips in a flash—and gave it a clearly audible smack. Right. Instead of the Major. Was that a proper *acte gratuit*, Parampion? No, that was not an *acte gratuit*, said Parampion. It was much more than that, replied Numbskull.

"Wait! . . . What's this? . . ." shivered the Colonel, frightened, taken aback, stroking the kissed cheek, wiping off the weird shame.

"What is the meaning of this, Major?" he addressed the Major sternly, but he was looking at all of them, shooting anyone who would dare laugh now. But it was all right, no one was laughing, they were all gaping in amazement. "Major, I asked you what this means!"

"I don't know, Colonel," replied the Major indifferently.

" 'I don't know' and that's that? Well, I'm not having it!"

"Perhaps the boy was trying to say he loves you . . ." the Major tried to explain, an invisible grin twinkling in a corner of his mouth.

"Permission to speak, sir?" spoke up Tartuffe.

"Go ahead."

"We think he's not sane, sir. Yesterday he kissed the sister . . ."

"Sister? Whose sister?"

"Ours, sir . . . the nurse."

"It was when he was dreaming, Colonel," she blushed all over.

"In his dream? What were you doing in his dream?"

"I leaned over to see if he was asleep and he suddenly raised his arms . . ."

". . . and thmack! wight on the mouth," Hermaphrodite completed the sentence with gusto.

"Shut up, you bastard!" snapped the Colonel at him. "Sorry you didn't do it, is that it?"

"That'th wight, thuh," guffawed Herma, "I'm not thaying I'm not thowwy . . ."

"Stop clowning," spoke up Menjou, "this is serious business. Sir, we think the man's really crazy . . ."

"Crazy? He's an idiot!"

". . . and we would not like him to remain here with us," finished Menjou.

"With you? Get this man transferred to Neurology straight away!" commanded the Colonel, striding out at the head of the procession.

That's right: not a madman—an idiot! Confirmed from the top! Melkior was glad to have been reduced to an impersonal *this man.* And so to Neurology . . . But what is it exactly? Presumably a madhouse, which might turn out to be interesting . . . meeting Napoleon and Martin Luther. I've already had the honor of being introduced to Caesar . . . er, from afar. Kissing the Major wasn't required for the *idiocy* degree; after all, this gesture was far more chivalric, magnanimous in a way: you're urged to spit into a face (we're not children), but you plant a kiss on it instead. You could smell the odor of the dentures. At night, the yellow false teeth submerged in the glass snarl at the Colonel from the night table, and he lies in his bed with his goatee, small, meek, sans stars, sans gold on shoulders, powerless and toothless like a newborn—can't even say *zzz*. His poor wife is forgetful due to menopause, possibly also squeamish and fearful and superstitious for her *special reason*, so she hasn't changed the crocodile's water for three days, and it consequently has a spit-in-my-face smell. And he, a high-ranking Medical Corps officer, Head of the Pulmonary Department and generally a prominent man, a soldier who knows Menjou's father the Guards general and all the other *fathers*, goes fishing with his index finger in the water glass in the morning, already buttoned up to his chin and with his boots on. Fishing for the yellow false teeth using his index-finger hook. The falsies somersault wriggle evade capture flip over, will not leave the comfort of their murky water for the smacking slimy mouth in which to masticate a freshly baked cheese pastry. And when they are angry enough in their water they nip the Colonel's stern index finger. In the end the Colonel nabbed them after all and slid them into his mouth with an irritated move-ment of his hand, disgusted, as if being made to eat a cold frog. But one day the yellow teeth will bite his index finger off and there will be one soldier fewer—a finger on the trigger is what makes a soldier, he said so himself, and he stood by what he said, stood firm as a rock, we're not children, damn it all.

"Pity, weally," said Hermaphrodite, "it'th going to be dead boww-ing in here with him gone."

"You thick bastard, you think it's funny, a nutcase sassing the Colonel?" Menjou was getting riled.

"He wathn't thathing him, he only kithed him, hoo-hoo-hoo . . . Nithe."

"What, you think he kissed him because he loved him?" Tartuffe joined in.

"It would be 'nithe' for you to shut your trap, you moron!"

"Mowwon, eh? Then you'wwe a cwetin!" flared Herma. "The Old Man wath hathling him, wight, and he kithed him, foww that? Would you have had the gutth? I know I wouldn't . . . tho I thay to him 'bwavo! bwavo!'"

His anger provoked laughter. (Melkior laughed, too, inside.)

"The Old Man was 'hathling' him, eh? Bwavo!" Everybody laughed.

"I thaid 'hathling,' not 'hathling,' you thilly thap! *You*'wwe the nutcathe, not him! It'th you they ought to put undeww obtherwathon . . ."

"Stop it, don't get all riled up," spoke up Little Guy in the low voice of a repentant. "I made all this happen."

"Made what happen?"

"Him kissing the . . ."

"You mean it was another one of your suggestions?"

"Yes," admitted Little Guy like an incorrigible sinner.

"Oh, go and . . . eat your mother'th cheethe pathtry!" said Hermaphrodite, his patience cracking at last, and there would probably have been a fight if Mitar had not at that moment entered the room followed by a huge, muscular young man in white who displayed awe-inspiring biceps under his rolled-up sleeves.

"Which one?" asked the young man.

"This one," Mitar indicated Melkior. "Come on then, get your gear. You're off to Neurology."

"So they got you then, eh?" he was asked by one of the three on the third day after he was moved into a vast white room with barred windows. Even now the person who asked was not looking at Melkior. He was looking at the wall behind Melkior's bed. Floating in his eyes was a dim look with which he dreamily stared at the bare walls, even at the empty space of the room, as if he had prepared himself for a patient and tedious existence for the rest of his days.

The other two had not yet spoken. The short chesty one went up to the window from time to time and snarled irately through the bars, and the endlessly long and lean type, in contrast to him, lived in exalted calm and dignity. His food was eaten by the short chesty one while he himself solemnly marched up and down the room, clearly performing an important function.

There were only four beds in the room (the fourth having been brought in for Melkior), one in each corner, bolted firmly to the floor, and nothing else, no other objects: bare white walls and emptiness. The acoustics of bare empty space, horrible, hopeless.

Melkior had spent two days on his bed as if he were on a raft, in absolute peace, alone with himself. The bed with ancient blankets, with no sheets, filthy, uncared for, with the condensed smells of the bodies which had been releasing their fumes there before him. But the stench had by now acquired his familiarity and warmth. He had adopted the despised and abandoned smells of the other people and drawn them with fraternal cordiality around his shoulders, like a beggar does a chanced-upon overcoat.

Skunk fashion, bedbug fashion, he had wrapped the stench around him and was now challenging all and sundry, derisively, like the Asclepian on the cannibal island: Come on, you delicate noses, approach if you can this impregnable circle of revulsion, this armor of safety, this halo of holy stink! He felt the stench on his person like a life belt before a storm, like the inebriation with a folly which made him light, transparent, invisible. If only I were no more! If only I were the smelly air hiding my existence so reliably!

"How did they get you?" the dreamer asked again, still looking at the wall above Melkior. "Were you making petals?"

"What petals?" asked Melkior politely.

"I don't know. It was something . . . I don't remember what." He lapsed into thoughtful silence, then heaved a sigh and cried out bitterly: "On Ombrellion, the barren mountain, he spake! I'm a melancholic, they say, the Tartars. What about you—are you mad?"

"No. I'm a complete idiot," replied Melkior gravely.

"What's that mean? Do you fight people?"

"No, I'm peaceful. I stink."

"They wanted to cut me in half over there. I was in the Artillery infirmary, where the hack-hack guns are, understand? Hack-hack, with a hyphen, you know, to hack one in two . . . one-two, left-right, one-two, three, four . . . I can count up to a billion. That's the count of the hairs you have on one half of your head, multiplied by two. Down with the King and Queen!" this last he added in a whisper, watching the beanpole fearfully who was doing his march past.

"Which queen?" asked Melkior.

"The King's wife."

"He hasn't got one."

"Down with his sister then."

"He doesn't have a sister either."

"Well, there has to be some female at court—so down with her then. You know," he slunk up to Melkior and whispered confidentially, pointing at the beanpole, "you can't say things like that in his presence—he's the Lord Chamberlain," he added with sly irony.

"At which court?"

"This one . . . the Royal Saccharinic Court," the Melancholic gave a cunning smile. "He's privy to court secrets. But he confers only with the top-rankers. Watch." The Lord Chamberlain was having a pleasant chat with the King, riding in the royal carriage (the King was sitting on his pillow), but the only intelligible words in the entire conversation were "Your Majesty," uttered with enormous respect; the rest was a highly confidential whisper. The Lord Chamberlain, with a sweet smile on his face, was waving to the people, pointing meanwhile, for the King's benefit, at various prominent persons in the cheering crowd. The carriage came to a sudden halt in one place, the Lord Chamberlain's index pointing resolutely at the Melancholic.

"It wasn't me, Your Saccharinic Sweet Majesty!" said the latter in fright, "It was he (pointing at the Short Chesty) who ate your bread and cabbage." But the Lord Chamberlain's index finger never left him. Moreover, the Lord Chamberlain hooted *hoo!* at which the Short Chesty yelled bloodthirstily:

"I am Rover, the eldest of five, let me at him, I'll skin him alive!" and snarled at Melkior showing small close-set teeth.

"Don't do that, Rover—I'll give you a two-rupee piece," the Melancholic held out a small white button with two holes, "and I'll let you have a four-rupee one tomorrow."

"Get it sewn on your own tomorrow! Gimme now!"

"I haven't got one now, Rover, I'm expecting one from my brother tomorrow. What you can have now is a bit of my fingernail."

"Gimme."

Rover quickly sawed off the Melancholic's thumbnail with his small sharp teeth and displayed it to the Lord Chamberlain. The latter nodded with satisfaction, dismissed Rover, and drove the horses on.

"You have to act like that with them," explained the Melancholic to Melkior, apparently in some embarrassment.

"Listen," said Melkior hopefully, "you can square with me: you aren't actually . . ."

"Mad?" the Melancholic smiled sadly. "Well, no, not in the way they are. Different category. They think . . . the Lord Chamberlain thinks (Rover doesn't know a thing) two and two make five; I know they make four (see?) but it's too much of a bother to think."

"What's there to think about?"

"Oh, quite a bit—you must get them to come together. Here, take two from one side and two from the other," he held up two fingers on each hand. "Now then, which two will join the other two? Why should one pair do the approaching while the other stands idle? They're equal, right? Ma-the-matically equal, so why should either pair approach the other? Well, they may be equal in terms of mathematics but not in terms of character. One set is perhaps too proud, or believes themselves to be a better sort, a higher class, and they prefer to keep themselves to themselves, and you have to waste your time arguing with them! And all for a four. But what can you do when they don't want four? See what trouble it is? You might say: they can meet each other halfway, come to an agreement . . . All very well, if they want to, but they seldom do. . . . You'd have to waste so much time waiting." He looked into Melkior's eyes with curiosity. "You're probably wondering at this, thinking I'm talking about people. No, I'm really talking about pure numbers, I majored in math at the university." Melkior was silent, looking at the floor to avoid embarrassing the other with his gaze. "Try playing roulette or buying a lottery ticket and you'll see numbers for what they are—all whimsy and deceit."

"All right, but how do *they* make five?"

"The madmen?" smiled the Melancholic in commiseration. "They take twice two fingers of the same hand, and since they're all connected with each other they bring the fifth—the little finger—along . . . so as not to leave him alone. Hence the misconception."

"You majored in math—but what do you do in life?"

"I'm a traveler. I pick hawthorn berries."

"And count them?"

"How did you know?"

"Something tells me . . ."

"Something tells you my foot. You must've read it in the papers. They wrote about me."

"So how do you 'get them to come together' when you count?"

"In my pocket. I have a hard time of it. Up to a billion. Want me to count your head hairs? I've counted his," he gestured at Rover. "Know how I do it? I divide his head in sectors . . . I had a pencil, but the Tartars took it . . . and then I work by sectors, easy as pie. Only I didn't finish—he wouldn't sit still."

"How will you do me if you haven't got a pencil?"

"There's another method—plucking. Only ten hairs a day. But you'll have to wait until it has grown back in. What is it they say— don't let grass grow under your . . ." All of a sudden, as if he had remembered something, he caught Melkior by the elbow and whispered in confidence: "See those windows across the way? Take a good look: three stories, five windows each. Tonight I'll show you something I'm quite keen on. Now hush, pretend you don't know me." He went off "craftily" and, walking up to his bed, suddenly raised his arms high above his head, crying out: "On Ombrellion, the barren mountain, spake he!" then lay down and closed his eyes.

Time had begun to peck at him. The day was now endlessly long, the third day among the insane. The Melancholic had taken him briefly back to the world of living words, then thrown him back into silent solitude again. Aroused by the sound of a human voice, his hearing now found the deaf silence more difficult to bear than during the previous two days. The Melancholic had left him with the fifteen windows across the way and a promise for tonight . . . But tonight was a long way off. Outside and up high, the day was still shining in the sky among tattered clouds, and above him (to make things worse) floated the sun in a glory of autumn blue. He hated the sun in the square of the sky and the clouds and the light and everything that made up the day. He was yearning for words, words to the hungry ear! Any words, any kind of words, just as long as it was the sound of a human voice!

He tried to listen to himself. But what should he say? *Romans, friends, countrymen* . . . But what if *they* responded? *Polyphemus the Cyclops, the beast* . . . No, he could not enunciate that either. Then it came to him in a flash merely to say *Parallelikins*, as if it were a name. Melkior said it aloud.

The Lord Chamberlain leapt up, cut to the quick. It was as if he had been awaiting that very word to get his terrible excitement going. Has someone dared utter it? was what his astounded look meant. Using a finger he sicced Rover on Melkior. Rover was off like a shot. He turned around with catlike speed and, hands outstretched, scampered toward Melkior.

"I am Rover, the eldest of five," he snarled at him.

Melkior remembered the Melancholic's trick of . . . He hastily tore two buttons off his striped robe and repeated his words:

"Don't do that, Rover—I'll give you these two four-rupee pieces . . ."

"Hah, two buttons!" leered Rover derisively. "Get them sewn on your own! Surrender!"

"All right, I surrender—here," Melkior put his hands up. What's this? They won't accept their own currency any more? "I surrender, Rover, take me prisoner."

"What've you got? Gimme a ten spot!" Rover stood facing him, short but broad-shouldered.

"Haven't got a ten spot—the Tartars took it," Melkior made another attempt to make some headway using the formulas of this weird world. But it suddenly appeared as if none of that worked any longer. Even the Melancholic laughed:

"Heh, how can there be any Tartars here?"

"Well, you said yourself they took away your . . ."

"I only said it . . . *tan-gen-tially*," specified the Melancholic and set up an ugly cackle, which Rover took up in a modified, animal version. Even the Lord Chamberlain laughed, a dignified and dry laugh.

Why, they are genuinely insane! thought Melkior, taking offense, now they're mocking me in the bargain. He went across to the Melancholic and sat down on his bed. The man used his foot to warn him to get off. This offended Melkior further; he now wanted to *clear things up* at all costs.

"Very well, I'll say it to you from here. You mentioned Tartars twice, and now you're laughing? Are you laughing at your own madness then? Unless you meant 'doctors' when you said 'Tartars.'"

"Since when do doctors have anything to do with Tartars?" laughed the Melancholic derisively. "I may be mad, but I'm not daft. Listen," he spoke to the other two, "doctors and Tartars—do they have anything to do with each other?"

All three were laughing at Melkior.

What's this supposed to mean, he thought in embarrassment, madmen laughing at me? And he was already prepared to think it was all just a con game played by disbelieving malingering clowns, a test to see whether his presence was not a trap devised by the army authorities, but their laughter suddenly stopped and all three pricked their ears in fright at a strange sound from the corridor.

Indeed, even Melkior could hear a kind of distant mournful wail, like the howling of a sick dog. Melkior tried to approach the door, to peek through the keyhole or at least put his ear to it—what was it that had frightened them so much?—but Rover blocked his way in a soundless leap and gave him a terrified look telling him to stop.

"Hssst, don't move," whispered the Melancholic, quaking.

"Why not?" Melkior whispered himself, without realizing it.

"Wolf," whispered Rover inaudibly, between his palms. "He's hungry."

"A wolf . . . here? If there are no Tartars, there are no wolves either," Melkior defied them.

"There is one . . . in Number Sixteen," the Melancholic implored him to believe. "We also thought at first . . . But later on I saw it: all black and warty. The tail . . . the teeth . . . !" he shivered like a man in a fever. Using his index finger he confidentially invited Melkior to come closer, and whispered in his ear: "You're right, there can't be a wolf in here—he made it up, the primitive. The only animals he's ever heard of are wolves and bears. He's never heard about alligators, so . . . never mind the moron. It's an alligator in

Number Sixteen," whispered the Melancholic in an even lower voice, "a dreadful one, huge, nine meters long, needs ten beds to sleep on, I saw it with my own eyes . . ." Now what was heard was a terrible roar. "Aha! Can you hear it?"

"But what's it doing in here?" asked Melkior in feigned confidence.

"Hah, 'what?' There's one in every town. A secret weapon. They crunch everything with their teeth, not even a tank can hurt them."

The Melancholic was speaking with the certainty of a man in the know. A silly kind of joy came to life inside Melkior: a momentary, quaint illusion derived from a mad story. A flash of hope. Against Polyphemus the cannibal there rose the dreaded Alligator. Samson, Achilles, the Golem, the national giant, crushing everything underfoot, invincible! . . . And his imagination began narrating to Melkior *The Great Victory*—an epic at the Central Military Hospital Neurology Department—fiddling all day long to the vengeful joy of the defenseless.

And when night fell and the smell of boiled cabbage died behind the locked door, in the lightless room, in that madmen's dark, there resonated the dignified sleep of the Lord Chamberlain and Rover's vehement snore. That was when the Melancholic crept out of his bed on a secret mission and quietly approached Melkior on tiptoe.

"Here, take a look," indicating *those* windows, "think I forgot? See?"

A window or two was lit on each floor.

"You mean, some of them are lit?"

"Some? Ha-haaa," he knew more, which was why he was laughing. "Try to remember which ones are lit now . . . it'll be quite different later."

"Of course it will—people go in and out, turn lights on and off . . ."

"Hah, in-and-out . . . And why do they go in-and-out at certain times only, eh? At night, hah? All night long. I've been watching it for a long time. While I had my pencil I took notes, well, now I memorize. About that other business . . . *doctors, Tartars* . . . I had to step in or *that fellow* would have killed you. It mustn't be known they're here, that's the whole thing. Hah, they took away my pencil but I deciphered it without one! Ha-ha, you Tartar bastards . . ." laughed the Melancholic with strange contempt. He mused for a moment, then spoke up again, offhand; it was as if he had not been saying what was really on his mind: "Do you like to smoke? I like to watch the ember in the dark . . . when I'm talking with someone. You know you're talking to a living man then; when he inhales, the smoker, his face gets lit up, his eyes shine, and all the darkness comes alive. All very well, but how are you to come by a cigarette in here . . . that is to say, you could get one, but the matches . . . *They* won't let madmen use fire or they'd burn the whole . . . One thing I've never understood is why it says 'Safety Matches' on the box. Why are they afraid of a fire if it's 'Safety'? And Nero set fire to Rome without matches. How do you suppose he went about it—rubbed sticks together? But it takes time, which means it was malice aforethought. Or used a flint and tinder . . . but that, too, is malice aforethought. Now, I like fire in general, I like to watch the flames . . . Devils dancing, sticking their long tongues out at each other. Licking and stroking each other, perhaps even in a sexual way (there's always a she-devil or two there), cracking and crackling, enjoying the fire all the time, damn them . . . Wait! Look out!" he suddenly took a firm hold of Melkior's arm and squeezed it tight in a state of expectation. He was looking at *the windows* opposite, really waiting for something: "Of course. There, I-3's off . . . III-5 is off next, and II-2 goes on, of course, exactly by the system!"

"What system?"

"Secret code. They're doing it again, damn them . . ."

"The Tartars?"

"Shhh! Don't interrupt!" whispered the Melancholic sharply, his gaze absorbed by the windows opposite: "One-five, five-two, five-four, ah-ha, five-five, two-five, ah-ha, ah-ha, ah-ha, of course, one-three, of course, that's what I thought, they're signaling about the Alligator."

"What? Signaling what?" asked Melkior eagerly.

"Arranging for the day . . . of release. That's why they are keeping it in here!"

"Why, isn't it ours?" asked Melkior apprehensively, while taking note of his own stupidity in action again, stripping away the selfsame hope it had offered him just hours before. He was not going to give up easily . . .

"Nah, we have no use for such a monster. It would eat us up along with everything else. We don't know how to control it . . ."

But he didn't seem to feel so strongly about the issue. He was too busy deciphering the signals in the lit windows to pay any attention to Melkior. He was muttering ciphers, delighting in his edifying discoveries.

Melkior saluted this bright morning: joy was twittering in his chest. She's here, she's here to see me! That was his first thought, the wave of happiness that had reared up inside him and was standing there, tense, looming, ready to engulf him whole. Darling, darling, he responded to the echoes of the long white corridors, to the footsteps of the burly dull male nurse walking behind him. C'mon, get up, you have a visitor—with these words the man had got him out of bed and into this bright motion. The trip seemed endless, and Melkior rejoiced at the small eternity of expectation. At this right-left, as the male nurse directed him, with her presence resonating around each corner and each window pouring on him another reason for joy.

On top of it, there was in the windowpanes some autumn sun, softly ruddy, there were little birds screeching on dried-up boughs, a rooster was greeting the morning from afar . . . all to her glory, all to her glory . . .

"Through here," the male nurse showed him a door, "your visitor's inside. I'll be back later to pick you up," he said walking on down the corridor.

Standing and waiting in the middle of the room was Numbskull.

Melkior's wave broke at once, as if all life had left it, and all of the promised happiness spilled away. A wretch's sigh was conceived in his breast and fluttered timidly, wishing to be born and to fly out of his mouth like a small luckless angel, but Melkior immediately strangled it and blew its soul through his nose, angrily.

"Are you angry I came?" Numbskull asked him with shyness, humbly.

"No. Only surprised," Melkior tried to explain himself, and a kind of lonely poignancy grabbed him by the throat. He let the sigh be born—stillborn. "How did you find me?"

"I have a brother over there in Pulmonary, he's a lab tech . . ."

"Mitar?" said Melkior in surprise. "He sent you for his money?"

"Money, heck! I came to see you . . . he told me they'd transferred you over here . . ."

"I got *myself* transferred," Melkior specified proudly.

"You kissed the Colonel? An interesting idea," admitted Numbskull, "but how are you going to get out of here?"

"Well, even if I don't . . . it's an interesting enough place. I don't care if I die here, I've been abandoned by everyone," Melkior put tattered tragedy on and felt like a good cry. All on my own shall I . . . his throat constricted, he was unable to finish the sentence even in his mind.

"Interesting my foot. I don't see anything interesting . . ." Numbskull looked around the room in mournful wonder. "You'll go to ruin in here, my old friend, that's what's interesting."

"Who sent you?" Melkior suddenly asked with aggressive suspicion. "Own up, who sent you?" He appeared to be pressing for a name. He shook Numbskull's greatcoat sleeve impatiently.

"Shake on—you'll shake out a heck of a lot," said Numbskull indifferently. "The Mikado of Japan sent me to say hello and to bring you these oranges from his own orchard," he took out an orange from each greatcoat pocket. He was already speaking to Melkior seriously, as one does to a madman.

Melkior was tempted to take up the manner. A thought was smiling fetchingly at him: it was she who sent them, in strictest secrecy . . . and he suddenly said like a certified lunatic: "I thank the dear Mikado! Give him my regards and tell him I kiss his hand."

Numbskull was watching with suspicion: is the fellow playing a game, or teasing me, or what? . . . or is he really off his . . .

"Look here, pal," he lost his temper after all, "let's cut this out, all right? Will you stop playing silly games with me—I'm not Nettle, you know."

"Very well, seriously now: did she give these to you in person?" and he indicated the oranges.

Numbskull was silent for a moment, watching Melkior with no hope at all, now. "What do you mean, she? The grocery girl across from the hospital?"

"Not . . . the nurse? . . ." Numbskull had shattered his last illusion. He hated him for it. This is the end, thought Melkior. He offered Numbskull his hand with the oranges in it: "Here, take them back, I don't need them," and took a deep breath to quell a sob.

Numbskull put his hand on Melkior's shoulder and, being short, looked in his eyes from below: "What the heck's the matter with you, man? They've driven you right off your rocker. You've got to get out of here double quick! You'll go nuts. As for the oranges, I bought them—I didn't get you any cigarettes . . . Throw them away if you don't want them, but talk to me, will you?"

"I don't need anything," said Melkior tragically. "A cubic centimeter of water (dirty water! he specified vehemently) to live in like a microbe, that's all."

"A microbe, he says . . . You're an intellectual, a clever man," Numbskull fussed over him. "Gosh, if only I had a grain of your salt in my head . . ."

"What would you do with it?" asked Melkior brusquely.

"Do? . . . I don't know . . . all kinds of things. Write books, think, explain things to dolts; salt the stupid world, in short. I'd be erudite . . . did I get that right?" he looked at Melkior in fear: was the man laughing at his ignorance?

Melkior was not laughing. He was angry at having to be embarrassed. He was pursing his lips as if about to spit on something.

How do I get rid of this "believer"—he thought cruelly—without disappointing him . . . unless he's doing a masterly job of pulling my leg? What is it he sees in me? Or was he sent to see what's wrong with me? By those from the barges . . . Then again, he may have come as a "follower." God, I'd now have to assume a role for his benefit, playact in public, be an ideal, a leader. . . . Rubbish! But what if he's mocking me? Trying to mount me on Rocinante . . . and canter on his donkey behind me, laughing and showing me up to the Medical Corps? Why, I've asked him after Dulcinea already! A dangerous idea flashed in his mind: were the oranges sent by her or by . . .

"Tell you what—give them to me!" He suddenly snatched the oranges from Numbskull's hands and shoved them down his shirt. "Right. Not too big, are they? No, they're just right," and patted his chest, insanely, girl fashion. "Then I'll put my belt on à la Récamier (that was a good idea you had!), it'll hold them in place. Ha-ha, what do you say? I'll keep the skirt . . . I really ought to be there when they let it out . . . and then I'll run down the corridors and shriek, shriek, a frightened Foolish Virgin. Tell me, how does that strike you as an idea? Is it good?" He trained his wide-eyed stare at Numbskull.

"Fine, fine . . ." Numbskull was backing in fear toward the door. All the same, just in case, he asked: "When they let out what?"

"The Alligator. Shhh, it's a terrible secret. Crunches everything in sight, not even a tank can hurt it," he whispered to Numbskull in the strictest of confidence.

"Watch out now, here comes a Tartar, pretend you don't know me . . ." Numbskull went out tearful and broken. Melkior saw it. He was broken up himself by inner tears over the friendship he had so crazily rejected. A belated discovery. Oh Lord, allow me to trust at least one man!

He felt the "silly" breasts against his body. A smile played on his lips, but his entire soul suddenly went dark and he wished, in fear, to run after Numbskull and shout "wait, I was only joking," to flee from the darkness . . . But there were already someone else's steps in the corridor—the orderly was returning. Fifty percent is certainly there, in these breasts, fifty percent pure madness, he thought in haste before the orderly came in, as if hurrying to hide a terrible secret.

"Brother gone?" asked the orderly.

"Gone." Melkior took an orange out from his shirt. "Here, take one. Look, I've only got one tit left," he was cracking jokes, establishing "relationships," giving the world back its banality.

The orderly gave him a weary look.

"What the hell did you go and kiss the Colonel for?"

"I don't know, really . . . Like he was a father to me."

"You were disrespecting him. Now you're rotting in here for it. As punishment. 'Under observation.' What's to observe, you nasty no-good? You could have got court-martialed."

The orderly was peeling the orange. A holiday fragrance filled the bare room. "You came out of it all right, considering—you didn't even get the showers."

"What showers?"

"The cold showers. Shocks . . . to bring you back to your senses." He was wolfing down the orange segments. Melkior watched his Adam's apple bobbing inside his throat and nostalgically remembered ATMAN, Ugo, Viviana—the far-off beings from "that other world." "I think your Major put in a good word for you . . . else you would've really been in for it."

"How do you know he put in a good word?"

"I just know. He spoke to our Major about you. They won't keep you in here much longer, just long enough for the Old Man to forget about you. They'll send you back to the barracks then."

"Why to the barracks? I'm not fit," complained Melkior and shivered at the dreadful image of Caesar. "Here, look at me," and he showed the orderly his arms bared to the shoulder.

"Don't know about that. Maybe they'll post you . . . Let's get a move on . . ." The orderly motioned him out with his head and followed in step.

They had sent him back to "his" Major. They took him directly to the examining room. *She* was not in the anteroom. She knew they were bringing me here, she doesn't want to see me . . . and that made it easier for him to harbor a feeling of suffering when he came before the Major. On top of that, he was filthy, in need of a shave, and so unkempt and miserable that he could not even imagine how he looked. He had refused to check out his reflection in the passing windows. I probably smell bad, too, it's better she shouldn't be here, really . . .

"Well now, what are we to do with you?" the Major tried to lend some military sternness to the question, but his warm, worried eyes betrayed him.

"I don't know, Doctor," said Melkior indifferently, at the moment he was indeed all but unconcerned for his life.

"Get you posted to the Quartermaster Training Course (there are no horses there, he added with a smile) . . . or perhaps send you home?"

"Whatever you think best, Doctor," said Melkior with uneasy shame as his heart started beating faster at the word "home," which showed ingratitude in a way . . . But he may only be testing me, he thought all the same, just in case.

"All right, we'll see," concluded the Major. "Now go upstairs to the ward, report to Nurse Olga. And clean yourself up, man!" added the Major informally. "You look a hideous mess! We do have a hospital barber . . . there's a bath available, too . . ."

Melkior reddened. I clearly reek . . . Good thing *she's* not here . . .

"I'm sorry I'm in such a . . ." he stammered, ". . . *over there* I simply had no opportunity to . . ."

"Yes, yes, I know." The Major stood up and, dropping a hand on Melkior's shoulder, said in an intimate and "confidential" tone: "Why are you ruining yourself? You're still a very young man, for God's sake, you've got your whole life ahead of you," then turned around and went out almost angrily.

A man feels his stench as a personal, homely, tamed odor. An atmosphere of confidence. The nose steeped in one's particular smell: olfactory solidarity—let's be helpful to one another . . . That was what Melkior was saying as he went up the stairs on his way to the ward, but his thoughts were not with the words. He was thinking: he has read me through and through. He's not sending me back to *Her*, but to Nurse Olga, *you've got your whole life ahead of you, man!* Let Olga be your life, man, and let *Her* be spared from your life which you've got in front of . . .

In front of you, see, is a female body, a rustling one, with the broad cheeks of a saint on an icon. Her eyes are mournfully surprised and she has a regulation voice as if it had been laid down in the Minaeon:

"Are you the one from Neurology?" Nurse Olga was saying with a wooden face. "Come with me, this way," and she set off down the corridor in the opposite direction from Room Seven.

Melkior had a feeling of being defeated in battle, on his way to a place of exile. The dirty, smelly prisoner of war, long unshaven, had been hiding out for days among lunatics . . . Numbskull "found me out." Perhaps he arranged my transfer with the Major. I've got my life ahead of me!

He sneered bitterly at his momentum. Oh where have they hidden her? *Her* presence will rustle any moment now around this corner, where the corridor bent with a fresh little hope. He stopped at a few doors: he thought he heard her voice in there in the cacophony of rasping, coughing, hawking, and spitting, he peeked through doors left ajar, but *she* was nowhere to be seen. *She* was nowhere to be found anymore.

"We'll put you in here . . . for now," said the white icon.

Two long rows of battered white beds with a lot of haggard pale faces above the army blankets. A rotten reek encountered his olfactory sense as the local worldview. Now to readapt. To tame this general smell, too, make it his own, familiar . . . he almost said "belief." Struggle for survival through olfactory adaptation. And he lay down immediately, the sooner to make the dirty rags reveal themselves to him, to exchange touch and warmth with them, to establish a close relationship. Melkior was settling in to live there, his whole life was ahead of him, man!

He shaved and bathed. I don't smell bad anymore, so where are you?

He took a tour of the entire ward . . . but *she* was nowhere to be found. Downstairs in the examination room now sat Nurse Olga, accompanying the Major on his rounds was Nurse Olga, temperatures were taken by the grave and austere Nurse Olga. *And She is no longer here. In the air fade the locks of her hair, on the floor, in the dust of my pining, her footprint is no longer there. . . .* He spoke automatically, but with the piety of a past, imagined happiness, which he believed in to the tears. *I have closed the window the more to be alone, with you to be alone . . .* and he watched himself meanwhile invent that poetic window, yet nevertheless closed it with a vast sorrow, as if nailing himself shut, and a torrent of weeping broke through the constricted throat. *Getting dark. Those are black shadows drinking my tears . . .* and Melkior dissolved into soundless sobs in the twilight of the hospital room.

He is saying *Can you hear me?* in an ugly voice, but the little girl doesn't seem to hear. She is standing in the middle of a deserted street staring straight ahead, meekly and somehow patiently, as if she trusts nothing but silence.

She is standing still like a big expensive doll with deep-set dark eyes. An arrow is embedded in her small plump back, all the way through, from one shoulder to the other, with a small caesura in the middle where it crosses the dimple in her back. The girl is standing slightly hunched, the better, presumably, to adapt her stance to the steel fibula that has pierced her back; her arms hang down her sides and her head is thrust forward in a kind of humility.

"Hey? Can you hear me?" he shouts, in fear this time, for he is thinking the little girl needs urgent care. But what is to be done? Still she is silent and motionless. He doesn't know whether he ought to touch her at all. Is she dead?

"Please tell me: does it hurt?"

"It hur . . . urts," he barely hears the little voice, frightened but somehow sustained and multiplied in echoes sounding from several directions simultaneously, as if a children's choir has sung it in canon. . . . It is only then that he looks around, his gaze sweeping the breadth of the streets. There are seven or eight more little girls, equally transfixed with arrows, equally motionless and silent and slightly hunched, with their heads thrust forward. And they are all staring straight ahead humbly, as if patiently expecting something. . . . Or . . . perhaps they expect nothing any more, having already surrendered to a horrible enchantment, motionless, pierced, abandoned like dolls after a mad, cruel game.

He tries to find out who has done it and why, and why little girls, but there is nobody to be seen. He sets off in search of someone, to call for help, for it is appalling to see the little girls standing there, staring humbly ahead with arrows in their small, innocent flesh. How strange, he thinks, there's not a drop of blood on them anywhere! And their wounds are not serious or fatal, as if this was done deliberately, so they could live, and they *are* alive and I could almost say healthy, they could move, pull the arrows out of their bodies and run back home to their Mamas. . . . Why are they standing still like that? This frightens him and he sets off down the streets in search of someone. But there is nobody to be seen anywhere in town. The town is empty.

The Alligator! flashes the most terrible thought of all.

"That's right," the Melancholic confirms from somewhere, invisible, "he passed through here this morning."

"This morning? And what time is it now?"

"Night. But the Sun stood still to light his way. He's a son of the Sun, being a victor. All victors are sons of the Sun."

"So those little girls have been standing there like this since this morning?"

"Hee, hee, the little dolls . . . stayed behind." That is Rover's animal smell, it is by his smell that Melkior knows him. "The Tartar archers passed through, everybody ran off, they shot the little dolls, hee, hee . . . and left." Shot and left . . . he repeats, but cannot understand why Rover is laughing like that, almost lasciviously. The poor little innocent ones . . . But he has no time to feel sorry. He hurries back: they must be helped as soon as possible. The arrows must be plucked from those small bodies, the little girls must be freed from the terrible reptile's thrall and returned to life. And then I'll tell them an amusing adventure story for children to entertain them. . . . Running back, he is singing the Paternoster . . . but when he reaches *the* street again the little girls are gone. From an old dilapidated house where living redbrick flesh is exposed under the crumbling front he hears the unruly laughter of women. The women are standing at the windows in various stages of undress, some of them quite naked, and laughing at him, tipping him winks and beckoning him upstairs. Draped over the windowsills are bed-clothes put out to air: white sheets; amber, blue, and scarlet silk eiderdowns; large white pillows trimmed with lacework; foamy, transparent, insubstantial negligees; lain-in, slightly rumpled pa-jamas that have retained the outlines and fragrances of those female bodies. . . . Lust's props with living naked laughing flesh sway lux-uriously above his head.

"The little girls . . . Where are they?" he asks, and hears repeated salvos of their laughter.

"It hur-urts, hee-hee-hee," the window women laugh *cantabile*, in canon. Above them, high up, coming out from the top floor, the coloratura laughter of a birdlike voice stands out by dint of its penetrating trills. *She* is beautiful, the most beautiful of them all. She has plumped out her lovely full bosom on the sill like two ruddy peaches and is performing her laughter with a kind of manic perseverance.

The laughter has been planted there by ATMAN as bait to the passenger through the deserted town. And she has been given the birdlike warble as a sign of his particular benevolence. She is Head Mermaid, the Honorable Mother in this house of sin for Tartar archers, the victors.

"Viviana, Viviana," he tries to call out to her from down below, in a pious whisper as if he were praying, but his voice is soundless, it is only a dead breath of his terrible grief.

He would have cried out loud had he been able to. He looks for the entrance to the house, but finds none. He then flaps his arms, powerfully, like a swimmer, like an eagle, dun-feathered sky-dweller, and up he flies, leaving the ground below him. . . .

"Look, this one's flapping his wings," somebody said, "he'll be crowing next."

And Melkior indeed crowed for all he was worth, in a desperate scream, as if shaking off the night. Then he heard tittering. Earth was laughing at him.

"Morning, Mr. Rooster!" Mitar was giving him a dull matutinal look from above. "What's the matter, did you give her one in your sleep?"

The heads above the blankets laughed flatteringly in honor of Mitar's witticism.

"Say what?" Melkior was still listening to Viviana's laughter.

"You were mounting a hen by the look of you," Mitar was consolidating his success like an actor. "Flapping your wings, crowing . . ."

"Oh, I was flying . . ." Melkior thought aloud, tying up the threads of dream and reality.

"And they say dreams mean nothing!" Mitar sat down on the edge of his bed and bent over his ear: "I've got it right here," he was pressing the top pocket of his white coat with his hand, "your ticket. You were dreaming about flying, well, it's come true. You're going home."

"Home?" repeated Melkior mechanically, but, oddly enough, he was not moved at all. He marveled at his indifference. Look, the "private" cannibal story had come to a sudden end! The red-headed Asclepian had assumed power, with no bloodshed, literally with love, and the castaways were saved. Very soon afterward the natives came to realize how fortunate they were not to have eaten them. Instead of the pleasure of several meals which they would have soon forgotten, they began to enjoy the lasting benefits of the small-scale civilization which those wise and experienced men soon established in the primitive conditions of the savage island. Melkior had no time at the moment to enumerate their achievements in full—

Mitar was watching. And shaking his head in offended amazement: what's the matter with the madman, it's as if he doesn't care . . .

Yes, why is it, in fact, that I don't care? The first mate no longer chews narcotic leaves: he has devoted all his time to the study of winds; he watches the clouds float and the stars fall (useful for hunting and agriculture) and composes verse which he presumably gets from heaven. And no one any longer despises the body or curses "the voracious animal." It has now become "human pride" (in its token garb of what used to be called the *fig leaf*), it has been re-affirmed as the source of the most glorious pleasures known to man. The native girls are able, through woman's intuition (congenital in the queen bee and Messalina alike), to assess properly certain skills peculiar to these unusual males. And the redheaded Asclepian, to cut a long story short, gets married! He concludes a political marriage with the chieftain's youngest daughter. He thus enters the ruling dynasty, first as an adviser and the ruler's son-in-law; later on, when the chieftain retires to devote all his time to his monkey tail collection, the doctor assumes full power. He proclaims himself king, subsequently to change his title to Emperor, of the state he called Asclepia in honor of his protector. While he does assign his former friends from the *Menelaus* to ministerial posts, they still have to pay full imperial homage to him and address him as Your Imperial Majesty or, on informal occasions, simply Sire. But Emperor Asclepius the First rules with a benevolent hand, all under the helpful influence of "our Major" who brings the story to a happy, if somewhat abrupt, end.

But Melkior was not made happy by the ending. Indeed, he watched Mitar with a tinge of hatred for bringing him his ticket like that, *in his pocket.* The happy ending in the pocket of a white coat.

"What's the matter—isn't that what you wanted?" Mitar was offended by his silence. Not to mention the look in his eyes . . .

"Of course it is . . . thank you so much . . ." but it came out unconvincing.

"Thank your sainted aunts! Think I would've bothered if I hadn't promised my brother? Well, you can . . ."

"Numbskull asked you to . . . ?" Ah, Mitar is expecting his *fee*, as the deal stood.

"That's right, call him names! And him pleading for you like a brother. Hadn't been for him, you'd still be rotting at the funny farm. He went to see the Major about you."

"The way I heard it, it was *she* who . . . asked the Major . . ." lied Melkior, wishing to be able to believe it.

"Acika?" laughed Mitar. "Oh sure, she was falling all over herself to help you. Never ate a bite, never drank a drop, never slept a wink . . . She went away ages ago! I think she left the same day you were transferred *over there*."

All may be well, say some characters in Shakespeare when they have lost all hope, thinks Melkior. Of course she left!!! They'd been treating me so inhumanely . . . What could the poor girl do?

"What did the poor girl do?" he listens to the echo of his romantic imagination. "Where's she now?"

"On the rolling main. Sailing. Honeymooning." Mitar was grinning maliciously.

"What? She got married?"

"To a seaman, ship's officer, whatever the word is. Merchant marines. Longtime romance, she'd been waiting for him faithfully. Nobody knew anything about it, except perhaps the Major . . ." said Mitar with an insidious smile.

"How come you know it all?" Melkior felt betrayed, what's all this now, out of the blue?

"She writes to the Major, sends postcards, Naples, Alexandria, and that island down there—not Sumatra, it's . . . you know . . . the Greek one, statues with no arms . . . Well, whatever it is, I don't give a . . . Anyway, that's where she is."

To the first mate, the castaway from the *Menelaus* . . . He doesn't chew narcotic leaves anymore. Another happy ending. Oh why didn't I let the cannibals cook the happy flesh in their cauldron?

In an instant he shrugged off the "hypocritical head cold," Atchoo! (he mocked her in passing), as if he had never met her, and Viviana lit up again with a distant life-saving glow. The lighthouse beacon after a shipwreck. He was fond of "shipwrecking" thoughts at the moment. . . . Down there, around Calypso's Ogygia, there must remain some of the vicious Aeolian winds which Poseidon had set in motion against Odysseus for blinding his one-eyed son, Polyphemus. . . .

He surprised himself with his malicious, vengeful hope and felt ashamed of his Love which had now turned its monstrous face to him. There's love for you: be mine or . . .

"Right, here's your century!" he threw the hundred-dinar note to Mitar with a kind of scorn.

"Taking it out on me, eh?" Mitar refused the money, leaving it on Melkior's night table: "Here, I want you to keep it. Have good food and drink, celebrate your return and good health to you! Put some meat on those bones."

"When do you think they might discharge me from here?"

"Tomorrow morning. Then you go back to the barracks, hand in your gear, and you're as free as a bird."

Melkior nearly chirped. He felt tremendous joy at the idea of going home. He abruptly felt freedom in his legs, in his arms, and an irrepressible instinct of motion propelled him from his bed. "Let's go" he said to Mitar and, hastily donning his greatcoat, all but ran out of the room.

"Wait up, what's the hurry?" Mitar couldn't catch up, he was lugging that great belly out in front of him, see?

"Let's knock back a couple downstairs in the canteen. I've got my ticket in my pocket. We're saying our farewells, Mitar."

"We are, but not like this, not on the run," gasped Mitar. "Also, I'm on duty, listen, I'm telling you . . ."

But there was no stopping Melkior. "Shot to shot—two shots," he shouted to the canteen-keeper from the door. She gave Mitar a questioning glance, and he signaled her with his eyes to get pouring. Pouring The Good Stuff, of course.

"You know what I regret? No, I really really regret it . . . No, you don't believe me, but I do regret it . . ."

"What the hell's there to regret? Here y'are, down the hatch!"

That was after the fifth round of "shot to shot—two shots." They were clinking their glasses, stuck to the bar like two wobbling jellyfish. Their hands were bypassing each other in the air, everything hovered around them in a state of levitation.

"No, listen, Mithridates . . . Be Mithridates, being just Mitar is too minor for you. You can call me Eustachius, I don't mind . . . Mithridatey, my old matey, see how it rhymes . . . matey, there's something I wanted . . . no, wait, what was it I wanted now?"

"Never mind. Wait, oh God, I'm on duty! If the Major calls . . ."

"That's it, right, that's what I regret: I didn't kiss the Major, I kissed the other one . . . ha, ha . . . And it was the Major I'd meant to kiss!"

"To make a fool out of him? Well, you're a nasty . . ."

"No, Mithridates, I'm not," whispered Melkior hanging his head in contrition, the entire world suddenly starting to spin in his field of vision.

Funny how everything spins. How things have dislodged from their peaceful existence. Everything is moving and traveling on a conveyer belt . . . Melkior had the idea that it would never come to rest again and was childishly overjoyed at his huge new toy. He kept reaching after it and it struck him as hilarious to be unable to get hold of anything. I'll just climb onto one of those chairs and take off. And he believed—even though it was comical, as if he were wakeful and watching his dream—that he was going to land at the Give'nTake before the Parampions on his *flying chair*.

"O Eustachius the Cosmic, I salute you on behalf of the Parampions!" exclaims Ugo in delight. "Did you have a good flight? No snags? There have been many chairs in the air today. Conferences, sir, conferences, held 'on the fly' as they call them. Whatever will they think of next?"

Also present are Viviana (without Freddie) and all the Parampions, and Maestro, being singularly pleased, is well and truly . . .

I'm drunk as a lord, thinks Melkior, laughing at the thought every time he encounters it. He no longer sees Mitar at his side. "Mitar has . . . mitared away," he says to some other whitecoats, who grab ahold of his arms and teach him to walk. "No, no, give me Mitar back . . . remitrify," he struggles with them, refusing to begin to walk.

"He took off from right here, I saw him! Flag him down, lob a shell at his seat, ha, ha . . . Let him open an umbrella, ha, ha. He'll come down then, Mitar the visitor from outer space! Have them roast him Caesar's heart!"

His legs would not follow the motion performed on them by a pair of very angry whitecoats: they, too, were laughing in their own way.

"Let go of me, pastry cooks!" shouted Melkior suddenly and stood mightily upright. "I'm off to kiss the Major," he said, seeming quite himself again; which was why they promptly grabbed hold of him again. "All right, all right, you can carry me if you insist," he said in a slyly conciliatory way, winking "craftily" at the canteen-keeper herself. "Go on ahead, one of you, and announce me. I can't very well barge in on the Major just like that, on your arms . . ."

"Okay, we'll be off to see him then," said one of the whitecoats, and he winked to a soldier who had happened to stand nearby: "You there, go on, announce him."

"Who to?" the soldier asked stupidly.

"To your aunt's aunt . . . You heard me—the Major!" one of the whitecoats lost his patience.

"Which major?" the soldier was still having trouble catching on.

"Ours, of course, not Major Attlee for heaven's sake."

The soldier went out of the canteen; he did not have the faintest idea what he was supposed to do. Which was precisely what was wanted from him: just for him to leave.

Melkior now let himself be led along. His legs trailed on the ground, knocking against each other. But he was in a way enjoying the incapacity to which he had relinquished his body. He was flying through strange spaces where everything was awhirl. He found the "earthly" disorder so wonderful that he kept smiling happily, as if ascending to heaven borne by two strong white angels.

Not even ATMAN knew yet! He had been living for four days above the palm reader's head, quietly, in slippers, leading a lazy, pampered life of sleeping, lounging in bed, stretching. Watching the flames in the pot-bellied stove . . . Devils' tongues, the Melancholic used to say, an intriguing little hell.

And the rain falls day and night . . . (the poet grabbed at the chance for a metaphor) . . . *as though asking if I'm all right.*

Am I all right?

A parrotlike, random question. He was luxuriating in his laziness like a loyal cat, and that was a question that was apt to provoke Fate. Remind it of *solutions*, reopen the file of the forgotten case. That is the way of the curious imagination of humans: troubling the peaceful waters again, poking at the coffee dregs in the bottom of the cup. Offering Fate small detailed recipes for its own demise. Making suggestions: this approach, I believe, has not yet been tried. Revealing to it, in metaphors, undreamed-of coincidences, inventive novel downfalls. Seductive, coquettish. Artistic.

He had arrived by an early train four days earlier, dead tired and bone weary. He had tiptoed upstairs, holding his breath past ATMAN's door. The entire house was still sunk in sweet winter sleep. From Mrs. Ema's room he heard the culmination of some terrible dream—she was again having knives plunged into her belly.

The bed was standing there snowy white and fragrant, ready to receive him. But Melkior felt himself unworthy of its chaste purity.

He wrapped himself in an old coverlet and dropped down onto the sofa, which greeted him pleasantly with its tired springs.

He lay there thoughtless and sleepless in a lethargy of vacuous idiotic elation like a dog come home to settle in again at the threshold. He yearned for a hand to stroke him. He stroked his own muzzle and gave the hand a loyal licking. And smiled at his own fidelity.

His thoughts kept reaching for Enka, but they were all half-awake in a stupor, in the image of a tongue of flame trying to reach the hem of a fluttering red patch of fabric which somehow "protected" itself, craftily retreating. He attempted to hold the fluttering with his hands, to catch hold of that *feminine-Enkish* something, that *feminenkish* something, wriggling, undulating, and giggling, elusive within his reach and glittering with a blazing gleam which made him feel a terrible thirst burn over his whole body. His arms, empty, fell down outside the coverlet into endless cold spaces and his teeth chattered with fear and chill. He pulled his arms back under the covers, sheltering his head there, too, from the storm which was already distantly roaring in his ears like a raging sea.

Then Viviana showed up, all in shivers of a small twinkling happiness, faceless and featureless, as a dispersed, hazy, blurred memory. But he quickly put Enka (as a flash of lightning) in her place and shivered all over from the tempestuous nearness of her. Again he tried to insert himself into the vortex, to embrace the whirlpool and give himself over to the passionate flood wave, but he felt an icy wind blowing cold once more across his skin, shaking his jaws as if it meant to crumble his teeth.

It's too early yet, I'll give her a ring later, decided Melkior, his teeth chattering. But later on . . . well, ideal, incorporeal spirals try to insinuate themselves into other spirals . . . They cannot fit—they are too big for the smaller spirals . . . and little *Quantities* keep struggling against large *Boxes* trying to enclose them in their empty *Voids* . . . and *Threads and Ropes* resist the ruthlessly long PROLONGATION, quaking before the *Great Scissors* which in ATMAN's hands snap their crocodile jaws, going *snip-snip*. . . .

The threads snap in the brief, hazy awakenings . . . But he knows that the insufferable heat has taken hold of him over "those unsolved questions" and again delves into the spirals, boxes, and threads, again arranging, disposing, unraveling, tugging, using the threads to tie together the *Two Infinities*. . . .

In a ragged clear patch through the dim cloud of a yellow light he recognized Mrs. Ema. She was saying stern things to him and feeding him bitter tasting button-shaped tablets (for how many rupees?), and pouring warm, sweet liquid into his throat . . . His stomach kept swelling, but he couldn't bring himself to throw up, out of respect for Mrs. Ema. The yellow light then went out again and she spoke no more. And Melkior was standing in hot water up to his ears, he only extracted his arms so he could swim, striking out toward a cool island where palm trees waved their green fans . . .

"You're absolutely out of your mind, boy!" Mrs. Ema chided him. She was sitting maternally at his bedside, wiping his face. "Why didn't you come to see me?"

"You were asleep . . . and I didn't know I was ill."

"Didn't know indeed—and he was burning like a piece of coal! Would you believe he lay down drenched with sweat in a chilly room, without undressing, without even taking off his shoes! Why didn't you undress and get into bed?"

"It was so white and clean," smiled Melkior. "I'd got out of the habit."

He was lying in bed, in his pajamas. The fragrance of cleanliness was everywhere. So she must have undressed me! he realized in a flash.

"Well, I never! He lost the habit of using clean things!" Mrs. Ema was putting on a tone. "You don't happen to have brought any vermin with you, have you?"

"Oh no, certainly not," Melkior assured her, for all that he was not so certain himself.

She put her palm on his forehead out of gratitude.

"See how I brought your temperature down?" she boasted. "You were still delirious only this afternoon. The doctor gave me those pills last winter, I thought they were past their expiration date—well, obviously they weren't. Are you hungry? Didn't they feed you in the army? You look like your bones will be breaking through at any moment."

Melkior reddened, she saw me naked . . . But he reached down under the eiderdown and found she had put his pajamas on over his underwear. He gave her a grateful look. As if understanding, she looked away at the window:

"Doesn't seem to be letting up . . ."

The rain was making a fine tattoo on the windowsill . . . as if asking . . .

"Falling day and night . . ." he said out loud, then answered the rain, inside: "I'm quite all right . . ." He thought he could do with a little Turgenev. Later, when Mrs. Ema left . . .

He saw her face in the light of the small lamp on the night table. Her skin seemed somehow tired; it was in a weak, resigned, sagging condition. O Lord, look at all the wrinkles she's got! Many indeed, said the Lord, indifferent (He had more pressing concerns).

She sensed his seeing her "unprepared" face with the wariness of a woman on the brink of old age: she sprang to her feet, patting her hair.

"I'm going to get you some hot soup," she was showing her goodness of heart instead of her face, "God knows how long it's been since you last had something to eat . . ."

Indeed, Melkior couldn't remember . . . yesterday at noon, porridge at the barracks, no appetite . . . He had traveled all night, chilled, feverish. . . .

"Madam, if anyone asks for me, please don't tell them I'm back. I would like to get some rest."

"To be sure. The fellow downstairs keeps inquiring . . ." she pointed her toe downward. "He asked me for your address, said he wanted to write to you."

ATMAN wanted to write me! Melkior shivered. ATMAN wouldn't have written just to say it was raining. Something must have happened . . . if *he* wanted to write.

But after the soup, later on, that night, Melkior relaxed. And read his Turgenev, *A Nest of Gentlefolk. White all over and a tinge of . . .* He was enjoying himself like a Russian landowner.

He had lived four days above ATMAN's head without ATMAN knowing. Melkior triumphed. He slept, lounged in bed, stretched . . . and watched the amusing little hell in the potbelly stove. And the rain . . .

. . . was not drumming a fine tattoo on the tin windowsill tonight. He already felt well and impatient to be out and walking along the wet streets. Also, it was amusing to sidestep ATMAN, to sneak by under his nose as if the man was a blind monster, to escape like Odysseus from Polyphemus. Why had ATMAN wanted to write?

His heart was pounding as he drew level with ATMAN's door. He had a strange feeling at his back: any moment now the bony long-fingered hand might drop onto my shoulder—thump!

But there was no *thump*, he got safely out into the street. The air was fresh and sweet, rinsed but still damp, undried. Melkior nevertheless inhaled it greedily, mainly for the symbolic meaning of *breathing freely*, or, as they also say, *breathing in the air of freedom*.

He found himself outside the Cozy Corner. Curious silence behind the yellow curtains. Has Else married the sergeant after all, he wondered. Which he wished for Kurt's sake with all his heart: congratulations, Kurt, and may the little centurions multiply in bliss . . .

"Look in, do look in at the misery, sir," he suddenly heard behind him a voice saturated with impatient pleasure, and the bony long-fingered hand was already resting on his shoulder.

When he turned around, the inseparable polyp eyes were looking at him from the dark and smiling, smiling . . . *ha-ha, sir.*

"Mr. Adam," ejaculated Melkior in fright, as if he had seen a ghost. "My God, man, how . . ."

"Quite by accident, on my way home," ATMAN hastened to explain.

". . . you frightened me!" finished Melkior. "Frightened me, devil take your . . ."

"Good heavens, why?" ATMAN was embarrassed. "Could it be because you thought I didn't know you were back? Well, I didn't want to disturb you—you were ill. The evening's damp, I don't think it's wise of you to . . . Look, why don't we go in? So you can see what it's like now. Here you are then," and he had already opened the door in front of Melkior and pushed him in.

Inside, a short, pale, nondescript man in black was standing among the unoccupied tables in a waiter's position (napkin over forearm), looking submissively down as though being rebuked by a demanding guest. When they came in he gave a surprised start but didn't seem glad to see them: with a hopeless civility, he offered them a seat, needlessly tweaking the tablecloth.

"Yes, gentlemen," he said unhurriedly, "what can I serve you?"

"What would you say to some hot wine?" ATMAN leaned toward Melkior across the table. "An autumnal drink, keeps the cold away. Or would you prefer something to eat first?"

"Cold dishes only," said the cold voice above them with an important flick of the napkin across the table.

"Sardines, cheese, and some salami," ordered ATMAN in the manner of a distinguished guest.

"No sardines, cheese homemade, cow's milk, low-cal salami only," said the pale man indifferently and again flicked his napkin at some invisible morsel on the tabletop.

"I won't have anything to eat," said Melkior. "I'll only have a hot brandy."

"Excellent idea!" cried ATMAN. "I'll have one, too."

"So, nothing to eat, just two hot brandies," said the pale man ambling off. "With customers like you, who needs enemies," seemed to be what he meant.

"More or less," ATMAN called wittily after him. "And his wife's reading *Secrets of the Russian Imperial Court* in the kitchen. Stupid fool, buying a business at a time like this."

"Oh, so Kurt has . . . ?"

"Natch. What's the use of holding on to it, now? You heard the man, 'cheese homemade, cow's milk.' They say there's going to be a shortage of wine, too, things are going to . . . well, you know where to. Anyway, the Cozy Corner has . . . cozened its guests . . . in every way." ATMAN put a particular stress on the last words, training his small derisive eyes onto Melkior's. And Melkior got confused, foolishly, not having yet caught ATMAN's drift.

"And why did you ask for my address in the army?" he asked suddenly, so that it appeared in some way connected with what ATMAN had been telling him.

"Ah-ha," blurted ATMAN unawares, as though a little bird had got snared in his trap. "I wanted to write you."

"Why . . . and what about?"

"Well . . ." ATMAN was smiling like a man hesitating before revealing something momentous, ". . . nothing special. I wanted to drop you a line, send you a parcel perhaps. It was her idea that we should send you a parcel."

"Viviana's?" All of Melkior's nerve fibers quivered, but everything subsided again presently, he's lying! ATMAN's lying! and aloud he said, "I don't believe you."

"Why not? She's got a kind heart. She even knitted you a pair of woolen gloves herself. That is to say, her Aunt Flora did, but she bought the wool and generally saw to it . . . But there was no address, so she gave them to me—here they are." ATMAN produced a pair of gray knitted gloves from his pocket and put them on the table as evidence. "Here, take them, they're yours after all. Only you'll find the fingers too long, she took the measurements from my hands, and I have long fingers, heh-heh, look," and he put his hands on the table—bony, heavy, with unusually long, hard fingers. Terrible hands. Poor Numbskull, thought Melkior, that must have hurt something awful. . . .

"I see you don't like my hands." He bunched his fingers, making his joints crack with an ugly sound. "Neither do I, believe me. I saw a film, a silent one, long ago, where Conrad Veidt played a famous pianist. He'd lost his hands in a railway crash. It so happened that a vile murderer was executed at the same time and the surgeons . . . I really have great respect for surgeons, they're the only ones I appreciate in the entire medical profession . . . grafted the murderer's hands onto the pianist's arms. That's where his suffering begins: wearing the hands of a murderer. He goes on playing, true—but with a murderer's hands! On top of which the murderer visits him in his dreams demanding his hands back. Now there's surgical charity for you! Must appreciate them all the same, don't we?" ATMAN gave Melkior a barely noticeable wink, then suddenly thrust his hands at him and laughed with an ugly cawing sound: "Horrible, aren't they? As if they'd been taken off a murderer. By surgeons. And the worst thing is I have to wear them all the time. Caressing and embracing women with these! That may be why women dislike me. You're all right. Not only are you able to caress them with words, you also have fine, white hands with delicate fingers . . . That's why they go for you so much, thinking they'd like to send you parcels, and gloves for your gentle hands. And yet—shame on you—you don't write to any of them. Not even to . . . hm . . . so she came around for a bit of soothsaying. But what could I say? The surgeons have been mobilized, too, called up for exercises, that is, the army's taken away all the joys: men, food, automobiles, the lot."

"Who came to see you? Why should I care about your customers anyway?"

"Unh-unh, this one you should, er . . . and it's only proper that you, er . . . I spoke to her in the . . . is it correct to say 'rosiest'? Well, those are the terms I spoke to her about you in . . . all flowery and rosy. When abandoned by men, these kinds of desperate women are apt to do anything."

"Such as hang themselves," said Melkior vengefully, malice oozing from his eyes, "and when you take them off the rope they hang themselves around your neck."

"Heh-heh, some truly are like that," ATMAN gave a flattered laugh. "Allusion understood—and a valid one it is. Only she's not really hanging around my neck; your informant (is that the right word?) was exaggerating just a bit. Anyhow, it's wise to have someone on hand for our physical 'needs,' and we are well able, are we not, to keep the dirty and vulgar stuff separate from our i-de-als, we who know ideal love—Platonic, if you'll permit. It's an entirely different kettle of fish from physical need . . . *off the rope*: We're masters of that pitiful parade there, indeed we are tyrants with terrible demands. We torment those she-apes of ours, do we not, Mr. Melkior, and enjoy seeing it make them even crazier about us. And then we take the notion—out of sheer caprice—to start ex-pa-ti-ating (God, what a word, I've got my tongue all twisted) as if we resent their being unfaithful to Coco—with anyone but us. Because we're but a guilt-less instrument of their sordid will in the whole affair; pretty nearly innocent victims of their lust, too."

He squeezed all this out of her, fool, Melkior fumed at Enka, he milked her dry. . . .

"You are so experienced in the matter." He resolved to respond in kind. "You must have suffered terribly over Eve."

"Over . . . Eve?" ATMAN was momentarily flummoxed and his fore-head went a shade pale; his lower jaw trembled slightly, as though with fear or a sour memory; but he presently accomplished his derisive smile and stretched it over his face like a mask. "Heh, because my name's Adam? Your catechist taught you well, that must be why you've remained so loyal to him."

"Unh-unh, I was not referring to the biblical Eve," triumphed Melkior at embarrassing ATMAN. "But it is true they called her Eve because of your name being Adam."

"Ah, so . . ." ATMAN almost said ". . . you know"; he was effecting a tactical retreat. "Stories from the Olden Days. It is a small world indeed." ATMAN was at a loss all the same, the fount of his eloquence had gone dry; he fell silent and seemed to be lost in thought. Mel-kior was sorry he'd told him—he might have done better to save this trump card for a more decisive moment, or simply to have kept his silence. He preferred ATMAN speaking to ATMAN silent. He was now afraid of the silence, who knows what the fellow might be up to?

"Ah, here comes the hot brandy at last," stirred ATMAN. "That was a good idea of yours—I've been feeling all frozen . . . inside."

They sipped the hot brandy in tandem, blowing "haah" from their warmed throats.

"Perhaps it wasn't nice of me to bring that matter up," began Melkior; he wanted to break ATMAN's strange silence.

"Nice or not . . . you wanted to get your own back at me," smiled ATMAN by way of a grimace. "All right, so be it. Did they at least tell you Eve was beautiful, very beautiful?"

"Like a goddess!" exclaimed Melkior jokingly.

"Goddess nothing! All the goddesses I've seen, in paintings and so on, are poorly built—childbearers, every last one, with no waist to speak of. Now she was well-filled yet slender; the legs, the bosom, the eyes, everything . . . no, she was a magnificent woman, if that isn't a ridiculous way of putting it."

"Why did you break up, then?"

"She was too beautiful for me," said ATMAN uncertainly, looking at Melkior with suspicion: does he know more by chance? He probably saw some tiny ironical twitch on Melkior's face; that was why he went on straight away, though not readily: "There were certain incompatibilities in our characters . . . For all that we were what I may well call madly in love, I suffered. Her beauty was simply too much for me to bear. She knew it and liked to torment me. Just for fun, on a whim, as women amuse themselves. She said such things were inevitable in a happy marriage. She used to tell me about men from our circle of friends molesting her, laughing at me behind my back. . . . She had me at odds with everyone. I had truly become suspicious and horrible. There was a boy I beat to within an inch of his life. She had complained about him propositioning her brazenly in public, what would people think of her, and once the rumors got started I was going to end up believing them myself, no, honestly, it had gone past being a joke, after all she didn't want me to be everyone's laughingstock, and so on . . . and I went and beat the hell out of the cur, or rather the pup—he was small, frightened, and miserable."

Poor Numbskull.

"What did you beat him with? A dog whip?" Melkior broke out in goose bumps.

"Whip nothing—I used these instruments," he thumped his

dreadful hands on the table. "She admitted later on she'd made it all up. Why? Well, she wanted me to thrash someone over her."

"But why the young man, of all people?" asked Melkior with an internal smirk.

"Because, would you believe it, she liked him!" replied ATMAN, as if still perplexed. "He was the most polite of them all—sort of admired her from afar. That was precisely what put her in jeopardy . . . and she wanted to remain faithful to me. That way she averted the danger . . ."

Oh how very classical it all sounds, as if Racine himself had had a hand in it, gloated Melkior.

"You seem to be smirking, Mr. Melkior?" ATMAN was looking at him inquisitorially. "I know what you're thinking. But if I'd beaten her up—'to be on the safe side' as you like to say . . ."

"I didn't say a word."

"Oh come on now, Mr. Melkior, I can see your brain laughing in there. But if I'd beaten her up I would've had to claim what I could never prove. *Coco* never has proof. It would all have been reduced to the classical 'He said—She said . . .' and so on to eternity. I didn't want to live under such conditions, did I? I'm a practical man, I wanted to go on living with her. Shall we have another round? Sir, same again please."

Poor ATMAN, thought Melkior in a moment of weakness. He watched the palmist twiddle his shot glass around and around in his long, hard hands, studying it carefully as though something were being revealed to him in the simple optics of the smudged glass. His eyes had come fearfully close to each other with a kind of grave concern, nearly fusing into a single Polyphemic Cyclopean eye. Who is this man to whom I gave the chiromantic name ATMAN as a joke? Once again Melkior felt a kind of queasiness at the question.

"It goes without saying, Mr. Melkior," spoke up ATMAN, still peering with concern into the empty glass he was rolling between his hands, "after all you have learned about my sen-ti-mental life, that you should raise the question (please don't protest, I can see it in your eyes for all that I'm not looking at you): how is it that I dare again . . . you know."

"No I don't."

"Oh, don't lie, Mr. Melkior, we understand each other only too well. I know I'm not at all . . . oh hell, it's hard to say bad things about oneself . . . well, not particularly attractive to women. No, no, I do have a mirror, you know. It breaks my heart to look at my reflection. Funny how the eyes mostly look at themselves in the mirror. Now what's there for my eyes to see in themselves? If only they could see my heartbreak! That, and my fear of the image of my hideousness, the miserable insecurity before women's critical eyes! But not a bit of it! When I'm *on the job* they quake at my gaze, like trapped birds . . . and that's all the com-pen-sation I get. But they then see me not as a male but as a god charting their destiny. She asked you— remember?—what com-pen-sation meant. Now when she wants to unsettle me she stares with her beautiful eyes at my simian ones . . . and that, it appears, is Destiny's way of warning me. But I defy it, you see . . . I fight back."

And Melkior again felt sorry for ATMAN.

"No, honestly, there is something evil in my eyes, as if they were forever scheming to commit a crime," went on ATMAN in desperate lamentation. "I've noticed you, too, avoid looking into my eyes— you're afraid of offending me. This kind of eyes, naturally enough, are to be found in apes and owls . . . and born criminals. On account of them (and my hands, of course) your Don Fernando would immediately sentence me to death 'to be on the safe side,' according to his theory of killing. Then again, who knows, perhaps I really am dangerous. Don Fernando may be right, perhaps I really ought to be put to death . . . 'to be on the safe side'; what do you think?" grinned ATMAN provocatively.

"You're talking gibberish, Mr. Adam; what on earth do you mean by the 'theory of killing'?" Melkior was alarmed: where the hell did he get that from?

"Why, it's Don Fernando's theory. Hasn't he set it out for you? I don't believe he hasn't—he takes you for one of . . ."

"I know nothing of it."

"Nothing, you say?" smiled ATMAN suspiciously. "Truth to tell,

Don Fernando's thinking is not entirely insane. Many an innocent man would go to the wall, but quite a few of the 'dangerous' ones would be eliminated as well. Through . . . what's the word for doing something to forestall an evil? Acting . . . how?"

"Preventively."

"That's it—through preventive killing. According to Don Fernando, that was—pre-ven-tively—how Hitler should have been done in, while he was still walking the Earth as a private citizen. As well as the others Don Fernando suspects—they ought to be done in, all of them . . ."

"Where did you get this all from? Did he tell you?"

"Of course he did . . . not me, we haven't met, but someone else. Perhaps an 'executioner' who . . . Because now he's looking for 'executioners,' naturally—he doesn't want to dirty his hands. And of course he's looking for them among desperadoes who no longer care whether they live or die—they've already sold their body to the Faculty of Medicine."

Maestro! it dawned on Melkior, Maestro told him all this in his cups. But could it be that Don Fernando had settled on Maestro? . . . no, Melkior couldn't bring himself to believe it.

"Very strange, is it not, Mr. Melkior, to sentence a man to death because of his 'appearance'?" ATMAN propped his chin on both palms and trained his terrible and (somehow) *dirty* gaze on Melkior: "I know I've been blacklisted on account of the look in my eyes, take a look, Mr. Melkior," he pointed both his index fingers at his eyes, "only the 'executioner' is missing, ha-ha . . . The man who was subjected to the prop-a-ganda did not take the 'preventive killing' theory seriously. He is, well, an irresponsible, crack-brained man. He promised to go through with it, for a joke (he doesn't care, he's going to kill himself anyway), only to sit down with the 'victim' and have a good laugh at the customer, ha-ha-ha . . . All right, but it wasn't merely 'we had a chuckle—end of story,' oh no!" finished ATMAN in a somehow threatening way, yet laughing still.

"So what else was it? Come on!" Melkior was purposely feigning anger. "What would make you 'dangerous' in anyone's book and why should anyone have you on a blacklist?"

"Why? The expression in my eyes, that's why! according to the theory," cried ATMAN, too, almost boastfully. "And I do know I've been blacklisted! If you want to know, there's a contract out on me . . ."

" 'A contract' out on you," laughed Melkior nervously, "as if this were Chicago! You seem fond of crime stories—that, or the 'shot-to-shot' lush has been feeding you his drivel."

"What lush, Mr. Melkior?" asked ATMAN with a fetching smile. "You know I can't abide drunks—I'm having this brandy at your suggestion, to ward off a cold, for medicinal purposes really. That's why I only appreciate you of all of your crowd—for not drinking, for being a serious, sober, and *concerned* man. Quite frankly, I'm disgusted with the whole Give'nTake mob. Did you know," he suddenly remembered, "that Maestro recently injured Ugo? He smashed glasses on his head—there are cuts all over his face."

"Did she tend to him again?" asked Melkior with hidden anguish.

"No. She wasn't there. She's not to be found *there* anymore."

"Oh?" went Melkior, his heart fluttering with excitement.

"Yes, didn't I tell you? You're next. I want it to happen as soon as possible . . . so that it can be over with as soon as possible. As you know, I help events come . . . and pass . . ."

"So you know I'm next . . ." Melkior gave a nervous laugh.

"I do. She's like a gourmet—she must taste every dish. Come on, Mr. Melkior, don't scowl, I'm sorry but you're not just any old dish. I wonder why I keep speaking in terms of food. You would indeed be dessert for such a woman—in the intel-lec-tual sense, I mean. You saw it yourself—she's primitive, a real spiritual orphan, so much so that she even takes pity on me sometimes—and you know my level such as it is. We are *exemplars*, she and I, that's why we belong together. But I'll go on waiting . . . until she comes to realize it, too."

"What if she never does?"

"Never . . . that's impossible," said ATMAN with conviction.

"Perhaps later, perhaps quite soon, but one day she will have to. I rather think that will be very soon . . . because there won't be any other options left."

Melkior shuddered at ATMAN's chilling prophecy. The old fear made itself known again: a raven croaking above its small consoling wakefulness. In an instant he dreamed again the deathly dream of his cannibal motif: facing the teeth of Polyphemus the Cyclops, the one-eyed beast. And he wondered, bitterly, where that eternal companion of a thought had been hiding these last few days.

Fear began to shake Melkior ("because there won't be any other options left"); his mournful gaze did a round of all the walls and objects in the establishment: here, all this will persist and the little old man will be here with that slurring speech of his (he's beyond "the dwaft," of course), I shay, *bud*, it'sh . . .

"Looking around, Mr. Melkior? You've spent many the evening here chatting with Kurt. Fond memories."

"I used to drop by, in passing, to have a bite to eat . . ."

"Well, even if it were not in passing, what could have been wrong with that? It's not as if I were reproaching you or anything. You might, for that matter, have become Kurt's drinking buddy and gone on binges here—well, that would be nobody's business, am I right?"

"I was not Kurt's 'drinking buddy'!" replied Melkior sharply.

"Well, what I'm saying is that, even if you did, what business is it of anybody else's? You presumably had your own personal reasons, and Kurt had his—(a bit less personal, muttered ATMAN with a smile)—well, each of you had your reasons, so what? It was to mutual advantage, that's your own business."

"There you go again with your innuendoes!" Melkior was angry; he sensed ATMAN trying to embroil him in "something." "What benefit could I have gained by eating the occasional sausage here?"

"Well . . . that of having eaten the sausage," laughed ATMAN. "Did you think I meant something else? Kurt's mother was a good cook, Styrian. Else was an agreeable hostess, Kurt a helpful lad . . . yes, it was a cozy corner in every way. The garrison sergeants found a really warm spot in here, a home away from home, almost in the bosom of the family. Isn't this borne out by their very absence now? The warm spot has been undone. The war, the war, Mr. Melkior, cheese home-made, cow's milk."

ATMAN spewed out the word "war" with malicious glee. Melkior watched him with disgust and fear as the man leered brightly in his face.

"So where's Kurt?" he asked purposely, to mask his fear. "What's he up to these days?"

"I really couldn't tell you where he might be . . . But if you need him for . . . anything, I'd be glad to . . ." ATMAN was ready to be of service.

"No, what could I possibly need him for?" Why am I getting caught up in this, snapped Melkior to himself. "Merely asking . . ."

"Merely asking . . ." smiled ATMAN. "Perhaps he's still here and *up to things* . . . and perhaps his Führer has summoned him . . . They're not like us with our medical boards and weighing machines and starvation cunning—they're burning with the desire to die for that swastika'd spider of theirs . . ."

"And you knew Kurt was . . . *up to things?*" Melkior asked suddenly and was alarmed at his own audacity, why the hell am I getting caught up in this?

"Are you telling me you didn't?" grinned ATMAN threateningly. "You really should have done something about it, Mr. Melkior, I thought about that all the time. You are a serious and almost *responsible* man, you house people clandestinely . . . (Has ATMAN reported it? Where's the Stranger now? flashed through Melkior's mind.) If only you'd told your Don Fernando . . . to put him on that list of his," joked ATMAN, his small eyes having a malicious good time. "I obviously couldn't have, they wouldn't have believed a palmist, it's a dodgy occupation . . . They could've thought I myself was one of . . . right? Don Fernando put me on his list, did he not? . . . But you, a man of confidence, an honest John, as they say . . . but you didn't— you were all wrapped up in your civilian purity, to the point of hermitage, and purportedly 'all for mankind, for social justice.' My dear Mr. Melkior! If you'd only left it at that—but no, you got . . ."

"Mr. Adam, your provocations . . ." shuddered Melkior, and instantly he found himself tongue-tied.

"Provocations nothing! In for a penny, in for a pound, Mr. Melkior," ATMAN gathered momentum like someone deciding to act, "you yourself got . . . well, yes, you did, to some extent . . . got yourself in deep with Kurt . . ."

It was as if ATMAN had meant to keep the last words to himself but oh dear, they had escaped him, what was done could not be undone. He smilingly watched pallor spreading over Melkior's face, followed by a flush, by pallor again . . . he was amused by the color changes. And Melkior knew what was happening on his face . . . Oh you scoundrel, you blackguard, you rogue! But what was the use? He couldn't silence ATMAN's craft by such pitiful cursing into his own ear. But neither did he propose to reward him by a "show" of anger, so he gave a laugh meant to speak more eloquently than words.

"All the same, I would . . ." began ATMAN and stopped as if he had changed his mind.

"You would what?" laughed Melkior while feeling a kind of cold horror welling within him. "You got in deep with Kurt"; he felt the wetness of the words on his skin. But now it was ATMAN's turn to speak.

"First of all, I wouldn't laugh," he said with genuine severity, "and secondly . . . listen to the important way I'm saying *secondly*, practically as if I'd invented the sewing machine . . ."

"All right, you did not invent the sewing machine. What would you do *secondly*?"

"Nothing," laughed ATMAN. "Or, if anything, perhaps just say we'd be well advised to . . . how shall I put it? pay a wee bit closer attention (*wee*, that's pure baby talk, *wee-wee*). Uncertain is our destiny in what the politicians call this part of the world."

"So what do you think we ought to do for our destiny? Pay attention to what?"

"A wee-wee bit of attention," ATMAN was amusing himself, "A wee-wee bit of attention to the fact that we all have our own destiny, wee-wee. You may have got away with it for the time being, but Destiny has other wonderful surprises up her sleeve."

"And you are insured against these surprises?"

"No, I'm not. How could I be? Where's the insurance? Do *you* know?" ATMAN held his face close to Melkior's. Melkior could smell his unpleasant breath.

Melkior sat back and said derisively: "You're asking me? You who have such a cozy relationship with Destiny?"

"Have a cozy relationship? Heh, I'd be delighted, if she were pretty."

"Well, being an expert, you presumably picked the prettiest one for yourself."

"Now you're poking fun at my occupation, too, Mr. Melkior," said ATMAN with a kind of sadness. "But you did do something for your destiny . . . by fasting, like a saint . . . and with the assistance of this . . . Kurt fellow," he was monitoring the impact of his words, squinting derisively at Melkior.

Melkior was now unable to laugh anymore: "What assistance of Kurt's? With what did Kurt assist me?"

"The pounding of your patriotic heart, ha-ha . . . What is it you dip the cigarettes in—do you remember, Mr. Melkior? it wasn't so very long ago."

"You spoke about that to Kurt?"

"It was I who told him that, not his *Vater*, heh-heh . . ."

"But I didn't. I didn't even ask Kurt about it—he came up with it. . . . Why did you go through him?"

"I wanted to lend you a hand. You wouldn't have taken it from me, you don't trust me."

"And I trust Kurt, is that it?"

"Well . . . I rather imagine you do. You do indeed—more, at any rate, than you trust me. He's on the side with the *upper hand*. Perhaps Kurt could help you still, I mean in 'crucial' things—after all, he's got a kind and noble heart."

"Well, speak to him, then," Melkior told him angrily. "Perhaps *you* could help *him*."

"How might I be of help to him, Mr. Melkior?" ATMAN feigned shocked surprise. "On the contrary, he might welcome some of your military ex-per-tise . . . oops, how did 'tease' pop up like that?"

"Now look here! . . ." but Melkior managed to restrain himself, why the hell should I shout? Who does this rascal take me for . . . or is he just winding me up? "May I impart some of that expertise to you instead?"

"Why, whatever could I possibly use it for, Mr. Melkior?" ATMAN went on wondering, "I'm not a warring party."

"No, but there is a secret, everyone is frightened of it," whispered Melkior in the strictest of confidence. "I learned about it while I was *out there* . . . Alligators, a new weapon, they keep one in each town. . . ."

"Oh, that's just an animal, an aquatic animal, a crocodile," laughed ATMAN, but with a watchful eye on Melkior.

"An animal, true enough. But what about Hannibal's elephants? And a crocodile is more awesome than even an elephant; it hides in the tall grass and then suddenly: snap! The fear and terror of any infantry. They were brought in from the Ganges and the Nile."

"And you've seen those crocodiles?" ATMAN was going along with the joke.

"No, but I've heard them. They howl worse than any beast. They're kept well hidden—top secret."

"You don't say . . ." said ATMAN rather vaguely, while keeping a close eye on Melkior: is he pulling my leg or is there really something in . . . "And you think that in case of war . . ."

"They'd make mincemeat of all those armored columns or whatever the things are called! They sweep tanks away with their tails like this," he flicked a matchbox with his little finger, sending it flying far away from the table.

He felt pleasure at the victorious gesture. With my little finger! And the words sounded warrior-like to him. He embraced the madness which made another assault before a bewildered ATMAN. "Yes, Mr. Adam, I could tell you about plenty of other very strange things I saw *out there*," so let the scoundrel snitch to whoever he reports back to—Kurt or his lame Scarpia.

"Very interesting indeed," ATMAN was saying, baffled: he now was truly at a loss. "It looks like you've delved quite deeply into these military matters."

"I didn't plumb the depth, but when it comes to signals in lights (this is how Gogol's Zhevakin II speaks, thought Melkior in passing) it's not just switching the lights on and off—you've also got to be careful which windows are lit, by number and floor, this last is particularly important. It's a special code, you see, and you can read all the signals to be sent about the alligator if you can crack the code."

"And you cracked this code?" asked ATMAN in a bored way, even with an unconcealed and impertinent yawn. But he liked repeating the phrase *cracked the code*.

"I studied it . . . with the aid of an expert." Melkior could not hide his smile: he had remembered the Melancholic. "I can't help laughing when I remember how we decoded it all wrong once. We got something really funny, swears and vulgar words. I expect the counterespionage boys were having a laugh, joshing with the enemy spies. Then again, perhaps they'd merely encoded the signals under a new system and we decoded them using the previous one. Most amusing it was."

ATMAN was yawning a great deal by now. His eyes were wandering in boredom, his gaze going hazy. He'll drop off any moment now, thought Melkior with pleasure. I've fixed ATMAN the Great with his own weapon!

"But I'm being a bore, Mr. Adam. Apologies."

"Not at all, it's most engaging," but nevertheless he glanced at his watch and gestured, "Bill, please."

"All the same I *have* bored you this evening, you've got to admit it," Melkior was not going to give up, I'll finish him off, if only for tonight.

"Oh, no, Mr. Melkior, whatever makes you say that? It's just that I'm rather tired, I've had a very long day to-hoo-hooo . . . day," finished ATMAN, with a long and seemingly strenuous yawn.

"Doing horoscopes?" Melkior was not letting go.

"No—two maniacal females. Brought by that woman of mine, the one 'off the rope' as you like to put it. So, Mr. Melkior," ATMAN suddenly asked in a very serious tone, "do you really believe in these . . . alligators?"

"What's there to believe?" said Melkior "sanely," as madmen are apt to speak. "I don't believe in death rays, but alligators are aquatic animals, you said so yourself."

"How strange." ATMAN looked at him in a "certain way." "I thought you were joking," he added in a low murmur and with a kind of morose disappointment.

Outside, Melkior offered him his hand, "Good night."

"You're not going home?" asked ATMAN with what was nearly pleasure.

"I feel like a walk. I've been cooped up for so many days now . . ."

"Only four, Mr. Melkior. Don't tell me you're off to the Give'n-Take—your crowd hardly ever goes there anymore. Thénardier's trying to get rid of them in stages—he won't let them drink on a tab, someone told him the police are keeping an eye on them. Have a nice time. After all, heh-heh, I spoke to her in the *rosiest* of terms . . . Help Destiny, Mr. Melkior, and she will reward you a hundredfold," laughed ATMAN out loud. "Knock, and the door shall be opened unto you, ha-ha-ha . . . Good night, you lucky man!"

Lucky man? He was left alone, lost in the cold dirty fog. There was nowhere to go, the fog had coated all the streets with a smelly cold barren wasteland. He decided to give ATMAN a good head start and then go back to his warm nest himself.

Or should I *knock* after all? It was not yet nine o'clock. Destiny was really imploring him to do his part. He responded with an adventurer's grin. The phone booth on the corner offered itself to him like a harlot, like an old reliable whore mistress: hey, boy, here's Ambulance Service, make the last digit 4 instead of 3, make the last digit 4, 4, 4 . . . What the hell, Melkior waved a hand, Destiny calls in person! ATMAN said so. Let's go and knock at the door! *Let this be the ruination of you and of me* . . . he sang defiantly inside.

That selfsame defiance drove him up the seventy-two steps, and Coco's honorable nameplate gave a gleam of shame, oh Lord! But Melkior did not look at the honorable face of the spouse and master of the house—he sent his masculine signal (Alligator's here! and he laughed cruelly): long-short-long.

Presently there was a sound of movement inside (female? male? which?) and then someone said "oh-oh-ohhh . . ." as if a hen had been disturbed. And Melkior said "co-co-cohhh" behind the door out of some silly need to tell the *nameplate*, See, there *is* a hen inside.

The small brass window set in the door opened; he heard her ragged, excited breathing inside. She's alone, concluded Melkior, relieved.

"Who is it? Th-that co-code . . ." he heard her quavering whisper from the dark rectangle. He trembled all over with the nearness of her, he felt the noise of his blood in his veins.

"It's not *Coco*, it's me," he said with as much co-cocky derision as he could muster.

"Kior!" she exclaimed madly. "Kior's back! He's back, he's back. . . ." she spoke to herself cuddling, confidential, out of her mind with unexpected happiness. She kept turning the key in the lock, right, left, nervously, she barely managed to unlock the door.

"Where are you, where are you, you naughty boy, ahh . . ." petite and all aquiver, she clung to him in a tight embrace, "Kior, ah, Kior!"

She had an emerald-green velvet housecoat on, closely fitting the body Melkior knew so well . . . and underneath it—"Here, nothing, I've just taken a bath, Kio, I had an intimation, I knew, ah Kio, I was waiting for you."

"How did you know? Did Adam tell you?" he asked suspiciously.

"Adam who? There you go again with your . . . Ah, you crazy man!" she got the point of the joke. "Yes, Adam, I'm waiting for you like Eve, see," she unbuttoned the housecoat, showed herself naked to him; she had not understood which Adam he meant.

He hugged her eagerly under the housecoat and vigorously fell to kissing her neck and breasts, belly, hips, leaving the matter of Adam aside for the moment.

"In here, Kio, come here," she pulled him into the room with the wide double bed. "I'm all alone, Kio, I've been alone for a long, long time, you all abandoned me, you bad, cruel men," her tears began to flow, she was feeling sorry for herself. "No, he's not bad, you're bad, you never wrote a word to me all this time. Ahh, Kio, how I've been waiting for you!" She heaved a deep sigh flinging herself onto the bed with panicky speed, as if fearing the elusion of the reward for all the suffering she had borne.

"I've had a tough time of it, Enkie, I'll tell you all about it," said Melkior throwing his clothes onto chairs, the floor, every which way, he, too, was in a hurry. "I wrote to no one, I've been through . . . all kinds of things . . ."

"Ssh, don't talk," she whispered from the bed, all but pleading with him, "I want us to be happy tonight, to forget everything. Turn off the ceiling light, turn off all the lights. We'll be watching each other and talking later, now I want to see nothing, to hear nothing. I just want to feel you in the dark, all of you, all of my darling. . . . Come, Kio. Ah, I can't see you, where are you? Ah, Kio, Kio . . ." and she laughed madly in his tempestuous embrace.

They were sharing (of course) a cigarette and lying there in silence. She had her head propped on his lean upper arm and was surrendering with indulgence like a small boat in a sheltered cove; he had one of her small breasts cupped in his splayed fingers, re-gally, like a monarch's orb. He felt on his chest the pleasing pres-ence of the heavy cut-glass ashtray, rising and falling on the waves of his breath. He was remembering the dream he'd had on his first night in the barracks. Had it been this one, Enka, or . . . he could no longer remember. "That's right, call me a liar!"—"I said *briar* . . . and anyway, you're not a liar—you're a fool, and that's not a dream."

"How could you go and spill everything like that?"

"I didn't spill anything. He already knew all about it. He's not a chiromantist for nothing."

"Chee-rro-man-tist," he enunciated mockingly.

"He got everything right—as if the devil himself was in him." She snuggled up to him, keeping under his mighty wing, poor, small, helpless, alone. . . .

"And you believe he can soothsay?"

"I told you—he already knew all about it; I told him nothing, it was he who did the talking . . ."

". . . and you did the confirming," he said angrily. "Did you mention that you love your husband?" asked Melkior with concealed irony.

"But of course . . ."

"But of course . . . You can now expect him to blackmail you for as long as you live."

"Why should he?"

"Why shouldn't he? He now knows you are anxious for your husband never to learn about . . . *this* . . . well, you can see for yourself, can't you?" He was ashamed to talk about it; he was getting irritated.

"But I paid what he charged!"

She paid what he charged! "Oh what naïve little creatures you women are!" He was angry and prepared to approve of ATMAN's behavior. "You think your *special* little fifty dinars bought you the privilege of enjoying your safety? Oh no, that's nowhere near enough, Madam! He hates you, he hates your pleasure and wants you to pay him for it!"

"Pay him for hating me?"

"You seem to be beginning to understand." It was again he who had grown tired of her; he enjoyed being in a position to torment her. A fresh arousal; he saw tears in her eyes.

"Oh, Kio, that's awful! You frighten me!"

"No fear . . . as long as you can afford to pay him."

"Well, how long will he go on demanding it?"

"He may not ask for just money every time, heh-heh. . . ."

"That's repulsive what you are saying!" she moved a little way away from him and removed the trophy ashtray from his hand; she gave a shiver and covered her breasts with virginal shame.

"Repulsive it may be . . . but there it is. He would do it to spite me, for one thing. Aren't you flattered that he should envy me?"

He pulled her to him again and made a round of his little kingdom with a ruling hand. She clung gratefully to him and put herself fully under his aegis.

"Oh, Kio!" she kissed his hairy chest. "But even if he told Coco something, Coco wouldn't believe him," she laughed in a way that Melkior hated.

"Well, did you tell him that?"

"Tell who?"

"Adam."

"Adam who?" she laughed; the conversation amused her.

"ATMAN. The chiromantist. Why are you laughing?" Her laughter irritated him.

"I'm laughing, oh God . . ."—can't he see the point?—"isn't it funny, a chiromantist called Adam, telling people's fortunes?"

"It's just a name. What's so funny about it?" But there is something, damn it! he was admitting to himself, it really was funny.

"I mean the Adam of Earthly Paradise, that's why I'm laughing."

"You mean his original sin, too . . ."

"That business with the apple, Kio?"

"Yes, with the apple," he firmly cupped her breast.

"Oh, Kio!" she was getting excited. She was imagining Eve, naked, with Adam, naked, in Earthly Paradise. Like the two of us here now—oh, Kio!

She sought the tree of knowledge that had grown tall and stiff in the midst of the garden.

"Oh, Adam, Adam . . ." whispered Enka in abandon, offering herself madly.

Adam the aphrodisiac, thought Melkior.

"Don't smirk at me, you tormentor!" Enka surfaced for an instant with a martyr's face and immediately sank back into the silt, as ATMAN would have put it.

"See how Adam works." Melkior was resisting ATMAN's "Destiny." He had knocked on the open door, given her *first aid*—he now wanted to lord it over her, to be a little god in this mini-paradise.

"Didn't ATMAN prophesy it . . . 'in the rosiest of terms'?" mocked Melkior.

"Yes he did, and you came back quick, quick, you're here, take me, Kio," she was writhing, possessed by the devil of Eden. "Kio, let's sin here like Adam and Eve in Earthly Paradise, let's sin, Kio. Come on!" The biblical tableau would not let go of her. "Don't you want it, don't you want me anymore?"

"And what if God were to appear and . . ." God nothing! she was not believing in God—the devil was tempting her with *the tableau* ". . . and to . . ." He heard a noise from outside the door ". . . and to shout: Adam . . ." The sound was now repeated clearly: someone was trying to put a key into the lock . . . *For dust thou art, and unto dust shalt thou return,* uttered Melkior inside through force of memory, with a strange feeling of wakeful cataleptic dying. His legs went icy, for he could clearly hear someone trying to unlock the door.

"Listen, someone is unlocking the door." But the meaning of the words was not getting through to her. "Someone is unlocking the door, do you hear?" At last she was present.

"He can't do that, the key's in the lock on the inside," she said carelessly and began sinking again.

"What do we do now?" Here comes the Lord! Melkior straightened his legs to get out of bed, but she turned him back preemptively, without a trace of kindness. She had taken the matter into her own hands.

"Do? Stay put, that's what. You had to invoke those gods of yours!" she whispered in a rage, swearing. "Why didn't he send word he was coming? He can go to a hotel, I'm fast asleep, he ought to know as much!" She was now raging at the man outside.

In the silence of the flat the bell sounded irresolute as it rang, tearful, open up, it's me. . . . But Melkior heard it as an angry scream, as the voice of the Lord, Adam, where art thou?—In here, Lord, naked, in thy marital bed. . . . The second round of ringing was anxious, what's the matter, why isn't she answering the door? and the third was already panicked: intermittent, long, short, chaotic. . . .

"All right, I'm not asleep anymore, I can hear you, dearest," she whispered with a smile of sorts. But she was not stirring from the bed. She had a firm grip on Melkior's arm, listening to *that thing* going on behind the door.

There was the sound of minor, muted demolition coming from the hall.

"Get dressed," she commanded.

"What's he doing?" asked Melkior, his foot missing the trouser leg.

"Smashing the door light . . ."

"It's too narrow—he couldn't even get his head through," said Melkior foolishly.

She gave a soundless laugh and waved a hand in dismissive contempt.

"He'll put his arm through, take the key out from inside," she said calmly, getting up deliberately slowly, "then he'll unlock the door . . ."

"Do you think I could get out somehow?" said Melkior, his fingers barely managing to find the buttons. "Is there another way out?"

"Yes there is," she said mockingly. She had put on some underwear, and her housecoat over it. And was listening again.

The demolition was now much more hurried, more impatient; the job was clearly progressing well under his deft fingers.

Unraveling his tie with fear-maddened fingers, Melkior tried to imagine poor *Coco* in his full dignity: at the clinic, surrounded by a suite of assistants, nurses, technicians, over a patient's wide-open innards, his calm, wise fingers carefully . . . smashing the door light at his own flat! He wished to save him in his mind, to lift him out of his embarrassment and shame, out of the bitter humiliation of a man betrayed and derided. . . .

"He knows someone's with you,"—you damned whore, Melkior added inside, outraged.

"He's imagining me with my veins slashed, seeing me poisoned, raped, slaughtered." She spoke with an odd kind of enjoyment. "He's hurrying, he thinks he may still have time to save me . . ."

"The wretched man!" sighed Melkior sadly.

"You're the wretch! Why do you want to feel sorry for him in front of me? Who are you? The bastard who's cuckolding him! He has such a . . . beautiful imagination," she said without irony, indeed with a brand of delighted admiration.

O Lord, what *is* this thing? asked Melkior. Mimicry, replied the Lord scientifically.

She had remade the bed (as if nothing had happened); she was preparing for *his* entry.

"Right," said Melkior after she had tucked in the sheets, "now go on and open the door to him. He's going to find me here anyway . . . Wouldn't it be more sensible if you opened it yourself?"

She gave him a glance and a contemptuous smile. She didn't bother to hide her contempt. She was unnaturally calm, composed, even certain she had nothing to fear. Why, she was innocent! . . . though the circumstances were a trifle . . . "unusual."

She's thought of something . . . but Melkior was leery of relying on her certainty. She had already "dethroned" him, dispatched him to the *outside world* where she had picked him up in the first place. He felt rejected, excommunicated from the family consecration, an intruder, "the fourth ape." What's this, she seems to be looking at me with surprise: what's *this guy* doing here? Who does he think he is, speaking to me *in such an intimate tone?* How dare he!

Coco had broken through the door light; the brass flap clanged on the anteroom floor. He's already reaching through, thought Melkior, the "encounter" is only minutes away. He'll strangle me, he thought, gulping air.

Enka had by then locked the bedroom door and gestured him on. She led him through cold dark rooms (. . . where to? wondered Melkior in a dungeon where languished incarcerated furniture). She locked each door behind her, giving a mumbled "hem" every time the key clicked in the lock.

Jumping over hurdles, poor Coco. Running from a pursuer in a dream, thought Melkior, bound to end at an impenetrable wall where to await Destiny's strike to come . . . but that is the point at which we wake up. In the cinema, too, there is a way out in the nick of time. . . . This is ATMAN pitting Destiny against me. "Knock," ATMAN had laughed. So I gave Destiny a hand and here I am— trapped!

Enka had turned a light on at last. They were in Coco's study. Floor-to-ceiling bookcases lining all four walls, a set of leather arm- chairs; a skull grinning on the desk. That was where Melkior's gaze rested: had Coco cut the head off?

Alas, poor Yorick! The dead man's mocking face watched him from the empty sockets.

"A chimney sweep," explained Enka as indifferently as a tour guide, stroking the dead man's pate. "Fell off a roof, probably drunk; you can still see the fracture."

Here's what they'll be saying about Maestro's skull: a journalist, a character, a terrible lush. Long before he died he sold his body to the Institute of Anatomy; we got his skull for a song from a lab assistant, a lush himself. . . .—What did he die of?—Syphilis, we think; rotted alive. There: it's like this, on a desk, my poor Maestro, that you'll be Yorick the jester in the dull day-to-day routine of some dolt who will now and then, yawning, say to himself *Alas, poor Yorick* and *Yorick, thou fool*, all thanks to the presence of your skull, to give himself a smidgeon of Hamletian subtlety. Anyway, who can be sure his skull won't end up on top of a wardrobe?

"Sit down for a minute, why don't you," said Enka insultingly coldly, her tone suddenly formal, "we've got to wait a bit."

"Wait for what?" asked Melkior, irritated. What do you know— we're formal, are we! He felt as if he was going to slap her face at last.

She had of course sensed the "great moment"; she smiled at him in that fetching way which had always worked wonders before.

"Don't be cruel, sir," she whispered seductively next to his ear. "We've go to wait before you can leave, you fool."

"So there *is* a way out!"

"Didn't I say so . . . back there?" she was smiling in a kind of sly triumph. "Why do you think I'm doing all this?"

"Why, you're an . . ." Melkior was about to give her a kiss in his delight, but she held him off with both hands. "Tell me, how do I get out of here? Am I to jump out the window?" He could see no other way.

"That would be the best thing all around . . . seeing what you're like," she said with a kind of serene malice. "Wait a bit more . . . and don't worry, big brave boy, you'll get out just fine."

Her showing off her own bravery struck him as ludicrous. It was like reproaching a trapped mouse for its cowardice. . . .

Over there, several rooms away, Coco was vainly calling out to Enka in a discreet, familial voice. In front of locked doors the frightened, worried man was crying for a breath, a single sign of her being alive . . . and had she said: I'm in here, darling, I'm alive and in bed with another man, he would have heaved a sigh of relief: never mind, sweets, so long as you're alive.

But there was no sound from her, and he tackled the first locked door. There were muffled breaking and crashing sounds (he was careful after all to make as little noise as possible), followed by his forlorn voice in the distant room, *Enka, where are you, answer me, Cookie* . . . and then another cry, a despairing scream of a hopeless man . . . *if you're still alive* . . .

Something repulsive flashed across her face, something like victorious jubilation. She was parading it *triumphantly* for Melkior: see how much I mean to him? What would *you* do for my sake?

"Would you be prepared to stay here . . . for my sake?" she asked him in her cuddly, insidious way, and laughed provocatively.

Melkior gave her an astonished look: "That's what you seem to have arranged in the first place! There really is no other way out!"

"Oh yes, there is," she laughed with pitying scorn.

He had no time to note the humiliating manner of her cinematic *rescue* (exit in the nick of time)—in the adjoining room Coco was going through a mad fit of utter despair: Cookie, please stop playing with me! Oh God, what is this? If only she's still alive! The hapless man was weeping as he forced open the last door.

Enka then soundlessly opened a concealed door in a bookcase; a black hole leading into darkness opened up in front of Melkior.

"Quick now!" she whispered hurriedly. "The anteroom's down the corridor, to the right," and she had already pushed him into the darkness. "The door's there, as you know . . . Here's the key to the front door . . . Give me a ring, Ambulance Service, as always . . ."

The door closed behind him and the darkness pressed his eyes with its black fingers. The wall responded with cold unpleasantness to the touch of his fingertips. Melkior was nevertheless heartened by the cold presence: he was able to orient himself by it. Curse you and your home! He cursed with hatred, feeling the inimical walls. I just hope I don't stumble over a box, a pot, a bell, these bourgeois types leave all sorts of things along their corridors . . . hurdles and traps for thieves, intruders, luvvah boys . . . he finished with mocking satisfaction. Oh where's the door—this gate, that let thy folly in, said mad King Lear. It seemed to him that he would never get out of the insanity which was pressing the darkness against him between the two icy walls.

She had defended herself Troy-like . . . Troy as he might, Coco had been hampered by having to force open three doors . . . or was it four . . . to reach Helen, the pretty harlot. Odysseus groped over the walls inside the horse seeking a way out of the abdominal darkness, like a piece of feces on its scatological journey down Enka's spry intestine. O damn you, damn you! cursed Melkior in the dark, where's the door that let my folly in? Menelaus must have entered Troy by now and is begging forgiveness for besieging it, pleading mercy on his bended knee. . . . There were no more sounds of breakage—all that was to be heard in the silence was, perhaps, sobs . . . hers, brought on by the joy of it being him, *Menelaus-Coco*, and not a murderer, robber, despoiling lecher, sex maniac. That was why she had put herself behind so many locked doors, trembling, trembling . . . oh God! . . . perhaps even fainting at the last moment. . . .

Finally there was a ray of light; ah, here we are, here was the anteroom and the gate that let . . . with the door light broken . . . And the staircase! Escape from the dungeon, ramparts, ropes, guards, the jailer's daughter, the hopeless love . . . the whole romantic bit. He broke out in goose bumps as he glanced down the dark abyss of the stairwell: no, sir, not a joke, going down that on a rope . . . For Viviana?—eh? eh? . . . but he made no reply.

He hurtled down the three flights of stairs with all the acceleration physics would allow, even on the turns, bumping into walls . . .

Freedom!

The street was slushy with uncertain snow that was attempting to hold his footprints. No go, it was nothing but water in a loose state of failing firmness; ha-ha, he triumphed treading on the signs of old December's impotence. Nevertheless he looked back: no, no footprints. . . . A lit window on the third floor was what he had left behind. A nighttime dispute in the study, long, insatiable, sucking the poor couple's blood and sleep.

He suddenly felt terribly unhappy. Sent out like a dog into the street, into the night and winter, while behind the lit window they warmed each other with kisses of *unexpected happiness*. Robbed, tricked, bamboozled, alone in the night . . . on top of which I happen to be convalescent! (this was a reproach to him, the doctor) and he nearly broke into sobs in the middle of the empty, slushy street. He felt wet, sticky coldness on the soles of his feet. Oh no, not that, too! Leaky shoes! They had dried up in civilian rest while the master was being borne by government-issue boots; the poor black orphans were squealing tearfully as they squelched their way through the dirty slush.

"Wanna come and get warm, boy?" the question came from a doorway out of a fiery rouged face peeking momentarily out from the warm nest of a large yellow fox-fur coat.

"You're freezing, too . . ." replied Melkior in passing. I've had enough of women, of woman. Less than an hour ago I was lying as naked as Adam . . .

"Let's you and me have a rub-a-dub-dub, eh?" the yellow fox fur voiced hope. "Wait a sec, I've got something to show you. . . ." Melkior turned and saw, from the open coat, a long beautiful leg in a provocative advertising posture.

"Take a good look—the other one's just like it, wanna see?" This is such stuff as dreams are made on, he thought hurriedly.

"Don't part them for my sake," he tossed to her, moving by, "let the sisters live in harmony . . . and say hello to their Mama."

"And you, dimwit, stop flogging the lizard!" she grumbled crankily after him.

"It's mine to do with as I please. . . ."

"Boil it for your girlfriend's birthday dinner!"

"Give me your address—I'll send you the soup. . . ."

Melkior let her have the last word, but the distance rendered what she said unintelligible. Who would ever go to bed with someone so . . . yellow? Mr. Kalisto, the papal namesake. He remembered the man's pink gums and spat in disgust. The father of *such* a son!

Hey, this must be magic!—he heard the son's voice from a distance. Melkior halted. The night was uncertainly transmitting the words of Ugo's pathos-drenched recitation . . . *to the queen of all women* . . . This was in honor of the "fox fur" in the doorway behind—she had bandied her legs about for him, too. . . . *To chrysanthemums' sister.* . . . Already she was sending him away and Ugo was, like a tenacious little dog, barking out further verses in her honor by the doorway. He ended his recitation with his arm high in the air. . . . *I raise this glass to your health* . . . (Melkior saw him under the lamppost as a black silhouette), then bowed deeply *Madam!* And went on his way with another poem. He approached with a drunkard's big uncertain steps, his galoshes squelching noisily as far as the pavement was wide. "And now I'm off to Khabarovsk," he announced boastfully out ahead, making wide and important sweeps with his hands in some sort of hurry.

Abruptly he halted. His expression was anxious, he was looking mournfully down at the ground. "I? What am I?" he asked himself bunching his fingers in front of his nose. "I'm a bug," he replied with a kind of false despair and went resolutely on his way, "but I'm off to Khabarovsk all the same."

Melkior moved into the shadow of the monument to poet Petar Preradović to let Ugo pass.

But Ugo halted in front of the statue. The bronze poet held a pencil and sheet of paper; awaiting inspiration, he was staring at the front of the building opposite.

"I say, Petar, sir, do you know what *tartalom* means . . . in Hungarian?" Ugo asked him; watching him provocatively from down below, he waited a moment for the poet to reply. "You don't, do you? You think it's some kind of Greek hell, ha-ha. . . . It means *content*. So much for today. Take it down," and he turned to leave, only to spin back right away: "One more thing, Petar—I'm a bug. That's off the record. Goodbye."

Melkior gave Ugo time to make some headway, then followed him.

Where's he coming back from? From . . . *her*? he thought with hesitation.

But "she is not there—she's not to be found *there* anymore," ATMAN had said. So, where is she now . . . now that it's my *turn*? The *turn* wrested a profound sigh from him.

"I? What am I?" asked Ugo of the entire city that slept on behind darkened windows and cared not a whit. . . .

Yes, indeed—what is he? wondered Melkior. All right, I'm Eustachius . . . although that's not quite clear either . . . but what is he, the Parampion, Ugo, Mr. Kalisto's son? And the city doesn't care, the city (Melkior was having his joke) which has the honor . . . who knows? . . . does anyone know what he is, the Parampion, Ugo, *Misterkalistosson?* Or what he might yet become? Approach with caution! Because later on, if he became a He, what might we be in for?—fear or shame, depending on whether he would be lenient or not. Today he's a bug—but what about tomorrow? Hey nonny noe, does anyone know?

"I? I'm a bug!" Ugo kept informing the sleeping city of his minuscule despair.

. . . Or his dreadful threat, hey nonny noe, does anyone know? went on Melkior with his joke, but less vigorously now—after all, who knows?

A thick jet of water had blocked Ugo's way and was hissing

threateningly, would not let him pass. The joking workmen had used their hose to stop *the bug*. He was trying to maneuver his way past the watery reptile, to distract its attention and scuttle away, but the arching reptile was rearing at him again and again. The little game had been going on for some time.

"Esteemed hose-wielding working men," Ugo addressed the workmen, opening the rally, "with this mighty weapon in your hands . . ."

Why did he cut his speech short? Melkior was unable to make it out from his distance. Look, he'd started a quiet conversation with them; the workmen had taken a break, turned the water off, they were laughing, thumping him on the back. There, he was already having a cigarette with them! Honestly, there must be some dark force on his side! What did I say? He'll win them over, too. He wins everyone over, men and women, Parampion the Conqueror! And he does it using what? His eyes, his mouth (his fillings!), his words, his gestures . . . all of it fraudulent. He felt like shouting *across there*: "The man's lying!" And what would have happened?—They'd only stone me, that is to say they'd sweep me away with the water from their *mighty* hose, the hosers!

Envy shook him, like that, at a distance. *He* was "in the circle of his family" over there, among people, among *his own*. They were patting him on the back and he was laughing at them in his snotty nostrils, amusing himself, mocking them. "Working men!"

What is it they see in him? Melkior was disbelieving ATMAN, now. What she sees in him is an entertainer, a monkey, a romp. He had drunk his fill at her place. They'd taken back sausages, bread, booze. . . . Two couches: now you come to me, *not* like that, visit me on my couch, Mr. Romper . . . wait, not right away, court me a bit first. Liver-paste smears on the white bedsheets, soak one end of the towel, what will the washerwoman say? Perhaps it was at the very same moment . . . as "Adam and Eve" (before Coco broke down the door) . . . perhaps it was at the same moment that we were *romping?*

Melkior fingered Enka's key in his pocket with pleasure. . . . But he's got the key to her flat! He showed it to me! he replied to a voice that was trying to console him.

But over there, around the hose, the idyll seemed to have ended. Well, there you are, I knew he was conning them . . . just to cadge a couple of cigarettes!

Ugo was quickly moving away from the reach of the hose; he was now revealing his deceit:

"Working men . . . proletariat . . ." he trumpeted at them with pursed lips, insultingly, sounding like an inflated balloon as it expels the air, "Come on, proletariat, spray me . . ."

They didn't hesitate: in the blink of an eye they pointed the hose his way, took aim and opened the valve. The mighty jet shot vengefully forth at Ugo. Will it reach him . . . will it reach him? . . . Melkior rooted for the avenging hose.

Then Ugo let out a cry of pain: he had been hit. His hat spun in the air. The workmen shouted "Hooray" like gunners hitting their target. The quickness of the revenge gave them back their self-assurance and a taste for malevolent cackling.

They laughed at their dripping adversary.

"Long live capitalism! Down with surplus value! Long live the First of May devotions!" shouted Ugo in a kind of hysterical despair.

The workmen laughed loftily at the shouts. "Howl on, bud." They no longer heeded him—they went on washing the street.

The pleasure of the victor, thought Melkior. He was no longer on their side . . . although . . . well, they were right. The wet clown in the arena. He felt Ugo's coldness on his own skin. That was what it had been like back at the stable with Nettle . . . wet, cold, next stop pneumonia, I shouldn't wonder. O Parampion, you jester, your place ought to be at the royal table. Who knows what oaf will be bumping into your skull with his spade . . . if, that is, your skull is still in one piece once *all this is over with and done*. And there will be no Hamlet to ask, "Whose was it?" "A whoreson mad fellow's it was. . . . A pestilence on him for a mad rogue! This same skull, sir, was the Parampion's skull." "Let me see (Hamlet takes the skull)—

Alas, poor Parampion!—I knew him, Eustachius: a fellow of infinite jest.—Where be your gibes now? your gambols? your songs? your flashes of merriment that were wont to set the table in a roar? Not one now, to mock your own grinning? quite chap-fallen?" Quite, good my prince.

Melkior approached the workmen with a pang of guilt: at least they're working . . . at that stupid wet job, while I . . . where am I coming from? As if they knew, he, too, expected to be drenched by the same human revenge. The rage of the deceived. Kill! Smash! Windows being smashed (a telling effect on stage), the acoustic symbol of revolt, revenge in the sound of shattering glass. You feel like the whole world is crashing down. An irritating sound, a sign of destruction and victory. What will the revolution be like?

Melkior made his contrite way past the jet of water sluicing the street. The water spurted noisily past his ear wishing him a good night and pleasant dreams.

You're a tired man, said the water to him.

"Oh when will spring, when will spring send forth its tender shoots," recited Ugo sadly, sniffling. (He had been sniffling all winter, ever since the night the hose got the better of him.)

Cold, gray, rainy days. Military, uniform days. Soldiers moving, olive drab, uniform, much like the days, monotonous, bundled, miserable, hopeless soldiers. Marching by day, pounding their feet bravely; stealing out by night, soundlessly, stealthily, keeping unit strengths, directions, dispositions TOP SECRET. Melkior listened to the muted commands and countless feet treading cautiously and with fear at night. Going somewhere . . . which may turn out to be nowhere, nothing. What Kurt had sowed on their path. Sprouting now as nettles and shattered glass: a terrible pilgrimage . . .

They will reach a certain line and be told *halt*. By Nettle. *Count off—one-two. . . . Face down!* And there will they await *that day, Kurtsday*. The name day of Polyphemus the man-eating Cyclops celebrated with fierce shooting by his thunder-loving twin brother. War.

It is impossible for the blossoms of spring to bloom. To send forth green shoots and the fragrances of the freshly awakened Earth. To stretch a blue sky overhead. . . . The milk brother is no longer riding down the Milky Way. . . . Huge is the boulder with which Polyphemus has plugged the world's door: ruling inside are silence and darkness and terror at the one-eyed beast.

Melkior unravels and spins long tangled thoughts. Hungry winter gnaws at roots under the cover of snow, hissing nastily: you, too, will be gnawing roots before long. . . . You'll wish you could hide in earth like a worm, in water like a crab, under stone like a green pepper. . . . You say spring will not be sending forth its tender shoots. . . .—No, it's Ugo who says that . . .—. . . well, you refuse to look at the greenery, you'll close your eyes so as not to see it. . . .

Winter spoke like a soothsayer, like a witch. Melkior feared the advent of spring. "They'll start marching on Russia after the snows start to melt," Don Fernando had said the other day. "And before they do they'll say 'Good morning' to us here in the Balkans. Protect their right flank. And Vissarionovitch shoved his generals aside and signed the Pact!" Don Fernando laughed bitterly.

They had been discussing this at the Corso Café. They were in the know.

"The snows, sure . . . but what about the Pripet Marshes?" said Melkior; he knew a thing or two himself.

Don Fernando laughed.

"The marshes . . . and the business with Napoleon—oh yes, now that is sure to stop them." Don Fernando was mocking him. "Berezina," he laughed.

Why did he strike this conversation up with me? Melkior had recently heard in the office, from the people on the Foreign Desk, about the Pripet Marshes. They can't have made that up—everyone was counting on the marshes.

"They are counting on the marshes," Melkior said.

"The marshes?" scoffed Don Fernando. "And Tolstoy's War and Peace."

Melkior abandoned the pointless conversation. He knew nothing apart from the marshes. Well, the Russians will bring them to heel somehow, won't they? There's a hundred and eighty million of them! A Chinese calculation. As for us (he thought of himself and shuddered), we'll only be a mere mouthful for Polyphemus the man-eating Cyclops. . . . *He grabbed another two men and devoured them for breakfast* sounded like a joke.

Once the snows melt . . . and they'll deal with us when spring sends forth its tender shoots.

ATMAN had gone, moved on goodness knows where. He might have known all about it, down to the very date . . . he was going by the calendar, spring had "officially" come. Kurt and ATMAN . . . Melkior was now putting two and two together . . . they had gone.

They'd "opened up for business" across from the 35th's barracks. . . . Hang on, when was it that ATMAN took up lodgings downstairs? . . . two years back . . . or was it three? Well, Mrs. Ema ought to know, she was one of his first clients. The Cozy Corner dated from that same time. The same "inspiration." Who would ever have figured that one out—a chiromantist and a tavern, worlds apart. An observation post at ATMAN's: the "clients" were keeping an eye on the barracks, every bit of information counts. No one was thinking about things that way. Apart from Don Fernando (had he really recruited Maestro?)—he would give *them* all their come-uppance. . . . He could sniff out the bastards from miles away. All— *preventively!*

While *she* . . . Melkior's heart contracted achingly . . . Mata Hari! Execution at dawn. The small courtyard of the army prison. Eight riflemen, Nettle in command. He has in fact asked permission to "finish off the bitch" himself. Eight gun barrels aimed at her heart. Her false, traitorous heart! Implacable Melkior. Really? she thinks quickly, cunningly. Are they really going to shoot me? She tries to wiggle her hips under the skirt; she thrusts out her chest, pushes her breasts forward . . . the sergeant's a man after all . . . Nettle sees only *the bitch*, he is no man . . . Melkior! . . . Melkior! . . . will give his blood, ATMAN said . . . Melkior . . .

Melkior looks away, gives the order—*Fire!* The salvo in him resounds dully, as if underground—Viviana is dead.

He stood up from the sofa with relief.

I have buried my dead love, said the poet Sima Pandurović . . . he said as he approached the window. Cold, cold, my girl, said Othello after he had strangled Desdemona. Cold, cold . . .

Rain was falling on wretched, bare, *dead* branches.

. . . without love and deceitful spring . . . he watched raindrops on the glass pane . . . sliding down . . . I have shot my false love . . .

News vendors were hawking a special edition. Passersby grabbed the papers from their hands and greedily thrust their heads between the pages then and there.

The animals are feeding . . . that was what it looked like to Melkior from up above. The pigs have had fresh swill poured into their trough.

He grabbed another two men and devoured them for dinner . . . because it looked like evening. The spring morning has gone dusky with rain, with sorrow, with eyes peering into the dark. The *little old man* is now saying to the *giant:* musht be shome shenshation or other, eh, *bud,* sheeing azh they've put out an ekshtra edition?—Gr, could be, replies the *giant.*—Perhapsh the Germansh have landed in England?—No. The *giant* is on the side of the English; he defended the *George Fifth* that time. . . .—What maksh you sho sure they haven't? You alwayzh know it all! the *little old man* is querulous. —I do.—You can't know everything.—I just do, see?—Shee, shee, shee, laughs the *little old man.*

There was the sound of conversation on the stairs; it was carried on the wave of some kind of mirth.

"Put up or shut up, heh-heh. . . ." That was the judge.

"Might is right, they ought to have known that from the start." The lawyer from the first floor.

"Better late than never. (Another proverb! Lovers of folklore.) What matters is now we're safe and sound. They could've squashed the lot of us like . . . They've shown considerable patience, if you ask me."

"Considerable indeed. After all, you can't sneeze over here without them knowing, heh-heh. . . ."

"Heh-heh . . ."

They parted in brotherly satisfaction. The judge was on his way up to the third floor, humming like a happy man. What matters is that now we're safe and sound.

Melkior let him climb up and enter his flat; he had no wish to meet the man. But he dropped his umbrella coming out. The judge stuck his head out at the sound: he was looking for someone to share his joy with.

"Did you hear the news?"

They've attacked Russia! In the same flash of thought he imagined the Stranger trekking his lonely unhappy way through the world. . . .

"You don't know?" the judge was fervently preparing his revelation. "We've signed on to the Tripartite Pact! Job done! Here, look, signed at the Belvedere Castle in Vienna," he was waving the newspaper.

"Now we're safe and sound," said Melkior ironically, but the judge missed the irony; being safe was a serious thing!

"Exactly what I said to that fellow downstairs!" he was glad to have found a kindred spirit. "Now, you see," he brought his voice down to gossip level, "he is more on Hitler's side, while I . . . frankly . . . so long as they leave us alone. What's the sense of small fry like us getting caught up in this, am I right?"

"Snug as a bug in a rug," said Melkior.

"You said it . . ." laughed the judge; the flash of humor rounding off the pleasure. "Hitler and Churchill can go to it and . . . why not?"

"Sure, they can indeed go and . . ."

"They might as well hash it out, I mean."

"So do I—let them put up their dukes. But it must be said Hitler *has* got things sorted out in Germany," Melkior offered him the thought wholeheartedly.

"Yes, that's the truth," the judge took it up readily. "You've got to give the devil his due. Only," he hesitated for a moment, watching Melkior with a tinge of suspicion, "they often go a little too far, don't they? On the other hand, that man with his Bolshevism . . ."

"That's why it's best to do like the Americans . . ."

"Yes! You took the words right out of my mouth!" exclaimed the judge in delight.

Heavens, why we agree on just about everything! Melkior sneered at himself. We are all for middle-of-the-road, no risk, no danger, all in the circle of the family . . . Bingo, Parcheesi . . . let the lunatics kill each other.

"We are all for middle-of-the-road," said Melkior out loud.

"You're so right! Not the left or the right—the golden mean."

"The soundest way there is."

"And the most prudent."

They said goodbye as wise men.

"Signed on to the Pact," and Kurt's gone, ATMAN gone . . . something weird is going on, all right. Signing on to the Pact means no war (here). . . . Does it? He was asking himself in a formal tone, as if it were Don Fernando doing the asking. He was smiling like Don Fernando did when putting questions to him, derisively. But to go back to our . . . So you think it does?—Well, given that we've signed on to the Tripartite. . . .—We who?—Well, we . . . the country.—"We, the country." Are you telling me you're a country?—No, I'm no country.—What are you then?—A *sensitive individual*, you called me that yourself.—All right then, *sensitive individual*, can you now go back to your third floor and knock on the individual-within-the-circle-of-his-family's door: Hey, how about a game of Parcheesi, now that we are safe and sound . . .

He very much wanted to run into Don Fernando.

He set off for the Corso; he's bound to be there at this historic hour. They must discuss the latest news, they must do it for the sake of mankind. Pupo despised them, the "café table revolutionaries," "anarcho-individualistic intellectuals." That's how his pigeonholes are labeled, said Don Fernando, but Pupo did turn to them when he needed them. And they listened to him. Don Fernando made fun of Pupo's "pigeonholes"—little monk, defrocked priest, careerist . . .—but he listened to Pupo all the same. What was the power that Pupo carried around in his "pigeonholes"? Don Fernando naturally refused to recognize any "forces" there, he was a *free agent*, and yet he complained about "slowness," about "cataloguing" (he seemed to have mentioned some such word once) while one should strike immediately—in advance, even, wherever there popped up the merest suspicion of any kind of *look* in any eyes that might betoken a possible criminal. He was impatient. He saw a man drowning; one should throw him a plank, or even a straw or at least a shred of *personal hope* . . . but Pupo said: one plank will solve nothing, the thing to do is cultivate a whole forest. And Don Fernando dutifully proceeded to plant saplings . . . but thinking all the while: who's going to bother if there's no personal hope at all? A forest is, Come on, old boy, sacrifice yourself for future people you don't even know! For Mankind. For someone named Kikuko who will be born two hundred years from now. Give a kidney, give an eye, give blood, give three meters of intestine . . . give, give, give your life for a future little Japanese boy. You drop dead—long live the future Kikuko! He will know the exact number of atoms in the dot on the *i*, he will be traveling at the speed of light, he will be eating pills for food. He will be manufactured in a test tube by Professor Bombashi, who will raise the pumpkin-head (for Kikuko will be more or less all head) under a glass bell. Under the bell will be, among other things, a library of miniature books. Kikuko will spend his youth in space colonies to familiarize himself with the universe. He will travel from planet to planet, engage in applied science. He will collaborate with Martians in vacuuming up moon dust, in draining extra heat from Mercury, he will take part in putting up an electromagnetic *cordon sanitaire* around our solar system for protection against the invading hordes from the upper galaxies . . .

There was commotion out in front of the Corso. A group of people had gathered, making a semicircle in front of the café windows. Melkior halted and took a casual look: he could see nothing above the heads.

"Has something happened?" he asked one of the spectators.

"It's this man . . ." this was all he knew.

"What man?"

The spectator gestured with his head: "The one at the window . . ." and accommodatingly stepped aside to let Melkior pass.

Standing there was Maestro. He had his hands pressed on the window and his face against the glass, as if watching something inside. A thin streak of blood was dribbling down the pane . . .

The bleeding is from his face. Melkior passed a palm over his own face; he was removing the blush of an irrational shame. Poor old Maestro . . .

"Where did he, er . . .? Did he fall?" he asked the man next to him.

"No. Somebody struck him . . . in there, in the café . . . punched him. Then the waiters threw him out. . . ."

"Punched him? Why?"

"Oh, something political . . ."

"Political? No way! The guy inside, the one with the woman, the young actor, what's his name . . ." the man nodded toward the café interior, "and the old geezer got caught up with them . . . that's why he got the knuckle sandwich."

Melkior looked inside. Indeed, there on the soft green settee under the long wall mirror, sat Freddie and, next to him, her legs crossed, Viviana. They were facing the window on which Maestro was glued, but were paying no attention to him; *that* had nothing to do with them. They were carefree and happy: laughing, chatting, displaying the luxury and beauty of their persons behind the glass . . . two laughs, two blossoms, two precious objects . . .

Melkior shared Maestro's pain and humiliation. "You're next"; why had ATMAN said that? She had never even broken it off with *this one!* There was the proof, in the lovable tête-à-tête after the inglorious bloodshed. Freddie had a dirty, insidious look in his eyes . . . according to Don Fernando. But Melkior remembered Viviana was "dead" and squelched his pain; there only remained the odor of the snuffed deathbed candle. . . . *If I quench thee, thou flaming minister, I can again thy former light restore, should I repent me* . . . Othello had said . . .

Maestro was still bleeding down the glass; the poor bug squashed against the pane.

"Has he been standing like this long?" he asked the political-explanation man.

"I don't know—I just got here."

"And yet you say it's 'something political'?"

"That's what they said . . . he'd been shouting in there that they were all spies, every last one of them . . . Well, he might not have been entirely wrong," continued the man in a whisper, looking out suspiciously into the glittering café, "this is where all kinds of city lowlifes hang out."

Melkior kept an eye out for Don Fernando. His "crowd" was not there in "his" corner, which was instead occupied by two corpulent ladies in expensive fox stoles who were browsing foreign illustrated magazines with café-esque dignity.

Lady spies, joked Melkior . . . but I wouldn't put my hand into the fire on it. . . .

A waiter was drawing the curtain in front of Maestro's face. The show was clearly over. Maestro, too, seemed to have taken this for the end (as spectator or actor?): he came unglued from the window. He left behind the imprint of a bloody mask on the glass. The audience gave a slight sigh of shock, surprise, possibly pleasure even: serves the drunken scum right—a good bashing's the best medicine! The "scene" was more engaging than the accession to the Tripartite Pact: they generally kept their newspapers folded on their behinds.

Maestro spitefully turned his bloodied face toward them and growled *sangrrre!* like a hardened bloodthirsty fiend. . . . Those in the front row stepped back in fear, moved aside, made way. . . . An awesome face, blood thirst; nose swollen, mouth bloodied; covered in blood up to the ears. A savage look—the vampire has guzzled his fill of gore.

It's all from the nose, concluded Melkior with relief. But where can he go now, with his snout all bloody? Of course he was drunk: he was walking like . . . what the hell, he knows only too well where he'll end up. He'll be arrested by the first copper who happens by, thought Melkior. They're aroused by blood like wild beasts. They'll run you in even if the blood is your own. Prove it! Where are your wounds? The blood's from my nose. And you'll get one on the nose, so there, as counterproof. So what if it's yours, blood is shed for Kink and countwy, not by brawling in cafés. Get your ass into the Black Maria! And in clambers Maestro . . .

Where the hell had he got to now? He had slipped out of Melkior's field of vision. The spectators were dispersing. Boring, really. All the fuss over a bloody nose. A nosebleed, hey!

"Something happened?" ask the latecomers.

"Nothing much. Somebody's caught one across the snout, spilled a little blood . . ." The informant even spat at that point, blood from the nose was disgusting, dirty cowardly blood.

"Oh. I'd thought it was . . ."

"So did I . . . Well, never mind, there'll be order imposed here soon enough," said the informant hopefully.

Melkior was about to ask him . . . but he was afraid for his own blood. Once order is imposed, no blood will be spilled from the nose. You will be able to show your wounds. You will display your severed head and your hands covered in pure blood, it won't be from the nose like this, disgusting. *The informant* will not spit in disappointment. That will be to his taste: pure and plentiful. And instead of those bloodied, the police will be arresting the pale, the bloodless: afraid, eh? And what're you afraid of, eh? A dissenter, right? . . . and they'll spill your blood to show that the thin, fear-diluted blood you have been carrying in your heart with such anxiety is proof of your having been on the *opposing side.* . . .

"Don't hold it against me, Eustachius, that I should be waiting for you in here," spoke a battered Maestro from a dark doorway. "Don't look so surprised, don't lie, Eustachius the Truthful, that you've only just discovered me. You were watching me *over there* already . . . I saw you, too, but I didn't want to compromise you."

"Sure, all right, but what we ought to do now is get some water to . . ."

". . . to bathe our wounds like chastened warriors," Maestro attempted a joke. "I'm well aware of it, dear Eustachius—all the same, I'd like to wear this mystagogic mask of cannibal religion a little longer. I'm sure it flatters me, aren't you? I saw myself in the glass, partly, over there, but it must be more impressive in profile—have a look."

"Leave it for now, Maestro, damn it!" said Melkior angrily. "Your nose is still bleeding. Have you a handkerchief?"

"A handkerchief? You're asking me the way Othello asked the all-pure Desdemona. Wait, I'm not joking. I have no handkerchief. What do you need one for anyway? This is a trick to put me from my suit."

"What suit?"

"Oh, that's a quote, Eustachius . . . but there is indeed a suit. It's because of you I fared like this. I'd been looking for you all evening and I ran into . . ."

"But why did he . . ."

"How do you know it was a he? Perhaps it was a she? . . . but with his fore hoof, so it was in fact a he, which puts you in the right. As to the how and why, it's a long story, Eustachius, and right now I'm not in the mood . . ."

"All right then, let's go."

"Go where, Eustachius? You're always keen on going somewhere. As if *somewhere* else was *something* else. And apart from that, I can't very well go anywhere before my nose subsides."

"Oh, I see—it'll subside right here in the doorway?"

"It won't, but it'll have a rest. People keep looking at it: the return of the wounded warrior. . . ."

"Here's my handkerchief, staunch the warrior's bleeding; it's dripping on you, you're bloody all over. Right. Now let's go."

"Not in this rain, shall we, Eustachius?" Maestro was reluctant about coming out. But he can't stay here either, not with this "mystagogic" mask, thought Melkior.

"It's not raining very hard. And we have an umbrella." He did manage to draw him out of the doorway.

They went down the street huddled under the umbrella.

"You know what, faithful Eustachius? . . . I'm going to bite off his ear, you'll see," muttered Maestro into the blood-stained handkerchief. "This blood shall be avenged."

Planning his revenge like a little boy . . . but how does he propose to bite his ear *off*?

"How do you propose to bite his ear off? That's not easy . . . not to mention that he simply won't let you."

"That's what I'm figuring out right now . . ."

Maestro was indeed thinking as he breathed damply, with mucus, through the sodden handkerchief.

"Here's how: first I'll pretend I've forgiven him, lull his suspicions . . ."

"Oh, give it a miss," said Melkior with a kind of disgust.

"Give it a miss and let evil reign supreme! Don Fernando's right —preventive action is in order." So he had been telling Maestro about his "science." But it was clear that Maestro was aligning himself with "science" temporarily only because of the insult . . . otherwise he didn't give a hoot for "science."

"So you think this *preventive action* . . ."

"Well, it has its weak points, of course, but in essence . . . the idea of eliminating a bastard before he's done some evil deed . . ."

"But what kind of evil deed could be done by that stupid . . ."

"Stupid, stupid!" cried Maestro, "it's precisely the stupid who are capable of it! You don't think Erasmus of Rotterdam would have smacked me one, do you?"

Melkior laughed.

"Funny, is it? Everything I say is funny to . . . Or is it my proboscis? Yes, well, I am a joker! Circus clowns wear snouts like mine. *Laugh and the whole world laughs with you* . . ." muttered Maestro through the handkerchief.

"Oh, look up, Eustachius, is this the moon showering its charms on us? Everything's gone blue, *au clair de la lune* . . . Marvelous . . ."

They had entered the realm of the Give'nTake's neon light. Maestro took a somnambulistic step toward the blue domain; with an alert motion Melkior pulled him back, stopping him at the very threshold of heaven.

"Oh how painful . . ." groaned Maestro.

"You're not going in looking like this, are you?"

"Just a peep, anxious Eustachius," Maestro all but pleaded. "I need Ugo urgently, for . . ."

"You stay here, I'll have a look," said Melkior somewhat sharply.

"Don't come back empty-handed, Eustachius, I'm badly on the down-and-out . . ."

Thénardier did not deign to spare so much as a glance at the "regular." Ugo was not there . . . and he'll be lying to me, saying he'd been with *her*, sighed Melkior.

"Has the Parampion been in tonight?" he asked sweetly of Thénardier.

"No," replied Thénardier arrogantly without looking up from his dirty notebook. "What are you waiting for? Get lost! And stop coming in here looking for each other! I'm sick and tired of the lot of you! Troublemakers!" he abruptly fell to shouting. "Rabble like this, you could end up in the poorhouse . . ." Melkior heard behind him Thénardier's remark to his *good* customers.

He came out disgraced and terribly unhappy. Why the hell did I get involved with *them* again?

"Eustachius the Indispensable, what about the shot to shot . . .?" asked a disappointed Maestro; he had been trembling all the time, hoping for his shot.

"Well, you said yourself you'd switched to beer!" snapped Melkior angrily.

"Did I mention drink?" Maestro was being innocently sheepish. "I only asked you about the crazy Parampion . . ."

"Why did you send me in to take a peek in the first place? Didn't you have a clash with him recently, cut him up with glass?" remembered Melkior suddenly.

"Glass, yes . . . but why? Anyway, it was drinking glasses, not just glass. But the reasons are nothing compared to the blood friendship that now binds us. We have already embraced each other and forgiven everything. It was precisely the spilled blood that bound us! Spilled for a common cause . . . For yours, for your cause, too, ungrateful Eustachius. But it galls me to speak of it now. Perhaps later . . . Tell you what—I'm going back to my abode," he declared suddenly and started off right away, only to turn back and pull Melkior along after him. "Come with me, Eustachius, I'm rather wobbly on my feet. Could be blood loss, what do you think? You asked me, what suit? The suit to come back to my place. You promised ages ago! You'll see everything is . . . simple there. I'll make you some hot chocolate, and I'll have . . . doesn't matter what I'll have. I'll be looking at you, if you agree, and won't open my mouth. If you don't feel like conversing, we'll just sit there in silence, like saints in a church. Me thinking my thoughts and you thinking yours; who knows, perhaps our thoughts converse by themselves as soon as they're out of our heads without us being any the wiser. What do we know about our thoughts anyway? We know they mean this or that, but how they come into being, how they move from one head into another, how they work their way into various pots (a Papin's digester, for instance) and books and machines. . . . Therefore, I say, it may not be necessary to flog thoughts with the tongue at all. . . . What matters is that two heads should be there in the same bag . . . or same dwelling, Eustachius the Wise, and by *dwelling* I mean a kind of sympathetic relation . . . or antipathetic, whichever you prefer."

"What do you say we take a tram?" interrupted Melkior, for Maestro was definitely having trouble walking. "Where you live is a long way from here."

"Never! Even if all my blood gushed straight out of my nose," protested Maestro most resolutely, indeed with some fear. "But it won't because . . . your magic handkerchief has done its job . . . and I'm not bleeding any more. And my nose feels like a tomato, it's mushroomed over half the world: I can only see up, not down. But if I look up I'll see the umbrella, and if I look down . . . what's there to see? Thénardier in the thrall of 'technological progress': the siphon . . . that great invention!"

Maestro was laughing bitterly, mocking with ruthless sarcasm. But, thought Melkior, what is it he's mocking? A pressure cooker? The pot calling the kettle black. . . . The senseless waste of spiritual energy in the manufacture of pots, machines, even books? Flogging thoughts with the tongue. Thoughts conversing by themselves in a sympathetic relation . . . it was clearly a flattering invitation to have a talk. Melkior wished to get him indoors, under a roof, as soon as possible.

Maestro was gesticulating, drawing the attention of the passersby to his blood-stained face. Melkior was using his umbrella to hide from people's looks, he was protecting himself from embarrassment. He was in a hurry to reach Maestro's "dwelling" and get rid of him.

"But you, fleet-footed Eustachius, have launched into a marathon race! What's your rush? You don't happen to be one of those impatient ones who are forever after some *solution* or other, do you? Easy does it, Eustachius, you need to walk at a thinker's pace, peripatetically."

"It's raining, man! We ought to get somewhere dry!" said Melkior impatiently.

"Somewhere high and dry? Man, we *are* under a roof! *Spreading far above our heads, black as dreadful night* . . . that's how the purple poem *The Umbrella* runs. Has anyone written the poem about the umbrella? No? Of course not . . . *black as night snuffed* . . ." declaimed Maestro using pathos to summon his next line. "Lend us a hand, Eustachius, I've hit a snag, it's a pathos-ridden ascent . . . *black as night snuffed* . . . never you mind, I'll write it later." He fell silent for a moment, wiping his nose. "Right—let Cyrano's humiliated comrade breathe his fill of the evening's rainy air," he took the handkerchief off his nose and inhaled greedily. "They're right—contact with Nature . . . even by way of the nose, is contact with—that is, a stab at—Nature . . . by which I mean nothing but the pure fragrance of dainty flowers. . . . Hey, I've come to the conk-lusion it's pretty stupid to tote about such a big conch of a conk. And duels are a thing of the past, more's the pity, I can't do a Bergerac and . . . I would have challenged him to one . . . without using a glove—just giving him a plain old slap in the face . . . *à la barrière* and may the best man win! As it is, all you get is Bergerac, an honorless hunk of nose, leaking snot beneath an umbrella. You rode to a duel in a coach: black redingote, top hat, pistol-case—heroism and toughened honor. Nowadays drivers stink of petrol and fight with their bare fists. En garde, sir, en garde! But the driver spits on his palms and then it's whack! in the chops—there's progress for you, Eustachius my dear companion."

"And you would challenge him to a fencing duel?" grinned Melkior.

"So I would, Eustachius! Whooosh! and off with his ear!" Maestro swung his saber at Freddie and took keen delight at the sight of Freddie's severed ear flying off. "And then a cat that was following us (cats can sense this sort of thing), that was on the lookout for scraps of flesh . . ." giving his fancy free rein, relishing his revenge. "Or what do you say I lop off his nose? The effect's even greater! and then the cat . . ."

He'll have read this in Edmond About, thought Melkior, a Croatian translation of *A Notary's Nose* was published not long ago. . . .

"A noseless Lothario, ha-ha," rejoiced Maestro. "Cat got his nose!"

They had reached the unpaved, muddy, dark reaches of the city outskirts.

Dogs started barking at them from small fenced front gardens.

"You'd better take the lead now, Maestro," said Melkior, "I can't see a thing, nor do I know the way . . ."

"This way, just follow me along these fences," Maestro directed him with assurance. "Only mind the barking guardians of private property, they're very eager. If you so much as touch the fence they'll think you want to steal a head of cabbage from their garden and they might trim your fingers for you. 'Hands off!' is what this barking means," prattled on Maestro tottering on ahead of Melkior. "And when an old muzzle starts snarling on the left, we're to turn right; he is the lighthouse in this nocturnal cruise. When he dies I don't know how I'll manage to find my way when in *a state of illumination*."

"They'll put up electric lights," chuckled Melkior.

"Electric lights . . . that's not *my* way," Maestro halted warningly. "If your *electric lights* was meant to provoke me, Eustachius, I can tell you it went wide of the mark." Although he was leading the way, Maestro was speaking very seriously. "I don't care much for people thinking my convictions backward and laughable. I'm capable of laughing better than any of you Parampionists, thank you very much."

"You took offense all the same, didn't you?"

"Well . . . not exactly. You can take offense if you're . . . disappointed, if you'd expected *something else* or . . . but that's beside the point. . . . That is to say, if you're promoting your ideas, seeking followers . . . and I don't give a tinker's for the whole ballgame, cherished Eustachius. I'm not being ironic at all when I say *cherished*, because . . ." Maestro seemed to hesitate for a moment before deciding to keep something to himself. "Careful now, there's a ditch here with a lot of mud in it, they're laying an idea of sewage-pipe order, ha-ha, you'll have to jump across it. Hop!" Maestro swung his arms and jumped across, "right, from now on it's all safe going, down along the fences." He was silent for a moment, struggling with the mud in which his feet were sinking. "I've got you into a nice mess, haven't I, Eustachius—quite literally so."

"Isn't there some other way?"

"Yes there is—a roundabout road. *Electric lights* and all—but I wanted to show you *my* way, my dark way. Perhaps it will help you understand me better. Here he is, snarling—now turn right, Eustachius, after me." Indeed a dog did heave a geriatric wheeze, as if too feeble to bark. "Did you hear that *memento* along my way? *Dies irae*. He's got nothing against me, he only gives voice to guide me. The lighthouse keeper. And up there, look up, Eustachius. . . . Ah, the umbrella! Fold the umbrella, look up . . . those black lines, those staves, empty of notes, across the sky, That's *It*—the Powerline. You, of course, find my hate of those copper wires ridiculous?"

"I'm already used to your bizarre views. . . ."

"But I'm not after anything bizarre, kindhearted Eustachius—I genuinely hate the thing," said Maestro very quietly, indeed with a kind of modesty.

For some time they trudged squelching on across the slippery mud. Maestro had trouble pulling his feet from the clay dough.

Melkior had to help his unstable guide several times. A kind of mud Inferno, thought Melkior, with Virgil somewhat tipsy and crazed. He has changed—he is not mad for the sake of madness but with a sincere and true madness. Perhaps the spirochaetae are adding to it by completing their arduous work. Gnawing asunder the last of the filaments for the proper connections, as in a telephone exchange . . . *wrong number, this is a private residence*, yes, yes, the last digit's *four, four* . . . I still have Enka's key . . . Put it in a small oblong box (toothpaste?) and send it by registered mail. . . . But leave that for tomorrow, leave it for tomorrow . . . without a word, thank you for *everything*, I think we are now *quits*. Even if she writes another letter, if her words bring those waves of goose bumps down the thighs and desire starts snailing up the spine . . . it should all be shaken off—*apage! apage!*—like Saint Anthony, the anchorite of Thebes. Very good, sir, but what if she appears in person? Shall we do *apage!* Like . . . the anchorite saint, chop off a finger on the block like Father Sergius . . . (the film with Mozhukhin, what rot!), shall we *refrain*, following the doctrine of the aged Count Leo . . .

"So, Eustachius," spoke up Maestro, "this is where we leave the fences. We strike out diagonally across this little field, down the path, toward that black silhouette—There Is My Home," he finished in a tuneless version of the Czech national anthem.

Over the herd of low hovels that had dug themselves into the ground up to their knees in modesty and impoverished shame there loomed self-assuredly but quite unconvincingly a dark five- or six-story monster . . .

"What's that thing doing here?" said Melkior in surprise.

"It used to be a storage facility for the bastards of the city's bon vivants," replied Maestro, the Inferno guide. "This is where unwed mothers used to wait for the fruits of their sinful loves to be born. Here bawled the unacknowledged counts, barons, dukes, in the arms of their mothers, crazy virgins. Of course, everything in noble penury, in rags worn with dignity. At this point, few of the old-timers are on speaking terms with each other, they're like Russian émigrés —it's beneath them to speak to *just anyone*. Now and then they jump from the top stories; they're the *real thing*, the ones who don't go for suicide notes and shit like that. But there are also the snobs—jumping from the second floor, feet first of course, into the grass. Breaking bones, getting their heads smashed . . . They leave their 'life stories' behind with detailed 'pedigrees'—eager for a headline, of course . . ."

"And you write them up . . ."

"Yes, I do them that small favor—they take some risk after all . . . Some of them actually succeed."

"Why, it's . . . How can you live here?" Melkior was horrified, ". . . it's a suicide house!"

"No, why? It's a kindergarten!" laughed Maestro with malevolent glee. "You say what you like, it has a certain charm all its own. The charm of the waltz. The *upper-story* types don't do it all that often, and the *lower-story* types . . . heh-heh . . . There's this 'Baron Sigismund.' *Si-gis-mund is not to blaaame for setting girrrls' hearts aflaaame . . .*" all of a sudden Maestro launched into a hoarse rendition of a number from the operetta *The White Horse Inn*, but presently grew serious again ". . . who has jumped grassward twice. The first time it was trouble with the ladies. He wears a pencil moustache and a monocle, all our fifty-year-old virgins (we've got a lot of those) are crazy about him; there was nothing for him to do but jump. The second time he jumped because of the fourth partition of Poland, the autumn before last. A nobleman and a knight! Knows all of Sienkiewicz by heart—but doesn't know a word of Polish. *Kobieta* and *herbata*—the two Polish words I know—mean *woman* and *tea*, respectively . . . I also know the word *bardzo* . . . it doesn't mean *quickly* the way *brzo* means in Croatian. . . . I forget what it means. *Szesdziesiat piec* means sixty-five. . . . Sigismund doesn't even know what *szesdziesiat piec* means, but that doesn't keep him from attempting suicide over Poland, Pan Podbipieta strike him. But what was I going to . . . oh yes, I was going to say this is a true 'home of the gentry,' indeed a house of knights."

"Speaking of which, how's the knightly nose?" Melkior halted at the entrance.

"I'd already forgotten about it. But it seems to be feeling quite well in its larger-than-life-size like a statue in the middle of a town square. But what have you stopped for, Eustachius? Afraid of the dark in the stairwell? Wait, I'm going to strike a light; you can go up after me."

"I'm not coming up with you, Maestro," Melkior barely managed to spit out the words; he knew they were going to sadden Maestro. "I'm sorry, but I really . . ."

"What, you don't mean to come up?" mumbled Maestro in poignant disappointment. "And I thought . . . You promised me so long ago! I'd been looking for you all evening, there was this Corso business, too . . ." he seemed to have pointed to his nose in the dark, "and now you won't . . ."

Melkior felt sorry. It was as if Maestro had put out a hand, begging for alms. . . . Fear of loneliness? The suicide house? What is it he wants tonight? To put himself to death in a *brand new original medicinally pure* fashion? He spoke mockingly about jumping from *upper* and *lower* windows. He's against jumping.

"Do come, Eustachius, for half an hour only," pleaded Maestro. He plucked a candle stub out of his pocket and lit it. "Here, I'll walk ahead and light the way. . . . I won't keep you long." Melkior followed him upstairs. "And the way back . . . there's a roundabout, over there, a proper road. Pavements and electric lights," he laughed in a way that seemed almost shy.

The stairwell reeked of stale cabbage, urine, and unwashed women. How can you have any kind of "medicinally pure" death in here? Melkior was nauseated by the cocktail of smells.

Clambering up the stairs on the wall behind them were two huge, terrifying hunchbacks. Melkior glimpsed their escort out of the corner of his eye. He turned around: he saw two quiet, patient gorillas, long-armed, noseless . . . we're following you to the zoo.

"Have a look, Eustachius. Behind each of these doors," he gestured at a row of doors in long dark corridors, "lives an exemplar, usually single, of those bastard gentlefolk *in noble penury, in rags worn with dignity*. The life of a convent—the cell being what is known as a *room with cooking facilities*; independence fiscal and otherwise . . . I now recommend a quiet ascent," warned Maestro in a whisper, "we're entering the habitat of street vendors of holy pictures, picture postcards, and writing paper—but at this late hour they might offer us interesting collections of pictures for the single man. They serve (for those who like them) as inspiration for solipsistic pleasures—*Ramona, give my soul its peace and quiet . . .*"

Melkior cast a furtive glance at his gorilla: what was it doing? It hunched its back, compressed itself, poised. . . . Maestro lifted the candle, the creatures crouched on the wall, bowing to the light.

"Here, Eustachius, behind this door," whispered Maestro, "breathes the knightly soul of Baron Sigismund. If we hold our breath we might hear Andrzej Kmicic decapitating Tartars. Ssss . . ." he put his ear to the door. "No, Pan Wolodiowski's wife is dead—he's crying."

"What is he—mad?"

"Depends on your viewpoint. Do you find Don Quixote mad? This one is fond of knights, too. We've strayed too deep, Eustachius the Myrrh-Exuding, into belle-esprit-ism of the ovine variety. Grazing on daisies in meadows—*she loves me, she loves me not*—exactly like sheep and goats, like meek Bethlehem sheep. Dainty souls in quatrains, in crowns of sonnets, ahs and ohs and *love that never palls* . . . what a load of balls! Whereas they charged tanks armed with spears, *credo quia absurdum. . . .*"

"Who did?"

"Who? The knights, that's who! The Pans! Skrzetuski, Wolodiowski . . . never mind their names, the awakened forefathers! At Kutno, at Kutno was where the spearmen, the cavalrymen . . . we carried the story in our paper . . . went in against the Teutons, like Boleslaw the Crooked Mouth in the Middle Ages," Maestro crooked his own mouth in honor of the royal moniker.

Crooked Mouth—that one is missing from my Great Rulers list, thought Melkior.

"How long have you been such a knightly person then?"

"Perhaps since birth, Eustachius. I may be a Porphyrogenite, too, or a Leopold the Landless—this remains to be seen. You'll know me in my full glory yet. Here we are, Eustachius." Maestro held the candle aloft: halt! In the flickering candlelight, with its presence-of-death paraffin odor, there was a photograph stuck on the door: a bon vivant with a pencil moustache and a smile under a rakishly angled Maurice Chevalier straw hat.

"And this . . ."

". . . is me, God bless the master of this house. Dating from the age of the Charleston, Eustachius: *adieu, Mimi*. . . . In lieu of a visiting card with a nobleman's boar or some other ferocious animal. Enter my kingdom, Eustachius!" But Maestro bumped into something inside, in the dark; his candle went out in the draft when he opened the door. "Ah yes, the warning. Wait a moment." He was striking matches and looking for the candle, but the matches went out, too, in the gust of air.

"Please stay where you are, Eustachius. There are certain small warnings here by the door. It's my sober self in the morning asking a wardenlike question of my drunken self in the evening: where do you think you're going, you nitwit? Thus the small *reality* of a common table blocks my way to the door opposite, which could take me to eternity. Can you see the sky? Because all this, dear Eustachius, is taking place on the fourth floor, and my angelic wings are quite stunted. . . ." explained Maestro from the dark, now using the blind man's sense to grope for the oil lamp.

He'll knock it over, spill the oil, set the house afire. . . .

But Melkior's fears came to naught. Maestro lit the lamp quickly and with amazing dexterity as if he had flipped on a switch. "*Buona sera*," he said with a bow.

An odd mix of coffee and lamp oil smells wafted over Melkior from inside.

"Do sit down, Eustachius, anywhere you like. Everything's clean in here, that is to say the chairs and the chest are—but don't look at the floor, it's fertile soil, I'm planning to plant it with tomatoes."

The room was with a cooking stove, as he said, and the floor coated with dried mud. Soil, that is, probably fertile at that. But the seats of both chairs were freshly scrubbed, as was the lid of the enormous chest. What did he keep in there?

Melkior sat down on a chair. Perhaps the dismembered body of a woman? A victim of sadistic lust. . . . Has anyone seen Viviana? He looked around the room as if with an eye to discovering clues . . . bloodstains, a hair or two, a torn shred of an undergarment . . . He surprised himself with the thought—God, what rubbish!—and looked back at Maestro, confused, with a pang of guilt.

". . . perhaps since birth, even," Maestro had been saying while Melkior was not listening. "And why am I one of the prize exhibits in this museum? You think I'm not authentic . . . oh, oh, oh, I merit preservation in alcohol—mind, body, and all! They call it *compote* up at the clinic. If you didn't know, how will you ever be able to eat canned fruit again, when the plums, cherries, peach slices will . . . ah, *merde!* Medical science has befouled all of life. Reposing in alcohol is my destiny, even if only in pieces: some details of me are bound to get into the . . . alcohol compote. Damn it all, I should now heave a sigh of longing as befits a true-blue tippler!"

Melkior felt uneasy: set out in his imagination as if on shelves were a row of jars with severed ears, tongues, penises. . . . He gave a shudder. He wished he could get away.

"You're chilly, Eustachius. I'll stoke the stove straight away, get you warm in no time at all."

In one corner of the room stood a folded iron cot with a rolled straw mattress in it. Maestro pulled a whole sheaf of straw from it, fed it into the stove, arranged some cordwood on top and lit it all. The fire set up a mournful mumble under the iron burner, came to life in its grave, thought Melkior.

"Do you always pull straw from your . . ." he nearly said *grave* ". . . from your bed?"

"Indeed I do. Stupid, isn't it? And you spotted it right off. I steal from myself, dear Eustachius, like an imbecile out of Molière, only to end up sleeping on what used to be straw, on nothing but the little souls of the burnt straw. Once I even dreamed the burning souls. There were tens of thousands of them. You can well imagine how many I've burned, tantamount to some Spanish Inquisitor. There were all these little burning candles going around and around my bed, singing in piping female voices *requiem aeternam dona ei, Domine, et lux perpetua* . . . the '*lux perpetua*' coming from the straw! What a ridiculous business. I woke up in cold sweat."

He was priming the oil stove while he spoke. First he warmed it using denatured alcohol, then he pumped air in. The stove suddenly hissed, having gone out, releasing puffs of gaseous petroleum. The room filled at once with a heavy, stuffy smell.

Melkior coughed. He was breathing with difficulty, choking. He remembered Nettle's stable and feared he might faint.

"Might we open . . ." he mouthed in what was nearly his last gasp.

"Why should we, Eustachius the Welcome?" wondered Maestro carrying a lit match across the room. The match went out halfway across. He went back and struck a fresh one, which also went out en route; meanwhile the primus stove was eagerly hissing as it released petroleum stench.

"It's been airing all day, I've only just closed the window," said Maestro carrying yet another match across the room. It, too, went out, of course. But he was not at all miffed—he went back to strike another one . . . Melkior followed the insecure little flame with anxiety. . . .

"Why don't you strike a match there by the Primus instead of carrying it over?" he said in near-irritation.

"Ah, seeing to that, too, are you?" Maestro resented interference in his habits. "The matches are duds. Incidentally, it's not really much of an invention: carrying a flame on top of a toothpick! Kitchen Prometheanship!" The "Prometheanship" was what he snuffed the fresh match with: he had blasted out the word with such seething scorn and the tiny flame passed away like a premature baby.

"Everything smells of petroleum in here. . . ." grumbled Melkior.

"Everything?" asked Maestro with curious irony. "Ahh, Eustachius the Sensitive, you're acting like a royal personage visiting a poor subject. Hold your royal nose for an instant . . . there, it's lit!"

"And your cursed nose is ripe for a splash. Have you got a mirror?"

"So that's what it is! You're afraid of me . . . bloody as I am? What a physiognomy, eh? No, I've gone without a mirror for two decades, give or take. Since . . . the days of the Charleston. Why do I need one? To study the reflection of my beauty?"

"Why should I be afraid of you?" and yet an icy snake slithered up Melkior's back, why was he out looking for me tonight?

"Just saying," laughed Maestro and the swollen red nose made his smile mournful, clownish. "Children are afraid of ugly faces. I'm fond of you, Eustachius the Artless, and . . . perhaps for that very reason . . . am giving you a wee bit of a scare, boo. . . ."

Maestro grimaced with his hideous face and bloody swollen nose at Melkior, like someone trying to scare a child. Melkior cringed with disgust and looked away.

"Oh, don't be angry, it's only my little joke," Maestro abruptly went serious. "It's beside the point anyway. I didn't invite you up here to show you the silly faces I can make. I say . . . that electric chair thingy in America—is it true the electricity kills the man instantly, or . . . does he remain alive for some time after all—perhaps a minute or even two?"

"I don't know," replied Melkior giving him a surprised look. "What's that to you now?"

"I read about someone having been brought back to life, no less than seven minutes after the jolt. As soon as they got him off the chair the doctor opened his chest and massaged his heart. He lived for a long time in Mexico afterward. His lawyer had it all arranged, bought 'the body.' So it appears all is not lost after the jolt, you can go on living . . . provided someone turns their hand to it, right, Eustachius?"

"Could be . . . I don't know," replied Melkior, bored, "I haven't read about it . . ."

"Well, I have. And I won't have anyone saying Tesla knows all about electricity! He knows how to make calculations and build motors, but it takes dying, dying from it, Eustachius, to understand the filth!"

Maestro was speaking in the middle of the room with prophetic awe, his arms raised evangelistically.

"Well, you won't be put in the electric chair," Melkior tossed off sarcastically, "here we hang people."

"Even that is more dignified . . . being strangled by your own weight! I could also understand being drowned like a pup, but being force-fed with electricity . . ."

"Who on earth is force-feeding you, man? What's the matter with you?" laughed Melkior nervously. No, honestly, what the hell was the matter with him tonight?

"You're right, man, nobody is force-feeding me," said Maestro thoughtfully and went back to the oil stove. "Do you like your cocoa strong, Eustachius the Kind?"

"I don't like it at all," replied Melkior, boorish.

"Well, I'm making you some as promised, Eustachius the Unkind. Now why are you going all principled on me all of a sudden?"

"All right, I'll have some," Melkior relented. In point of fact he felt he could do with a hot drink; indeed the aroma of cocoa had aroused his appetite, too.

Maestro went about serving his guest with joy:

"Here you are, my dear Eustachius. I've got some biscuits in the box as well. It's all hermetically sealed, don't feel squeamish. No insect could penetrate in there. Not even the positively most cunning among them—the bedbug, as suffering mankind knows all too well. But I'm free of them, they suddenly disappeared, oh, something like three years ago. Too frightened to go on living with me. . . . Or is it that I was too much for them?"

"What?" Melkior choked on his mouthful in nausea; he suddenly felt the bedbug smell all around him.

"Well," went on Maestro with a lovable nastiness, "perhaps I've got some fratricidal bugs in my blood, heh-heh. . . . I'm sure people have been gossiping to you about that: I'm a microbe breeding ground, Wassermann with three crosses. Those three crosses are a Golgotha, a small, personal, and very intimate Golgotha. They believe that one day, or night, I'm going to fall apart, disintegrate, melt into a poisonous gas, colorless, tasteless, and . . . well, not odorless certainly, there will be odor . . . that of brandy, of course. So mind how you go, adorable Eustachius!" Maestro poured himself half a glass of brandy and took a goodly sip, but with a sensible smile, like someone stoking his greediness, then tilted the bottom up and knocked back the rest. "Right. This is to preserve my spoor—or *breath*, it makes no difference which."

"Didn't you switch to beer?" asked Melkior.

"Oh yes, for nightly practice," Maestro gave a mysterious smile. "I've got a whole crateful over there," he pointed at the corner of the room, where necks of beer bottles were indeed sticking out from a crate.

"Practice? What sort of practice?"

"Ballistic. Can't you see the shells ready for action?"

"I've no idea what you're talking about."

"You will, good Eustachius, if my ballistic arc reaches eternity, ha-ha," he was laughing, but the laughter congealed on his lips, some dark rictus was strangling his gaiety.

Cold horror licked Melkior again.

"Don't laugh like that!"

"How else should I laugh, Eustachius extraordinaire? Prescribe a manner, I can't laugh any other way." He went across to the crate, took out two bottles of beer: "Good thing you reminded me," he tilted the bottle and drained it with extraordinary skill. "Glug-glug-glug and it's done, in one go, without a pause for breath," he boasted and turned the empty bottle upside down, "like a waterspout."

"I think I'll be off now," said Melkior standing up. "What is it you were wanting to bring me here for?"

"Why it's been ages, Eustachius the Incorruptible, since I asked you to come around for a talk! But no, you're not at all easy to catch! I had to use my bloodied nose for bait, that's the kind of fish you are! And now you won't even let me laugh. . . ."

"So, go ahead and laugh," said Melkior, laughing.

"Yes, but only in a way you approve of. You want it to be tasteful, to be according to Bergson, your nerves can't take it any other way, you're very choosy. Hah, if only I could do it her way," he tilted his head in the direction of the wall, "if only I had that force of derision! And you never even glanced her way." Maestro held the candle aloft, illumining a darkened, soot-covered Gioconda on the wall.

Melkior barely turned his head. He had come to feel unbearably irritated, he wanted to leave.

"How long has it been hanging there?" he said casually. "It's all black from the fumes."

"From the infernal fumes is what you mean, all blackened from hell itself! For this is the hell of my life, and she sits there smiling above the hell, the damned femina!"

Maestro had got quite agitated, he was speaking with hatred of the picture.

Melkior chuckled at the unexpected outburst of rage.

"No, that's not funny, Eustachius the Heartless!" Maestro rebuked him gravely. "I'm not talking about the picture. I hung it there myself, of course. But what's a picture? just a symbol, a breath, of art—indeed a poor job of printing—but she herself, the femina, I did not hang her up so she would sit smiling above my life! She sneaked in on her own and parked herself there. . . . We all know it, she has parked herself in the lives of us all, and all we do is laugh at each other. What's the matter, exalted Eustachius—not laughing anymore?"

Melkior had indeed grown serious. Maestro's sarcastically scowling face was quite near his, plashing it with brandy breath. In a daze, like someone about to faint, he sat back down and made no reply. Inside him Viviana revived, a painfully wanton, loud image of lust.

"What, shall we have ourselves castrated, virile Eustachius, out of the pride and nobility of the male spirit? Well, what if all our power is implanted right down there, in that trouble spot, in that masculine humiliation? Who's going to risk it, lovely Eustachius? One stands to lose all. Becoming a eunuch, yuk-yuk-yuk . . . an all around progeny-free creature, a belly with a chassis of loose flesh." Maestro was being torn by an ugly forced laugh which made spittle spray from his grimy black teeth. "Here, I'm laughing, with your permission, most illustrious Eustachius, if that can be . . . if that's what . . ."

He's lost his train of thought, mused Melkior with pleasure, he's drunk again. Or is it the "fratricidal bugs" hacking away in there . . .

". . . what her smile is?" Maestro was having trouble pulling his thoughts together. "Why hers? Is it on that little minx, groomed to be bait to lecherous lust (do you notice the Shakespearean style here, Eustachius?) that there should twinkle such a manifestation of the mocking spirit? Only a Voltaire could be so derisive. But who gave a femina the male right of derision?—that is the question, most wise Eustachius! She who cries out so blatantly with this or that side of her flesh (and most delicate flesh it is—let us bow before the curves!) has all of a sudden wrapped herself—that is to say, enveloped that exclamatory flesh—in some kind of inscrutability, in the mythical veil of *the eternal feminine*, and proceeded to mock male mankind from within. O, Leonardo, I'm not forgiving you for that!" exclaimed Maestro in bitter resentment. "Unless . . . unless he was wanting to do some mocking himself, using the little minx to have a laugh at his own expense. . . . Well, never mind, Master Genius can well allow himself that."

At this Maestro drained another bottle of beer.

"Would you like one, too, Eustachius, seeing that you don't seem to go for my cocoa? Here, look, it's brewery sealed, hermetically indeed . . . cap and all . . ."

"No, thank you. I say, why do you so hate women?"

"Stuff and nonsense, Eustachius. And besides, the words 'you hate women' are a woman's way of putting it, and that I do hate. Me hate women? That's like telling me I hate brandy. But we're not going to go hiding the truth for the sake of our untameable sympathies, are we? Science is science. You're a progressive man, Eustachius, and naturally a humane one. In the name of science and humanity you frown on witch hunts. You're horrified at the notion, right? You can't see how people could have believed that a woman had hopped onto a broomstick and flown off for a rendezvous with the devil. Heh-heh, that's where your science shows a measure of naïveté—in thinking *they* believed it. The big-nosed scholars with their caps over their ears and their hands tucked into their wide sleeves, and in there, their fingers crossed . . . you think they believed in witches?"

"Many people believed, the backward masses . . . Martin Luther, for one, believed in the 'Devil's whores,' as did Keppler himself. A cousin of his was burned as a witch, his mother was persecuted . . ."

"There, you see—the great Keppler, too!" took up Maestro with delight. "They burned his cousin and the genius took fright! Eh? Now do you think, Eustachius, that cousin wasn't a little whore? And Frau Keppler a nasty old harridan . . . hairy wart on chin? Even now they would be calling her a witch."

"And you would have her burned?" Ugo's fiancée: hairy wart on chin, romping, a witch—to the stake! To the stake! Ugo would be bringing armfuls of dry twigs, *auto-da-fé*, a blow for freedom, a blow for freedom! Now, what about Enka? Well, Enka, too, would . . .

"Madam Keppler? I don't know, she wouldn't have been so amusing. But the little cousin . . . heh-heh, now she would've made a tasty roast duckling . . . Don't be horrified, I'm only teasing, you're egging me on . . . Seriously now, *they* had found how to get rid of the women, because these females were really dangerous—never mind whether they were witches or not. Some innocent ones died, too, of course, but which of them, tell me honestly, which of them was completely innocent? Which of them would not have let the devil mount her . . . if only out of curiosity? According to the *Malleus maleficarum* they would dance around him kissing him on the bum while he, the swine, farted with relish, ha-ha!" Maestro had clearly brought the scene to life in his mind and was enjoying himself devilishly.

"I don't believe, sweet Eustachius, that there have been no bitter mouthfuls in your love's flask. Indeed you may have had your fill of that very bitterness, the bitterest of all, the one that forever poisons the heart. You see (I'm giving an example to clarify my views, even though they may disgust you—what do I care?) the whole world mourns for Desdemona—but not I. If she'd been completely innocent she would've tickled her husband's armpit when he came in to strangle her. Why didn't she tickle him, eh? I may be the only one in the world who thinks she was strangled fully in accordance with the rules of masculine prevention. You haven't yet, you little whore, but you will . . . if I don't strangle you first. For the time being I persist in you, Desdemona, shot to shot you have knocked again—shots twain (look, rhyming verse!), you're still drunk . . . but we know all too well, glorious Eustachius, how long their inebriation lasts; so make with the prevention—klklkl! (Maestro made a strangling gesture) and be done with it. And rest assured you won't have made a mistake."

A weird thought tickled Melkior hard.

"You must have discussed this long and loud with Don Fernando?"

"Discussed what?"

"Why . . . *preventive action.*"

"Could be, I don't know really . . . He wants to save mankind, no less, and I want mankind to *leave off.*"

"To be destroyed . . . by war?"

"Nonsense, sensible Eustachius! Wars nurture it, multiply it. War is a sign of rage. I want a peaceful liquidation, a sort of bankruptcy— everyone realizing the deal's off . . . and joining the ranks of eunuchs. Infertile women no longer give birth to living dolls; as for everything else, let microbes devour the lot. Let them eat all the books and the museums, the cities and the machines, they'll devour each other in the end . . . only the Spirit will remain to move upon the face of the waters as in the opening chapter of Genesis."

"But what's the point of all that?"

"What's the point of all *this,* life-saving Eustachius? Perhaps you're hiding meaning in your pocket? So, show it to me!"

Maestro bared his teeth at Melkior like a dog at a helpless man, feeling the advantage. Melkior was alarmed: he may go for me next with those teeth . . .

"Don't fear, Eustachius," laughed Maestro quite mildly, "we won't start with you. We'll start somewhere much closer, heh-heh, much, much closer . . . Here, see for yourself—no books. I've gone without long since. I gave them to someone downstairs—a Russian, a count, a general, a relative of the Grand Prince. Not to read though—he's even forgotten his Russian—but . . . he cuts and pastes paper silhouettes and presses them with books. That's how the general makes his living, in noble penury, in rags worn with dignity. Here's another use for books—to press the imagination of the Grand Prince's relative. *Habent sua fata libelli.*"

ATMAN never returned the Adler book, remembered Melkior with regret, which presumably reflected in some feature of his face.

"Don't frown, bookish Eustachius—the book does not deserve our respect. Verily, verily I say unto thee that thought, imagination, feeling, have gone dull in lead and resin. The book has imposed on the spirit a stupid, heavy (particularly heavy!) and totally unsuitable corpus. Did you ever wonder, featherweight Eustachius, why the book needed such weight? If there's anything ridiculous in this world, it's that weight. We glorify Guttenberg . . . for what? For transforming thought into a brick. To conserve the thoughts inside! Mummies, dried cods. *Bourgeoises, garamonds, minions, italics* . . . for thoughts to be 'clear,' to be preserved for generations to come. Homer and Socrates never wrote a single letter between them, and yet they were preserved for generations to come. Did Socrates need italics to make his thoughts clearer? While our Don Fernando drives typesetters up the wall with his italics and boldface, the better to set out some par-ti-cu-lar thought for posterity. Pharaoh Don Fernando (life—health—power) wants his mummy to be prepared carefully for distant centuries . . . but what of it? In a year or two it'll be nothing but a dried cod—with no head, of course."

Melkior was grinning. He was enjoying the image of the "headless dried cod." A malicious imp of revenge was having its field day inside him. He tried to set his own "modesty" against Don Fernando's "pharaonic grandeur" and bask in it.

"Smiling, Eustachius? You think his mummy will be anything more than a dried fish?"

"It will indeed," replied Melkior ambiguously. "Don Fernando has some engaging notions. He has expounded them to you, too . . ."

"Expounded . . . yes . . ." Maestro's mind had already moved on to something else. "Death disgusts me, Eustachius. I'm imaginative enough, I can picture my own skeleton, and it's a horrible sight. Take a look, Eustachius—is my bald spot dirty?" he bent his head low: the denuded pate featured a mud-dirtied bruise, "I like cleanliness."

"Why, they hit you on the head, too!"

"No, no, of my own volition I lay down on my back . . . in the middle of the road, in lieu of a protest rally, for freedom of movement . . ."

Maestro was speaking rapidly, in a muddle. He meant to hide from Melkior that he had been thrown out of the café head first. His "protest lie-down" was an ad-lib.

"But you've got a bruise on the top of your head?"

"Never mind, it's not a bruise, it's my beret leaking blue dye . . ."

"It's muddy. You should clean it. The nose, too."

"The pate I'll clean, of course. But not the nose!" he declared defiantly.

"The nose is not dirty—it's bloody, which makes all the difference. Tomorrow I'll appear, bloody nose and all, at the Corso when the whole crowd is there."

"But what's the use of parading it in public?"

"What's the use? It'll be a public indictment! I'll show the culprit up (as nose is my witness), I'll thrash him, I'll raze his nose to the ground! Right there, in front of everyone! Perhaps even Meštrović will be there!"

Again Melkior felt the burn of the evening's café tableau: Freddie with Viviana. "Why did Freddie go for you? Was he alone?"

"What do you mean, alone? Everyone was on his side! All the waiters, the cooks . . . even the cleaning lady in charge of the restrooms. Aah, if he'd been alone, then *his* nose would have looked like this!"

His nose is now grazing on her fragrances . . . his imagination tormented Melkior.

"I mean, did Freddie have company?" he was purposely stoking Maestro's hatred.

"What's the thrust of this diplomacy, Eustachius?" Maestro gave a sly wink. "Trying to set me up, eh? You know who he was sitting with, heh-heh, and that's why you're asking."

Melkior felt a blush sear his face. Well, it's a lucky thing the old boy's so drunk . . . also, he was relying on the poor light of the oil lamp.

"Don't go red, Eustachius. Or perhaps white, I can't see in this light, but it's just as nice. Out with the soul, that's what I like."

Melkior was crestfallen and silent as a sinner. Maestro sank a brandy, then poured an entire bottleful of beer down his throat. Where does he find room for it all, wondered Melkior in passing, but he was not really giving it much thought. Again he felt the disorder *inside* him. He keenly wanted to get up and leave (he'll get me all confused), if only to go back to his room, or to walk through town in the rain, to count his steps and his thoughts . . . to think alone, walled in by the ramparts of his endless solitude. Maestro now appeared to him, in the dim lamplight, to be an unreal man whom he had invented and projected out before him cinema style. Maestro was still talking, but what reached Melkior was only sound in the strange acoustics of a dream; the words themselves he couldn't follow.

"Have you ever thought about it, Eustachius?"

Melkior said nothing. He watched Maestro's pale skull move up there, above his own head and, how strange . . . thoughts are happening "in there," words emerging, moving through space and ringing in my ears, but my brain is no longer taking them in. He wanted to get up and go, but instead he stretched his legs under the table and, yawning, raised and lowered his elbows like a crowing rooster. Indifferently, *I couldn't care less* . . .

"I'll brew coffee forthwith, fragile Eustachius. You'll fall asleep at the table in the end, and we haven't even got to *the subject*. I'm purposely beating around the bush. Do you think I give a fig about the burning of witches? Hah . . . although I was not speaking off the top of my head. Sometimes I think—for such is my life—that I was born conjoined to a twin. They cut us apart, but one of us had to die. It was he who died. And so, you see, he has been pestering me ever since. Dead alongside me, he keeps saying: let's face it, you're only half a man. That's how I feel, Eustachius—I drag behind me a skeleton."

The aroma of the coffee brought Melkior back to the real presence of things. He heard the oil stove hissing; he heard something about a skeleton, too. Who knows if Dom Kuzma is still among us? Ask Ugo, his mother might know . . . Well, what's it to me even if he is . . . ? Hey, let him live . . . until Polyphemus the beast grabs ahold of the whole Earth . . .

"That goes for all of us nowadays . . . everyone's dragging some sort of skeleton around," said Melkior.

"Easy for you, youthful Eustachius, to speak in metaphors. But my dead man is no poetic image. Oh . . ." Maestro was about to exclaim, but suddenly changed his mind and beckoned Melkior to get up, "follow me, faithful Eustachius. Dante called Virgil 'Maestro,' too."

He led Melkior to a small balcony "which looked out (Melkior was composing a description and chuckling at the way the balcony was 'looking out') over the empty outlying fields sunk into the dense wet night." The freshness of the moist air caressed his cheeks; he inhaled deeply the smell of wet soil. From away in the darkness came the barking of dogs, and from somewhere near by, a strange buzzing sound, as if a mechanism were finely grinding the silence.

"Can you hear that, quiet Eustachius?" whispered Maestro in a kind of fear. His voice was trembling, but that could be merely due to his being drunk and chilled, thought Melkior. "Can you hear the *zzeee . . . zzeee . . . zzeee . . .* the villain's sinister meditation! You'd say it was the night, speaking with the many voices of Nature . . . crickets, cicadas . . . but that's not what it is, Eustachius, listen carefully. I listen to it night after night . . . It's praying to the devil, its master . . . or, if there is no devil, it is praying to the stupid Power that shakes it—that's why it's buzzing so. Like a sinner set to trembling by God acting in him . . ."

Maestro was shaking all over with a kind of horror; the shakes broke his voice every now and then.

"Whatever are you talking about?" The terror moved over to Melkior. "Can't you see its claws and tendrils? Look over there, in the distance." Maestro was pointing a shaking hand into the dark. "Over there, over there, can't you see the stripes scoring the sky, that's its trail. It leads to the . . . country from whose bourn no traveler returns, as the Prince of Denmark once said."

Only then did Melkior see it: quite near and level with Maestro's balcony, perhaps only three or four meters away, was a transmission line. The black cords of thick, powerful cables boldly sliced the darkness. And the buzzing sound was coming from the pylon jutting up nearby, as tall as the building. Lightning must strike there often, thought Melkior.

"So what is there for you to be afraid of?" he said to Maestro as he would to a child, "it's an electrical cable."

"A *po-wer ca-ble*," emphasized Maestro, "'high voltage, danger of death.' Down at the bottom of the pylon there's a skull and crossbones as well, a courteous warning: don't play with this. Then again, it could serve as an enticement. Imagine a shepherd, for instance. . . . Could it be that you're cold, tender Eustachius? (he himself was trembling like a leaf), let's go back in, Eustachius, let's go back in. So the shepherd is up on a mountain, a sodomite, a dolt, living among the lightning bolts, and out of boredom he shimmies up the pylon to grab that porcelain cup, possibly to bring it as a vandal's trophy back to his village. Or just to spite the warning, displaying some preposterous form of heroism, think I'm scared of you?—and there he is up top, a fried imbecile, his abandoned sheep bleating down below. A folk fool."

"Why 'folk'?" protested Melkior without enthusiasm, "a fool, an *individual* fool."

"Oh no, dear Eustachius, a folk fool. An individual fool is Freddie for one . . . and let's say Ugo, too. Or . . . let's not say Ugo, he's more of a nut case, a concept which has some charm to it. But folk stupidity is thick. It's as if it were a general duty to be a standard folk fool to a certain ethnic degree; it's of a piece with folk costumes and songs and dances. Folklore and 'patrimonial treasure.' Just take a close look at those dull, cruel, ugly (particularly ugly!) 'folksy' snouts. They're all of a pattern: mouth mindlessly half-open as if they were forever listening to Latin Mass; and eyes small, cunning, ready for cheating and theft. Find me a single 'folk belle' if you can. Yes, you'll only find one in the cow's-milk cheese ad! No, no, country folk are ugly, cynical, and dirty."

Melkior looked around the room with an ironic smile, then fixed his stare on Maestro in stubborn derision. Maestro looked over himself, confused, but his rhetorical certainty soon returned.

"Sure, I get the point—who am I to talk about tact and cleanliness? Everything about me is dirty, inside and out," admitted Maestro contritely, even with a touch of embarrassment. "I'm immersed in filth, pure Eustachius, in every way. . . . But at least I don't stink with the timeless stench of humanity, not with horse shit and animal rut the way barracks and schools stink . . . with that eternal soaked-in-pissedness. . . . My stench is the vile smell of an indomitable individual who doesn't give a hoot for the rules of hygiene; my stench possibly contains poetic inspiration, the poetry of bohemianism, an aroma of freedom. Do you think a nicer . . . forgive me, but this is a necessary question . . . a nicer smell came from—all right, I'm not saying Baudelaire, but Verlaine, for instance? He would have stunk just as badly as I do and Louis XIV if they hadn't kept splashing him with scents. Incidentally, my dear Eustachius," sighed Maestro, melancholic, sluicing his throat with brandy, "there was a time when I used to shave as often as three times a day! I, too, used to yearn for things *tender, pure, white* . . . things like dainty arms around my neck, whispers of 'darling'—'dearest.' And the rest of love's liturgy . . ."

He was standing miserably in the middle of the room as if on trial. His eyes were cloudy, wet . . . with brandy or possibly tears,

Melkior could not tell. But all this can just as well be a dreadful drunken bug's labyrinth of cynicism into which he intends to draw me, only to laugh in my face if I start to believe him.

"So why didn't you fall in love . . . back then when you used to shave three times a day?" added Melkior derisively "to be on the safe side"—he did not believe him.

"I . . . did love, Eustachius, I did love!" Maestro waved his arms weirdly, his head thrown tragically back in the manner of the grand pathetic school of acting (thought Melkior). "And what was it I loved? The rosebush, the twigs, the thorns! My sighs, my kisses ended up spiked on thorns, while others plucked the flower!" Maestro was all but howling by the end.

Damn this—it's genuine! thought Melkior in fright, feeling another kind of horror. The *stench* business had had him disgusted, but at least it had been at the level of Maestro's superior-in-its-own-way cynicism, which Melkior sometimes admired for its insolent originality, but this "laying the soul bare" turned his stomach in a completely different way. He disliked intimate confession; this one was all the more odious coming from a man with a bloodied nose who had often declared himself old enough to be Melkior's father. There was something sad and dirty at the same time in Maestro's avowal which made Melkior ashamed, and the shame made him avert his eyes to avoid looking at the wretch standing before him . . . as if he'd been declaring a homosexual love for me . . . ptui, damn it all!

Maestro wasn't looking at him, either. Head turned away, swollen livid hands pressed against his chest, he was overcome by a spasm of despair, *here, judge me* . . . Stupid, stupid, stupid! raged Melkior.

"You despise me now, Eustachius," spoke up Maestro timidly, in the voice of a spurned lover. "Well, I never really expected you to fall on my neck and join me in tears. Although, ahem . . ." he abruptly pulled free of the spasm and went on in his "old" derisive tone, "that would be like a scene from a French vaudeville. . . ."

"What would be like some scene from a French vaudeville?" asked Melkior, his eyes still away.

"Well—the two of us weeping in each other's arms," (Melkior shuddered at the thought) "and our beloved serviced—or for all we know *being* serviced—by a third, hollow Frederick! Ha-ha-ha . . ."

All of a sudden Maestro broke into dreadfully mocking and unbridled laughter, thumping Melkior on the shoulder—"fraternally."

Melkior startled at the touch, at the laughter, but Maestro's words appeared not to have reached his mind yet. He was staring at Maestro in dull amazement.

"Yes indeed, Eustachius—which is why I've chosen you for this ceremony."

"What accursed ceremony?" Melkior was angry. He had a flash of "revelation": he was setting me up all along! Priming his "despair" as a trap, to have me fly into his embrace with "avowals."

"It's not 'accursed,'" Maestro went serious again, "it's a sad ceremony, perhaps even a *last tribute* to a man . . . or a former man."

What's *this* piece of buffoonery for the benefit of? Doesn't sound like a joke . . . but then he's a past master of hoaxes . . . Melkior was being cautious. He waited in silence.

"My laughter has misdirected your thoughts, Eustachius, which is a pity." Maestro sat down heavily on a chair and dropped his head between his palms. ("The Great Confession posture," thought Melkior with alarm.) "You will now find it hard to believe what I have to say, and there's a great deal to be said." Maestro filled his glass with brandy. Melkior also filled his (Might make it easier to listen to him). "That's the spirit," smiled Maestro. "Your good health, then. Only I'll have to cut the brandy with beer, for I wouldn't want you, sober Eustachius, to take this for drunken prattle . . . and also because I have . . . other reasons," he added with a kind of worried hesitation. "She was married at the time to a colleague of mine, he used to work for our paper as sports editor. A young, cheerful, shallow journalist; spent more of his time at stadiums, swimming pools, playing fields, than at the office. The cult of the body. That's how he found her, body and all—at some playing field or other, or was it at a swimming meet, breaststroke or backstroke, it now makes no difference which, but it would have been a . . . backstroke kind of thing, and married her . . . rather, he took the precious body home and put it in his bed. Like a sporting health deity, *mens sana in corpore sano,* that was a frequent tag in his athletic articles. But don't think I hated him, honorable Eustachius . . . I only envied him, for reasons which are presumably still clear to you. He seemed to have a great deal of respect—you might even say liking—for me. He was forever inviting me, dragging me home for coffees, lunches, dinners, being a pest . . . in the beginning! But later on she joined in, and I came to look forward to visiting with them: a 'home away from home' (I'd become something of a household pet), not to mention the wonderful hostess, you'd think every object would like to caress her as she went by . . . (Melkior failed to stifle a sigh) . . . anyway, I got to dropping in uninvited, at all times of day, just to see her. She would receive me with childish delight, laugh at my every word, even when nothing I'd said was funny: she thought it was 'witty' and wished to show she had got the 'point.' Only later on did it dawn on me that I'd been playing the role of prattling entertainer . . . I was good at it then, I was inspired, made happy by her laughter, by the enjoyment of the superb body, I was seeing 'soul' there, would you believe it? I didn't drink much in those days, just enough to get my tongue loosened and my fancy prancing, but even that was very genteel, always strictly within the bounds of bourgeois good manners. I tell you, I used to shave and bathe, change my shirts . . . I didn't look like this at all."

Maestro rubbed his forehead in a spasmodic gesture of despair, finished his drink and dropped his head between his hands again. He then gave a cruel and dry laugh: "Love . . ." he scoffed. "No one speaks to us with such feather-brained fickleness as love: it makes of us Apollos one moment and losers the next. In her company there, it seemed to me she was finding me 'interesting' (of course, I use that cautious term now that it's all 'water under the bridge'), and when she saw me out with a 'do come again' I felt dismissed as a servant who had done his day's work. But I was grateful to her even for that: my love found in that invitation some 'slyly concealed promise.'"

"Well, did you tell her eventually?" said Melkior, unable to contain himself.

His voice woke Maestro: he raised his head, looking at Melkior with a strange hatred—look who's here!—as if he had only then remembered Melkior's presence. He then laughed with scoffing viciousness:

"Did I tell her what, Eustachius . . .?" Melkior heard the implicit attribute "the Blockhead," too. And said nothing.

"Tell her, indeed . . ." went on Maestro maliciously. "I didn't have to, did I? She saw it herself . . . and proceeded to have fun."

"At your expense?"

"No, at the expense of the City Savings Bank!" snapped back Maestro in irritation. "Don't mock me, Eustachius. I may be floating in formaldehyde tomorrow," he went on gloomily, his voice breaking with agitation. Melkior's heart constricted. I mustn't leave him alone tonight, even if it means sitting up until . . . "So please restrain, if you can, your pleasure at my disgrace. I'm sinking to lizard level under your very eyes, and all you can think of is cracking jokes!"

"My dear Maestro," cried Melkior magnanimously, "nothing could be farther from my mind . . ."

"Good, because I'm not addressing what is far from your mind," went on Maestro with kind composure, "I'm addressing your mind itself, the very center and core of your reason, capable of full understanding. Too late did I get wise to her perfidious little game, that is to say only after I'd given my hopes and fantasies free rein: well, why not? Women had been known, in certain exceptional cases, suddenly to appreciate spiritual qualities as well, perhaps for originality's sake, or simply out of defiance . . . I was imagining with sweeping breadth."

"Well, perhaps she did appreciate you?" said Melkior timidly.

"Eustachius, if you're not making fun of me and looking only to console yourself, then I suggest you turn around and spit three times, as though a black cat had just crossed your path. Appreciate me? Ho, ho, ho . . ." ho-ho'd Maestro out of his poisoned gorge. "She appreciated athletes proficient in various disciplines. As I found out when it was too late. Legs, shoulders, biceps. . . . Even good coxswains—good in the literal sense, I mean. As to how highly I was being appreciated . . . or, since we're using business terms, depreciated . . . well, listen and I'll tell you. I was alone with her in their flat, on a Saturday evening, her husband had left for somewhere out in the sticks to cover a Sunday match, that was why I'd chosen that particular day. 'Chosen' for what? Well, I couldn't answer that one even today and yet I still say 'chosen.' I had been alone with her before, late into the night, sipping a drink or two, chatting away, entertaining her, and everything had been so, well, *normal.* . . . But that evening some demon got hold of me: I kept feeling I had to make a move, I have no idea which way. Do something? Say something?—I don't know, but it had me hobbled, I couldn't move, I kept shoving my hands into my pockets, in shame, in fear, spouting drivel, lamely, being boring. Looking all the time, unblinkingly, at her knees, well-rounded, full (you've seen those knees!) and watching out for the moments when she crossed her legs, to slip my gaze into that holy semi-darkness . . . She noticed this and got going with her rotten game. She'd worked it all out while I was sitting there across from her, you'll see." Maestro took a sip of brandy and cleared his throat; the butt in the corner of his mouth had gone out long before and was dangling from his lip like a slimy grub. "Interesting, eh, Eustachius . . . (Melkior had his attention stretched from ear to ear) and instructive for the coming generations of men. She might have been in a bit of a fix herself, as you will see later, well, she could always have sent me off, asked me to leave, said she was tired . . . but no, she decided to play a little game. And so she did. Her legs began crossing and recrossing a bit too often as if competing, offering themselves, showing off; and meanwhile her skirt was getting shorter and shorter—she never once tugged it down over her knees as women will do in that kind of leg game when they're being decent . . . I mean sincere . . . about seducing a man, but I was a stranger to that kind of thinking at the time—and on her face there was a nervously twinkling smile 'brimming with desire for me.' Well, how else was I to see it? I pounced wildly on her knees and started kissing them like a man demented; I wanted to make up for everything at once, for all the yearning, the waiting . . . I was going on mindlessly, grunting as I rootled in her lap like a ravenous piglet, and she was laughing quaintly, even stroking my head and scratching me exactly the way you scratch a piglet, in among the hairs . . . there was a lot of hair on my head in those days. . . . Suddenly, as if she'd made up her mind, she whispered soulfully in my ear 'Wait, we'd better get undressed,' and she glanced at her watch as she rose . . . I remembered that bit only later. She went to the bathroom to get undressed. I waited for her, naked, in the sitting-room, trembling . . . you can well imagine! There, I'm telling you all, Eustachius the Privileged, all, down to the very last mortifying detail, because that's where her whorish triumph was—in those very details! She took a long time coming back, I could hear the sound of water in the bathroom, and I was trembling . . . I thought: why must they wash and groom so much for it . . . but with another part of my mind I was exulting in her wish for purity . . . of the first touch, my dearest, my great love. . . . That was what I was tremblingly muttering, straining my hearing for every sound in the house, frightened like a thief. . . . Suddenly I thought I heard someone inserting a key into the door from the outside! And true to form she came back running, flushed, 'it's *him*,' she whispered in despair. She took me by the hand and led me to the bedroom and pushed me inside a cupboard full of men's clothes; came back again, threw my clothes in there, too, then locked me in and took the key out of the lock. And now, Eustachius, begins the cruel vaudeville . . ."

Maestro paused. He spat the butt to the floor and lit a fresh cigarette, which he immediately moved with his tongue to a corner of his mouth to keep it from impeding his speech.

"And the most miserable thing, honorable Eustachius, is that I'm sitting there in the wardrobe among the rags, choking from the smell of mothballs—and terrified I'll give myself away . . . fearing for her sake! Word of honor, I didn't give a thought to myself (fine, I'll get through this . . . or choke to death, it doesn't matter really)—it's because of her that I've become all darkness and silence. Here they come, into the bedroom . . . I never move an eyebrow, I don't breathe! But what's this? It's not his voice, the colleague's, the husband's! Then again, perhaps it's only the acoustics of the wardrobe . . . anyway, there wasn't much time for checking: they were at it before long. That's how it was, Eustachius . . . me listening inside to the entire . . . entire charade . . . until the last gasp. I don't remember what kind of sound I made, but it must have been some vengeful cry, because he jumped out of bed right away and began looking for me in the room. I then thumped an elbow against the wood, 'here I am.' "

"What?" Melkior was flabbergasted, "weren't you afraid?" He remembered his own "retreat" from Enka's. . . . "He could have killed you there and then."

"He could have indeed . . . but the desire for revenge was stronger, Eustachius. After all, a naked man in the wardrobe (and I'll have you know I was a *man* in those days), locked in from the outside, and the key out of the lock!—what better evidence of a woman's harlotry do you want? He started shouting (like the Moor demanding the handkerchief) 'The key! The key! The key, you God-damned whore!' and she kept giggling wildly in the bed for all she was worth—it was all a lark, you see. Try to picture the scene, Eustachius! At last, when he was utterly beside himself and lurched to strangle her, break open the cupboard door, she gave him the key. He pulled me out by the ear like a schoolboy. . . . But what happened? It wasn't him, the husband—it was someone else, a huge fellow, an athletic superman! The revenge had misfired! Never mind me being pulled out by the ear, never mind me being naked (asthenic, intellectual build, with a bit of paunch in the bargain), never mind her laughing (and why shouldn't she: just imagine it— two naked fools!) . . . the revenge, the revenge had fallen flat! God, why did I ever bellow inside that cupboard? In the end, after he'd taken a better look at me, he joined in the laughter himself. He crawled into bed next to her and the pair of them, covered, proceeded to jeer at my naked self. . . . In that case, I thought, miserable and bare-assed as I was, retrieving my clothes from the cupboard, in that case, the whore's ball will come to an end one day. And I did put an end to it."

"You got your revenge!" exclaimed Melkior aligning himself wholeheartedly with Maestro.

"You bet I did, Eustachius, of course I did! Very soon, too!"

"How did you do it?"

"Through a second vaudeville, one with a dramatic ending and this time directed by me!"

"How did you . . ."

"The end justified the means. Don't hold it against me, Eustachius—I used an anonymous letter. Instead of me, it was the avenging husband who hid in the cupboard. Fully clothed, of course. And armed with a toy pistol, just to be able to throw them out into the street naked."

Melkior was listening with a feeling of personal satisfaction: he was entirely in the "avenger's" shoes; he didn't even mind the "anonymous letter."

"Surely you invented that bit?" He wished to be sure of his satisfaction.

"Do you think, Eustachius, that I could deprive myself of such an occasion to gloat? I was standing right there as Adam and Eve were evicted from the Garden of Eden . . . and I cackled like an infernal demon, I assure you, I howled to make it sound as malevolent as possible."

"Did he see you?" Melkior was hankering for the details.

"The spouse? No, he slammed the gate shut as soon as they were out . . . it was only then that I appeared, hee, heeee . . ."

"Did the fellow recognize you?"

"Hah, that was the only fly in the ointment. It was not *the same fellow*, it was someone else again, a subtler type, a master of the racquet . . . Word has it that he's now coaching an African ruler in the game."

"And how did she behave?"

"Innocence incarnate. Covering her instruments with her hands . . . Oh, it was one of the greatest scandals of the day! You can imagine how I wrote it up for Yesterday in Town: 'Adam and Eve Hit the Street'! The Old Man commended me. . . ." Melkior was not enthused by Maestro's gloating. So this is the story of Viviana . . . (It was as if this were a source of "fresh relief" and "final liberation") . . . unless Maestro'd invented it all? Well, hadn't I buried her already? Oh yes, *I have buried my dead love* . . .

"So he actually kicked her out . . . naked . . . into the street?" he asked all the same. Perhaps the old boy did invent it. . . .

"Precisely. It was as if he'd taken my advice. As a matter of fact, there was a wee suggestion to that effect in the anonymous letter, if my memory serves me well—it has been a good number of years since."

"She'd have been very young?"

"Very, very, veracious Eustachius. If you want to find an excuse for her in it. . . ."

"I want nothing!" said Melkior, irritated. "Why would I care?"

"Ah, on the subject of 'care,' I've been meaning to ask you—how well do you know her?"

Melkior gave him a sullen and distrustful look:

"We spoke once at Adam's, the chiromantist's . . ."

"Well, did they, heh-heh . . . take you into the partnership?" squinted Maestro maliciously. But this may have been from the cigarette smoke in his eyes, thought Melkior, anxious: the question had been all too clear.

"I'm not with you . . . What partnership?"

"Don't listen to me, Eustachius, I'm a nasty fellow," said Maestro and gave another inexplicable squint. "But verily, verily I say unto thee: beware of the magician Adam. This is my testamentary advice to you: A perfidious bastard is capable of doing what no one else can. Remember, mortal, that dust thou art . . . he'll get his neck wrung yet. . . ."

"Get his neck wrung," that's *preventive action!* Melkior detected Don Fernando's fingers in this. So he's exerting his influence all right . . . but only as fingers, Melkior dismissed.

"And as for the bait," went on Maestro in a kind of hurry, "I've told you: spit thrice. I used to shave three times a day, and you, Eustachius, should spit three times in a row!" he lifted an ATMAN-like index finger, "those are the words of your ruined parent on his deathbed."

Maestro looked at the folded-up cot with regret.

"It would be meet for me to lie down full length upon it and give you my blessing . . . but I can't be bothered to open it out . . . not merely for the sake of ceremony . . ."

"I'll do it . . ." hastened Melkior only to bite his tongue, "I mean, it would do you good to lie down, it's late, you're tired, also you've had a lot to drink. . . ."

"What, and let you escape? Uh-oh, I won't have it, Eustachius! Your testimony will be my protection against slander."

"Who would slander you . . . and why?"

"The Corso humanists . . . for 'defeatism.' I told them, over my shoulder, that I didn't give a fig for their Future. I don't give the toenail from my little toe for their hydroelectric power plants. Anyway, I haven't even got toenails on my little toes—what I have is hooves that have become corns . . . from walking. There, I don't give a single pedestrian corn of mine for all the electrical powers of the Great Future. What use are they to us pedestrians? I respect human walking."

"You said so to Don Fernando?"

"To him . . . and to the rest of them. I respect perpendicularity, human dignity! A huddled fool in a tin bucket hurtling up and down the street—is he still a man? Staring in front of him, his eyes bulging from their sockets like those of a mad believer; he mustn't turn around or he'll be turned not into the biblical pillar of salt but into a pile of iron and shit . . . and he in such a hurry to reach the FUTURE, heh-heh, my dear Eustachius!"

"So mankind ought to relinquish technological progress?"

"Mankind . . ." Maestro gave a mournful smile. "Perhaps 'mankind' would give it up after all, if anyone were to ask. But who ever asks 'mankind' anything, Eustachius? 'Mankind' has only hands, the *energy* of its ten fingers. . . . Mankind does not know what 'horsepower' is . . . unless it's the power of a four-legged horse. Now do you, Eustachius, know what 'horsepower' is? Well, you don't! You will look it up in the *Petit Larousse Illustré* when you get home. In this powerful horselike day and age, Eustachius, it's a shame not to know what horsepower is. HP. Now do you know, you delegate of mankind, what *energy* is?"

"The capacity . . ." Melkior was laughing, the night had taken an amusing turn, he thought, "the capacity to perform an action . . . something like that . . ."

"Wrong, Eustachius! Sit down!" cried Maestro tutorially. "The ability of a *body*—yes, *body*, you silly lad—to perform an action! You must emphasize the body, with a focus on the substance. The soul doesn't come into it at all—that comes under theology. Here, my body is getting up and walking," Maestro took several resolute steps, "and that's ENERGY: a body being capable of performing an action. Right, but what about that *invisible* thingy which courses through a wire, has no body and is not the soul of a dead tightrope walker . . . eh? You think this is . . . no more than a folk riddle?"

Maestro made a rhetorical pause, watching his "lad" with derisive expectancy.

"Even the religion of the Future, dearest Eustachius," he went on didactically, since his "lad" had failed to come up with an answer, "has its own incorporeal, invisible deity, present in all things, in Heaven and on Earth. Danger of death! Thou shalt not needlessly touch thy God!—That is the first and supreme commandment. Old God-the-Creator can no longer frighten anybody; he used to frighten people naïvely with fire, which firemen can nowadays put out in no time flat. But The Invisible One coursing madmanlike along wires (Maestro gestured at the window with his thumb over his shoulder), well, just try pointing your hose at Him!—He'll fry you like a fish. There you are, Eustachius, that's the distinctive feature of the new theology." Maestro gave a sigh of relief. He had done a meaningful job: winkled out that "new piece of human folly," that "mystical entity of inestimable importance for mankind" from science's mystery. . . . Using persiflage and extravagant metaphors all the while . . .

because he, as everyone knew, did not care a rap for anything in this world. Or the next . . . if you wanted to know that, too.

He was satisfied. Melkior saw his chin tremble slightly with a happy smile, but he would not let his face glow with visible pleasure. He had to sustain his role of sufferer.

"Demanding sacrifice," Maestro went on, taking evident satisfaction in the malicious pathos of his own voice and filled with an urge for contrariety. "Put your fingers on Future's anvil so we can smash them! So we can tear off your arms, fracture your legs, use your skull for a flowerpot! Be a martyr! We shall give your name to the gigantic hydro-temple of our God, ELECTRON! My dear Eustachius! But I'm an atheist! I don't fall for ditties sung to marching tunes."

Maestro was laughing bitterly, staring sardonically into Melkior's eyes as if challenging him. His hair stood up like the plumage of a rooster enraged.

His eyes were quite glazed, demented from drink; his nose featured a cracked crust of dried blood, his face swollen, red, with purple blotches and a dense web of swollen capillaries. Faces like this loom in imagination's horrible projections before sleep, thought Melkior.

"Please lie down, Maestro," (if only he would, he'd fall asleep). "I'll be sitting here and talking to you. Let me open your bed . . ."

"No, Eustachius," Maestro raised a resolute hand, "I won't have it. If I lie down I'll fall asleep like a foolish virgin. I must be awake, Eustachius, I'm not giving up this night. I want to share it with you like Socrates with . . . the one who tried to persuade him to flee. But you're more like the other one . . . what was his name? . . . the tearful disciple. Socrates was killed by hemlock and I'll be killed by the invisible God ELECTRON! What an honor, ha-ha . . . God strike me! God nothing!" Abruptly he was angry, it seemed. "Nnoo, this is no honor! Some God, coming from resin, amber (the ancient Greeks called it *elektron*); we would therefore render it as Gum God, my kind Eustachius. By gum, I'll come to a sticky end, I will."

Melkior was alarmed:

"What are you saying, you lunatic?"

"What's wrong, Eustachius? Heh-heh, afraid of me shaking your faith? We can't even tie a shoelace any more without believing in something. Don't be afraid, most kind one, there will always be one sort of bait or another in front of your nose, just close enough to tease your sense of smell, but your teeth will never reach it. Well, go ahead and believe in that Eternal Sausage (Melkior remembered Kurt and shuddered), follow it . . . but bear in mind: *you* will never sink your teeth into it."

"Perhaps I'm not after anything," Melkior tried to justify himself, at the same time irked: "If you think I'm a fool . . ."

"You're no fool, wise Eustachius, but you don't know how to live in *in-dif-fer-ence.*"

"And you do?" said Melkior, irritated.

"Don't be angry, Eustachius, even heads wiser than ours didn't know. They've left behind temples, children, pyramids, symphonies, books . . . mummies. You, too, would leave a mummy behind, even if it is only this big, so long as the embryo of your glory reaches the Future in a jar of alcohol. *Ambitious* types like you imagine . . ."

"Leave me out of this!" interrupted Melkior angrily: had he not himself thought about . . .

"All right, not you—the . . . others, the fu-tu-ristic lot," conceded Maestro, in a placating tone, "picture the Future as a Final Ceremony, a Grand Parade: everyone will be there, sporting their decorations . . . and afterward—nothing, just a dream. Everything will stop in incantation, in apotheosis—something like Gundulić's dream, painted on the stage curtain at the Zagreb Opera House, a tableau vivant, for eternity. Ha-ha, most kind Eustachius, the picture of Judgment Day is every bit as naïve, but at least there's some dynamic and fear in it, something earnest . . . Oh why didn't I have the acquaintance of all men!" sighed Maestro with pathos.

"What use would that be now?" laughed Melkior. "So you could leave them a memory of you?"

"All I wish to leave them now is my undamaged skeleton, Eustachius," said Maestro gloomily and, it seemed, with reproach, "as stipulated in my contract with the Institute . . . So that students may study me and become doctors, eventually to become skeletons themselves. There's *equality and fraternity* for you, Eustachius!"

Maestro's head then dropped with fatigue and drink, first to his shoulder, but finding no support there it slid powerlessly forward and thumped against the bare wooden tabletop. The sound was dull and probably painful, but he seemed to feel nothing anymore.

He'll drop off now, hoped Melkior. He watched the dried mud on Maestro's bare pate: "the grimy bald spot." They threw him about and beat him before her very eyes. Freddie thrashed him and she, in all probability, enjoyed it. Viviana.

Melkior pronounced the name with mournful scorn and this concluded all he had to think, completed all he had to say. Over and done with. Shot dead. He ordered the volley himself. Fire! He repeated the punishment with a listless and miserable despair.

He was tired. How long the nights still are in March . . . His eyes closed of their own accord, they had nothing to see anymore, they longed for sleep. *But the head is not abed . . .* he repeated mechanically inside, yet the words remained meaningless, *in-dif-fer-ent.*

He noticed that, too. Maestro is not moving: dead or alive?— everything is now *in-dif-fer-ent,* as if this were a dream. And the words were an echo from a fast forward, agitated image sequence on the borderline between fancy and dream . . . a park with a dead man in white floating in a pool . . . a jet of water spouting between his legs . . . a silent screening, no splashing to be heard. (The rain had stopped.)

Dogs barking: night agitated; train squalling: faraway places sobbing; a young, vernal wind sighing outside Maestro's balcony. . . . Melkior was explaining everything to his numbed senses.

Zee-zee-zee . . . piped up outside the house in its nocturnal, homely hum, like the Dickensian cricket, It, the Powerline.

"Can you hear that, Eustachius," spoke Maestro all of a sudden, sullenly, without lifting his head, "can you hear the siren song? Plug my ears . . . with wax, Eustachius."

"Go back to sleep, Maestro," Melkior reassured him, "it's the breeze, soon it will be day."

"The proper phrase is *a new day*, Eustachius . . . for the sake of ex-pec-tancy and mi-ni-mum optimism . . ."

He stood up and stretched, in a seemingly sober way.

He wasn't asleep, concluded Melkior, he was only resting his thoughts on the knotty tabletop. Embossed on his forehead was a starlike imprint of a knot in the wood: there, he's one of the marked . . . *a star on his forehead, a sparkle in his eye* . . . thought Melkior by way of the poet's line.

Maestro opened the balcony door, fragrant fresh air burst into the close, smelly room.

"Can you smell the breath of spring, Eustachius?" he asked with concealed irony. "That's why I feel the torrents of spring inside me. I'm not partial to Turgenev, are you? I'm off to point my hose, Eustachius," he said going out onto the balcony, "perhaps I'll touch Eternity with my arc. Adieu, adieu! Eustachius, remember me . . ."

"*Remember thee! Ay, thou poor ghost, while memory holds a seat in this distracted globe,*" recited Melkior with pathos. He noticed his voice had gone hoarse. It's the waking and the smoking, I'm going to take it easy all day tomorrow . . . and sleep, sleep . . . This "tomorrow" struck him as exquisitely lovely and he smiled.

Maestro had already "pointed his hose" powerfully, there was the splashing sound of a waterfall . . .

A boyish game, the little Brussels piss-kid playing with his wee fountain in the park. Melkior was smiling as he listened to the noise of the cozy little cascade. A-ahh, *mannequin-pisse* . . . he said yawning. But before he could close his mouth he noticed his hearing turn around with an earnest interest in the sound outside . . . he saw a glittering arc rearing defiantly, shooting across the night, bound for somewhere far away: it aimed to sprinkle its badmouthed, symbolic water over the whole of the Future and all it concealed . . . to reach Eternity with its defiance.

From outside the house there came again the ingratiating, warm stridor *zreee . . . zreee . . .* as though wishing to offer the warmth of the home fires and the comfort of sleep.

Melkior was suddenly illumined by horrifying clarity! As if the walls of some *other, common, everyday* consciousness had broken down inside him, as in the flash of a spark, he instantly intuited Maestro's "brand new," "original," "medicinally pure" death. He did not have time to scream, to rush out on the balcony . . . Maestro had already *reached Eternity* with his "arc." He heard the altered, thick, and somehow surprised voice, as if the man was angrily trying to clear his throat for a new speech with "honorable Eustachius." But all it came to was a labored mumble, a death rattle, and then a soft and seemingly cautious thud which seemed to mean, "There, that's all."

Massage the heart, massage the heart . . . Everyone is saying it. They are gathered around the *sleeping* and seemingly *deceased one* who has apparently forfeited his retirement benefits. . . . He is draped across the balcony's wrought-iron railing, with flowers strewn over him, as if decked out for a celebration. . . . He is being funny: eyes closed, he is twitching like a dead body on a clattering cart, as though shaken by electric shocks. Electric fever persisting, thought Melkior. Numbskull is giving him artificial respiration: *that's the thing to do*, he says raising and lowering Maestro's arms, *pump the air, he's nothing but a pump now, a diver must have air* . . . Ugo is laughing: *a pump! By my father, the lecherous Parampion Kalisto, this is the only thing that will help him!* and sprinkling brandy over him from a watering can. *Look, his ear is moving* . . . "On Ombrellion, the barren mountain, spake he!" cries out the Melancholic from inside the room. Who speaks? asks Melkior. *He who is bent double out there . . . and who shall be resurrected before the cock crows thrice . . . for we know why the cock crows,* he adds to Melkior in a whisper, with a confidential wink. "No you don't! No more on tab!" The shout comes from Thénardier, who is wrestling with Ugo for the watering can. "Who's going to pay me for what he guzzled alive? Let the Earth . . . devil take him! . . . let the Earth soak it all!" "On Ombrellion . . . Give him belfry bats and a spinning top, he's got to be brought back to life!" shouts the Melancholic stamping his foot in a quarrelsome way. "And when we hear the Alligator tonight (he whispers to Melkior) I'll show you the winks. There are nine of them. Shh, it's a Scale Six secret. Now walk on, pretend you don't know me."

Chicory is weeping: *Master!* . . . He's the only one who loved him, thinks Melkior and reproaches himself for being cold-hearted.

"Take this—now you'll see for yourself how hollow you are!" Freddie has suddenly sprung up from nowhere and is leering over *The One Bent Double Across The Railing,* "and I'm a sugar cane, ha-ha." And he flings at his eye the thorny stem of a rose. "Fred, sugar—my sweet," exclaims Viviana.

A great multitude has gathered around him, the small balcony is chock-full. The room, too, is filled to bursting, and so are all the corridors, the staircase, all the way down to the main door. Outside the house the crowd shouts: Hang the whore on the wall! Spit on her! (This is a reference to the Gioconda; she is there above him, the smile never leaving her face.)

Freddie is saying to Viviana: "Don't be afraid, they can't hurt you—I am here."

"All the same, Fred, what if they put me in a frame and spit on me?" trembles Viviana.

"They won't—I'm here!" This time it is ATMAN speaking. In the housecoat, with the white muffler, with the spider. She snuggles up to him, "Oh, Mac!" He pushes her back gently: "Wait, I've got to massage his heart." He points his long, bony fingers at the doubled-up Maestro and starts incanting mumbo jumbo, "So, father? Bare-foot, was she . . . So, father?"

"You're not going to revive him, are you, Mac?" she asks in great fear.

"Re-viiive?" drawls ATMAN looking Melkior derisively in the eyes. His own eyes come quite close together, flow into one (like two drops of water) to form a large, hard, bulging eye, blue as a plum.

Polyphemus! Melkior goes numb with fear.

"Uh-ah, no, no," laughed ATMAN with his wide-set teeth. "Not Polyphemus! The embryo of glory in alcohol, right? While taking the animal to be weighed every now and then: a bone and a skin. . . . The drum gets the skin, right? And what does the Motherland get—

a fig? Ah, no, no, you'll make a dinner for the *Croco-dile!* Alligatorrr!" he summons the monster.

"Didn't I tell you it was still *over there?*" whispers the Melancholic, almost breathless. "Wink to wink—nine."

In reply to ATMAN's call, the endless *Length* of the Great Worm begins to undulate. Lightning flashes and thunder booms from every movement. . . .

"It will be the ruination . . ." howls Melkior, but with a singsong lilt as if there were gaiety in it.

"And I pissed on it, Eustachius, ha-ha," says Maestro bent over double (with laughter) over the railing. "That night, remember *reaching eternity?*—well, it was that very night that I . . . ha-ha-ha, lightning strike me dead!"

"But what am I to do, Maestro? It's my turn now, *he's* coming, infuriated, horrible . . ."

". . . and pissed on! Retreat into the Vatican Library for six years . . . in noble penury, in rags worn with dignity." After some thinking: "Have yourself castrated! You'll be Saint Eustachius the Eunuch, what more can you ask? Ooh, ooh, ooh . . ." Maestro is having a marvelous time.

At that point, issuing from afar as if it were the echo speaking, comes Don Fernando's drawling voice beseeching: "Do not drink the water . . . capture whoever poisoned the reservoir . . . do not drink the water."

Downstairs among the crowd a panic spreads, cries, commotion, they rush off straight away to nab the poisoners. "It's their agents poisoning us." And I've just had two full glasses, thinks Melkior with a desperate man's pleasure; he is feeling bravery in his stomach, like a small boy who has swallowed a button.

Then there is another voice, sober, accommodating, from quite nearby, from the adjoining room: "Citizens, this is not an exercise. Our country is under attack. We are at . . ."

Melkior pronounced the word himself, inside, his eyes still closed, and repeated it.

"Good morning," he said without relinquishing his dream. He

wished to retreat into the labyrinths of false sounds, the echoes of amicable distances; to let the sleeper go on toying with words; to grant waking the benefit of another morning from *the other world* . . . but the voice from the adjoining room was tenaciously repeating its lesson, practicing a difficult language: *Citizens, this is not an exercise. What you are hearing is our guns. Our country is under attack. We are at war.*

Our guns! heard Melkior with emotion. He sees hardened warriors, our men, intrepid, smiling self-confidently . . . *O-ri-en-ted* . . . by moss, "Listen up, look at him . . ." disarray in the image of the stable: Caesar's croup . . . Nettle; barking at the lightbulb . . . piss off, I don't want to see you again, ever . . .

Early this morning our capital city was . . . something like a thunderclap covered the voice from the adjoining room. The announcer cleared his throat, composed. "He's overcome with emotion at the roar of our guns!" Melkior was trying to retrieve the emotion, but the very words disbelieved their own sentence, scoffed at its sweetness.

"That's anti-aircraft," could be heard from the street.

They are shooting at Kurt. Melkior sees him up there, high in the sky, "Duty calls, Herr Professor," keeping an eye on his Cozy Corner around the corner . . . Well, well! muses the delighted Kurt.

"Call this shooting? The man must be blind!"

"It's the height, man, the aeroplane's way too high up. Reconnaissance, he's not carrying bombs."

"Of course, he's carrying bonbons for the little children. What did I tell you—there he is, dropping chocolates, they've got chocolate to spare."

"He's dropping leaflets, leaflets!" shouted the judge from the window, educating the imbeciles in the street. Why be rude—it might make them go back for real bombs.

"Parcheesi," said Melkior.

Do not drink the water, the announcer came on again. *There is reason to suspect that the water has been poisoned by enemy agents. Do not use water until we have broadcast the laboratory report* . . .

"Utterly ridiculous propaganda!" the lawyer was saying angrily on the landing. "Why, they'll be here by tomorrow . . . what do you think they'll do . . . poison themselves? Preposterous. Danica, get me a glass of water!"

"Oh, please, Dad, don't . . ."

"Get me a glass of water, you ninny! Take a big one from the kitchen!"

"Doctor, perhaps you really shouldn't . . ." came the landlady's anxious voice.

"Shouldn't nothing," the lawyer was shouting angrily. "I'll show you who's poisoning the population! They poison the water? As if they had nothing better to do . . . Ptui, this is mineral water! You want me to crack your skull? I said, pour me a glass of water!"

"I was so scared, Daddy . . ."

Not to fear, daughter, said Melkior to her, your Daddy knows their plans did not include poisoning . . . Kurt and ATMAN and Dad and Auntie . . . Viviana . . . they all knew. Perhaps Don Fernando was right after all . . .

"There—has anything happened to me?" The lawyer had performed an ad hoc analysis on the landing and achieved the desired effect. The tenants were looking at him with respect as a man knowledgeable about *this new thing that was happening* . . .

God knows what else things will come to . . . They were retreating to their nests; their locks went click . . . to be on the safe side.

"Poisoned the water, indeed," the lawyer was yelling after them, "well, just let me see if there's anyone else to say they did!"

Melkior felt like shouting: yes, there is—I do! But he nevertheless tucked his head under the blanket and fell to gnawing his already well-gnawed bone: *O body of mine* . . . In the intimate darkness, erotically, cannibalistically, he sensed the odor of his body. This is presumably what cannibals and women feel when close up to a man . . . does that mean I wish to eat, and make love to, myself? The bones (he happened to have a kneecap in hand), gnaw the bones, copulate with the shadow.

The self-abusing autophage. The thrilling presence of one's own

518

body. And (like that night on the train's hard bench) he fell to exploring his strange structure. So: an undamaged skeleton . . . ay, thou poor ghost, is still lying here with me. It knows the lever and scale laws and walk, jump, run, get up, lie down, sit down; knows what "we could fall" means when on a sheet of ice, knows what means a polite bow or a kick (with the right foot, or indeed the left, as you wish), what means the hand moving easily across paper, leaving in its wake black, bent, intertwined, broken threads of tortured thoughts. All those pipes, valves, bladders, pumps, membranes, filaments, communications networks; mechanics, optics, acoustics: the world broken down into tones and colors, odors, tastes, into rough and smooth, hard and soft, warm and cold, sweet and bitter. All those laboratories, cabinets, institutes, precision instruments for a fine reading of life's safety. . . . In here, lying with me, is this perfect world: wisely ticking its little time in its little darkness . . . and outside there's a war on. And that lethal insect has already been released from Essen, homing in on this perfection . . .

The door opened noisily and somebody burst into the room.

"Ha-ha, will you look at him?" Ugo bared his black fillings. "Worlds colliding outside, and he's caught up in self-abuse! Hey," he yanked the blanket off Melkior, "we're under attack! Sir, there's a war raging out there!"

"How did you get in?" wondered Melkior pulling the blanket back up to his chin. "Wasn't the door locked?"

"You failed to take the first precaution for safety in time of war. First you lock the door and only then do you pull the blanket up over your head. This is what the mentally retarded bird known as the ostrich does."

What the devil brought him here now?

"I'm not in a mood for joking. Leave me alone, let me sleep."

"Perchance to dream? What about the war then—nothing, a mere joke? Why, this is against mankind!"

Everything's a joke to him, damn his . . . Melkior was irritated by the eccentric, irresponsible "Parampionic style" at a time like this . . .

"Will you for God's sake leave me in peace!" he finally shouted.

"Wouldn't that be nice! I, too, would have preferred 'in peace' . . . along with Immanuel Kant, but they won't let me. Did you hear me: we have been attacked."

"I know, so what? Shall I set up dominoes for them?"

"Well, that's not a bad idea in fact . . . as the first line of defense. You match three to three, five to five, laying them in different directions to confuse things, set up traps . . . bravo! Tell me, did you see that in a dream?"

Melkior did not answer. Lying on his stomach he was looking over the edge of the bed at his slippers on the floor. Old, faithful, scuffed. There they are, waiting, motionless ever since the night before, patient, indifferent to anything that is not me. They have no idea they have experienced war. And when I descend from the bed they will piously kiss the soles of both my feet and come with me, rustling prayers for the warmth of my feet, for my comfort, for the happiness of my solitude. How I have worn them! O good my Slippers, never before have I noticed your dedicated and quiet life down there on the floor. . . .

"Come on, Eustachius, get up and let's go."

"Go where?"

"Why, out, to watch the war. That kind of thing you only get to see once in a lifetime."

"And what do you think you'll see?"

"What do you mean, 'what'? Everything's changed now. My Kalisto put in a large supply of salts and ten packets of toilet paper first thing in the morning. There'll be a shortage of them, says he. In addition to Eros, he's a great worshipper of his anus. You should see how piously he breaks wind—word of honor, you'd swear it was Saint Francis talking to the pigeons. It's easy for you to laugh, but I have to live in that atmosphere."

Melkior was not laughing—he appreciated Mr. Kalisto's worries. There, at least he's concerned about the future, if only in that way, whereas his son . . .

"And another thing," the son was saying, "it's fun to watch the bourgeoisie lose their composure. With their shops out there, their houses, and the bombs dropping from above. Making a rush at the banks, trying to withdraw their deposits, only to find the banks are closed—it's Sunday. They'll be buying chocolate and toothpaste tomorrow. There's a war on, sir. My mother tearfully says there'll be a shortage of flour and soap (you're familiar with her cleanliness complexes), and my Kalisto, ahh, he is hoarding toilet paper! So much for the war as reflected in my family. In the street, everyone walks sniffing at the air, as if the war were exuding a smell—and a pleasant one, too. And everyone's looking up at the sky . . . That's where the main celebration is expected to come from. People say they landed last night outside the city, they're all over everywhere in plain clothes."

"*And* they've poisoned the water," smiled Melkior nervously, his jaw trembling.

"Laugh on, do. . . . But the language of Johann Wolfgang Goethe is to be heard abundantly all over town, and the women—the per-fumed ones—are pricking up their ears in cafés at *guten Tag.* I've already stunned one with a line of poetry, plus two tears for good measure, well, you know me . . . *O Grille, sing, die Nacht ist lang . . .* and after that, in another line, there's this word *unbedacht*—know what it means? Well, never mind, we'll be chirping about that lyri-cism tonight, the night is long. . . ."

"Oh," Melkior's throat constricted, "what about our (sure, 'our') er . . . the one you used . . . *October's gentle breath . . . ?*"

"The one I used gentle breath? What do you mean?"

He knows, the brute, he knows all right—he's just being . . . "The one I called *Viviana* . . . don't tell me she's looking forward to *guten Morgen,* too?"

"She's off to meet them halfway, I think," said Ugo casually. "But it hurts, mournful Eustachius—she went away without a goodbye kiss, without leaving me two hairs or at least a nail-paring to remem-ber her by forever . . ."

"Went away . . . with Freddie?"

"Does it matter? She's gone, the dove's fluttered away."

"Unless it's with ATMAN?" wondered Melkior aloud.

"Batman who?"

"The palmist . . . the one living downstairs . . ."

"Hah, ATMAN. Was it you who first gave him that name? Or the late Maestro? Tell me, you were actually with him the night he . . . scorned technological progress? Anyway, the idea was . . . you must admit . . . What symbolism—to piss on electric current! Worthy of a . . . of that Greek who threw himself down the crater of Etna."

Maestro couldn't remember the name of the Socrates' pupil, either. . . . "The one who tried to persuade him to flee."

Melkior's head was still hanging over the edge of the bed. He was no longer looking at his slippers, he had his eyes closed. He saw Maestro's dead arms dangling from the railing; stretched out, long, straight, as if—extended toward the Earth—they wished to show their scorn for the sky above. Arms . . . with no head; the head had been swallowed by the jacket—it had slid down and devoured Maestro's head. That was the image in the blurred grayness of Melkior's memory.

"Death most likely instantaneous" was the sentence on Maestro's "City Page" with which Melkior tried to console himself. A minute or two—how long was that to a dying man? Perhaps a vast and emotion-laden duration . . . which the City Desk reporter had slashed to zero—"instantaneous"—presumably to make it all seem *easy* and *simple*, no thought, no hope. A consolation for his own future? And yet Maestro had remembered reading about a man who survived electrocution! Seven minutes afterward, a huge chance! "So it appears all is not lost after the jolt, you can survive . . . provided someone turns their hand to it, right, Eustachius?" Yes, massage the heart . . . my dead soul!

Melkior shuddered. Why didn't I see it at the time? He moved his head to the pillow; he looked at Ugo with wondering and irritation and again closed his eyes.

"Had a bad dream, sir?"

"He'd worked it out ages ago, drinking beer, practicing," Melkior was saying without opening his eyes. " 'A pure death.' Against bodily mutilation as performed by scoundrels and rogues . . . He'd sold his cadaver, too . . ."

"Yes, 'Snip,' we do remember, 'Anatomy, or My Person on Sale' . . . Ahh, our poor bug! He knew all the animals in Dostoyevsky. So, Eustachius . . . did he really . . . aim and hit at his first go?"

Melkior scowled in disgust and made no reply.

"Don't frown, I have serious reasons for asking." Ugo's face was really serious, even thoughtful.

"You and your 'serious reasons'—bah!" Melkior dismissed him scornfully.

"All the same, dear Eustachius . . ." smirked Ugo mysteriously, "perhaps I do possess certain facts, eh? Why did he choose that very night for his great outpouring of scorn, eh? Now, now, don't get upset, it has nothing to do with you. He only took you along as a witness to the . . . gesture, for the sake of his legend . . . But try to remember: what state was he in when you found him outside the Corso? Yes, all right, 'illumined,'" Ugo replied immediately to his own question, "but that was hardly unusual—he'd been, as you know, inebriating himself with that joy before . . . but what other state was he in? Bloody, or rather bloodied . . . and do you know who'd done that to him?"

"Why, Freddie the actor, of course."

"Oh no—just goes to show how much you're in the dark. That is, it wasn't Freddie alone, and that crowning, bloody blow was not Freddy's doing, he hasn't got such a remarkable hand. It was a heavy, bony hand, shovel-like, that did that. You must know," Ugo lowered his voice theatrically, "Maestro was at the Corso that evening *on assignment*, to borrow a phrase from the parlance of revolutionaries."

Melkior gave an angry snort:

"You're out of your mind!"

"No, you are! Did you hear what he was bellowing in there?"

"No I didn't—I came too late."

"Well, I did! I didn't want to miss the spectacle."

"So you knew all along?"

"Naturally. I'd spent the whole afternoon at the Give'nTake assisting in rehearsals for the feat. That's where it all began. He accused Thénardier, too: you're an informer, you've sold your soul to the fifth column; he gave him a squirt of soda from a siphon right in the eye, massacred rows of enemy glasses on the bar . . . And so, presumably enraged by the tinkle of broken glass, he went off to carry out the *assignment*."

"What assignment, God strike you?"

"His assignment . . . presumably patriotic . . . He was to draw public attention to the suspicious characters at the Corso . . . but it turned out all wrong. While on the spot, old wounds reopened—love wounds, as you know—and instead of sowing panic among the fifth columnists, stirring the public to action, in a word, instead of striking terror into the hearts of the spies he got his proboscis bashed in by a heavy and bony hand."

"By a hand . . . ?"

". . . well known for its cracking finger joints . . ."

"ATMAN!" Melkior shook with rage. Now it was all becoming clear to him.

"You said yourself you called the magician by that name."

"But why did Maestro think it was the actor who struck him?"

"Yes, well, he wasn't far from wrong. He'd been shouting at her and him and his entire clientele that they were blackguards, spies, traitors, fifth columnists . . . he knew the litany by heart. Given that there was a lady present, Freddie only offered him a couple of slaps in the face and pushed him into the dark behind the cloakroom, into the magician's hands. Thus did Fredegarius the actor shine in yet another supporting role."

"Now, those . . . slogans—that *assignment*, rather—it was Don Fernando's doing, wasn't it? Pre-ven-tive action . . ." added Melkior and gave a malicious smile.

"I beg your pardon?" affected Ugo, while bursting with suppressed laughter. "With your permission, Eustachius, I will refrain from making any declarations or comments. I offer only my observations. I may add, for what it's worth, that the Central European thinker just referred to by you was monitoring the diversion from the phone box faking a telephone conversation. Unless he was really reporting the development of the operations to some headquarters or other. . . . This of course I add with great reservation."

"But how did he drive him into it?" mused Melkior aloud. "What did he lure him with?"

"Despair, Eustachius," replied Ugo somberly, "medicinally pure despair. And with shot after shot. He'd been feeling . . . you know how . . . to begin with, and when he saw her with Frederick the Hollow in the bargain . . . well, you don't need me telling you—you followed the squashed bug's last twitches yourself. That's why he selected that very day: two birds, one stone, adieu!"

"He was looking for you afterward, sent me in to scout the Give'nTake . . ."

"For the big farewell scene. He was a theater lover. A pathos-ridden individual."

Melkior was now hating the tone of glib irony. They were discussing a man, after all, a mutual acquaintance, the "Mad Bug," the *noble* Maestro! He wished to raise the memory to the level of his present state of mind. Maestro had started the cycle. "Now it's your turn." Melkior shuddered.

"Anyway, who knows what's written in the stars about us?" said Ugo looking "tragically" out the window. "Did you ever ask your star-gazer to read your destiny for you? Who knows . . . well, you've seen his eyes."

She doesn't need dead men, remembered Melkior, and he said nothing.

"Come on, get up," said Ugo with sudden impatience and tried to pull the blanket off of Melkior again. "You're behaving like a sickly dauphin being told in bed there's a war on."

"You go on ahead, I'll catch up," Melkior defended himself with all his might. "I'll look for you at the Give'nTake," he promised without meaning it, just to get Ugo to leave.

"At the Give'nTake? Where do you live, my child?" said Ugo in theatrical consternation. "You don't know that Thénardier the monster has issued a reward for my insolvent head? Apart from that, there has appeared at the Give'nTake an ad for Bayer aspirin to replace the jovial tippler with the snifter of Courvoisier."

Melkior laughed absentmindedly.

"Don't laugh—I'm in no mood for joking in these critical times!" Ugo wished somebody would believe in his "earnestness" if only once . . . "Aren't these dangerous symptoms? Weird metamorphoses are going on there, everything's already stinking of the most glaring Fascism."

"I'll look for you somewhere else, then," said Melkior.

"Perhaps at the Theater Café. . . . Because there's no room for us at the Corso; the headquarters of The Concerned is in permanent session there, and we are just . . . well, magpies . . ."

"At the Theater Café, then . . ." The leech! fumed Melkior, latching onto every word you say.

"Why 'then'?" (There he goes again.) "Planning to stand me up?"

"All right, strike the 'then' and see you later, damn you!" flared Melkior in the end.

"Well, is it see me later or damn me?" Ugo bared his black fillings above him. "Come to think of it, you're right: damn me if I know if anyone can hope to see anyone else later, in times such as these . . ." He made a skeptical grimace and went out, launching into a vehement whistled rendition of the Radetzky March on the stairs.

These streets were already lying down in submission. Waiting patiently for the tramp of army boots. "They've already occupied Varaždin," he heard in passing a snatch of conversation between the windows.

The gray, cold, colorless April Sunday was blinking, ill-tempered, at the betrayed city. Down the arbored avenue the bare trees were too anxious to bud; they were returning the sap to the wretched Earth beneath: no, thank you, I really can't accept . . . (Poor mother, why did you ever give birth to us?) They did not wish the sun to warm them: please don't bother; they were returning their green to the sunlight. We don't want to make a triumphal arch over their heads, do we? Let's hibernate a bit longer, they were saying to the spring.

Patriotic trees! spoke Melkior with comic pathos walking under the bare black boughs which were shivering in the cold. Each beech, oak, and elm that none can o'erwhelm! he recited under the bare boughs, seeking strength in words, with a sour smile playing around his lips. . . . And brushwood and brambles . . . all the brackens across the land . . . Melkior felt comically moved by the piece of nonsense and gave a mournful laugh. He nevertheless raised his head in honor of the sumptuous plane tree in front of the University building: "Your Imperial Majesty," he said to it and thought of Empress Maria Theresa. Sparrows were chasing each other all over it in what looked like raucous merriment. A prominent old professor of theoretical physics was coming down the stairs; he, too, noticed the sparrows' festivity. Melkior saluted him, lifting his hat. "Having a time of it," he said to him. "Yes—at just the right moment, too," replied the professor, raising his soft black hat "Good morning."

From a side street came the newspaper hawker's nasal chant; he was selling his *Morning News* with mechanical apathy.

"Oh look, 'Situation Improving,'" laughed a man gesturing with his chin at a banner-type headline on page one of his paper, "'Certain signs suggest . . .' ha-ha!"

Melkior responded with a vague smile—who knows what he meant? And when he turned around for another look at the man (what a funny . . . *sweeping* walk), he bumped into a soldier who was in great hurry. The soldier took hold of his shoulders and held him at an arm's length:

"Watch out: eyes to the fore!" The man was smirking. Melkior stared at the familiar face, his mouth agape, but it was a bit odd . . . dressed like this . . .

Pupo, in a private's boots and rough cloth but with the epaulettes of a reserve lieutenant. He smelled of military storerooms: mothballs, leather, urine . . . Of course, he had to tack on the political lesson, noted Melkior morosely. But he instantly felt a surge of joy at the encounter: there, a fighting man, in boots . . . no glasses . . .

"You're a soldier?" he said in confused, senseless amazement.

"Well, what would you want me to be . . . a seducer?" retorted Pupo haughtily, with self-importance. "We're all soldiers now. So will you be, too . . . if you want to live!"

"Live?" repeated Melkior mechanically. Which pigeonhole did he pull that cliché out of? Somewhere it must've been decided to . . . "What's the use—they'll be here by tomorrow."

"What about us—won't we be here, too?"

"Be here like this . . . with epaulettes?" Melkior cast a derisive glance at the gold on Pupo's shoulders.

Pupo turned his head to glance at it, too, but nevertheless with a hushed pride: "This? These are just the necessary rigmarole. This kind of gold's very precious right now," he added with a smile.

"You can command men," teased Melkior.

A cloud of rage flashed through Pupo's eyes. He was about to say something hard, insulting, but he changed his mind, gave a patient smile: "It has its points, too . . . if it's useful for the cause I serve."

"What you do is always useful." Melkior did not want to talk this way, but something inside him was rebelling against the respect he held for Pupo, a vicious and cynical voice . . . as it had against what he felt moments ago for the trees. Brushwood and brambles . . .

"Look, I'm in a hurry," Pupo got moving all of a sudden, taking leave of the *incurable one*. Still, out of habit, he did not fail patiently to donate a warning at least: "If you're doing nothing, at least don't deride those who are doing something."

"Well, what am I to do?" Melkior gave a helpless shrug. "Spit on Hitler's tanks?"

"You seem to think only in large-scale terms . . ."

"What, should I go after their tanks with something small-scale?" laughed Melkior spitefully. "Like the Polish nobility with their spears at Kutno?"

"Stop flailing about with desperate gestures," Pupo cautioned him with all-but-spent patience. "What the hell do you think *I'm* doing? Going from one barracks to another, speaking to the men, preparing them for combat! That's why I wear these stars on my shoulders . . ."

"What combat?" smiled Melkior hopelessly. "It's a complete rout already. They've occupied Varaždin!"

"The real combat is yet to begin," said Pupo with muted pathos. "The thing to do is to stow away as much equipment and weapons as possible. I'm getting my hands on rifles, grenades, boots, that's what I'm doing, small things, fair knight; and as for Varaždin . . . sorry, not my department."

Collecting bees, thought Melkior, and right now we need the honey. I'd rather believe in the Melancholic's alligators . . .

"By the way, that chap I put up . . . do you know where he is now?"

"What do you want with him?" said Pupo sternly. "I don't know where he is . . . and it doesn't matter, anyway."

It doesn't matter . . . Again there was that something that put him off of Pupo. What a perfect dutiful instrument! That other man was quiet, modest, sensible, presumably he was dutiful enough, yet in addition to that he had a strange expression of concern in his eyes . . . "If I didn't work, I wouldn't believe . . ." Pupo would be unable to muster such a thought.

"So," concluded Pupo with a smile, "don't meddle in things which don't concern you . . . and find your place in these times. You're an honest man," he added before leaving and shook Melkior's hand firmly: he understood and forgave.

Melkior took the handshake as an insult; that, too, was dutiful . . . as was the "You're an honest man."

At the main entrance he was greeted by a familiar cap with large golden letters on it spelling PORTER. Behind the large glass panes of the courtyard building it was dark and quiet, no lead was running into moulds, the print rollers were lying still on their axles. The clock in the porter's lodge had stopped.

"Your clock stopped," said Melkior to the Cap.

The smooth red face with a thick yellow moustache and golden eyebrows (which had earned him the nickname of Carrot) nodded worriedly:

"Everything's stopped today, my dear sir. For the first time in the twenty seven years I have been sitting here."

"What, are we having the day off?"

"We haven't come out with an edition at all. Did you see the *Morning News*—'Situation Improving . . .' and the capital city gone! They're all laughing about it upstairs." He laughed himself, loyally. "You going up? They're all there. Rooms full of cigarette smoke, everybody smoking like . . . Nobody's doing anything. The compositors went and got drunk first thing in the morning."

"So the situation's . . ."

". . . 'bloody offal,' as our Russian gal likes to say."

"Carrot, don't tell me you, too, are propagating defeatism!" Coming down the stairs was a tall cowboyish individual, the Foreign Affairs Editor. His head was unsuitable for any kind of hat and stood out with an air of importance, vast and bare as it was. While still on the stairs he attacked the red-headed porter: "I'll shove that damned cap down your throat, gold letters and all! Already preparing to serve the new masters, are you?" He then spoke to Melkior with unspent rage, which had made his head swell further still: "Send the lot of them out to the border, let them spout their shit there! Defeatist damned nits! Already watching out not to get off on the wrong foot with the new masters, fifth-column scum!" His strong hands seemed to be looking for something to break and crush . . . and they unconsciously crushed between their fingers an innocent little Morava cigarette.

The porter had taken timely refuge in his cubicle and went about winding the clock.

"Why didn't we come out with an edition today?" asked Melkior with accommodating naïveté.

"Why?" bellowed the editor again. "Didn't I tell you—out of consideration for the enemy! I brought them news from the front, from the Fourth Army Headquarters, but no—the gentlemen want to check it, we can't publish he-said she-said, they grumble. So what I bring is he-said she-said, is it? God damn you all!"

"Perhaps it's because the news is bad . . ." Melkior was playing the fool.

"What do you mean, bad?" yelled the editor (Melkior took a step back).

"Our army's already taken Rijeka, Zadar, Skadar! The northern frontier is firmly in our hands. The young King has left for the front line in person. The operations are moving ahead favorably . . . and in their book that is he-said she-said!"

Perhaps it's true after all, hoped Melkior foolishly. He watched the little Morava, crushed between the mighty fingers, and it struck him as symbolic . . . those awesome, invincible fingers . . . and brushwood and brambles, all the brackens . . .

"And what does the Old Man say?"

"The Old Man's invisible as never before! Hidden himself away in the Black Room, the Jesuit! Phoning left and right, demanding to be put through to Lord God! Asking for top guarantees for his career! Why take risks, right? Oh, God damn him!"

And off went the editor, striding hurriedly as if he had decided to undertake something elsewhere which would make all of "them up there" wail in mortal anguish. Melkior waited until the furious editor had left. He no longer wanted to go upstairs, he preferred believing our boys had taken Zadar, Skadar . . .

"The creep must be thinking the King will send him a decoration for this," grumbled the offended porter. "Why don't he go fight himself? He's strong as an ox! Instead of taking it all out on me like . . . There he goes," he jerked his head angrily to the other side, "off to the bar . . . to guzzle cognacs and liqueurs . . . and the rabble can damned well go to the wall for their lordships. No, honestly— am I right?"

"I gather you're against . . ."

"Me? Neither for nor against," the porter hastened to cut the question short. "How much is my head worth? As long as I've got this cap on it . . . that's what it's worth. If the cap goes, the head goes with it, as the late Maestro used to say. PORTER," he pointed a finger at his golden letters, "it doesn't hurt nobody's political feelings. Look after your cap, Carrot, the late Maestro he used to shout to me when he passed by. He called me that on account of these hairs of mine."

"He was a good sort . . ."

"Polda? Now there was a man!" exclaimed Carrot respectfully. "Many's the time he'd tell me, in confidence, like: You, Carrot, you're the only real man in the bunch! So, honest, was I a match for him—an ordinary porter? He knew each of us like the inside of his pocket, and a nice word for the ordinary man always on his lips . . . All the brains and all, and look how he goes—by the electricity, like a gangster. No funeral and no grave, but such a man! No, honestly—am I right or am I right?" Carrot actually brushed away a tear. "Why don't they take that ox instead, have the vets study him?" He then asked confidentially: "Is it true they're gonna put his skeleton on show? I'd like to take him a bunch of flowers . . ."

"What exhibit?"

"Up the Faculty of Medicine . . . he left it for the poor students to learn on . . ."

This is already Act Five, at the cemetery. Yorick's skull. Prithee, Eustachius, tell me one thing . . . Melkior felt a chill in his bones: why this conversation just now? He felt a superstitious fear at his presentiment, left the astounded porter and hurried out into the street.

And there's a war on again! He didn't know which side to join—both were equally pointless. A staff automobile with a high chassis zipped past him. Inside were red lapels, white moustaches, gold: generals. He set out after them. Follow the commanders (he said) in times of war! They're making for the front, where the young King is . . . Or fleeing, perhaps—leaving the King in the lurch? Whatever the case—after them!

The automobile had long since disappeared but he moved on with resolve: he had decided which direction to take. "I may be floating in formaldehyde tomorrow." That memory, now? He tried to chase it off by means of a pretty picture postcard: city panorama—green spring, arborways, park—a view from the railway station. . . . A small square pool in the middle of the park: a naked pale corpse floating face down; posterior flashing white, formaldehyde reeking. . . . Ay, thy poor ghost, while memory . . . Release me from my promise!

I'm off to where the war is, he said inside with a kind of firmness —follow the generals! "Everyone is bound to fight if of hero stock he be," they sang at school outings, children's patriotic piping voices, the teacher with beautiful neck walking at the head, the boys following, in love with her . . . "Lay down his life like a knight for our homeland's libertee!" And little Melkior was ready to "lay down his life" for the teacher-homeland with her beautiful arching neck, him unhappy at being a child, her neck full and soft, with dark tender folds. . . . It gave Melkior goose bumps. . . . When I grow up I'll marry her. . . . "For our homeland's libertee." And now I'm following in the generals' footsteps. . . .

Before him he saw: a deserted street. A squad of ragged soldiers with outdated long rifles. Hey, where are the generals? He felt their disappearance as treason. Poor soldiers, abandoned in the middle of the street, tramping their hobnailed boots in dead earnest. Where are they off to? With those knee-length rifles? To get dry straw for Caesar at the front? Which way do you go when you go off to war?

Look, he's still there with those ears! exclaimed Melkior almost aloud. At about ten meters ahead he had spotted that pair of huge ears and the familiar scrawny neck . . . Making for the invalid's weighing machine. The desperate warfare for every gram was still on! "Everyone is bound to fight," sang Melkior inside.

He approached the machine as if he were the "next customer"; he waited patiently for his turn.

"Now then, in God's name," said the catechist, removing the ballast from his pockets. About to float away, thought Melkior. "But do pay attention (he had stepped onto the machine)—precision, precision!"

"Not to worry, Reverend," the invalid cajoled him. "Nothing but the best for a regular such as yourself. . . ." The invalid was missing his left arm right up to the shoulder, and the left side of his face was poorly patched together. A trench bomb, explained Melkior with expertise.

"What? It can't be!" the catechist was astonished. "Sixty grams down since last night! No, you've got it wrong."

"No way, Reverend, no way," said the invalid with scientific certainty, "that's what it is and no mistake."

"But, hey, man, sixty grams since last night! You weighed me yourself."

"I know, Reverend, I know," shrugged the invalid indifferently, "but there's nothing I can do—it's what the equipment shows." ("The equipment"—that's what executioners call the guillotine, the gallows . . .) Melkior loathed the invalid's indifference. "After all, what's sixty grams, Reverend? It's only a tad over two ounces . . . just running a light sweat would have been enough."

"Running a sweat, indeed," the catechist snorted. "I'm shivering with the cold! Look, it's beginning to snow!" Indeed, there was the odd snowflake here and there to heighten Dom Kuzma's suspicion.

"Well, there are losses beside sweating," the invalid smiled at Melkior, "I don't have to spell it out, do I?"

"Losses beside sweating . . ." repeated Dom Kuzma, unthinking. Having noticed Melkior by his side, he began to stuff his belongings back into his pockets in embarrassment. All of a sudden he raised his head toward the invalid, radiant with joy: "You were right, friend, I had an orange in my pocket last night! That's the sixty grams!" He stepped down with a smile, full of unexpected optimism. But the devil relished spoiling his joy: "All the same, I do have my doubts about your machine . . ." He went off entirely unhappy.

"God give me strength!" sighed the invalid with relief. "Yes, sir."

Melkior lay a one-dinar coin shamefully on the cover of the little box and went away without stepping onto the machine.

"What about the weighing?" said the owner of "the equipment" in surprise: it takes all kinds . . .

"No need," said Melkior, more or less to himself. Davos, the glaciers . . . *white all around and a tinge of illness* . . . there was no need for anything. He felt shame and anger. The Cyclops Polyphemus, the beast, now treads the Earth! (He was foaming at the mouth.) A stinger and wasp's venom . . . so I could stab his gorge . . .

He noticed what he was saying and it struck him as comical. But laughter was deaf at his observation. Laughter is a robot anyway! he said angrily.

But the sound of laughter came . . . from somewhere close, so near as to surprise him: where did the echo come from?

"Your attention, heh, heh, heh . . ."

All of a sudden there materialized before him a leering drunken face with dark fillings. Ugo was leading a mob of drunks picked up in dives along the way . . . a noisy and motley crew, from ragamuffins like Four Eyes to the elegant dandy Freddie. What's this combination, now? wondered Melkior. As a matter of fact, Freddie was rather standing "aside" (not his crowd), but Four Eyes kept addressing him as "Your Highness" and attempting to fling an arm around Freddie's shoulders.

"Your attention, lowlifes," spoke Ugo to the mob, "here's our Conscience—bow down!"

Four Eyes bowed humbly, who knows, it might turn out to be a wise move. An unshaven and dirty individual laughed in his face.

"Cut the cackling, Shitface!" Four Eyes warned him. "He's got more in his little finger than . . ." He was remembering the drinks on Melkior at Kurt's Cozy Corner . . . ahh, those had been the days!

"Shut up, Basilisk!" Ugo snapped at him, "you always ruin everything!"

"Yes, Master . . ." Four Eyes looked around the mob, honored: he had acquired a moniker.

"Welcome at long last to our midst, oh, Sun!" Ugo waved his arms fawningly, "we're lost without you! Just say the word and . . . Where shall we go?"

"To . . ." Melkior opened his mouth, but rage rent all his words. In his dry, bitter mouth he felt the vexing taste of a kind of spite; a brackish vengeful hatred which had long been gathering momentum inside him burst its inarticulate, savage, animal-like, speech-deprived way into his mouth, and he spat it out unconsciously, dryly, almost symbolically, right in Ugo's face which was grinning fetchingly before him in confident expectation.

This is what Freddie had been waiting for: he rushed in first (to settle accounts with the pen-wielding artist at last!), the others followed. . . . Get the weirdo!

Ugo elicited Melkior's admiration once again. He never even winked after being spat on—he only gave him a moist, blurred look. He then calmly turned to face the mob and stepped in front of Melkior spreading his arms in protection:

"Over my dead body!" he said resolutely. "Shitface," who had been spoiling for a fight, cursed. "Quiet! And everyone to his proper place! There's a higher form of justice, this is not your calling. Fredegarius, resheath your pinewood prop sword! Open the ranks, make way for Eustachius the Magnificent!"

The mob parted obediently, and he made a gracious gesture, waving Melkior through.

It's a hoax . . . thought Melkior, distrustful. (Freddie was smirking insidiously from the side.) But there was nothing to be done, he had to go . . . His back broke out in goose bumps, expecting blows . . . He passed halfway through the gauntlet; nothing happened (this is how people used to be flogged); he reached the end; this is where it starts . . . But there was nothing, not a thing, not even a single nasty poke . . .

O Parampion! He felt like turning back and giving Ugo a hug. But he was still not convinced. And once he'd been convinced he still thought: it could just as well make the madman regret what he'd just done . . .

"And now, you crew of good-for-nothings, forward to new adventures!" he heard Ugo command behind him. But there was a despondent and sad undertone to the voice, like a desperate call after something that had been lost . . . or so it seemed to Melkior.

He now wished only to move on around the next corner, as if there were a different world there.

Everything was the same around the next corner. The street, the infrequent passersby with half-frozen noses. (It was the sixth of April —some spring!) They were watching the random Sunday passersby with indifference. Idle, useless watching. . . . Was that war—people looking on, indifferent, dull? Had they stared at Sunday mornings before?—He could not recall. Ugo is talking gibberish—the war is invisible.

An aeroplane droned very high overhead. There it is, said Melkior. Solitary onlookers were gathering into knots as if an accident had taken place, raising their noses. "Reconnaissance," explained an expert (everybody was listening trustingly), "he's flying solo at a great altitude—he must be on a reconnaissance flight. Photographing. The bombers follow later . . . And our anti-aircraft fellows are not lifting a finger . . ."

The man barely said the words before guns started booming. The aeroplane was a tiny toy high among the clouds. Small white cloudlets blossomed beneath it. . . . "He's too high—they're wasting their ammo," said the expert.

Should they save it for Christmas then? thought Melkior irascibly. Let them boom on!

Funny, the rumbling . . . (he walked away with derisive thoughts) . . . as if we were celebrating something down here . . .

"It's not very wise to stand around in the street," he heard the expert behind him, "shrapnel comes down all over." Melkior drew closer to the façades . . . as if it were raining, he laughed at his prudence.

"Keep away from the wall!"

A soldier—a sentry—was standing in front of him, on his rifle a bayonet, on his head a helmet. Over the gate was dejected gray lettering on a dirtied gray background: GARRISON COMMAND.

"Keep away, you hear!" The soldier was already unslinging his rifle.

"I'm going in," Melkior told him uncaringly and tried to enter.

"Wait!" bawled the sentry rudely, then yelled into the gate: "Sarge!"

Out came a young, emaciated man, his face sickly but his eyes keen and feverish.

"This one here," the sentry tilted his head at Melkior.

"What do you want?" asked the sergeant, irritated.

"To see the Orderly Officer," replied Melkior importantly. This must be the place, he thought.

"You're looking at him."

"Your superior," said Melkior.

"Can't see you. He's busy. There's a war on, if you hadn't noticed."

"I'm on official business."

"What kind?"

"Important." Saying this, Melkior smiled and, so it seemed, gave a slight wink.

"C'mon in." Outside one of the doors the sergeant said: "Wait."

A long empty corridor with a floor scarred by army boots, a row of gray doors opposite which tall windows looked out on a barren, mournful yard. Why is everything so hopeless in here? Melkior was about to leave, but then the door opened and the sergeant said: "Come in."

The room smelled of garlic and brandy. It appeared to be empty. On the desk, under a picture of the young King, were a half-full bottle, an inkwell in a wooden holder, and the remnants of some processed food among several sheets of paper scattered helter-skelter. It was moments later that Melkior noticed an army bed as well, and on it a man under a gray blanket.

"Well, what is it, you . . ." came the voice from underneath the blanket, only to be overcome by a volley of sneezes so it couldn't curse at Melkior, which it most probably had been about to do judging by the tone of the question.

Atchoo. Melkior waited for the sneezing to stop. He then sensibly thought: how can I say this to a man under a blanket? I haven't even seen his face . . . He's clearly got the flu—seeing as he's eating garlic and drinking brandy; now he's sweating under there . . .

"You still here?"

"Yes." It suddenly seemed to Melkior that he was talking to a man dead and buried.

"Well, speak up . . ." this time he managed to get his oath in. "Can't you see I'm damned near death's door here . . . Make it snappy!"

"I believe you need hot tea and aspirin." Melkior approached the bed meekly: "Have you got the flu?"

"What's the matter, did you come here to make a monkey out of me?" The officer threw the blanket aside in a threatening gesture.

Melkior remained in place. He watched the man with pity. A young second lieutenant in a wrinkled old (field) uniform with cracked epaulettes. The eyes feverish, turbid, the face burning with heat, the hair wet, plastered down over the ears and forehead . . . poor lieutenant! They had left him, sick as he was, under that blanket, with a bottle of slivovitz and a bulb of garlic . . . and off they went, fled . . .

"Well, what the hell is it?" He didn't have the strength to get up, he only propped himself on an elbow.

Careful! You still have time to say: I'm looking for So-and-So, he's a staff captain, a relative of mine . . .

"I came to report for service," enunciated Melkior nevertheless. Who knows why he was now reminded of Numbskull . . . the man brought me oranges . . .

"Draft-dodger?" asked the lieutenant with accustomed boredom. He closed his eyes in pain, his head was splitting.

"Volunteer," said Melkior with resolute clarity.

"What did you say?" the lieutenant seemed not to have heard him right.

"I'm reporting as a volunteer," repeated Melkior clearly.

"Why?" the lieutenant let slip unthinkingly.

"To fight . . ." Pupo slapped his back: see, you're an honest man.

"How come you're not . . . Wait," he remembered something, "I'll take you to see the captain, this is not my business."

He did not wait long outside one of the doors in the corridor. The lieutenant came out and said go in, and off he went, probably to get back under the blanket again, to sweat . . .

Melkior suddenly found himself facing a lean officer, grave and morose under a drooping black moustache. Four stars: captain first class, interpreted Melkior. He was sitting at a bare army desk and staring with boredom through the window.

"Don't you know how to close the door after you?" the captain muttered sternly without even a look at the newcomer.

When Melkior had closed the door: "Over here, come closer." He now turned to cast a glance at Melkior, superficially, with a strange smile.

"So you want tooo . . ."

"Yes."

"What?" the captain snorted angrily; his moustache shook.

"To enlist as a volunteer." Melkior could no longer recognize his own voice (everything here was *stern, brief, regular* . . .), the words came out of their own volition, as if under hypnosis.

The captain was now examining him with a cold, mocking gaze. Melkior felt like a comical worn-out object offered at the Kikinis pawnshop: he's bartering to lower my price with that gaze . . .

"How come you weren't drafted? You're young enough and you look fit," he was gauging Melkior's legs and shoulders, chest, arms, head . . .

"I was discharged . . . unfit for service," said Melkior with a tinge of shame. It's a disgrace here. . . . Why did I get into this? He wanted to turn and go.

"Unfit for service. . . . So you haven't done your stint. No rank. Intellectual?"

Melkior nodded mechanically, looking over the captain's head, at a map of the kingdom, for the town of Varaždin. So that's where they already are? Near enough . . .

The captain took out a sheet of paper and dipped his pen into the inkwell:

"Last name, father's name, first name? Year and place of birth? Military district and unit where you served?"

Melkior duly told him everything. He then addressed Pupo: there, see?

"Now there's another thing I want you to tell me," the captain raised a kind look at Melkior and said in a seemingly fatherly voice: "Why are you enlisting?"

"Well . . . the country has been attacked!" He now really meant to feign ardent patriotism (Pechárek, Kink and Countwy), but instead he was thinking of Pupo: rifles and ammunition, boots . . .

"And you care an awful lot for this country, is that it?" The captain's smile was twinkling with insidious distrust. "Anyway, I'd like you to tell me, in confidence . . . look, it's not that I object or anything—no, you're doing a fine thing . . . you were told to enlist, were you? Come on, tell me, there's nothing to be afraid of, everything's fine, see, I've taken down your statement, but who sent you here?" Melkior's blood stopped running for an instant: this is an interrogation! But Pupo did not send me . . .

"Why would anyone send me? I came on my own." Some common decency protested inside him.

"To fight, eh?" The captain went on looking at him for some time, with the same twinkling smile.

He's studying me, he's thinking: does this simple fellow really want to lay down his life in vain? The scoundrel doesn't believe in patriotism, he's got civilian clothes stashed in the locker, he'll skedaddle when they get here, shave the moustache . . .

"Goood," concluded the captain. "If that's what it is, young man, fiiine." He stood up and took the sheet of paper from the desk: "Wait here a minute. Here, have a smoke," he gave him a wink, "good man," and left the room.

Sure, they offer you cigarettes to gain your confidence. . . . Just like in the cinema: pushing a silver case under his nose, "Cigarette?" lighting his first (such manners!) and then his own afterward, with the same flame, fraternally. Both smoking, blowing smoke away, their clouds of smoke merging in the air (so, a pipe of peace, you might say) ahh, never mind which smoke is whose, believe me, my dear fellow . . . I've nothing against you personally (switching to a more intimate tone) but there you are, you've got to handle this boring piece of business, it's orders from above, if you ask me I'd much rather down a couple of shots with you (the damned fools have banned alcoholic beverages on the premises) and go for a game of cards (that's forbidden, too, everything that's any fun is forbidden) or just have a good old chat, ha-ha, about you know what. . . . I've seen you with that dame, you sly so-and-so. . . . Now, the surgeon fellow, isn't he her hubbie, heh-heh? Coco? That's what she calls him? Hang on a second, finish the cigarette, back in a jiffy . . .

A telephone was jangling somewhere in the building. Call Enka. Coco has been "called up." War, wounded men, torn flesh, surgeons in their element. . . . What am I sitting here waiting for? He's now speaking to the police, *goood*, send a man over, *goood*, an intellectual, having a smoke, yes of course, I'll keep him here until you arrive, *goood* . . .

Melkior stole on tiptoe to the door: silence in the corridor, silence in the army building . . . and there's a war raging out there along all the frontiers! A voice in the adjoining room was elocuting confidentially over the phone: it was he, the captain, supplying Melkior's description . . . nose: regular, moustache: clean-shaven, beard: clean-shaven, distinguishing marks: none. . . . He pressed the knob and gave the door a slight push . . . it squealed, a stool pigeon, everything's set up this way here, purposely not oiled . . .

The empty corridor stretched away in both directions . . . To the right, of course! The captain was still chatting into the telephone on the left . . . Behind the lieutenant's door came the sick man's groans, burning up with fever, brandy and garlic, folk remedies. Smells. He tiptoed along. Heels pound straight from the coccyx, from the spine, from the head, with the entire weight of the body; on tiptoe the body loses weight, moves on light springs—ballet . . . The way thieves, spies, lovers walk, the way people who are skulking and escaping walk, with fear crawling over their skin.

Once in the doorway he treaded on his whole feet. Within reach of salvation: street, corner, broad urban expanse—tiny needle in haystack, *adieu, mon capitane*, regards from the volunteer deserter, now there's a paradox.

"All OK, mate? Sorted it out with the brass?" asked the sergeant at the gate, already with a grin of familiarity.

"Yes indeed, sssergeant! Sssee you! Sssee you, too, sssentry!" he hissed mischievously.

The sergeant replied "See ya," the soldier clicked his heels mechanically. He was in for a dressing-down by the sergeant: What did you click your heels for, nitwit? Saluting a civilian!—A volunteer deserter, Sergeant . . . if you've heard of that arm in the royal forces.

Melkior was in a great hurry to get around the next corner.

But why should I call her?—He halted in front of a telephone booth—that *four, four, Ambulance Service* business . . . I've forgotten the number anyway. I'll go straight there. Coco has, as we said, been "called up." That officer must be looking for me now, *goood* . . . Yelling at the sergeant: Why did you let him leave, you cretin! And the Black Maria standing in front of the Garrison Command gate, wide open . . . its bowels stinking of Lysol . . . waiting for the volunteer deserter—apparently, in vain.

The tram was chiming with holiday courtesy, greeting acquaintances on the street—hey there! It did not care that the day was cold and bleak. Coming calmly to a halt, its windows smiling: won't you come in? It took Melkior aboard, too, ting-a-ling, let's go. The traveling burghers were morose, angry, call this Palm Sunday?—You've got to wear a winter coat, snowing like it's New Year's Eve! No, honestly—everything's gone haywire!

A burgher was venting his anger at the weather, heh-heh. . . . Off to his Sunday lunch, potage, plaice, poultry, pork, pies, puff pastry, pancakes, pass the port, pop the cork, let's have a bit of a singsong . . . aah, they've spoiled it all, the idiots! Who can eat under these circumstances? The brutes went and hung a war overhead—

go on, knock the plate with your fork if you can! And all that on Palm Sunday, if you please! Chose the right day for it, that's for sure!

Back, in childhood, there blew a close, hot, moist, so-called *passion day* southerly wind; the sky without a trace of blue, with ragged rapid clouds, the sea lead-gray, mournful . . . It gave you a foretaste of the Savior's passion and death. Dom Kuzma had explained at school beforehand that it had been like that, too, during that long-ago week (which we now call the Holy Week) from Palm Sunday, when Jesus had entered Jerusalem, to Holy Saturday, or rather Holy Sunday, Resurrection Day, when He was resurrected. (Melkior was never clear on whether Jesus had been resurrected on Saturday, at the second peal of the bells, or on Sunday, when Easter is celebrated . . . but nobody dared ask Dom Kuzma). The boys in the white sailor suits, the girls in the white dresses, with braided palm fronds and olive twigs in their hands, under the tall church vaults, in the fragrant smoke of incense, in the sounds of the organ . . . a grand occasion. Now and again the bishop himself, under his miter, crosier in hand, would serve Mass, the Pontifical, and they would undress him and put on his robes, put his shoes off and on, and Dom Kuzma appeared to be a valet to a lord. Melkior was amazed: how could Dom Kuzma be such a . . . a nobody, just someone who put the Bishop's slippers on for him?

But then on Good Friday, when they showed Jesus' Passion in Church, Dom Kuzma was Jesus! They all shouted in his face: crucify him, crucify him! Annas and Caiaphas the high priests, scribes, customs men, Pharisees and servants in Caiaphas's palace. . . . Dost thou answer the high priest so? an officer said to him and slapped him on the cheek. And Dom Kuzma, in a long white robe with a palm branch over a mighty shoulder, his ears jutting out alarmingly, took it all in stride and replied, mild, meek, humble: If I have spoken evil, bear witness to the evil: but if well, why smitest thou me? Pilate, the Roman procurator, was the only one who did not shout. He was indeed prepared to release him. What he saw was just a harmless fellow spouting drivel . . . Art thou the King of the Jews? he asked the poor dreamer with seigneurial irony . . . he was at a loss for what to do with the crank. And Dom Kuzma again said meekly, humbly: My kingdom is not of this world . . . Pilate went out to face the Judaean mob: shall I crucify your King? The occupying potentate was mocking the enslaved people divided by political passions. We have no king but Caesar! bellowed the mob mindlessly. Away with this man, and release unto us Barabas! Pilate did as they demanded and washed his hands diplomatically: that was how it was with the dirty business of politics . . .

Melkior had been incensed by the injustice.

. . . And Dom Kuzma could have crushed the entire churchful of them with his bare hands . . . only nobody dared mention anything about his ears!

"It's all some big business deal or other and spit in my face if it isn't." The burgher (he had a gold watch-chain across his belly) was very angry at "this war": this is only the beginning, there's no telling what we're in for next . . .

"I daresay there are loftier things: after all, people die for their ideals!" The other was disgusted at the vulgar approach: "That's materialism, that is!" he exclaimed accusingly. "It's all the rage with the hotheads these days . . ." he was looking suspiciously at Melkior (or so it seemed to Melkior), this chap's eavesdropping on our conversation a bit too closely . . .

"No war has been anything but a business deal since year one, and you can call me a jackass if you like! It was always a case of someone making a bundle . . . and someone else biting the dust."

"Oh!" cried *the idealist* cut to the quick, "and what about the honorable victims, what about the fallen heroes?"

"It's all about biting the dust, call me an ape if you like. It's all savagery . . . wheeling and dealing."

Melkior was getting off at the next stop. Pity. Will *the idealist-warrior* spit in his face?

"How many wise men have perished at the hands of savage soldiery? Ever since ancient Greece and Rome. Carthage . . ."

"Syracuse!" shouted Melkior jumping off the tram. "Archimedes murdered! Lepanto, Cervantes' arm crippled!"

The tram was already pulling out, *the materialist* smiled at him behind glass in gratitude for his help.

Arm . . . the right or the left? Actually cut off . . . with a sword? Longin Podbipięta. Those were Turks at Lepanto, Damascus sabers . . . Where's this Lepanto place anyway? Perhaps he wrote all of *Don Quixote* with his left hand . . . and in a dungeon at that, on bread and water. A cripple. Don Miguel Saavedra. "Do you think, gentlemen, that it's an easy job to inflate a dog?" says the madman in the preface to Part Two. "Do you think, sir, that it's an easy job to write a book?" adds Don Miguel, the cripple of Lepanto.

He was in front of Enka's house.

"I have often walked down this street before . . ." he hummed in a low voice (there was a song that went like that) and halted at the door. What on earth's the matter with me? He knew there was no reason at all to go upstairs. None at all?—No! he replied resolutely and turned his back to the door.

Yes, but where to? The street is short, empty, morose. Closed in on either side by the questions *right? left?* He spared each side a contempt-inspired look. Weak motives as motives go: one corner with a sundries shop (a loping deer—Zlatorog soap), the other a stunted bare sapling tied protectively to a pole—authority. Enter *motive-following action.* Buridan's ass finally met its death in plenty (the pampered creature), indeed it had two haystacks to choose between (luxury!), but it died for a principle like some heroic character out of Corneille, hail to him! Hail to Buridan's ass between the two haystacks . . . whereas I wasn't given so much as two straws to decide between, not a hollow straw to clutch at . . .

Numbly he watched the descent of the sparse snowflakes: disappearing before even touching down. The brief life of a snowflake. Flutter and die. And yet, how the duration may seem long to the flake! A life of insubstantial weightlessness, a floating, a white dream on the way from sky to Earth . . . And the Earth spells the end of that masterpiece, the fallen star made of lacy crystals.

He was looking at the tiny perfection on his sleeve. The minute six-pointed wonder! (All snow stars are six-pointed . . . it's presumably prescribed by a celestial canon of beauty.) The white star shining on a dark sky of unworthy cloth. Displaying a peaceful, wise, meek dignity of its orderly whiteness in this world of black, disorderly, back-to-savagery things. The Cyclops Polyphemus, the beast, now treads the Earth. You can feel his contagious breath . . . The tiny white star winkled out, melted into a dewdrop.

Right or left? stirred Melkior. Here are your motives: the Zlatorog soap-ad yellow deer and the stunted young tree next to its warden, the dry, self-righteous pole. He opted for the pole. It was after all some kind of authority, was that prideful male vertical. It was advancing to meet the events . . . while the deer (yellow to boot!) was rearing in panicky flight, a clear picture of fear, run for your life!

Melkior approached the runty sapling: all of its buds were still firmly closed, the little one was still afraid to face the world. He patted the pole: hello, Stoic! Seneca, in burning Rome!

On that side of the street the houses were sparser. Two-story family houses in the middle of small decorative garden plots protected by dogs and iron (bars).

From the houses came music, jaunty, bright, holiday-like, middle class; after a heavy lunch, a siesta by the gramophone: operetta, pop hit, *march tran-tam, ran tan-tam . . . Baron Trenk. Once more to offer you my hand before we paaart. When you're all alone and far from home* . . . A flashing thought of Viviana, bitter solitude, envy of *home and hearth* . . . "A home of one's own." A *homeland have I* . . . What's "my homeland"? The street, the Give'nTake, Enka's bedroom, the "separate-entrance room" at Mrs. Ema's? They're already looking for the deserting volunteer there . . . The "New World Order" will by now have been established at the Give'nTake, there's likely to be a new *Kio* at Enka's . . . Let us go, then, you and I to the broad expanses of our Homeland! To the meadows, to the fields with the shepherd's pipe . . . *thy flatlands dear* . . . To the pampas, gaucho, to the prairies! To the deserts to gnaw at the roots of prophets and catch grasshoppers in preparation for the great temptation . . .

He was already striding along outside city limits, through the fields, down well-trodden muddy lanes. He still heard a tram's *ting-a-ling* from the suburban terminus. Goodbye, Melkior said to it, the time for joking is over, I'm not accepting the *ting-a-ling*. I'm off to face Polyphemus the man-eater who now treads the Earth . . . in order to scuttle between his legs before he plugs the cave entrance with his rock. And when I'm out (if I'm out) I'll shout for all I'm worth: Cyclops, you one-eyed bloodthirsty brute . . .—*Why do you go and taunt the savage again?—If only I could rob him of life and soul!*

In the distance there resounded a loud crack. At nearly the same instant an angry insect in furious flight whizzed past Melkior's ear. He hugged the Earth in a trice.

That's the one from Essen, ha-ha, laughed Melkior's nose in the wet grass. Missed me, ha-ha! Let the Earth hear, whispered Melkior into the mud beneath, let the pipes play: *Polyphemus the Cyclops, the one-eyed bloodthirsty brute, Polyphemus the Cyclops, the one-eyed bloodthirsty brute* . . .

A light was glowing around him, as if a setting sun had pierced the clouds. But Melkior was not lifting his head: he was prostrating himself before his great good fortune which had lain down along his back, pressing him to the Earth. Don't stir, don't move a finger, play dead, said Fortune.—I will, I will, I will, he panted obediently. . . . Because that thing may still be after me, right? asked Melkior sensibly.—Where are *you* off to, he said to an ant which was clambering up a leaf of grass and using its feelers to examine the strange thicket above its eye (*and brushwood and brambles and brackens,* says the ant perhaps), why do you go and taunt the savage? Don't move, play dead. But the ant is not heeding Fortune . . . there's nothing that can touch it . . . it is counting the hairs in Melkior's eyebrow. Irritating, tickling . . .

Melkior is not even blinking, not betraying Fortune: if she says you're dead, that's it—you're dead. The main thing is you know it and can tell yourself you're dead, you mustn't even blink. To live, now there's the challenge. So tell the grass (Fortune advises him): don't grow, spring won't put forth its buds here. What is the point of flowers and green leaves? *He* leaves nothing behind, *he* will trample everything underfoot, browse everything bare . . . scoff at all of spring. And tell the Earth: don't wake up . . . be a cold, icy, darkness-bound, hard, unfriendly rock. Be a dark home to the dead. Be a grave. And tell yourself (Fortune tells him): don't breathe, don't stir—he will guzzle your breath, break your movements. Crawl underground to gnaw the roots of hermits, crawl underwater, under the stone like a beetle . . .

Look, one had just crawled out from under a stone. Making straight for his eye. Horned, hairy on the belly and sides, weighed down by the hard plate glistening metallically on its insidious bent back. Moving awkwardly, clumsily, on long articulated legs—six all told, Melkior counted. The huge monster had filled the field of vision of his one eye (he has closed the other one).

Melkior did not blink.

The giant insect—an omnivore, a pantophage (as described by Edgar Allan Poe) was having trouble pushing through the thicket. It was hampered by its legs, its horns, it was pressed by the heavy armor of its backplate . . . but it had its eyes thrust exploringly forward, outside its head; it was pushing its greedy way to its target—Melkior's eye.

Melkior did not blink.

Hear me, ghost . . . he launched into his speech at the last moment (it's going to pierce my eye with its horn!), but the unstoppable insect had already covered all of his vision, snuffed the light out, blocked out the world. . . .

He's shoved his stone in place as a plug, said Melkior and let his head drop helplessly to the Earth's bosom: oh, Mother . . .

He heard a rumble deep below. The Earth trembled beneath him.

The rent, wounded Earth was groaning, his hooves tearing her flesh. "Here comes Polyphemus the Cyclops!"

And when he regained his sight . . . the sky was burning along the horizon.

Crackling stars were spewing fire from high above.

He heard the bellowing of frightened beasts in the distance.

"*Zoopolis!*" he said forlornly and an odd smile lit his face with insane glow. "The fortified city!"

"To make petals . . . in rags worn with dignity . . ." The body stirred by itself. The legs . . . the arms . . . he could no longer tell the difference . . . The uprightness of the pole—hello, Stoic—the dignity of the foot, the thumb, the index finger . . . Nothing. Four trotters, hooves, an earthbound life . . . on the Earth's bosom . . .

He gave Earth a lover's, fiery kiss.

The beasts once again put up a demented bellow: hey, what's this? Over here! Help!

"Coming . . ." replied Melkior.

He nuzzled a leaf of grass, tenderly, first with his left cheek then with his right: we'll never meet again, he'll trample you, too; and to the ant he said: go underground, you wretch! He kissed Earth again—goodbye—and set off on all fours in the direction of the bellowing of the beasts—don't shout, I'm coming—and he crawled fraternally into the frenzied city of Zoopolis.

Born on the island of Vis in 1913, **Ranko Marinković** attended high school in Split and Zagreb and earned his degree in psychology and pedagogy at the Faculty of Philosophy in Zagreb in 1935. He briefly edited his own literary magazine, *Dani i ljudi* (Days and People), later joining Krleža on the journal *Pečat* (Stamp). Marinković's first play, *Albatros*, was staged in 1939.

The Italians held Marinković prisoner at a camp in Ferramonte for two years during World War II. Then, after fleeing to Vis with many thousands of Dalmatian refugees after Italy capitulated, he and the other refugees were sent by the British, who were then with the Partisans on Vis, to El Shatt, Egypt, under British control, where he spent a year and resumed his writing.

As soon as the war was over, Marinković first worked for the Croatian Ministry of Education, then the Nakladni Zavod publishing house. He was director of the Croatian National Theater from 1946 to 1950, and in 1951 he became a professor at the Zagreb Academy of Dramatic Art in 1951, where he taught until his retirement.

Marinković quickly made a name for himself as a short-story writer with the publication of his acclaimed book *Ruke* (The Hands) in 1953. Several of his short stories have appeared in anthologies in English translation, including the title story from the 1953 work, "The Hands" (in *Death of a Simple Giant*, 1965), "The Bone Stars" (in *Yugoslav Short Stories*, 1966), and "Badges of Rank" (in *New Writing in Yugoslavia*, 1970). When his play "Glorija" was premiered in 1955 at the Croatian National Theater, he was recognized as a leading playwright ("Gloria" in *Five Modern Yugoslav Plays*, 1977).

Cyclops was a best seller in 1965, making Marinković one of the leading writers of Yugoslavia.

He published another play, *Inspektorove spletke*, in 1977 ("The In-spector's Intrigues," *Most/The Bridge*, 1978) and two more novels subse-quently, *Zajednička kupka* (Shared Bath, 1980) and *Never More* (1993), but these works did not enjoy the success that marked the reception of "Gloria" and *Cyclops*.

Ranko Marinković died in 2001.

Ellen Elias-Bursać has translated novels and nonfiction by Bosnian, Croa-tian, and Serbian writers for the past twenty years. Among the Croatian writers whose novels and essays she has translated are Slavenka Drakulić, Antun Šoljan, and Dubravka Ugrešić, and plays by Slobodan Šnajder and Miro Gavran, and poetry by Tin Ujević and Ivan Slamnig. She has also translated prose by David Albahari, Slobodan Selenić, and Karim Zaimović.

Her translations have appeared in periodicals and anthologies such as *Best European Fiction 2010*, *Words Without Borders*, *Harper's*, *Draw-bridge*, *Two Lines*, *Context*, *Playboy*, *The Bridge/Most*, *Agni*, *Granta On-line*, and *Leopard*. With Ronelle Alexander she coauthored *BCS: A Text-book for the Study of Bosnian, Croatian, Serbian*, which won the 2009 AATSEEL award for best work of language pedagogy. She has also pub-lished a monograph on poet Tin Ujević and his work as a literary translator.

Elias-Bursać is the recipient of a National Endowment for the Arts translation fellowship. Her translation of David Albahari's novel *Gotz and Meyer* was awarded the National Translation Award by the American Literary Translators Association in 2006.

Vlada Stojiljković (1939–2002) was a journalist, poet, prose writer, trans-lator, and artist. He was born in Zagreb in 1938, attended elementary and secondary school in Niš, and earned his degree in English Language at the Faculty of Philosophy in Belgrade. He was a member of the Writers' Association of Serbia and the Association of Applied Artists of Serbia. He started his career as a journalist at Radio Belgrade on its program for foreign countries, and spent most of his working life at the Radio Belgrade Children's Program, where he also served as editor.

He is the author of eleven books for children and adults. He illustrated many of his books himself and also provided illustrations for the books of domestic and foreign children's writers. He wrote ten radio plays for adults and nineteen for children, many of which won awards and several of which were performed abroad in Hungary, Czechoslovakia, and Austria. He wrote more than eighty teleplays and several synopses for cartoons. He published his work in a number of children's magazines and also exhibited his artwork. His writing has been included in anthologies of both adult and children's poetry.

His poem collection *Blok* 39 was given two awards, and in 2001 he was given the Zmajeve Dečje Igre award for his exceptional contribution to literary expression for children. His fondest professional memories as a writer relate to his work on the children's magazine *Poletarac* and collaboration with Duško Radović.

He translated many books from English, some of the most notable being *Brave New World* by Aldous Huxley, *1984* by George Orwell, *Lassie Come Home* by Eric Knight, *Gulliver's Travels* by Jonathan Swift, *Ubu Rides Again* by Alfred Jarry, *Pincher Martin* by William Golding, *Nonsense Songs* by Edward Lear, and *Monty Python Speaks* by David Morgan. He was a member of the board of SIGNAL, an international review, and in the 1970s he was an active participant in the Signalist movement.

He died in Belgrade in 2002.